The
MX Book
of
New
Sherlock
Holmes
Stories

Part XXI – 2020 Annual
(1898-1923)

THE MX BOOK OF NEW SHERLOCK HOLMES STORIES

STORIES

PART XXI
2020 ANNUAL
(1898-1923)

SOUTHAMPTON STREET

359

EDITED
By
David
Marcum

OFFICES

TRADITIONAL HOLMES
ADVENTURES
COMPILED FOR THE
BENEFIT OF THE
RESTORATION OF
UNDERSHAW

First edition published in 2020
© Copyright 2020

ISBN Hardback 978-1-78705-569-8
ISBN Paperback 978-1-78705-570-4
AUK ePub ISBN 978-1-78705-571-1
AUK PDF ISBN 978-1-78705-572-8

Published in the UK by
MX Publishing
335 Princess Park Manor, Royal Drive,
London, N11 3GX
www.mxpublishing.co.uk

David Marcum can be reached at:
thepapersofsherlockholmes@gmail.com

Cover design by Brian Belanger
www.belangerbooks.com and *www.redbubble.com/people/zhahadun*

CONTENTS

Forewords

Adventures

(Continued on the next page . . . .)

(Continued on the next page . . . .)

These additional adventures are contained in
Part XIX: 2020 Annual
(1892-1890)

These additional adventures are contained in
Part XX: 2020 Annual
(1891-1897)

(Continued on the next page . . . .)

These additional Sherlock Holmes adventures
can be found in the previous volumes of
The MX Book of New Sherlock Holmes Stories

(Continued on the next page . . . .)

(Continued on the next page . . . .)

Part V – Christmas Adventures

(Continued on the next page . . . .)

Part VI – 2017 Annual

(Continued on the next page . . . .)

Part VII – Eliminate the Impossible: 1880-1891

Part VIII – Eliminate the Impossible: 1892-1905

(Continued on the next page . . . .)

Part IX – 2018 Annual (1879-1895)

(Continued on the next page . . . .)

(Continued on the next page . . . .)

Part XII: Some Untold Cases (1894-1902)

Part XIII: 2019 Annual (1881-1890)

(Continued on the next page . . . .)

Part XIV: 2019 Annual (1891 -1897)

(Continued on the next page . . . .)

The Poisoned Regiment – Carl Heifetz
The Case of the Persecuted Poacher – Gayle Lange Puhl
It's Time – Harry DeMaio
The Case of the Fourpenny Coffin – I.A. Watson
The Horror in King Street – Thomas A. Burns, Jr.

Part XV: 2019 Annual (1898-1917)
Foreword – Will Thomas
Foreword – Roger Johnson
Foreword – Melissa Grigsby
Foreword – Steve Emecz
Foreword – David Marcum
Two Poems – Christopher James
The Whitechapel Butcher – Mark Mower
The Incomparable Miss Incognita – Thomas Fortenberry
The Adventure of the Twofold Purpose – Robert Perret
The Adventure of the Green Gifts – Tracy J. Revels
The Turk's Head – Robert Stapleton
A Ghost in the Mirror – Peter Coe Verbica
The Mysterious Mr. Rim – Maurice Barkley
The Adventure of the Fatal Jewel-Box – Edwin A. Enstrom
Mass Murder – William Todd
The Notable Musician – Roger Riccard
The Devil's Painting – Kelvin I. Jones
The Adventure of the Silent Sister – Arthur Hall
A Skeleton's Sorry Story – Jack Grochot
An Actor and a Rare One – David Marcum
The Silver Bullet – Dick Gillman
The Adventure at Throne of Gilt – Will Murray
"The Boy Who Would Be King – Dick Gillman
The Case of the Seventeenth Monk – Tim Symonds
Alas, Poor Will – Mike Hogan
The Case of the Haunted Chateau – Leslie Charteris and Denis Green
        Introduction by Ian Dickerson
The Adventure of the Weeping Stone – Nick Cardillo
The Adventure of the Three Telegrams – Darryl Webber

Part XVI – (1881-1890)
Foreword – Kareem Abdul-Jabbar
Foreword – Roger Johnson
Foreword – Steve Emecz
Foreword – David Marcum
The Hound of the Baskervilles (Retold) – *A Poem* – Josh Pachter
The Wylington Lake Monster – Derrick Belanger
The *Juju* Men of Richmond – Mark Sohn

(Continued on the next page . . . .)

The Adventure of the Headless Lady – Tracy J. Revels
Angelus Domini Nuntiavit – Kevin P. Thornton
The Blue Lady of Dunraven – Andrew Bryant
The Adventure of the Ghoulish Grenadier – Josh Anderson and David Friend
The Curse of Barcombe Keep – Brenda Seabrooke
The Affair of the Regressive Man – David Marcum
The Adventure of the Giant's Wife – I.A. Watson
The Adventure of Miss Anna Truegrace – Arthur Hall
The Haunting of Bottomly's Grandmother – Tim Gambrell
The Adventure of the Intrusive Spirit – Shane Simmons
The Paddington Poltergeist – Bob Bishop
The Spectral Pterosaur – Mark Mower
The Weird of Caxton – Kelvin Jones
The Adventure of the Obsessive Ghost – Jayantika Ganguly

Part XVII – (1891-1898)
Foreword – Kareem Abdul-Jabbar
Foreword – Roger Johnson
Foreword – Steve Emecz
Foreword – David Marcum
The Violin Thief – *A Poem* – Christopher James
The Spectre of Scarborough Castle – Charles Veley and Anna Elliott
The Case for Which the World is Not Yet Prepared – Steven Philip Jones
The Adventure of the Returning Spirit – Arthur Hall
The Adventure of the Bewitched Tenant – Michael Mallory
The Misadventures of the Bonnie Boy – Will Murray
The Adventure of the *Danse Macabre* – Paul D. Gilbert
The Strange Persecution of John Vincent Harden – S. Subramanian
The Dead Quiet Library – Roger Riccard
The Adventure of the Sugar Merchant – Stephen Herczeg
The Adventure of the Undertaker's Fetch – Tracy J. Revels
The Holloway Ghosts – Hugh Ashton
The Diogenes Club Poltergeist – Chris Chan
The Madness of Colonel Warburton – Bert Coules
The Return of the Noble Bachelor – Jane Rubino
The Reappearance of Mr. James Phillimore – David Marcum
The Miracle Worker – Geri Schear
The Hand of Mesmer – Dick Gillman

Part XVIII – (1899-1925)
Foreword – Kareem Abdul-Jabbar
Foreword – Roger Johnson
Foreword – Steve Emecz
Foreword – David Marcum
The Adventure of the Lighthouse on the Moor (*A Poem)* – Christopher James
The Witch of Ellenby – Thomas A. Burns, Jr.

(Continued on the next page . . . .)

The Tollington Ghost – Roger Silverwood
You Only Live Thrice – Robert Stapleton
The Adventure of the Fair Lad – Craig Janacek
The Adventure of the Voodoo Curse – Gareth Tilley
The Cassandra of Providence Place – Paul Hiscock
The Adventure of the House Abandoned – Arthur Hall
The Winterbourne Phantom – M.J. Elliott
The Murderous Mercedes – Harry DeMaio
The Solitary Violinist – Tom Turley
The Cunning Man – Kelvin I. Jones
The Adventure of Khamaat's Curse – Tracy J. Revels
The Adventure of the Weeping Mary – Matthew White
The Unnerved Estate Agent – David Marcum
Death in The House of the Black Madonna – Nick Cardillo
The Case of the Ivy-Covered Tomb – S.F. Bennett

The following contributions appear in the companion volumes:
The MX Book of New Sherlock Holmes Stories
Part XIX – 2020 Annual (1882-1890)
Part XX – 2020 Annual (1891-1897)

Editor's Foreword
Not Just "Always 1895" –
A Hero for *Now*
by David Marcum

In late 1887, Dr. John H. Watson finally accomplished what he'd been promising to do for years – to publish an account of the first case that he'd shared with Mr. Sherlock Holmes.

It had occurred back in early March 1881, when Watson had known Holmes for about nine weeks. They had first met a couple of months before that, in the laboratory of Barts Hospital on New Year's Day, a Saturday, after being introduced by a mutual acquaintance – simply because both had mentioned in this friend's hearing that they were in need of someone to split the cost of affordable lodgings.

The following day they examined the rooms at 221 Baker Street and, finding them acceptable, Watson moved his own possessions around that very night, with Holmes doing the same the next morning.

Watson's physical assets were limited. He'd only recently returned from Afghanistan, where he'd received a grievous and nearly fatal wound while serving at the Battle of Maiwand, only to further face the trials of enteric fever during his subsequent recovery. He states that after he and Holmes agreed to share the lodgings at 221b Baker Street, he was able to move his possessions from his hotel in a single night. Holmes's were a bit more extensive, consisting of several boxes and portmanteaus. No doubt these included materials for his scientific research, records of past cases, and his extensive commonplace books.

From early January to early March 1881, the two settled into a tolerable existence, mostly as adjacent strangers. Holmes turned twenty-seven a few days after they moved to Baker Street, and Watson was then around six months past his twenty-eighth birthday. However, in spite of this similarity in ages, they were vastly different individuals. Holmes, always brilliant, had been earning his bread and cheese as a consulting detective for a number of years, living in Montague Street by the British Museum while pursuing various studies to broaden and deepen his professional experience. Watson had trained as a doctor, and after receiving his degree in 1878, had eventually ended up in military service in India and Afghanistan, leading to his injuries and severance from the British Army.

In Baker Street, they each carried out their separate lives while trying not to bother the other. Watson was simply concerned with recovery, having neither the energy nor the inclination to do much more than stay around their rooms and wonder what his new flatmate was up to.

For Mr. Sherlock Holmes was something of a mystery to him. Watson, with nothing better to do, nowhere to go, and no other friends, began to try and learn more about this mysterious person. He wasn't very successful. In those early days, Holmes kept regular habits – early to bed, and gone before Watson rose in the morning. Holmes's trips away from Baker Street involved long walks through London, or to Barts. Some days he was energetic, and others found him lethargic, barely moving or speaking – just as he'd warned would happen when he and Watson first met and described themselves to one another.

Watson once made a list of Holmes's skills and limits, but after realizing that it wasn't really telling him anything, he threw it in frustration into the fire. He wanted to know more about this unusual person who seemed to be educating himself toward some specific but unknown goal, and who was visited by so many interesting people – for it wasn't long after they started sharing rooms that a curious collection of individuals began dropping by to consult with Holmes – although about what Watson didn't have a clue.

There was a young fashionably dressed girl, and an excited and grey-headed seedy visitor. And a slip-shod elderly woman. And an old white-haired gentleman and a railway porter. As Watson recalled, one of the visitors who came three or four times in a single week was a "*little sallow rat-faced, dark-eyed fellow*", introduced simply as "*Mr. Lestrade*". And every time that one of these callers arrived, Holmes would politely ask that Watson withdraw to his own bedroom so that he could use the sitting room as his "*place of business*" to see his "*clients*". And Watson would climb the stairs for a while to his room – which was probably good therapeutic exercise for him – and then return a little while later, never quite willing to simply ask Holmes just what his business actually was.

This changed on March 4th, 1881, when the two flatmates had a discussion about a magazine article, written by Holmes, regarding observation and deduction. Watson was inclined to dismiss it as "*ineffable twaddle*" . . . although it was true that Holmes had demonstrated his skills at their first meeting when he'd stated that Watson had been in Afghanistan – an action that puzzled the doctor greatly.

That morning, Holmes had revealed to Watson that he was something called a "*consulting detective*", so now Watson knew what and why Holmes did what he did – but he didn't really know anything at all. Not yet. Who can say what would have happened if this conversation had simply ended then and the two of them had gone about their normal daily business?

We are told that in a quantum universe, *all* possibilities exist. Schrödinger's cat is alive *and* dead. Every choice isn't an either/or proposition – rather, *both* happen . . . somehow. Somewhere there's a world where Holmes received a message from the police that morning of March 4th, 1881, in the midst of that conversation with Watson, and then he retrieved his hat and coat, departing to examine a murdered body on his own, while the invalid physician remained in the Baker Street sitting room, purposeless as he had been for the previous two months. Life in that universe continued along the same lines, with Holmes going out on his typical errands, and continuing to meet clients who came to obtain his armchair advice, while Watson continued to politely retreat upstairs. In a few months, Watson probably tired of this and sought another residence, while Holmes was likely making enough money from his consulting practice to no longer need anyone else to share expenses. After moving out, Watson might have continued to get better, or he might have slid into a life of profligacy and drunkenness. Holmes would certainly have continued to develop his skills, and to those that knew of him, he would have provided a great deal of help. But without anyone to make him known to a wider world, a lot less people would have known of him.

But in *our* universe, in the midst of their conversation about deduction and being a consulting detective, Holmes received the message from the police regarding a murder across the Thames in Lambeth, and instead of simply leaving, he curiously invited Watson to join him. Luckily we live in *that* universe where Holmes said, *"Get your hat."*

"You wish me to come?" asked a surprised Watson.

"Yes, if you have nothing better to do."

And so, after having been acquainted with Sherlock Holmes for sixty-three days, Watson finally actually *met* Sherlock Holmes – the *true* Holmes, and not just the random bits and pieces that he'd seen and tried to list over the previous couple of months – with just enough data jotted on a sheet to indicate that all the important questions were still unanswered. Finally, after seeing Holmes in action, Watson began to understand the *true* Holmes for the first time.

Of course this initial investigation was a success, and at the end Watson learned another thing – Holmes did this work for the sake of *the game*, and not for the public glory. Watson was amazed to see that the public records of the case gave credit for Holmes's work to the official force. Holmes didn't seem to care, but Watson felt otherwise. *"Your merits should be publicly recognized!"* he cried. *"You should publish an account of the case. If you won't, I will for you."*

"You may do what you like, Doctor," Holmes replied. One wonders if he knew what he'd actually allowed with that one simple statement, for Watson – doctor and stalwart friend – was also an incipient writer. He faithfully recorded the facts of this case, and so many others that followed.

"I have all the facts in my journal," he told Holmes, *"and the public shall know them."*

Which brings us back to late 1887, when Watson, with the assistance of a literary agent, Dr. (and later Sir) Arthur Conan Doyle, finally published his version of that first investigation, initially relating his own personal history prior to January 1st, 1881 (in less than four-hundred words), and then telling of his meeting with Holmes, the empty days of January and February 1881, and finally the events connected with the murder in that empty house in the Brixton Road. But between early 1881 and late 1887, when *A Study in Scarlet* (as Watson's narrative was titled) was published, Holmes was involved in hundreds – nay *thousands* – of other investigations, many of which were shared with Watson. The good doctor kept notes about these, as well as additionally recording what he could learn concerning other adventures that took place without him, and also those that had occurred before he and Holmes were introduced. And thank heavens that he did make notes about these, and then find time to write them up, because one way or another, they've been finding their way into print by various paths ever since for those of us who want to know what else Mr. Holmes did besides what we're told those wonderful and yet pitifully few sixty stories that make up the official Holmesian Canon.

Initially there was a contemporary immediacy about the Holmes tales. When Watson first published *A Study in Scarlet*, he was narrating circumstances that had occurred less than seven years earlier. His next published volume, *The Sign of the Four*, appeared in early 1890, approximately seventeen months after that case took place. In June 1891, less than two months after Holmes was presumed to have perished at the Reichenbach Falls, further revelations of Holmes's adventures began appearing in *The Strand Magazine*, itself having been in business only since January of that year. Again, these records of Holmes's investigations were relatively immediate. "The Red-Headed League", published in August 1891, begins with Watson explaining that *"I had called upon my friend, Mr. Sherlock Holmes, one day in the autumn of last year . . ."* Further internal evidence places this narrative in October 1890 – less than one year before Watson's version of what happened appeared in print.

Imagine the thrill of Londoners reading these stories and finding out the complete facts in relation to what they may have already known, but without comprehending the full truth. For instance, "The Speckled Band" was published in February 1892 – not quite ten years after the business that it related. Certainly many who lived in the area of Stoke Moran still recalled the mysterious death of Dr. Grimesby Roylott in April 1883, but here was where many of them discovered for the first time – by way of Watson – what *really* happened on that terrifying night.

From the beginning, Watson's motive for recording the facts related to Holmes's investigations was to tell the public of this heroic figure. Of course, Holmes wasn't one-dimensional – he had faults, and uncertainty, and failures. But without a doubt he was a *hero*, which is certainly one of the most important reasons that he is still so well-known today, in the 2020's, decades after his death. And yet we are a great distance now from when Watson was writing of contemporary investigations for people who were aware of them as "current events". As of this writing, the investigation that made up *A Study in Scarlet* took place over 139 years ago.

When certain noted and legendary Sherlockians such as Christopher Morley and Vincent Starrett began assisting in the care and protection and promotion of Holmes's legacy and reputation in the 1920's and 1930's, Holmes and Watson were still with us, and Watson was still, with the assistance that same literary agent, publishing new accounts of Holmes's cases – right up until 1927, although they were no longer contemporary by that point. The last time that Watson released a narrative close to when the action actually occurred was when "His Last Bow" appeared in October 1917, telling what Holmes and Watson had done at the beginning of The Great War in early August 1914. After that, between 1921 and 1927, he wrote and published a further twelve Canonical cases (later collected in *The Casebook of Sherlock Holmes*) that occurred between 1896 and 1907, with most of them grouped around the turn of the century. And from the first published Canonical effort in 1887, *A Study in Scarlet*, to the last in 1927, "The Adventure of Shoscombe Olde Place", Holmes was presented as the hero that he truly was.

Too often of late, it has become fashionable to try and redefine Holmes as someone broken – from small instances to having him be a full-on sociopathic murderer. No doubt this is due to the need of some individuals to tear down heroes rather than admire them – For how can they who are not heroic themselves ever make a connection with someone that is? Better to replace the hero with someone damaged and with whom they can identify than have someone provide an example. With these motivations, some have tried to drag Holmes a long way from the hero that we first met in the publications of the late 1800's. And this is a mistake.

This can be blamed to a certain degree on the nature of the world in which we now live. Lately I've been seeing Vincent Starrett's poem *221b* referenced by Sherlockians quite a bit more than I usually do – often with a whiff of desperation. It's very familiar to those in the Sherlockian community, as it's often recited at the close of various Holmes-related gatherings as something of a benediction before returning to the responsibilities of daily modern life. Perhaps, with its nod toward times past, it provides a comfort as the world seems to be moving in an increasingly speedy express line in the proverbial hell-bound basket.

For those who don't know Vincent Starrett's well-known work:

221b

Here dwell together still two men of note
Who never lived and so can never die:
How very near they seem, yet how remote
That age before the world went all awry.
But still the game's afoot for those with ears
Attuned to catch the distant view-halloo:
England is England yet, for all our fears –
Only those things the heart believes are true.

A yellow fog swirls past the window-pane
As night descends upon this fabled street:
A lonely hansom splashes through the rain,
The ghostly gas lamps fail at twenty feet.
Here, though the world explode, these two survive,
And it is always eighteen ninety-five.

The concluding line – *And it is always eighteen ninety-five* – is often referenced amongst Sherlockians as if there is something particularly special about *that* year. As I've written elsewhere, (in the editor's foreword to Parts XI and XII of *The MX Book of New Sherlock Holmes Stories,*)1895 is definitely of Holmesian interest, as it's a year that falls squarely during those years that Holmes was in practice in Baker Street – but it certainly wasn't his busiest or most famous year. Canonical cases that occurred then – although agreement amongst Holmesian Chronologicists is by its very nature an impossibility – include "Wisteria Lodge", "The Three Students", "The Solitary Cyclist", "Black Peter", and "The Bruce-Partington Plans". But 1894 was a year that Watson specifically mentioned (in "The Golden

Pince-Nez") when discussing just how busy Holmes had been then, with three massive manuscript volumes required to contain both his and Holmes's work. And if one is looking for those cases that are often more remembered as reader's favorites, then one must examine the 1880's for all of those beloved tales recorded in *The Adventures* and *The Memoirs*. (For example, the highly revered "The Speckled Band" took place way back in 1883, when Holmes was only twenty-nine years old.) All four of the longer published Canonical works, *A Study in Scarlet, The Sign of the Four, The Valley of Fear*, and perhaps the most famous, *The Hound of the Baskervilles*, occur chronologically a number of years before 1895 – the first in 1881, and the other three in 1888.

And yet, 1895 is still the representative year most mentioned by Sherlockians – where *"it is always eighteen ninety-five"* . . . .

Vincent Starrett wrote these lines in 1942. While I cannot place myself in his mind, I can – as the holder of a Liberal Arts degree that involved numerous hours in English and Literature classes, teasing out various (and often ridiculous) themes and interpretations and speculations from honored literary works, and then going one step beyond to manufacture extensive entangling constructs from the vaguest of gossamer threads of guesswork and pretentious projection simply to impress teachers who became weak and giddy from being fed that kind of thing – be tempted to speculate that Starrett was looking around at the complicated and dark world of 1942 and wishing for the "simpler" times of 1895. Starrett himself was nine years old in 1895, so looking back, it probably represented a period that seemed less complex, less dangerous, and less depressing than what he was reading about in the 1942 newspapers. (And it didn't hurt that, as a poet, he'd found a year that rhymed with *"survive"*.)

In 1942, Starrett was fifty-six – just a year or so older than I am right now as I compose this essay. While our experiences were completely different – he was a Canadian born in the late 1800's who moved to Chicago as a small child, where he spent the rest of his life as a newspaper man, while I was born in the 1960's in the southern United States, where I still live and have ended up as a civil engineer – I can't help but think that there is some commonality among people of any historical period who reach a certain age and obtain any kind of earned wisdom. Thus, looking around now at the madness in today's world, I sense something of what Starrett felt when he expressed a wish for past days of the better and more innocent variety.

In 1942, Starrett must have thought that the world was falling apart. The Great Depression had started in 1929, and had continued throughout the 1930's – some say right up to the beginning of the World War in 1939,

7

the event which forced the world economy to re-tool and get back to work for such a terrible reason. The war itself began in Europe in the fall of 1939 after a crazed period involving the unimaginable rise of vicious and evil nationalism across the world. While the war's initial spark might have started anywhere, in fact it was due to the actions of a diabolical madman, a seemingly unstoppable juggernaut of evil who had seized dictatorial power, inch by inch, in plain sight, and with the enthusiastic consent of both the ignorant cheering masses influenced by the dictator-controlled press and a group of equally evil, self-serving, and corrupt people within his own government who thought that they could control him, only to find that he was carrying out the Devil's own work with their assistance. How could such a thing happen?

1942 was the first full year that the United States had officially been involved in World War II, although support had been given to England and other allies for quite a while before then. The start of 1942 was just a few weeks after the events of Pearl Harbor, when America was suddenly in a race to bring its industrial machine to a war footing, and all over the country patriots rushed to volunteer for whatever service that they could provide. And sometime during this same year, as all around him America went to war, Starrett was prompted to write his famed poem, which is still referenced and recited at Sherlockian meetings across the U.S. – now seemingly more than ever.

But was 1895, particularly in Victorian England, really worthy of such idealization? Obviously not. 1895 was just seven years after the Ripper Murders, which had thrown London into a frenzy of panic while exposing the vast and disgusting gulf between haves and have-nots. It has been pointed out that The City in the center of London, which was probably the wealthiest place on the planet, was literally next door to the most vile and diseased part of London, where the Ripper rampaged amongst the poorest and most pathetic who existed in unimaginable conditions.

By 1895, England was still incredibly polarized in terms of politics and division of wealth. There was no diminishment of the fear of foreigners, and intolerance within the country took many other forms as well, as evidenced by the trial and imprisonment that year of Oscar Wilde. Additionally, the British were certainly aware of equally unpleasant conditions across the Channel, such as the ongoing miscarriage of justice against Alfred Dreyfus.

But as Starrett rightfully pointed out, there were two men of note living at 221b Baker Street during that time: One a detective, the other a doctor. Both were men of their times, but also enlightened and committed to seeking justice – which wasn't always defined by the actual law. As

8

Holmes remarked to Watson during a notable trip that they took to the Continent in late April and early May 1891:

I think that I may go so far as to say, Watson, that I have not lived wholly in vain. If my record were closed tonight I could still survey it with equanimity. The air of London is the sweeter for my presence. In over a thousand cases I am not aware that I have ever used my powers upon the wrong side.

There are many casual Sherlockians who try to pigeon-hole Holmes and Watson into a specific era, while forgetting that they lived lives encompassing multiple decades. Both were born in the 1850's and lived well into the Twentieth Century. They saw the best and worst of those times – the continuing rise of industrialization and the various quality-of-life improvements that such could provide (for some), the increasing influence of Britain and its Empire upon the rest of the world, and advances in science with their theoretical benefits for mankind. But each of these had their substantial drawbacks, such as population displacement and the increased divisions between wealth and labor caused by new more efficient manufacturing methods, and the inevitable evils of greedy colonialism that went hand-in-hand with empire-building, and the losses of feeling toward humanity as cold science sometimes became the be-all and end-all goal of those in responsible positions.

Is it any wonder, then, that knowing Holmes and Watson were working on the side of *right* in 1895 – and for several decades on either side of that as well – that Vincent Starrett looked back from 1942 and a world at war and wished for what seemed to be a simpler time? And is it any wonder that we do the same now from our own snarled and grim days? For Watson wanted to let us know about a *hero* when he first published in the 1880's, and Vincent Starrett needed to *remind us* of that hero in the dark days of World War II. It's no mystery that, in today's inundation of daily spiraling disasters, we need to know about him too.

We live in an age of immediately available and constant information, which is forcing us to evolve as a species – whether we want to or not. I recently heard of a study that showed that the use of electronic maps through various online sources actually causes a part of the brain that affects one's sense of direction to atrophy – Why bother to try and keep track of where you are, or how to get from here to there, if you can simply look it up on your phone? Likewise, we don't have to memorize things anymore – We can simply look up a state capitol or a recipe. It's sad that human beings, who developed *reading* as a way to store information outside of our heads, have now reached the point where we store so much

9

information that way (because there *is* so much information) that if we had to, it might be impossible to go back to the way things used to be.

While we used to have time to process information, we now have immediate news (as well as immediate opinions from countless scads of yapping heads to interpret it for us), and we can binge every episode of a television show, one episode after another, without ever going away and thinking about each separate piece and examining it this way and that to ponder and appreciate the development or the inherent puzzles. In the midst of this, our current world, there are people – some, but not all – that yearn for the simpler times. Maybe not 1895, but certainly a step back from the madness of today. And this can be found in the adventures of Mr. Sherlock Holmes.

Some are happy with the original sixty tales of The Canon. Others want more. I fall squarely in the latter camp. And while I complain about the crazed frenzy of the modern world, I can't argue that today's technology has allowed for more of Watson's narratives to be newly discovered than ever before.

When Watson first started publishing, *A Study in Scarlet* and *The Sign of the Four* appeared without much fanfare. It was only in mid-1891, when his efforts were placed in *The Strand*, that excitement spread. Over the next four decades, Holmes's adventures appeared at a very irregular rate. There were two-dozen in the initial *Strand* run from 1891 to 1893, and then nothing from Watson's pen (by way of the literary agent) until *The Hound of the Baskervilles* was serialized in 1901 and 1902. In September 1903, further short stories appeared in *The Strand*, beginning with "The Empty House", with thirty-two short stories and one novel appearing between then and 1927. And for those wishing to know more about Mr. Holmes, the pickings were slim – the Canonical stories appeared at a very uneven pace. Those seven collected in *His Last Bow* were published between 1908 and 1917, *The Valley of Fear* was serialized in 1914 and 1915, and the twelve in *The Casebook* between 1921 and 1927.

There were some other bits available for those who wanted more Holmes during these times, but not much. The countless parodies that appeared through these decades, as collected by such able scholars as Bill Peschel in his *223B Casebook Series*, don't really count as actual cases. A true early extra-Canonical story was William Gillette's 1899 play, *Sherlock Holmes*. Others were few and far between. In 1920, Vincent Starrett discovered "The Unique Hamlet", which he wisely brought forth years before his scholarly work *The Private Life of Sherlock Holmes* (1933) – showing that his skills at setting priorities are a shining example to us all.

In 1930, Edith Meiser brought Holmes to radio, correctly recognizing that the detective's cases were perfectly suited to that medium. But after several years of repeated adaptations of The Canon, she began to pull other tales form Watson's records, including an account of The Giant Rat of Sumatra, and another called "The Hindoo in the Wicker Basket" (broadcast January 7th, 1932). These narratives from beyond The Canon, both by Meiser, and later by Leslie Charteris, Denis Green, and Anthony Boucher, helped pave the way for easier acceptance of cases that didn't have to be presented by first crossing the literary agent's desk. But there were still far too few of them.

Through the 1930's and 1940's, extra-Canonical Holmes stories appeared in films starring actors such as Arthur Wontner, Basil Rathbone, and Reginald Owen. In 1948, the world was shocked to learn of a new Holmes story, apparently found in the literary agent's files, thus giving it some kind of supposed extra legitimacy. This story, "The Case of the Man Who Was Wanted", was actually determined to have been brought forth around the turn of the Twentieth Century by a man named Arthur Whitaker. The excitement that this one new story caused shows just how hungry the world was, even then, for new Holmes adventures.

In 1952 and 1953, twelve newly discovered chronicles, later collected as *The Exploits of Sherlock Holmes* (1954) were published in *Life* and *Collier's* magazines. These, as presented by the literary agent's son Adrian Conan Doyle and famed mystery author John Dickson Carr, were very authentic – although received with caustic hostility at the time in the Sherlockian community because of the well-earned animus directed toward Adrian by his past greed-directed actions in trying to "own" Sherlock Holmes.

In 1954-1955, the world was blessed with thirty-nine half-hour episodes – only a handful of which were based on Canonical tales – of the television show *Sherlock Holmes*, starring Ronald Howard. As is often the case with film presentations of Holmes and Watson, one must look past poor screen-writing or abysmal casting to see the Watsonian Truths underneath – but for 1950's television, and following those years when Watson's reputation was so terribly damaged by Nigel Bruce's portrayal, these are actually very good Holmes stories.

Scattered through the years were occasional stand-alone stories that kept the Holmes-fires burning. There were several films and early television broadcasts that presented new adaptations of Canonical stories. In 1965, something new arrived on the scene with the premiere of *A Study in Terror*, the first time that one of Holmes's many encounters with Jack the Ripper, a massively complex case from 1888, was widely revealed to the public. And then for the most part, except for the occasional

11

appearance of a new and random Holmes short story, there was nothing until 1974, when Nicholas Meyer's *The Seven-Per-Cent Solution* was published, igniting a Sherlockian fire that has only grown ever since.

Meyer made people aware that Watson's manuscripts were out there – in attics and old trunks and stacks of family papers – just waiting to be found and presented to a public starving for more about Sherlock Holmes. Meyer found a few more, including his most-excellent 1895 exploit, *The West End Horror* (1976). In that same period, John Gardner uncovered some of Moriarty's journals – not those of the Professor, but instead his younger brother. In 1976, Nicholas Utechin and Austin Mitchelson discovered *The Earthquake Machine* and *Hellbirds*. Sean M. Wright and Michael P. Hodel found one of Mycroft Holmes's early investigations, *Enter the Lion* (1979).

Through the 1980's and 1990's, the flow of newly discovered Watsonian adventures continued, growing a little each year. Interest was fueled by the Granada television show (1984-1994), in spite of its steadily declining quality. (Sadly, except for a few stand-alone Holmes films, there have been no ongoing series about Sherlock Holmes on British or American television whatsoever since the end of the Granada series.) In the 2000's, the rise of the internet and the opportunities that it presented allowed for the dam to burst, and a very welcome surge of discovered Holmes history began to appear in the form of hundreds of online-stories, as well as books that could be prepared and sold without the strangling baggage that had been associated for so long with the publishing industry. A new paradigm washed away the old, where before a Holmes story might sit in limbo for a year or more before being published – if it were to be published at all. Now one of Watson's works could be found and brought to the public nearly immediately. And for someone like me, who has collected literally thousands of Watson's narratives for over forty years, the amount of Sherlock Holmes stories in the world was finally on the right track to being correct. But it isn't there yet, because truly *there can never be enough tales about the* true *Sherlock Holmes*.

And why? Because Holmes is a *hero*, and we need him now more than ever. As we're assailed by corruption, ignorance, intolerance, and pure evil at the highest levels – criminals and perverts and cheats and traitors of Biblical proportions – we need an essential example of someone who *thinks* and seeks knowledge instead of relying on superstition and ignorance and hunches and prejudice. We need someone who doesn't see facts as hoaxes, and someone who searches for the honorable path to justice, and not ways to subvert it. We need someone who *helps* rather than *destroys*, because of completely self-centered narcissistic greed, or simply for the warped and deviant joy of chaos. And like Vincent Starrett – who looked around in 1942 thinking that *"though the world explode"* and wished for a simpler time – we too need someplace where, though imperfect, we can look for inspiration – not finding Holmes as a broken criminal, the way that some now try to present him, but rather as the true heroic figure whom Watson wanted to honor in the 1880's, and whom Starrett wanted to remind us about in the dark depths of the early 1940's.

We may look back on Holmes where *"it is always eighteen-ninety-five"* – or several decades on either side of that – but in fact the *true* Holmes is a hero for *all* ages, and never more necessary now, and in as many stories about him as we can find.

* * * * *

As always when one of these sets is finished, I want to first thank with all my heart my incredible wonderful wife of nearly thirty-two years (as of this writing,) Rebecca, and our amazing son and my friend, Dan. I love you both, and you are everything to me!

Also, I can't ever express enough gratitude for all of the contributors who have donated their time and royalties to this ongoing project. I'm constantly amazed at the incredible stories that you send, and I'm so glad to have gotten to know all of you through this process. It's an undeniable fact that Sherlock Holmes authors are the *best* people!

The contributors of these stories have donated their royalties for this project to support the Stepping Stones School for special needs children, located at Undershaw, one of Sir Arthur Conan Doyle's former homes. As of this writing, these MX anthologies have raised over $60,000 for the school, and of even more importance, they have helped raise awareness about the school all over the world. These books are making a real difference to the school, and the participation of both contributors and purchasers is most appreciated.

Next is that group that exchanges emails with me when we have the time – and time is a valuable commodity for all of us these days! I don't get to write as often as I'd like, but I really enjoy catching up when we get the chance: Derrick Belanger, Bob Byrne, Mark Mower, Denis Smith, Tom Turley, Dan Victor, and Marcia Wilson.

There is a group of special people who have stepped up and supported this and a number of other projects over and over again with a lot of contributions. They are the best and I can't express how valued they are: Larry Albert, Hugh Ashton, Derrick Belanger, Deanna Baran, S.F. Bennett, Andrew Bryant, Thomas Burns, Nick Cardillo, Craig Stephen Copland, Matthew Elliott, David Friend, Tim Gambrell, Jayantika Ganguly, Paul Gilbert, Dick Gillman, Arthur Hall, Stephen Herczeg, Mike

Hogan, Craig Janacek, Steven Philip Jones, Michael Mallory, Mark Mower, Will Murray, Robert Perret, Tracy Revels, Roger Riccard, Geri Schear, Brenda Seabrooke, Shane Simmons, Robert Stapleton, Subbu Subramanian, Tim Symonds, Kevin Thornton, Charles Veley and Anna Elliott, Peter Coe Verbica, I.A. Watson, and Marcy Wilson.

I also want to thank the following:

- John Lescroart – While many know John as the best-selling author of the Dismas Hardy books (as well as a number of others also set in the Hardy Universe), I first encountered him by way of his novels relating adventures of young Nero Wolfe (although not quite under that name) during World War I – *Son of Holmes* (1986) and *Rasputin's Revenge* (1987). Holmes is very much a part of these books, and I later discovered that John had also written his own version of "The Giant Rat of Sumatra". It was only natural that I would ask him to write a foreword for these books, and he very graciously wrote a really good one. I've been a fan of his works – both Holmes-related and the highly-recommended chronicles of Dismas Hardy – for a very long time, and it's my personal thrill that he's a part of these volumes. Many thanks!
- Roger Johnson – I'm so grateful that I know Roger. His Sherlockian knowledge is exceptional, as is the work that he does to further the cause of The Master. But even more than that, both Roger and his wonderful wife, Jean Upton, are simply the finest kind of people, and I'm very lucky to know them – even though I don't get to see them nearly as often as I'd like! In so many ways, Roger, I can't thank you enough, and I can't imagine these books without you.
- Steve Emecz: I had the great good fortune to communicate with Steve way back in 2013, when I was interested in placing my previously first-published book with MX, the fast-rising superstar of the Sherlockian publishing world. It was an amazing life-changing event for me, and ever since, Steve has been one of the most positive and supportive people I've known, letting me explore various Sherlockian projects and opening up my own personal possibilities in ways that otherwise would

14

have never been possible. Thank you Steve for every opportunity!

- Brian Belanger – In January 2020, I was able to attend – for the first time – the Holmes Birthday Celebration in New York. I met a number of wonderful people there in person after getting to know them through emails over the last several years, and I was especially glad to meet Brian, one of the nicest and most talented of people. He's amazingly great to work with, and once again I thank him for another incredible contribution.

And last but certainly *not* least, **Sir Arthur Conan Doyle**: Author, doctor, adventurer, and the Founder of the Sherlockian Feast. Present in spirit, and honored by all of us here.

As always, this collection has been a labor of love by both the participants and myself. As I've explained before, once again everyone did their sincerest best to produce an anthology that truly represents why Holmes and Watson have been so popular for so long. These are just more tiny threads woven into the ongoing Great Holmes Tapestry, continuing to grow and grow, for there can *never* be enough stories about the man whom Watson described as *"the best and wisest . . . whom I have ever known."*

David Marcum
March 4th, 2020
The 139th Anniversary of
Holmes telling Watson to
"Get your hat."

Questions, comments, or story submissions
may be addressed to David Marcum at

thepapersofsherlockholmes@gmail.com

Foreword
by John Lescroart

Ironically enough, Sherlock Holmes entered my life as a respite from literature. At the time, I was majoring in English at UC Berkeley, with an emphasis on *The Continental Novel In Translation*, immersed in the works of Tolstoy, Dostoevsky, Stendahl, Goethe, Flaubert, Camus, Thomas Mann, and many others of the all-time literary greats.

The problem was that they may have been superb stylists, but they were often not exactly easy to read. So, for example, I would have just spent five hours and three-hundred-and-fifty pages getting to the point in *Anna Karenina* where somebody's long-lost aunt dies (Not really, but you get the idea), and I found that I couldn't force myself to read another word of this high literature. Of course, in those days, I had neither a television set nor a computer – entertainment at my apartment came only in the form of more reading.

Fortunately, I had somewhere and somehow acquired the two-volume set of William S. Baring-Gould's *Annotated Sherlock Holmes*, and one day in the midst of my required reading of another of the classics, I couldn't take it anymore and, in despair, I reached over to my bookshelf to see what Dr. Arthur Conan Doyle was up to with this Sherlock Holmes fellow.

The answer was: Plenty.

I'd of course heard of Holmes, who after all is perhaps the most well-known fictional character in human history. But the discovery for which I was completely unprepared was the sheer accessibility of these stories. They were in many ways the polar opposite of the books I'd been laboring through. They were, in fact, eminently readable and plot driven – and yet there was an elegance and approachability in the writing itself that, in my opinion, stood up to the best of what my continental novels had to offer.

Beyond the "English Major" stuff, though, from the very first words of the very first book, *A Study In Scarlet*, Holmes (and Watson) come alive not just as interesting characters, but as fully realized human beings, imbued with depth, great intelligence, irony, humor, bravery, and sensitivity. These are wonderful people we come to know and yes, even to love. We want to spend more time with them, hang out with them, and be part of their lives, which are so familiar and yet so unique and remarkable.

Hence, this volume of new and original Sherlock Holmes stories.

One would be tempted to think that enough had already been written about Holmes and Watson and the world they inhabit. Surely, with Conan

Doyle's original sixty stories, with literally hundreds of pastiches published over the past century and more, the trove of Holmesiana must be close to exhausted.

But this is the miracle of Sherlock Holmes. It is not so.

Sherlock's appeal is so universal, Watson's language is so identifiable, the mysteries they encounter speak to all ages and to the human condition, that it is small wonder that writers, like the talented contributors to this latest volume, continue to be driven to visit and revisit Holmes and Watson, and to add their narrative voices to The Canon as nothing less than a universal tribute to the original.

Holmes comes fully alive again in these stories and, indeed, from the evidence presented herein, he will never die.

Enjoy.

John Lescroart
May 2019

"What Could Be Better
For the Purpose?"[1]
by Roger Johnson

Arthur Conan Doyle was generally tolerant when his work was parodied. In his reminiscences *Memories and Adventures*, he cheerfully quotes in full "The Adventure of the Two Collaborators", a short and very funny spoof written in 1893 by his friend J.M. Barrie. [2]

He was less amenable to more serious imitations. The French author Maurice Leblanc appropriated Holmes as the only detective worthy to challenge the famous *gentleman-cambrioleur*, Arsène Lupin, but Conan Doyle understandably took exception, and the name was changed to "Herlock Sholmès" – or in some English editions "Holmlock Shears". On a lower literary level, Sherlock Holmes quickly became a hero in the European pulp magazines, where he was given a young assistant named Harry Taxon in place of Dr. Watson. From 1907, innumerable stories appeared on the bookstalls in Germany, France, Denmark, Spain, Poland, and even Croatia. Russia developed its own more intelligent and better written series. None had the approval of Conan Doyle – but he could be generous in his rejection. Consider "The Case of the Man Who Was Wanted".

After Conan Doyle's death in 1930, the family made no proper effort to examine his papers. It wasn't until 1942 that Hesketh Pearson, researching what was intended as *the* authorised biography, discovered among them the typescript of an unpublished Sherlock Holmes story. In 1948, "The Case of the Man Who Was Wanted" was published in *Cosmopolitan*, but upon its British publication the following January the Conan Doyles received a letter from a retired architect named Arthur Whitaker, claiming that he had written the story in 1910 and sent it to Sir Arthur, who had given him ten guineas for the rights to the plot. And despite furious denials and threats of legal action from Sir Arthur's sons, Denis and Adrian, Whitaker easily proved his claim, as he had kept his carbon copy of the typescript and the letter from Conan Doyle. "The Case of the Man Who Was Wanted" is not at all a bad story, written in a fair imitation of the Watson style.

The Conan Doyle brothers' almost fanatical opposition to imitations of their father's work had been demonstrated in 1944, when Ellery Queen's anthology *The Misadventures of Sherlock Holmes* was published in America. That outstanding collection of parody and pastiche – which

18

includes stories by Anthony Boucher, Agatha Christie, S.C. Roberts, Vincent Starrett, and Mark Twain – was short-lived. Denis and Adrian detested the tongue-in-cheek scholarship of the Sherlock Holmes societies, and jealously guarded their legal rights in his characters. After two printings, *The Misadventures of Sherlock Holmes* was withdrawn from circulation.

Ironically, the major contribution to Sherlock Holmes pastiche came in the early 1950's with a series of twelve stories by Adrian Conan Doyle himself, six of them written in collaboration with John Dickson Carr. They appeared in book form in 1954 as *The Exploits of Sherlock Holmes*, and despite the dismissive comment of Edgar W. Smith, head of the Baker Street Irregulars, that they should be called "Sherlock Holmes Exploited", they are about as close to the real thing as any writer has got.

Denis and Adrian's sister Jean outlived them both and achieved far more in her life, becoming head of the Women's Royal Air Force (the first Director to have risen through the ranks), and ADC to the Queen. Her relationship with Holmesian enthusiasts was gracious, courteous, and supportive. As an Honorary Member of The Sherlock Holmes Society of London, she happily attended the Annual Dinners and even took part in pilgrimages to Switzerland. In 1991, she became the first woman to be admitted to the Baker Street Irregulars *with all rights and privileges*. Her investiture, most appropriately, was "A Certain Gracious Lady".

Dame Jean was never entirely happy with Holmesian pastiche, believing that authors should create their own characters. It's a simplistic view of a rather complex phenomenon, but understandable. Now, of course, the afterlives of Holmes, Watson, and the rest have become vastly more complex since the expiry of the original copyrights, everywhere except the United States, in 2000. (Under the USA's unique copyright law, some stories were never protected there, while a few of the late ones will not enter the public domain until the mid-2020s – which has made the situation even more complicated.)

Nevertheless, I fancy that Dame Jean would be pleased with the success of this remarkable series of books. The contents are evidence of worldwide affection and admiration for her father's work, undiminished ninety years after his death. And she would surely approve of the reason for the books' creation and publication: To help support the regeneration – you might say the *rejuvenescence* – of The House That Conan Doyle Built.

Roger Johnson, BSI, ASH
Editor: *The Sherlock Holmes Journal*
January 2020

NOTES

1 – From *The Sign of the Four*, Chapter XII.
2 – Thanks to *Arthur Conan Doyle: A Life in Letters*, edited by Jon Lellenberg, Daniel Stashower and Charles Foley, we know that Barrie was also responsible for the equally neat "My Evening with Sherlock Holmes", published anonymously in 1892.

An Ongoing Legacy
for Sherlock Holmes
by Steve Emecz

Undershaw
Circa 1900

The MX Book of New Sherlock Holmes Stories has now raised over $60,000 for Stepping Stones School for children with learning disabilities and is by far the largest Sherlock Holmes collection in the world – by several measures, stories, authors, pages and positive reviews from the critics. *Publishers Weekly* has been reviewing since Volume VI and we have had a record thirteen straight great reviews. Here are some of their best comments:

> *"This is more catnip for fans of stories faithful to Conan Doyle's originals"* (Part XIII)

> *"This is an essential volume for Sherlock Holmes fans"* (Part XI)

"The imagination of the contributors in coming up with variations on the volume's theme is matched by their ingenious resolutions" (Part VIII)

MX Publishing is a social enterprise – all the staff, including me, are volunteers with day jobs. The collection would not be possible without the creator and editor, David Marcum, who is rightly cited multiple times by *Publishers Weekly* and others as probably the most accomplished Sherlockian editor ever.

In addition to Stepping Stones School, our main program that we support is the Happy Life Children's Home in Kenya. My wife Sharon and I are on our way in December for our seventh Christmas in a row at Happy Life. It's a wonderful project that has saved the lives of over 600 babies. You can read all about the project in the second edition of the book *The Happy Life Story.*

Our support of both of these projects is possible through the publishing of Sherlock Holmes books, which we have now been doing for a decade.

You can find out more information
about the Stepping Stones School at:

www.steppingstones.org.uk

and Happy Life at:

www.happylifechildrenshomes.com

You can find out more about MX Publishing
and reach out to us through our website at:

www.mxpublishing.com

Steve Emecz
August 2019
Twitter: *@steveemecz*
LinkedIn: *https://www.linkedin.com/in/emecz/*

The Doyle Room at Stepping Stones, Undershaw
Partially funded through royalties from
The MX Book of New Sherlock Holmes Stories

A Word From
Stepping Stones
by Lizzie Butler

Undershaw
September 9, 2016
Grand Opening of the Stepping Stones School
(Photograph courtesy of Roger Johnson)

Undershaw continues to develop during this new era as Stepping Stones School. The school is going through a very exciting time of change in 2020, with our student cohort at full capacity of ninety-five students across both our lower school and upper school sites, making daily life here at Undershaw rewarding, exciting and busy.

We really appreciate the support and donations received from MX Publishing and we look forward to another successful year as we fulfil the wants and needs of our students and their families.

"I didn't want to get up in the morning and go to school but now I love school. Everyone accepts each other and we're like a family, we trust, look after and understand each other, I think that's very special. This is now my happy place, where I can be who I am."

– Stepping Stones Student, 2019

Best wishes,

Lizzy Butler
Fundraising Manager, *Stepping Stones,* Undershaw
February 2020

"Undershaw," Hindhead, Conan Doyle's House.

Sherlock Holmes (1854-1957) was born in Yorkshire, England, on 6 January, 1854. In the mid-1870's, he moved to 24 Montague Street, London, where he established himself as the world's first Consulting Detective. After meeting Dr. John H. Watson in early 1881, he and Watson moved to rooms at 221b Baker Street, where his reputation as the world's greatest detective grew for several decades. He was presumed to have died battling noted criminal Professor James Moriarty on 4 May, 1891, but he returned to London on 5 April, 1894, resuming his consulting practice in Baker Street. Retiring to the Sussex coast near Beachy Head in October 1903, he continued to be associated in various private and government investigations while giving the impression of being a reclusive apiarist. He was very involved in the events encompassing World War I, and to a lesser degree those of World War II. He passed away peacefully upon the cliffs above his Sussex home on his 103rd birthday, 6 January, 1957.

Dr. John Hamish Watson (1852-1929) was born in Stranraer, Scotland on 7 August, 1852. In 1878, he took his Doctor of Medicine Degree from the University of London, and later joined the army as a surgeon. Wounded at the Battle of Maiwand in Afghanistan (27 July, 1880), he returned to London late that same year. On New Year's Day, 1881, he was introduced to Sherlock Holmes in the chemical laboratory at Barts. Agreeing to share rooms with Holmes in Baker Street, Watson became invaluable to Holmes's consulting detective practice. Watson was married and widowed three times, and from the late 1880's onward, in addition to his participation in Holmes's investigations and his medical practice, he chronicled Holmes's adventures, with the assistance of his literary agent, Sir Arthur Conan Doyle, in a series of popular narratives, most of which were first published in *The Strand* magazine. Watson's later years were spent preparing a vast number of his notes of Holmes's cases for future publication. Following a final important investigation with Holmes, Watson contracted pneumonia and passed away on 24 July, 1929.

Photos of Sherlock Holmes and Dr. John H. Watson courtesy of Roger Johnson

The MX Book
of
New Sherlock Holmes Stories

Part XXI – 2020 Annual
(1898-1923)

The Case of the
Missing Rhyme
by Joseph W. Svec III

I sat trembling with pen in hand,
At my paper, staring o'er the land,
Wondering what word to use,
To complete the rhyme that I did choose.

Yet, I could not find it.
I could not never mind it.
Who could help me in this chore?
Is it like a Sign of Four?

Or a scarlet thread upon the chair,
Where to look I knew not where.
Would it be in the valley of fear?
Is there a vicious hound? Oh Dear!

T'would be a Scandal, Bohemian, I am sure
If the rhyme I could not procure.
I'd blush like a league of red heads you see.
Or even lose my identity.

Could it be in Boscombe Valley somewhere,
Beneath five orange pips over there?
Really, I must get a grip.
Should I ask the man with the twisted lip?

Or perhaps the goose that ate the carbuncle blue,
Would know exactly just what I should do.
I had the rhyme almost at hand,
But it slipped away like a speckled band.

Perhaps if I have just a wee bit o' rum
I can nail it like an engineer's thumb.
Or if I search the world global
I will find it like a bachelor noble.

If I were trying to rhyme with beryl coronet,
Ha! It t'would really be no sweat.
As easy as rhyming with copper beeches
Just a bowl of tasty peaches.

But here I stand without my rhyme
What to do, truly lost I am.
About it make no bones at all,
Sherlock Holmes is the one to call.

The Problem of the
St. Francis Parish Robbery
by R. K. Radek

Reconstructed from Notes of the Late John H. Watson, M.D.

Foreword

During the many years of our association, I witnessed quite the parade of diverse clients march into our sitting room to consult with or to offer a commission to my friend Sherlock Holmes – dignitaries, businessmen and working people, wives and husbands, the forlorn and the desperate, statesmen, politicians, police, and an occasional scoundrel. The one thing that all of these different men and women held in common was a need to avail themselves of my friend's special powers of ratiocination and deduction.

One morning a few days ago, with a howling storm discouraging any venture out-of-doors, I decided to spend some time with my notes pertaining to Holmes's cases with a view towards their organisation. Near to the fire seemed the best location for the exercise, so I pushed my chair slightly closer to the hearth and settled down with a sheaf to begin the process.

After some few minutes so engaged, I came across an entry in my journal concerning a small matter Holmes and I had handled together at Christmastime last, and lost myself in a pleasing reminiscence about it. It had been an unusual affair, and although it took but two days to resolve, the problem did have a residual effect for all of us who had participated in it. The note Holmes had received inviting him into the affair I had stuck between the pages, and now I perused it. I was pondering for a moment whether the matter could be an appropriate addition to the line of his cases I had memorialized when his voice broke in on my thoughts.

"I see you're deciding whether to burden the public with another of your over-dramatised accounts," he said. "Which one, I wonder? Ah! Of course! It's the little business we cleared up at St. Francis last year about this time. I'll bet you dinner at Simpson's I'm right!"

Holmes was standing at the deal table swirling a clamped vessel of some dark substance over the Bunsen. Thankfully, this wasn't one of his more malodorous experiments, as with the windows closed tightly against

37

the storm, the atmosphere would have suffered, and I along with it. Holmes was right, of course, although a thought raced across my mind to mention some other matter. Simpson's was well worth the small deception. But he'd likely catch me up in it, so I resigned to tell the truth. With a sigh, I admitted, "Precisely, Holmes. Although with notes of eight or ten cases in my lap, I don't know how you hit on the one."

Holmes walked to the sideboard where I had left my coffee cup, picked it up, and carrying it in one hand, the clamped flask in the other, set the cup down on the table to my side, chuckling. "Coffee, Watson?"

Now it was my turn to chuckle – the experiment was to reheat our coffee. "Yes, please, and with it, an explanation?"

"About the case? Or the coffee?" my smiling friend queried. "Since the two are interconnected, you'll have both. I observed that shortly after you ensconced in your chair, you paused at a point in your journal. This lasted a full two minutes. There was a hint of a smile on your face, and you shot passing glances at the sideboard where you had left your cup and at the bell-cord you could pull to summon our page to bring you coffee. I know your talent for organization, and it was only a year ago I witnessed you last going through your journals. Thus I knew the cases you were reviewing dated no earlier. That established the temporal context. Lastly, and most conclusively, I caught a glimpse of the note card you removed from the book. It's distinctive heading, with its rendering of St. Francis posed with a group of animals, made the final deduction elementary."

"All right, then, Holmes. What say you to my writing an account of the matter? You must admit it would be unique in the annals of the published cases."

"Watson, old friend, you have me at a bit of a disadvantage. This is the season we become imbued with feelings of good will towards men. I am not fully immune to its effects, so I am disinclined to say no. I ask only that you concentrate on relating the investigative and deductive features of the case and pass over the purely *outré* or emotional elements."

"Of course, Holmes, just as I always do."

"Hrumpf!" was his grunted response. Unfazed, I rose from my chair, threw a scupper of coal on the fire, sat down at my desk, took out pen and paper, and began to write.

Chapter I – Season's Greetings

Christmastime is a paradoxical time of the year. Many people, whether religious or not, Christians or otherwise, rich or poor, extend cheerful and charitable regard for one another. An aura is generated by festive decorations in the windows of homes and shops everywhere one looks. The street lamps are festooned with boughs and bells, and there is a bounce in the steps of pedestrians absent most other times of the year. Even the cabmen's horses are dressed for the season. But while the public basks in the glow of the season, the criminal class takes no break that I can discern from the nefarious enterprises in which they ordinarily engage.

One evening, a few days before Christmas last, while I was dressing to go out with Holmes for dinner, I heard carolers somewhere on the street below. When I opened my window slightly to hear them a bit better, there was a sudden dissident intrusion to their song. Someone was ringing the bell at our front door so loudly that I worried it would be knocked from its mounting. I decided to head quickly downstairs to investigate the clamour. When I reached the sitting room, my tie dangling from my collar, I saw Holmes had already come from his room for the same purpose – to find an out-of-breath Mrs. Hudson. Handing Holmes a small envelope, she cried, "Mr. Holmes, I must have climbed these stairs twenty times today! Mercy, me! I am winded! This is from a cleric I have waiting on the doorstep. He insists he's here on an urgent errand, and he prays you will accept his note and see him despite the hour." I joined them, and Holmes, after reading the card he took from the envelope, handed it to me.

It had a neatly stylized image of a friar, presumably St. Francis, piping to a group of animals at its upper left corner. At the bottom of the card was printed "*Church of St. Francis of Assisi, Notting Hill.*" In a handsome hand was written:

> *Mr. Holmes,*
>
> *I deeply regret this untimely intrusion upon you. However, if you could kindly admit Brother Innocent, he can explain our predicament and our urgent need for your assistance. I would be so grateful to give you such particulars as I know, should you agree to help us.*
>
> *Msgr. Thomas Burley*

"Perhaps we should have the messenger up, Watson, and learn what calamity has occurred at St. Francis that sends this summons."

"By all means. I'm curious to learn what's the fuss." I looked at Mrs. Hudson, and I could see that she wasn't relishing escorting Brother Innocent up the stairs, so I volunteered to go down and show him up.

I went down and let in a young man in cleric's dress with a red-lined cape folded over his arm, hat in hand. Brother Innocent was a bright-eyed lad of perhaps twenty-three years, slightly taller than average, with dark hair, a strong, square jaw, and athletic build. I guessed he was of Irish descent, and in that I was soon proven correct. I directed him to take the stairs, and I followed after him.

Holmes had remained at our doorway, and as soon as we reached the threshold he bade the young cleric welcome and motioned him to a chair near the fire. Holmes introduced himself and me, and Brother Innocent wasted no time in beginning his explanation for the visit.

"I am so pleased, Mr. Holmes, and Monsignor Burley is, too, that you have granted this audience. To come directly to the point, there has been a burglary at the Church. Someone has stolen one of the statues in our Nativity scene, and we pray to God, Mr. Holmes, you can recover it."

"With the Nativity so central to the Christmas celebration in the Church, I can quite see the concern that is has been molested," Holmes remarked. "Tell me, what facts of the matter can you relate?"

"Not many, I am afraid. I know this much: The entire collection – the figures, manger, wooden rail fence, everything – was loaned to St. Francis by the Bishop. He celebrates Mass at a different Parish each Christmas, and sends the Nativity scene to each Church in advance of the Mass. It really is a beautiful rendition. Not quite life-sized, but the pieces are so well done, they almost look real from just a short distance."

"Watson," Holmes interrupted, "Perhaps you could take all this down." I grabbed my notebook and pen and began to make notes. "You see, Brother Innocent, Dr. Watson assists me in much of my work, and I would want him to – "

"Of course, Mr. Holmes," interjected the cleric. "It need not be said that Dr. Watson's assistance is equally welcomed by the Monsignor, and he emphasised to me to make that clear, should you agree to take up the matter. Indeed, sir, I have reached the limit of my knowledge, but if you could come back with me to Notting Hill, the Monsignor could give you a fuller explanation than I."

"Then I suggest we do that. Watson, if you're game – "

"I am."

" – we could finish dressing, accompany the good Brother to the church, and look into the problem. And there are some fine dining establishments nearby as the church is not far from Kennsington and High Street, so we shan't go hungry."

"A fine plan," I enthused.

"The Monsignor sent me here in his conveyance, and it is waiting below, gentlemen," said Brother Innocent. "I will wait outside for you."

"Pshaw! You wait right where you are, by the warmth of the fire," insisted Holmes. "We will be with you momentarily."

Soon, the three of us were down and into the provided coach and off for Notting Hill.

We had some conversation along the way, learning that our messenger was the Monsignor's secretary and was studying to one day become an ordained priest. Most amusing was his relating how he was given the name Innocent. His mother, Mrs. Malloy, it seemed, felt Mr. Malloy was guilty of many offenses. She gave her son his name so that he could, were he to follow in his father's footsteps, in all circumstances, claim to be *"innocent"*.

Chapter II – Audience, Examination, and Invitation

Upon our arrival at St. Francis, I saw that the church was constructed in yellow brick, with matching annexed buildings. We were ushered into the Monsignor's library. Introductions were made, and the Monsignor asked Brother Innocent to stay, telling us at the same time it was his desire that the Brother be our liaison in the matter. Brother Innocent collected our coats and hung them in a closet almost invisibly set into an oak-paneled wall.

The library served as his office as well, and was comfortably furnished without reaching ostentation. There were bookcases on two walls, a fireplace in use, numerous chairs, tables and lamps, and the usual things one would expect to see in an ecclesiastical setting – a familiar portrait of Jesus, a copy of DaVinci's *Last Supper*, some statuary, and above and behind the Monsignor's desk, a painting portraying St. Francis, his arms outstretched, praying among animals.

As for the Monsignor himself, he was not taller than average in height. I judged him at five-feet-six or seven, and tending towards stocky in build, perhaps twelve stone in weight. He had attained middle age, his graying, somewhat receding hair and slight crow's-feet at the corners of his eyes giving evidence to that fact. Despite the obvious stress that he was under, his demeanor was congenial, without a hint of officiousness or formality. In short, he struck me as a pleasant, likeable man.

"I am deeply appreciative, Mr. Holmes, Dr. Watson, that you have come to our aid. I'm sure Brother Innocent informed you of our predicament."

"Only to the extent that the missing figure is part of a special collection of the Bishop's," answered Holmes.

"True. It is extraordinary in that the figures are beautiful renderings, quite artistically painted. It was a gift to the Bishop on his appointment from Cardinal Newman, and pecuniary value aside, it has great personal meaning for him. Needless to say, it is virtually impossible to replace the

41

missing piece, and I would like to avoid suffering the great embarrassment that would follow from the fact it was lost while in our custody."

"I assume that you haven't referred the matter to the police?" asked Holmes.

"Actually, we contemplated doing that, Mr. Holmes, but Brother Innocent suggested that since the object stolen was not of tremendous financial value, the police might not energetically pursue the matter. And if they then were unsuccessful in recovering it, we would be asking your assistance, but probably too late to allow for the timely recovery of the piece. You see, we hope to have it back in time for the Bishop's Mass, which is just three days hence. Therefore, we decided to ask you in at the outset."

"Whether I can satisfy your timetable. . . ?" Holmes responded. "That is something I cannot promise."

"Of course, we understand," the Monsignor acquiesced. "But we do have hope. Now, if you would like, Mr. Holmes, I could take you into the church, and we could continue our conversation at the scene." Holmes nodded.

Brother Innocent led the way. We followed him through a doorway that opened into the Sacristy and through another that opened into a side chapel of the church sanctuary. The Nativity scene was situated at the front of the side chapel and was cordoned off several feet from its border. In the subdued lighting, I saw only a few people scattered about the sanctuary, sitting or kneeling in pews.

As the four of us stood before the scene, I quietly asked Monsignor Burley whether our voices would be disturbing to the parishioners in the pews. He said as long as we spoke quietly, there would be no problem. People are used to activity in the sanctuary – weddings are planned, funerals, baptisms – all sorts of things happen, and speech, he said, is expected.

Looking at the scene, I noticed the principal figures were present: Mary and Joseph, the infant Jesus, three Wise Men, a shepherd, several lambs, and even an ass. Holmes must have noted this too, because he remarked that all pieces appeared present save the usual second shepherd, the one commonly depicted kneeling. Holmes asked us to step back several paces so he could begin an examination of the floor and the area abutting the scene. Brother Innocent suggested we three sit in the front pew as Holmes had dropped to all fours, making a minute examination of the floor, the side of his face at times very close to or directly on its surface, as I had witnessed so many times before. Eventually rising to his feet, he asked to pass the cordon for closer examination of the scene, itself. The

Monsignor told Holmes that he certainly could, and that he could go anywhere in the building he felt he needed to go. He need not ask.

The floor of the manger was, of course, straw, and Holmes was in it, once again on all fours, making as careful an observation as he had the floor previously. After several minutes, he stood, lifted a few of the figures slightly, and then thoughtfully swept the straw he had disturbed back into position with his feet. Once he had brushed the remnants of straw from his trousers and sleeves, he joined us in the pews. "Other than the remaining impression in the straw of the missing shepherd," pronounced my friend, "I found no trace left behind that could help identify the perpetrator, and in leaving with the figure, no straw was deposited on the floor."

"Since we only noticed today the shepherd was missing, it is possible the floor was swept since the time of the burglary," Brother Innocent speculated.

"This much, at least, I know," Holmes asserted. "We're looking for a very neat, careful burglar, and given the pieces have considerable heft, a fairly strong one. Well, we may as well take our investigation to the street, although I doubt we'll find much in the way of physical evidence – too much wind, too much pedestrian and vehicular traffic, and no snow to show footprints," Holmes lamented.

"Brother Innocent will take you back to my office for your coats, gentlemen. When you're finished outside, would you please stay and have dinner with us? We eat in the rectory which is just next door, and our cook does splendidly, let me assure you," said the Monsignor, stretching his waist band.

"Very kind of you," said I. "Are you certain we aren't imposing?"

"Quite certain," the Monsignor assured. "Brother Innocent, please bring Mr. Holmes and Doctor Watson to the rectory after Mr. Holmes has concluded his work. In the meantime, I'll let Mrs. Vaughn know we have two more at the table tonight, and", his eyes twinkling, "maybe hunt for a bottle or two in the cellar to honor our famous guests."

"Please go to no extra bother for us," Holmes implored.

"No bother, Mr. Holmes. I expect it will be some bother for you two, however. All the staff is aware of your celebrity, and I'm sure you're going to get plenty of questions about the cases that have appeared in *The Strand!*" Holmes shot me a covert pursed-lip glance.

The front doors of the church opened into a small courtyard and walkway leading to the Lane. Holmes first inspected the walkway, and then Pottery Lane, lingering only briefly as he looked up and down the street. He crossed to the opposite side and did likewise, after which he rejoined us. "Nothing learned here," said Holmes. "An army could have passed by, and the pavement and the swept walks wouldn't reveal it. Also, there are no windows across the street would that provide a direct vantage point from which anyone could observe a person moving up and down the street. And the Lane curves sharply away from the church, so someone exiting in that direction would be quickly out of the view of anyone in this vicinity. Given all this, it would have been blind luck had some passer-by seen the shepherd being carried off and reported the unusual occurrence to the police or someone at the church."

"I trust that you're correct, Mr. Holmes," agreed Brother Innocent. "Many of the people who come and go here are parishioners and would have recognized instantly a piece of the Nativity being carried away. There would have been intervention or, at the very least, we would have been informed. That there was not I believe supports your conclusion."

"Tell me, Brother," continued Holmes, "are there side doors that open away from the Lane that could have served as the exit?"

"There is a side door, but it leads you to the walkway that, in turn, leads to Pottery Lane, and, thus, anyone using it must enter upon the Lane as anyone who had used the front doors. Also, the side door is always locked except after Sunday Masses. After the final Mass, the door is locked again and the key returned to its hook in the Sacristy."

"Well then, with a dearth of physical evidence, we may better approach the case from the standpoint of motive. It may not be the most scintillating dinner conversation, but there is presently no other thread to pull."

"Indeed, Mr. Holmes. If you'll both come with me please, I'll take you both to the dining room."

Chapter III – Pleasant Conversation, An Excellent Dinner – Rudely Interrupted

We hung our hats and coats on a tree in the small foyer of the Rectory, then accompanied Brother Innocent to the dining room where we were introduced to the company and directed to chairs. Including ourselves and Brother Innocent, there were eight of us: The Monsignor, and Fathers Murphy, O'Donahue, Wexler, and Sullivan making up that number. The large Irish contingent didn't surprise me, as I knew the neighborhood to have a significant Irish population. Father Wexler said grace, after which we were seated, passing around a large basket of soda bread while Mrs. Vaughn ladled vegetable soup from a serving cart that her assistant, Mrs. O'Keefe, wheeled around the table. I remarked what a wonderful aroma it gave, and my reward was a proud smile and an extra portion!

The discussion came around to the burglary as the soup bowls were cleared from the table. Holmes remarked that the physical layout of the building and grounds necessarily funneled egress to the relatively small area of the courtyard, but he'd found no trace of the burglar there or in the Lane. He asked whether anyone had any idea why the shepherd would have been taken. Had the church offended a parishioner who wanted a form of revenge? Had there been incidents of vandalism to which the burglary could be related? There were no answers given. Father Sullivan, I thought, made a valid point – if someone wanted to demonstrate malice, wouldn't they have removed the Holy Infant? I offered that the theft of the shepherd was perhaps a matter of easiest opportunity, as the shepherd was nearest the cordon. For his part, Holmes appeared to be listening, but his fidgeting with a dessert spoon told me his mind was mostly elsewhere.

Soon Mrs. Vaughn and O'Keefe returned with the cart and began plating dinner. Monsignor had Brother Innocent pour the wine that had been opened before dinner. When everyone was served, Monsignor Burley offered a toast and a short prayer for success in recovering the stolen piece. Then we settled into a meal of delicious roast pork and potatoes (that only Mrs. Hudson could match) and more conversation. I remarked about the striking appearance of the church and the connected buildings. From that, Monsignor told us that the church had been designed and built by John Bentley, "that same John Bentley who built Westminster Cathedral, don't you know!" Then we learned of a period of vice and degradation through which a large part of Notting Hill suffered, but happily – at first gradually, and now in great strides – the area was eliminating the blight. It was at this point our evening took quite the turn.

There came a series of knocks, and standing at the open door to the room was a nun responsible for them. "Fathers, Monsignor!" she said with alacrity, "I am so sorry to break in on your dinner, but we all know you are entertaining Mr. Sherlock Holmes and his associate Dr. Watson, and we thought you should have the news straight away. Another figure of the Nativity is gone!"

Holmes was up in an instant, and muttering some words of excuse, bolted by Sister Eugenia so quickly she had to twirl to avoid being bowled over. I followed, hoping that with quick action it might be possible to apprehend the thief. Brother Innocent said that he'd better come, too, and with Sister Eugenia now standing aside, we rushed through the door after Holmes. In his hurry Holmes had left the foyer door open, leaving his hat and coat behind. Brother Innocent and I closed the foyer door behind us and entered the church. We espied Holmes, but he had already turned and was running back to the front door.

"Watson, Innocent!" he cried. "Quickly – to the street!" We turned on Holmes's heels and, in a few seconds, we were all standing in the middle of Pottery Lane. Looking at Brother Innocent, Holmes shouted,

"You go down the Lane. If you see anyone remotely looking like the thief, yell for us. Be careful, but make haste! Watson, you come with me!" Holmes was off even as he finished barking the directives, and I followed in his footsteps. Pottery Lane turned to the left as we chased up the street, and Holmes was outdistancing me with each stride until there were fifty yards or more separating us. Abruptly he stopped, and that allowed me to join him.

As I began to catch my breath, Holmes quickly put his finger to his lips. No longer interested in running down the street, he cupped his hands to his ears, listening for our quarry. I tried doing the same. After a few moments, Holmes said *sotto voce*, "Watson, do you hear that?" I admitted that I heard nothing, but I was uncertain what I should be listening for. "Dogs, Watson! Two or three of them, barking. They're disturbed, possibly raising the alarm. We go towards the noise."

We were in an area of row houses, so we first had to come back up the street to find an opening between them. Next we were impeded by the fences closing in the minuscule gardens, clotheslines invisible in the dark threatening to garrote us, and then we were faced with the backs of additional tenement houses. I worried, too, we might ourselves happen upon some large, unfriendly dog. Holmes stopped, put his arm out to stop me, and then again cupped his ears. "The dogs have quieted, Watson. Too bad. We were to the chase only a minute or two late. We may as well make our way back to the church. With more attention paid, I might learn something from the few footmarks that I saw."

With a light snow beginning to fall, we weaved our way through the row house maze and back to the street. A sign affixed to a lamp post indicated the street was now "*Princedale Road*". Somewhere in the crook the name had changed in the London manner, where a contiguous street is differently named every few blocks, as is Baker Street. Whatever its name, we were greeted by Brother Innocent, who had come up looking for us. He told us his effort had been for naught. Holmes told him of our adventure among the row houses and the ultimate escape of the protagonist. "You were quickly closing in on a very rough region, Mr. Holmes," the Brother informed. "There is an increasing deterioration the further you go, and some very rough people in it. It was for the best, especially in the nighttime, that you abandoned your pursuit."

We walked briskly back to the church, Holmes wanting a second look at the grounds before the snow obliterated them. As it was, a light fluff had already obscured the pavement, walkway, and the courtyard pavers. Holmes announced he would stay with it, despite the snow. Brother Innocent volunteered to bring us our coats, and Holmes made a request that he come back with a broom, not of the push type. In no time, the

46

Brother was back with our coats and the requested broom. The Monsignor, he said, would like a report, if possible, when the opportunity presented.

What, I wondered, did Holmes want with the broom? Sweeping away the snow would surely sweep away also the footmarks that he wanted to see. As he began wielding the broom, my question was answered. He swung it to and fro in an arc extending to a few inches above the ground, and like a fan, it blew away the fluff leaving what was beneath it visible. However, there was not much visible to my perception. "Watson, here I've cleared the pathway. You can barely make out the marks of some footfalls as the little dusting of snow was compressed. You see more clearly the front of the boots, much less so the heel. That's because the thief was already running, and the heel doesn't touch down. And here," he went on, "the space between footfalls increases as the pace of the runner increases. And here, hallo! Here is another mark. Yes, a bit larger than the first. Now we know we have two people involved."

Holmes took us to courtyard near the entry doors of the church where he repeated his broom technique. "Ha! We see them again, Watson, but they come from the side, not directly out the front doors. And here – these are the Sister's footprints. They are in a direct line to the Rectory. And, of course, the others belong to the three of us as we rushed to the church when the alarm was raised.

"The Sister's bootmarks appear much the same as the thieves," observed Brother Innocent. "They may have been left at the nearly the same time, before much more snow had fallen."

"Brother Innocent," Holmes cried, "if you decide to change your calling, you may well have a career as a detective!"

"Oh, my goodness, Mr. Holmes!"

"Well, let's put you to the test! Look at the impressions – first the perpetrators, then Sister Eugenia's. Judging by their relative shape and size, can you draw any conclusion?"

"They are awfully faint, but again, they have some similarity. Nuns wear very practical footwear, and that could explain a similarity of shape. As the thieves were running, Mr. Holmes, as you pointed out, we see Sister Eugenia's heel, not the thieves'. I can think only the evidence is that Sister was not running."

"Quite true," said Holmes, flatly. "Now I think we must revisit the Nativity scene to see whether we can learn anything more about the absquatulation." We entered the church, which at this hour was empty of parishioners. Holmes asked us to follow behind him, as he wanted to examine the floor carefully and, in this manner, we slowly made our way to the Nativity scene.

Brother Innocent and I took our previous seats. I could see at once, and Brother Innocent's gasp indicated he did, too, that this time the thieves absconded with the figure of Mary. Holmes didn't pass the cordon, as his attention became focused to the side of the manger nearest the side door. "They were not as careful tonight, gentlemen. We have bits of straw on a line to the side door." Holmes walked to it and pushed it open. "Hello! Plainly there is more than a single key, and the thieves had access to it."

"And they must have left in such a hurry, perhaps hearing Sister Eugenia at the front door, that they didn't relock the door after passing through," Brother Innocent interjected.

"And I deduce," I hastened to add, "we left glasses of particularly good wine, and possibly dessert in the Rectory dining room, not forgetting the Monsignor is awaiting your report, Holmes. Perhaps you two detectives might continue your cases inside?"

Holmes came and sat in the pew with us. He remained quiet for a minute, gazing pensively at the now more depleted Nativity scene. Finally he spoke, as though thinking out loud, "The shepherd remaining is standing with his staff. The shepherd missing was kneeling, Brother Innocent, was he not?"

"Yes, that is true," was the reply.

"Curious, is it not?"

"How so, Mr. Holmes?"

"That the figurines taken have a singular commonality." Neither Brother Innocent nor I replied. Personally, I was having difficulty imagining what a shepherd and Mary had in common. Assuming we were stumped, Holmes completed his thought. "Both were in a posture of prayer." Holmes fell silent in thought. Then, with a shrug of his shoulders, he said tersely, "We may as well deliver the client the bad news, gentlemen," and we began a somber procession to the Rectory.

Chapter IV – Report to The Monsignor, A Next Day Visit To The Tenements

On our return to the dining room, we found the Monsignor, the wine, and a tray of nicely decorated Christmas cookies waiting for us. The priests had since gone to their rooms. I didn't hesitate to finish the wine, but I passed on the cookies. Although not actively religious, I found the thought of eating cookies in the shape of angels troubling. Monsignor Burley received Holmes's account of our most recent efforts with resignation. He had seen us return empty-handed from a Rectory window, he said, and Brother Innocent briefly mentioned our lack of success when he grabbed up the broom. His mood was decidedly gloomy. "Well, I suppose I will have to send a note to the Bishop in the morning. We certainly cannot have him discover the thefts when he arrives to say Mass. Lord help us! He will not be happy."

"I suggest you withhold that information as yet," said Holmes. "We came close tonight to ending the affair. I have a new avenue of inquiry that, I believe, may hold some promise. We may yet come to a successful conclusion."

"You give me hope, Mr. Holmes. We will not lose faith," the Monsignor declared, although his voice was tinged with apprehension.

"We will pray for you and Dr. Watson," Brother Innocent promised, "and that tomorrow the clouds shading this affair will part."

"It has become late, gentlemen, and I'm sure you have earned the comfort of your room in tonight's exertions. And for Brother Innocent and me, the day begins early, and we should be getting our sleep, too. Brother Innocent, would you please rouse Mr. Fortney and ask him to bring around the brougham for our guests?"

"That is most kind," said I.

"Yes," Brother Innocent replied, "and I will see that the side door of the church is locked."

It wasn't long before Holmes and I were being driven to Baker Street. As usual when he was knee-deep in a case, he spoke very little during the trip, only remarking how painfully close we had come to an apprehension, if only the alarm was raised a minute – even half-a-minute – sooner, *etcetera*. Back again in our rooms, I was thankful that Mrs. Hudson had banked the fire for us, and I soon had it up, quickly taking the chill from the air. Holmes hung up his hat and coat. "A nightcap, Watson?"

"I could certainly stand for one," said I. He went to the gasogene and prepared two whisky-and-sodas, handing me one, and we took our usual chairs by the fire.

I sat silently recollecting the events of the evening, finally deciding to ask Holmes about his thinking of the matter. "It has been an unusual series of events. I cannot get my arms around it. Why would someone take individual pieces of a display that have little meaning apart from the collective. What value would they hold?"

"They won't be turning up at a pawn shop in Tottenham Court, if that's your gist. The pieces must have value to the thieves," Holmes replied, swirling his drink, its amber colour illuminated by the light of the fire. "The question is *why*. Why did they take only the praying figures? Once we have the answer to that question, we'll be much closer to a solution."

Holmes quaffed the remainder of his drink. "We must have an early start in the morning, Watson. Can you manage six?" I replied that I could.

Holmes took my empty glass and placed both on the sideboard, then began walking toward his room. "One more question, Holmes?" My friend paused at his door to field it. "You mentioned a new avenue of inquiry. What do you have in mind?"

"The second key, of course. Good night, Watson!"

At precisely half-past-six, with only coffee and a scone to sustain us, Holmes and I were in a cab heading back to Notting Hill. The temperature had noticeably dropped overnight, and snow was gently falling. Pulling up our carriage rugs, we weren't uncomfortable on the ride. Holmes this morning was in a particularly jovial disposition.

We pulled up to the church and, in the daylight, Pottery Lane and its environs didn't appear as foreboding as it seemed during the events of the previous night. Holmes rang the bell of the rectory and we were admitted by Mrs. O'Keefe. She explained that everyone was at morning Mass, but we could wait in the Monsignor's office, or if we preferred, the dining room, where we might have a breakfast of oatmeal porridge, toast points, and coffee. I opted with enthusiasm for the latter.

Some twenty minutes later, I heard the front door swing open and the voices of the priests and Brother Innocent in conversation as they made their way to the dining room. Last to enter was the Monsignor. Everyone was happy to see us again, and setting down his coffee cup, Holmes began to address Monsignor Burley. "Coming straight to the point, Monsignor, I want to ascertain what you told me yesterday – that I might go anywhere in the church or the Parish buildings." Holmes more asserted than asked.

"Absolutely you may," he replied.

"And with that license, I may talk with or question anyone, clerical or otherwise, with respect to the matter under investigation."

"Again, the answer is yes, Mr. Holmes."

"Thank you." Turning to me, Holmes said, "Sorry to whisk you away from the table, Watson, but we have work to do." I followed after him to the foyer where we picked up our hats and coats. Holmes, however, didn't put his on. Going outside, he turned to enter another of the contiguous Parish buildings. "We're on our way to the second key, I hope. This is the first stop." One of the signs on the door read "*Office*" and listed the hours that it was in operation, "*8 a.m until 1 p.m. Closed Sundays and Holidays*". We entered into a corridor, and a few steps brought us to the office door. Although the words "*Please Walk In*" were stenciled on the door, Holmes nevertheless tapped twice before we let ourselves in. Sitting behind a desk was a middle-aged lady dressed tidily in a black smock with a white collar, a name plate pronouncing her to be Mrs. Elizabeth O'Roarke.

"Madam," began my friend, "my name is – "

"Sherlock Holmes, of course!" she interjected, slapping closed the ledger book in which she had been writing. "And with you, the gentleman with notebook in hand, is Dr. John H. Watson. I am so thrilled to meet you! We all know you're working on the Nativity scene thefts, Mr. Holmes, although I can't imagine there is a clue to be found here. But if I may be of service in any way, you need only ask."

"Thank you, Mrs. O'Roarke, you are very kind. And you may be able to assist us. We were told yesterday that there is but one key to the Sanctuary side door, the door opposite to Pottery Lane. However, certain events that took place late last night lead me to believe there could be a second or spare key. Have you any knowledge of this you might share with us?"

"Wish to heaven, I did, Mr. Holmes, but I'm afraid not. You see, I am secretary for the schools – we have both Infants and Junior – and if your inquiry pertained to this building, well there is little that I don't know." At his moment Brother Innocent entered the office.

"Sorry I didn't keep up with you, Mr. Holmes, but you left rather abruptly, and I must admit, I did want to finish my porridge . . . Good morning, Mrs. O'Rourke."

"And to you, too, Brother Innocent. I am being interrogated, Brother Innocent! By Mr. Sherlock Holmes! I wouldn't have dreamed! "

"Yes, indeed, you are, madam," said Holmes. "You were explaining, I think, you do not know of a spare key."

"True." Mrs. O'Roarke paused, looking away for a moment, searching for a thought. "But, you know, Mrs. George – she's the lead cleaning lady, for the church and everything – she might know whether there are spare keys. Maybe one for the Sanctuary."

"Excellent, Mrs. O'Roarke!" exclaimed Holmes. "Do you know where we might be able to find her?"

"Well, with the schools closed for the holidays, I doubt that she's here. But she might be in the church getting things in shape for the Bishop's visit. That would be my guess." Without waiting for further comment or question, Mrs. O'Roarke sprang from her desk, grabbed a shawl from a coat-hook, and pulling the office door open, practically yelled at us, "Let's go! If we find her, I can introduce you, and we don't, I know one or two other places we might look."

Brother Innocent flashed a grin as we accepted the inevitable and joined in the secretary's wake. "If this isn't something! Wait until I tell my sister Gladys that I helped Sherlock Holmes with a case! She will just die!" Appreciating her enthusiasm, as I know we all did, we were happy nevertheless that we found Mrs. George straightaway upon entering the church. "Vivian! Vivian!" Mrs. O'Roarke called out. Mrs. George emerged from the side-chapel, holding a feather duster in one hand while straightening her apron with the other.

"Oh, Betsy, why so the commotion?" Mrs. George asked, now looking with consternation at the unfamiliar, for the most part, crowd trailing behind her.

"Vivian," the secretary gushed, "this is the famous detective Mr. Sherlock Holmes, and his associate, Dr. Watson. You know," she added, as Mrs. George's blank expression belied that she recognised our names at all, "the ones in *The Strand Magazine* . . . from Baker Street." Each successive hint produced no sign of recognition. Mrs. O'Roarke, sensing the futility of further clues, then simply introduced us as the people trying to recover the missing pieces of the Nativity Scene. The cleaning lady's face relaxed as understanding replaced perplexity. "They want to ask you some questions – "

"Betsy . . . I had nothing to do with it! I just saw the shepherd was missing, and I told the Monsignor – "

"Mrs. George, please do not worry," Brother Innocent reassured. "No one suspects you of anything. Mr. Holmes simply has a question or two he would like to ask. Isn't that so, Mr. Holmes?"

"Perfectly so," my friend sedately responded. "It is simply this: We are trying to find out if there is a key to the side door," Holmes asked calmly while pointing in that direction, "other than that which is kept on the hook in the Sacristy?"

Mrs. George reached into a pocket of her apron and removed a ring of several keys. Selecting and holding up one, she said, "Here is one." She handed it to Holmes, who looked at it and then handed it right back to her.

"Mrs. George, did you loan this key to anyone? Or did it go missing at any time in the last twenty-four hours?"

"No, sir. It was in my pocket on my keyring all day. I was here 'til after Vespers, then went everyone left, I replaced some candles, checked the pews for things – people always seem to be leaving things – and swept the floors. "'Twas when I swept up around the manger that I saw the one shepherd was missing, and I ran to tell them at the Rectory."

"Can you recall the last time you saw that shepherd in the manger before it went missing?"

"No, sir. I think it was there early in the afternoon, but I can't be sure. It's always there, and I don't pay attention every time I come in."

"Naturally. While you worked after Vespers, did you notice anyone lingering in the church?"

"I don't think so. I wasn't noticing on 'count of I wanted to finish my work and go home. Brother Innocent, I think . . . yes, I remember Brother

Innocent was speakin' with an older couple, then they all walked out together."

"Thank you, Mrs. George. Just one more thing. Besides yourself, would anyone else have a key to that door?"

"Why, sure, sir. The other two charwomen have a key, just like mine."

Holmes looked piqued. He shot a glance at my way and said "just one key" under his breath. Engaging Mrs. George again, he asked, "Pray, could you tell me the names of the other two, and where we might go to talk with them?"

"Well, there's Miss Splyver, she lives with her parents. And there's Mrs. Wilson, but she wasn't in yesterday 'cause she's been sick these last two days, the poor woman. I don't know their addresses, I'm afraid, but they're in the Parish somewhere."

"I could look them up in the Parish records, Mr. Holmes," Brother Innocent volunteered.

"And I'm sure we have Mrs. Wilson in the school records," said Mrs. O'Roarke. "Her son attends our Infant School – the fourth form, I think – and the older boy finished from the Junior School two or three years ago."

"Both fine lads," Brother Innocent added, "those Wilson boys."

"Well liked by their classmates, too," Mrs. O'Roarke added.

"*Basta!*" Holmes exclaimed. "Let us waste no time looking up the addresses."

We thanked Mrs. George for her cooperation, and bade her good day. In the school office once more, Mrs. O'Roarke looked up the two needed addresses and copied them for us. Blotting and handing them to Holmes, she opined, "I may not be much of a detective as yourself, Mr. Holmes, but were I you, I'd check on Miss Splyver first. You'll be wasting your time with the Wilsons. I've been secretary here for twenty-five years, and I can tell you the Wilson boys are as fine in character and scholastics as anyone we've had here. And Mrs. Wilson, why she's raised those boys by herself ever since her lout of a husband abandoned them."

"I can echo what Mrs. O'Roarke just said, gentlemen," Brother Innocent agreed. "Although I joined the staff here too late to know the older brother, I know the younger boy quite well. He is a sincere and devout lad. He could not possibly be involved in the theft of a matchstick."

Holmes looked at the addresses he'd been handed and smiled. "I think there is less than a mile between these two locations. Brother Innocent, I hope that you will be coming with us." He nodded his assent. "Excellent!" continued Holmes. "You are known to everyone, and will have a settling effect after the anxiety that Watson and I will surely generate."

The Monsignor's brougham was brought around on the Lane, and as Brother Innocent and I boarded, Holmes handed the address of our first destination to Mr. Fortney. Once underway, we followed a rather circuitous route: Princedale Road, Penzance Street, finally coming to a stop in front of a tenement on Wilsham. Holmes directed us to a common entry and told us we were going up to No. 337 G. The building was in a sorrowful state of disrepair, the principal features being walls denuded of paint or vestiges of it peeling everywhere any remained, the smell of rotting wood, and a lack of illumination. Where there were lamps, their oil reservoirs were empty. We reached our objective floor and found the door bearing a dingy "G". Holmes suggested Brother Innocent knock, and presently the door was tentatively opened by a young lad of nine or ten years. I knew then that Holmes had brought us first to the Wilson residence, opposite of the intelligence we had been previously given. Brother Innocent said, "Hello, Thomas," and asked if we could step inside. The boy didn't speak, but stood away from the door, which we took as a tacit "Yes." I closed it behind us.

I was struck immediately upon entering the markedly different appearance of the rooms from what we witnessed gaining access to them. To begin, they couldn't have been neater or better kept. We were in a modest front room that served as a sitting room, kitchen, and dining area. The windows were clean and allowed in the light, and with the pale yellow wallpaper, the room was quite bright. The floor, though only plain boards, shone. The hearth was swept but held no fire, despite the cold. There was a small fire burning in the cook stove against the back wall, and this seemed to be the only source of heat for the room. To the right and left were doors leading, I assumed, to the bed chambers.

Brother Innocent began the conversation. "Thomas, is your mother here that my friends and I might speak to her?"

"She's asleep in her room," the boy replied sheepishly. "She's been sick, and Billy said she should stay in bed to rest and get better. I'm not supposed to bother her."

"I see," said Brother Innocent. "And is Billy here? Maybe we could talk to him."

"Billy left to fetch some coal for the stove. He isn't back yet."

"Thomas," Holmes began, in as gentle a tone as I imagined him capable, "would it be all right if we talked about the manger scene at St. Francis? There are two pieces missing, and we're trying to find them."

"I can't . . . I'm not supposed to . . ." the lad stammered, first wiping a tear from his eyes, then breaking down into a full-fledged cry. In between sobs he tried to speak, but I could only make out a few words, "Mother" being one of them.

Brother Innocent went to the boy, giving him his handkerchief. "Now, then, Thomas, you don't need to be upset. Mr. Holmes and Dr.

Watson are only trying to bring back the shepherd and the Blessed Mother to the church, so that everyone can enjoy the Nativity. They don't want to get anyone in trouble. Why don't you sit down in that chair by the table and we can fix it all."

As the boy did what Brother Innocent asked, our attention was diverted to the front door, where an older boy had entered, a small sack slung over his shoulder. He slid the sack in the direction of the stove and went directly to his younger brother's side. "Don't worry, Thomas. I'll take care of this." The older boy turned to Brother Innocent. "Are these the police?" he asked.

"No, they are not," replied Brother Innocent. "They are Mr. Sherlock Holmes and Dr. John Watson, who Monsignor Burley asked to find the missing Nativity pieces."

"Well," Billy said resolutely, "you cannot have them."

"Can't have them?" Brother Innocent uttered, clearly taken aback.

"No," the young man retorted. "They are needed more here."

"Why would you need them more here?" an incredulous Brother Innocent asked.

"Ah! Here comes our 'why', Watson," Holmes whispered.

Thomas, under the protection of his older brother, had regained his composure. It was he who gave Brother Innocent the answer. "Because of what you told us, at school," he piped up. "You said if we pray, the Holy Spirit will come to help us. I told Billy that we had to pray a lot for Mum, so she could get better, and the shepherd and Mary from church would pray, too. So we went to get them. Even when we go to bed, they pray."

"There you have it, Brother Innocent. What do you say to that?" Holmes asked.

Brother Innocent was at a loss for words. He looked up, possibly to Heaven, before speaking. "I . . . I don't know what to say."

I injected myself at this point in the proceedings, speaking directly to the brothers. "Boys, I am a medical doctor. Why don't you let me look in on your mother. I may be able to help."

"We have no money to pay you, Doctor Watson," Billy said matter-of-factly. "Had we money, Mother or I would have called one in before now. I spent our last shillings on coal. Mother is very chilled, and that much I could do. Once I got the fire up, I was going to St. Francis or St. James to ask for charity, a last hope, but the three of you showed up."

Billy, I thought, possessed a great deal more maturity that one would expect from a fourteen or fifteen-year-old. "There will be no charge for my services. Please show me to your mother."

Billy opened her door. Inside the chamber, Mrs. Wilson was asleep in her bed, the purloined praying figures beside her, about head-high.

Curtains of some dark but fading hue were drawn to darken the room. I had no instruments, but even without them, Mrs. Wilson, I immediately knew with a touch to her forehead, was a very sick woman. "Holmes, this woman is burning with fever. She has profound swelling on the right side of her throat, and the side of her face – all signs of infection." Without a stethoscope I had to lean my ear on her chest. Her breathing was shallow, but the lungs sounded clear. "Not pneumonia, at least," I could pronounce. My examination had roused the woman, and she began to speak, but what she said was nonsensical.

"Delirium. We are going to have to bring down the fever. Billy, do you have a bathing tub?"

"We do. It's in the other bedroom."

"Good. Please show my companions where it is, and they will place it next to the kitchen sink. Now, here," I continued, reaching into a trouser pocket, "are two sovereigns. I want you and Thomas to go downstairs. You will find Mr. Forney and a brougham on the street. Tell him to take you to the nearest pharmacy. You will buy six ounces of salicylic acid powder, and a package of gauze pads." I scribbled a note in my pocket notebook, tore it out and handed it to the lad. "Here, give this to the pharmacist. Come right back with it. Knock before you re-enter the rooms."

"I understand, Dr. Watson."

Quickly the boys were gone on their errand. Once the door had closed behind them, I instructed Holmes and Brother Innocent how they would assist me. "We first fill the tub with cold water."

"Only one spigot, it will obviously be cold," Holmes remarked.

"And while I fill the tub, you two will undress the woman and carry her here to the tub."

"Dr. Watson," Brother Innocent said hesitantly, "It should be better, I think, that I fill the tub and you . . . ."

"Bull rot! I ejaculated. "Aren't you some sort of soldier of the church? Soldiers execute their missions, just as you will do now. Think about saving the woman – what she means to those boys. We haven't time for petty modesty."

"Of course," he confessed. "I was being stupid."

"Well," said I, on second thought, "you may leave her in her undergarments. The nightdress and stockings can come off."

In a matter of minutes, we gently placed down the woman in the tub, continuing to fill it with water. I found a small pot, and used it to pour water over the woman's head and shoulders. The water came from the spigot a bit rusty. Cast iron pipes, I thought. At least the tenants here are spared lead poisoning. Meanwhile, Holmes loaded the stove with the coal Billy brought, and the room temperature rose to tolerable.

We waited apprehensively, but after twenty minutes or so, she began to rouse, became conscious of her surroundings, and looked at me with understandable trepidation. I leaned over. "Mrs. Wilson, I am Doctor John Watson. We were here with Brother Innocent for a home visit and found you to be quite ill. You had a very bad fever, and that is why you're in the tub. Is the water feeling too cold for you?"

Opening her eyes wider to look about the room, she asked, weakly, "Where are my sons? Brother Innocent, I am embarrassed I have put you through this ordeal."

"Not to worry, Mrs. Wilson," the good Brother said gently. "All that matters is that you recover."

"We have sent your boys out for some medicine, madam," said I, "and we expect their return soon."

"Thank you, sir," she replied. "I don't know how I can repay your kindness."

"We'll let you soak another few minutes," I told her, "then you can return to your bed, and I can finish your examination. Have you a robe?"

"It hangs on the back of the door to my room." Brother Innocent retrieved her robe and draped it over her shoulders as Holmes and I assisted her to stand, step out of the tub, and return to her bed. Reaching the bedside, she noticed for the first time the two kneeling figures next to it. "My word," she professed, "where did those come from?"

Brother Innocent spoke up. "Now I do know what to say, Mr. Holmes. Mrs. Wilson, they are a gift from your boys. They were helping the Holy Spirit to make you well, and together, they have been magnificent."

A series of raps announced the brothers' return. I took the supplies they purchased and went directly to Mrs. Wilson, pausing only to fill a cup of water to use to administer the salicylic. I found the cause of her illness to be an infection in the lower jaw, most likely due to an impacted tooth. I relieved some of the pressure, again because of the lack of instruments, with a toothpick. In the morning, I told her, I was coming to take her to St. Mary's where, despite it being Christmas Day, there would be an oral specialist who would give her the proper treatment. Finally I instructed her on the further doses of salicylic she was to take.

With the woman now resting comfortably, and confident the drug would do its job, I returned to the main room, where there was a discussion in progress concerning the figurines. With Mrs. Wilson out of danger, the boys agreed the shepherd and Mary could return to the manger, their work at 337 G being completed. With Mrs. Wilson's blessing, we removed first Mary and then the shepherd and hauled them down to the brougham. It took all three of us to carefully negotiate the stairs, impressing us that the boys were able to transport them and carry them up without assistance.

Holmes attributed it to great determination. Mr. Forney was sworn to secrecy concerning the entirety of the day's activities, and we returned to St. Francis.

Brother Innocent went off in search of the Monsignor while Holmes, Forney, and I restored the statues to their proper points of occupancy within the manger.

Soon Brother Innocent came after us, saying the Monsignor was overjoyed by the recovery of the figurines, but was wanting to see us. There were questions he wanted to put to us.

"It is a miracle, your recovering the Nativity pieces, Mr. Holmes," began the Monsignor once we joined him in his library, and he motioned us to chairs, "but I must know how you came to do it. Where did you find them? Who took them?"

"We've heard a confession, and granted absolution, and so Monsignor," Holmes chortled, "I am not at liberty to divulge that information. Let us just say they fulfilled a special spiritual purpose, and now they will continue to put Christmas in the hearts of all believers."

"Very cryptic, Mr. Holmes," the Monsignor said as he took a cheque-book from his desk and began to write. "I hope this will be sufficient compensation for the fine work you did for St. Francis." He handed Holmes the cheque.

It looked at first as Holmes was going to refuse it, but after a moment or two, he put it in his breast pocket. "Thank you very much, Monsignor. I think I have just the perfect use for it."

"Well, now, Brother Innocent, Mr. Holmes deflects my questions. Are you sure you're not all hiding something?"

"Monsignor, in this you must forgive me. I am, and have since the day of my birth, been perfectly innocent!" We were still laughing when the Monsignor rose, and we with him, to shake hands. Warmly smiling, the Monsignor wished us both "Merry Christmas," and we bade the Monsignor and Brother Innocent the same tiding.

On Pottery Lane, Mr. Forney was waiting to carry us home. A minute into the trip, Holmes took out the cheque the Monsignor had presented him. Holding it up so that I could see it, he said, "Fifty Pounds, Watson! Not a fortune, but a fair recompense for the small effort. You, it seems again, had more to do bringing about the favourable outcome than I."

"I didn't do very much, Holmes," I protested.

"Of course you did. You saved the boys' mother."

"Infections can become fatal. Thankfully, her condition is no longer life-threatening, and tomorrow, with the proper treatment, the episode will soon be forgotten."

"I doubt that Brother Innocent or the boys will be forgetting anything, my good man. I must tell you, while you were ministering to Mrs. Wilson, and I and the others were negotiating for the release from custody of the shepherd and Holy Mother, a thought crept into my head. Mrs. Hudson is aging, Watson. You've seen lately how she has been struggling on the stairs – especially these days, with larger numbers of clients at our door."

"Yes, go on."

"I think the time has come we hire a page – at my expense, of course – to see clients up. He could also run errands, handle the post, bring up the papers, do some of Mrs. Hudson's bidding, that sort of thing."

"Capital idea, Holmes. You have a certain lad in mind for the position, dare I guess?"

"I do indeed. In the morning, I'll have some words with Mrs. Hudson. Assuming that she has no problem with the plan, I will then accompany you on your return to 337 G. Wilsham, run out my idea, and make Billy an offer of the position. If Mrs. Wilson has no objection, Billy becomes the page straight away!"

"It's a marvelous plan, and knowing that he can thereby help his family, he'll leap at the opportunity." I saw a smile broaden across my friend's face. Holmes was quite pleased with himself, and he had every right to be.

Grabbing his stick, he knocked for Mr. Forney's attention. "Mr. Forney," shouted Holmes, "a change in destination. Do you know the way to Simpson's? On the Strand, near Covent Garden?"

"That I do, sir!" he hollered back, and instantaneously, the carriage lurched, changing direction.

"Are you all right with that, Watson?"

"I am already thinking of the saddle of lamb!"

Holmes rapped again for our driver. "And Mr. Forney, pray tell me, where in Notting Hill can we buy coal?"

The Adventure of the
Grand Vizier
by Arthur Hall

During my long and extraordinary association with my friend, Mr. Sherlock Holmes, we shared many adventures of a nature that I could easily have accepted as having a supernatural or unearthly basis. He, however, would have none of that, always maintaining that every event, no matter how unexplainable or unusual it seemed, would be found in the end to have a perfectly ordinary and logical explanation. Some situations, as my friend was always pleased to point out, were made to appear to be products of the occult or something contrary to natural laws quite deliberately, in order to bring about circumstances that would profit the perpetrator of the delusion. As I search my dispatch box to unearth such a tale at my publisher's request, I find myself drawn to the documented description of one of my friend's cases that has long been overlooked, in favour of the more dramatic incidents that have built his well-deserved reputation.

It was, as I remember, a fine autumn day that found me enjoying my first pipe after breakfast as I immersed myself in the early edition of *The Standard*. Holmes stood gazing down from the window, his face expressionless and his cigar unlit.

"What has arrested your attention in Baker Street?" I asked after a few moments, lowering my newspaper.

He replied without averting his gaze. "I am observing the antics of a most indecisive fellow. Apart from the fact that he appears to be in great fear of something, I can make nothing of him. He has three times made to cross to our door between the passing hansoms, and three times altered his intention at the last moment."

"Is he perhaps pursued by someone from whom he wishes to conceal his destination?"

My friend shook his head. "Unlikely I think. I have been watching him for at least five minutes, and he hasn't as much as looked around him or behind him. No, he is suffering an internal conflict over whether or not to consult us, which suggests that the matter is something of which he is embarrassed or uncertain."

I returned my attention to the newspaper. "Doubtlessly you will tell me if he decides to visit us."

"A-ha!" Holmes cried. "I think he has come to consider us as his best course of action. Whatever his difficulty may be, we are to get the opportunity to assist him. The door-bell will ring within the next thirty seconds, Watson, since he has run headlong between a hansom and a landau in his efforts to arrive on our doorstep." As always, my friend was correct. Mrs. Hudson must have been nearby, since the door was opened before the final peal had died away. We then heard hurried footsteps upon the stairs before she opened the door for the man to enter.

"Mr. Randolph Pindler to see Mr. Holmes," she announced. "I will serve tea in a moment, gentlemen."

"Well anticipated, Mrs. Hudson. Thank you."

Mr. Pindler stood looking confused. His eyes went from Holmes to myself then back again. I concluded that he was in a frantic state.

My friend rose and approached him. "I am Sherlock Holmes, and this is my friend and colleague, Doctor John Watson. I see that you are suffering some anxiety, which I'm certain that we will be able to dispel. There is a slight chill in the air, is there not? The chair on your right, nearest the fire, you will find to be most comfortable. Pray be seated."

I fancied that I saw Mr. Pindler tremble slightly as he took his seat. A small man, clean-shaven except for a rather unkempt moustache, he carried no hat and wore a pea-coat that had evidently seen much service. "Thank you, gentlemen," he said in a wavering voice. "I don't know how yourselves, or indeed anyone, can throw any light on my strange experience of last night, but if you will hear my story, you will at least understand why it is that you see me in such a fearful state."

"Don't distress yourself on that point," my friend replied. "Many fantastical accounts have been heard in this room, but few have remained so after some little investigation. Proceed, please, for you have our undivided attention."

The little man shifted in his seat. "Well, gentlemen, to begin I should explain that I am the night watchman of the Egyptian Gallery at the British Museum. Recently the mummy of a man, not a Pharaoh I think, was added to the exhibits. There was little left of it, so it was displayed upright in a glass case rather than enclosed in an ornate coffin as is usual. Last night, as I completed my first rounds, I noticed that another exhibit that has been on display for some months now was missing from its place. It was the fabled Sceptre of Anubis, and I had hardly recovered from the shock of its absence when I heard footsteps approaching along the adjoining corridor. Thinking that this must be Mr. Thomas Glowry, the curator who occasionally calls in unexpectedly at all hours, I rushed to meet him at once to tell him of my discovery, but I was completely unprepared for what confronted me as I turned a corner."

"What could it have been," I asked him, "that has caused you such distress?"

Our visitor's voice rose almost to a shriek. "It was the mummy, sirs – the one I mentioned. I swear to you that it was walking down the passageway with the Sceptre of Anubis held before it, as if intending to make an offering of it to the gods."

At that moment, after knocking, the door opened to reveal Mrs. Hudson laden with the tea tray. I took it from her and thanked her, and she withdrew after a curious glance at our guest.

After I had poured each of us a cup, Holmes held up a bottle of brandy.

"I believe that a little of this in your tea will help to calm you, Mr. Pindler," he said, before adding some to the beverage.

"Why, thank you, sir. I'm sure it will."

In less than five minutes, the cups were all returned to the tray, and our visitor did indeed seem to have regained himself somewhat. "My dear Mr. Pindler," Holmes began. "Whatever else might be discovered during our investigations, I assure you now that a living mummy will not feature in it. The dead remain dead sir, no matter for how long. Clearly then, you have been subjected to some sort of trickery. Pray tell us of your actions immediately after witnessing this extraordinary sight."

Our guest became downcast at once. "I lost my senses as the apparition drew nearer. I am ashamed to say that I have always been prone to such a weakness. I fainted dead away like a schoolgirl."

"Which, I have no doubt, is exactly what was intended, so that the stealer of the Sceptre could escape unobserved. You see what we have learned already – that the person responsible knew that you would be on duty alone, is aware of the value or significance of the Sceptre, and that you are of a nervous disposition. Therefore, he reasoned, because of this last, some sort of shock was necessary in order to remove you as an obstacle. No, it isn't to the realms of the supernatural that we should look here, but rather to those who are familiar with both you and the museum. A colleague, possibly, I think."

"You dispel my fears so effortlessly, Mr. Holmes." Mr. Pindler looked distinctly brighter. "But I fear that there is something else."

"Then kindly elaborate."

"The curator, Mr. Thomas Glowry, suspects me of taking the Sceptre. Inspector Lestrade of Scotland Yard was called in this morning, and he gave me the same impression."

"Other than the fact that you were present during the robbery, have they any other reason for believing this?"

Mr. Pindler averted his eyes. "Yes sir, I'm afraid they have. Five years ago, I was convicted of stealing from a baker's shop where I worked. My wife and child were starving, sir. We couldn't pay our rent and live on the pittance I earned. I took two or three loaves of bread, and we hadn't had a mouthful each before the constables arrived. My family died while I was in prison, but after my release I managed to find this job at the museum, where I've worked ever since. Mr. Glowry knew of this when he took me on, he gave me a chance that he will be regretting now."

Holmes and I murmured our condolences at our visitor's double loss.

"Very well," my friend said after a moment of thought. "We will see what can be done. You have only to disclose to us any details that you may know about this mummy, and then I think we need to detain you no further. You can be assured that we will spare no effort to get to the bottom of this curious affair."

Mr. Pindler's relief was evident. "I will tell you all I know, gentlemen, but I fear that it is very little. The mummy is always referred to as that of Em-Todeh, and it was discovered during an excavation three years ago at a place called el-Amarra. The Egyptologist who led the expedition was Sir Oswald Hendrie."

Luncheon that day was Mrs. Hudson's excellent shepherd's pie, of which I ate the greater part. Holmes consumed his share mechanically, his mind elsewhere. When at last I laid my knife and fork upon my soiled plate, awareness returned to his eyes.

"We can be at the British Museum within the hour, Watson." He glanced down from the window. "Be a good fellow and pass me my hat and coat."

We had no difficulty in securing a hansom, and alighted at our destination after a journey that Holmes spent deep in thought. We had made no arrangements for an interview with Mr. Thomas Lowry, and had impressed upon our client that he should ignore our presence if he was recalled to the premises on the instructions of Scotland Yard. It appeared as if Inspector Lestrade had already concluded his investigation, for there was no sign of him or his men.

We made our way through rooms of natural history, and galleries of skeletal remains of animals that once roamed the Earth and those that still inhabited places far away. After passing through an array of armour, weapons, and many insights into civilisations long past, we came upon a square room bedecked with Ancient Egyptian discoveries. All signs of activity had gone. We were quite alone in there.

Holmes stood quite still, his eyes taking in the death masks and mummy caskets surrounding us. After a moment, he walked slowly around the perimeter, staring intently at the floor.

"It has been many a century, Watson, since such as these walked the Earth. I take it that this vacant plinth is where the mummy of Em-Todeh formally stood."

I peered at the panel nearby. "That is correct."

He then whipped out his lens, carefully examining the floor and crawling on his hands and knees towards the exit.

"A-ha!" he cried. "Much of it has been disturbed and swept away by Lestrade's clod-footed blunderers, but still traces remain."

"What have you discovered?"

"The remains of the wrongly accused, I think." He produced an envelope from his pocket and proceeded to scrape a tiny quantity of a fine brown leaf into it.

"That is from the body of Em-Todeh?"

"Probably. I shall confirm it later. He is hardly in a condition to steal anything and walk around with it, wouldn't you say?"

"It seems to me that there must be very little left of him. But what was it then than Mr. Pindler saw?"

"We will get to that shortly. For now, let us attempt to follow this hardly visible trail to its conclusion."

He then got to his feet, bending low so that he could continue to see the floor with his lens as he crossed the room to a corner. An unmarked door stood before us, and he looked around for assistance from any museum staff within earshot. Seeing none, he called out twice. We waited, but no response was forthcoming. Holmes gave a slight shrug and produced his pick-lock. The door was opened in seconds.

"The mummy's destination is revealed, Watson," Holmes announced, "but the fate of the Sceptre is still to be determined."

I looked past him into what was little more than an alcove, apparently used for storage. The crumbling remains of Em-Todeh lay in a heap in a corner. Holmes bent to examine them, but stood up more quickly than I expected, to transfer his attention to a bundle of brown paper that had been crushed into a ball and forced into a sack.

"Who has done this?" I asked.

"That we will doubtless discover, but you see what has occurred here? The thief removed the remains of Em-Todeh, leaving a trail of his crumbling body leading to this cupboard, where he hid them. His purpose, I am sure, was to take his place on the plinth until Mr. Pindler's rounds were completed and the opportunity presented itself for him to abscond with the Sceptre of Anubis."

"But," I protested, "how could anyone adopt such a disguise?"

"This happened during the hours of darkness, did it not?"

"During the night, according to Mr. Pindler."

"And, as I'm sure you've noticed, at least half the gas lamps in this gallery have been tampered with. It would have been a very shadowy form that our client saw – if indeed he did see it before encountering it in the corridor after the theft."

"Mr. Pindler didn't mention the lamps."

"He was overwhelmed by what he had witnessed. He would surely have reported it to his superiors otherwise."

"So how do we proceed?"

He consulted his pocket-watch. "It's getting late, and the museum will close soon. I suggest that we return to Baker Street, where I'm sure we will find that Mrs. Hudson has prepared for us an excellent dinner."

We ate our roast pork and apple sauce with relish, I more than he, as is often the case. He did little justice to the following treacle steamed pudding.

No sooner had Mrs. Hudson cleared away the plates and cutlery than he began chemical experiments on the scarred table that he used for the purpose. I retired to my armchair with a glass of brandy and a newly-arrived medical journal until he followed and sat near the unlit fire.

"How was it?" I asked.

"Much as I expected. The powdery substance from the museum floor was indeed part of the remnants of both the mummy and its wrappings, so it would appear that my reconstruction of the theft was accurate."

"But to where does that lead us? Are we to interview the museum staff tomorrow?"

He considered this. "Later, perhaps. First I would like to know more about both this ancient Egyptian and the Sceptre of Anubis. I recall that Mr. Pindler mentioned that the Egyptologist who discovered the tomb of Em-Todeh was Sir Oswald Hendrie, during an expedition of three years ago. Be a good fellow and look him up for me. Our copy of *Who's Who* is just above your left shoulder. His address will be sufficient."

I put down my brandy glass and picked up the volume. "'*Number 11, Cheam Passage*'," I quoted.

"Which is just off Berkeley Square, as I recall. Very well, we'll pay Sir Oswald a visit after breakfast. As for tonight, I'll join you in a glass of brandy as we discuss some of the previous cases about which you have persistently enquired about lately. Afterwards, we should retire early, for tomorrow is likely to be busy for us."

65

Holmes was finishing his breakfast with a slice of buttered toast as I joined him. His expression told me that he had given our current case much thought already and I, also, had ceased to eat before he emerged from his distraction.

"Drink your coffee, Watson. I think you'll find that it has now cooled sufficiently. We will need to make other calls after we have spoken with Sir Oswald, I think."

Cheam Passage proved to be a row of identical houses with pillared porticos in white stone, near Berkeley Square as Holmes had said. I paid off the hansom and we approached the door numbered eleven after casting our eyes around us. Our surroundings were deserted and the only sound was of distant traffic.

Holmes rapped upon the door, which was answered quickly by an elderly white-haired man with the most elaborate moustache that I have ever seen.

"Pray tell me," said my friend, "is Sir Oswald Hendrie at home?"

The old man smiled. "Indeed he is, for I am he. I live alone, you see. I have no need of servants." He stretched out a tanned arm to shake hands with Holmes. "And you are Mr. Sherlock Holmes, I think, and your companion will be Doctor Watson. I have read with great interest of your exploits, which I find almost as fascinating as the mysteries of Ancient Egypt." He shook my hand with equal enthusiasm, before stepping aside to let us pass. "But come in, sirs, come in."

We entered a spacious room with laden bookshelves on every wall. As I had expected, there were souvenirs of Sir Oswald's expeditions all around. When we were seated in the leather armchairs that surrounded a highly-polished table, he offered us port, which we both declined at this early hour. He poured himself a large glass but left it untouched, seemingly eager for conversation.

"I get few visitors these days, gentlemen, other than fellow Egyptologists now and then. My brief moments of fame have passed, and I am largely forgotten. But I have my memories and my books, and the freedom to walk around London if I wish, so I am content." His glance fell briefly on a folded newspaper upon the table. "I have read in *The London Gazette* that there has been some trouble at the British Museum involving the mummy that I brought back from the el-Amarra expedition. Presumably that is why you have called?"

"Indeed," Holmes replied. "And the Sceptre of Anubis has disappeared in most extraordinary circumstances. In order for me to begin an investigation, it is necessary to know something of the background of both the Sceptre and the mummy of Em-Todeh. Both Doctor Watson and myself would be most grateful for any assistance from you in this matter."

"Yes, I see." Sir Oswald let his head fall onto his chest for a moment, as he collected his thoughts. "First I must explain that el-Amarra was the capital established by Akenhaten, the 'Heretic Pharaoh'. He was the ruler who rejected the traditional Egyptian gods in favour of a single deity – Aten. Em-Todeh, as far as we can tell from our studies of the remnants of various hieroglyphics – painted on tomb walls and similar surfaces around the site, you understand – was one of a number of high-ranking officers in the Pharaoh's court, probably what we would recognise as a Grand Vizier, or similar rank. The Sceptre of Anubis was a ceremonial tool already ancient around 1340 BC, the period of Akenhaten's rule."

"Has its significance been established?" I asked.

The old man's face lit up. "It has, and I'm not boasting when I say that I, myself, played a large part in that. The inscriptions, when translated, revealed that the Sceptre was traditionally believed to be the key used by Anubis, the god of the underworld, to unlock the way to transport the Pharaoh into the afterlife. One of the mysteries attached to all this is how it came to be in the court of Akenhaten, who believed only in a single god. It is generally supposed that it was allowed there exceptionally for another person, possibly a concubine."

"So Em-Todeh was made the official guardian of the Sceptre?" Holmes enquired.

"Indeed. He was charged to protect it from all harm, with his life if necessary, in this world and the next."

"My thanks to you, Sir Oswald. Just one more question, if you please, and then we will disturb you no longer."

Our host nodded. "Of course. Please continue."

"Is the Sceptre of monetary value – that is to say valuable to a common thief? Could such a thief dispose of it as he would, for example, stolen pearls or diamonds?"

Sir Oswald seemed surprised at this. "Good heavens, sir, no. It is true that the Sceptre is inlaid with coloured stones, but these are not such as we consider valuable. They are merely for decoration and wouldn't be worthy of appraisal. The value of the Sceptre lies entirely within its historical concept, and is meaningless except to those who appreciate the treasures of history. I recall a similar discussion with Mr. Thomas Glowry, the museum curator."

Holmes and I rose as one, to shake hands again with Sir Oswald.

"My thanks to you again, sir." Holmes repeated as we left. "You have thrown much light on this matter."

We hailed a hansom shortly after emerging into Berkeley Square. Holmes seemed rather pleased with the interview. The frown which often dominated his features in the midst of a case was, I noticed, entirely absent.

"It went well, then?" I remarked, to encourage him to speak.

"It was satisfactory."

"But what, apart from some interesting history, did we actually learn?"

"The essence of the entire conversation was concentrated on my final question."

"I cannot follow your reasoning."

He turned from observing the passing scene. "We now know that our robber moves within circles other than those of the common criminal. Only someone who appreciates the historical value of the Sceptre would have gone to such trouble to possess it. Also, my original suspicion that someone connected with the museum and Egyptology is confirmed, for what would a commonplace thief want with something that he couldn't dispose of profitably? Sir Oswald stated as much – the Sceptre has no value except to someone who appreciates its historical significance. We are looking for a collector of sorts, I think."

We alighted near the entrance to the British Museum. Once inside, Holmes turned away from the corridor leading to the displays and exhibits, following instead a narrow passage that brought us to a number of storerooms and offices. We came to an abrupt halt before a door on which was proclaimed, in ornate script, the name of the Museum Curator.

My friend knocked and opened the door carefully to reveal a chamber lined with bookshelves and pictures of historical or natural significance. A small desk with a typewriting machine, presumably used by a secretary, stood empty to our left. The man sitting at the much larger desk to our right stared at us, surprised at our sudden entry.

"I fear you have taken a wrong turn, gentlemen," he intoned in a hoarse voice. "The public rooms are entered by means of the adjacent corridor."

"Not so, Mr. Thomas Glowry," my friend replied. "Or purpose here is to see you."

"I was not aware that I had an appointment."

"There was no appointment. We are here to put things to rights."

Mr. Glowry showed a flicker of interest. "Who are you, sir?"

"My name is Sherlock Holmes. My companion is Doctor John Watson."

"Ah, the thief-taker. I have read of you occasionally. What does this supposed wrong of which you speak concern?"

"The theft of the Sceptre of Anubis."

"You have recovered it?" he asked hopefully.

"Not yet, but I believe I am close to doing so."

Mr. Glowry sighed, and moved awkwardly in his chair. Against the wall behind him leaned a heavy wooden crutch, and I knew that Holmes also would have concluded that the man was a cripple.

"Very well. Pray sit down and we'll discuss the matter."

We settled ourselves in the upright chairs in front of his desk, and I studied the man as we did so. Mr. Thomas Lowry was tall, heavy-set, and had a sombre expression. His hair was black with the first signs of grey visible, and he was clean-shaven except for his side-whiskers, which he had allowed to grow down to his jawbone. His clothes were worn but of good taste.

"I must tell you, gentlemen," he informed us at once, "that the thief is known to me. The only reason that he isn't at this moment in the hands of Scotland Yard is that I cannot prove his dishonesty, for I am unable, in good conscience, to condemn him on mere suspicion. However, this man has before now been convicted of a crime, and it is difficult to see how anyone else could be responsible. He was alone in the museum at the time in the course of his duties, and seeks to excuse himself with fantastical stories. I have no doubts that Inspector Lestrade will form the same conclusion, and that will be the end of it."

Holmes had listened intently. "Very much to the contrary, sir. I think the good inspector will absolve Mr. Randolph Pindler, if he hasn't already. Although my investigation isn't yet complete, I have established to my satisfaction that he is quite innocent of any wrongdoing. He appreciates that you employed him knowing of his past, and would never consider jeopardising his income."

"But what of his ridiculous story?" Mr. Glowry was clearly surprised that Holmes did not concur with his understanding of events. "Surely, Mr. Holmes, you aren't of the belief that the mummy of a man dead since ancient times can arise and walk off with one of our exhibits to heaven-knows-where?"

"Not at all. But to Mr. Pindler this appeared to happen. I have already ascertained how it was done. His delicate nervous state played an essential part in the plan, for little strain was required to induce a fainting spell."

"You astonish me, sir." The curator shook his head in bewilderment.

"To your knowledge, Mr. Glowry, has anyone else taken an undue interest in the Sceptre of Anubis?" I asked. "Perhaps someone has visited the display on an unusual number of occasions?"

"Excellent, Watson," I heard Holmes mutter beside me.

After some small consideration, Mr. Glowry explained. "There have been some visitors who came out of curiosity to see Em-Todeh – there usually is with any new exhibit. A few parents with schoolchildren, but on the whole the response had been disappointing. Egyptology is a fascination only to some, outside of those with knowledge of the subject or with a passion for it." He shook his head in a hopeless gesture. "The most frequent visitors, of course, are members of past expeditions and lecturers, and a young fellow from the British Egyptological Society."

I sensed a quickening of Holmes's movements. He leaned forward in his chair, his eyes glittering.

"And who is that, pray?"

"Oh, our regular student of all things Egyptian, Mr. Lionel Watting. I don't think you need concern yourself with him, Mr. Holmes, for his connection with the museum is of long standing."

My friend rose and I followed.

"As I have stated, Mr. Glowry, my enquiries are as yet unfinished. I have every reason to expect a satisfactory conclusion before too long. I thank you, sir, for allowing us this interview."

After that, I can recall only a hurried shaking of hands before we found ourselves once more in the streets of London.

"Is our next call to be on this fellow Watting?" I enquired as we awaited a hansom.

"Most likely, but first I must consult my index. It is, in any case, nearing the time for luncheon, and I recall that Mrs. Hudson was in the process of baking a chicken-and-ham pie as we left earlier. I'm sure that it will satisfy you until dinner, Watson."

Holmes went straight to his scrapbooks upon our arrival at Baker Street, treating our luncheon as a momentary diversion from his purpose. As I consumed my own meal and the stewed apple that followed, I watched him as he kneeled to turn pages and dismiss their contents impatiently.

"Ha!" he cried triumphantly. "I knew the name was familiar to me."

I left the table to peer over my friend's shoulder. He held a cutting from *The Evening Standard* from a few months earlier, with a detailed sketch of a thin young man holding a stone sculpture of a cat.

"At any rate, Holmes, it seems that this Lionel Watting is exactly who he represents himself to be. He is indeed a regular visitor to the British Museum, in one capacity or another."

"I had expected nothing different."

"Do you believe him to be somehow involved in this?"

"I suspect so, but I'll be certain only when we have seen him." Without replacing his scrapbooks he got to his feet and took up his hat and coat. "Come, I feel that we are nearing the end of this affair."

He must have obtained an address from his index, for he had no hesitation in planning our route. We travelled to Harrow, and there we hired a four-wheeler, directing the driver to travel north, eventually passing into increasingly rural surroundings. After several farms were left behind we turned into a well-kept park – the edge of an estate I discerned – but our conveyance came to halt near a long low building of impressive design that stood some distance from the main house. Holmes requested the driver to wait, and we both noticed the movement of the curtains as we approached the single entrance.

"I don't anticipate a friendly reception here, Watson," he said as he rapped upon the door with his cane.

He was immediately proven correct, as the door was flung open to reveal the young man who had featured in the sketch. His expression was hostile and his jaw held rigid in an aggressive stance.

"I know you. You are Holmes, the busybody detective! Why are you here? I should tell you that you are trespassing on the estate of Lord Galtacre, and that I am under his protection."

My friend's expression remained unaltered. "I am flattered that you have heard of me. It's no surprise that his Lordship protects you, since you evidently reside upon his property. However, we are here to request your assistance in recovering the stolen Sceptre of Anubis."

"I have heard of that icon only in the course of my Egyptological studies, but never laid eyes on it" Mr. Watting spluttered, his face reddening with obvious guilt. "Whatever has befallen it is no concern of mine."

"Come now," Holmes said reasonably. "You cannot claim to be innocent in the face of so much evidence to the contrary. All is known. I doubt that Lord Galtacre will appreciate being dragged into the scandal that will surely result, if you don't take advantage of this chance to put matters right. You'll find that it is far easier to deal with me than Scotland Yard."

The young man's angry expression was replaced by a furtive look. "What do you imagine that you have against me? There is no proof that I have committed any crime."

"You may well think that, but my entire strategy is without fault. It is based upon the fact that your preferred newspaper is *The London Morning News.*"

"Such impeccable reasoning," Mr. Watting replied sarcastically. "If that is the extent of your perception, then clearly I have nothing to fear. It might interest you to know that the only newspaper I ever read is *The Times.*"

The door was slammed in our faces, but Holmes wore a grim smile as we returned to the hansom. We were well on our way back to Baker Street, before I asked:

"What is this evidence that you have against Mr. Watting, Holmes? I was completely unaware of it."

"Apart from what we have just learned, there is the bandage on his left wrist, and the tiny remnants of the mummy from the museum floor adhering to his boots."

"I confess to learning nothing except the name of the newspaper that he takes."

"Precisely. I deliberately stated another, and he was kind enough to correct me. I fear that Mr. Watting has not proven to be a very worthwhile adversary.""

I looked out into the street, my attention attracted by the cries of a group of urchins begging outside a bakery.

"I can make nothing of any of this," I admitted, turning to face him.

"Then," he said patiently, "cast your mind back to when we discovered the remains of Em-Todeh's mummy at the Museum. Do you recall that anything else had been left in the same place?"

"Surely there was nothing more in that alcove than a sack of brown paper."

"Indeed. The paper was the costume used by Mr. Lionel Watting to make it appear that the mummy had stolen the Sceptre. It was composed of newspaper cut into strips and dyed to resemble burial wrappings, probably with tea. I noticed that it was spattered with a small amount of blood – hence the significance of the bandage that we have seen. Probably Watting cut himself, either on the sceptre or some other sharp object, during the theft. I recognised the type face used by *The Times* at once, and Mr. Watting's confirmation, together with his knowledge of Egyptology and of the museum, was immediately suggestive, since Mr. Thomas Glowry, as a cripple and the only other possible thief besides our client, is clearly incapable of such acts.

"Mr. Watting, having entered the building undetected, hid in the alcove until he was certain that only Mr. Pindler remained in the building, before putting on the makeshift costume and stealing the Sceptre. He was undoubtedly well acquainted with Mr. Pindler's condition of nervous weakness, and knew that this would result in a fainting spell long before he drew near enough to determine the true nature of the apparition before him. Mr. Watting then rid himself of his disguise in the alcove, before leaving the building unseen. It seems likely that he also knew of Mr. Pindler's past crime that was certain to cause him to be blamed for the theft."

"But what was the purpose of the robbery? Does Mr. Watting intend to keep the Sceptre for his own satisfaction?"

"I think not, but for confirmation I must make a few calls after breakfast tomorrow, and then perhaps a visit to Mycroft."

Holmes began his calls early, for Mrs. Hudson had already cleared away the remains of his breakfast as I entered our sitting room. A *locum* who had temporarily assumed the practice of my colleague, Dr. Mayfield, had struck me as rather inexperienced so, in Holmes's absence, I seized the opportunity to visit his surgery to conduct a check on the fellow. I was pleased to see that the he had managed extraordinarily well, and I returned to Baker Street earlier than I had anticipated.

I had hardly had time to settle myself in an armchair, much less to light my pipe or call to Mrs. Hudson for tea, before the front door slammed and Holmes's footsteps rang heavy on the stairs. He burst into the room and quickly shed his hat and coat.

"I perceive that you have visited the surgery of one of your friends, Watson. I hope all was well there."

I rose, surprised by this unexpected observation. "Is there nothing that can be hidden from you?"

"Many things, I'm sure, but nothing as simple as the traces of mud on the side of your boots and the borrowed medical journal bearing today's date that you have left sticking out of your bag. I know that no such publication was delivered here this morning."

"You never cease to amaze me," I scowled. "Was your own morning successful?"

He lowered himself into one of the other chairs. "Extremely so. I have spoken to several underworld acquaintances, and met briefly with brother Mycroft in the Stranger's Room at the Diogenes Club. Everything is as I suspected and," he consulted his pocket-watch, "as it is scarcely past the hour of three o'clock, I see no reason why this affair cannot be brought to its conclusion this very day. Assuming, old fellow, that you're willing to accompany me."

The second journey to Lord Galtacre's estate seemed shorter than before. Mr. Watting's residence appeared unoccupied as we passed it on our way along the gravel drive to the imposing Tudor manor house that stood ahead.

An elderly butler answered Holmes's rapping on the iron-studded front door. At the sight of us, he announced immediately that his master was not at home, whereupon my friend wrote "*The Sceptre of Anubis*" on a scrap of paper and asked the man to deliver it. A few minutes later we found ourselves in a drawing-room bedecked with landscapes and portraits

73

on every wall, while Roman and Egyptian artefacts stood on marble plinths among the furniture.

For the first few moments we were alone, and then the door was flung back and a short man in hunting clothes strode in. His anger was immediately apparent, the eyes that stared from above the full beard that hid much of his face were filled with fury.

"What is the meaning of this intrusion? Who dares to suggest that I have stolen this bauble? Who are you?"

Holmes answered in a mild, even tone. "My name is Sherlock Holmes, Lord Galtacre. I am, as you may know, a consulting detective. I have been given the task of retrieving the Sceptre, but have not, as yet, accused anyone of its theft. It has come to my notice however, that Mr. Lionel Watting whom you employ, has obtained many works of art and historical significance on your behalf, sometimes resorting to crime to do so." He glanced around the room. "I wonder, how many of these excellent examples are copies, and how many are originals long since thought to have disappeared after theft. I don't think it will be long before the truth is extracted from Mr. Watting during a police interview, and the resulting scandal will swiftly follow. I'm here to advise you to return the Sceptre, and distance yourself from his fate."

The effect of Holmes's words on Lord Galtacre was increasingly evident. His face had turned a deeper red and his expression hardened with anger. When he spoke, the words came out with much effort, as from one who has difficulty breathing. "How dare you, sir! By God, I will not tolerate this!" He raised the riding crop that was clenched in his right hand, holding it as if to strike my friend a heavy blow.

"I would strongly advise against that, your Lordship," Holmes said calmly. "Such an act would do nothing but make matters worse."

"Get out of my house, before I have you thrown out!"

"We are glad to acquiesce, but I should perhaps mention that the official force, as well as myself, are aware of your past dealings with professional art thieves and the circumstances of your dismissal from your club. The outcome of all this is entirely in your own hands."

"Leave my house immediately!"

"Goodbye, your Lordship."

Holmes bid the driver of the hansom that we had procured during the walk towards Harrow to stop and wait for us while he despatched a telegram to Lestrade.

"I've told the inspector that he can safely arrest Mr. Watting," he told me on resuming his seat. "Enough evidence was provided by my underworld acquaintances to establish that the man has used his knowledge to organise thefts before now. It would be interesting to find out how many discoveries have disappeared from the store room of the British Museum before they could be catalogued."

"He has acted as an agent, in that respect, for Lord Galtacre before?"

"So Mycroft assures me. Apparently his Lordship is quite notorious, an obsessive collector of culture. He is singularly ruthless in his methods, often offering large sums to the owners of artefacts that he wishes to make his own. On several occasions, a refusal to sell has been followed by the theft soon after of the icon concerned. It was one such incident, although his responsibility was never proven, that resulted in him losing his membership of his Pall Mall club."

"They wished to avoid any connection with a possible scandal," I said as the driver brought the horse to a halt near our lodgings.

"Precisely. Lord Galtacre is not popular among his peers."

We heard nothing more of the affair for three days. Mrs. Hudson had barely cleared away the remains of our breakfasts when she reappeared bearing two telegrams for Holmes.

"Ah, yes," my friend said as he identified the senders. "Everything has turned out exactly as I hoped."

"I am glad to hear it."

Holmes dropped the torn envelopes onto the unlit kindling in the fireplace. "The first message is from Lestrade. He has looked into Mr. Watting's activities as I suggested and found ample evidence for a successful arrest. Apparently Lord Galtacre's agent didn't cover his tracks well, doubtlessly in the belief that his employer's position made the effort unnecessary. As for his Lordship, he embarked on a long sea voyage, and when Lestrade's men visited his residence they found not a single work of art."

"He must have disposed of his collection rather quickly."

"I would imagine that he had made advance preparations, in case his methods of acquisition ever came to light. Not that it matters now, for Lestrade tells us of a report received from the French police. It seems that Lord Galtacre's first stop was the port of Marseilles, which is the hunting-ground of much of the local criminal classes. Possibly his prosperous appearance caused the attack upon his person, for he was certainly robbed of all that he carried. He did not survive. However, it is expected that the stolen art will soon be recovered."

I leaned forward in my chair. "What of the second telegram, Holmes?"

"That is from our former client, Mr. Randolph Pindler. He thanks us for restoring the faith of his employer, Mr. Glowry, in him, and for the increased salary he has received by way of apology. He also states, and this is especially satisfying, that a plain wooden box was delivered anonymously to the British Museum yesterday. It contained, among much careful packing, the missing Sceptre of Anubis."

"A most satisfactory conclusion to your investigation." I observed.

Holmes reached for his clay pipe and proceeded to fill it from the Persian slipper. "I would agree, old fellow. That being certain, it occurs to me that it has been some little while since we have allowed ourselves dinner at Simpsons. What do you say to giving Mrs. Hudson the evening to herself, while we again sample their cuisine?"

The Mummy's Curse
by DJ Tyrer

The boy in buttons had handed my friend an invitation that had arrived in the post and Sherlock Holmes was holding forth in disdain, jabbing it towards me as he spoke.

". . . an insulting imposition upon my valuable time, Watson," he was saying.

Trying hard not to chuckle at his words, I said, "Holmes, it is intended as a reward for your services in retrieving Lady Montalban's diamonds. I should think you would be glad of the recognition."

"Well, there is that," he conceded, "but, it does seem a waste of my time. Unwrapping an ancient mummified corpse has nothing to offer my knowledge of criminality."

It was the irony of my friend that his status as a great detective offered us many opportunities to experience society, yet he had little interest in other people unless they provided him with a case against which to pit his wits, or information that would assist him in the solving of such cases.

"But it might. You could examine the corpse and conjecture how it was that he happened to die. Or it could be that the gathering will offer you the opportunity to observe some interesting people."

Holmes leaned forwards and steepled his fingers and looked at me with a smile.

"I see, Watson. As a medical doctor, this is a subject that fascinates *you*. Hence your wish that I would accept the invitation so that we might attend together."

I could hardly deny it.

Holmes stood. "Very well, Doctor. You shall go to the unwrapping party."

The horizon was beginning to blotch with inky stains as we approached Dorbury House, the home of Lord Montalban, which was located on the eastern edge of the city where it shaded into the fields of Essex. Our carriage deposited us before the doors of the grand house and a footman ushered us inside.

"Welcome, Mr. Holmes," called Lady Montalban with effusive waves as she joined us in the entrance hall upon the despatch of a servant to announce our arrival. "Welcome, Doctor Watson."

"It was very kind of you to invite us," said Holmes. Although the banalities of social intercourse were anathema to him, my friend could play the delightful guest with gusto.

"It should be a fascinating evening," I told her.

"Quite. Well, come through and allow me to introduce you to our other guests."

She took us both by the arms and led us through to the dining room. Where the long table would ordinarily have been lay a large wooden sarcophagus, the lid of which had been set aside against one wall to reveal a mummy case laid within, gaily painted with the image of a handsome young man, and images of deities and daily life painted in panels down the torso. An empty board had been placed atop two packing cases next to the sarcophagus, which I guessed would serve as the work-surface for the evening's entertainment, whilst a series of side-tables along the rear wall of the dining room had been laid out with an array of light food for our nourishment during the evening's proceedings.

Aside from Lord Montalban and one of his manservants, who was stood to attention beside a platter of sandwiches, there were six people in the room awaiting our entry alongside our hostess – three men and three women. I was most struck by a woman wearing a dark-blue dress and veil that reminded me of my time in India, whose deep and soulful eyes were her only visible facial feature, staring out through a gap between the top of her veil and the scarf that covered her hair.

After providing our names, Lady Montalban introduced each guest in turn as the manservant poured us sherry.

"This is Reverend Dowson. He is quite the expert on Pharaonic Egypt, you know?"

We exchanged greetings, then she led us on to the next guest, a slight young woman with a washed-out appearance who blinked at us with the nervousness of a baby deer.

"My niece, Miss Angelica Bradburne."

"Pleased to meet you, sirs."

I took her hand and was rewarded with a wide and hopeful smile.

Holmes glanced sideways at me, his right eyebrow ever-so-slightly arched, but Lady Montalban was already showing us on to the next two guests.

"Mr. James McKinnon, of the Royal Historical Society, and his wife."

McKinnon inclined his head towards each of us.

"I know you, of course, by reputation, Mr. Holmes. In many ways, of course, our callings, that of the consulting detective and the antiquarian, are quite similar – the way in which we tease meaning out of the disparate clues granted us."

There is no doubt in my mind that my friend disagreed most profoundly with such an assessment, but he held his tongue and offered the man and his wife a genial air.

Lady Montalban then turned to the woman in the dark-blue veil whose eyes had so caught my attention. There was a sudden unease about her, as if she were uncertain how to introduce the woman.

"Hawwa was the . . . *companion* of my late brother, Angelica's father."

"Delighted to meet you, Miss –?" said Holmes, bowing low and guiding one of her henna-painted hands to his lips. I wished that I could discern what emotion flashed in the bright, mysterious eyes.

"I am known as Hawwa. Just Hawwa."

"Delighted." He looked at her intently.

"And, this," said Lady Montalban, "is Doctor Frederick Monksbridge, the man who shall be performing the unwrapping."

"Doctor Monksbridge," I said, "I read your recent article in *The Lancet*."

"And, I, of course, have read your pieces in *The Strand*. Most fascinating." He nodded, appreciatively, at Holmes.

"And, now, our guest of honour . . . ."

I must admit to a feeling of bemusement, until she pointed at the sarcophagus and its inhabitant, and said, "Prince Amunhet of Thebes."

"You will like this, Mr. Holmes," said McKinnon, stepping over to the sarcophagus and pointing at the smaller mummy case within. "The shell that protects the mummy itself is made from what we call 'cartonnage', something similar to *papier-mâché*, but made of layers of linen covered with plaster. Do you know, Mr. Holmes, that, in Ptolemaic times, they often used papyrus in place of linen, and it is possible to recover the strips and read what was written upon them? As I said, detective work . . . ."

"Indeed." Although Holmes looked and sounded entirely civil, I caught the faintest trace of acid in his tone, whilst McKinnon smiled as if complimented.

To forestall the possibility of Holmes loosing a direct barb, I asked the antiquarian what was known of Prince Amunhet.

"Very little. What evidence there is indicates that he was a junior scion of the Eleventh Dynasty some four-thousand years ago, and we know he held a priesthood of Amun at Thebes. His tomb was untouched."

"Until it was uncovered by my father," Miss Bradburne said.

79

"Your tone seems to imply it would have been better had he not," I told her.

"Quite so. You may have noticed my father isn't in attendance at the unwrapping of his greatest find . . . He was a victim of the mummy's curse."

"Mummy's curse?" I couldn't help but echo the words in surprise.

"The reason why the tomb had been left untouched," she said. "It was written upon the entrance – '*Those who disturb the rest of Prince Amunhet shall suffer certain death*'. My father failed to heed the words – and, he died shortly after the tomb was opened and the mummy removed."

She looked around at the others. "All those who took treasures from the tomb or who received them as gifts are at risk. Those of us here today, too – especially you, Doctor Monksbridge."

The medical man chuckled. "Poppycock, my dear. It was a tragedy that your father died but, as I told you at the time, his death was due to the sting of a scorpion, not the ministrations of a vengeful ghost."

"What say you, Mr. Holmes?" Hawwa said from behind her veil, her tone challenging. "I am led to believe you are a wise and learned man. Would you deny the power of the curse?"

"It would be false modesty for me to disagree with you, madame." Holmes paused to consider the point. "I'm forced to take a sceptical view of the supernatural, as it is predicated upon neither leaving evidence nor obeying rules we understand. Of course, if, after eliminating all other possibilities as impossible, a seemingly-supernatural one were the only one left, then I might entertain it as the answer to a mystery, although I would, perforce, hold it then to be within the realms of fact and science and amenable to further investigation and, thus, not meeting the layman's meaning of the term 'supernatural'."

"I think what my friend is trying to say," I interjected, before he could continue his speech, "is that, when one has a scorpion as the plausible culprit in a man's death, it is unnecessary to add in any sort of magic."

"Indeed," said Holmes.

"Quite right." Doctor Monksbridge nodded vigorously.

With a clap of her hands, which caused us all to turn, Lady Montalban announced, "Attention. There is food for those who wish it. Doctor Monksbridge will prepare his tools and, when he is ready and you have eaten your fill, we shall proceed with the unwrapping."

There was a murmur of interest: To see the preserved face of an ancient prince revealed from beneath his wrappings represented a tremendous opportunity.

I believe that Lord Montalban and I were the only ones there with an appetite. Holmes seldom eats much and the others seemed nervous with anticipation.

As we waited, Doctor Monksbridge unfolded a small table and placed it beside the board laid across the two packing cases and proceeded to lay out his tools upon it: A selection of knives, scalpels, and shears. As soon as he was done, he called us over.

"As my good friend is no longer here to complete his discovery of this inestimable treasure, it falls to me to carrying out the unwrapping of Prince Amunhet."

"Well said," called Lord Montalban.

With his assistance of the manservant, Monksbridge removed the cartonnage lid from the mummy case and put it on the floor beside the sarcophagus. They then took out the mummy itself and gently laid it upon the board ready for the doctor to get to work.

Picking up a long and slender blade from the table, Monksbridge used it as a pointer to gesture toward elements of interest upon the surface of the linen-wrapped mummy, indicating where he would cut and the nature of the ancient corpse's bindings.

With a flourish, he then took up a scalpel in place of the long blade and prepared to make his first incision into the stiff-linen bandages that wrapped the corpse. Within minutes, we would have our first view of the ancient flesh concealed beneath – following the evening's work, the prince would be denuded of all his wrappings.

"Halt!"

Holmes lunged forward and seized Monksbridge's empty hand from where he was about to lay it upon the mummy's shoulder, ready to guide and steady his work. The scalpel slipped out of the man's fingers and clattered on the floor as he stared at my friend in startlement. I must admit that the rest of us were equally shocked and perplexed.

"You very nearly became a second victim of the supposed curse," said Holmes.

Monksbridge spluttered at him and Lady Montalban, hands at her mouth, gasped through them, "It's not an Egyptian asp, is it?"

Releasing his grip on the doctor's wrist, Holmes shook his head and said, "No. There is no need to worry about asps, scorpions, or tarantulas here, Lady Montalban."

"Then what?" Monksbridge rubbed at his wrist as he spoke and glared at Holmes for interrupting his moment of glory.

Holmes didn't answer directly, saying instead, "You have removed the wrappings of a mummy before?"

Monksbridge nodded. "Of course. Several times, in fact. Bradburne was skilled at unearthing them."

"And you would say you always begin in the same place." Holmes gestured to where the man had been about to make his first incision.

"Of course. I begin approximately at the centre of the collar bone. It is a good position from which to work."

Holmes nodded. "And you always rest your hand on the shoulder of the mummy you are uncovering?"

"Well, yes. Look, what are you getting at?"

"Your attention was focused upon where you were about to cut, but my gaze was taking in the entire mummy, and I noticed here – " Holmes pointed to the shoulder. " – someone has commenced the act of unwrapping before you."

Looking closely, I thought I could discern what my friend was getting at.

"No! The tomb and the mummy were untouched."

"Until you and the late Mr. Bradburne opened it," said Holmes. "Look closely, but don't touch the mummy, and you will see that the linen bindings have been snipped away in places at the shoulder quite recently. If I might have a scalpel, Watson?"

I passed him one from the folding table.

Holmes used the fine blade to nudge back a small flap of bandage from the shoulder.

"So? A little linen has come loose. What does it matter?"

"It is quite literally a case of life and death. A piece of loose cloth, naturally, would pose no risk at all. But, beneath it . . . ."

Using the scalpel, Holmes drew back more of the linen bandages before guiding out a tiny black object no larger than the nail of my little finger.

"What is it?" asked Mrs. McKinnon as we all leant a little closer, trying to discern the answer.

"A thorn. It was sticking up through the linen." Holmes looked at Monksbridge. "Had you laid your hand upon the shoulder, as is your habit, you would have been stabbed in the palm – with fatal results."

"Your concern is unnecessary. I fully understand the risks and always give myself a dose of the tetanus antiserum prior to commencing work such as this. The effects last for a few weeks and leave me resistant to the virus."

"I am not talking about disease, Doctor Monksbridge, but poison."

"Poison?" He stared at Holmes, then his eyes flickered towards the tiny thorn. I found my gaze aping his. It seemed so innocuous.

"Poison," Holmes repeated.

82

"And you say it is fresh?" Angelica Bradburne asked, hands clasped over her chest. "Might it not have been inserted millennia ago?"

Holmes nodded. "I am certain. Yes, a poisoned thorn would have worked to ensure the rumoured status of the tomb as cursed, but this was placed here only recently, once the section of linen had been drawn back. An ancient thorn would doubtless have dried up long ago and any poison upon it have become inert. This one," he nudged it a little with his scalpel, "is still damp and you are a lucky man, for the slightest cut produced by this thorn would, I am sure prove deadly . . . Just as the poison proved for your friend, Mr. Bradburne."

"You don't mean – ?" Angelica gasped.

"Yes," said Holmes, "Murder and attempted murder."

Monksbridge gasped. "Surely not!"

"Without a doubt."

Lady Montalban let out a cry and her husband the manservant swiftly guided her into a chair.

"Ridiculous," muttered Monksbridge, but his face had grown quite pale.

"I'm sorry to say it, my dear lady," said Holmes gently, ignoring the man, "but given what we have just discovered, I'm strongly inclined to suspect your brother was the victim of murder."

"Surely not!"

He turned back to Monksbridge. "You say it was a scorpion, but others imagined he died due to the curse – I take it you couldn't definitively prove the cause."

"There was a tiny . . . a tiny puncture wound." From the look of him, I thought Monksbridge was about to swoon.

"As might have been left by a thorn? No scorpion visible?"

"No . . . ."

"Did anyone see a scorpion?"

None owned they had.

"But, a thorn..." murmured Monksbridge.

"Chemical tests will indicate what type of poison it is, but should you truly be unwilling to trust my deduction, please, jab it into your fingertip and let us see what effect it has upon you."

The man stared down at the thorn, but his fingers didn't twitch towards it.

"Good," said Holmes. "Very good. Now, we must catch a killer – "

Lord Montalban laughed. "Here? At Dorbury? Surely not."

"Yes," said McKinnon. "Surely, whoever did this was in Egypt?" He sniffed. "Assuming you're right and it isn't ancient."

His wife nodded. "Yes, if Angelica's poor father was the target . . . ."

83

"It's possible that it was emplaced back in Egypt, but did Mr. Bradburne handle the mummy?"

McKinnon shook his head. "I believe not. He looked inside the coffin, of course, but didn't touch it to my knowledge, as he planned to unwrap it upon his return to England."

Holmes gave a curt nod. "As I suspected. Had he been killed as a result of touching this thorn, I'm certain that it would have been removed. After all, if someone else were to pierce his or her finger and die, it might be attributed to the curse, but would potentially lead to the method of murder being discovered. But if he never touched the mummy, he couldn't have died from its effect.

"Further," he glanced at Monksbridge, "you and McKinnon have both indicated that the man intended to unwrap the mummy himself."

"That's correct. I've unwrapped many, but this was his great discovery."

"And did he rest his hand upon its chest in the same way that you do?"

Monksbridge considered a moment. "No. He always took a more delicate approach to it than I." He gave a nervous chuckle. "I used to joke he didn't wish to disturb their rest."

Holmes gave a curt nod. "Then, we can conclude that the thorn was placed specifically to kill *you*." Monksbridge paled further, but Holmes ignored his shock. "Whoever put it there knew that you would be unwrapping this particular mummy and knew of your habit of placing your hand just there. Anyone else handling it – " He glanced towards the manservant, who blanched. " – was unlikely to place their hand anywhere close to it."

There was an audible sigh of relief from the manservant, but Holmes continued without pause: "Likely they knew, too, that you give yourself a dose of the tetanus antiserum, meaning you would be unconcerned by the prick of the thorn, even if you detected it."

He cast his eyes over those assembled in the room. "All of which indicates that our killer is both someone known to the doctor and who has had close contact with the mummy, either here or in Egypt."

"Which means," said I, "that we can rule out native diggers and the like."

"So this isn't some native conspiracy to prevent the ransacking of their ancestors' tombs?" asked Lord Montalban.

"That is correct," said Holmes. "Had Egyptians wished the members of the expedition dead, they might have poisoned their water supply or just attacked the camp. No, this is selective, premeditated, and targeted."

His expression pensive, Lord Montalban said, "Then Mr. Holmes, you must do what must be done." He shook his head. "The less police involvement, the better."

"I will." He took out his pocket watch. "Now, it is late and you have all suffered a shock, so I shall question you tomorrow. Nobody is to leave the house for any reason."

That brought a flurry of nods and Holmes continued, "Tonight, I shall look over the mummy case and see if it has any clues to offer."

Lord Montalban nodded and summoned his servants to escort his guests to bed, save Doctor Monksbridge, whom Holmes asked to wait in the library so that they might speak.

Once the room was empty, my friend looked over the case and mummy.

"Anything?" I asked him.

"No – not that I expected to find anything."

I raised an eyebrow.

"Misdirection. Let the murderer think my attention is here and that he or she may act with less reserve elsewhere."

He took a pair of tweezers from amongst the doctor's tools and removed the thorn from the mummy wrapping, dropping it into a glass vial.

"Best put this somewhere safe. I shall ask Lord Montalban to lock it in his desk."

Straightening up, he said, "Watson, I want you to patrol about outside the house." He slapped me on the shoulder. "I know you doubtless were looking forward to a fine feather bed, but this is necessary. It's possible that our killer will attempt to flee rather than face interrogation, or might seek to dispose of evidence of his or her involvement, and I need you to be there to intercept whomever it is."

I nodded and headed outside. It was a chill night and I had to slap my arms a little as I walked to warm myself.

The moon was a full ivory globe high above, and there were but a few wisps of cloud in the sky so that I had no need of a lantern to guide my way, but could instead walk the perimeter of the house by the bright silvery light. It would have been a quite romantic scene with the pleasant grounds and the gothic decoration of the house, had my presence there not been due to such sinister reasons.

I kept to the lawn as I patrolled about the house, rather than the gravel path, in order to pass as quietly as possible, and where I could stayed near to the trees that edged it so that I wouldn't be too easily observed. After all, if I could see thanks to the light of the moon, so could the killer, should he or she choose to step outside.

Not that anyone seemed so inclined. The entire house appeared to be asleep, and I rather wished that I could have joined them. I suspected that the entire exercise was a waste of time and didn't think my friend thought it very likely that anyone would try to flee – after all, doing so would only reveal him or her, and someone cunning enough to plot such a murder would likely imagine that he or she could outwit the great Sherlock Holmes.

As the night passed, my formerly brisk march grew slower and I took to pausing and leaning against trees as I yawned with the boredom of the night's operation. From my military experience, I knew that this was the greatest difficulty in such situations: Tiredness and boredom led one to cut corners.

Perhaps the killer had thought of just such a thing, or maybe he or she had the sense to sleep first, but it was near to dawn when I heard the soft sound of a sash window opening.

Slowly I headed towards the direction of the noise, looking up at the windows on the upper floors of the house.

I spotted a hint of white and movement and looked at the open window as something small dropped from it. Then, the white-clad arm withdrew and the window closed. I had been unable to see to whom the arm belonged.

Having waited a couple of minutes, in case anyone was watching, I crept over to the bushes beneath the window, horribly aware that I must be easily visible from it.

Even with the moon, I knew that I would have trouble locating anything amongst the thorny leaves, especially without making a noise, so I drew my handkerchief from my pocket and hung it from the bush as a marker, before resuming my weary patrol.

"Good morning, Watson," said Holmes, as I entered the breakfast room where he was just starting his meal.

I sat down before him, asked the servant for a plate of eggs and bacon, and placed a box on the table between us. "This was dropped into the bushes last night. I haven't opened it."

Swallowing, Holmes leaned closer. "Well done."

He opened it and examined the contents, then showed them to me.

"A selection of thorns and a bottle that must contain the poison."

They sat within the padded interior. There were six slots for the thorns, two of which were empty.

"Four thorns, Holmes. Does that mean four more murders were planned?"

"We can only conjecture. They may have been held in reserve in case an attempt failed."

Looking it over closely, Holmes added, "I would be willing to place a bet upon the thorns being from Egypt or Arabia, but beyond that, I doubt our murderer has left us any clues. The box is English and unexceptional."

"So any of our suspects could have procured the box with ease and obtained the thorns from the east, either directly or indirectly."

"Precisely."

As he set the box down and returned to his meal, I said, "I checked which window from which it was dropped, but it was at the end of a hallway, and could have been accessed by anyone."

"And, of course, whoever dropped it was invisible to you?"

"Naturally. All I saw was a brief flash of white, but that tells us nothing – most nightshirts and nightdresses are white."

Holmes nodded, but said, "Still, it might assist us." He pushed his plate away. "I spoke to Doctor Monksbridge last night, but he cannot believe that anyone would wish him dead."

"It must be nice to be certain of such a thing," I said drily.

With a smile, Holmes rose and, saying "Enjoy your breakfast," he left the room.

The others filtered down with a dispirited air at the previous night's unexpected turn and their forthcoming interrogations. Despite his certainty that he had no enemies in the world, Doctor Monksbridge looked quite shaken, barely touching his breakfast.

Finishing my meal and wishing that I had time to lie down after my nocturnal patrol, I stepped out into the hallway. A maid approached me and bobbed a curtsey, saying, "Mr. Holmes requests your presence in the library, Doctor Watson, sir."

I nodded, thanked her, and headed for the library.

"Ah, there you are." Holmes was reclining upon a chaise longue amidst that temple of knowledge. "The box yielded nothing, but your 'white flash' has proven most useful."

"How?"

"I asked a maid to find out the colours of the nightdresses and nightshirts, and the dressing gowns or drapes, of our fellow guests and hosts. Being able to rule out those whose habiliments are not white as the person who disposed of the box is quite useful."

"And were you able to rule anyone out?" I asked.

"Yes. I initially questioned his Lordship's staff, in case one had been asked to dispose of the box and, having ruled them out, we can also of course rule out Monksbridge as the intended victim. I was also able to eliminate our host, who favours regal red, Reverend Dowson, who possesses a pair of blue pyjamas and a red robe, and Hawwa, who has a nightdress of green and a robe of black. We can also put Mr. McKinnon and Lady Montalban lower down the list of suspects, for he affects a brown robe and she a red robe matching her husband's. Although it's possible that one of them ventured out without their robe, between propriety and the chill, it seems unlikely."

"So, Miss Bradburne and Mrs. McKinnon are at the top of your list?"

Holmes nodded. "Two potential white-clothed killers – although in the latter case, it is possible she was disposing of evidence on behalf of her husband, so we cannot rule out Mr. McKinnon and, likewise, we cannot dismiss Lord Montalban entirely, for his wife could have left her room without her robe to dispose of it upon his behalf."

"Still, Dowson and Hawwa seem to be innocent," I said.

My friend nodded again. "So it would seem."

I sighed. "You know, I rather inclined towards Hawwa as our killer."

"An exotic murderess?" Holmes smiled.

"Less that she is exotic and more that the method of murder is. A poisoned thorn is certainly an unusual means of murder, and better suited to someone playing upon a mummy's curse. As a foreigner, she seems more the sort to employ such a method, and I did wonder if it might yet have a connection to anger at the opening of the tomb. As an Egyptian, she might have taken offence."

"A logical surmise, if lacking in a firm foundation in evidence."

"Well, had the evidence not ruled her out, she would have been top of my list."

Holmes smiled. "We have yet to eliminate her, or anyone, entirely from our list. Her guilt might be improbable, but is not yet impossible. What we have learnt so far is merely a guide to our further investigation.

"Speaking of which," he added, glancing at his pocket watch, "our first suspect is due."

There was a knock at the door and he stood, calling, "Enter."

The door opened and Lord Montalban entered. Holmes and I sat behind his Lordship's desk and he sat on the far side, opposite us.

"Mr. Holmes, Doctor Watson," he said with a nod.

"Lord Montalban." Holmes steepled his fingers. "I trust that you won't be offended if I ask you a few questions in order to rule you out as a suspect in this awful business."

I had to force myself not to smile at the way he put the man at his ease.

"No, indeed not. Has to be done, wot."

"Indeed. Now, I know you weren't in Egypt, which strongly indicates you weren't involved in your brother-in-law's death, which would, in turn, indicate that you played no part in the plot against Doctor Monksbridge."

"Thank you," said Lord Montalban.

"Although, of course," Holmes said, causing the Lord's smile to drop from his face, "it is possible that you intrigued with someone else to kill him. I say 'intrigued', but it's highly unlikely. After all, only a fool would invite Sherlock Holmes to witness a murder."

By this point, Lord Montalban looked quite confused, unable to tell if Holmes suspected him or not. I couldn't tell either.

"I wonder if you could tell me about your late brother-in-law?"

Lord Montalban shrugged. "Didn't know him that well. He and my wife weren't that close, and he spent most of his time chasing antiquities and women, so we seldom saw him. What I did see of him didn't endear him to me. Our relationship was . . . correct."

Holmes nodded. "Family."

"Yes."

"And Doctor Monksbridge?"

"An acquaintance, nothing more. He was a friend of my late brother-in-law."

"I think that is all that I needed to know," said Holmes, allowing the Lord to make a grateful retreat.

Lady Montalban was next, and her words agreed with her husband's, save that she expressed warmth for her late brother.

I looked at Holmes after she left. "Well?"

"I believe they are both telling the truth. Add to that the unlikelihood of their disposing of the box and the fact that they would be fools to bring me here to observe the murder attempt, I think we can safely exclude them from our list of suspects."

"My thinking, too. So, we have five left."

Reverend Dowson was the next to enter and sat before us, ill at ease, wringing his hands and gulping nervously.

"Such unpleasant business," he said, shaking his head. "Terrible, terrible. I have been quite unable to sleep."

"Really?" I asked, quickly. "Did you leave your room?"

"No."

"Did you hear anybody else moving about?"

"I cannot say that I did."

"Thank you, Watson." Holmes took control of the interrogation, asking about the man's connections with both the deceased and the doctor, but it seemed he had only a passing acquaintance with either.

"As something of an expert on ancient Egypt," he said, "it seems that he wished for me to see his discovery being unwrapped."

"You may leave," Holmes said.

"Oh, thank you, thank you."

Almost tripping over a low ottoman, he hurried from the room and I looked at my friend.

"Well, unless he is a great actor, I think that he's innocent."

"That was certainly my impression. I asked Montalban about him last night, and there seems absolutely no reason to believe he has any connection to events. So yes, cross another name off."

Mr. and Mrs. McKinnon were the next to enter the library.

"Anything that you have to say to me," said the antiquarian, "you may say to my wife – and vice versa."

Mrs. McKinnon sat primly by his side, and I had the impression she wasn't entirely happy about this shared interrogation. As Holmes would often say, many a seemingly-respectable life concealed its secrets.

"How did you sleep?" Holmes asked.

The antiquarian blinked. "Um, well, thank you."

"And you Mrs. McKinnon?"

With the hint of a shrug, she said, "Well."

"Do you recognise this box?" Holmes held it up for them to see.

"No." McKinnon glanced at his wife, who shook her head.

Placing the box back on the desk, Holmes proceeded to quiz them about their relationship with the late Mr. Bradburne and with Doctor Monksbridge.

"I've known them both for many years, through our mutual love of history. My wife has, naturally, met them both several times. I think that I could, without exaggeration, call both of them my friends."

"And, how would you describe them? As men, I mean."

"Erudite, decent, honourable fellows, both of them," McKinnon said with an emphatic nod. His wife turned to look into the fire.

"Can you think of any reason someone would wish to do them harm?"

"None at all. There might be some professional jealousy in our field, but nobody would resort to violence or murder. Such behaviour is simply unthinkable."

I could see that Holmes held that opinion in little esteem, but he nodded and allowed them to leave, asking them to send Lady Montalban's niece in next.

"Your impressions?" he asked me.

"The man is an ass, but I cannot see him as a murderer. However, his wife definitely knew something. She'd seen the box before, I'm certain of it." Holmes nodded his agreement. "And I suspect that she knew something about what happened last night. I also formed the impression she didn't share her husband's high view of Bradburne and Monksbridge."

"Yes. I'd like to talk to her alone, but her husband is either unlikely to allow it, or to leave her side long enough to facilitate such a conversation."

"Do you think he's keeping a secret for someone?"

"No," said Holmes, after a moment's consideration. "He paid her no attention. I doubt that he's aware that his wife knows anything."

"So we can cross him off the list?"

"Yes."

"But she stays on it?"

Holmes nodded. "She is either involved or knows something pertinent. I'm inclined to the latter view, but we cannot rule her out yet."

"Of course, there is another whose name has gone unmentioned. Indeed, I confess I do not even know his name."

"Really, Watson?"

"Yes, Holmes." I felt a warm glow of pride at having noticed something my friend had overlooked. "The manservant. He was in contact with the mummy."

My friend smiled and I felt the glow brighten inside me. "Very good, Watson. Full marks for observation, if a little late in the proceedings. Yes, the manservant – his name is Walters, by the by – was also on my list." I felt the glow dim. "However, his reaction when he thought he had a close call with the poison thorn was quite honest and, questioning him, which I did along with the other staff, revealed a quite dull and unremarkable man incapable, in my opinion, of falsifying such a natural reaction. In addition, he was here at Dorbury House when Mr Bradburne was murdered in Egypt.

"Of course," he added, "that doesn't necessarily rule him out entirely, but there are more plausible directions to look in before him."

I must admit I still felt a little disheartened when Miss Bradburne entered the library a few minutes later.

"Mr. Holmes," she said with a curtsey, before seating herself opposite us, her hands hidden in her lap, trembling a little. "Doctor Watson."

"Miss Bradburne." Holmes smiled indulgently at her. "This must all be quite distressing for you, learning that your father was likely murdered."

"As awful as it was, murder seems worse than a curse," she said with a sad smile. "Or, perhaps, it was that I had set aside my loss and find it now reopened."

"It's certainly more personal," I said, and she nodded.

"How did you sleep?" Holmes asked.

"About as well as you might imagine." She shrugged. "I tossed and turned for some time."

"You have our sympathies," said Holmes and I concurred.

"Thank you."

I couldn't help but feel it somewhat ungentlemanly to put the poor child to our questions in her current state, but Holmes handled her with masterful tact.

"And, your peaceful rest disturbed, did you happen to hear or see anyone else up and about in the house?"

"None at all."

"Good. Now, may I ask, have you ever seen this box before?"

He held it out towards her and she glanced at it, before looking away. "I've seen boxes like it, although I cannot say if I have seen this specific one."

"It would have been in the possession of one of your fellow guests," I prompted.

"Sorry, no."

Holmes turned the box over in his hands. "It is quite ordinary, isn't it?"

Still looking away, she nodded with a sniff as Holmes laid it aside.

He was silent for a moment, studying her, before asking about her father.

"He was an excellent man," she said in a fierce tone, as if merely bringing up his name were to besmirch it.

"Did he have any enemies?"

Miss Bradburne shook her head. "No. When he died, my only thought was that he was the victim of the curse. I never once considered that he might have been murdered. Never."

The poor girl was trembling.

I felt compelled to interject. "I say Holmes – steady on."

But, he ignored me and pressed on, asking, "And Doctor Monksbridge? He was a friend of your father's?"

"Yes." She looked to the ceiling, as if recalling the past. "He is my godfather, and often we would visit him when in England, or he would come join my father on his digs."

"Can you think of any reason why someone might wish to kill him?"

"No, no, none at all." The words came in a rush.

"And Hawwa? Your father's companion? Might she have harboured either man enmity?"

"No!" The young woman half-rose from her seat, affronted. "You would never meet a kinder, gentler woman than her. I have come to love her as a mother. If anyone is innocent, it is her."

She sank back as if drained of energy, and Holmes smiled.

"Thank you. I am sorry for your distress, but you may leave now. Please ask Hawwa to come in, and be reassured that we shall treat her with gentleness."

She exited as swiftly as she could and Holmes turned to ask me my opinion of her.

"A distraught young woman. A victim in her own right."

"I believe you are correct in that latter assessment."

Before I could thank him, the Egyptian woman entered and Holmes bade her sit.

Although her veil gave her an enigmatic appearance, her eyes flickered nervously from side to side, taking in the room whilst avoiding looking directly at either of us.

"Hawwa, you were the companion of the late Mr. Bradburne. I take that to mean lover, correct?"

She nodded. "Concubine would probably be the word."

Holmes returned the nod.

I had known men in India to take a native woman as a wife in all but name, but never had I heard of one being brought back to England.

"Did you desire to marry him?"

Hawwa shrugged. "He paid my father for me. My wishes were irrelevant."

"Did he love you?"

Her hand twitched up towards her veil, then fell back to her lap and she shrugged.

"Yet his daughter has come to love you."

Although her lips were invisible to us, I had the impression that she smiled behind her veil.

"And I her."

"Could you suggest anyone who would wish him dead?"

She blinked. "No. He was widely respected."

"Were you awake last night?" Holmes abruptly changed the subject and she blinked again.

"No."

"Finally, let me ask, have you seen this box before?"

Her eyes widened, then closed and shook her head and I noticed that her henna-painted hands had gripped the arms of the chair.

"No, I have not."

"You may leave."

I glanced at Holmes, but he gave me the slightest shake of his head and I said nothing.

When she was gone, I told him without hesitation, "She's guilty."

"Really?" he asked with an impish twitch to his lips.

"Oh, come now, Holmes, you cannot tell me you failed to notice the way in which she reacted when you showed her the box. She clearly is guilty."

He didn't answer, but steepled his fingers and looked at the fire.

"I believe that I have the answer," he said. Then, he surprised me by sighing.

"Holmes?"

"I fear that revealing the guilty party may do more harm than good."

"Well, that has my mind baffled," I told him.

"I must consider this a little more. Watson, find Lord and Lady Montalban, Miss Bradburne, and Hawwa and bring them here in ten minutes time."

"Doctor Monksbridge?"

"Let him remain in ignorance, for now."

"Very well."

Precisely ten minutes later, I led the four of them into the library, where Holmes had resumed his position upon the chaise longue.

"You know who killed my father?" asked Miss Bradburne, hands clasped before her.

"Yes, Miss Bradburne."

"Who?" asked her aunt.

"Miss Bradburne."

Lady Montalban blinked. "Sorry?"

"Your niece killed your brother."

"What?" spluttered Lord Montalban. "That's . . . that's simply preposterous!"

"It's the truth," said Holmes, simply.

The young woman looked away, but didn't deny it. She quivered like a fearful deer.

Holmes sat up. "Watson was quite convinced it was Hawwa and, I must admit, she certainly seemed likely – there was no love between her and your late brother, Lady Montalban. Only she seemed to have no reason to kill Monksbridge, and we ruled her out as responsible for the disposal of this box, which contains the poisoned thorns, last night – Although she certainly knew of it.

"But your niece, whilst she made a good attempt at lying to me, gave herself away in her reactions to my questions – words and actions never quite matching."

"I don't understand," said Lady Montalban. "Why would Angelica wish to kill her father? She loved him."

"Perhaps, once. I never met your brother, but whilst you cared for him, I don't believe that he was the kind and decent man that you imagined him, nor the honourable one that Mr. McKinnon described. Not in private, at least."

He stood and began to pace. "Lord Montalban, you intimated that he was not a likeable man."

The Lord coughed, awkwardly.

"And although her husband clearly approved of both Mr. Bradburne and Doctor Monksbridge, it was evident that Mrs. McKinnon disagreed. Woman often have a different view of men than other men.

"And, lastly, Hawwa clearly had no love for the man who had bought her as a lover."

"But wait," I interrupted. "Miss Bradburne was quite fierce in her defence of her father when you questioned her."

She glanced listlessly over her shoulder at her name, then away, again.

"Yes, Watson, only there was nothing to defend. Such an outraged response clearly betokened a sense of guilt. Clearly, her feelings for her father were ambivalent at best. As for Monksbridge, her response indicated dislike there, as well."

"It was me!" cried Hawwa. "I killed him!"

Holmes shook his head. "I approve the sentiment, but no. You may have provided her with the knowledge of the poisoned thorns that she used, but your only real involvement was in hiding the box for her, or perhaps *from* her, last night. I noticed your startlement when I produced the box, yet you were not the one who ejected it from the window in the early hours. No, that was Miss Bradburne. But, although you were not party to her act of murder, I believe that she killed him for you as much as her herself – perhaps more so."

He turned to Lady Montalban. "Your niece was protecting the woman she had come to see as a mother from a wicked man who harmed her. Perhaps she remembered him harming her real mother as well?"

"He was an awful man," whispered the young woman.

"No!" Lady Montalban looked about wildly, as if seeking something with which to disprove the words as lies.

Holmes turned to Hawwa. "Show her."

The Egyptian woman cast her eyes down. "I cannot."

"Show her!"

With trembling fingers, she unhooked her veil and let it fall to hang away from her face. The Montalbans and myself all gasped in shock to see the hideous scarring of its right side.

"When she displeased him, my father took a fire-iron to her. He was a cruel beast."

"I thought that I noticed a hint of scarring behind your veil when first we met and, when your hand went to your veil as I questioned you, I understood and, knowing what I was looking for, it was easy to discern."

Hawwa nodded and Miss Bradburne repeated, "He was a cruel beast."

"So you killed him?" said her aunt in a soft voice.

"Yes. I had to." She turned and lifted Hawwa's veil back into place. "Dear Hawwa never could have saved herself, so I did it for her."

"But Monksbridge?" asked her uncle.

"My godfather knew what my father was like, and not only turned a blind eye, but abetted him in his cruelties to Hawwa and myself."

She began to pace.

"As you said, Watson, a victim in her own right – doubly so, for she shall surely hang for her crime of ridding the world of a terrible man.

"Unless . . ." said Lord Montalban.

"Unless?" echoed his wife.

Lord Montalban swallowed. "We have it in our power to save her life."

Holmes steepled his fingers and looked at him, his expression grim.

Lord Montalban swallowed again.

"How?" I asked, unable to see the answer.

"Only we six know the truth," said Lord Montalban. "If we are of one mind, we may yet lay the blame upon the mummy's curse."

"But what about Monksbridge?" asked his wife.

"Even the great Sherlock Holmes errs at times," replied her husband, glancing nervously at my friend. "We tell him and the others that you were wrong – that the thorn was clearly placed there millennia ago. He cannot believe anyone would want him dead and, I think, will be easily convinced. I'm sure the others will concur."

Holmes didn't speak. As inscrutable as his face was, I was certain there was a conflict within between the justice of the law and that of the avenging angel.

Whatever decision he had reached, Miss Bradburne cut him off as he opened his mouth to speak.

"It matters not." She held up her finger, a drop of blood upon its tip. In her other hand was a thorn – the box was open on the desk behind her.

Hawwa ran to her with a shriek and hugged her, but Miss Bradburne pulled away to stand proudly before us.

"A hat pin may work as well as a thorn to administer the poison. Despite Hawwa's entreaties, I knew I must have the means to administer it if you came to suspect me. My godfather is likely already dead. As for me . . . ."

Lady Montalban gasped and looked at the ceiling, and then at her niece.

"Terrible things, these mummy curses…" she said in a quavering voice.

"Indeed." Holmes said with a slow nod. "Indeed."

The Fractured Freemason
of Fitzrovia
by David L. Leal, PhD

"Are you aware that today is the 24th of June?" asked Sherlock Holmes as he sat in his chair near the cold fireplace. "It is St. John's Day, the feast day of John the Baptist, and one of the principal holidays of the Masonic Order."

I will confess that I did not know the date, and I could not have sworn even to the day of the week. The long-awaited summer was underway, and the days had begun to blend together in their characteristic, dreamy way. I avoided a direct answer by replying, "I have never given the 24th of June, or such a feast, a second thought."

Indeed, very little was taxing my mind that month. No cases had lately occupied the attention of my friend, so to quote the psalmist, Holmes had not called upon me in any day of trouble. My patients were not unduly challenging my skills. The newspapers conveyed no worrisome developments in politics. I reflected that an element of routine, perhaps even boredom, had crept into the summer.

While I enjoyed such days, I knew they could be dangerous for Holmes. His mind needed activity, and without new cases, he might turn again to artificial stimulation of the most destructive type.

His uncharacteristic mention of Freemasonry, however, suggested that his mind was not unoccupied. Could it involve some aspect of a new investigation? Holmes wasn't a member of this order, and secret societies and their rituals were contrary to the nature of a man who treasures rationality. In addition, his personality was not one that welcomed new friendships or acquaintances. His only social activity, if one can call it that, was his membership in the Diogenes Club, which forbade conversation among its grateful members. A new case would be most welcome, I reflected.

Trying to disguise my relief, I replied in an offhand manner. "Holmes, are these Masonic dates attracting your attention for a reason? Might you, the least sociable man in London, be soon undergoing its ancient rites?"

"Do not be absurd, Watson" he replied, although with some good humor. "Can you imagine me with a rope around my neck, a pant leg turned up, riding a goat? Such antics hold no interest for the rational mind."

"I don't know how you can credit such rumors," I replied rather stiffly.

"My apologies if I have offended you" said Holmes, "but fraternal rituals are really something *outré*. You will be interested to hear that I've been contacted by a Freemason, and not just any member. I received by the first post a letter from the Grand Master himself, the Earl of Devonshire, about a delicate matter. He hoped that the police could clear it up, but with each passing day, I'm afraid the deficiencies of Scotland Yard became more manifest. Inspector Lestrade took me into his confidence about this case last week, and he isn't holding up well under the strain. I was already aware of the basic facts, of course, but I couldn't act until the main protagonists engaged my services. And if I am not mistaken, I hear a four-wheeler pulling up across the street."

Muffled sounds were soon heard on the seventeen steps of our stairway, and I perceived that a man was making his way up to our rooms. Our landlady, Mrs. Hudson, knocked on the door, opened it, and announced in her light but still discernable lowland Scottish brogue, "A gentleman to see Mr. Holmes."

The Earl of Devonshire

"Show him in, Mrs. Hudson, show him straight in," replied my friend with a smile. He took the letter in hand and removed a number of books from the couch. "We have assisted members of the fraternity before, but never such a distinguished individual."

I recalled that one of our cases, the Red-Headed League, involved a Freemason. Holmes had immediately observed that Mr. Jabez Wilson was a member. Wilson was taken aback by his powers of observation, but Holmes explained to the surprised man that a Masonic pin was visible on his lapel, contrary to the rules of the order. Mr. Wilson replied that such powers of observation were "really a small thing", to the annoyance of Holmes.

The Earl of Devonshire entered our chambers. He was a tall and elegantly dressed man, with the mien of "*a nobleman who was in truth noble*", but his fatigued face told of recent sleepless nights. His Lordship peremptorily asked which of us was Mr. Holmes. My friend replied in that soothing manner he could instantly adopt, "I am Sherlock Holmes, my Lord, and welcome to 221b Baker Street. I don't believe that we have been previously introduced, but your reputation as an enthusiastic Freemason, not to mention as a supporter of many worthy causes, precedes you. Your letter was rather short on detail, but let me assure you that I will provide any assistance within my power."

99

After an embarrassed pause, our guest said, "I forget my manners, Mr. Holmes, but the stress of the last few days has been extraordinary. I will explain fully, but first I must thank you for seeing me. If I tell you that my closest friend was murdered last week, and the murderer may be someone I know well, you will understand why courtesies are far from my mind.

"As you know, I am the Grand Master of the United Grand Lodge of England. It would be unseemly for my cousin, the Prince of Wales, who was himself initiated into Navy Lodge No. 2612, to lead such a private organization. I have gladly accepted the role, but I have many calls upon my time. The position is an active one and not at all honorary, so I need the assistance of a worthy second. Colonel Alfred Carlton-White admirably led the 12th Indian Lancers and is now my Pro-Grand Master. As such, he presides in my absence and takes care of day-to-day affairs."

"You mentioned my charitable work, which is focused on the good works of the Church of England. The Reverend Tobias Brooks is the Bishop of Barking and directs the Church's largest charities. We have worked together on a variety of causes for many years, and he is also the chaplain of my own Masonic lodge, Quatuor Coronati No. 2076."

"As our landlady, Mrs. Hudson, will soon appear with our tea, I hope that we can establish the basic facts before that happy moment arrives."

"I will get to the facts, but as you will see, this mystery involves both of these gentlemen in a very intimate manner. The murder that I mentioned was of Arthur Savile Garrick, more recently known as the Duke of Lansdowne. We have all known each other since our days together at the Abbey School under the headmastership of the legendary Dr. Thorneycroft Huxtable, MA, PhD, *etcetera*. My unfortunate friend was originally from the English Midlands, but when in London he lived at his mansion in Fitzrovia. His untimely death was a shock that has deeply saddened his many friends. However, I must admit that a recent decision of his caused much dismay among those same friends, and he had even received some threats through the mail. In short, he was converting to Rome, and as a Catholic, he was not only leaving the Church of England, but also resigning his membership in Freemasonry."

After a pause, he continued. "Every Englishman is free to change his religion, and the Sacramental Test Act of 1828 and Roman Catholic Relief Act of 1829 removed most of the old restrictions against members of the faith. He need not have resigned from the House of Lords, for example. Yet his decision was controversial, and many of his friends and colleagues saw it as a betrayal. In their eyes, he was renouncing his faith, his friends, his family, and even, in a sense, his nation. As the twelfth person in line to the throne, he was giving up a chance, however remote, of becoming King.

100

As you know, both Catholics and those married to Catholics are excluded from the line of succession. Not that long ago, a person might forfeit his life for such religious beliefs, and I worry that someone saw his convictions in that light."

"But would anyone see such actions as justifying murder?" I said. "Who would be willing to kill over a decision honesty made by an honorable man?"

"I admit that this reasoning may seem fantastic, yet I can see no other explanation. As you may know, our Masonic oaths do involve some rather gruesome penalties for betraying the order. These are today taken as allegorical, not literal, but it is possible that some unbalanced individual developed the wrong idea. As for religion, we aren't very far removed from times when religious opinions were hotly held, and I don't believe that the embers have completed cooled. Not too long ago, Roman Catholics endured many penalties, prohibitions, and tests. These prevented them from matriculating at Oxford or Cambridge, serving in Parliament, assuming civil or military office, practicing law, or working in the judiciary. My recommendation is to focus your attention in this direction, but of course you are the expert in detection and I should not presume to instruct you. If you require any assistance, my friends the Colonel and the Bishop will help you to explore the masonic and religious aspects of the case."

My friend considered the matter for several minutes in silence. I wasn't surprised when Holmes replied that he would be happy to look into the matter, and that he first required a clear account of the murder and the life of the unfortunate man.

The Earl replied that he himself had discovered the body. They had planned to meet at the Duke's home to further discuss his religious conversion and planned resignation from Masonry. He was admitted by the butler, a middle-aged man named Crockford, and shown into the study. They were shocked to find the man lying on the floor near an open window. A grievous wound was upon his head, and a candlestick lying beside him was smeared with blood.

"The butler rushed toward his master, while I ran into the hall and telephoned my doctor, who lives nearby. When I returned to the room, my friend was dead. The butler relayed his final words, 'It was the sun on the window,' which is a possible cryptic clue to his death. I inspected the window panes and frame but saw no signs of blood. On the windowsill sat a candlestick, a twin of the apparent murder weapon, but there was nothing unusual about it. We saw nobody outside in the garden, although the wall was low and the butler reported that the gate was not always locked."

"What do you know of the butler?" replied Holmes.

101

"He has served his master for two decades and is the proud father of ten children. He replaced Pratt, an old soldier who had been with the family since his discharge from the Guards. I've always found Crockford sensible and reliable, not the sort of man to lose his head in a crisis. He served in the Crimean War with the Royal Irish Mallows and received the Distinguished Service Medal, which should say something."

"Indeed it does, but what do you make of the dying man's last words?"

"I cannot say, but there must be a commonplace explanation. I observed that the sun was bright and the sky was cloudless. Perhaps the light reflected off the glass in such a way as to obscure the approach of the murderer. At the last minute, the Duke may have found the man upon him, leaving no opportunity to defend himself. These words may reflect his surprise at being taken by surprise, so to speak, but I am hypothesizing before assembling all the facts."

"Then I will work on assembling those facts, my Lord, and keep you informed if we pick up a trail."

After he departed, Holmes turned to me and asked what I thought of the clues. I replied that I saw few clues, and those in our possession provided no clear direction. The murder scene, the means of murder, and some possibly misunderstood words seemed like a weak foundation for an investigation.

"Perhaps, perhaps," was his only reply, and then he lapsed into a silence that I knew from long experience would not be broken for at least several hours. To pass the time, I began to read a remarkable account of exploration and adventure by Allan Quatermain, whom I had seen at a rather raucous public lecture some years earlier. Holmes was engrossed in thought and started another of the fine crusted ports he obtained from Berry Brothers and Rudd on St. James Street. By the time I retired to bed, the lamp was down to its wick and I couldn't tell if Holmes was asleep or still pondering the day's events.

Colonel Carlton-White

On the next day, our first step was to interview the Pro-Grand Master, Colonel Carlton-White. We stepped outside into the warm sunshine, hailed a dog-cart, and traveled to Freemason's Hall in Great Queen Street. The ride took some time, as the throngs of people, animals, carts, and carriages that clogged London streets were as thick as ever. The original buildings had seen considerable renovations in the 1860's, but it was a familiar location to me. I led my friend through Freemasons Tavern and into the upstairs offices of the United Grand Lodge of England. We met

102

the Colonel and he took us to the new banqueting hall, an extremely large room where we couldn't possibly be overheard.

He began the interview in a somewhat censorious tone. "I have read your stories, Dr. Watson, and I believe that our fraternity hasn't come across in an altogether positive light. Jabez Wilson is a member of 'Three Golden Balls Lodge No. 1891', which meets in this building and was founded for members of his particular trade. He is an honorable man and well respected among his *confrères*, who scarcely recognize the 'obese, pompous, and slow' character described by your pen. I can only hope that your future portrayals will be more positive – perhaps of a respectable young attorney from a good family and with a bright future."

I was inclined to respond to these comments with some asperity, but Holmes must have decided that conciliation was in order. He responded that, "I have often remonstrated with my friend and colleague about the license he takes in his stories. He feels this is necessary to reach the average reader, whereas I would write these investigations as instructional texts. He may have exaggerated the slowness of Mr. Wilson in order to accentuate my skills, but I hope you will forgive him and allow us to assist you in solving this difficult problem."

This explanation appeared to satisfy the man, even if it caused my face to turn a darker shade of crimson. The Colonel made a grunt that somehow expressed approval and replied, "I cannot exaggerate how important this is to English Freemasonry. The newspapers have only reported the basic facts, but I am worried about what may yet come out. If it is proved that a member of our order killed him, we would see no end to the scandal."

"Is it possible that a member of this order is responsible?"

"I will not deny that many of his Masonic friends were upset by his recent decision. They thought he brought discredit to the order by, in effect, choosing the Roman Catholic Church over this venerable English institution. If a fishmonger had made such a decision, it would be of no consequence. When a member of the House of Lords does so, we should expect reverberations. I was prepared for a certain amount of gossip and mockery, but a murder is beyond the pale."

"Are fishmongers frequently found in Freemasonry?" asked Holmes.

A somewhat surprised Colonel answered, "They do have their own lodge, Cod Lodge No. 3154 at Fish Hall, and there is some overlap in membership between Freemasonry and the Worshipful Company of Fishmongers, which received its Royal Charter in the thirteenth century. The Duke was a patron of the company, but he was involved with many such groups, and I only mention them as an example."

"If not a Freemason or fishmonger, who might have killed him?"

103

"That I cannot answer. I have known him for many years and was a frequent guest at his homes, but I cannot speak to his private affairs. As I understand that nothing was stolen, it may be an act of personal grievance. I would suggest you look in that direction, although you may discover other lines of inquiry as the investigation continues."

"If this act did reflect some enemy out for revenge, why did he use the candlestick, instead of bringing his own weapon? The murder, as it was actually done, suggests an impulsive decision."

"Again, I have no answer to your questions."

"Can you tell me anything about his private life – his business dealings, family, and any particularly close friends?"

"As far as I know, he lived quietly. He had a private income derived from landholdings, as well as funds invested by trustees. I never heard him discuss money, although he was less rich than commonly believed. The family fortune was once among the largest in the nation, but the value of agricultural holdings has declined rapidly in our age of industrialization, free trade, and competition from America. In addition, the old Duke broke the entail and the new but now deceased Duke inherited the estate but with considerably less money than anticipated. Keeping up the manor house and his two London households, as well as continuing the charitable contributions and other forms of generosity appropriate to his position, had somewhat drained his bank balances. They aren't at the level of country squires, of course, but in another generation the family might find itself with more social prestige than ready cash.

"The Duke was a widower with two children, Selwyn and Clare, both now grown and living in London. Selwyn works in the City for a well-known firm, but you will hear rumors of its rather sharp business practices. Clare was frightfully filled with facts at Cambridge and is now an organizer with the emerging Labour Party movement. The Duke spoke of both children with affection, and I heard no whispers of any estrangement. While none can know what is in the mind of another, I would swear that they were as happy a family as can be found."

"I think we would be well-advised to interview these individuals," said Holmes, as we took our leave. "Would you be so good as to inform them of our inquiries? Otherwise they may be naturally reluctant to discuss this case with strangers."

Bishop Brooks

We arranged to meet the Bishop at his see home, Felix Lodge, in Battersea. His curate, a young man who introduced himself as Harold and wore a Harlequins cricket sweater over his clerical shirt, admitted us into

104

the house and led us to the study. The Bishop was a man of late middle age, with a friendly but melancholy mien. He wore pressed black trousers, an over-clean black frock-coat, and a stylish waistcoat with an elegant chain. In every way, he was the very model of a slim, modest, and intelligent English clergyman.

As Holmes wasn't above disguising himself as a man of the cloth, I couldn't help but smile upon seeing the genuine article. My friend never saw the inside of a church with the exception of funerals, particularly for individuals associated with his failed cases, so I'm certain he found the meeting a unique one. I thought back to the Greek Orthodox services for Paul Kratides, the Church of England funeral for John Openshaw, the American Protestant service for Jefferson Hope, and the impressive Norfolk Cathedral funeral for Hilton Cubitt. Holmes enjoyed learning about different rituals and beliefs, although he had little regard for organized religion. In later years, he had even tried to reconstruct the manuscript of Professor Coram, which threatened to "cut deep at the very foundations of revealed religion", but to no avail. The scholarly blade proved rather dull, and I believe that Holmes was forced to reevaluate some of his prejudices. He used to make merry over the cleverness of bishops, saints, and prophets, but I have not heard him do it of late.

The bishop welcomed us to his home and informed us that, "I gave my other servants the day off, ostensibly to celebrate the Western Feast Day of Cyril, Bishop of Alexandria. Please come into my study and we can discuss this most disturbing case in complete privacy."

"I understand that many of the late Duke's friends were distressed by his change of religious affiliations. Do you suspect any individual of taking such a view to its illogical conclusion?"

"I do not, Mr. Holmes. The days of intolerance are well behind us. We read about such times in history books, but no one today believes that violent punishment is merited for even the most heretical religious views. Today, my main chore is to convince a diminishing flock to participate in any way in the life of the church, not to deter the fanatical from excesses."

"Can you think of any individual in your circles who is unbalanced in any aspect of his life, religious or otherwise?"

"That I cannot, although I know little enough about the private life and thoughts of my friends, let alone my parishioners. My mutual acquaintances with the late Duke are all respectable people, hardly prone to assaulting their friends over a Pope. My own theory is that we are on the wrong track – that a robbery gone wrong is the most likely explanation."

This earnest man couldn't believe that anyone he knew was involved, and he seemed unwilling or unable to provide pertinent information about the friends and acquaintances of the late Duke. As the good Bishop continued his well-meaning discussion of alternative theories, each less likely than the other, I noticed that Holmes was losing interest. I knew that my friend would soon stare up at the ceiling, close his eyes, or otherwise embarrass our host. I therefore brought the interview to an end, pointing out that we had a busy schedule and must not keep the new Duke waiting. We stood up and exchanged pleasantries as we walked to the door. Before leaving. Holmes asked where the Bishop's cook obtained her fish. The man was surprised, mumbling that he didn't know the answer and only rarely ate the dish. "It is a point of no account," replied Holmes, and we looked for a cab.

The Family

It was arranged that we would meet the new Duke at his home in Mayfair. His sister, Lady Clare, would also be present.

We rode to the address in a hansom and rang the bell. A maid admitted us, took our cards, and asked us to wait. After almost half-an-hour, we were shown into the Duke's study. His demeanor conveyed an attitude of suspicion, boredom, and superiority. Perhaps to distract us, he pointed to a musical box on a side table and began a dissertation on the subject. "This has been my main hobby for many years, and I am particularly fascinated by the machinery. Artisans have devised mechanical animals that make realistic noises – look at this metal bird that tweets when you open the box."

As the discussion of this unusual hobby progressed, Holmes and I lost our train of thought. Whether this distraction was innocent or intentional, we perceived a need to return the discussion to more productive ends. Holmes cleared his throat and said, "I am fascinated by your collection, Your Grace. Allow me to introduce my friend and colleague, Dr. Watson."

"Of course. May I introduce my sister, Lady Clare?"

"I seem to recall the name," said Holmes. "Were you not involved in what we would only describe as a *fracas* at Cambridge several years ago?"

"Why, yes, that was me," she replied, bold as brass. "I accidentally ingested too much Pedro Ximénez at a Newnham College Gaudy and threw the college cat at my preposterous tutor. I was rusticated by the Principal for the Lent term and spent the time working to advance the socialist 'impossibilist' cause in Clydeside." She sniggered in a most disconcerting way.

Holmes ignored the boastful confession of the sister and addressed the brother. "My Grace, I'm sorry to meet you under such circumstances. It is now our painful duty to investigate the circumstances of your father's

106

death, and I hope you can provide information, no matter how trivial it may seem to you, that will allow us to narrow down the list of suspects."

The man relaxed slightly and replied, "But I know very little of my father's personal life. Even his closest friends were mere names to me. My sister and I had much respect for him, but I wouldn't describe him as warm. His relations with his own parents, as you may know, were strained. Between his father's strict English demeanor and his mother's love of the more open Continental life, he always felt rather unsettled. We were away at school when our mother died, and while father was kind to us in his own way, we had no wish to move back home. Since coming down from Corpus Christi, I have lived in London, but saw father only on holidays and birthdays."

"Can you think of anything out of the ordinary over the last month or two?"

"Nothing at all. My life revolves around the City, and my sister's around her efforts to bring the 'submerged tenth' into politics. Our routines are well established, and nothing has intruded of late, save the tragedy you are investigating now. We shared neither my father's interest in religion nor his love of fraternalism, and nobody from those worlds has entered into our lives, even briefly."

"Everything that my plutocratic brother says is true," added Clare, albeit with a smile. "We had no inklings of danger, and father communicated nothing out of the ordinary to us."

Holmes asked a variety of additional questions, to which the brother and sister provided only the most minimal answers. As the clock chimed, we took our leave and hailed a dog-cart. We were quite hungry after a long day of interviews, so we ventured to Simpson's in the Strand and ate our usual roast beef and potatoes. After a tawny port in the nearby Coal Hole, we returned to our rooms and read until late in the evening. Holmes was engrossed in the latest issue of a Royal Chemical Society journal, while I kept up to date with the latest issue of *The Edinburgh Medical Journal*, edited by Dr. Joseph Bell.

Baker Street Reflections

I awoke early the next day but Holmes was gone. I went to my club and enjoyed an excellent halibut for lunch. At the end, I drained my glass of club claret and walked to Soho's Golden Square for a coffee at Fourmi Bleue before gradually making my way back to Baker Street. When I returned to our rooms, several dozen books were scattered about, and Holmes was lounging in his chair with the air of a man who has been rewarded for his labours.

"I really must commend to your attention the literature on Freemasonry," he said. "It is remarkable for including so much writing that contains so little of value. I have read page after page of esoteric ramblings, dull lodge histories, and fanciful historical claims. Many of the brethren have discovered a longing to be philosophers and historians, even if they are ill equipped for such endeavors. I imagine that the Freemasons who are fond of action, and we can see innumerable examples of Masonic charities throughout London, must be both bemused and frustrated by these dreamers.

"Nevertheless, I have been rewarded by my researches. Despite the order's strict injunction for secrecy, some of these authors have included elements of Masonic ritual and terminology, and that is of the utmost importance to this case. We were all confused by the last words of the Duke, and the police were therefore inclined to dismiss it as a reference to the weather. As you have so often noted, the official police cannot cope with any detail that does not fit within their rather limited world.

"By contrast, I immediately placed myself in the position of the dead man. If he left an obscure clue, that in itself might be important. To my mind, it meant that he *didn't* want to clearly identify his killer. Why? In order to avoid a scandal that would hurt an institution and individuals that he still valued. Unfortunately, that doesn't narrow down the list of suspects, as we know he valued Freemasonry, the Church of England, and his own family members. He would hardly want to cause a scandal for any, so we must turn our attention to the clue itself."

"And who is the guilty party?" I asked.

"I will reserve the answer until our meeting with the Earl," he replied. "But I warn you that the outcome will be less than satisfactory. As with the case of the famous missing racehorse, it may be that no prosecution will be possible."

Dénouement

The next day, we traveled by carriage to the Earl's home in the West End. We were shown in to the study by the butler, where his Lordship – as we had arranged beforehand – was alone.

"I believe I've solved this mystery," began Holmes, "although you will undoubtedly be frustrated by the outcome. I can identify what happened, and why, but you will almost certainly decline to take my findings to the police. I also believe that the victim himself would urge you to keep my conclusions within these four walls."

"Am I to understand that the outcome is consistent with my original fears – that a member of my order is responsible?"

"Quite so, my Lord. I tested thirty-three separate hypotheses until I arrived at the answer. I believe that Lord Lansdowne was murdered by Colonel Carlton-White, and in quite cold blood. Lord Lansdowne didn't want the name of his murderer to become public, however. At stake was the honour of Freemasonry, and to reveal your Pro-Grand Master as the culprit would bring scandal to this group."

"My first clue was the mysterious words spoken moments before his death. While you were busy inspecting the window for clues, I thought it more likely that this sentence constituted a puzzle. He could have easily named his killer, and yet he did not. This indicated that he was protecting either an individual or an institution. I saw no person that he would wish to protect, especially one who had just attacked him. But an institution can itself be blameless yet shoulder unfair opprobrium from the actions of an individual. And because the organization most likely to be harmed by scandal was Freemasonry, which is already viewed with suspicion in many quarters, I concluded that the murderer was a Freemason."

"Lord Lansdowne may have been leaving Freemasonry, but he was a man of the most exacting principles. I believe that it was the work of a moment for him to decide that justice for an individual should be sacrificed for the honour of the many. He wouldn't let a desire for revenge harm his former brethren, whom he loved despite his religious conversion."

Holmes continued. "He therefore gave a clue that the butler would not understand but that a fellow Freemason could interpret. I spent many hours reading historical and philosophical works of Freemasonry. While much of it was useless – some Masonic authors are less discrete about their order than they probably should be – I learned that his words "It was the sun on a window" were more likely to be 'It was the son of a widow.'

"The latter, as you know, is a Masonic reference to a fellow member, an insider vocabulary unlikely to be known by the uninitiated. However, you and Crockford took him too literally and were certain that the answer lay in understanding the play of light on the glass. My guess is that a glare was present, and it gave Lord Lansdowne the idea as he lay dying. It is to his credit that he thought of his fraternity and brethren above any ideas of personal revenge. It is unfortunate that this knowledge must unavoidably be concealed from the world, for this aspect of the case would certainly do credit to your order."

The Earl reflected on these conclusions for a few minutes. When he finally spoke, it was with a voice of resignation. "I can attest that he was an honorable man, and his actions do not surprise me. His decision to convert to Rome was not made from hatred of Freemasonry but his conviction that the Church of England didn't have the authority to represent Christ on earth. This was no mere fancy of his. I knew from my many conversations with him that his new ideas followed from a careful study of the history of religion. He could no longer support a church that was birthed, so to speak, by Henry VIII's creative application of 'till death do us part' in his quest for a son.

"Do you have any other evidence, Mr. Holmes, especially of the type that could be admitted in a court of law?" asked the Earl.

"I am afraid that I do not, although this further justifies our keeping such speculations from the public. My belief about the true meaning of his words couldn't possibly send the Colonel to the gallows. Such a charge could only embarrass the order while not bringing about any public justice."

"You said the Colonel murdered the Duke in cold blood, yet you originally thought that the use of a candlestick indicated a crime of impulse. How do you account for the murder weapon?"

"The Colonel was familiar with the victim's study, which he had visited many times. He would have noticed the candlesticks, which themselves were symbols of the two allegorical Masonic pillars, Boaz and Jachin. He therefore knew that a weapon would be at the ready, and the fact that it represented Freemasonry would make it especially appropriate.

"My Lord, I will leave you with these conclusions and allow you to do what you think is best. Nevertheless, I believe that Watson and I have heard the last of this mystery, which will be officially unsolved. We have brought Inspector Lestrade to positive public attention many times of late, however, so a defeat will do his career no real harm."

Back at Baker Street

Within the hour we were at home, sitting in our usual chairs near the bearskin rug. I had begun to read a mystery novel but was troubled by the outcome of our real-life case. The words swam indistinctly on the page, and I broke the silence by asking Holmes, "If what you said is true, then evil has won and justice has lost. Can there be no judgment for the murderer to face, barring that of the next world?"

"I think that you will find that the Freemasons have their own form of punishment. The responsible members will eventually take action against the hothead, as the murder of a prominent member can hardly be tolerated. I have heard rumors of similar cases, where an offending member was punished by his own brethren. Although the punishments in the ancient charges are now said to be merely allegorical, the initiate learns that wayward behavior leads to 'no less a penalty than that of having my throat cut across, my tongue torn out by its roots . . . my left breast torn open, my heart plucked out . . . my body severed in two, my bowels taken

110

from thence and burned to ashes.' Yes, we may read of a gruesome and fatal accident befalling the man, but you and I will know the truth about the fate of Colonel Carlton-White."

Two months later, the post brought an anonymous clipping about the accidental death of the Colonel while on a hiking trip in the Hebrides. The story (in the typeface of *The Dundee Currier*) reported that he drowned while wading across a river with a rapid current. His traveling companion, a Past Master of Light of Justice Lodge #45 in Skye, was unable to rescue him.

The Bleeding Heart Mystery
by Paula Hammond

Holmes was lounging on the sofa, his tall, spare form swaddled in a purple dressing gown, his long, thin hands moving with grace and precision. I'm no musician, but I didn't need my companion's unique skills to guess that he was replaying, in his mind's-eye, Sarasate's *Zigeunerweisen*, which we had heard performed at St. Johns' Square the previous evening.

In such reveries, Holmes was no longer the man I had so often caricatured in my case notes. Instead, his keen features were transformed. With eyes closed and a gently smiling face he was, at that moment, at the zenith of the metronome's swing. I knew that, in an instant, the pendulum could swing back and my dear friend would once again be the determined sleuth-hound of fond acquaintance.

"My dear Watson" he said lazily, "do be seated. Mrs. Hudson has been in a whirl all morning, and should you continue to lurk in the doorway I fear she will be compelled to sweep you up."

I'd often heard Holmes's clients tell their extraordinary stories, but now that I was possessed of a tale of my own, I found it wasn't such an easy task. So there I remained, paused on the threshold, contemplating how best to broach the subject.

Something about my inaction caught Holmes's interest and he bolted upright, every inch the detective once again. "I take it from your attitude that this morning's excursion to Leather Lane was more fruitful than you'd hoped?"

I'd risen early and left our rooms while Holmes was still asleep. I certainly hadn't mentioned any appointments. It was true that, by now, I was used to such remarkable pronouncements from my friend, but my amazement remained.

"I honestly have no idea how you deduced that," I exclaimed to Holmes's evident delight.

"Ah, Watson! The notes on today's expedition are written very clearly. You are, as I'm sure you'd agree, a creature of habit. You generally do your rounds on foot, leaving and returning at much the same time every day. In the evening, you polish your shoes and lay out your bag, ready for the next day. Today you rose early, and leaving your bag behind, took a hansom to Leather Lane."

"But – " I began.

"Your shoes" Holmes chuckled. "They still have their shine. And, as to the location – well that handkerchief you keep in your sleeve, in fine military style, shows traces of mustard. Put that together with the sesame seed on your collar, and I'd hazard you've partaken of a breakfast of that famed Yiddish delicacy, a salt beef beigel. A speciality of Leather Lane eateries."

"I admit to everything you say. But you couldn't possibly know my frame of mind."

"Oh, come, you do me a disservice." Holmes exclaimed, clearly enjoying every moment. "I would be a poor companion if I hadn't noticed your prolonged silences. Your sighs. The well-thumbed text books. You've been vexed by a problem, and it's not too much of a leap to believe that this morning's unusual expedition has something to do with it. Now, my dear fellow, pull up a chair and don't keep me in suspense any longer."

I did as instructed and, in our customary positions, with Holmes on one side of the fireplace and I on the other, I began.

"You've heard, no doubt, of the great American inventor, Dodson Hughes?"

"The whole world surely knows that gentleman's name." Holmes said. "Don't tell me he's a patient?"

"Not exactly. This isn't widely known, for fear of spooking his shareholders, but for the past year Hughes been suffering from increasingly severe bouts of bronchitis. I have a young patient similarly afflicted and I had, in truth, begun to despair of ever finding a treatment which would ease her distress. A few days ago, an old friend from my Barts days mentioned that Hughes was rumored to be working on a new inhalation device. Now, it sounds like pure quackery. Even if he has been haunting the lecture halls, the man has no medical training. But it's a terrible thing to watch a child fade before your eyes and feel helpless to stop it, so I determined to see Hughes and this miracle device of his."

"He lives in the country, does he not?" Holmes asked, his interest piqued.

"West Norwood, I believe, but his workshops are in Hatton Garden, and he commutes to the City regularly to supervise the work. As you know, most of Hatton Gardens' businesses are diamond cutters and jewelry-makers. Visitors are strictly forbidden and, given the nature of Hughes' work, he adheres to the same rules as his neighbors, so that all business meetings are conducted in local cafés."

"Hence the beigal?"

"Indeed."

"And his inhalation device?"

"Still in development," he said. "But you'll be amused to know that he calls it his 'Peace Pipe'! It is only right that after creating so many murderous machines, he should do something to try and save lives. It will, I think, be some time before it enters production and he was violently protective of its secrets. However . . . ."

"That isn't what brought you to rushing back to Baker Street with mustard on your whiskers?"

"No," I laughed. "That was something infinitely stranger."

Sandwiched between Kings Cross and Farringdon, Hatton Garden is one of London's few remaining villages. No doubt its cobbled byways, timber-framed buildings, and tightly-packed lanes will soon be brushed away, as the city continues to replace wood with stone, quaint beauty with brash commerce. But, for now, this Medieval remnant clings determinedly on. Indeed, just as Scotland Yard once belonged to the kings of Scotland, this part of London once belonged to the Bishops of Ely, and is still technically, if not actually, in Cambridgeshire.

It was the great Tudor queen, Elizabeth, who grabbed part of the Bishop's estate for one of her favorites, Sir Christopher Hatton. Down a narrow alley, hidden behind rows of marble-fronted homes, still stands the tiny tavern where the young princess is said to have danced around a cherry tree in the courtyard one May morning. Walk down Ely Place, past the church where Henry and Catherine of Aragon famously feasted, and you enter Bleeding Heart Yard – a warren of dark backstreets that will, with many twists, turns, and dead ends, eventually lead you to Leather Lane. It was there, in a cozy corner of a kosher café, that my tale began.

As I spoke, Holmes leant forward, regarding me with eyes kindled. It was unusual to find myself on the receiving end of such fevered scrutiny and I must admit, it wasn't an all-together comfortable experience.

Fifty-years of age, with a shock of snow-white hair and an overgrown Van Dyke beard to match, Dodson Hughes was a man in whom passions ran deep. Several times during our interview he accused me of trying to steal his secrets. It was only when I'd shared my own researches into the bronchial disease that afflicted him that he visibly relaxed – realizing, perhaps, that I could provide the expertise he lacked. However, our interview had barely begun when the day took a distinct turn for the bizarre.

The café door flew open and a small, red-haired man, blanched with terror, gave a strangled yell and fairly fell across the threshold.

He was gathered up and deposited at a spare table with all the efficacy you'd expect from an establishment that serves all-day breakfasts to the hurried and the hungry. I rose to offer my services, for he was much

114

excited, with the sort of wide-eyed near-hysteria I'd often seen in those who've endured a sudden shock.

"She's back!" he whispered "Back . . . with death at her heels!" The café fell silent. A small clique had gathered around the table, but now, even those who'd remained seated turned to regard the agitated speaker.

"There! There in the Yard! Drenched in blood!" he sobbed, his voice cracking "There will be death. Mark my words! Death!" And with that final cry, he fell into a dead faint.

A waft of smelling salts brought him round and a small brandy did the rest, but the fellow was a mess – sweaty-faced, pale, trembling, and clearly embarrassed to have made such a spectacle of himself. Indeed, no amount of cajoling could compel him to elaborate on his curious pronouncement.

Hughes dismissed the whole thing as occasioned by "too much drink and too little learning". The café owner spoke witheringly of "soft-brained men repeating tales told to keep children a-bed". The patrons returned to their business dealings and the whole thing was quickly brushed under the table.

"I naturally insisted on escorting my new patient to a cab and Hughes – irritable at the interruption – hastened off to his place of business in something of a funk. But there's a mystery here, Holmes! I can taste it."

Holmes raised his eyebrows. "The case does have some interesting elements. Yes. Very interesting . . . If you would permit me?"

He took hold of my left sleeve and proceeded to examine the cuff.

"This stain – was it here yesterday?"

"I hadn't noted it. Oil from the hansom's step, no doubt." I commented.

Holmes said nothing, but I could tell from the flush of his cheek that his keen mind had found something of interest in my curious tale.

"You think there's something in it?"

"Yes" Holmes said quietly. "I do."

"Off to Hatton Garden, then?" I hazarded.

"Naturally! Holmes chuckled. "Who am I to argue with a client? Especially when he also happens to be my dearest friend."

There's been a Bleeding Heart Tavern in Hatton Garden for at least four-hundred years. The current building is a mere one-hundred-and-fifty years old, but its small, round, sunken bar tells of an older history, and of one pub built on the ashes of another. The bricks and mortar may be Georgian, but the design testifies to a time when bears were baited in the pit while the patrons sat atop, drinking and laying bets. Today, it still has

115

a bad reputation: *"Drunk for a penny. Dead drunk for two-penny."* was the disquieting boast emblazoned over the door.

We stepped down into the main bar and Holmes made a bee-line for a rickety table inhabited by a baby-faced man in worn tweed who had the look of one permanently delighted by the world.

Joseph March was what Holmes terms a "cultural historian", specializing in London's myths and legends. How he knew Holmes I never did discern, but then, given how reluctant my flat-mate could be to leave Baker Street at all, the fact that he knew anyone beyond myself and Mrs. Hudson was a source of constant surprise.

"Pleased to see my telegram reached you, Joe", Holmes began. "What do you have for me?"

"Well, Mr. 'Olmes, with your love of the grotesque, I'm surprised you don't already know the tale. It's about a murder too. Right up your street."

Holmes laughed heartily. "Ah, Joe, but you're the expert. Please. Watson and I are all ears."

"Well, you asked if there might be any tales about the area that could account for the good doctor's curious experience. Truth be told, it didn't take much digging. It's a fairly well-known tale, tho' the legend mixes things up a bit. In reality, the supposed victim – Lady Hatton – lived a long life, but of the fact that a murder took place here there's no doubt. Places don't get named Bleeding Heart Yard on a whim!"

March closed his eyes, lent back, and began to weave his tale, his tone, just as a story-teller's should be: Low, warm, and enticing.

"Now, this was in the time of good Queen Bess. Holborn Hill, on which we sit, was still an actual hill, with trees and pathways winding down towards the valley floor. Today that's where the viaduct stands, but back then you would have found the River Fleet. Today, that great waterway is nothing more than a boarded-over sewer, but then it was fast and deep enough for the Queen to sail her barge all the way up to the Clerkenwell. But some things haven't changed. This tavern was still a tavern, not long since built. And the courtyard outside was still a popular place for festivities. And this is where our story starts. In these streets, under these stars, but many, many lifetimes ago . . . ."

One evening, or so the story goes, Lady Hatton was hosting a feast. She was an ambitious lady, keen to impress the Queen and the Court. Desperate, in fact. So desperate that she'd made a pact with the devil. In exchange for one glorious evening – a ball, the greatest names in the land in attendance – she would sell him her soul.

116

This was to be the evening. Everything would be perfect. Every dish, every drink, every moment. And at the centre of it all, there she would be. Stylish. Beautiful. The belle of the ball. At the end of the evening, it was promised, everyone would know her name. She would be the talk of London. Her future seemed assured, and all it would cost was something that she'd never seen and didn't believe in.

Fiddlers! Fiddlers! Fiddle away!
Resin your catgut! Fiddle and play!
A roundelay! A roundelay! A roundelay, I say!
Fiddle, fiddle, fiddle, away!

The musicians strike up a tune. The Lady opens her doors. And the ball begins.

And what a ball! It's like a waking dream. Live birds cut from the belly of a roasted boar whirl aloft, dropping gold leaves into the laps of the guests. Gem-encrusted tapestries glitter under the flickering candlelight. Jugglers and acrobats perform impossible feats. Dancers appear to walk on air. And everyone who is everyone is here.

As midnight approaches, the doors are thrown open once more and the musicians lead the guests out into the courtyard – the courtyard that's just outside this tavern. And as they dance and sing, a strange sound is heard. A deep clattering, like hooves running across the rooftops. But no matter. The party's in full flow and no one even notices the stranger who suddenly appears in their midst. At least, not at first.

Tall, dressed in black, he joins the dance, leaping, bounding into the courtyard. He throws himself into the air, pirouettes, lands with the surety of a cat, then leaps again. He leaps, he pirouettes, lands. Again. And again. The musicians take their cue from him. Faster and faster they play, their fingers getting bloody – seemingly unable to stop even if they'd wanted to.

Here's Lady Hatton, resplendent in white silk and ermine. He grasps her by the waist and springs into the air. Again, and again, and again. Lady Hatton is delighted. Swirling high over her guests' heads, she's laughing, gasping. She glances down and sees the party-goers begin to scatter. She turns, dizzy with exaltation, looks at her dance partner and finally sees what her guests have seen. The devil in all his satanic glory. His hands – claws. His feet – hooves. His face twisted into a wide, wide, smile and, on his head, a pair of vast horns, burning with the fires of damnation.

And the next morning, when the guests returned to see if what they had seen was a dream or not, what did they find? No signs of the sumptuous feast. No signs of the night's revels.

Of poor Lady Hatton, needless to say,
No traces of her have been found to this day,
Nor of the terrible dancer who whisk'd her away;
But out in the courtyard – and just in that part –
lay, throbbing and still bleeding: A Huge Human Heart!

It was just as March had concluded his tale – thumping the table and laughing heartily – that an eerie cry rocked the tavern. Holmes vaulted across the room and was at the door almost before the call had died out. I followed, fast on his heels, dreading, in the thrall of March's singular narrative, what we might find. We weren't disappointed. There, standing in the courtyard by the old water pump, was Lady Hatton herself. Her robes had once been white but now they were drenched in blood. A dark, gaping hole lay in her chest and in her hand she was holding her own heart. She looked at us, smiled with a sort of rapacious desperation, then threw the heart into the air. I scanned the dark sky, but could see nothing, and when I'd glanced back the Lady, too, had vanished.

We stood for some time in the chill air, considering this unexpected turn of events. Holmes said nothing, but in the half-light from the tavern's windows, I distinctly saw him smile.

Needless to say, news of the apparition spread quickly and, within the quarter-hour, the tavern was packed with locals jostling for position at the pewter-topped bar. With ale to loosen their tongues and lessen their fears, there was none of the reticence to speak that the patrons in the café had displayed. The talk was wild, and several times I overheard a newcomer loudly proclaiming that he'd "seen it all" while credulous onlookers *Ooh*-ed and *Ahh*-ed at his tale.

March was as giddy as a schoolboy, jogging from table to table, noting down every half-recalled tit-bit of "the Bloody Lady" in a voluminous notebook. Holmes, no less intrigued, sat quietly, soaking it all up in his own inimitable way.

Eventually the crowds began to disburse and Holmes and I headed for Lincoln's Inn, where the small, green cabman's shelter would be sure to provide a driver looking for late-night trade.

The hansom dropped us at Baker Street just after midnight and, although the day had been long and wearying, I was too eager for Holmes's take on events to feel sleepy.

My companion ensconced himself in the fireside armchair, pulled a cigar from the coal scuttle, and began to puff complacently.

"Well?" I asked.

"Well, Watson?" he replied, grinning at my obvious impatience.

"Well?" I repeated.

Holmes glanced at me mischievously, and I feared we would spend the whole evening in a round-robin of "Wells", when he suddenly he slapped his thigh and burst into a paroxysm of amusement.

"Watson, this has, I think, been one of the most entertaining evenings I've had for many years!"

"Entertaining? Horrifying I would have said!" picturing the lady and her bloodied dress with a shudder.

"Oh, my dear doctor – "

"No, no" I interrupted, hotly, feeling more than a little chagrin at being the subject of so much levity. "I know the great Sherlock Holmes doesn't believe in ghosts – "

"Oh, no, Watson. Please forgive me!" Holmes composed himself. "My humor wasn't aimed at you. And as for whether or not I believe in ghosts, you know my techniques. I deal in facts, not faith. Should someone present me with unequivocal proof of the existence of ghosts, goblins, or even the Easter hare, then I would accept it wholeheartedly. No, as entertaining as this evening's events have been, that's all they've been. Entertainment. A distraction. And very well done it was too."

"But I saw – ?"

"You saw, but you didn't observe."

Holmes walked over to the scuttle, took out a fist-sized piece of coal, and began tossing it in the air. Higher and higher.

I watched intently as the small piece of carbon flew from Holmes's hand, into the air, then back again. "Now," Holmes said, "watch carefully." The coal vanished. I saw it leave his hand – thrown into the air – I would have sworn to it.

"But how?" I ejaculated.

"Simple" Holmes replied, pointing to the carpet where I could see that the coal now lay. "Your mind sees what it expects to see. It expected me to throw the coal, and the smallest movement of my hand was enough to persuade you that's what had happened. But, just like in the courtyard, it's classic misdirection."

"Everyone watches the heart, while the Lady makes her exit."

"Just so. But it's all been misdirection, don't you see? Everything. The piece of theatre in the café and tonight's materialization, everything. You recall that greasy-stain on your coat cuff? Almond oil and starch, I'd vouch – face cream and powder. The tools of the actor's trade. You did note how sweaty and pale the man appeared . . . ."

"But why?"

"Now that is the question. Who knew of your meeting with Hughes?"

119

"I'd written to his place of business several times before he granted me an interview."

"Did you specify why you wanted to meet?"

"I didn't feel it prudent to mention that his new project was being openly discussed. I merely noted that it might be mutually beneficial if we met.

"So it's possible that someone on his staff knew he would be meeting the renowned Dr. Watson of 221b Baker Street, for reasons of 'mutual benefit'."

I began to see where Holmes's train of thought was leading. "But this is all-too wonderful!" I exclaimed. "And the episode in the café . . . ."

"Presumably to stop whatever discussion it was imagined that Hughes and yourself might have."

"And tonight?"

"A piece of last-minute theatricals."

"You think that all this fuss has been to draw my – *our* – attention elsewhere?"

"I think, Watson, that's a question that will best be answered after a good night's sleep."

And with that Holmes retired to his bedroom, leaving me to stare into the fire and wonder.

Bleeding Hart Yard was as gloomy during the day as it had been the previous evening. The brick was dark – slick with grease and soot. The hustle and bustle of Leather Lane was just few streets away, but the close-packed buildings muffled all sound and overhung the narrow passage in a way that made the place eerily claustrophobic.

"March mentioned that the Fleet runs nearby," Holmes said, all the time talking to himself rather to himself than to me. "This pump is rusted solid but doubtless drew water from the Fleet back in the day. Hmm, but now that venerable river has been repurposed, I'd wager that there's a manhole cover nearby. Ah, yes, yes. Here it is. Making a very handy getaway route for our Bloody Lady. And ha, ha! What have we here?"

He threw me an object, plucked from the ground, which proved to be a lump of shiny, red wax. The Lady's eviscerated heart!

"The joke of it is," he said "that it was the elaborate nature of the thing that aroused my interest. If it hadn't been for the command performance in the café, your meeting with Hughes would have been a footnote over morning coffee and toast."

As he spoke, his brows drew into two hard black lines, his eyes shining from beneath them with a steely glint. I saw him glance down at the manhole cover, then back up, seeming to scan the path that led from the courtyard to Leather Lane.

"Look here! It was dry yesterday evening, with a sudden downpour overnight. I'd not expected to find our Lady's footprints, but see this! Hobnails. And look how they've been smudged. The movement of manhole cover being dragged back into place. Someone has been here this very morning. Hmm. I wonder?"

Not for the first time in our long acquaintance, I was confused, and admitted as much.

For an answer Holmes gave a distracted nod. "You know, Watson, I think I may take a short constitutional. Care to join me? Oh, and if you would slip your revolver out of your pocket, I'd be very obliged."

With that, he hoisted off the manhole cover and threw himself into the dark void beneath.

The ladder complained bitterly as I climbed down. Its creaks and groans were such that they created the impression of an army of specters eagerly waiting in the oubliette below. I had to remind myself several times that everything we'd seen so far had been mere mummery.

I was a foot or two from the bottom when the fastenings finally gave way and I was forced to jump the remaining distance, landing hard on my game leg.

The ladder landed on top of me, adding insult to injury, and it took some time for Holmes to help me disentangle myself from the wreckage of rusted iron.

"Are you hurt?

"I'll live," I replied, gingerly testing my weight on my old war injury. It hurt like the blazes, but I was determined not to be the laggard.

Although the narrow tunnel curved above our heads, with many feet of London clay on top, we had no need for Holmes's flashlight. Besides, the dry cell batteries wouldn't last long and, for now, we were better off relying on the fat lamps someone had helpfully hung at intervals along the tunnel wall.

Holmes lit one and the flickering light revealed what he seemed to have already guessed. The route of the old River Fleet, culverted by brick, ran straight for a while, following the path of Gray's Inn Road, before curving down towards the Holborn Viaduct. But there was another passage, which had been roughly cut into the tunnel walls. The work looked to be old and I was reminded that every part of London has tales of such secret passageways. There had been a convent here once. Maybe these had been used by Catholics to escape the wrath of mad Queen Mary? Maybe they were built during the Civil War, or by rum smugglers? Or

121

maybe to allow some rich Lord to visit his mistress unobserved. Who knew? But now . . . .?

Holmes had pulled one of the fat lamps from its sconce and we let its fitful light guide us. I could discern very little in the gloom, though I thought I heard noises ahead. We slowed, Holmes extinguished the light, and for a while we stood, crouched together, in that tomb of wet earth – listening. Yes! Without doubt: Voices.

We edged closer but, in my eagerness, I stepped without thought and my leg, still aching from my earlier tumble, gave way beneath me. I fell with a thud and this time it did not go unnoticed.

A shout. Feet cannon-balling on hard earth. Then, a sound that I shall take with me to my grave. The noise of a lever, much rusted, being thrown and, quick on its heels, a roar like thunder, as a large body of water – the run-off from the evening's storm, now channeled by some unseen force – began to race down the tunnel behind us. Good Lord! Someone had opened the sluice gates!

Holmes pulled me to my feet, but my leg buckled beneath me and I went down again. A rat brushed past my outstretched shoe. Another, then another followed, and as I struggled back onto my feet, I could hear their terrified squeals as they raced to escape the approaching torrent.

With Holmes near carrying me, we backtracked – by unspoken agreement, making for the little passageway we'd seen cut into the tunnel wall.

Even through the water was only still only ankle-deep, the force of its flow testified to the power of the oncoming deluge. Yet, it wasn't the water itself I feared – rather what it would bring with it. A fetid smell had begun to fill the tunnel, and I had in my mind the horrible deaths of the six-hundred-and-fifty people onboard the Princess Alice when it sank in the Thames. Not drowned, but burnt and suffocated by the raw sewage which had been flushed into the river, ready to be taken out by the tide.

Already I was gagging, my eyes beginning to sting, and I knew that should I smell the tell-tale rotten-egg scent of hydrogen sulfide we were dead men.

Finally, with cold fingers doing the work that our eyes couldn't, we found the entrance to the little passageway. Holmes hoisted himself up and I clambered after. I could still hear sounds in the tunnel ahead. For a second, the voices became louder, the footsteps panicked. Then, a cry, long and agonizing, was suddenly extinguished. It was that silence, I think, that spurred me on. The blood in my veins turned to ice, and I ran like the very devil himself was at my heels.

Holmes veered left, and left again, following some instinct or mental map – I knew not which. Dizzy with pain, I followed where he led. At some point he had clicked on his flashlight, but in my fever, I hadn't noticed until I saw his face in the strangely yellow and distorted glow of the bulls-eyes lens, set in an attitude of grim determination.

"There!" He shone the electric torch and, ahead, I saw a little ladder leading up into a brick alcove. He helped me scramble up, following fast on my heels. In front of us was a small wooden door and there we crouched, hammering and hollering as though our very lives depended on it – which at that moment I truly believed they did.

It seemed to me that we spent hours hunkered there, in the dark, with the threat of certain death in every breath. Holmes turned his knuckles bloody with the force of his knocking and, in truth, I thought we were done for. Hoarse, frozen, and cramped, we had just decided to risk returning to the passageway when the hatch opened and a grizzled-faced man, spat, cursed, and hauled us out into the warmth of Dodson Hughes' machine room.

Hughes himself quickly appeared, red-faced and blustering at what he took to be thieves caught in the act of stealing secrets. Upon recognizing myself and, by association, Holmes, however, his attitude became one of studious attention.

"Why, I'd heard of the great Baker Street detective", he said, "But I hadn't known he was psychic! Just this very morning I'd missed some vital documents and, having made the acquaintance of the good doctor, was on my way to consult with you."

The grizzle-faced man busied around. Blankets and hot chocolate were procured and a place cleared for us by the little stove. There, Holmes – though much abused and still wan from our subterranean adventures – began to put together the missing parts of the puzzle.

"May I ask", Holmes said "exactly what it is you've been working on?"

"A gun, Mr. Holmes. A gun like no other. Single-barrel, belt-fed, capable of six-hundred-and-sixty-six rounds a minute."

Having seen what just one bullet could do to a man, there was something horrifying about the evident pride that Hughes' took in his latest invention, but I held my peace.

"And these documents were plans for that gun? But if I'm not mistaken, you've missed them before, have you not?"

"Why yes!" Hughes replied, much amazed. "Played holy hell with the staff. Threatened to get the police involved. I was quite the tyrant for days afterwards!"

"Then they turned up mis-filed?"

"Exactly so!"

"And what about your visitors? The ones you've been lodging at the Bleeding Heart Tavern?" Holmes asked.

"Why, my brother-in-law and his business associate. But how in blazes did you know?"

"It stands to reason a stranger wouldn't be allowed into your sanctum, and any employee who left his post without signing in or out would soon be missed. As to where they've been lodging, well, one of them – a small man, red-haired, with a fondness for hobnail boots and theatrics – left his trail clear for all to see."

Hughes' face turned to a stony glare. "That would be Taverstock. Never met the man myself, tho' Henry – that's my brother-in-law – has spoken of him. Local man. Fingers in lots of pies, and, yes, he does have a fondness for what they call amateur dramatics. Crazy for it, apparently. But I won't believe my own family has been trying to steal from me. George," he said turning to the grizzle-faced man "go fetch Mr. Henry for me. Quickly now."

George, as the elderly engineer proved himself to be, shrugged non-committally. "He ain't here, that's for sure. Was looking for 'im when I heard all 'ell breaking loose and found these here strays."

We could see that the hatch from which we'd been plucked had been hidden away behind a set of heavy shelves and scuffs on the floor showed that they'd moved many times before this morning.

"These tunnels, George . . . ." Holmes asked.

"Ah! I'd heard tales about the vaults and passages that them diamond cutters were said to have dug, so-as to move stock without being robbed. Regular den of thieves round 'ere. Hatton Gardens being in Cambridge, the City police don't have no jurisdiction, see? Can't be too careful. Never would have believed it, though!"

"Are you saying," Hughes' said, slowly, clearly confused, "that Henry and this Taverstock fellow have made off with my plans?"

"Almost certainly. I'd say Henry, having spent some time examining your work and determining which plans were the most valuable, initially tried to have them copied. The doctor's sudden desire to speak to you probably spooked him, so he returned them and decided to bide his time and try again. I'm afraid that our appearance at the Bleeding Heart Tavern yesterday evening may have forced his hand. So he simply stole plans, leaving the way we arrived, meeting Taverstock in the tunnels to make their getaway together. I'd hazard there's a boat moored on the Thames by the sewer outlet at Blackfriars' Bridge."

"Well, good Lord, man! What are we doing standing here? Let's have after them! I'll – "

Holmes held up a hand, cutting Hughes off mid-sentence. "That", he said in a voice, quiet and low, "won't be necessary. See to your sister. She'll need you now."

The weight of Holmes's words seemed to hit Hughes like a brick wall. He reeled, recovered himself somewhat, then nodded soberly. "My God! It's like that, is it? Oh, my poor Edith . . . and the children. Lord, what will I tell them?" He looked at Holmes with a sort of desperation.

"As little as you can. As much as you dare. The police will want to speak to her, but they'll be discrete. I can vouch for that."

"Thank you, Mr. Holmes! I'll go to her right away."

Holmes brushed off any attempts by Hughes to pay for his services and we left the factory in silence, walking once again down Leather Lane towards the small, green, cabman's shelter. There, Holmes turned to me with a look heavy with melancholy.

"Oh, Watson, how I envy you," he said.

"Whatever do you mean?"

"My mind is such that it obsesses over the smallest details. Like a kinesigraph, I see the events of this morning, replay themselves frame-by-frame. I analyze each frame as it flickers past, noting this and that. And do you know which frame sticks most strongly in my mind? The one I see replayed, even now, as we sit in this cab?"

"Why no. What is it?" I asked, alarmed. "Is it something we've missed?"

"No, no. Not at all. It's just a number. A silly, inconsequential number. Six-hundred-and-sixty-six."

"Yes", I whispered, with a rush of that same horror I'd felt earlier. "The number of the beast."

Holmes nodded heavily and tapped the top of the hansom. "221b Baker Street, driver, if you would please. And don't spare the horses."

NOTES

There is indeed a Bleeding Heart Yard and Bleeding Heart Tavern in Hatton Garden.

The cherry tree that the young Elizabeth I is said to have used as a May Pole was in the courtyard of the Mitre Tavern. The tavern is still there and the tree is preserved in the corner of the front bar. It still bloomed until the end of the last century.

The church where Henry VIII and Catherine of Aragon feasted in 1531 is St. Etheldreda's Church. Built in 1291, it is England's oldest Catholic Church, and the only surviving part of Ely Palace, which provided the setting for John of Gaunt's "*This scepter'd isle*" speech in Shakespeare's *Richard II*.

The pieces of poetry that March quotes are from "The House-Warming!!: A Legend of Bleeding-Heart Yard" which appeared in Richard Barham's *The Ingoldsby Legends* (printed in 1837).

In one version of the legend, it is Sir Christopher Hatton's wife who makes a deal with the devil so that Sir Christopher might be a success at Elizabeth's court. In a different account, the victim is Lady Elizabeth Hatton (Sir Christopher's daughter). This version places the murder at Hatton House in 1626, where Elizabeth is murdered by the mysterious Spanish Ambassador, with whom she'd been dancing. When found, her body was torn limb from limb, with her heart still pumping blood onto the cobblestones. Neither of these murders happened but, as Joe says, places don't get called Bleeding Heart Yard for no reason.

Dodson Hughes is based on Hiram Maxim, inventor of the Maxim machine gun. Maxim had a small factory at 51 Hatton Garden where, in 1881, he started work on his prototype automatic machine gun. In 1891, the British army adopted his invention and it was used to devastating effect during World War I.

Maxim did suffer from bronchitis, and in 1900 began work on the precursor to the modern-day inhaler, which he called his "Pipe of Peace".

Hatton Garden has been the centre of the jewelry trade since medieval times and still boasts a tight-knit Jewish community. Sadly, the kosher cafés, where business was conducted, have all but vanished, as gentrification wipes out another piece of London's distinctive character. The area is believed to have a maze of underground tunnels and vaults. How extensive they are, only the business-owners know.

At the boundary of Clerkenwell and Hatton Garden there's still a manhole cover through which you can hear the sound of the River Fleet, which flows beneath.

The torch that Holmes uses was an 1899 Ever-Ready electric flashlight. Samples were given out to law-enforcement agencies as promotion, which is presumably where Holmes acquired his. The name "flashlight" refers to the fact that they were designed to be used in flashes rather than continuously, which quickly exhausted the battery.

The kinesigraph Holmes references was invented by the wonderfully-named Wordsworth Donisthorpe in 1876. A sequence of prints, mounted on a strip of paper, was rolled on cylinders and passed before the eyes at the same speed as the recording, with electric sparks lighting each print. The only surviving results of his moving picture experiments are ten seconds of a scene in Trafalgar Square, produced around 1889-1890.

The Secret Admirer
by Jayantika Ganguly

It is no secret that my friend Sherlock Holmes is a man of great knowledge and many talents. And while he can be flamboyant when circumstances require him to be, he is rather reserved about his skills in general, and it was only after many years of companionship that I discovered most – if not all – of them. For him, it is perhaps not a matter of modesty or shyness – nor does he go to great lengths to hide his talents. It is more a matter of utility, perhaps, of using a skill when required, and if there is no need of a particular skill, it will lie dormant, perhaps hidden even in his own consciousness.

Of course, the one time I managed to have a discussion with him on the subject, he chuckled bemusedly and offered me a glass of whisky (probably in exchange for my silence, though he was too polite to say so directly). We had just concluded a matter which required Holmes to show off his ballroom dancing skills. And while I had been shocked to see him waltzing across the floor like an expert, in hindsight, I realised that it shouldn't have been such a surprise, especially given his musical prowess and fencing skills.

"I didn't expect you to be a better dancer than half the professionals," I ploughed on, determined.

Colour suffused his pale cheeks. "Enough, my good doctor," he replied. "Haven't you amused yourself at my expense long enough?"

I laughed. "It is a rare opportunity." Teasing Holmes was more fun than I had expected. For a moment, I could commiserate with his brother Mycroft, who had told me this.

Holmes poured me another glass wordlessly.

A retort died on my lips as our door was thrown open violently and a large, florid man barged in, his face contorted with rage.

"Which of you is the scoundrel, Holmes?" he demanded angrily.

Mrs. Hudson, who had rushed upstairs in his wake, stood by the door anxiously. My eyes met hers and she raised an eyebrow, silently asking if she should contact the police. I glanced at Holmes, who shook his head. Mrs. Hudson withdrew.

"That would be me, Lord Ellsbury," Holmes said jovially. "How may I help you?"

Lord Ellsbury . . . the name sounded familiar.

The nobleman let out a wild roar and rushed at Holmes, grabbing his collar. I sprang from my seat, ready to defend my friend.

"Stand down, Watson," Holmes said casually. If anything, he looked bored. "It appears that hunting lions in South Africa has left you with the temperament of one, Lord Ellsbury," he drawled.

I suddenly remembered – Lord Norbert Ellsbury, known for his hunting skills, had recently returned from South Africa, where he had been living for most of his life.

"How do you know me?" he demanded, his grip on Holmes loosening.

Holmes shrugged and shook himself free. "It is my business to know things." He smiled ruefully. "Besides, we met in Khartoum a few years ago. You might remember a Norwegian explorer named Sigerson. You were rather kind at the time."

The nobleman reeled back and fell into a chair, his mouth open in shock. "You . . . *you are Sigerson*?"

"In the flesh."

"But then, how . . . ? Why would you . . . ? How did you . . . ? Why did it have to be my Stella?"

Holmes frowned. "I'm afraid you aren't making sense, Lord Ellsbury. Who is Stella?"

"My fiancée!" Lord Ellsbury exclaimed, and glared at Holmes with red eyes. "Lady Stella Aster! You have stolen her from me!"

"I assure you that my responsibilities do not include abduction," Holmes said dryly.

"You have been exchanging letters . . . love letters!"

"Of course not," Holmes retorted. "Watson here will attest to the fact that I am one of the most unromantic humans that he has ever come across, and he knows me better than anyone, except perhaps my brother."

Lord Ellsbury reached into his coat pocket, withdrew a sheaf of papers, and flung them at Holmes. "Then explain these!" he cried.

The papers scattered all around us. A few fell on my shoes as well. I picked them up and glanced at the first one . . . and froze in shock. The letter was rather was signed "*Sherlock Holmes*".

I was quite familiar with Holmes's handwriting, so naturally I knew that this wasn't his hand behind this lovelorn epistle. It was addressed to "*S*". I quickly looked at the second one in my hand. This was addressed to "*My loving Sherlock*" and signed by "*S*" – and the contents were rather florid in their declarations of affection.

Holmes, who had looked through a few sheets himself by now, appeared flummoxed. He glanced up at Lord Ellsbury's red face.

"Lord Ellsbury," he said. "Where did you find these?"

"In Stella's drawer, right next to the letters that she and I have exchanged. She keeps a copy of each letter that she writes to me, and arranges everything chronologically, along with my replies. Apparently she has done the same with the letters that the two of you have exchanged." His voice broke. "I . . . I love her, Sigerson. Please don't take her away from me!"

"Did you ask her about these?" Holmes queried.

"How could I?" Lord Ellsbury roared.

Before Holmes could reply, there was a knock on the door, and Mrs. Hudson came in with a rather lovely young lady. She was well-dressed and elegant, and her eyes widened when she spotted Lord Ellsbury and the papers scattered across the room.

"Norbert?" she asked softly. "Why are you here?"

Colour receded from Lord Ellsbury's face. "Stella, I . . . ."

The lady laughed humourlessly. "I saw when you found the letters and rushed out of the house. You thought that it was I who wrote them. I called to you, but you didn't answer. I heard you tell the driver to hurry to this address – I suppose to tell Mr. Holmes that he should stay away from me?"

Her fiancé flushed.

"I followed as fast as I could, but it seems that I'm too late to stop you from embarrassing yourself."

"Men do foolish things in love," Holmes remarked.

"How true," Lady Stella said, smiling softly. "I apologise for my Norbert's actions. I also apologise for the embarrassing letters. I hope you will forgive them as a child's fantasies. Both of my younger siblings eagerly follow Dr. Watson's accounts of your adventures, and one of them is a particularly great admirer of yours. That is the source of the letters – both those to you and also the fabricated replies. Childish romance. I discovered them and felt that they shouldn't be left lying around, in case our father discovered them. They were never meant to be seen, and they were certainly never meant to be delivered to you." And she turned a frown upon Lord Ellsbury.

"Oh," he murmured. "I am such a fool." Then he turned to Holmes. "You have my apologies as well, Sigerson."

"Sigerson?" Lady Stella's expression changed, and she said to her fiancé, "Your Norwegian friend?"

Lord Ellsbury gave her a boyish grin. "Turns out that he was the great Sherlock Holmes in disguise."

Lady Stella smiled again. "A small world, indeed." She took a seat next to her fiancé and faced us with determined eyes. "Mr. Holmes, now that I'm here, I feel that I should mention that I'm in need of your help. I may be wrong, but I believe that I'm being harassed. Someone has been sending me anonymous letters, written in some sort of unusual code. I assumed that it was initially a prank, but now I feel anxious, especially with another of the notes having appeared just this morning. Norbert and I are to marry next month, you see, and then I will move to South Africa with him. In the meantime, I don't wish for any disturbances."

Holmes pressed his fingertips together and leaned back in his chair. "Pray continue, Lady Stella."

"It started a few weeks ago, soon after Norbert returned to England," she said. "I received a letter with what I thought were a child's scribbles."

"Did it arrive in the post?"

"It did. A plain envelope, mailed from the Post Office not far from my home. I ignored it. However, a few days later, I received another one. This time, my twin siblings – Stephen and Sarah – happened to see the letter and asked me if I had run afoul of an American gang." She paused. "They are young and immature, and I gave no credence to that outrageous statement. However, they continued to insist that it was something sinister, and it was them who suggested that I consult with you, Mr. Holmes. Two more letters arrived after that, which my siblings also asked to see, having kept an eye on the postal delivery each day, and recognizing when one of the letters would arrive. When I received yet another one this morning, they again urgently insisted that I should consult with you. Of course, I had no intention of doing so – but then Norbert's impulsive action led me here anyway.

"Receiving mysterious messages does feel somewhat threatening," she stated wryly. She withdrew five envelopes from her purse and handed them to Holmes.

Holmes examined them closely with his glass, as well as holding them up to the light, and even smelling them. Then he chuckled and passed them to me.

They were numbered one through five, with the figure written faintly in pencil at the left side. I glanced at Lady Stella and she understood my unspoken question. "When I received the second, I thought that it might be important to know the order in which they had arrived."

I flipped through them quickly and was quite surprised, for I recognized these little "dancing men". Holmes's deciphering of them had been one of his more notable, if tragic, recent cases. The first note was simply one word, with the end of a word denoted by a flag:

131

Then is became a bit more complex, with four words:

[dancing men cipher figures]

This was followed by a six-word phrase . . .

[dancing men cipher figures]

. . . and then one of five words . . . .

[dancing men cipher figures]

. . . and finally the longest of all, eleven words:

[dancing men cipher figures]

Holmes shook his head ruefully while I puzzled out their meaning. "These are the consequences of revealing my investigations to the public," he murmured. A shadow swept across his face . . . he was probably remembering our unfortunate client, Hilton Cubitt, whom we had been too late to save. The loss of a client always hit him particularly hard.

I recalled when Cubitt had visited our rooms in Baker Street, bearing similar messages that he'd found around his Norwich home, all apparently left for his wife, and contributing to a sense of growing unease. Holmes had decoded what was being conveyed by these little "dancing men", and we had rushed to down to Ridling Thorpe Manor, but it was too late. However, Holmes used the same figures to construct a coded message that trapped the criminal. The matter had been widely reported in the newspapers, and there were various versions of the cipher that were published at the time. Clearly whomever was writing the notes to Lady Astor had seen them, as I hadn't published my account of the affair – and I was uncertain that I would ever do so, considering the tragic nature of the case.

After I understood what the messages said, I wrote down the decoded text and passed the paper to Lady Stella and Lord Ellsbury for their edification. The five messages (in order) said:

Beware.

Stella I see you.

He is not a good man.

Do not go to Africa.

Danger lurks. Ask Holmes to help or else blood will flow.

Lady Stella appeared mildly surprised. "'*Ask Holmes to help . . . ?*' she said.

Lord Ellsbury, who had been peering over his fiancée's shoulders to look at the decoded messages, exclaimed passionately, "Who dares threaten my Stella?"

Lady Stella put a gentle hand on his forearm and urged the large man to be seated. His eyes glittered fiercely. Good man or not, Lord Norbert Ellsbury was clearly very much in love with his betrothed.

"What do you make of this, Watson?" Holmes asked me.

"Perhaps someone wishes to sabotage their marriage," I said, looking at the couple. "Can you think of anyone?"

Lord Ellsbury and Lady Stella exchanged a meaningful glance.

"I trust him," Lord Ellsbury said quietly.

"Very well," Lady Stella replied. "Then so shall I." She fixed her bright blue eyes upon Holmes. "There are several who oppose our marriage, although I find it unlikely that any of them would resort to such childish methods." She sighed heavily. "My stepmother wishes for me to break this engagement and marry one of her relatives instead. One of my former suitors still writes to me regularly to convince me to change my mind. My siblings dislike the idea of my moving to South Africa." She glanced at her fiancé. "On Norbert's side, there is an actress to whom he was close that still stalks him in the hope of preventing our marriage. Two other ladies who also each believed that they should be his wife are quite resentful. Some of his South African friends seem to dislike me immensely, and they appear to be under the impression that Norbert would permanently leave South Africa and shift to England if I asked him to."

"And I would!" Lord Ellsbury said fiercely and clasped her soft hands in his much larger ones. "You know I would even go to the moon for you, my dear."

Lady Stella blushed delicately.

I was reminded of my own dearly departed Mary, whom I still greatly missed. A sympathetic glance from Holmes brought me back to reality. After all, my friend had an uncanny knack for deducing my thoughts.

There was a knock at the door and the couple sprang apart, their faces red. I couldn't help but smile.

"Come in," Holmes called.

Mrs. Hudson opened the door and showed in yet another visitor. From his attire, the man could only be the butler of a noble house.

"Richard?" Lady Stella asked curiously. "Why are you here?"

"My apologies, Miss Stella," the man called Richard said, bowing formally. "Miss Sarah told us you were here, and when the Master heard, he sent me to urgently request Mr. Holmes's help." He looked up then, his expression wooden, but his dark eyes betrayed his distress. "Young Master Stephen has been abducted."

Lady Stella stood with a cry of anguish. Lord Ellsbury threw a supportive arm around her shoulders.

"Was there a ransom note?" he asked sharply.

The butler nodded and held out a sheet of plain paper. Lord Ellsbury grabbed it and without a glance tossed it to Holmes. "More of that rubbish," he growled.

Holmes looked at the note and sighed before handing it to me. I quickly decoded it.

Stella your brother now belongs to me.

"The ink – and possibly the pen – is the same, but the writing is slightly different," Holmes murmured. "This was written by a different person. A rather agitated one, I believe, from the strokes."

Lady Stella blinked. "So the person sending me these notes and the person who abducted my brother are different?"

"It is likely," Holmes replied. "However, I don't wish to theorise without sufficient data."

"Sigerson," Lord Ellsbury said quietly. "You can find the boy, can't you? Spare no expense."

"Please, Mr. Holmes," Lady Stella pleaded.

"Very well," Holmes said. "Shall we visit your home, Lady Stella?"

Soon after, we found ourselves in a magnificent estate south of the city that had clearly seen better days.

"Stella!" came a distressed cry as we approached the front door, and a young girl of about eight or ten threw herself at Lady Stella.

Lady Stella stroked her hair gently. "Sarah," she said softly. "Tell us what you know. Mr. Holmes is here to help find Stephen."

The young lady turned around abruptly and grabbed Holmes's hands in her petite ones. "Thank God!" she said fervently. "Thank God that you actually came, Mr. Holmes! Please save our brother! They want to kill him!"

"Sarah!" Lady Stella cried reproachfully.

Lady Sarah glared at her older sister. "You know that I'm right, Stella," she said coldly. "You know that they want to get rid of all of us – especially Stephen, since he'll be the one to inherit father's title! Father pretends to be blind to our suffering, and now you're going to abandon us and go off to South Africa with that wild man. But Stephen and I . . . we both – " She burst into tears.

Lady Stella shot her fiancé a helpless look.

To our surprise, Lord Ellsbury knelt on the ground in front of Lady Sarah and spoke in a soft, gentle voice. "My Stella would never abandon her beloved little brother and sister. We were already considering either taking both of you to South Africa with us, or sending you to a good school in on the Continent. I'm sure that your father will readily agree, what with his interest in his new wife . . . ." He scowled and pursed his lips, likely having said more than he'd meant to reveal about what he thought of the girl's father. Then he continued. "We have even identified a few schools, should you decide that you'd prefer that, rather than coming with us to Pretoria. We wanted to keep it a surprise and tell you when all visit my family's estate in the south of France in a few months, for your summer holidays, but . . . ."

Lady Sarah stared at him in shock, and then turned her eyes to her older sister. "Is that really true?" she whispered.

Lady Stella nodded.

The girl looked back at Lord Ellsbury, with a look of incipient joy in her eyes. But before she could speak, we suddenly heard loud arguments emanating from behind the closed doors of a nearby room.

"Robert!" a high-pitched, unpleasant female voice shouted. "You cannot possibly be serious! I am telling you, it is the boy's own doing to gain your attention. No one in their right mind would abduct that hellion!"

"Regardless," came a deep baritone, "he is my son and heir."

"You cannot trust him!" said the woman. "Richard has heard them talking. They hate me – "

"Not trust my own son?" replied the man. "I have no trust in Richard. He is clearly loyal to your former husband. I don't know why I ever let you convince me to let him replace Bates." He cleared his throat. "I will get to the bottom of Stephen's abduction."

"Wait for a couple of days and he'll be back by himself," the female voice countered. "There isn't even a ransom note. How are you going to find him?"

"I have written to a detective – that Holmes fellow that Sarah and Stephen speak of so often."

"And how will you pay for his expenses? You can't even afford to buy me a new dress anymore, let along take care of this estate. And yet you have money to waste on the foolish pranks of a deranged child?"

There was no response from the man.

Her cheeks flushed with embarrassment, Lady Stella looked at us and murmured softly, "Stephen is not deranged. He is an intelligent boy, at top of his class. He – "

Her thought remained unspoken as the door flew open and a distinguished-looking middle-aged gentleman stormed out of the room from which we'd heard the voices. Upon seeing us, he stopped short. A lady with far too many cosmetics came behind him, and her face hardened when she saw us.

Perceiving who we were, she snarled coldly, "We have no need for a detective, nor can we afford one. Our apologies for the trouble, but we request you to depart immediately."

"Mr. Holmes's fee is not your problem," Lord Ellsbury spoke up. "He is my friend, and I will take care of it."

"Sherlock Holmes?" the woman – who was certainly Lady Stella and Sarah's new stepmother – screeched. "I'm sick to death of that name. The twins are always gushing about that infernal detective!"

"Yes, he's the very same," Lady Sarah replied. "Stephen will be safe now." She glared at her step-mother.

While his wife was enraged, Lord Robert Aster, on the other hand, appeared rather relieved. "Thank you for coming at such short notice, Mr. Holmes," he said politely. "I was unaware that you were acquainted with Norbert."

"We met in Africa several years ago and became friends," Holmes replied vaguely. "When was your son last seen?

"This morning," answered Sarah for him. "When Stella left, Stephen followed her out of the house. We knew that she was going to see you, Mr. Holmes, following after Lord Ellsbury, so he decided to go too. I wanted to go with him, but he told me to stay put. After a few minutes, I decided that I wanted to go as well. I went outside and started down the road, and almost immediately I found his traveling cloak and one of his shoes, just outside the wall on the east side. There were boot marks in the mud showing the signs of a scuffle. That's when I knew that he'd been abducted."

"And the note with the message?"

The girl's father interrupted. "Sarah found it on the front steps when she returned to the house. She said that it was the same sort of gangster code that you had encountered before in one of your cases. She was able to tell us what it said. At that point I knew that we were out of our depth, but I was afraid to summon the police. That's why I sent Richard to ask for your help."

Holmes nodded. "May I see the boy's cloak and the shoe?" They were quickly brought, and just as quickly discarded. I knew that he'd observed nothing of interest. "And now may I examine his bedroom?"

"Yes, of course," Lord Aster replied, leading us down the corridor, and then up several flights of stairs. We stopped in front of a carved wooden door that wasn't in the best of conditions, just like the rest of the manor. Upon a handwritten board that was hanging from the knocker were the words "*Lasciate ogne speranza, voi ch'entrate*"

"'*Abandon all hope, ye who enter here.*'" Holmes murmured. "Dante Alighieri, *Inferno*, Canto 3. Interesting."

Lord Aster coughed lightly. "My son is a little . . . precocious."

"He is a gloomy, broody child," his wife spat, "with the temperament of the devil himself."

"Enough, Helen," Lord Aster warned.

A dark flush stained the lady's cheeks, but she remained silent.

Lady Sarah stepped forward and pushed open the door, ushering us in. Holmes immediately began examining the room, while everyone else watched him with different expressions on their faces. I was quite used to my friend's investigative method, but other people weren't, and thus, instead of watching Holmes perform his usual acrobatics around the room looking for clues, observing and deducing, I observed the other spectators.

Lady Helen Aster's mouth was tight with contempt, and Lord Aster appeared to be a little shocked, but still in control of himself. Lord Ellsbury looked quite amused, with the corners of his lips turned up in a smile, and

137

Lady Stella looked mildly interested. Lord Ellsbury started to whisper something about how he'd seen Sigerson do the same sort of thing years before in Africa, but his fiancée held up a hand to quieten him. Meanwhile, Sarah watched Holmes unblinkingly, taking in each movement, completely enthralled. Her eyes gleamed with fascination and adulation for the detective.

"He really does look like a bloodhound," she whispered softly, almost to herself. "I wish that Stephen could see this."

I suddenly recalled the letters that Lord Norbert Ellsbury had flung at Holmes earlier in the day – Sarah must have written them! The contents of those letters had . . . . I looked away from her childish face, embarrassed. She was still a child, no matter how romantic were her fantasies. No one in their right mind would imagine Holmes gazing dreamily at the moon with stars in his eyes and the tinge of roses on his pale cheeks . . . I shook my head when considering the flowery contents of what I'd read that morning. The imagination of a child could be fearsome, indeed.

Holmes, meanwhile, had looked closely at a number of papers on Stephen's desk, and was now digging through the rubbish bin beside the desk, collecting torn bits of blotting paper. I spotted several dancing men codes printed on them, which confirmed my own suspicions that the notes had been written by the young twins.

Holmes finished his examination and stood up. "Lady Sarah," he said quietly, "a word with you alone, if I may."

I sighed. Holmes really spared no thought to the young child who was so infatuated with him. Would she not think of it as an encouragement if he spoke to her without anyone else in the room?

To my relief, Lord Ellsbury seemed to have reached the same conclusion. He stepped forward and whispered to Holmes. "That might be inappropriate."

Holmes blinked and nodded. "Watson will be here." He glanced at the child. "Lady Stella may stay as well, if Lady Sarah permits. I believe there are certain things that she might not be comfortable sharing with the rest of you."

I could literally see hearts and stars shining in Lady Sarah's eyes at the thought of conversing with the object of her childish affection.

"Sarah?" Lady Stella asked softly.

"Stella can stay," the young girl replied.

Lord Ellsbury ushered Lord Robert Aster and his wife out of the room, the latter complaining vociferously.

When the door had shut, Holmes turned and said grimly, "Sarah, please answer truthfully. When was the last time that you saw your brother?"

138

"As I told you, when he followed Stella out of the house. When he was abducted."

"And yet you were the one who wrote the note with the Dancing Men, saying that *"your brother now belongs to me"*. Is that not so?" Holmes asked archly. "And then you gave it to your father and said you'd found it outside the house. You pretended to decipher it for him so that I would be summoned."

Sarah nodded sadly. "What else was I supposed to do?" she cried. "I was the only one who knew that Stephen was in real danger, and no one would have believed me!"

"Wait a moment!" Lady Stella said, her face very white. "Sarah, have *you* been the one who was writing these threatening notes to me?"

"It was fairly obvious," Holmes replied, "but I believe the hand that wrote those was actually your brother's. Yet I have no doubt that Lady Sarah was helping him." He pointed toward the desk, where the various blotting sheets covered with dancing men figures were still resting. "You said that both Sarah and Stephen are interested in my work. The code was published in the newspapers after the crime was revealed, so making use of it was no difficulty at all. The first five messages that you showed us, Lady Stella, were all written with certain characteristics, while the latest, announcing the abduction, was different. It was never much of a leap to realize that the twins were writing them."

"But why?" Lady Stella cried. "Why would you do such a thing?"

"Stephen really wanted to meet Mr. Holmes," Sarah said, looking a little guilty. "And besides, we thought . . . we thought that you . . . that you were . . . ."

"Abandoning you?" Lady Stella asked softly.

Her younger sister nodded silently.

Lady Stella sighed. "I wish that you'd spoken to me."

The girl lowered her head, but raised it again when Holmes stated, "The question now is whether this kidnapping is true, or instead another more elaborate attempt to lure me here."

A tear ran down the girl's cheek. "It's real, Mr. Holmes. We wouldn't have done anything like this to get your attention."

Lady Stella seemed convinced by her sister's story, turning to Holmes and asking, "How can we possibly find Stephen without a single clue about his abductors?"

Holmes smiled slightly. "There are plenty of clues," he said quietly. "Sarah, why don't you show us where you found your brother's cloak?"

The young girl nodded eagerly, grabbed the detective's hand, and rushed out. Her father, stepmother, and Lord Ellsbury, who had been

139

waiting in the hallway outside the room, hurried after them. Lady Stella smiled sadly at me and we followed as well.

We passed the butler Richard near the door, and when I glanced back a few minutes later, he had inexplicably followed us. By the time that we'd all reached the public road outside the east wall of the estate, Holmes was examining the area and Sarah was eyeing him with fascination again writ upon her young face, her earlier embarrassing confessions forgotten. Lord Ellsbury and I exchanged a troubled glance. He had also spotted the girl's intent gaze.

"A-ha!" Holmes said suddenly, picking up a small piece of cloth. He looked straight at Lord Robert Aster. "You have a dog, I believe."

The nobleman nodded.

"An Irish wolfhound?" Holmes asked.

"Yes, but how – ?" Lord Aster appeared flabbergasted.

"It is my business to know things that others do not," he murmured enigmatically. "May I trouble you to bring the hound here, please? He ought to be able to lead us to the culprits."

"No!" Lady Helen Aster said firmly, stamping her dainty foot. "I refuse to let you lead us on a wild goose chase!"

Holmes glanced at her speculatively. "Then it would certainly be easier if you led us to the boy yourself," he said mildly.

"What?" Lady Aster screeched, her face distorted, but her guilt poorly hidden. "How dare you?"

Holmes turned to the butler with a small smile. "Or, perhaps, Mr. Richard, you would like to do the honours? You have certainly aided in this abduction – there are clear signs of your presence here, where a struggle most definitely occurred. The boy's footprints are here, with characteristics similar his shoes that I examined in his bedroom. There is one other set of footprints here as well – *yours*, Richard. And this piece of cloth –" He held up the fragment that he'd discovered. " – matches the piece that is missing from the tail of your rather shabby coat."

Richard started to look, but stopped himself, Instead he peered at Holmes with wide eyes. "No doubt," continued the detective, "you put your mistress's plan into action when you perceived that Stephen was leaving, thinking that if he was already away from home, his continued absence after being abducted wouldn't be noticed for a while. Having overheard that you were connected with Lady Helen Aster before her arrival at this household, for whom else could you be acting but her? I don't know what your long-term plan was – and I doubt that there is one – but you certainly don't wish for your young master to be killed as well as kidnapped, do you?"

140

"Killed?" Richard whispered faintly and turned suddenly to Lady Helen. "My lady, you promised!"

"Don't listen to that trickster, you fool!" Lady Helen cried.

Lord Robert spoke up. "Mr. Holmes, Helen has no reason to harm my son."

"She does now," Holmes said simply and glanced at me. "How many months along is she, Watson?"

"About three, I should say," I replied, eyeing the lady carefully. I had naturally, thanks to my medical training, noticed the small signs of her pregnancy when first we met the objectionable woman.

Lord Robert eyed his wife warily. "Why didn't you tell me?"

"Because you are blind!" she cried. "Could you not see that your children detest me? Would my own child ever be welcomed into this family?"

"That is no reason to harm my son," Lord Robert said.

"I suspect that the cause is seamier than that," said Holmes. "With young Stephen is gone, you could be convinced that he'd run away, and if Lady Helen produces another son, then you have a new heir."

Lady Helen broke down and clung to her husband, who stood stiffly at her touch and looked at Holmes helplessly. I didn't need my accumulated understanding of women to perceive that her tears were overly dramatized and false – and also that this weak man was still uncertain as to how he would proceed.

Holmes fixed his raptor-like gaze upon the butler. "Is the boy held close by?"

Richard nodded fearfully.

"Then lead us," Holmes ordered.

Lord Aster pulled his arm loose from his hysterical wife, telling her sternly to go back inside the manor while the rest of us would follow the butler into the nearby forest which lay behind the manor, stretching from the house to the boundaries of the estate. We were soon under the trees, following a narrow and meandering trail. It wasn't long before we came within sight of a small shack and an adjacent well. We continued to the house, but Richard stepped to one side, stopping instead beside the well, and hanging his head in shame. "It's dry," he said. "He wasn't in any real danger."

"Find a rope!" Holmes cried urgently, understanding instantly and then stopping to unlace his shoes. I watched in horror as peeled off his socks as well and then quickly topped the low wall surrounding the well's opening. Within seconds, he was nimbly climbing down the walls until we could see his thin figure no more.

"Holmes!" I shouted, my voice echoing as I bent over the dark opening. A dank vapour rose to meet me. I could see nothing but his vague in the blackness below.

"I'm here, Watson!" came a faint echoing voice, much to my relief. "I've found the boy."

Richard, under the watchful eye of Lord Ellsbury, had found a rope in the shack – likely the same one he'd used to put Stephen into the well in the first place – and we lowered it into the blackness. It took some time, as his ascent was much slower and more careful then when he went down, but Holmes eventually climbed up with a shivering boy in his arms. The lad was soaked – the well hadn't been so dry after all.

I checked him quickly. The child was very cold, but overall he would be fine. We had found him in time.

"Stephen!" Lady Stella cried, pushing past us and, taking off her cloak, wrapped it around the boy as soon as I released him. Sarah reached to touch the boy's face, weeping all the while. Throughout, Lord Aster simply stood and watched, as if the lad in the well was a stranger.

Lord Ellsbury leaned forward and picked up the boy effortlessly. "Stella," he said, his voice determined, and with his eye on Lord Aster, who sadly made no counter-argument and failed to react whatsoever at the unspoken accusation of his ineffectuality. "We are taking the twins to South Africa."

Lady Stella nodded tearfully. "Yes, Norbert. Yes we are." And she glared at her father as well. He'd clearly decided to throw in his lot with his new wife, choosing her – in spite of her guilt – instead of his own blood kin.

As Richard, the butler, ran back through the woods toward the manor house, Lord Ellsbury turned to Holmes, saying, "Thank you, Sigerson. I doubt that I can ever repay this favour, but if there is anything that I can ever do for you, I will be at your disposal."

Holmes waved away his gratitude, nodding toward the trail leading back to the manor. "It's time for us to go home," he declared. "Come along, Watson."

I was exhausted by the time that we returned to Baker Street. Thankfully, Mrs. Hudson had a warm dinner awaiting us. We ate with relish and then took our seats near the fireplace with a glass of brandy.

"What an unpleasant affair," I muttered, leaning back in my chair. "That Lord Aster would forgive his wife and refrain from pressing charges on the butler . . . ." I shook my head. "At least those children will be going to a better home." And then I smiled. "And you, Holmes – you even managed to get yourself a fine young lady as a secret admirer!"

Holmes raised an eyebrow enquiringly.

"Sarah," I said, nettled. How could he have put the letters out of his mind so soon? It was only a few hours before that Lord Ellsbury had barged in with those insipid and flowery concoctions.

"What of her?"

"She has feelings for you," I said. "She was writing imaginary love letters to you – along with those equally over-the-top replies!"

Holmes smiled and shook his head.

"It wasn't just the girl that felt that way, Watson, and it wasn't she who wrote those letters," said he, chuckling, as he lit his pipe. "The boy was the author."

"How do you know?" I demanded.

"The penmanship. As always, you see but do not observe. Do you recall the Italian quote hanging on his door, and the papers that I examined on his desk?"

I nodded.

"Plenty of evidence."

I nodded again, and our conversation turned to other matters.

The Invisible Assassin
by Geri Schear

"The world is mud," Sherlock Holmes said, his voice heavy with disapproval. "That fog is so thick that I vow one could eat it."

"Cold, too," I agreed. "Why don't you come and sit here by the fire, Holmes? There is nothing to be gained by standing at a window through which you cannot see."

He sighed heavily, glanced at his silent violin and at the notes of his most recent investigation that lay upon the desk.

"You have to stay alert," I said.

"Oh? Why so?"

"This seems perfect weather for a case."

Holmes remained quite still, and I thought he was giving my words some thought. "Even if a crime were to be committed on a vile night like this, I doubt that it would be discovered until a man can see more than a foot in any direction."

It was Monday, the 4th of November 1901, and London had been shrouded in fog since Saturday. We, like the rest of the city's inhabitants, did not stray far from our fireplace. Traffic halted, and the city came to an almost complete standstill. Our protracted confinement had caused my friend to become increasingly irritable as the days passed, and the fog persisted.

I was searching my thoughts for a rejoinder when a harsh clamour on the door below made me start.

The flames in the hearth flickered as a cold draft gusted up from the hallway, and a moment later a heavy set of footsteps thundered up the stairs, followed by a fist hammering upon our door.

"A client!" Holmes cried with unsavoury glee. He leaped across the room to his armchair, his dressing gown billowing behind him as he sat, then he closed his eyes and tented his fingers. "Watson, the door, if you please."

Our visitor was a middle-aged man whose features were almost entirely obscured by the thick woollen muffler that circled his mouth and neck three times. He wore a brown woollen coat that had been patched and mended many times by an indifferent seamstress, knitted gloves, and a pair of black boots. A cloth cap was pulled low over his forehead and a pair of anxious blue eyes peered out from beneath it.

"Mr. Holmes!" the man cried as he crashed into our room. "Mr. Holmes!"

"I am Sherlock Holmes," my friend replied.

"Please, sit down," I said, hoping to calm the man's agitation.

"No time! No time!" he cried. "You don't understand. The man is dead!"

Holmes's eyes glittered with delight. "Who, sir?"

"My passenger! 'Take me to the War Office,' says he, and so I does, but he don't get out. I open the door to see what's delayed him, and there he sits. *Dead!*"

"How perfectly delight – ah, that is, how extraordinary!" Holmes barely managing to suppress a chuckle. "Where is he now?"

"In the cab below, sir."

"Get your coat, Watson. We must see this remarkable sight."

We hurried down the stairs and found the cab, a simple growler, standing idle in the street outside.

Holmes took the lantern from the front of the cab and we peered into the ghastly cabin. The passenger was a young fellow, certainly no more than thirty. He was neatly dressed in dark suit, a shirt that was once white but now was spattered with blood, a dark tie, a knitted scarf, and a heavy woollen coat. A bowler hat and a copy of the morning edition of *The Daily Telegraph* lay on the seat beside him. On top of the newspaper lay a bloody knife. The passenger sat facing forward, slumped toward the window. He was ashen, and his body was already starting to cool.

I followed my training and checked for a pulse. Predictably, I found none. I continued to examine the corpse as well as I might, but the cramped cabin and dismal light limited my efficiency.

"There's a lot of blood. No doubt there's a wound somewhere, most likely in the lower back, but we won't find it until we get him to the morgue. There is one curious thing, though."

"Yes?" Holmes's voice was eager.

"He has two deep cuts across his left palm and fingers."

"Interesting," Holmes suddenly blew a piercing whistle and through the swirling fog we heard the patter of footsteps. A minute or so later, a young lad emerged from the toxic mists.

"Yes, Mr. 'Olmes?" he said.

"Ah, Jacko. See if you can find a policeman. Constable Parry should be in East Street by now. Tell him we have a dead man who looks to have been murdered and ask him to come here at once. A shilling for your trouble."

"Murdered!" Jacko said, stretching his neck into the vehicle to see. "Is that blood? Cor! That is, right-o, Mr. H."

145

As soon as the boy scampered away, Holmes handed me the lantern and said, "Be good enough to hold that for me. I am unlikely to find much of any moment – the light is wretched – but this will be my only chance before the constabulary join us."

Very carefully, Holmes examined the knife and the newspaper. He handed me the latter. It was the early edition of *The Telegraph*, and there, scrawled on the front page in blood, was a trembling letter "*K*". I shook my head in bewilderment. Holmes had already turned his attention to the body. He spent some time looking at the man's hands and then, apparently oblivious to the sticky blood, plunged his long fingers into the dead man's pockets. A moment later, he produced a silver cigarette case, and then a wallet. Holmes counted and then muttered, "Twelve pounds, ten shillings, and nine pence. A good sum. No identification . . . But what is this?"

From the gory turn-up of the dead man's fashionable trousers, he drew a fronded leaf.

"Looks like it's from a palm," I said.

"Yes, indeed," he said in a distant voice. "It confirms my suspicions."

My physical discomfort dulled my interest, I confess. I felt the cold seeping into my very bones, and even with my nose buried in the collar of my coat, I couldn't escape the struck-match stink of the fog. I longed for the warmth of our hearth and a hot cup of coffee, but Holmes seemed oblivious. The cabby stood close at hand. He breathed into his cupped fingers and stamped his feet on the frigid pavement. We exchanged a sympathetic look.

"Well," Holmes said, "we cannot do more here. At least we have enough to help us make an identification."

"We do?"

"And as you yourself observed, we cannot know more about the fatal wound until he is in the morgue. Watson, why are you standing out here in the cold? Take the cabby into our apartment and ask Mrs. Hudson to bring up some coffee."

I handed him the lantern. "You aren't joining us?"

"I shall be along directly."

I wasted no time arguing and took the cabby indoors. I asked Mrs. Hudson to bring us a pot of coffee, and then we went upstairs and warmed our backs at the cheery fire. Once we had thawed sufficiently, I said, "Mr. Holmes will want to ask you some questions, Mr – ?"

"Jasper Monk is my name," said he, shaking my hand.

"Mr. Monk, why did you come to Holmes instead of going to a police station?"

"I panicked is the truth of the matter," he replied. His words were muffled by the thick woollen scarf that still covered half his face. "I

146

thought if I went to the police, they would arrest me immediately. A man hears of such things," he added in a confidential whisper.

"Did you know the dead man?"

"No, I ain't never seen him before. Truth to tell, I hardly saw him when I picked 'im up, the fog being so thick."

"But he seemed healthy enough when you stopped for him?"

Mr. Monk paused and thought about that. Then he said, "He were breathing hard, like he'd been running, but I reckoned he were anxious to catch the cab, what with there bein' so few on the road, what with the fog and all."

"Did you have any conversation with him?"

"No, sir, I did not. He said, 'The War Office, and step lively!' And so I did. Didn't take but about quarter-of-an-hour to get there, neither. Not much on the road, as I say. This were going to be my last fare, and all. I was away home as soon as I'd dropped him off."

A few minutes later, Holmes joined us. After vigorously washing his hands he joined us at the fire to claim his share of the heat. "Constable Parry has taken charge of the vehicle and we are awaiting the arrival of one of the Scotland Yard inspectors."

Mrs. Hudson arrived on Holmes's heels. She set a tray of coffee and buttered scones on the table. We sat and sipped the blessedly hot drink. As we did so, I had Mr. Monk recount everything that he'd told me. Holmes listened intently.

"Where did you pick him up?" he asked.

"At Waterloo, along York Road. I were stood at the taxi rank, like."

"I understand," Holmes said. "How many cabs were there at the time?"

"I were the only one, sir. Everyone else had gone home the weather being so bleak. Hard to see your hand in front of your face, much, less the road. The others reckoned it were calling for disaster. As I told your friend here, I was about ready to give up myself, and would have excepting for this bloke coming out of the fog like he did."

"From which direction did he come?"

"I couldn't say, sir. Didn't see him at all until he spoke to me. Put the heart across me, as my old mother would say."

"And you did not know him?"

"Not I, sir. Though, to be sure, I hardly got a decent look at him. He were nothing more'n a fare, and a fare ain't usually worth looking at, less'n they be a maid with a shapely ankle, like." He grinned.

We finished our coffee and I poured refills for all of us. Our repast did not last long, and there was nothing but crumbs and dregs left by the time we heard a knock at the door below. A moment or two later, Inspector Lestrade joined us.

"What's going on, Mr. Holmes?" he asked. "Young Parry shows me a body in a cab – said you could tell me all about it. A gent, I'd say, from his clothing. You've already had a look, I suppose?"

"I did, Inspector, as did Dr. Watson."

"The man was stabbed, Inspector," I said, "but I'm sure you probably saw that for yourself."

"Couldn't find the wound in the dark, but there was a fair amount of blood. We'll get to the bottom of the story, right enough. How did you happen upon this case, Mr. Holmes?"

"Mr. Monk here is the owner of the cab, Lestrade," Holmes said. "It was he who brought this matter to my attention."

"Oh yes?" the inspector replied, giving the cabby a stern look. "And why did you not go to the nearest station?"

"Baker Street was a fairly straight run, and, therefore, easier to find in such poor visibility," Holmes said, casually. "But perhaps it is best he tells you his story himself."

The unfortunate cabby related his tale yet again. Lestrade, for all his faults, is a good listener, and he did not interrupt once.

"You say you never saw the man before?" he asked, when Mr. Monk concluded.

"Never, sir. That is to say, I hardly saw him this evening, what with the fog, but nothing about him seemed familiar."

The policeman gave Holmes a look of disbelief. Holmes addressed Monk.

"Did the cab stop at any point in the journey?"

"No, Mr. Holmes, sir. Like I said, there weren't much on the road. We went direct from the station to the War Office."

"Well, I don't see how that's possible," Lestrade said. "A perfectly healthy man gets into a cab, it never stops along the journey, but when he arrives at his destination he's been murdered – unless he topped himself."

"Succinctly put, Inspector," Holmes said, genially. "Your conclusions are precise and accurate with one exception: The dead man was unquestionably murdered."

Lestrade shook his head in bewilderment. However, he was familiar with my friend's skills and had learned over the years not to doubt him. He turned back to Mr. Monk and said, "We'll have to hold onto your cab for examination for at least a couple of days, I'm afraid."

"A couple of days!" exclaimed the cabby. "You can't do that. That's my livelihood, that is! When do I get it back?"

"We have to examine it, Mr. Monk, and the body that it contains," the inspector said. "One of the officers outside shall give you a receipt and you may claim it in a day or two. In the meantime, you must go to the Yard with Sergeant Hill and give a formal statement. Go on. The sergeant is waiting for you."

Mr. Monk gave us a nervous look.

"You need not be alarmed," Holmes said. "It's been many a long year since the inspector arrested an innocent man."

Seeing the cabby did not look appeased, I added, "Just give the police your statement, Mr. Monk, and all will be well. In a day or two, you'll have your cab back and this fog will lift."

"A day or two," the poor man groaned, leaving the room and stomping down the stairs. The sounds of his protestations continued to rail until at last the front door closed behind them, and he was gone.

"Poor chap," I said.

Lestrade opened one of our windows and stood peering through it. "You got 'im, Hill?" he hollered into the street.

A distant cry in the affirmative came at once. Lestrade slammed shut the window and shivered. He turned back to us with a contented sigh, and then said, "Apologies, gents. I needed to be sure the fellow did not run off. Did you find anything of interest when you examined the dead man, Mr. Holmes?"

"As you yourself observed, there was little enough to see in these conditions. However, I did determine that the man probably worked at the War Office, most likely in a highly confidential role. His initials were 'S.B.', he smoked Players cigarettes, had a female friend or relative who cared a great deal for his comfort, and he started his journey in an exotic location. Oh, and he was right-handed. I believe the killer is South African, possibly a Boer. He has killed before, probably more than once."

Lestrade stared. "I should be used to you by now, Mr. Holmes," he said, "but I confess I am bewildered."

"It is simple enough, surely? The dead man asked Mr. Monk to take him to the War Office. It is reasonable to conclude, therefore, that he had business in that building."

"And his initials?"

"There was a cigarette case in the dead man's pocket engraved with the initials 'S.B.' and containing ten Players cigarettes. The hand-knitted scarf around his neck suggests a woman in his life who cared for his comfort, and the presence of a palm leaf in his trouser turn-ups indicates he had recently been in a location where such an exotic plant grows."

"Well, that all makes sense," Lestrade said. "But what about the Boer connection?"

149

"The spring-loaded blade on the seat contained an ivory handle which was engraved with the word '*afskeid*' and the year 1899. The word is Afrikaans and means '*farewell*'. The blade was extremely sharp and well kept. It is likely, is it not, that a man who possesses so fine an object and takes care to maintain it, expects to use it?"

"And the dead man being right-handed?" I asked.

"Mr. S.B.'s right hand is slightly larger than his left, indicating he used the right most often. There were also no fewer than three small ink stains on his right index and middle fingers, indicating he recently wrote something with that hand."

"But it's his left hand that was cut," Lestrade said. "How do you explain that, Mr. Holmes?"

Holmes lit a cigarette and inhaled before waving the match out and replying, "Given the blood was on the fellow's lower body, I surmise that his fatal wound is in his lower left back. A man so injured would be inclined to reach around to draw out the weapon with his left hand, especially if the blade were angled in that direction, as I believe this was. We'll be able to tell more once he's in the morgue."

"And he cut his hand when he pulled the blade out of his back," I said, following my friend's reasoning.

"Precisely, Watson. His hand was slick with blood, and I surmise the blade went deep."

"I see," Lestrade said, rubbing his chin. "Well, that certainly makes sense when you explain it. Is there anything else to which you would draw my attention?"

"Yes. There was a copy of the first edition of today's *Daily Telegraph* on the seat beside him. In itself it is interesting – more so because of the letter '*K*' scrawled in blood on the front page. Oh, and the leaf in his trouser turn-ups." Holmes lay the palm leaf on the table.

"A newspaper and a leaf?" Lestrade scoffed. "I cannot see how they help us."

"You may be right, Inspector. However, you did ask. Do you object if I keep the leaf, and try to identify the plant from which it came?"

"No, why should I mind?" He looked at his pocket watch and rose. "Only four o'clock. It feels like it's been midnight for days. Well, I suppose I must get back to the Yard and see if we can identify this fellow. You will, ah, let me know if you learn anything further, Mr. Holmes?"

"As always, Inspector," Holmes said, shaking the policeman's hand.

"Poor fellow," I said.

"Hmm?" Holmes was preoccupied with the leaf.

"Mr. Monk," I said. "Hard for him to be without his livelihood for a couple of days."

"It's not like he'll do much business in this wretched weather, in any case," he replied. "Can you identify this plant, Watson?"

I took it and studied it closely. "I'm afraid not. All I can tell you is it's a palm leaf – an exotic one, I'd guess."

"My thoughts precisely. I'm afraid I shall have to go out, my dear fellow. No, no, you stay here. That fog is extremely unhealthy. I may be gone some time. Don't wait up."

Much later that evening, just as I was thinking about retiring, Holmes returned.

"Good gracious," I exclaimed. "Where have you been?"

He sank into the armchair opposite me and held his hands to the fire. "It is a bitter night to be out," he said.

I poured him a glass of brandy, and he took a sip. "Thank you. Well, as to my exploits, I don't have much to report. True, I have identified the dead man, and I now have a very good idea of the events that lead to the unfortunate fellow's death. Beyond these trifles I have little to report. Oh, except to say that the oysters at the Diogenes Club are excellent."

"Didn't you once say that there is nothing so important as trifles?"

He chuckled. "That is certainly one of my axioms. Well . . . I began by tracing that peculiar palm leaf to its source. I theorised it could not be found domestically, and so I sought the advice of an expert. The botanist in the Palm House, Mr. Prosperity Longford by name, told me everything I needed to know.

"He identified the plant as *Ceratozamia Mexicana,* otherwise known as the Mexican Horncone. It's native to the Americas and is a relative newcomer to Kew. Mr. Longford tells me it arrived in 1880 and has grown there ever since."

"And the plant doesn't grow anywhere in Britain outside of the Gardens?" I said. "So Mr. Monk's passenger had been there shortly before he was murdered."

He took another sip of brandy. "Precisely, Watson. Knowing that fact was significant, though, thanks to the newspaper, I suspected that was the case even before I left Baker Street. You may not be aware of it, but the Palm House is a frequent rendezvous point for people whose business is secrets."

"You mean espionage," I said.

"Quite so. Given that the dead man's journey originated at the Palm House, and that his intended destination was the War Office, I surmised that the victim was a member of that most secret fraternity."

"And the newspaper? I don't understand its significance."

151

He chuckled. "The paper in question was the early morning edition, but Mr. Monk found the dead man around half-past three. The visibility was not conducive to reading in the cab, so why did he keep it? Indeed, why not discard the early edition in favour of the most recent? There is a newsagent at the railway station, after all. No, the paper was intended as a pre-arranged signal, so that the fellow he was meeting would be able to identify him. A specific newspaper is often used as a signal between strangers."

"So, you were right – S.B. did work at the War Office?" I put more coal on the fire and held out my hands to the flames.

"He did, indeed," Holmes said. "Furthermore, Mr. Longford was able to confirm that he had seen our victim speaking with a dark-haired man dressed entirely in black."

"That's splendid, Holmes," I exclaimed. "Will Longford be able to identify the other man?"

"Once we have him in irons, yes – though, of course, that doesn't necessarily mean the man is the killer."

"It's suggestive, surely?"

"Oh, indeed. And if we find the man is South African, that will pretty much confirm it, at least to my own satisfaction. Proving the point to a jury may be another matter. Still, it's early days yet."

"You haven't been at Kew all this time," I said as I suppressed a yawn.

He chuckled. "Well deduced, my dear Watson. Do you care to guess where I went after I left that home of the botanical sciences?"

"Given your hints about espionage and the Diogenes Club, I imagine you went to visit your brother."

"You are on sparkling form this evening," he replied. "That is exactly what I did. Thanks to the letters on the cigarette case and my description, Mycroft was able to identify our unfortunate victim as one Sebastian Barraclough."

"Did Barraclough work for your brother?" I said.

"Mycroft did not say so, but I inferred as much. He would only confirm that Barraclough was a government employee, one whose job lay in the darkest shadows of our empire's operation. When I related Longford's description of the man in black, Mycroft suspects our killer is one Frederick, or 'Fritz', Joubert Duquesne. The business between them was, I surmise, of an extremely sensitive nature. Something went awry, and Barraclough realised he was in danger. He fled, anxious to report to the War Office."

"Poor fellow. What sent him back to his office instead of seeking help? Do you know?"

"I have some theories," he began and then paused as I yawned loudly. "I think the rest must keep till morning, my dear Watson. You look done in. Get you to bed and we shall continue this discussion tomorrow."

My spirit, I confess, was eager to hear the rest of Holmes's tale, but I was utterly exhausted. I bade Holmes good evening and went up to bed.

In the morning when I came into our sitting room, I found him still sitting there by the fire. Mrs. Hudson brought in breakfast and I sat down to eat.

"Holmes, do you care to join me?" I said.

"Hmm? Oh, I am not hungry, but I shall certainly join you for a cup of coffee."

Once our cheery landlady left us, and I had eaten enough porridge to take the edge off my appetite, I brought up the matter of the dead man in the cab.

"What lurid name have you given to the affair?" Holmes asked, with studied indifference.

"I thought 'The Case of the Invisible Assassin'," I said.

He groaned. "I suppose it could be worse," he said. "No, I shall not give you any ideas. I will say, however, that this case may lead us into matters of national security. Write the tale if you must, but do not attempt to publish until you get approval from me or someone in government."

I buttered some toast and said, "How long do you think it will be until it is safe to tell the story?"

"Oh, fifty years should do it, I think."

"Fifty!" I exclaimed. "I cannot imagine either of us will be even remembered in fifty years."

"You think not?" He filled his cup and sipped the coffee. "I certainly have hopes of being remembered, at least by those members of the public with some wit and interest in *outré* crimes."

"Speaking of which, you never finished telling me about your adventures yesterday. Did you find out if Barraclough happened upon his killer, or if their meeting was prearranged?"

"It was certainly an arranged meeting," Holmes replied, "during which I suspect that the agent learned something that alarmed him. He fled from the Palm House with his killer on his heels."

"How much did Longford see?"

"Just a conversation and Barraclough leaving in some haste." He drank another sip of coffee and then continued.

"After I left the Gardens, I headed to Mycroft's office. It was nearly seven by the time I made it back to the city, but I was confident I should find my brother still there. Thanks to this war with the Boer, he hardly ever leaves."

I saw the troubled look in his eyes and said, "He's a stout fellow, Holmes. I'm sure that he's fine, though it's understandable that you should worry. Was he able to help you?"

"Yes, indeed. Barraclough was an experienced agent, solid and dependable. He was unmarried, but lived at home with his mother, a widow. Mycroft was very distressed to hear of the man's murder. He had a glittering career ahead of him, and his death is a grievous loss to the department, especially as so many good men have signed up to join the war effort.

"Mycroft gave me Barraclough's address and I went there to see what I could learn. He lived in a flat not far from Pentonville Prison. Indeed, from his bedroom window, one could see directly into the prisoners' yard. I wondered fleetingly if the horrors he saw there had played a part in his career, but I have no evidence to support that theory. Perhaps some of your romantic ideas are rubbing off me, Watson.

"His mother let me in. She was, as you can imagine, deeply distressed to learn of her son's demise. She showed me a photograph of him which removed any lingering doubts to the dead man's identity. I confess that I longed for your presence when I spoke with her, Watson. You have a talent for comforting people that I do not possess."

"You do yourself a disservice," I said. "I have often seen you offer solace to distressed people. Was Mrs. Barraclough able to add anything to your information?"

"Sadly, no. Barraclough, being a most punctilious agent, didn't discuss his work with anyone. His mother allowed me into his bedroom and left me alone while I searched it.

"Every surface was clean – the drawers contained nothing but his clothing and other such personal items. However, I did discover one curious thing: A stack of *London Gazette* newspapers, with the oldest dated three weeks ago. I spent an hour or more examining these papers. I discovered they all had one thing in common: Personal messages from an 'S.B.' to '*The Black Panther*', and an equal number of replies."

"'The Black Panther'? Who or what is he?"

"You are skipping ahead, my dear Watson." He sat back in his seat and crossed his long legs at the ankles.

"I stopped at Scotland Yard and told the inspector what I had learned. Then I went back to Mycroft. He was able to tell me a little more about the suspected killer.

"'The Black Panther', it appears, is a spy who hails from South Africa – one of the Boer, as we suspected. As I mentioned last night, his real name, as far as anyone knows – he has several aliases – is Frederick, or 'Fritz', Joubert Duquesne. He is notorious as a liar, a swindler, and a killer.

He has been arrested and incarcerated at least twice, but both times managed to escape. What he's doing in London we can only surmise. Mycroft has some suspicions. He is going to do some research on his end. If Barraclough suspected that he was exchanging messages with this fellow, he may well have felt justified in arranging to rendezvous with him."

"A shame he went alone to the Gardens," I said. "Two men might have had a better chance of capturing the brute."

"True," he said. "But we have the benefit of hindsight. Barraclough, at the time, had no way of knowing who he might encounter there. A meeting in a public place during the day must have seemed safe enough."

I downed my coffee and poured another cup, then said, "And he ended up being stabbed to death for his trouble."

"All the indications point in that direction, certainly. However, I thought that we might go to the morgue this morning. You know I will take nothing for granted."

"You mean, there is nothing more deceptive than an obvious fact?" I quoted his own axiom.

"Precisely, my dear Watson. I would be grateful for your opinion, if you can spare the time."

"Certainly."

We fell silent, occupied with our own thoughts. Several minutes later I said, "How is your brother?"

"Overworked and distressed about this accursed war. I persuaded him to join me for a late dinner at the Diogenes Club. I think the break did him much good. I later escorted him back to his rooms and extracted a promise that he would take some rest." He chuckled. "I threatened that you would hospitalise him if he didn't comply."

"Holmes, really," I protested.

"Oh, he knew it was an empty threat, but he did at least agree to have an early night. I stood across the street for twenty minutes after I left, and saw his light go out. I'm satisfied that he behaved himself."

"That is good. So, what is your plan to capture this 'Panther' fellow?"

"I have sent a message of my own to *The Gazette* inviting him to meet me on Friday at three o'clock in the Palm House."

"Do you think he believes Barraclough is still alive?"

"He has no reason to believe otherwise. Lestrade and Mycroft have agreed to keep Barraclough's death quiet for now, and I have no doubt that our Scotland Yard friend has put the fear of God into Mr. Monk if he dares breathe a word of what he knows. Before I left Mrs. Barraclough, I extracted a similar promise from her. I know it will be difficult, but she understands that her silence may help us to capture the man who murdered her son."

"Do you know how Barraclough was killed?"

"Of course. It is surely perfectly obvious."

"I think that I follow," I began, but he was already on his feet.

"If you have dined sufficiently, my dear Watson, I should like to get to the morgue early."

We decided to walk as the weather hadn't improved. On the way, Holmes bought a copy of the most recent *Gazette*. He smiled and handed me the paper.

"*If 'The Black Panther' wishes to learn something to his advantage,*" it read, "*he will meet SH at the usual place on Thursday at 3 p.m.*"

"Nicely done," I said. "Do you think it will work?"

"I think he'll find it irresistible, but we'll have to wait and see if our fish will bite."

It was still early when we arrived at the morgue. The body had been washed but not yet examined. It didn't take long to confirm our suppositions.

"There's a considerable amount of bruising," I observed. "The wound is deep and angles downward. It appears the left renal artery was severed."

"So, the killer was taller than the victim," Holmes added. "Another piece of evidence against him, should the case ever come to court."

A little after noon on Friday, we prepared for our encounter with "The Black Panther". "Don't forget to bring your service revolver," Holmes said. "Our friend may find that a blade is no match for a Webley No. 2."

I patted my pocket. "I'm prepared."

We went downstairs and climbed into the growler that stood outside our apartments. I was surprised to see Inspector Lestrade sitting inside, waiting for us.

"Good afternoon," he said.

"Inspector," Holmes greeted him. "I must ask you gentlemen not to discuss the case until we are in a safe location. Even in a noisy machine such as this, voices carry." Then he pulled his hat down over his eyes and seemed to fall asleep.

With conversation limited to trivialities, I, too, dozed off as the carriage made its dreary way to its destination. I lurched awake when we came to a halt.

"We're here," Holmes said, already opening the door and alighting into the eerie swirls of yellow.

"Keep close together," he said. "It wouldn't do for any of us to go astray in this muck."

The policeman and I followed on his heels as he led us unerringly into the blessed warmth of the Palm House.

The air inside the glass enclosure married heat and moisture and the cloying smell of humus. Holmes whispered, "No sign of our bird yet. Gentlemen, I must ask you to make yourselves as unobtrusive as possible."

Holmes and I took our positions behind a giant palm tree, the genus of which was unfamiliar to me. The policeman melted into the fronds of yet another impressive species.

"We must be quiet," my friend whispered. "I don't think we have long to wait, but we must be prepared for every eventuality. Keep your revolver at the ready."

I nodded.

We remained as we were, obscured by the greenery, and kept watch. I was surprised to see the Palm House wasn't as deserted as I would have expected, given the inclement conditions. From time to time, people straggled by our hiding place – a chance to get out of the weather and into somewhere warm, I supposed.

Time trickled by. I glanced at my watch and saw that we had only stood there for twenty minutes. It felt like hours. Though the wait was long, and the stifling heat made me tired, I confess I thrilled to be part of the chase.

Another dreary twenty minutes passed, and then I felt Holmes tense with excitement. "There's our bird, Watson," he whispered.

The man in question was young, no more than twenty-four or -five. Despite the season, he was deeply tanned with features that wouldn't have looked amiss on a poet. He wore all black and carried a newspaper.

"That young fellow? Are you sure?"

"Decidedly so. Don't take your eyes off him. We already know that he's deadly with a blade. If you see him draw it, do not hesitate to fire."

This said, he then strolled up to the man in question with a copy of *The Daily Telegraph* in his hand and greeted him, "The cycads are extraordinary, are they not?"

"As magnificent as they are ancient," the man replied in an accent that I might have taken for Dutch. Looking around, and as there seemed to be no one to overhear their conversation, the fellow continued, "You are S.H.?"

"I am. My name is Sherlock Holmes – ah, I see you have heard of me."

The fellow hissed like an angry cat and raised his hand. I fired my revolver and he yelped in pain. The blade fell to the ground and Holmes grabbed the man before he could flee. The assassin was instantly surrounded by the men that I'd observed wandering about the Palm House.

157

"An exceptional shot, my dear Watson," Holmes said as I stepped out from my hiding place. "I'm much obliged to you."

I wrapped the man's wounded hand in a handkerchief. He snarled at me in a language I didn't recognise. Holmes picked up the deadly knife from the ground and handed it to Lestrade.

"Be careful, Inspector," he said. "This one's bite is far worse than his bark."

"He'd better not try biting me," Lestrade said with feeling. "I bite back."

Back at Scotland Yard, the man refused to talk to any of us. While he sat in a cell being asked the usual questions – his name, country of origin, and so forth – Holmes sat at the inspector's desk and made several telephone calls.

Lestrade, well used to my friend's ways, and more indulgent in his maturity than he would have been when he was a younger man, was inclined to allow Holmes considerable latitude. He waited until Holmes concluded his calls before saying, "Well?"

"Ah, Lestrade, thank you for allowing me to use your telephone. I wonder if I might question the prisoner."

"You may, of course, Mr. Holmes, but I doubt you will get much out of him."

Holmes made no reply but went down the stairs into the bowels of the Yard, where the cells were situated.

The guard at the door unlocked the cell and Holmes stepped inside and sat facing the prisoner.

"Fritz Joubert Duquesne," he said. "Or is it Frederick?"

"Fritz will do." He smiled genially. "You know my name."

"And you know mine."

"You have no cause to detain me, Mr. Holmes."

"I believe that you have been tried and convicted twice already by the courts. Both times you escaped the cell where you were incarcerated. By my reckoning, you have a great deal of time left to serve. That's not to mention the murder of Sebastian Barraclough."

"Who?" the prisoner asked with a laconic air.

"You were seen talking to him at the Palm House on Monday."

"Oh, that fellow. I didn't get his name. He's murdered, you say? How terrible." He sat back and smirked.

Holmes's face didn't change expression. "We've recovered your knife, which you were unfortunate enough to leave behind. Your obsession with the death of a particular military gentleman is known. Your freedom has come to an end. Indeed, your very life is in jeopardy."

Still, Duquesne didn't react. Making sure that he was secured in his cell, we returned to Lestrade's office. The inspector said, "Do you really think that we can bring a case against him, Mr. Holmes?"

"I'm afraid that's irrelevant, Lestrade," Holmes said. "I cannot see the case ever coming to trial. The government doesn't want Sebastian Barraclough's activities to be made public, nor the reason Duquesne arranged to meet with him in the first place. I've telephoned the relevant parties. You may expect someone to discuss it with you within the hour."

"Well, I can't say I'd be sorry to hand this case over to someone else." Looking somewhat embarrassed, Lestrade added, "I don't suppose you'd care to tell me how Mr. Barraclough came to his death? I've been mulling it over and I still can't fathom how a man steps into a carriage, a carriage which doesn't stop until it reaches its destination, by which time the unfortunate fellow is found dead."

"And you have formed no theories?"

"I've been trying to follow your process, Mr. Holmes. I remember you always say if you have eliminated the impossible, whatever remains, no matter how improbable, must be the truth. You see, I do pay attention."

"You do, indeed, Inspector," I said, as Holmes seemed unable to reply. "So, if the statement as you put it is impossible, some part must be incorrect."

"You mean the cabby is lying and the cab stopped somewhere along the way? Or did Barraclough kill himself?"

"No, no, that's not it at all," Holmes said. "The fact that the dead man was right-handed should tell you everything you need to know. Watson, be so good as to explain." He lit a cigarette and sat back in Lestrade's chair, with his eyes half-closed.

"As you wish. Well, Lestrade, the cab driver, Mr. Monk, told us the passenger was breathing hard when he got into the cab. He thought it was because the man had been hurrying, but it seems evident that Barraclough had been stabbed *before* he got into the cab. Probably only seconds before. Monk couldn't clearly see his passenger because of the fog. He was, therefore, even more unlikely to see the killer."

"Splendid, Watson," Holmes murmured.

"It's likely Barraclough didn't realise how badly injured he was. He was focused on reaching the War office. He managed to pull the knife out of his lower back and placed it on the newspaper beside him. Frankly, he may have lived a little longer if he'd left the knife *in situ*. Its presence may have contained the bleeding. He removed the blade, possibly magnifying the damage already done, and allowing the blood to flow freely. He bled to death in a matter of minutes."

159

"Well, that's clear enough. Poor fellow. I wonder he didn't go first to a hospital."

"The end result would probably have been the same," I said. "The renal artery was severed."

"And he was anxious to make his report to his superior at the War Office," Holmes added.

"What did he have to tell them?" Lestrade persisted. "And what did that letter '*K*' have to do with it?"

"I'm afraid I can say no more, Inspector. Perhaps the government official will expand."

The fog had, mercifully, lifted by the time we left Scotland Yard. London bustled with the early-evening traffic, and we had no difficulty catching a cab back to Baker Street.

"I suppose you can't tell me any more than you did Lestrade?" I asked as we relaxed that evening in front of the fire.

"A little," he replied, "Though my earlier admonishment about the story not finding its way into print still stands."

"You have my word."

"Well, then, this is what Mycroft told me: 'The Black Panther' is Duquesne's soubriquet. He is merely twenty-four years of age and already has an ignominious history. Many of the tales about him come from his own mouth, and as he is an inveterate liar, we must treat them with a healthy amount of scepticism.

"Fritz Duquesne was born in London, but his family moved to South Africa not long after he was born. He had an excellent education here in London and in Brussels. He speaks several languages. He joined the Boer army as a commando in '99 and reached the rank of Captain. He was captured twice, once by the British, and once by the Portuguese. Both times he escaped.

"Duquesne's family home in Nylstroom was destroyed by the British Army. Most of his family was wiped out in a horrible manner, and his mother was interred in what Kitchener calls 'concentration camps'. Grotesque places of brutality, hunger, and disease if the reports are to be believed.

"After learning what befell his family, Duquesne developed a deep hatred of the British, and of the army's commander, Kitchener, in particular. Mycroft tells me he has already tried to kill Kitchener twice. He is nothing if not indefatigable."

"So '*K*' stood for Kitchener? Duquesne was trying to get information from Barraclough about Kitchener's movements?" Suddenly, the reason for the dead man's determination to report to the War Office became clear.

160

"His movements, and any possible weaknesses in his defences. That is Mycroft's theory, and I believe he is correct. In the beginning, when Barraclough began exchanging messages with 'The Black Panther', I think he had some suspicions of his correspondent's identity, but there was no proof of anything, and Duquesne was extremely careful to avoid detection.

"After a few weeks' exchanges, the two men agreed to meet, and we saw the tragic consequences. Duquesne was prepared to take a risk to get the information he desired. Possibly, Barraclough hoped to trap his killer with some promises, but Duquesne was too wily for him. I suspect Barraclough said the wrong thing or could not conceal his disgust. In any case, Duquesne decided the poor fellow was too dangerous to live. He followed him from the gardens into the city and stabbed him moments before Barraclough climbed into Mr. Monk's cab."

"And Barraclough was trying to write Kitchener, but blood loss prevented him from writing more than the first letter. Poor soul."

Two days later, Holmes returned from a meeting at the War Office in as bad a temper as I have ever seen.

"What on earth has happened?" I asked.

"That blackguard Duquesne has escaped. He was being transferred from the cells at Scotland Yard to what Mycroft would only describe as 'a more secure location'. Somehow, he managed to pick the locks of his manacles and the vehicle that was transporting him, and he has fled."

Fifteen years have passed since that foggy November day when we were summoned to the case of the unfortunate Sebastian Barraclough. At my friend's request, I didn't write up the story until today, but I shall not publish it. Word has come that Kitchener has died aboard the HMS *Hampshire*. The newspapers report the ship went down when it hit a mine. Perhaps. And yet I cannot help but wonder where Fritz Joubert Duquesne is. Did he get his man at last? Perhaps we will never know.

The Deceased Priest
by Peter Coe Verbica

Chapter I – The Deceased Priest

It was early evening in London and blustery. Blackbirds fought against the wind and sought shelter in the elms. In contrast, I found myself replete after supper – safely cocooned in our bachelor's apartment on Baker Street for the evening. The gaslamp behind Holmes illuminated his elongated and brooding features. The eccentric detective wore a gold-embroidered Turkish cap and stood next to the hearth mantle. His smoking cap owed its heritage to the Crimean War and the storied battle of Balaclava. When I asked, Holmes refused to go into great detail about the memento. He demurred, saying that enough controversy had swirled around the Earl of Cardigan and his infamous Charge of the Light Brigade. The fire of that war had been settled when Holmes was but a child, but he believed its embers continued to smoulder. The fez, he confessed, was a token of his involvement in a recent Balkan intrigue. When I pressed him further, he explained that it was bestowed upon him by one of the Queen's most trusted advisors. As I say, exact details as to the oddity's provenance remain cloaked by Holmes's steadfast discretion.

A craving for tobacco beckoned to me like a persuasive mouse upon my shoulder, urging me to indulge in an evening cigar. I opened the wooden cigar box and lifted out a colored postcard of a fanciful underwater scene, a damsel being saved from a giant squid.

Admiring the whimsical art, I dove into a fresh row of cylinders. While Sir Walter Raleigh may be credited for tobacco's popularity, Holmes would opine how Spanish and Portuguese sailors were more likely the initial ambassadors for the "brown gold". And, despite the Papacy's aspersions, its popularity has held fast, to the relief of good British gentlemen and the glee of landed Virginians. The Crown has become the richer for the custom as well, since the habit's persistency is a steady source of tax revenue. Without cigars, the Empire would also miss out on Jean-Marc Côté's illustrations of sea creatures and flying firemen. But I digress.

Turning my attention to Holmes once again, I observed that my friend held what appeared to be a small Anglican Book of Common Prayer and hymnal. I recognized the gilt lettering, deep red leather binding, and silk page-marker. Knowing Holmes to be a student of science more often than theology, I was surprised to see him leafing through the dog-eared pages.

He looked up from the book and his eyes followed horizontally past his scattered scientific beakers, his card cabinets, and an ashtray in need of emptying before he returned his intense gaze to me. Inner gears in the great mechanism of his mind whirred a myriad of hidden wheels and cogs.

"Watson, would you be able to take a brief leave from your medical profession? I have begun a case which manifests some perplexing elements."

"My practice is quiet at present." I told him.

"Capital! An Episcopal priest passed away recently. He was of some prominence, a widower from an illustrious family. I've been asked by his young protégé, the Reverend Thomas Wilson Taff, to provide insight. Though Inspector Lestrade has ruled the death was of natural causes, Father Taff feels otherwise."

"Murder? I remember reading about his passing. He presided over St. Paul's for many years, then took up a smaller parish away from London."

"Correct. Allow me to fill in a few details with which you may be acquainted: The reverend to whom I'm referring is Sir Francesco Bartoni – raised a Catholic and one of the more famous Anglican converts. He was exceedingly popular while in London, and an amateur biologist of some repute. He changed parishes, I've been advised, in part because the bishop and deacons found the priest's homilies bordering on the heretical."

"Ceremonies involving goats, like the Masons?" I mocked.

"Not quite. The reverend was friends with a certain beetle collector – by the name of Charles Darwin. Both studied divinity at Christ's College, though Father Bartoni attended years after the controversial and well-known scientist. Father Bartoni came from means – his family owned a

163

series of successful jewelry shops. To his relatives' dismay, I'm told, he helped underwrite a few of Darwin's endeavors. Both men enjoyed ornithology and would have animated discourse over finches."

Holmes removed a small card from between the pages of the prayer book and handed what appeared to be a Christmas greeting to me.

"What do you make of this?"

"A well-done likeness of a dead robin," I commented, observing the colored etching's detail.

"Rendered by the priest, Holmes explained. "Examine the back if you would."

I flipped the card and noticed the following gibberish, scribbled neatly in blue-black ink:

etewttXc h ssXa,ttuuXfd iddX ao Xyetfro.hrnootntbu fnr t uuftnu:
toaronde eu enrt trka aueoa ueorft,owh thstu; urt odoa ethnh thltutulta o
oa hlrthhnslgstsI i a

"I can't make sense of this, I'm afraid."

"Watson, once you understand how the cipher was composed, it's rather child's play. You remember, for example, the substitution technique used in the case you refer to as 'The Dancing Men'? And, you know my hobby of scanning for secret messages hidden from time to time in our newspapers."

"Yes," I answered, handing the card back to him.

"The code is easily solved if you realize it is a rotation cipher, composed by using a box with twenty-four columns. If you rotate the box to the left ninety degrees, and ignore the extraneous X's," the answer comes to life."

"Goodness. Please enlighten me."

"You will recognize it as a quotation from the King James Bible:

> *In the sweat of thy face shalt thou eat bread, till thou return unto the ground; For out of it wast thou taken: for dust thou art, and unto dust shalt thou return.*

"The book of *Genesis* . . . ." I said, thinking aloud.

"Yes. Chapter 3, Verse 9."

"An odd choice to encrypt. It foreshadows his own demise."

"It does, but I believe that there's more to this than a lesson regarding our temporal bodies."

"It's a mystery to me."

Holmes placed the prayer book down on a footstool next to him and

164

took up his pipe.

"The ether has begun to take shape, but much still perplexes me as well. Tomorrow, we shall pay a visit to the priest's protégé."

Chapter II – The Friendly Stranger

Early the next day we stood at the train station, which was bathed in gray. Steam from the locomotive's boiler escaped through the engine's dome and around its wheels. The conductor stood at the base of the Pullman coach's steps. He wore a dark coat affixed by a top button and busied himself with his watch, which was attached to a heavy chain. The train manager checked the time on a metal wall clock, then returned his gaze to his timepiece. A train whistle pierced the air and we boarded the outbound line. I hung my hat on a hook above our table and sat in an upholstered chair. Though there were only two of us, it was a four-seater adorned with a white tablecloth and a small silver-plate vase of flowers. The car's narrow walkway cleared as passengers hurriedly took to the diner's seats.

A short man with a bald head and full beard dabbed his forehead as he stood next to Holmes. As the train began to move, the man shifted his feet unsteadily under him, and he appeared disoriented. With all the seats taken, he looked enviously through his eyeglasses at our comfort. Tardiness is a quality punished by a variety of consequences, including who gets the best seats on a train.

"Please join us," Holmes said affably, pointing to the open chair next to him.

"Gentlemen, gentlemen!" the man exclaimed with relief as he seated himself. "My sincerest gratitude!"

"Would you like a glass of water?" I asked, leaning toward the bottle on the table.

"Why, yes! Yes, indeed. That would be just the tonic."

He gulped it quickly and I refilled his glass.

"Thank you! That hits the spot. Quite a jog to the station. I'm off on an important errand today and became distracted by my preparation. I dread a late start. Only scorned women are more unforgiving than a train which leaves on time."

As the man spoke, I tried to observe minute details of his dress and mannerisms, as I had seen Holmes do in prior instances. The man's fingernails seemed in need of a trim, but weren't dirty. The cuffs of his shirt were mildly frayed, and hailed from an earlier or foreign style. Also of some distraction, he had a strong floral odor, which I discerned from across the table. His spectacle lenses needed cleaning, and his coat

165

handkerchief, though clean, was un-ironed. He was bald on the top of his head, but his hair at the sides of his temple was full and tamed with oil. Were I to guess his age, I'd place the man in his mid-forties. Though slightly overweight, he seemed to move with agility. I surmised he must be a clerk of some sort.

He pulled a newspaper from inside his jacket and unfolded it in front of his place setting. Some rail travelers have perfected the art of halving a newspaper vertically while reading in tighter, public spaces – this art had escaped our fellow traveler. Despite his glasses, the man put his face close to the newsprint. He pawed at the pages noisily.

"Catching up on last week's news, I see . . . ." Holmes offered before turning to peer out of the carriage window.

A white-jacketed waiter filled our glasses and handed us small menus. Our uninvited guest continued to peruse the broadsheet in front of him, rather than his menu.

"Big breakfast already!" he explained, moving his head slightly from side to side. "Perhaps I'll have a roll and some jam in a bit."

Holmes ordered smoked trout and cheese and I copied him. Our stop would soon be reached, interrupting a more elaborate meal.

Our breakfast was served and we proceeded to enjoy the sustenance. Holmes, though often contemplative, seemed to me to be quieter than usual. When presented with new company, he could be conversational and animated, but this morning he kept to his thoughts. Our visitor focused on his reading, holding the text close to his nose.

I turned to look behind to see if I could catch the waiter's attention when I heard an unexpected commotion. Our tablemate had accidentally knocked over the water bottle and vase and was doing his best to retrieve the items. He patted the water off of my coat with a napkin with energetic apology and stood up.

"Let me retrieve our waiter!" the man exclaimed. His forehead and cheeks were flush with embarrassment. "I'm aghast, just aghast!"

To my surprise, Holmes grabbed the man by the scruff of his neck and abruptly forced him back down into his chair.

"You'll do nothing of the sort," Holmes said coolly. Holmes leaned across the small table and jerked the sides of the man's jacket down, effectively disabling his arm movement. Holmes then pulled items from the man's interior pockets. An assortment of gentlemen's wallets and coin purses of various shapes, sizes, and colors were quickly produced.

Other passengers took notice of the commotion and a determined guard made his way down our car's aisle.

"Watson, I think that you'll find one of these familiar."

"Good grief!" I looked down and recognized my wallet, emblazoned with my initials. I quickly retrieved it and slipped it inside my coat.

"Gentlemen, we can handle this rogue from here!" the guard declared, enlisting the waiter's help. Other patrons in the car rose and clapped a loud applause.

Our waiter apologized for the inconvenience and graciously insisted that breakfast would be courtesy of the London and Northwestern Railway.

As the train slowed to our station, Holmes stood, tipped his hat, and turned to a service employee. "Thank you for your hospitality and a stimulating meal."

Watching our train depart the rural red-and-salt-stained bricked station, I turned to Holmes. "I suppose you knew what that reprobate was plotting the whole time?"

"The dated newspaper was but one clue of his intent. A humble word of advice, Watson: I've found that the friendlier the stranger, the higher the probability he is a card-sharp, a petty thief, or bond salesman. And, in terms of damages to one's pocketbook," Holmes resolved, "the last of the three can be the worst."

Chapter III – In Search of a Fortune

We arrived at an impeccable gabled rectory behind the main church – clay spikes ruled its rooflines like dragon's teeth and corrugated brickwork gave geometry to the multitude of its chimney caps. Bright white window frames accented the honey-stucco. We walked along a neatly organized, white-gravel stone path lined by squat hedgerows. By the main entrance of the priest's home, I saw a small belt-driven steam contraption, perhaps used to power the irrigation. A riveted boiler stood next to it. There a small pile of what looked like decomposed granite sat near, along with a square shovel propped against the wall.

Father Taff greeted us with firm handshakes. He was bright-eyed, with a strong jaw and the upright carriage of a man in his thirties who took his calling seriously. A white dog-collar punctuated his traditional black attire. Though formal in manner, his voice resonated affably. He seemed to be one who could put others at ease, and proved this ability by ushering us in through a wide hall with waxed floors to a drawing room, and subsequently past richly-varnished pocket doors to a larger parlor with white-plastered walls, a high ceiling, and windows which flooded the room with a warm ambiance. After our salutations, we sat in matching rosewood-and-needlepoint armchairs. The height and width of the chairs were more modest than I would have preferred, lending to my self-consciousness of appearing all knees and elbows. Thankfully, I was distracted when we were promptly offered tea and biscuits.

Despite the light meal on the train, we found ourselves enjoying the communion of yet another. I noticed a crown high-backed oak parlor organ against one of the plain interior walls. It was flanked by two small kerosene lamps held by built-in, silver stands. At the contraption's center was a mirror above an embedded sheet music holder. The room, though more than fifty years of age, looked as if it had been freshly scrubbed. Oil paintings of men of the cloth neatly hung from the textured walls. The room's starkness was relieved by a horizontal paint-line the color of saddle leather, approximately one inch wide and at eye level. While the premises were flawless, none of the decorum leapt out as ostentatious.

"A gift of one of our wealthy parishioners," the reverend said after noticing my observation of the organ. "It was built abroad by the eponymous George P. Bent Piano and Organ Company – its founder won medals at the World's Fair. Not as rich in tones as the one in the church proper, but it has its own personality. This musical instrument doesn't boom with resonance or reverberation. Instead, it beseeches with a finesse. A few of the upper registers border on shrill, but slowing and speeding the delivery of notes helps distract the listener. Reverend Bartoni was a master at such subterfuge when he played. After his wife died, I think the pipe and parlor organs helped him best express his sorrows."

"What makes you believe that the reverend met with foul play?" Holmes asked, placing his steepled fingers to his chin.

"It's my conviction, Mr. Holmes, that the reverend was mysteriously killed in a foiled attempt at robbery."

"What engenders this severe opinion, Father Taff?" Holmes asked.

"He died with a tortured look upon his face, Mr. Holmes, as if he had been strangled, or had been gasping for air. I found him in his room, lying upon the floor entangled in the area rug, as if he were trying to get to his bedroom door, but unable to make it."

He cleared his throat and continued. "The reverend served not only as our main parish priest, but also as its treasurer. This was, from time to time, a bone of contention with the deacons. In particular, of late, they had concern over a large balance sheet item labeled '*Accrued Savings*'. Father Bartoni despised banks. He viewed them as rapacious, especially when it came to foreclosing on farms and estates of the distraught and ignorant. One of his favorite sayings was, 'I trust dead metals over live bankers.' Of great concern to me, we have yet to determine the custodian who holds these assets. The reverend insisted there was no worry, as his wife also knew who held the money. But she predeceased him and no other confidante had been chosen, to my knowledge."

Holmes looked up to the ceiling, as was common when he laid out the pieces of a puzzle in his mind.

"Aside from the fiscal concern, which should be solved by reviewing his correspondence, I'm trying to determine the kernel of your suspicions as to his demise. Is there more than his *post mortem* grimace?"

"There is more than one seed from which sprouts my doubt, Mr. Holmes. I continue to find certain things subtly moved or ajar. Books. Furniture. Paintings. Objects of worship. Cistern lids in the garden. As if someone is quietly searching for something. Turning over stones, as it were."

"Did you notice anything plainly unusual at the time of his passing?"

"Unfortunately, no. His garments were neatly folded, his Bible was by his bedside, his papers and wallet were untouched – nothing was out of place. The housekeeper did have a start when tidying – she discovered a dead bat."

Holmes rose and slapped his hands. "The fog is beginning to dissipate. You've been tremendously helpful. Has the sheet music on the parlor organ been changed since the good father's passing?" Holmes inquired as he leaned over the bench to inspect the keys and stops.

"No, Mr. Holmes."

Holmes picked up the top page and cleared his throat:

> *That we may feed thy poor aright,*
> *And gathering round thy throne*
> *Here, in the holy angels' sight,*
> *Repay thee of thine own.*
> *For so our sires in olden time*
> *Spared neither gold nor gear,*
> *Nor precious wood nor hewen stone,*
> *Thy sacred shrines to rear.*

"From Benson's 'O Throned, O Crowned with All Renown' hymn. You have an ecclesiastic cadence, Mr. Holmes. You would make a worthy deacon."

"Thank you, Father Taff, but I'm more at ease with chemicals than with congregations. May I trouble you to escort Dr. Watson and myself to Father Bartoni's bedroom?

"Certainly."

The consulting detective opened the curtains of the room and surveyed the spartan contents. The walls were whitewashed and had a rough texture, like the rest of the residence.

At a simply appointed desk, a folio of drawings was neatly arranged with an array of pencils, pen nibs, and ink wells.

On the shelf was a variety of books that showed the man's eclectic tastes – on sermons, India, Africa, gemology, mining, smelting, music, natural selection, steam engines, ornithology, and law.

"A polymath like you, eh, Holmes?" I remarked.

"Has his room remained untouched, other than what you described? I see his Holy Book, but no lamp by which to read it at night."

"I suppose you're correct, Mr. Holmes. Father Bartoni used an old hurricane kerosene lamp. Perhaps it was placed elsewhere. We're still in a bit of a shock, like a ship unmoored, without its captain."

"Pity the curious, Watson. If I believed in reincarnation like the heathen, I should like to return wholly contented and unquestioning."

Holmes pulled a magnifying lens from this coat pocket and examined the plaster. "Watson, note the garlic," Holmes said, pointing to a dried braid hanging on the wall next to the bed.

"A superstition from the old country to ward off evil spirits?" I asked.

"There's more to it here than mere superstition, Watson. Does Father Bartoni have surviving relatives, Father Taff?"

"Yes, a younger brother and sister. The brother, Abel, is affiliated with Sir William Ramsay at University College, London. The sister lives with her husband and their three children on a significant estate in Cumberland.

"This visit has proven most fruitful. Please get me a list of the parishioners and staff, and their respective professions, won't you?"

"Certainly, Mr. Holmes. Straight-away."

Holmes shook the hand of our host, as did I, and we bid him a good day.

"Watson, before we leave, let us visit the chapel," Holmes said, making a beeline past the parish cemetery to the slate-roofed building.

Holmes opened the main door and we stood in the cool quietude, taking in the whitewashed plaster walls. The faintest hint of incense informed my nostrils of a preceding service. The floor was a zig-zag arrangement of large rectangular stones the color of sandstone. Rows of pews lined each side of the aisle. Beams of light streamed through the clear leaded windows, reflecting off of the plaster and adding to the sanctuary's brightness. Icons of saints were placed economically – a large gold eagle near the lectern, an homage to St. John the Apostle, was the most intriguing feature, save for a stained-glass window over the altar and the organ pipes.

Holmes put his hand to the rough wall and stared at the floor. I could see him smiling inconspicuously.

"Are we hiking up the bell tower?" I asked, my old war wound pulsating around my joint.

170

To my mild relief, he replied, "No. That won't be necessary. Let us walk back to the train station, shall we?"

As we left, I noticed a gardener in overalls working a spade in a flower bed. His head was bent and I was unable to discern the features of his face, which were hidden by the shadow of his cap.

The sky darkened as we made our way along the pathway. Though I'm not superstitious, I shivered involuntarily when a large raven croaked above us.

Chapter IV – The Irate Pianist

The following day, we approached the Bartoni family estate, with its impressive Georgian architecture and wrought-iron fences near Hyde Park Corner, a few blocks past the Wellington Arch's new location. Like the famous duke who passed to the Great Beyond at Walmer, the enormous and maligned statue of his likeness was long gone. The massive bronze of Wellington holding his baton had been moved near Garrison Church on Round Hill in Aldershot – the metal tribute had been saved from the Queen's ire and smelter by no less than the British Army.

The familiar sound of horses' hooves bouncing off cobblestones changed as we traversed a crushed-stone path to the main entrance. A bower of trees softened the edges of the manor and we made our way past the columns and a series of urns set atop brick pedestals. The estate was crisscrossed by paths and hedgerows, but its owners had a practical side as well: I observed rows of fruit trees, no doubt for jams, jellies, and pies concocted by the kitchen staff. The residence proper had a commanding view of a substantial pond and a far-reaching park. Of clarity to me: These generations of jewelers had fared well. Wisteria blooms filled the air with their luxurious scent.

A gloved butler with pronounced jowls who looked more hound-like than human greeted us. We were escorted through a number of wide hallways punctuated by wooden columns with gilded capitals to a large salon. This room continued the theme of wood, and gold-leaf accented the friezes, showing a preference for the ornate. The walls away from the windows were lined with bookshelves. A gleaming Bechstein grand piano filled one of the corners.

A lightly olive-skinned woman with eyes as green and bright as emeralds greeted us. Her face was classically Roman, and she looked to be in her early thirties. Dressed in a simple but elegant gown, she met us with a business-like curtsey, but refrained from extending her hand. Her brunette hair was tastefully arranged in a high bun nested with miniature accessories. A bejeweled choker adorned her elegant neck, and from it

171

hung a large, pear-shaped pink stone. She waved a fan slowly at her face and then set it down on an end table. Her eyes surveyed us unhurriedly and then narrowed. We were not invited to sit. Before her rested a series of neatly folded newspapers – the top one featured a headline regarding *The Scotsman*, a passenger ship which had sunk two months prior.

"Thank you for seeing us, Mrs. Ross," Holmes said, bowing slightly.

"Mr. Holmes," she said, with surprising forcefulness, "I prefer my maiden name of Bartoni. Now, I'm told by the Reverend Taff that you are investigating my brother's passing. I know that he believes there's been some kind of foul play. That, to me, sounds melodramatic and fanciful. I think he's simply a sycophant going through the shock of realizing that his inconsequential church has lost its greatest benefactor."

"Your brother was generous to his church, I take it?" Holmes asked, raising his brow with his hands clasped behind his back.

"Generous!" she exclaimed. "The church, Mr. Holmes, is but a leech that latches onto the fattest calf it can find. It is a vulture which circles the carcasses of the dead. It is but a wolf on a leash which does Her Majesty's bidding. In my estimation, divinity school erased any sense from my brother's head. Our father, God rest his soul, did his best by establishing trusts to stanch the flow of blood. But after my oldest brother reached his thirty-fifth year, he was able to spend not only the income, but also the *corpus*. While bankers are discreet, because of our family's long-standing relationship, I was quietly informed that my brother imprudently had withdrawn all of his substantial inheritance. And, over time, he divested his landholdings as well."

"His parish is well-cared for, but by all appearances, impresses me as a modest one. The structures are in good repair and the grounds well-maintained. The fences are mended, and I saw no evidence of the roofs leaking," the detective said. "Wouldn't you agree, Dr. Watson?"

"Yes. Nothing disproportionate to the general area."

"Gentlemen," she said, "my brother had the financial wherewithal to build a cathedral if he wanted to do so. But, I will confess that this conversation wears on my good temperament. It is the fodder of family dinners and should not be the grist of debate with strangers – especially a pair such as yourselves, who manage to capture newspaper headlines with your sordid capers. Is it not sufficient to allow the dead to rest in peace, no matter how foolish they were while living?"

She reached out and grabbed a silver bell which I hadn't noticed earlier and rang it with authority. Then, she walked directly to the piano, pulled out the sleek bench abruptly, and swept her dress so that she could sit in comfort. She opened the fall and placed her hands upon the keyboard. Her hands began to vigorously strike the keys and she bowed her head

172

with the determination of a jockey coaxing a horse into full stride. I recognized it as Verdi.

The butler cleared his throat and we followed him out of the room. As we walked towards the main foyer, Holmes turned to me with the thundering notes of the enormous piano behind us.

"The *Requiem* is full of defiance and frustration isn't it? It's an angry epitaph to Rossini and Manzoni. Our modern world is a steady march away from subtlety. It will only get worse."

"I'm not sure about that, but I am sure that her rendition provides a spirited exclamation point to our exit."

"You might say she gave us the musical boot. Such drama is but a map of her Italian heritage." Holmes winked imperceptibly.

"Indeed," I said, realizing slowly that his pun referred to the shape of that country's famous coastline.

Chapter V – A Cry for Help

"Did I ever share with you "The Mystery of the Blind-folded Prince", Watson? Perhaps you can include it in your journals, along with *A Study in Scarlet.*

"I don't believe so. I'm sure that I would remember it."

"The young man was from one of the Northern African countries which the French love to colonize. He was taken in the dead of night, blind-folded, read a list of demands and threats, then released."

"Released? Why on earth would the kidnappers do that?"

"They wanted the prince to collect various Algerian antiquities from storage where only his presence was accepted as security so as to prevent fraud."

"Not a trusting lot, I take it."

"When they're from the old country, they rarely are. The nobleman sent for my assistance, nearly paralyzed with fear. When I asked for details of his apprehension, he was unable to provide descriptions of his captors. He could only account for an approximation of the time of his journey to-and-fro, that the men had muffled Gallic accents, and that he had been taken roughly down a set of stairs where the temperature dropped noticeably. And he noticed the smell of coal."

"The carriage could have been driven in circles, so time wouldn't assure the winnowing of possibilities. Correct?"

"Precisely."

"The one additional detail which he was able to relate was the horrific sound of either a woman or child periodically screaming for help. The kidnappers said that it was someone whom they planned to kill later, and that the prince should obey their explicit instructions or suffer the same fate."

"How on earth did you prevent more travesty with so few facts?"

"I solved the case with a telegram to a friend who ran the Rotterdam Zoo."

"A zookeeper helped you? I will confess I do not follow."

"If you've visited a Rothschild house as I have, you would understand my line of thinking."

"A banker's house?"

"A prominent feature in most of the Rothschilds' estates is the aviary. I telegraphed my friend to inquire as to who dealt with exotic birds, including peacocks. They have a habit, when loose, of perching upon chimneys. Their eerie calls can sound very similar to a cry for help. For the shriek to be heard in a cellar, I summarized that a chimney shaft would be the best medium."

"Thus, the steps and change in temperature?"

"Correct. I was able to determine eleven potential locations throughout the Greater London and then dispatched our Baker Street Irregulars. Most pass these street orphans by without notice. They are underestimated, but I've found the lads to be remarkably observant. In short order, one reported to me that he had overheard a strange language near Waddesdon Manor. I promptly notified Lestrade. The main instigator turned out to be one of the prince's staff."

"Do you anticipate a similar outcome with respect to Father Bartoni's death? I noted only the housekeeper and a gardener on our visit."

"Domestics and workmen have been associated with crime, though most are of good moral character. An instance which comes to mind, of course, is George Joseph Smith, the 'Brides in the Bathtubs' murderer. He would enlist his wives, who were also maids, in his criminal activities. But our conversation is about to be interrupted, for I hear Mrs. Hudson bringing supper."

"Let us speak of a cheerier topic then."

"If you must," Holmes said, clamping an unlit, oily clay pipe between his teeth. He turned his attention to a treatise entitled, *Investigations in the Toluic and Nitrotoluic Acids*. No doubt he would eat his dinner cold hours later, but such were the habits of my eccentric friend, who elevated scientific esoterica above the demands of his stomach.

Chapter VI – The College Visit

Holmes invited me to accompany him on a visit to Father Bartoni's brother, Abel, a professor who taught at the University College, London.

174

I readily accepted the opportunity, though in the back of my mind, I knew I would soon need to return my energies to medicine. I selfishly hoped Holmes would soon make his conclusions and close the net.

The secular college was anchored by its main building and featured a classical covered entrance and dome. Holmes seemed to know his way as we walked briskly to the Chemical Laboratory and Lecture Theatre. Unlike other parts of the college, which were more domesticated, the room reminded me of a rough barn with its high ceiling and cross beams. Windows in the ceiling helped illuminate the facility. Scores of glass chemical bottles of various sizes on shelves lined the walls. Next to the lecturer's countertop, a fire extinguisher provided testament that not all of the gases studied by the students were inert. The whole theatre was heated by a single, round Gurney warm-air stove.

A man in a worker's coat hunched over a brass alcohol burner, observing a bubbling, oddly shaped flask which bristled with glass tubes and clamps. At first, I took him for a foreigner, with darkened skin as if he hailed from the tropics. He had a full head of black hair. His manner was catlike – as he preoccupied himself with his experiment, he moved swiftly and quietly about the apparatus.

"Professor Bartoni, please allow me to introduce myself. I am Sherlock Holmes, and this is my associate, Dr. John Watson."

Though the man didn't look up, I could see enough of his face to recognize the resemblance to images that I had seen of his sibling. His features, though, were profoundly more masculine. "Insufficient to bother my sister, gentlemen? Is your mission complete only upon the annoyance of our entire family?"

"How is your work with noble gases progressing?" Holmes asked.

"You'll have to ask 'the Chief'," the professor answered flatly, pointing to a lectern which was labeled "Sir William Ramsay" in gold lettering.

"If this college really wanted to pursue something noble, it would fund research for the cure of syphilis besides toxic mercury pills," he continued.

"As a physician, I couldn't agree more," I offered.

"My dear brother believed it could be prayed out of existence," the professor said, with a huff of exasperation.

"If prayer brings about better habits, that is certainly true," Holmes proposed.

The professor looked at the flame before of him and then set a down a clamp to one side as if it were a chess piece.

"As a scientist, you can understand better than most our wanting to meet with you," Holmes said. "Your brother died intestate. With his wife predeceasing him, and no offspring, you and your sister are his main and equal beneficiaries as blood relatives."

"Holmes, I have no need for my brother's money. My wants are simple. I am a man of science. One can spend only so much on phials and sulfites. I agree with my sister that Father Taff's speculation that my brother met with foul play is preposterous. Now if you don't mind, I would like to focus on my experiment."

"May I suggest you can achieve improved results by not using hot metals? Perhaps," Holmes proposed to the chemist, "you could use a solution of potassium nitrite and ammonium chloride, and heat it in a water bath."

"Mr. Holmes! I do not need the input of an amateur! Now, gentlemen please take leave."

"As you request, Professor Bartoni."

Exiting the college, Holmes looked up at the gray cloud cover and stopped to examine an arbor of small trees behind fencing in the square.

"Watson, remind me to share my thoughts with Sir William Ramsay in the near future, won't you?"

"Of course," I responded.

"Forgive my wit after our visiting a chemistry lab, but I do see a 'solution' to this conundrum," Holmes said. "As our role in this matter is unofficial, soon we shall let in Lestrade and company pocket the credit."

Chapter VII – Staring at Stones and Walls

"Watson, our modern time, perhaps more than any other, enables us to cull curios from about the globe to fill glass cabinets. Rather than simple *objet d'art*, I think that we are at our best when we collect wisdom from ancient and widespread cultures as well. Though it is peculiar to us, understanding from abroad has its own sensibilities and refinements."

"Are you harkening to Egypt?"

"I was pondering the sayings of an Oriental. One mystic warns, 'The ignorant mind, with its infinite afflictions, passions, and evils, is rooted in the three poisons: Greed, anger, and delusion.'"

"A pessimist about human nature, then?"

"You might say so. But, I might describe the mystic more as dogged. Legend has it that he stared at a wall for seven years."

"Surely he could have come up with a better pastime . . . ."

"On my visits to Bartoni's church, I have been engaged in the mystic's practice."

"Staring at walls?"

"Indeed. And stones. I have found it extremely enlightening. Most

176

people see, but they do not observe."

Holmes tapped his oily clay pipe firmly into his palm and tossed the ashes. He deftly scooped fresh tobacco from a vest pouch and clamped the mouthpiece between his teeth. Igniting a match, he drew the flame into the bowl. A blue cloud formed about his visage and he brushed his hands together, revealing his excitement. I realized that he was well on the trail of his quarry.

"On another topic, what do you know of The Lloyd's Act of 1871?"

"Frighteningly little, I acknowledge. Lloyd's of London. Something to do with insurance, I suppose. A topic sure to put even the most wide-eyed listener to sleep!"

"True, though it does remind one of eggs and bacon. The hen, as it's said, is interested, but the pig is committed. Lloyd's Act, at its simplest, is an attempt to lower risk in exchange for a fee. Groups of financial backers – or 'Names' – underwrite various activities, including those crucial to import and export. These 'pools' are called 'syndicates'. The 'Names' are those wealthy families who get to eat at a gilded trough."

"A circumstance of fat hogs getting fatter?" I queried.

"A necessary evil to keep commerce vibrant. But catastrophe can strike driving a dagger into the best balance sheets."

"Men plan and God laughs, I suppose."

"Nicely done Watson – a Yiddish proverb, no less. We might recognize it as '*A man's heart deviseth his way, but the Lord directeth his steps.*' It is the key for solving Father Bertoni's death – as it illuminates the motive."

How mystics, underwriting of risks, and proverbs fit into the death of a priest confounded me, but I kept quiet as I pondered Holmes's cues. Lloyd's, given its prominence, would undoubtedly be involved in the insurance of ships which chugged to various ports in the Americas and the Orient. Did the company underwrite railway risks as well? Bridges? Mining operations? I recalled the Combs Colliery mining disaster in Thornhill. There was the Norwood Junction rail accident after a girder cracked due to bad casting – I witnessed the aftermath. Luckily, none were seriously hurt, but I had to treat the brakeman for a head injury and a passenger for a dislocated ankle. The Board of Trade enlisted General Hutchinson to investigate the under-bridges for defects. I didn't know the man well, but I remember him at the scene – squarely bearded, in military attire with dark circles under his eyes, evidence of his solemnity.

Chapter VIII – The Man with One Shoe

It was early morning when Lestrade pulled open the door at Baker

Street. He moved with some agitation and gave the appearance of a man who had been inconvenienced. He was followed in by one of his detectives, solidly built as a rail worker.

"Just in time for morning tea, I see, Inspector," Holmes said, waving the man into the room. "Please come join us."

"Mr. Holmes," Lestrade replied, "I have better things to do with my morning than discuss a case which has been closed."

"Very well, we shall utilize your time efficiently. I took the time to invite Father Bartoni's brother to visit as well, but before he arrives, let me share with you my findings. Your jail will have two new occupants when I'm finished."

Lestrade narrowed his eyes, as a creature might when a bright light is shone upon it in the darkness. "Proceed, Mr. Holmes."

"My first clue that something was amiss turned on a misplaced lantern. Such a trivial, commonplace item, inconsequential in and of itself, but in this instance, of utmost poignancy. Was it picked up by the housekeeper or another member of the staff? Alas, it had disappeared completely from the premises. Why would anyone wish to steal such a petty and worthless object?"

"Perhaps because it no longer worked and was thrown away or sent out for repair?" Lestrade posited.

"Plausible," Holmes responded. "Ah, I hear the faint footsteps of either a skilled prowler or our professor of chemistry."

The professor entered. "I see that you've troubled others to visit besides myself," he announced. "Now, you wrote to me that you have news of my brother's missing fortune."

"True," Holmes responded. "Watson, would you be kind enough to mind the door? I'm expecting an important guest by the name of Mrs. Hudson."

I followed his Holmes's instructions, surmising my role was to block an unwanted exit.

"Professor, did you visit your brother the day of his passing?"

"If you must know, Holmes, we weren't on the best of terms. So, the answer is 'No'."

"Have you returned to the parish since?"

"The bulk of my time is spent at the college," the professor replied. "Again: 'No'. This has nothing to do with why you asked me here. You said you knew where his assets lie."

Studying the professor, I noticed that he had a mild case of *aniridia* – the irises of his eyes were nearly enveloped by his dark pupils. It gave him an appearance of alerted prey.

"All in good time," Holmes replied. "Let's remove any pretense. You killed your brother by polluting the fuel of his lamp with poison. When he lit the wick by his bedside, the action atomized the toxin, disorienting him. As the fuel burned uninterrupted during the night, it caused him to expire. Unfortunately, the instrument of his death is missing. But you knew that already, as you must have returned to remove it."

"Spurious and outrageous conjuncture. My brother passed of natural causes."

"Though you removed the lamp in the dead of night, you missed another item, which unequivocally confirms my theory. May I ask you to turn your attention to what's behind you on the table?"

Everyone's attention turned to an item under glass.

"It appears to be a mouse, gruesomely drawn and quartered," Lestrade said, thinking aloud.

"Though similar in appearance, Inspector, it is from the order *Chiroptera* rather than *Rodentia*. It is the dead bat which the housekeeper disposed of the day Father Bartoni's body was discovered. I exhumed it to confirm that there are traces of cyanide its blood. Unfortunately for you, professor, you had no way to know a dead bat had been retrieved from the scene of the crime."

"Still conjecture!" the professor said exclaimed. "Traces of cyanide may be found throughout nature."

"True, Professor, but not in the concentrations present in the bat's corpse."

"Speculation!" he responded, his face becoming flushed – he began to animate like a boxer. "You have no evidence that I was on the premises."

"The parish is wound by stone paths and hard surfaces, making it more difficult to link your footprints to those on the grounds. Moreover, congregants' comings and goings throughout the week, especially on Sundays, corrupted any available evidence. Given your love of chemistry, I ask you to join me in an experiment if you would. May I trouble you for one of your shoes?"

"Certainly not! I've had enough of your accusations!"

The professor moved towards the door, but I obstructed his exit.

"Though Mr. Holmes's methods are unorthodox," said the inspector, "and I fail to see the benefit, I must insist you provide him one of your shoes."

"Ridiculous! I shall do nothing of the sort!"

"Detective, restrain Professor Bartoni, so we can finish this escapade," Lestrade said.

The professor tried futilely to wiggle from the detective, but the policeman held the man fast. He was as a trout caught on a line. I removed one of his shoes quickly and handed it to Holmes.

"Luckily, the professor kept returning intermittently to investigate where his brother may have hidden his immense wealth. But the visits were unpredictable and the professor was on the alert. Rather than spend weeks in the cold, on watch during the early hours, I decided to sprinkle the surroundings of the parish with common starch."

"Whatever for?" Lestrade asked.

Holmes turned to the table. Next to the dead bat was an open beaker filled with clear liquid, a dropper, and a small brown-glass container.

"Shall we can ask the professor what happens when we combine starch with tincture of iodine and water?"

"You meddlesome incompetent!" the professor yelled at Holmes.

"I see he is refusing to answer," Holmes responded, as he mixed amber droplets of iodine into the water.

"Watson, since the professor is silent, given your medical training includes chemistry, would you care to speculate?"

"I believe the concoction should turn a different color, Holmes."

"Precisely! May I trouble you to dip the sole of the professor's shoe into the solution?"

"Certainly."

The five of us stood looking at the beaker as the liquid turned a deep hue of blue. "*Res ipsa loquitur*," Holmes said. "The thing speaks for itself."

"Damn you and your schoolboy chemistry to Hell, Holmes!" the professor snarled.

"All right, Mr. Holmes, you've convinced me," Lestrade responded. "But why on earth would he murder his own brother? To what aim?"

"A dramatic reversal of fortune, Inspector. He and his sister are both Lloyd's of London 'Names.' Their pool underwrote the *Scotsman*, the liner that ran afoul on the rocks southeast of the Change Island. Due to a seaman's strike, the crew largely was inexperienced and drunk the night of the wreck. You should pick up his sister as well, though she will be harder to pin down as merely a co-conspirator," Holmes advised. "But, it is conceivable she will confess if told her brother turns on her to avoid being hanged."

Lestrade and his detective left with the one-shoed professor. We could hear the suspect's protestations fade as the officers and their newest prisoner distanced themselves from No. 221b Baker Street.

Chapter IX –A Fortune in Plain View

The following day, Holmes, Father Taff, and I sat in the neatly organized parlor of the parish priest's residence. In front of us rested a pot of hot water and three cups. Holmes had finished explaining the facts which led to solving Father Bartoni's murder. He placed the tips of his fingers together and sat in silence, his preferred natural state of contemplation.

"We are most grateful that you've helped bring justice in this instance, Mr. Holmes," Father Taff said, the warm resonance of his voice breaking our quietude. "While it doesn't bring back our beloved friend, it will provide some peace to this parish and its congregation. I'm still at a loss as to how we're going to discover where Father Bartoni deposited his largess for the benefit of our church. He was the anonymous benefactor who supported our capital improvements and efforts of goodwill."

Holmes burrowed his hand into his jacket pocket and removed a small, angular stone. "I plucked this from one of your stone paths. Watson," he said, handing it to me. "Can you identify it?"

"A piece of quartz, Holmes?"

"If you study it from the top, you'll notice that it has four sides, rather than six. A quartz stone has six."

"Gracious, Holmes! A rough diamond!"

"Undeniably, Watson. They are interspersed with common stones around the parish birdbath, where four paths intersect. Collectively, they hold immense value."

"Mr. Holmes, we are forever in your debt," the Reverend Taff exclaimed. "Your powers of observation will ensure the good fortune of our humble parish for years to come."

Holmes waved a hand as if he were distracting a gnat at his face. "Please, think nothing of it. It was easy enough to deduce once I understood the family's background and Professor Bartoni's proclivities. The irony for the professor is that he surveyed the grounds at night in search of some secret chamber or treasure cache. The mind sees what it wants to see, and he was unable to observe a fortune in plain view."

"Certainly nothing can surpass what I've learned this morning thanks to you."

"Allow me to differ, Reverend Taff."

Holmes removed a small envelope from inside his jacket, and a folding knife from his pants' pocket, he walked to the wall. He began scraping at the milk paint and collecting some of the gritty flakes. He dropped the powder in the teacup closest to the priest, added hot water from the pot, and stirred it with a teaspoon. Holmes then took out his handkerchief and lined his teacup with it. He then transferred the milky water from the priest's teacup to the lined cup, allowing the water to drain through the handkerchief. He handed me the cup with his linen square.

181

"Watson, kindly tell us what you see before you."

"Why, it appears to be gold powder," I stammered, dumbfounded.

"Indeed. The walls, up to eye level, are layered in it. Father Bartoni purposely bifurcated the rooms with an umber horizontal line – below the demarcation, for ease of access, should it be needed, is the gold-laced paint. When I saw the small steam-powered ore crusher outside the rectory, I thought it an odd contraption for a parish – until I noticed Father Bartoni's personal library on mining and smelting. The grit on the interior chapel and residence walls is caused by Father Bartoni's adding an abundance of gold dust to the milk paint."

"A strange indulgence," Father Taff offered, his face relaxed and wonder-filled.

Holmes stood, his thin frame making him appear taller than he was. Father Taff and I followed suit.

"Well, as Father Bartoni's cipher and the Good Book advise, '*unto dust shalt thou return*'. Watson and I should take our leave. May I suggest, Reverend, as time permits, you remodel your parish premises with a smoother white paint," Holmes advised, smiling.

"I believe that we shall, Mr. Holmes!" the priest exclaimed shaking each of our hands. "I believe that we shall!"

As we left the parish and passed the garden hedge rows, I thought of the intersections of the four paths upon the bird bath and the clarity of mind which enabled Holmes to unearth truth. It was early afternoon and the sky was clearing. The sun's crepuscular rays descended from the clouds and seemed to touch the hillsides. The scent of roadside lavender triumphed briefly over that of fall leaves' and their damp decay – but perhaps I was simply being influenced by the resolution of Father Bartoni's passing.

Just before the bucolic train station, I noticed Holmes quietly repeat to himself:

> *For so our sires in olden time*
> *Spared neither gold nor gear,*
> *Nor precious wood nor hewen stone,*
> *Thy sacred shrines to rear.*

The Case of the
Rewrapped Presents
by Bob Byrne

A blustery wind hurled itself at our shutters on Baker Street, for the holidays had brought snow and cold to London this December. While I could not deny that it lent a sense of Christmas cheer to the season, it was also an imposition upon me. In the mornings, my leg ached from the Jezail bullet I took at the Battle of Maiwand. Fortunately, once the circulation was properly restored, it was no more than a minor annoyance. I had been perusing an article on preventative measures for influenza, but dozed off, probably due to the warmth of our fire. The wind had awakened me and I looked over to Holmes, slumped deeply in his chair. His eyes were closed and he appeared to be sleeping. There was an air of lethargy hanging over our accommodations.

"Ah, Watson – does the criminal mind stop functioning in honor of the holidays? It certainly seems so."

I was startled to find that he was awake. Holmes hadn't been presented with a case of note for some weeks now, and this had brought on a bout of depression and boredom that was diminishing the cheeriness of our abode. In truth, I had noticed very little in the newspapers each morning that would appeal to my brilliant friend. I knew it was weighing more heavily on him with each passing day. The inclement weather and my leg had prevented me from doing more than making my daily rounds, which kept us in close quarters. Even comfortable lodgers such as ourselves found our constant company somewhat suffocating, upon occasion.

"Well," I ventured, "is there nothing in the agony columns? You can usually find some chicanery there. I should think Christmas would provide cover for some diabolical purpose."

"Bah!" He slumped even more dejectedly into the depths of the chair. "'*Baritone seeks Tenor for holiday music*'." He tossed today's paper aside. "There is no crime here. I long for the challenge of a devious mind."

"Holmes, this is too much!" I protested. "It is the one time of the year when all are expected to care for their fellow man. Thousands of people throughout the city are spending cherished times with friends and loved ones, and you wish for misfortune to occur. What of them! Should they suffer hardship and despair at Christmas so you are not bored?" I realized that I had stood and was clenching my fists. I sat back down with an audible, "Harrumph."

The flicker of a smile crossed Holmes's lips. "You are entirely correct. Although my keen intellect requires stimulation, it is unfair of me to wish trouble upon others so that I might be challenged. Once again, you have seen through my shallow concerns to view the good of all. I am properly abashed. I would be lost without you."

Mollified, I shifted in my seat and resumed a placid countenance. Holmes closed his eyes again and I resumed reading my article. After a few minutes, I set it aside.

"Yes, Watson, I do believe that Mrs. Hudson still has some plum pudding left for an evening snack."

I started at this. "How could you possibly know what I was thinking? My stomach made no telltale sounds, and I haven't spoken of food since dinner. In less enlightened times, you would have been burned at the stake."

My friend smiled at me and waved his hand in a deprecating manner. "I shall tell you, though it will be obvious once I do so. I noticed earlier that you were reading an article on preventing that cold-weather malady, influenza. Even a non-medical man such as I is aware that a healthy diet is important to avoiding illnesses during the winter months. Of course, warm foods are preferred when the weather is brisk. You then looked out the window and shrugged your shoulders. I deduced that you were thinking about the chilly temperature. Your medical journal having already placed the thought of food in your mind, you turned to the table where we supped a few hours ago.

"Now here I admit things were less certain. You could be thinking either of Mrs. Hudson's excellent plum pudding, or also quite possibly a warming cup of tea. Your occasional limp makes it obvious that your wound from the Afghan Campaign is not taking kindly to the cold. That explains why you took a small libation at half-past eight. As it is only now nine, you would not likely be thinking of tea so soon thereafter, so it was a natural to deduce you were wondering if Mrs. Hudson could be prevailed upon for a late night pudding repast."

He sat back and steepled his hands together in front of his face. It made perfect sense to me. "Well then, I can see how you came to that conclusion. It's only logical when you put it all together. No mind-reading at all."

He smiled at that. "Yes, a definition of deduction is to reach a conclusion by reasoning. There is no magic involved. It merely requires that one look at all the available evidence and try to see a pattern. Unfortunately, many people, including our good friend Lestrade, form a conclusion based on a partial facts. Then they try and make the remaining facts fit a pattern that reinforces their conclusion. I've oft said that it's a capital mistake to theorize with insufficient data."

Before I had time to remark upon that, we heard the bell ring downstairs. "Now, who could that be at this late hour? Surely you haven't forgotten to mention some appointment?"

He had left his seat and was attempting to revive our faltering fire. "No, this is an unexpected surprise. For someone to pay us a visit now, rather than waiting until the morning, indicates that it may be important. Perhaps an interesting tale is ascending our stairs."

Mrs. Hudson opened the door. Before she could say anything, a stranger brushed past her and looked anxiously between Holmes and myself. Our landlady started protesting these rude manners, but Holmes assured her that all was well and she left the room, muttering about late-night visitors.

As she exited, I looked at him He was about my height, though considerably thinner. He wore a grey overcoat with no hat, nor did he have a have a walking stick. His face was flushed, as if he'd run some distance. That was all that I had time to notice before he spoke.

"Please, which of you is Mister Holmes?"

"I am Sherlock Holmes, and this is my friend and trusted confidant, Dr. Watson. Anything that you say to me you can say in his presence. Now, please sit down. You've obviously come here from Birmingham, in some haste. You are a right-handed clerk, you are unmarried, and you wear spectacles when you work."

Our visitor, who had radiated a frantic energy and anxiety since his arrival seemed struck with paralysis. He dropped into my vacated chair and looked at Holmes in wonderment. "I'm certain that we have never met, yet that is all correct. How could you possibly know?"

"It is obvious to anyone who takes the time to observe. You have ink stains between your thumb and forefinger. Though you remove them frequently, their constant reapplication has caused some permanent residue, common to account clerks. Your collar isn't pressed, and you cut yourself shaving two days in a row. Only a bachelor appears in such a state. As for the spectacles, your nose bears equal indentations on the upper sides. Since you aren't wearing glasses now, it's reasonable to assume you wear them while at your office. Your pants aren't tucked into your boots, and you have snow and mud splattered on both boots and trouser leg. That indicates a rush to get here, as does your flushed complexion, though that could be due to the cold. Regarding Birmingham – your ticket stub is showing in your breast pocket, where you placed it.

Our visitor relaxed, assured that Holmes didn't somehow know him, and was in fact only using the skills that made him the successful consulting detective that he was.

"Tell us of your problem. For you to come at this late hour, you must be quite concerned."

"My name is Henry Thomas, and I am an accounts clerk with Grigsby and Bradshaw. I've been there for slightly over two years. Every holiday season I return to Birmingham, where my family still lives. The firm is quite reasonable about this, and I arrived at my childhood home on Tuesday. I believed that it would be a normal Christmas for all of us, but now I know it isn't to be so, and I have sought out your help."

He seemed to have wound down at the end of this, whether from exhaustion or due to the weight of his problem, I couldn't guess. Holmes was leaning back with his eyes closed, not yet intrigued. Our visitor had not as of yet actually said anything that indicated my friend would be challenged by this potential new case. I knew that Holmes remained aloof until he was certain a problem was worthy of his talents.

"So something, or several things, happened between your arrival on Tuesday, and your return to London today, on a Friday. What occurred?"

Henry Thomas composed himself and resumed his story. "I come from a common family. My father is a locksmith, my mother a housewife. They are regular folks in the town. I left two years ago, after finishing University. I was fortunate to immediately gain work with my current employers. I mean to convey to you that there is nothing special about my family, and no extenuating events that could explain what is happening.

"Mister Holmes, our family has a long-followed holiday tradition. We get our presents for each other, wrap them in secret, and then lock them all in a spare room. There are no windows and only one door. My father has the sole key."

Holmes interrupted by raising his hand. "Your father has the only key. I am then to infer that he alone places the wrapped gifts in that room." A nod of our visitor's head confirmed this. "The room has no windows. Is it an interior room, or does it share a wall with the outside of the house?"

Thomas thought on this for a moment. "It is an interior room with a wooden door."

"Proceed."

Our guest looked over at me, and then resumed. "Father had put gifts in the room during the week, as always. He securely relocked the door each time. Then, Tuesday morning, my sister gave him another present. When he opened the door, he immediately noticed that two packages were missing. He is sure that the key never left his possession. As you can imagine, it caused some considerable consternation the rest of the day, but my father vowed that no one in the family entered the room and removed the presents."

"On Wednesday afternoon, I gave him a present that I'd bought for my youngest niece. I stood and watched as he opened the door. This time, one gift was missing. My father was completely beside himself."

"It must have been a bit crowded in the hallway then" I mumbled. Holmes's keen ear heard my comment and he gave me a sardonic glance. I crossed my good leg over bad and said nothing more.

Holmes leaned forward in his chair and focused his gaze on Henry Thomas. "So Mister Thomas, on Tuesday morning, your father discovered two packages were missing from the locked room. On Wednesday, another present was found to be gone. He is certain no one in the house removed them. Correct?"

"Yes, exactly. But that is not the strangest thing. This morning, father opened the door to ensure that nothing else had happened overnight. The missing packages were there! But one other was missing. It is truly a mystery. I thought that perhaps it was some little joke by one of my sisters, but I have talked with both of them and I'm sure that they know nothing about this. It is unexplainable."

"Nothing is unexplainable. Some things are merely more difficult to ascertain than others." Holmes had been hoping for a problem worthy of his supreme skills, and this instead was likely a case of Christmas hijinks. Therefore I was caught completely off-guard by his next words.

"Well, this is a curious problem you have. I believe your assertion that your father hasn't let the key out of his possession. Upon the morrow I shall journey to Birmingham and see what may be discovered there."

Henry Thomas was absolutely delighted at this news. He looked in my direction. "And will Dr. Watson be joining you as well?"

Holmes spoke before I could answer for myself. "Yes, we shall both arrive in the late afternoon. Please write out your address on this card. It would be best if you yourself journeyed there in the morning and presaged our arrival."

With more effusive thanks and an exchange of pleasantries, our guest departed down the stairs and out into the night. I looked at Holmes with confusion upon my face. "This hardly seems to be a problem worthy of your time. Somehow a family member obtained the key and is using it. Or perhaps they had a duplicate key made, and are simply switching the presents. Or his father is stirring up excitement for the holidays."

"No, there is more to it than that. My instincts tell me it is not one of the daughters pulling a holiday joke. Nor is it the Senior Thomas. Surely they would have admitted to their actions before allowing our visitor to travel all the way here late at night to seek my services. That would be a waste of time and money. If in fact the elder Thomas hasn't allowed someone to gain access to the key, then I suspect some type of deviltry is afoot. This may even be a case worthy of putting down to paper before it's over. That's why I volunteered your attendance tomorrow. I was certain you wouldn't want to miss it."

With that, Holmes said no more. It was late, and I shortly retired up to my room. As I burrowed further under the blankets, I wondered why Holmes believed that this was a noteworthy case.

Bradshaw's showed us that we could be in Birmingham by two o'clock the next afternoon. That venerable guide, which no traveler from London should be without, was absolutely correct. We had an uneventful trip in our own first-class carriage, alighting in Birmingham, a short cab ride away from our destination. To my surprise, Holmes started walking away from the station.

"Come Watson, we must do a little research before visiting the Thomas' residence. Waltham's Safes and Locks is just around the corner. A walk will do us good."

I followed Holmes a few blocks to the business that he had named. It had rained earlier in the day and there was no snow left on the ground, though some slush remained in the streets. Kicked up by passing horses and carriages, I attempted to avoid it, with only modest success. It looked as if London was receiving a harsher winter than Birmingham. Church bells pealed from steeples adorned with Christmas wreaths. The holiday season had settled heavily upon this industrial town.

A bell rang as we entered the store, a small brick building situated between a tailor's and a pawnshop. A middle-aged man with muttonchop whiskers was behind a counter and greeted us. "Hello gentlemen. How may I help you?"

There were a few small floor safes in front of the counter. The wall was covered with various locks and different types of keys, and Holmes was examining one of the safes. "Yes. Mister Waltham, I presume." The shopkeeper nodded his head and asked again how he could help us.

"My partner and I recently purchased a warehouse on the west side of town." Here he indicated me. Since I had no idea what Holmes was up to, I gave a small nod of affirmation and tried not to look confused. "It contained a safe in one of the back offices. However, we have no idea of the combination. A business associate recommended a local locksmith named Thomas. Do you know of him?"

"That would be Richard Thomas. His shop is just a few streets over on Mill Ridge Street."

188

Holmes acted very pleased that Mister Waltham knew this. "Excellent. This property we have obtained may have been involved in some less-than-upright dealings. We intend to clean it up and lease it out to a wine procurer, but we have no idea what might be in the safe itself. If it is improper, we shall turn it over to the authorities. Regardless, we need a locksmith who we can rely upon not to spread word of what is found. It could make the renting of the warehouse more difficult. Would you say this Mister Thomas is of good character?"

I believed that I knew why Holmes had made this stop. To the proprietor's credit, he responded with no hesitation. "Mister Thomas certainly is a fine man. His work is first rate, and he is the administrator of our neighborhood Christmas fund. I'm aware of no one who has had a poor encounter with him."

My friend smiled and let out a sigh of relief. "Excellent, excellent. That is very good news indeed. It sounds as if he will do splendidly. Thank you for your insights. They have been most valuable, and we will certainly keep your establishment in mind for future business dealings. A fine holiday season to you and yours."

I added my thanks to Holmes's and followed him out of the shop. Though the sky was gray, it didn't look as if snow were imminent. "So you came here to verify that Henry Thomas was telling us the truth about his father being a locksmith?"

He looked at me slowly and dashed my hypothesis. "No, that information wouldn't be very useful. What I did find out from our good shopkeeper was that Richard Thomas is a man of upstanding character. The only harmless explanation for this mystery is that he was playing some joke on his own family and hiding the presents himself, and then returned them yesterday, but I don't believe such is the case. Something more sinister is at hand, though I don't yet know the particulars."

We hailed a carriage and headed towards the Thomas residence. However, we stopped and alighted short of our destination. I glanced up and down the street to see what Holmes was looking for. "We shall take rooms on this street, Watson. After a leisurely dinner, we can walk to the Thomas home and begin our investigations in earnest."

As it was closing upon supper-time, I wholeheartedly agreed with his plan. We found a warm-looking inn called The Knight's Chalice. The sign above the door bore the symbol of a dented silver goblet. Once we were settled into our lodgings, we entered the common room and ordered a very good roast chicken with potatoes and a passable red wine. Holmes talked of inconsequential things during dinner and addressed not at all the Thomas case. I knew that inquiries on my part wouldn't be answered, so I set aside my questions and concentrated on my meal. We followed dinner with a pipe. I suspected this was to let the Thomas family enjoy their own dinner before we visited.

Finally, at half-past-six, Holmes and I walked to the Thomas house. It was less than ten minutes from the inn, and the lack of humidity in the air left my leg feeling better than it had in days. The Thomas home was a one-story brick structure in a middle-class neighborhood. It wasn't very wide, but stretched back further than most houses of its type. There was a wrought-iron fence to the front that ran out along the sides to the backyard. We entered through the swinging gate and ascended to the front door. Holmes knocked sharply and we quietly awaited an answer.

Henry Thomas himself answered the door. "Ah, Mister Holmes and Doctor Watson. I'm so glad you have arrived. All through dinner I waited vainly for a knock on the door." Our client was definitely relieved that we had arrived and seemed confident his puzzle would soon be solved.

We were ushered into a cozy room where Richard Thomas was sitting in an overstuffed chair, reading *The Birmingham Press*. He rose and shook our hands as his son introduced us. Henry had his father's prominent forehead and slightly puffy cheeks. We heard sounds in the kitchen, which I took to be Mrs. Thomas. Holmes and I sat down in chairs by the fireplace, and the elder Thomas spoke.

"Gentlemen, I'm glad that you've come. While I certainly consider this a minor matter, I admit that it has me totally perplexed. No one else has a key to that room, and I'm convinced none of my family would perpetuate such nonsense."

"Mister Thomas," said Holmes, "have you examined the lock to determine whether or not it's been forced or otherwise tampered with?"

"I've been a locksmith for forty-four years, Mister Holmes. I apprenticed when I was thirteen. It's been my life's work. The lock is in perfect condition. I keep all of them in my home that way, and use only quality bolts. No one has picked, jimmied, or opened it without the key. I'd stake my reputation on it."

Holmes seemed pleased with this answer. "I have no doubt that a man of your experience would instantly detect the like. That means either someone has used your key, made an impression of the lock and created their own key, or is entering the room by another way."

Richard Thomas chuckled at this. "I know your reputation, Mister Holmes, and would cast no aspersions on your ability, but all three seem equally unlikely. I have the key with me at all times, and rest it on the bedside table at night. Could someone get an impression of the lock? Well, the house is rarely unoccupied. As for another way into the room, that is the least likely. It is solid, and has no windows. Of course, you'll see it for yourself shortly, and can deduce that on your own."

190

Holmes wasn't at all put off by these words. "The fact remains that the presents have been removed, then replaced. When the impossible has been eliminated, whatever remains, however improbable, must be the truth. We simply need to eliminate the remaining impossibilities to determine the truth."

I had often heard him state this. It was certainly logical. He felt it was the essence of his method of deductive reasoning. I hoped that it wouldn't fail us here. I still had some belief that this was a prank of some variety, though Holmes was certain that wasn't the case.

Henry Thomas had sat quietly during this exchange. His hopes were clearly pinned on Holmes. He excused himself to help his mother in the kitchen. After he left, Holmes continued his queries.

"Tell me – since your son left to consult with me yesterday afternoon, has anything else untoward happened?"

Our host looked uncomfortable as he stared at the fire before meeting Holmes's eyes. "Yes, it happened again. Before dinner. Knowing you would arrive shortly, I checked on the gifts. One of them was gone. Everything else was as it had been the day before, when last I checked."

Holmes rubbed his hands together and his face was suffused with life. "Very good. At present, two gifts are missing. How many different presents have been placed in that room?"

The elder Thomas closed his eyes and moved his lips as he counted, though no sound came out. Then: "Seven."

Holmes looked at me with no expression and said, "Then when we open the door shortly, there should be five presents in the room. Of those five, three have been taken and returned, while two have never left the room. That is correct, is it not?"

Thomas listened to Holmes's words, thought for a few moments, then agreed.

With that, Holmes rose to his feet. "Let us look at this mystery room." We were led down a hall to a wooden door. Further along were more doors. Upon arriving at the proper place, Holmes took out his magnifying glass and examined the door from bottom to top. He paid special attention to the lock and said nothing as he finished his scrutiny by rapping his knuckles on the door.

"Your expert assessment is correct. There are no telltale signs of forced entry around the lock. The door itself certainly is stout enough. I think that it's time that we inspected the room itself."

With that, Richard Thomas removed a key chain from his pocket, selected one, and inserted it into the lock. There was an audible click and he swung the door inward.

We found ourselves in an earthen-floored room with an old bearskin in the middle. It was originally a sleeping room, though it had become a storeroom over the years. There was a safe slightly set out from one corner. The opposite wall had a dusty chest of drawers and a small table, with the presents sitting on the latter. As expected, there were five of them in the room. Holmes eyed the safe for a few moments and then opened the drawers in the chest. There seemed to be some old garments and assorted odds-and-ends. He turned away from it with a dismissive grunt. The walls were of stone, and he picked up a cane leaning in one corner and tapped at various points. Every blow rang solid. He also poked at the ceiling to the same result.

"You have a well-built house here."

Thomas smiled. "Well, as you know, Birmingham is a damp city, and thick stone is necessary to keep interiors dry. The missus would certainly not tolerate a dank home." He chuckled at the thought.

"It's no surprise to find that a locksmith has a safe in his own home." Holmes's comment prompted me to glance at the square, steel object. It appeared quite ordinary to me.

"Yes, I keep a few items in there: Financial papers, my grandfather's watch, and the like. I use it so infrequently that sometimes I forget that it's here."

Holmes twirled the dial a few times, and then attempted to push the safe along the floor. It moved a few inches. "Solid enough for home use by a locksmith, certainly."

With that, he turned to the presents on the table. "Now, which of the three have been taken from the room and replaced?"

"Why, the blue one, the red one, and the green one."

My friend picked each one up and examined it in turn. Then he looked at the other two, which were covered in gold and yellow. "Have you carefully inspected each one to see if it has been opened, then wrapped again?"

I saw by the look on his face that Thomas hadn't thought of this. I was a bit chagrined to realize that I hadn't either. Someone could have been taking the packages, inspecting their contents, and then re-wrapping them and returning them to the room. Presumably they would remove anything they chose to before replacing them.

"Mister Holmes, such a thought never occurred to me. I myself wrapped the blue one here, and as best I can tell, it hasn't been opened, though I didn't pay much attention when I wrapped it. It looks the same. The other two that have been removed belong to my daughter, Sydney. I will have her inspect them when she returns this evening. She takes piano lessons on Saturdays and Tuesdays."

Holmes turned towards the door. "I believe that we've seen all there is to see here for the evening. There are promising signs that convince me we will solve your mystery within a day or two. For now, carry on as you have been. We shall be in touch soon."

We made our farewells and left the Thomas' residence. There was still no sign of snow in the air, though the temperature had dropped noticeably since our arrival. This was probably due to a stiff wind blowing from the south. Holmes set out towards our inn and I hurried along, my collar turned up.

"Tell me," I asked, "what do you make of it? I didn't notice anything particularly helpful."

My friend just smiled at me and replied, "On the contrary. I believe that I know how the gift thief made his entry into the room. However, I have not quite yet determined what he is after."

I stared openmouthed at him. "Surely if you know how the thief got into the room, you should have told Thomas so that he could prevent it from happening again."

"The family is in no danger. I have some inquiries to make before we spring the trap on our holiday villain."

We arrived at the inn, where retired to our rooms. I fell asleep quickly and woke long after sunrise the following morning. Apparently our trip had worn me more than I expected. After knocking on Holmes's door and receiving no answer, I dressed warmly and asked the innkeeper if there was a message for me.

"Yes sir. Your travelling companion was off early this morning and asked me to give this to you"

I opened the note: "*Watson, I'll be out all morning, and will meet you back here for a late lunch at 2:30. I suggest visiting a few sites in town. The university has a fine medical library. I believe that a doctor here is working on some groundbreaking research regarding respiratory ailments. H.*"

I knew that Holmes was off on one of his frequent fact-finding excursions. Though he didn't have access to his disguises, or even his usual informants in this foreign city, I had no doubt that he would gain the information which he sought. I did know that Doctor Allen Casper was making some excellent progress related to lung capacity and illnesses characterized by shortness of breath. While he wasn't available, the library did in fact have several of his more recent papers. I ensconced myself onto a settee and started reading his works.

I admit that I was quite absorbed by his basic, yet new, research. It was a little past two o'clock when I turned my attention from my reading. Realizing that Holmes would soon be at The Knight's Chalice, I gathered myself together and stepped outside to hail a cab back to the inn. I arrived shortly before our appointed time, and a check of his room established that he hadn't yet returned. I went downstairs and took a seat, occupying myself with the latest newspaper.

Finally, a little after three, Holmes returned. "Capital, Watson. Sorry to keep you waiting. The information I sought wasn't easily obtained. However, I now have a clear picture of events. Let us eat."

He turned with a flourish and was out the door. I stood rooted to the floor. His capacity to continually surprise me increased with our time together. I hurried to follow, not wanting to lose him. We stopped at a nearby tavern and ordered a roast with the fixings. The meal was frustrating. Rather, Holmes was – the food was fine. While my friend discussed some relevant points, he didn't share enough that I could determine what was actually happening, nor who was behind it all.

"You stood beside me in the room," he said. "Surely it is obvious."

Once again, I could only look at him, questioningly. "Perhaps if we knew that the packages had been opened and wrapped again, we would have a better idea. But as the daughter, Sydney, wasn't available, we don't know that. Or was that something you discovered today?"

"I have had no dealings with the Thomas family today – at least not directly with them. Much of what I learned was about the father, however. Tell me, did you notice the dust while we were in the room?"

I thought about this. "Yes. There was dust on the chest, but not on the table."

"Very good! The lack of dust on the table was due to the activity of placing and removing the gifts. That lack of dust in that room is what allowed me to solve the case."

I was at a loss to see how this could be a breakthrough clue. "The lack of dust means nothing to me. How could that be the key?"

"I am reminded our adventure involving that fine horse, Silver Blaze, and the dog that did nothing in the night time. Likewise, the missing dust tells all."

I stood, perplexed. My writer's mind is always working, and the thought popped into my head that "The Adventure of the Missing Dust" would not do.

"The firm of Thomas and Jacobs is in financial difficulty. Though our client doesn't know it, his partner has borrowed against the business. If you cannot deduce matters from the information at hand, you will have to wait until events play out."

He would tell me no more on that subject. He did say that we would resolve matters that very evening, and that I would be involved in apprehending the culprit, so we visited the university's botanical gardens for the remainder of the afternoon. After a light meal of cold cuts and vegetables at our inn, we prepared to visit the Thomas house again.

"Bring your service revolver with you tonight. I don't believe that we shall need it, but a surprised man can be unpredictable."

At nine o'clock, we found ourselves standing at the front door of Richard Thomas' home. He himself answered our knock and it was clear that Holmes hadn't informed him beforehand of our coming.

"Mister Holmes, Doctor Watson! I certainly didn't expect you to visit so late in the evening. Do come in, please. What news have you?"

We once again entered the front room and sat down as he looked at us, hopeful but uncertain. Holmes started the conversation. "I trust that there hasn't been another unwanted visit since we left last evening?"

"You're correct. I checked the room less than an hour ago, and all is as it was last night when you examined it."

"As I expected." Holmes leaned forward with a mischievous glint in his eyes. "In a few minutes, I want you to let myself and Dr. Watson into that room, then lock it up again, as you always do. I assure you that your family is in no danger whatsoever. But I do ask that you all remain in your rooms until I call for you to unlock the door. At that time, open the door and you will find that your mystery will be solved."

He certainly was confused by this rather odd request, but he quickly replied. "It will be as you direct, sir. It will be a relief to all of my family when this affair is over."

When the door was opened, Holmes looked carefully about the room. "Watson, you are to sit on the chest. As we have done on adventures past, we must maintain a silent vigil here. However, we'll be rewarded with the solution to a crime that hasn't yet occurred." Holmes himself settled into a sitting position to the left of the door, resting on some winter blankets that weren't yet in use.

"If you would kindly lock the door, all will proceed according to plan." Our host for the evening shut the door, and then we heard the lock click. It was completely dark in the room. Though my eyes did adjust a bit, I couldn't see the presents on the table next to me, but I knew that was where the action would occur, so I sat upright against the back wall and stared into the darkness.

I couldn't even hear the sound of Holmes's breathing. This was another of the many amazing feats of which he was capable: Absolute and total silence. Time passed. I had read of experiments conducted in which the subject was placed into a sealed box that was then lowered completely below ground. While air was plentiful, it was totally dark, with no light rays of any kind. The subjects told of becoming disoriented and of losing all sense of direction and time. While I did not feel disoriented, I had the sense of being in a vacuum, where all motion and time had stopped.

I don't know how long that we sat there. Eventually, I heard Holmes whisper, "Watson, get ready!" While I had briefly dozed off earlier, I was wide-awake at this time. I heard nothing. About a minute later, I did detect some type of scratching noise. The darkness was still absolute.

The scratching noise continued, getting slightly louder. Then I heard a more distinct sound, as of a heavy object shifting. Though I couldn't see, I realized it was coming from the area of the safe. I peered in vain at Holmes, sitting near the door, but could see naught. A small shaft of light came up from the floor. Momentarily puzzled, I realized the shifting noise was the safe being moved sideways, and the light was coming from below the floor. I moved not a muscle as I watched.

The safe continued to slide over. When it had moved about three feet, an arm came up and set a lantern down in the room next to the newly formed hole. It was shuttered almost completely, so it lit the immediate area around the hole, but didn't reveal either Holmes or myself. I saw a dark shape clamber up from the hole and settle beside it. The figure then reached an arm down and helped another man climb up.

At this point Holmes sprang up, saying "Now, Watson!" and pushed the safe backwards, partially covering the hole. The two figures were totally stunned.

"Don't move!" I said. "I have a revolver and you are both covered."

After shoving the safe, which certainly helped startle the intruders, Holmes had grabbed the lantern and partially unshuttered it, allowing us to see more without blinding either of us. My vision quickly adjusted and I had a look at the two captives. One was older, perhaps in his mid-fifties, while the other man was younger – no more than thirty, if that. Holmes addressed the older man.

"Your plan is thwarted, Silas Jacobs. And I assume your companion is in fact your eldest son."

The older man let out a long breath and looked totally crestfallen. "Who are you, and how do you know my name?"

"I am Sherlock Holmes. You will not get what you came after tonight." Holmes then called out to Thomas and pounded on the door. It was less than a minute before it was opened and Richard Thomas stood in the doorway.

"Mister Holmes, Dr. Watson, I heard your call. Are you all . . . ?"

He stopped speaking as he saw our two visitors. A look of despair settled on his face. "Silas. Jeremy. What in the world are you two doing here? Why . . . ." Richard Thomas didn't finish his sentence. He seemed at a loss.

Silas Jacobs was absolutely miserable. He didn't say a word. By this time, the rest of the Thomas family had crowded into the hallway, with Henry at the front.

"Allow me to explain," said Holmes. "I admit that my first thought was that someone had somehow made a copy of your key and was entering the room when the house was empty, but I couldn't understand the taking of only one or two presents, then returning them and taking others. This would involve a higher degree of risk, as simply taking all the presents at one or two different times would have involved fewer visits.

"Also, if someone was looking for something in the presents, he could have just ripped them open, taken what was sought, and left. That led me to surmise that if it were the case, the culprit didn't want the searching of the presents to be known. But why take them and put them back, which surely would raise suspicion?"

So far, Holmes's explanation made perfect sense. However, I had no idea where this would lead. Jacobs looked down at his feet, while his son stared sullenly at Holmes. I kept a steady eye on him, aware that cornered culprits are often the most desperate and dangerous.

"I felt that the taking of the gifts was simply a diversion to shift attention from something else. When I inspected the room, I saw that the chest was dusty, while the table was not. Likewise, most of the floor also had a thin layer of dust. There were two exceptions. The first was a path leading from the door to the table where the presents were. This was to be expected. However, the floor was also clear next to the safe. It is partially in shadow and would likely go unnoticed."

My friend had been pointing to the floor as he discussed the lack of dust. Now he cast his gaze upon Richard Thomas.

"You told me that you rarely used the safe, and in fact sometimes forgot it was there. Even if you used it frequently, it seemed unlikely to me that you moved it very often. I was now convinced that someone was gaining access to your room via a tunnel dug underneath the safe."

"Earlier today, I visited a house agent who verified that the house directly behind you is vacant. I managed to inspect it and found a hole dug in the back wall of the cellar, which had been concealed with some crates. I knew the tunnel had to come into this room."

"Since I didn't believe the gifts were the reason for the visits, but were merely a diversion, I was sure that the thieves were after something in the safe. Your accountant told me that earlier this year you received some bearer bonds for services rendered to the Bank of London here in Birmingham."

197

Richard Thomas spoke. "Yes, that's true. I showed them that they had an inadequate lock system on the main vault and recommended replacements. They paid me with those bonds."

"You did well to lock them up, as whoever has them in their possession is the legal owner. Your partner, Jacobs, knew you had received these from a job you performed independent of your business. He also knew that if he could obtain them without your knowledge, he could redeem them, likely in London, and you would never trace the theft to him – had you even suspected they were gone."

Holmes now turned to face the Jacobs. While the son maintained a look of glowering defiance, his father was completely defeated. He couldn't even look at his accuser.

"So, with the help of his son, he dug a tunnel from the abandoned house into this room. He has frequently been a guest here and knew the layout of the house. He was coming into this locked room at night and attempting to crack the safe. He had no interest in the presents, but that little trick of taking them diverted attention from the safe, in case you detected that someone had been here. Even I was drawn in initially. However, he was unable to open it. He would have continued trying and I suspect eventually have succeeded, had your son Henry not sought my services."

With that, Holmes stepped back. Richard Thomas looked at his partner and asked, "Why?"

"I'm in debt, Richard. I've borrowed heavily on my half of the business. I needed money to get it back. You were just sitting on the bonds, doing nothing with them. I needed them to stay in the partnership. I would have found a way to pay you back!"

The elder Thomas looked at both of us. "Mister Holmes, thank you very much for helping my family. Please charge us whatever fee you determine is fair and I will pay you. I would like to be left alone with Silas. I don't know what I'm going to do, but we need to discuss this sordid affair."

Holmes held up a hand. "There is no charge for my services. Think of it as a Christmas present. It was a case not without some interesting features. Dr. Watson and I wish you the season's greetings."

We left, a disappointed Richard Thomas looking at a downcast Silas Jacobs and we walked back to our inn.

"Come, Watson. We shall catch a few hours of restful slumber, then take the 9:10 back to London. It's the Jacobs that I pity most in the world. They are good people at heart, but allow circumstances to force them into poor choices. I don't know if Thomas will turn them over to the police. While we've ensured that the family shall have all their presents for the holiday, I doubt that the elder Thomas, or Jacobs, will have a pleasant Christmas."

The Adventure of the Incessant Workers
by Arthur Hall

"When a doctor goes wrong, he is the first of criminals"
– Sherlock Holmes.

During my long association with my friend Mr. Sherlock Holmes, I was privileged to witness his dealings with clients of all classes and from many walks of life. Not all visitors to our lodgings in Baker Street sought his attentions, however. I recall a stormy morning when our landlady, Mrs. Hudson, ushered a windswept lady with quite a different purpose into our sitting room.

"Mrs. Clementine Durrell, to see Doctor Watson," she announced. "Shall I bring tea, gentlemen?"

Holmes assented, with a faint air of disappointment. "You seem to be more in demand than I today, Watson," he said. "If you and your patient have no objection, I will remove myself to the far side of the room to continue reading while I drink my tea."

"Please don't inconvenience yourself on my account," the lady said at once. "There is nothing of a personal nature to be discussed. I merely seek a second opinion about something which my own doctor is unable to clarify."

"Very well." I gestured to her to take one of the armchairs. As we seated ourselves Mrs. Hudson brought in the tea-tray, and I waited until she withdrew before pouring for the three of us. Holmes took his cup and resumed his perusal of *The Standard*.

"How is it, Mrs. Durrell, that you have come here to consult me, rather than at my practice?" I asked her then.

She replaced her cup in its saucer, which she stood carefully on the tray. I noticed that her hand shook. "I should explain that my usual physician is Doctor Selby, whom I have consulted several times about my ailment. He is an elderly man, due to retire soon I think, and appears perplexed as to my condition. He suggested that I seek a second opinion but was not specific and, knowing of no other medical men or anyone who could make a recommendation, I was at a loss to know where to turn. Then I read a newspaper article about one of Mr. Holmes's cases and you were mentioned. I resolved then to visit you here, as I knew no other address, in the hope of receiving the benefit of your advice."

200

While she had been speaking I noticed Holmes look up briefly at the mention of his name. I had no doubt that he had heard every word, and made his usual observations about my patient.

I would have placed Mrs. Durrell at about thirty years of age. There was a delicate air about her, and indeed that described her looks also. A tall woman, her dark hair was unfashionably long, surrounding strong features and lying easily on the shoulders of her green costume. Her eyes appeared slightly sunken, and her expression one of weariness.

I put down my own cup. "I understand. Pray tell me then, what it is that troubles you?"

"It seems so absurd when put into words," she said after an embarrassed hesitation, "but it is simply that I awake every morning in a state of exhaustion. I am more weary then than on retiring the previous night. Doctor Selby prescribed a tonic at first, but it had no effect."

I nodded. My first thought was possible that this lady had fallen prey to somnambulism. Previously, over the years, I had been consulted by several sufferers, usually former military men haunted by memories of violent action.

"Perhaps you have been walking around the room in your sleep. Has your husband been disturbed by your movements during the early hours?"

"I am a widow sir," she said sadly. "My Richard was taken by consumption three years ago. Nevertheless, I am able to tell you that I have considered this and found nothing to suggest it. Nothing is out of place throughout the house, and I haven't ventured outside – the front door remains locked as I have left it."

"I'm sorry to hear about your husband," I said with feeling. "For how long has this tiredness persisted?"

"Almost four weeks, and I'm aware that my appearance has begun to show it. I suspect that it could have been longer, and that I may not have been aware of it at first."

There was a long moment of silence as I considered Mrs. Durrell's account. Clearly the tonic prescribed by Doctor Selby hadn't helped, nor could I see that a stronger preparation was the answer. Laudanum, perhaps? No, for that would simply be a temporary solution that wouldn't attack the source of her complaint.

Suddenly, Holmes put down his newspaper and strode across the room.

"Pray excuse my interruption," he began, his eyes moving from my patient to myself, "but I feel that I may have something to contribute here."

I glanced at Mrs. Durrell, who nodded her acceptance of my friend's inclusion in our conversation, and concurred. "Do join us, Holmes, please."

When he has settled himself in his chair, we looked at him expectantly.

"I believe that this may be in my province as well as yours after all, Watson. During the past two weeks, I've been consulted twice by prospective clients with exactly the same symptoms, if I may put it like that. Mrs. Durrell, if you could tell us what you are able to recall of your dreams throughout the nights before awakening in a state of exhaustion, it would be most helpful."

The lady appeared somewhat surprised by this request, and looked to me for confirmation that she should take this seriously.

Then a new expression crossed her features. "It has just now occurred to me as strange that my dreams have not varied at all. I dream of the same event each night."

"And what event is that, pray?"

She shook her head in dismay. "My only impression is of sitting at a desk or table, surrounded by banknotes of a high value. I am sorting the money into piles of equal number and someone is watching constantly. The only sounds that I recall are of being urged to work faster, ever faster."

"Precisely the descriptions of the two men who previously asked my advice!" Holmes cried triumphantly. "You mark my words, Watson, there is something strange afoot here."

"What advice did you give to these men?" I enquired.

"My first inclination was to recommend that the first client seek out a priest, for I have had many similar situations put to me to which that was the solution. When the second man approached me, however, I realised at once that more was involved because his account was identical to the first. I then resolved to treat both as unsolved cases, which would bear investigation when additional evidence came to light. Mrs. Durrell has now supplied such evidence."

"Then I'm not going mad," she said in a voice heavy with relief. "I considered that as a possible explanation, for these experiences are distressing and I haven't known their like before."

"That is certainly not the case," I reassured her. "But Mr. Holmes and myself will spare no effort until the true cause is found."

"That there is some human agency behind this I have no doubt," Holmes added. "I have no inclination as to how this can be as yet, but you may be sure that no stone will be left unturned until all is revealed."

The lady got to her feet. "I'm so grateful to you both for setting my mind at rest. Is there anything more that I can tell you?"

Holmes looked thoughtful for a moment. "You are a widow, are you not"?

"I have said as much, sir."

"Then tell me, pray, has the loss of your husband compelled you to earn your own living?"

"It has."

"What then, is your present occupation?"

"I work in a laundry."

"That was one of the possibilities that presented themselves to me after examining your hands as we spoke. Thank you, Mrs. Durrell. You will hear from us presently."

It was left to me then to show our client out. On the stairs, she gave me a glance that told me she hadn't understood the relevance of Holmes's observation, and that she found him to be curious among men. I was glad to see that the storm had subsided somewhat as I secured a passing hansom for her.

I re-entered our sitting room to see Holmes watching from the window as she departed.

"It seems we are on the same track, Holmes."

"It never ceases to surprise me how the situations that confront us can alter in an instant, after facts are brought to light during discussion." He lowered his head, still peering through the window. "But I see that the dark clouds are passing and the wind has definitely dropped. I think, Watson, that with your permission, our enquiries can begin immediately."

Within the hour we found ourselves in the waiting room of Doctor Selby's surgery. The three patients ahead of us had been dealt with quickly, emerging from the doctor's presence after far less time than I would have allowed. I recalled that he was elderly and on the brink of retirement.

The last of them, a one-legged man with a crude crutch fashioned from a tree branch, re-entered the waiting room and sullenly limped out into the street. The doctor called for us to join him.

Doctor Selby was indeed elderly. A grey and bleary-eyed man, he sat half bent over his desk. At our approach, he looked up sharply.

"I hadn't expected two patients at the same time. Which of you gentlemen requires my attention, or is it both?"

We removed our hats.

"That is not the cause of our visit, sir," said my friend. "My name is Sherlock Holmes, and this is my friend and associate, Doctor John Watson."

"Ah, a fellow medical man. But if there is no ailment, what can have brought you to me?"

At Doctor Selby's invitation we settled ourselves in the two worn chairs before us.

203

"We are making enquiries about one of your patients," Holmes began. "Mrs. Clementine Durrell, I understand, consulted you recently regarding her exhaustive state."

The elderly physician nodded. "Yes, I recall the lady. She did indeed appear exhausted. My examination revealed nothing to be physically amiss, so I prescribed a tonic of herbs with a recommendation that she should drink plenty of strong coffee. She returned not long after, but I felt there was little else I could do for her, apart from adding a sleeping draught to be taken on retiring to increase the depth of her slumber. She declined this, and I haven't seen her since."

"Did she mention the repetitive dream that haunts her?" I enquired.

He was briefly still before the recollection came to him. "She did speak of something of the sort, but I attached no significance to it. I am not a doctor of the mind, but it seems obvious that an unhealthy obsession with money is involved, having no connection with Mrs. Durrell's excessive tiredness."

"Did she disclose anything more – about her dream or general condition?" Holmes asked.

"I can recall little else of what transpired during our interview." Doctor Selby shook his head slowly. "Her ailment is most peculiar, though."

Holmes and I rose together.

"Strange indeed," my friend said. "Our thanks to you, Doctor, for a most informative conversation. We will now take our leave and wish you a very good morning."

Holmes's remark about the time of day was only just correct, for it was almost mid-day. We returned to Baker Street to consume our luncheon, which was for me a good helping of Mrs. Hudson's curried fowl. Holmes, as was usual when he was in the midst of an enquiry, dealt with his food less enthusiastically.

"We seem to have learned little from Doctor Selby." I observed as I pushed away my empty plate.

"To the contrary," Holmes replied thoughtfully. "We've had confirmation of much that Mrs. Durrell told us."

"That would seem to be so, but I cannot see how we can proceed."

"A visit to Mr. Michael Brewer would doubtlessly help to set us on the right path."

After a moment, I shook my head. "I haven't heard that name before."

"That is because I haven't mentioned it. He is one of the two previous clients whose account was the same as that of Mrs. Durrell."

At my friend's direction, the driver brought the hansom to a halt near the entrance to a decrepit alley somewhere in Whitechapel. The decaying buildings on either side were tall enough to prevent much of the newly-appeared early afternoon sun from lighting our path, and the smell from the plentiful piles of rubbish caused us to take only shallow breaths.

Holmes's knowledge of London has always been a source of amazement to me, and now he led us through what became a maze of narrow backstreets as if they were thoroughly familiar to him. Presently we emerged into a tiny courtyard. It was a dismal place, containing six houses in poor repair with tiny barren gardens before them. My friend peered at the faded numbers briefly, then opened a low and rickety gate to approach a nearby front entrance. He rapped upon the door with his stick, receiving no response at first. I was about to suggest that he repeat the summons when it swung open, its hinges squealing in protest.

"What do you want?" asked the dowdy and solemn woman after a moment of staring at us suspiciously.

"Mrs. Brewer?" enquired my friend.

"What if I am?"

Holmes put on his most charming smile. "My name is Sherlock Holmes. Your husband may have mentioned to you that he consulted me on an unusual matter concerning his health."

I noted that he made no reference to his true profession, doubtless because any connection to the law would automatically be met with resistance here.

"He said something," she replied unsmilingly, "but it seems you did him no good. He acts as if he's worn out all the time, and I can't get him out of his chair. We'll have no food soon, if he doesn't change his ways."

"Does he, by any chance, leave the house during the night?"

"I don't know how you found that out, unless he told you. It's true, but how he can do it when he says he hasn't the strength to stand up during the day, I don't understand."

"It may be that I will soon be able to throw some light upon this curious condition," Holmes told her. "Can we now come in and speak to him?"

"If he's awake, you can." She stood aside and we entered the dwelling. Halfway along a dusty corridor, she pointed to a door ahead and said, "There," before disappearing into a nearer, shadowy chamber.

We approached the room she had indicated and Holmes knocked on the ill-fitting door, announcing us. The reply that came from within was more of a weary growl than a bid to enter, but we took it to mean the same. The room held little that was unexpected – tattered curtains hung around smeared windows, and the single armchair contained a sprawled figure.

"Mr. Brewer," Holmes began, after introducing me. "I'm sorry to see that your situation hasn't improved. We're here because we've learned something more, and are getting closer to a solution."

Mr. Brewer made a gesture which Holmes interpreted as permission to sit, and we settled ourselves in the two straight-backed chairs near the worn table. This man did indeed look tired to the point of being ill. He was in a worse state, I thought, than I had observed Mrs. Durrell to be. His unshaven face and disarranged hair contributed to his appearance of absolute hopelessness, and I would have wagered that his shapeless trousers and collarless shirt had adorned his body for many days.

"Have you yet discovered the cause of this?" His voice was barely a whisper, like someone who is barely conscious.

"We have made some way forward," Holmes answered. "You may be assured that what ails you isn't natural, but is caused by the actions of another."

In the gloom I saw Mr. Brewer's eyes widen. "But how is that possible? And why? To my knowledge, I have no enemies."

"Those are among the questions we seek to answer. Pray tell us, are your dreams continuing as before?"

"They are, and worse than ever. In the midst of a restless sleep, I'm surrounded by more money than I've ever known, and on awakening my strength, and my will to live, grows less every day."

Holmes nodded. "Your wife had said that you leave the house every night, and you refuse to explain how this is possible. What have you to say to that?"

"I cannot explain it. Neither can I remember doing this. As I told you before, Mr. Holmes, I go to my bed exhausted and awake the next morning feeling ten times as weary. I know nothing more."

"When you consulted me in Baker Street, you didn't mention the recommendation of your doctor. What was his advice?"

"Doctor Queller insisted that these effects are part of the normal process of aging for some men. He assured me that they would pass, after some little time."

"Then he must have rare knowledge indeed," I said. "Never in all my years in medicine have I come across such nonsense. Has he perhaps travelled in the East, and adopted some of their attitudes towards healing?"

"That I do not know, Doctor. I am mostly unfamiliar with the man. He has recently taken over the practice of Doctor Freshwater, who is now deceased."

"Be so good as to describe Doctor Queller for us," Holmes requested.

Mr. Brewer hesitated, as if the effort of recalling Doctor Queller's appearance was immense, as it probably was to his sluggish senses. "He is tall, and very thin. His nose is sharp and pointed, and his hair is longer than is usual, and grey. His manner is what you might call aloof."

I saw a glimmer of excitement in my friend's eyes. "Did he, by any chance, have a missing left forefinger?"

"I'm sorry, Mr. Holmes," Mr. Brewer shook his head slowly. "I was in no condition to notice."

"No matter." Holmes hid the impatience in his voice well, I thought. "You have given us a new line of enquiry, for which I thank you. I have every expectation that matters will be put aright soon, and you have my word that I won't rest until then. May your recovery be swift. Good afternoon to you, Mr. Brewer."

Holmes took us back through the labyrinth of alleyways, and as we regained the streets of Whitechapel I saw that the look of triumph that I had come to know well had entered his expression.

"Have you found the solution to this curious business?" I asked him as he raised his stick to attract the attention of the driver of a passing four-wheeler.

He made no answer, but I saw a secretive smile steal across his face as we took our seats. He shouted the address of our lodgings and the carriage moved off at once.

"Yes, I believe I have it now," he said as we passed a group of urchins who were begging from passers-by. "I will however require confirmation, but that should be settled by means of a couple of telegrams." He then instructed our driver to stop at the nearest Post Office.

That evening we ate an excellent dinner, and I was pleased to see that the solving of this affair had improved my friend's appetite. About two hours must have passed, and we sat in our usual armchairs reading, he the latest *London Evening News*, and I a medical journal, when the answers to his telegrams arrived.

"Capital!" he exclaimed as he tore open the envelopes. There was a moment of silence between us when the only sounds were of a passing carriage beneath our window and Mrs. Hudson's retreating footsteps on the stairs. "Mr. Stephen Lang confirms that he also consulted Doctor Queller, and that he noticed his missing finger."

"I take it that Mr. Lang is the other client who previously consulted you on this matter?"

"You take it correctly, Watson. The other message is from our current client, Mrs. Clementine Durrell, who informs us that a man of similar description to Doctor Queller was present as an unidentified observer during one of her visits to Doctor Selby. This is all taking shape rather well, I think."

"Who is this Doctor Queller? That you have had previous dealings with him is obvious, since you knew of his missing finger. I cannot recollect you mentioning him before now."

My friend reached for the Persian slipper on the mantel-shelf and filled his clay pipe. "You will recall Barker, the private enquiry agent with whom I have had some dealings?"

"Of course."

"It was he, not I, who encountered the so-called Doctor Queller in the course of a case of extortion. I understand that Queller narrowly escaped a prison sentence, due to the disappearance of a vital witness."

"Could Queller have done away with him?"

"Most probably. It was suspected by Scotland Yard but never proven." Holmes blew out a cloud of smoke and leaned back in his chair. "However, if Queller was innocent of that, I'll wager that he had it done. He is no more a doctor than I am. In fact, he was dismissed from the Royal College of Physicians while still in the early stages of training. His real name is Elisha Cobb, but he hasn't been known by that for years. During the case involving Barker, I added much that the dailies reported to my index."

"Should we not inform Inspector Lestrade of this man's activities?"

Holmes shook his head slowly. "As yet, we have little to charge him with. However, if you would care to continue reading for a while, I believe I may have the means to set things in motion."

I took up my medical journal again, as I was bidden. Holmes sat in silence until he finished smoking, and then returned his pipe to the rack before crossing the room to stare out of the window. After a short while he suddenly exclaimed "A-ha!" and dashed out into the street. I rose and looked down at the passing hansoms and people out for an evening walk, in time to see my friend in conversation with a ragged urchin who saluted smartly and ran off. Seconds later, I heard Holmes on the stairs, and he quickly resumed his seat.

"I was fortunate enough to see one of the Irregulars out there. They have been instructed to watch Doctor Queller's house from now until the early hours. That should be sufficient time, I think, for him to take the action that he must if my presumptions are correct. As for us, my dear fellow, we have work to do this evening."

"What have you in mind?"

A quick smile. "A little matter of burglary."

"My dear Holmes!" I exclaimed, surprised.

"You really shouldn't be so shocked, Watson. We have, in the course of some enquiry or other, undertaken such action before, have we not?"

"Yes, but – "

"Are you with me now, as you were then?"

I allowed myself to smile, at the memory. "As ever."

"I thought I knew my Watson."

A distant church clock chimed eleven as we took up our position beneath a sprawling beech in a well-to-do side road off Hammersmith High Street.

"We're in deep shadow here, Watson. Even from a few yards away, we are invisible."

"That is reassuring, although the street is deserted."

"Yet the Irregulars are here somewhere. I gave Winters, the boy you saw, most specific directions."

From a while we stood in silence. An occasional fellow, dressed for an evening out, walked or staggered along the street, and once a cat ran madly across, but at no time was our presence detected.

Presently the clock chimed again. It was now midnight, and no more than a few minutes later the front door of the house we watched opened to reveal a man in a tall top hat who struck off smartly along the street in the other direction.

"That was Queller," Holmes whispered when the man was almost out of sight. We saw a shadow detach itself from a distant wall, and move quietly in pursuit.

"Your unofficial detective force hasn't failed you," I said quietly.

"We will enter by the front door, I think, since the street remains deserted."

"Holmes, what if the man has a wife, or there are servants within?"

I sensed his eyes upon me, in the darkness.

"You surely do not imagine that I would have brought us here with such intentions had I not first ascertained that Queller lives alone. An elderly couple attend from morning to late afternoon, to care for his needs and the maintenance of the house, but that is all."

We spoke no more until my friend had produced and made use of his pick-lock, while I kept watch in both directions. We entered slowly and without a sound. The house was quiet except for the loud ticking of a tall casement clock standing in the hall. Holmes ignored all four of the doors facing us and noiselessly climbed the stairs two at a time. Three more doors on the landing were opened and quickly closed again, until he entered the fourth room and beckoned me to follow.

"The study," he whispered. "That is where it will be."

"What do we seek?"

"Proof of my theory. Proof that Queller is responsible for the exhausted condition of Mrs. Durrell and the others."

He produced a dark lantern, and by its light examined the contents of the bookcase and those of a locked desk drawer, which again required the use of his pick-lock. After a surprisingly short time, but to my relief, he announced that we were leaving.

"Already? Have you found what you were searching for?"

"Everything."

"Is it as you supposed?"

"Exactly as I supposed."

"Then we can return to Baker Street?"

"By the first carriage that presents itself."

We took our leave of the place, ensuring that everything was as it had been before.

Holmes seemed in an extraordinarily cheerful mood the following morning. I attributed this to the obvious satisfaction he derived from bringing some understanding to this strange affair, and on my mentioning this, he immediately concurred.

"It is always gratifying to be proven correct in one's suppositions," he answered. "The final piece of the puzzle will be within our grasp when my unofficial force bring me the results of their activities."

"What is it that you expect them to have discovered?"

"The location of the factory."

I looked up from the morning edition of *The Standard* at this unexpected development. "The factory? How does such a place concern our investigation?"

"It is where Queller was bound for, when we saw him leave his house last night. If not that, it has to be a fairly large room to contain all his victims. You can be sure that the three of whom we are aware don't represent the extent of his villainy."

The steely look in my friend's eyes told me that it would have been unwise for me to enquire of him further for, as was usual for him, he would enjoy revealing all at the time he considered appropriate. Showing a little impatience, he wandered across to the window before resuming his seat.

I was about to ask when he expected to hear from the Irregulars when the door-bell rang, responding to my question before I posed it. I heard Mrs. Hudson answer the summons and her voice rose critically, before quick footfalls echoed on the stairs and a hurried knock sounded upon our door.

"Come in, Wiggins!" Holmes cried, and I knew that he had seen our visitor approach from the window.

The leader of the Irregulars entered, looking slightly taller and older than when I had last seen him. He snatched his cap from his head and stood stiffly at attention before us.

"Did you succeed?" Holmes asked him at once.

"We did, sir. It was just as you said."

"And where was the place?"

Wiggins produced a crumpled paper from his pocket and handed it to Holmes. "There is the address. It's some distance away, in Hammersmith. The gentleman arrived not long after half-past-midnight as far as we could judge and spent about twenty minutes inside the building, which was a place that used to make bicycle clips. When he came out, he was with a big man, a really nasty-looking cove, I can tell you, and together they sent twenty-two people, both men and women, in different directions. Did we do well, sir?"

"You conducted yourselves without fault or error," Holmes assured him. "Here is twice our agreed rate, together with enough money to cover the additional inconvenience of travelling further afield. Kindly express my appreciation to your companions."

Wiggins gave a slight bow as he accepted he coins before mumbling his thanks. A moment later we heard the front door close as he departed.

"I presume he spoke of the factory that you mentioned earlier," I enquired, as Holmes glanced at the paper.

He nodded. "I think we can safely spend today reading, or perhaps partaking of some exercise. I may take it upon myself to conclude the series of chemical experiments that I've been conducting of late, for we can do nothing more until tonight. Then, I have great hopes that we can bring this affair to its conclusion."

As it was a fine day we passed the morning in a pleasant stroll in Hyde Park, and the afternoon as Holmes had suggested. Our mealtimes came and went, slowly for me as I found myself eager to discover the true nature of this adventure. I would have certainly liked to add it to the chronicles intended for my publisher, but whether Holmes would allow this was, as usual, quite another matter.

After dinner, we had begun a long discussion concerning the current political situation, particularly the rising influence of Imperial Germany, when Holmes paused abruptly and took out his pocket-watch.

"It is time, Watson. If we leave now, we will be in Hammersmith just after midnight."

So involved had I been in our discussion that the lateness of the hour had quite escaped me. We rose and retrieved our hats and coats before leaving quietly so as not to disturb Mrs. Hudson.

211

Because of the lateness of the hour, hansoms were not so much in evidence, and we had walked almost to the end of Baker Street before one drew up beside us in answer to Holmes's call. I formed the opinion that the cabby was anxious to get to his bed, so rapidly were we conveyed to Hammersmith.

Before long we stood at the end of a long street, poorly lit by the glow from regularly-spaced lamp-posts. The departing hansom left in the direction of the High Street, and we exchanged no word until the sound of the horse's hooves on the cobbles had ceased.

"There appear to be no houses here," I observed with difficulty. "These buildings are factories and business premises, some of them disused I would think."

In the poor light, I saw him nod. "And there is but one showing any sign of habitation. I can just make out a lighted window above those rather decrepit gates. Come, I see a deep doorway a little way further on. From the opposite side of the street we should have a clear view."

"But what are we looking for?"

"We are watching for the workers to leave, of course."

"I was under the impression that we were waiting for Doctor Queller."

"And so we are. Have patience, Watson, and all will be revealed soon."

We stood still and in silence in the doorway of the old building. The only sound, apart from an occasional bird-cry, was the faint throbbing of machinery from the lighted factory before us. It seemed an age, but in reality was probably less than an hour, that we waited. I felt cramp in my shoulder, a legacy of the Jezail bullet from my service days, and shifted my position to ease it as Holmes spoke.

"Any moment now, Watson. Try to limit your movements, if you can."

Before I could reply, the doors opposite were flung open. A burly roughneck who was probably the man described by Wiggins stepped out into the street and looked cautiously in both directions. Seeing that he was apparently unobserved, he made impatient gestures accompanied by a series of oaths, shouting back into the building.

For a few moments nothing happened. Then a procession of about twenty people filed out. I recognised at once our client, Mrs. Clementine Durrell, and Holmes murmured the names of his two recent clients also. The little group arranged themselves along the pavement with no word having been spoken, and I became aware of the unnatural posture of them all.

"Holmes," I whispered. "They are sleepwalking."

"As I suspected. Ah, here is Queller."

The man who Holmes and I had briefly seen near his house strode out and ordered the group to be ready to leave. About five minutes elapsed before several carts drawn by black horses appeared at the end of the road and approached. The instant that they came to a halt, Queller, the other man, and the driver roughly pushed the group forward until everyone was loaded aboard. I noted that they were about to embark on an uncomfortable journey, for there was little room in the cart for half their number. But not a sound, not a cry of complaint, came from their lips, as they passed slowly out of our sight.

Queller and the other man, whom I presumed to be some sort of factory foreman, exchanged a few words before going their separate ways, each in search of a cab. Only when the street was empty did we emerge from our concealment.

"Holmes, those people looked more dead than alive. What does it all mean?"

He smiled grimly. "First let us see if we are to be fortunate enough to find a hansom at such a late hour, for the second time tonight. A brandy, I think, would be in order on our return to Baker Street."

I knew that to press him for an explanation would be pointless, for it had long been his custom to decline to disclose his theories and deductions until his own chosen moment. Hammersmith High Street was devoid of traffic and we were about to resign ourselves to a long walk with the prospect of finding a cab on the way when the doors of a tavern burst open and a thick-set and obviously drunk customer was forcibly ejected onto the pavement. We watched as he staggered to his feet and shook his fist at his assailant, and then made his way to an open cart nearby. The tethered horse scraped the road impatiently with well-shod hooves, and his master murmured words of affection into the animal's ear and took up the reins.

"Come, Watson." Holmes strode across to the other side of the street and I followed closely. In minutes he had come to an agreement with the man and we were on our way back to our lodgings. My friend constantly issued instructions, and despite the inebriated state of our driver we arrived without incident. We thanked him and my friend rewarded him handsomely. Then we were climbing the stairs to our sitting room.

"Will you now explain to me what this man Queller has done to those people?" I asked when we were settled in our armchairs with glasses of a fine cognac.

Holmes took a sip before placing his glass on a side-table and leaning back in his chair. "Ask first the purpose of our visit to his house last night, and I will reply with one word which will reveal much to you."

"Very well. What is the word?"

213

"*Mesmerism*."

"That is how Queller controls them?"

He nodded. "I suspected it almost from the first, and on examining his notes and books on the subject in his study last night, it became a certainty. By means of that practice, he is able to cause these individuals to rise from their beds and work for him in that place we watched tonight. I suspect that the work involves the processing and packing of large amounts of counterfeit notes, but that is something for Inspector Lestrade to confirm when I lay the full facts before him."

"This certainly explains the weariness of Mrs. Durrell and the others."

"That was to be expected, when they were allowed so little rest. The dreams of course, were the fragments of memories of their unpleasant experiences. They were returned to their homes where, after a few hours, they would awaken exhausted with no recollection of having ever left."

"And the labours of the day to contend with," I finished. "Little is known of mesmerism as yet, but I wouldn't have thought it possible to manipulate others to that degree."

"It seems that it is, old fellow. You cannot have forgotten that scoundrel Marcus Davery, who employed a similar technique."

"No, indeed," We sat drinking in silence for a while, Holmes's mind elsewhere and mine on the incredibility of this affair.

Presently he drained his glass and rose, and I did likewise.

"I do believe we will visit Lestrade at Scotland Yard tomorrow before we confront Doctor Queller. But for now, I wish you a very good night and a peaceful sleep during the remaining hours."

He turned and disappeared into his room before I could reply. I realised then that fatigue had claimed me, and followed his example.

With Lestrade beside us, we set out for Queller's house immediately after breakfast next morning. Holmes had hardly rapped upon the door with his stick when it was opened by Queller himself, his top hat in his hand.

"Ah, I see that you were about to go out, Doctor," said Holmes. "Pray spare us a few moments of your time, beforehand."

Queller stared at us, surprised. "I do not see patients in my home."

"We are not patients. My name is Sherlock Holmes, and this is my friend and colleague, Doctor John Watson. And this is Inspector Lestrade of Scotland Yard."

"The consulting detective," his eyes narrowed with suspicion, "and a Scotland Yard man. I cannot see that either of you could have dealings with me."

214

"Perhaps things would become clearer if I mention mesmerism, counterfeit banknotes, and the exhausted state of twenty people or more."

"You can prove nothing." He adopted a sly expression. "If it were true, of what crime do you accuse me? I know nothing of mesmerism, nor of the production of false money."

"We have a client who will be an excellent witness," said I.

"I doubt that. He or she will remember nothing."

"And how, knowing nothing of mesmerism, would you have ascertained that?" Holmes enquired. "And what of murder?"

I saw Lestrade's expression sharpen.

Queller's eyes were now full of alarm. "To what are you referring?"

"I am simply stating that we intend to pursue the disappearance of a witness in a case that would certainly have resulted in your conviction," Holmes answered. "You may recall Mr. Elisha Cobb."

At this, Queller's thin face contorted with shock. Doubtless he had thought that the case investigated by Barker was behind him and no longer a threat. He made as if to reply and raised his top hat to his head, and for a moment I thought that he was about to accompany us, but then he suddenly retreated into the house smartly after slamming the door.

"Quickly, Watson!" Holmes cried. "He knows that he's finished! That gate at the side of the house will lead to the garden – it's his escape route. Hurry and intercept him, while Lestrade and I wait here in case he attempts to retreat."

I was prepared to use my service revolver on the lock, but it proved unnecessary. I flung the gate wide and rushed through to find Queller in the act of leaving by the rear entrance. He spat out a foul oath and turned back, once more slamming the door with a mighty crash. I fired my weapon and blew out the lock. I was about to cautiously enter when sounds from above reached me. Surprised, I stepped back outside. Queller stood above me, framed in the full-length window. I imagine that his intention was to leap to the ground while I searched for him within. He was balanced precariously, his expression fearful and uncertain.

"Queller!" I cried. "Stop! You will not survive!"

I was about to call again, but Holmes and Lestrade appeared by my side in that instant. Before we could do anything more, Queller turned back into the house was gone from our sight.

"Back to the front of the house!" cried the inspector.

We followed Holmes at a run as he ran full-pelt. There were no large windows on that side of the house to accommodate Queller, but he had already used a chair to smash his way through before we arrived. This time we had no opportunity to make an attempt to reason with him, for he had launched himself into the air with his arms outstretched. We watched in horror as we realised that he would never reach the ground, his jump going awry and falling far short from of where he intended. He screamed once as he became impaled upon the iron railings that ran along the front of the building. Then his body writhed briefly and was still.

His blood pooled around him as we approached.

"An awful way to die," I commented after the briefest of examinations.

"Indeed." Holmes turned away.

We finally departed the premises, leaving the inspector to continue. The white-faced driver of our waiting hansom said nothing, but instead took up the reins at once.

"However," my friend said, seeing that the incident had unsettled me, "I wouldn't waste too much sympathy here, Watson. The way my accusation was received suggests that he *was* guilty of murder, and his criminal use of others reveals a cruel and insensitive nature."

I nodded as the driver urged the horse onward. "I suppose, Holmes, that justice is not always decided by the courts."

"It may be that fate sometimes takes a hand in our affairs," he said thoughtfully, "although I doubt that it will be recorded that way in Lestrade's report in any case. I think that a Turkish bath before lunch is in order, if you would care to join me."

When Best Served Cold
by Stephen Mason

"Holmes, when will you accept that your parlour tricks no longer impress me?"

"Considering the enlargement of your eyes and the sudden intake of breath, I will assume my 'parlour tricks' are still an amazement to you."

"Fair point. But how did you determine that I've taken up a new pastime, since I've left no obvious clue, and I haven't spoken a word of it in these past several months?"

"Quite easily, once I spared a moment to *observe* my friend and not just *see* him. First, I noticed that you have developed a tan line along the midpoint of your brow. Never have I seen such a demarcation before on your forehead. I must deduce that you've begun an activity that keeps you outside on a more regular basis, and you are wearing some type of headwear to help protect you from the baking rays of the summer sun. Additionally, I behold a very slight but noticeable indentation upon the inner side of your fingers, particularly your left hand, along the proximal phalanges. I recognize those deformities as someone who is gripping too tightly the leather of a golf club – specifically, the over-exaggerated grip of a bulger club can cause these tell-tale marks on a golfer's fingers. How is your game? I assume you're trying your luck at either Sunningdale or Walton Heath?"

"Sunningdale is one of the more recent courses built, and so is in its growing-pains stage. Walton Heath is still under construction and is due to be officially opened within a year or two. I favour the London Scottish Golf Club near the railway station in Wimbledon. The course meanders over the existing landscape, with large, lovely mature trees, severe gorse areas, and challenging roughs that take several strokes to regain the fairway. Fortunately at that course, I don't feel the need to challenge the professionals, who are trying to earn their keep on the links. I've decided the term 'duffer' was created to best describe my game.

"But back to your ability to deduce my newly found interest . . . as in so many other instances, I'm inclined to believe that in another age you would float if tested."

"There are many who would surmise that I would bob on the surface of the water such as a piece of driftwood. Others favour that I'd simply melt when covered by water, such as described in that recent children's work by the American author, Baum. In any case, the increased exercise will help reduce the slight bulging around your equator."

"Not just a touch," I responded with a smile, "but a direct strike to the lower abdomen, I would say."

"My dear Watson, my intent was not one of harm. My mention of your slight weight gain is simply to remind you as we enter the years of middle *age*, our ability to carry out many of our investigative techniques may be limited by a widening of the middle *stage*. We are no longer spring chickens. I daresay a couple of old hunting dogs may be more apropos."

The year was 1902, in which Holmes had already succeeded in several other cases – though none were exceedingly taxing. Over eight years had elapsed since I had returned to our established lodgings after Holmes's three-year hiatus.

"Returning to our discussion of my new athletic hobby," I said, "part of my feigned surprise is explained by the point that I was about to ask a very large favour of you, which is remotely connected to my golf game. As you're aware, each month I take a quick jaunt up to York to visit an old university friend, William Hardy. He's the administrator of a clinic in York, and cajoled me into taking up the grand game. For several months, I've joined him in a round or two at the Knavesmire Golf Club, just outside the central part of York."

"I am aware of that particular course."

"Why would you have an interest in a golf club?"

"Believe me, the sport itself doesn't draw my interest. However, for many years, most public hangings in York were located within the confines of Knavesmire. As those grounds are situated in a very low position, they're liable to major flooding during periods of sustained rains. Thus, the area wasn't inhabited or built up as were other parts of the city. The gallows were erected in in the late 1300's. The actual location of the executions was known as 'York Tyburn', named after the original Tyburn Gallows in Middlesex.

"The hangings there continued until the beginning of the nineteenth century, when the gallows were moved closer to the castle. Evidently, executing people right on the door step of your city is not considered good for tourism. Many of the victims of the executions were buried on the spot. The locale would seem to be an idea area for use as a golf course."

"I'm playing golf on a cemetery?"

"It appears that way."

"Be that as it may, I was scheduled to take my monthly trip to visit William this week. Just this morning, I received an interesting telegram from him that I was about to reveal to you. What do you make of it?"

John,

Golf is postponed. Unusual events occur at clinic. Could use wisdom. Also use your friend's help. Please hurry.

William
The Retreat

"Watson, while your friend's request is very sparing in details, it does appear that he's in dire need of assistance. Fortunately, my plate has some empty space upon it at present. I would recommend that you refer to the *Bradshaw* to determine when we can catch the correct train, and reply back to Dr. Hardy that we will be there tomorrow around noon to provide what 'wisdom' we can.

A tap on my bedroom door stirred me from a restful sleep. Dear Mrs. Hudson had set out a light snack of tea and toast for us, which I welcomed after finishing my morning ablutions. While Holmes perused the early editions of the newspapers, I hurriedly packed a small valise, which I considered to be sufficient for an overnight trip.

During the journey, I was able to provide Holmes with a very short biography of Dr. William Hardy. "It's easy to see why we became friends at an early age, and have continued the relationship to present. He was one year behind me at University, and was dispatched to Afghanistan, such as myself. Fortunately, he wasn't on the receiving end of a bullet as I was, but he did suffer a debilitating case of dysentery. While he didn't succumb to the disease, with the assistance of the bark of the kapok tree, he was discharged to come home due to prolonged weakness.

"Once he had built his strength back up, he joined Blackheath Club, where he played next to me for a couple of seasons. He practiced under two other doctors in Cavendish Square before becoming assistant administrator at an institution, the Hanwell County Mental Hospital. He then took over The Retreat just before the turn of the century."

A few-hour rail excursion deposited us at the York station, presently the largest in the world, where we secured rooms at the adjoining Royal Station Hotel. Interestingly, we were placed in the Klondyke Wing, named after the Klondike gold rush. Each of our rooms was appointed with bed, sofa, writing table, and two chairs.

After a late breakfast of eggs and fresh rashers in the dining room, we were then whisked by hansom to The Retreat for an eleven o'clock appointment. The cab pulled into a circular drive in front of the primary building, with wings to the left and right of us. From previous visits, I knew that extensive gardens occupied much of the posterior sides of the structure. One of the more significant features of the clinic is the fact that the windows don't have the normal bars that one typically encounters in similar institutions. From the outside, they appear to have routine frames.

An assistant escorted us to the Administrator's Office, providing us with an obligatory cup of coffee. A few short minutes later, my old friend William Hardy entered the room and proceeded to shake Holmes's hand and give me a quick hug before taking a seat behind his humble desk against the far wall. William was middle-sized, with a pleasant, well-tanned face. He was dressed in a simple white-linen coat, which had become more and more popular with physicians who wished to connote the scientific aspects of medicine.

After a few minutes of pleasantries, during which time Holmes quietly drummed his fingers upon his own chair arm, William initiated the discussion for which we had been requested.

"I trust, Mr. Holmes, that you'll be able to spare our facility a few hours of your valuable time. We've experienced a couple of painful incidents in the past few days, and I'm at a loss as to what should be done."

"Dr. Hardy, I would be very much obliged if you would give us the particulars of these incidents. Pray focus to give a clear and concise account of what has befallen this house of healing."

"I will attempt to do so. First, you should know that William Tuke established our facility in 1796 as an alternative to the barbaric asylums which had sprung up across England. It originally only treated Quakers, but later opened its doors to anyone in need. We started with a thirty-person bed capacity, but that number has steadily grown. Most of our patients are single, male, and under the age of fifty.

"Two things separate us from other such facilities: First, our humane treatment of our clientele. Second, the complete anonymity of the residents. I alone am aware of the true identity of each patient. All other staff only know the patients by fictitious names, and the files are kept locked.

"We have completely banned the use of severe physical restraints and punishment. We employ the use of strait-jackets only in extreme circumstances, instead focusing on bringing patients back to their own self-esteem. You may not be aware, but part of our unique treatment methods stem from a client who died here late in the previous century. Hannah Mills was a recently widowed young woman suffering from depression, or known then as 'melancholy'. She had been admitted to the asylum, and was dead within a month. The doctors at the time confirmed that they kept her in isolation, not even allowing her family or friends to visit her to buoy her spirits. Now we stress occupational therapies, such as

220

working in the farms and gardens located throughout the grounds. Finally, unlike other institutions, we allow the clients to wear their own clothing, in lieu of typical patient outfits.

"Simply stated, two deaths have occurred in the past few days which appear slightly irregular. Both were female patients, known here as 'Jean' and 'Claire', approximately forty years of age, with no discernable physical health issues. They had both eaten regularly on the day of their demise, had quiet evenings, and went off to bed with ease. But each passed during the night – peacefully, I might add, with no sign of any acute affliction when discovered the next morning."

"When did the two women expire?"

"Jean left us on Thursday, three days ago. Claire went just last night. We didn't see any apparent signs of catastrophic injury or illness, although both women were beginning to exhibit the early symptoms of a common cold, or perhaps influenza. We provided both with plasters to their chest area, as well as a sedative to help with their sleep."

"Where are the bodies?" asked Holmes.

"In our medical exam room. The undertaker will be receiving them later this evening. In each case, there were no family members to notify, so as yet we haven't identified anyone that we can tell of their passing."

"And have you alerted the police?" I asked.

"Not yet. The chances of suicide in such an institution are much higher than the general population. We estimate that approximately one in ten of our patients are considering taking their own lives when first admitted. While we believe our treatments lower that possibility significantly, we still do have rare instances where someone is beyond our reach, and find that their only salvation through the end of life. While we make no attempts to cover up the manner of death of any of our clients, we allow the coroner to make the final decision on whether a death is natural or self-inflicted before we notify the local Constabulary. This is the case for the two women, and the autopsies have yet to be scheduled."

"Can you tell us what was in the plaster?" asked Holmes.

"It was a simple mustard plaster, prepared by mixing ground mustard and warm water to a proper consistency, and then applied to both the back and chest areas."

"This type of poultice," I added, "can help to sweat out any 'ills' that the body may contain. The treatment can also assist in drawing out congestion from the lungs."

"For most patients," William said, "we apply a layer of petroleum jelly to the skin first in order to prevent blistering."

"It sounds routine as a treatment. I assume that Watson and I both have permission to examine the bodies?"

"If you believe that it's necessary for you to determine if anything untoward has happened, then by all means."

We were escorted down the hallway to the examination area which, while sparse, was exceedingly clean and had the necessary equipment for this type of facility, including recent additions such as a sphygmomanometer and ophthalmoscope, alongside the more usual thermometer and reflex hammer. Dr. Hardy excused himself to check on another patient for a few minutes.

"Watson, while I may have a theory or two, a diagnosis of cause is much more within your realm. Please examine the woman known as 'Claire', the more recent death, and tell me what you think."

I slowly and thoroughly examined the body from head to toe, noting the normal body deformities, discolorations, and other imperfections to be expected from a person around forty years of age. Claire was of average height and weight, with brownish hair, mixed with just a few wisps of grey.

"I observe no signs of outward trauma," I reported. "There are no extreme contractions exceeding the usual *rigor mortis*, and I see no unusual discolouration around the lips or nose that would indicate some type of poisoning. I believe that she may have simply died in her sleep of natural causes."

"And yet, another has also died within days and in a similar manner. While I fully accept your expertise in these matters, I will amuse myself with a cursory examination of certain parts of the body."

He quickly pulled out his lens and proceeded to conduct a cursory viewing of the corpse, focusing mainly on the extremities. At one point he pulled a very small mass off the inside of the woman's lower calf, rolled it between his thumb and forefinger, and then placed the object within an envelope that he'd procured from a side table.

"What did you find?" I asked.

"See for yourself," he said, and handed the envelope to me. I walked toward one of the windows and held it open. There was a small brown object within, not much bigger than a flake. It looked rather like a small scab or skin tag.

Holmes was replacing the sheet over the body when I handed him the envelope without comment. At that moment, William returned, stating, "I assume that you both will need to now inspect the other body."

Holmes quickly replied, "I believe a very quick glance on my part will be sufficient."

He proceeded to the other bed, lifting the section of the sheet covering the lower extremities, and after only a second or two, lowered the sheet.

"Holmes, whatever did you see in such a short time?"

222

"Just what I expected to see. Doctor Hardy, I believe that the next step will be to examine your employee files, if you would be so kind?"

"I hope you don't suspect any member of my staff in any wrongdoing . . . ."

"Just being thorough. I believe a glimpse of the files might strengthen a possible supposition."

"If you must . . . However, I'm due to start treatments with a few of our more critical clients. One of our procedures here is to keep to a strict schedule upon which the patients can rely. Can we agree to meet back in my office in a couple of hours? In the meantime, you may want to enjoy our gardens, as well as review the books that we keep in our library. You might have suggestions for additions that would benefit our clients."

We separated and slowly made our way outside. While William hadn't dissuaded us from doing so, we kept our interactions with the residents to simple pleasantries, with no mention of their present circumstances.

As we toured the gardens, I took the time to provide Holmes with some more details about what I'd learned of the facility. "For the last twenty years or so, the majority of patients have been younger, and tend to be un-married. About one-third of them are considered suicidal, and thus are in dire need of acute therapies. Some of the patients have been diagnosed with delusions, and as you can imagine, those are here for longer-term care. However, many others are admitted for more simple disorders. The patients tend to be discharged within one year, with medicinal therapy providing a great deal of relief."

We took time to visit the dining area and library facilities. The books were all fictional, with most being light-hearted adventures or comedies. Gothic tragedies, as well as volumes dealing with social issues, were very limited. I couldn't discover any novels which dealt with mental issues as a major theme.

Late afternoon found us returning down the primary hallway to the Administrator's Office. Beams of sunlight filtered through the sheer curtains, brightening the wooden furniture and darkened Axminster carpeting.

"I hope that the two of you were successful in entertaining yourselves during my absence?" said William.

"Yes," responded Holmes. "You've maintained a model facility, from which many others could take a lesson. Now let us proceed. Dr. Hardy – how many patients, other than the two recently deceased, do you currently have in residence?"

"Actually, for the first time in years, we are severely below capacity. The number presently stands at sixteen – three women and thirteen men. Obviously, the two deceased women lowered the total from eighteen."

"And the number of staff personnel?"

"Also very limited. One counselor, two nurses, three aides, and one maintenance worker. Most have been here for years and are as respectable a staff as could be hoped for."

"Interesting. There are no other doctors here?"

"No, we've adopted the belief that more doctors does not necessarily lead to improvements in the mental stability of our clients. All of our staff live on the premises, take their meals with the clients, and even work along-side the residents in the gardens and farms. All inhabitants here share in the day-to-day chores and help with preventive maintenance activities."

William then directed Holmes to the wooden cabinet behind his desk, indicating where the employee files were kept locked in one of the drawers. Holmes quickly began flipping through the folders.

"Hmm . . . *Ashdown, Brewer, Gedge, Kaylock, Sheills, Stanbury, Wanhopes, Youngblood . . . .*" He spent a few minutes looking through the files, and then something seemed to occur to him, and he reopened one that had been previously set aside. He read through it for several minutes and then fell silent, tapping his lip with a finger while he considered what he'd read. Then finally he laid aside the files and said, "You indicated 'most' of the employees have been here for a long period of time. Which have been here for a shorter frame?"

"Miss Wanhopes has been here just one week, while Miss Kaylock arrived only last month. Both of them came to us with solid references and a strong work record."

"References and records can be easily forged, if need be."

"Mr. Holmes, as you can imagine, keeping staff employed in such a facility is constantly a challenge. Wages are routinely lower than at normal hospitals, and stress is high when dealing with the type of patients that we have here. With a shortage of administrative help, following up on the information that we're given during an employment interview is unfortunately rarely accomplished."

"I understand. Now, I must also ask for the patients' files."

"Mr. Holmes, I am sorry, but that is going beyond the realm of propriety. We must keep the confidentiality of our clients first and foremost."

"Dr. Hardy, I can understand your reluctance, but if it will help ease your mind, I am now prepared to state to you that both women died, not naturally, but from the hands of a murderous individual. Seeing those files may be our only chance to prevent further mayhem."

"All right, but I will have to ask upon your honour you will protect any information that you see."

"I agree, and I'm sure that Watson will take the same vow." I promptly nodded my assent.

"Can you please allow me until tomorrow morning to put the files in a more orderly manner? Unfortunately, tidiness of files is one of those luxuries for which I simply don't have time."

Holmes hesitated. "I only hope such an extension may not prove to be disastrous."

William's assistant retrieved a cab for us to return to our hotel in the centre of the town. Holmes then took the time to write out a message and asked one of the hotel pages to promptly have it sent. Afterwards we walked to The Golden Fleece, a small pub known for simple but tasty fare. Due to the warmth of the evening, we were pleased to secure a table near an open window, enjoying a light breeze which aided in moderating the temperature inside. The establishment's owner, a Mr. Parker, joined us for a pint, showing interest in our reasons for being in York. Holmes established us as two artists from London, hoping to find landscapes in the surrounding counties to paint as part of an exhibit for later this year. Of course, Holmes's artistic French bloodline helped him play the part perfectly, while I simply nodded or responded in one or two word answers to inquiries directed toward me.

With a full day of activities and an even fuller stomach, sleep came easily on the comfortable hotel bed. I met Holmes in the dining room the next morning for breakfast. While enjoying the eggs and ham, a messenger approached our table.

"Is one of you a Dr. Watson?"

"I am."

"Message for you from The Retreat."

After tipping the messenger, I opened the envelope to reveal the words inside. I felt my stomach lurch.

John,

Come as soon as possible. Another female death. I will have to bring in police. Again, please hurry.

William
The Retreat

"Watson, I shouldn't have left the facility yesterday without insisting on examining those files – or at least recognizing the danger still lurked there. Let us not delay."

Upon our arrival at the hospital, we were led immediately to William's office, at which time he removed the patient files from a locked drawer within his own desk and placed them on the surface of the bureau.

"Do you wish to see the latest patient? I choose not to refer to her as a victim until we know for sure what is transpiring here. 'Ada' was similar to the other two patients – thirty-eight in age, in relatively good health, but showing the beginning signs of a respiratory infection. She was given a mild sedative to sleep, as well as a syrup containing a tincture of belladonna to help alleviate coughing. As before, she seemed to be resting quietly and with no acute issues when the nurse checked on her before retiring for the evening."

"I don't need to see the third victim. I'm sure that I'd find the same as the other two."

"By the way, Mr. Holmes," said William, reaching for an envelope on his desk, "a message addressed to you was delivered by messenger just before the two of you entered the facility."

Holmes accepted it, scanned the contents, and quietly nodded his head. "There's one bit of information confirmed."

There were eighteen files for Holmes to potentially comb through, but he shuffled through them until he found one labelled "*Hudson*" on the outside. He read it quickly, put it back in the pile, and assured Hardy that he could replace the files under lock and key.

"Did you find what you were looking for?" I asked.

"Yes. I now believe all the pieces to this puzzle have been revealed, and I've been able to fit them all into the right places. Dr. Hardy, I'm afraid that tonight there will be a further attempt to end the life of another of your female patients."

My gasp was audible enough to interrupt my companion. "Holmes, surely you can't believe that someone is trying to murder *all* of the female patients here? Why would they desire to do so?"

"That is exactly what I am suggesting. There are two female patients – listed under the names 'Emma' and 'Ruth' – still residing here. However, to ensure that I don't unintentionally risk the welfare of either patient, with your agreement Dr. Hardy, I'd like to implement the following plan . . . ."

Holmes and I returned to the hotel for a late lunch, consisting of buttered-bread, a piece of meat, cold pudding, and coffee. The same as the day before, he dashed off another quick message to be wired from the nearest Post Office, after which we walked to the local Constabulary to discuss the situation with the rural police force. There we were directed to Constable Browning, stocky and ruddy-faced, who greeted us with unabashed enthusiasm. A moustache and shadow of a beard outlined his facial features, which were accented by bright blue eyes, several shades lighter than his uniform.

"Mr. Holmes, Dr. Watson, I'm honoured to have the two of you within my territory. I'm also pleased to say that I've adopted a few of your tactics in my own policing efforts. Your adventures have been a godsend to many of us in the hinterlands."

"I hope that my suggestions will continue to serve you well. In the near future, I plan on finishing my own textbook on detection which will equip you with even more weapons to combat crime – " He glanced my way. " – without all the trappings of an embellished narrative."

Amazingly, Holmes's jabs no longer crawl at my skin, and I simply smiled and let him continue.

"Constable, I'm not sure that you're aware of the circumstances surrounding the events at The Retreat, but three women have been murdered in the preceding days, and a potential fourth death may occur tonight unless we act to stop it."

"I've just now received a note from Dr. Hardy, asking that I accompany the two of you back to the facility. However, I feel that I'm out of my league and should send a message to London, asking for support from the Yard."

"You may do so, but I'm inclined to think that their assistance would only arrive in the morning at the earliest, which would too late to prevent another death. Our efforts tonight will not only stop this from happening, but should also determine for sure who has been behind these crimes."

"Sadly, because of unexpected illness and injury, I'm the only active member of my force available at this time. We cannot count on any support, if needed."

"With Dr. Hardy, the four of us should be sufficient. After we've eaten dinner, and nightfall has arrived, we'll return to the facility, ensuring that no one is aware of our presence."

Thus, after dark I found myself sitting in a dark corner of Emma's private room, holding a vigil to ensure her safety throughout the night. William and Holmes had staked out a similar position in Ruth's room. When we'd arrived a few minutes earlier, William had provided Holmes with another envelope, which I assumed must be an answer to his earlier message. Constable Browning was stationed in Dr. Hardy's office, placed so that no one was able to escape down the hallway and through the front door. All the other entrances had been secured to ensure that egress was impossible. Holmes's admonition still rang in my ears: "Do not go asleep – her life may depend upon it!"

The bedroom held only a scant amount of furniture – the bed, writing table, and chair. Near the bed was a walking stick – apparently belonging to the sleeping woman. The walls were adorned with small portraits that I assumed were of family members, as well as a few sketches done by Emma herself. While she would never be considered a true artist, one could easily see the challenges that she had bravely faced. The most dominant sketch was of a small village cemetery, with the tombstones angled at many varied degrees. In the forefront was a tombstone lacking an inscription, which I could only assume was reserved for the name *"Emma"*. I hoped that she would never reach the point where she felt as if she must fill it in.

A bit of light penetrated the room from the rays of the moon peeking through a narrow slit in the window shutters. The only sound was Emma's regular breathing as she slumbered in the sleep of the innocent. Both Emma and Ruth had been provided with light sedatives during dinner to make certain that we didn't disturb them while keeping watch.

Around midnight, my limbs were becoming weary and stiff, yet I dared not stand and give up my hiding spot. Then, without warning, the hallway door slowly began to open, and in a few moments a shadowy head leaned in. The intruder obviously felt comfortable enough to enter. I held my breath, scared to inhale or exhale too loudly.

Even in the room's limited lighting, I recognized the figure as an employee, one of the aides by her attire. Yet she didn't seem familiar and I realized that I hadn't yet met her. Peering through the darkness, I watched as her vague outline crept toward Emma's bed. She walked so close to me that, with just a little effort, I could have reached out and snared her in an embrace. However, Holmes had cautioned me not to make any move or sound the alert until the intruder had made a definitive threat against my charge. Obviously, the aide was ignorant of my presence as she reached Emma and bared her lower leg, similar to the procedure taken by Holmes when examining the deceased patients.

Suddenly, I was able to discern the glint of a needle in the moonlight, and recognized that the aide was holding a very large hypodermic syringe. I had no idea what she planned to inject into her victim, but she would have to subdue me before carrying out her deed. With a cry, I jumped to grab her from behind, but in the darkness I didn't see that she had turned, lashing out with her fist toward my face. I saw the glint of the hypodermic in her clenched fingers, and I involuntarily jerked away. As I flinched, my leg twisted, and my old injury, combined with the extended period of sitting perfectly still, caused my legs to fail at the most inopportune time.

The best that I could do was grab at the intruder's midsection, while she fought to escape me. I tried to see if she would again make an effort to thrust the hypodermic in my direction, but instead of doing so, she suddenly leaned forward. Then she twisted in my grip and immediately I felt a shattering pain across the top of my head. As the sound of something made of wood hit the floor, my grip loosened and she stepped away. Then a kick to my chest sent me to my knees.

As she ran from the room, I cried, "Holmes, come quickly! Emma has been attacked!"

I was already pulling myself up by the bed frame when Holmes and William entered the room. I saw Emma's walking stick, which I noticed earlier, was now shattered into two pieces and tossed onto the floor. I wanted to confirm that my own injuries weren't severe, but instead I turned to make sure that Emma was unharmed. Amazingly, she had slept through the entire ordeal.

"Where is she, Watson?" asked Holmes.

William followed close behind. "Did you see which direction she headed?"

"No." I straightened to face them. "I was completely focused on Emma's safety."

Holmes quickly responded. "I imagine that she has retreated to the perceived safety of her own room. Quickly, Hardy – take us to Miss Wanhopes' lodgings."

"What makes you believe it is her?" William asked. "You didn't see her escape."

"I'll explain later. We have no time to delay. Make haste!"

William led to the main hallway, where we found Browning standing outside the office, tense and ready for action, but uncertain as to how to proceed. Holmes told him to accompany us, and William started down the south hallway to where the aides and nurses resided. I trailed slightly behind the others, the tingling in my scalp and the pain in my chest receding, and feeling slowly returning to both legs.

William led us to the third door along the corridor, but when we tried it, we discovered that it was closed and locked. Two or three attempts by Holmes to knock it open proved useless. I found a hat rack with a very sturdy base nearby, and we were able to force open the door after several strikes with our make-shift battering ram. Then Holmes charged through with the rest of us close behind. One door along the hallway showed a light underneath, and without knocking or announcing himself, Holmes burst in, the door slamming against the wall. Looking over William's shoulder, I was able to witness Miss Wanhopes sitting on her bed an unusually calm look upon her face.

229

"While I've never had the pleasure of meeting you in person," she said, "I assume that I'm addressing the famous Mr. Sherlock Holmes, and your trusty chronicler, Dr. John Watson."

I responded, "This is correct, but you have the advantage of us. Who you are, and more importantly, why did you undertake such a deed?"

"I believe that Mr. Holmes has figured out what my goal was," she replied. "How else could you have anticipated my efforts tonight?"

"Miss Wanhopes," replied Holmes, "as you have chosen to be known, I comprehend a great deal of your intent, based on what I've learned in the past two days. If you'd like, I can provide a summary of what has transpired, and you may be willing to fill in any small details that I've yet to determine."

At this point, William intervened. "Before we initiate discussions of motives, can you please let us know the method you undertook to murder these three women?"

She sighed, as if explaining a basic fact to a dull student. "I believe that you'll find that there's nothing very sophisticated in the procedure. As an aide, I was able to introduce a small amount of strychnine into the meals of the three women. A ready supply is always available in one of the medicine cabinets, and I believe that your institution at one time prescribed it for depression, as well as other medical issues.

"In very small amounts, over a few days, strychnine can mimic the beginnings of influenza – muscle stiffness, sore throat, and respiratory distress. The staff administer always sedatives to assist the patients in sleeping, and the suggestion of oncoming illness caused them to administer a little extra, so that they wouldn't awaken during the night. This made my work ever so simple.

"Every night, I entered each room and injected a very large amount of ordinary air into a vein of my victims. They were sleeping so soundly that they never felt a thing. In only minutes, the embolism had done its job."

Her statement left me cold with horror. "As an aide," I asked, "how did you come by the skill and knowledge to inject anything into the vein of a patient?"

"I'm not untrained, Doctor," she said with a touch of contempt. "I've spent some time during the past couple of years helping the wounded who have returned from the war. You can imagine that, with the shortage of medical help, any assistance, even from an untrained person such as myself, was not only needed, but very much appreciated. Injection skills have become very handy for me, as you may surmise.

"If you examine those oranges in the bowl on the side table there, you'll see that they have been most useful in practising the procedure.

Injecting just below the skin without rupturing the fruit can be as daunting as hitting a vein, especially in very little light.

Constable Browning interrupted with a certain amount of frustration. "I am still completely in the dark concerning this entire event. Can someone please let me know what has just happened before members of the Yard arrive later this morning?"

"Yes," said Holmes. "I can walk through the steps that I undertook to solve the puzzle. I will begin by stating that while three people have lost their lives as a result of Miss Wanhopes' actions, I was able to piece together the motive behind the crimes fairly simply. The first clue was presented to me when we examined the first two victims' remains."

"Holmes," I said, "I thought we determined there were no signs of foul play."

"You are correct that our initial assessment didn't reveal any obvious indicators. But as you recall, I focused on their lower legs, where I found a small item on the inner calf just above the ankle on the first body." He pulled the envelope from his pocket and handed it to me. I looked at it again, but it was no different than what I'd seen the other day. I showed it to both William and Browning, but they looked puzzled as well.

Holmes took back the envelope and slipped it into his pocket. "It's a small bit of actor's clay, Watson. As you know, I've used that same material in many of our cases to alter my facial features, and it's particularly useful when adding to the size of one's nose or chin."

"But what would be the purpose of putting a speck of clay on their legs?"

"To hide a very small pin prick, where a needle had been inserted into their legs. The use of the clay provided me the evidence of a needle stick, an intentional act to cause harm. This was murder. When I next scanned Jean's legs, I found the same small piece of clay covering a needle insertion – which I've left in place as evidence. At this point, I determined that both victims had been mortally injured, using the same method. The idea of an embolism, which leaves no apparent trace, was the obvious explanation. And that could have only been accomplished by someone on the staff."

"As Miss Wanhopes indicated," I added, "the sedatives were given to the patients helped them sleep. It appears that the additional dosage did the trick to ensure the prick of a needle wouldn't stir them in the night. In fact," I said with a sudden realization, "we gave them even more tonight, so that they would sleep while we hid in their rooms."

"They will be all right," William interrupted. "We use chloral hydrate – the slightly greater amount will simply cause them to sleep deeper for the entire night."

Holmes continued. "Next, having established that the murderer was an employee of the hospital, I needed to find who was executing these actions. A quick scan of the personnel files provided me the clue I needed. After reviewing each one, Miss Wanhopes' file caught my eye. Dr. Hardy, you stated she had just started within the past week. That alone was an interesting fact. But more importantly, I recognised two other things: 'Wanhopes' is Middle English word for 'despair'. Quite unusual – and one that I considered might even be false. Next, I saw where she had listed as her place of origin: Horsham."

"I don't understand."

"At first, I didn't either. It was simply a fact, as were the towns listed in the other employees' files. But that name, *Wanhopes*, was unusual. I can't recall ever seeing it as a name at all, although I suppose that such a thing is possible. And yet, even as I scanned through the files, I continued to mull upon it. There was something that just didn't ring true about it. Then my mind made the connection between *Wanhopes* and *Horsham* – for it was from that rural locality where our former client, John Openshaw, had hailed."

"I don't see – "

"It's an anagram, Watson. *Wanhopes* can be unscrambled to *Openshaw*."

Beside us, William and Browning struggled to follow our conversation, but I saw that a look of defeat had entered Miss Wanhopes' eyes as she listened to Holmes explain how he had come to understand the solution.

"Openshaw is a family name tied to one of our former cases," I explained to William and Browning. "It concerned a warning sent in the form of orange pips by the American criminal organization known as the *Ku Klux Klan*, or *K.K.K.*" I perceived that the explanation hadn't helped to remove their confusion whatsoever.

Holmes looked at the woman. "Do you have anything that you wish to share with us?" She gave a wan smile and shook her head. "No matter." He turned back to face William, Browning, and me. "As Miss Wanhopes – or Miss *Openshaw* as we should call her – assumed that no one would figure out the puzzle of her unusual name, she carelessly listed her previous address as Horsham, in Sussex.

"You will recall that I sent several messages during the past two days. Over the years, I've found it extremely advantageous to develop relationships with the clerks of most of the counties. Therefore, the first message was sent to the clerk in Sussex. The response, which I received yesterday, confirmed my suspicion. Miss Sophronia Openshaw was the daughter of Joseph Openshaw, and the younger sister of John. We were careless, Watson. When John Openshaw was killed by the K.K.K., we followed that thread, and never bothered to look into his background in Sussex. Just because he didn't mention having a sister didn't mean that he was an only child as we assumed."

He spoke to William and Browning. "This woman's family was terrorized by the K.K.K from America following their Civil War. As a result of that, her uncle, father, and brother were murdered. I was informed by the Sussex clerk that their mother had committed suicide years ago by drowning herself, similar to the manner in which her brother-in-law and son met their deaths. And my friend indicated the last surviving member of the family, Miss Openshaw here, was briefly institutionalized herself after the slew of tragedies destroyed her family. However, she escaped the asylum and hasn't been seen since."

While it had been almost fifteen years since Holmes and I had met with her older brother, John Openshaw, I could now discern a faint family resemblance in the nose and eyes.

"So now we have two parts of the puzzle: The method, and the murderer. But I now needed to determine who the intended victim would be. It will be one of my everlasting regrets that I was unable to examine the patient files in time to identify the possible victim. Once I saw the files, I only had to reach the fifth before I found what was possibly the answer."

"Which was?"

"The name *Hudson*."

"And the relevance – ?"

"Watson, you know that the details of many of our cases are no longer stored within my brain-attic. However, the Openshaw tragedy is one of the exceptions. I've always felt that I failed young John Openshaw, this woman's brother, in preventing his tragic murder that night by Waterloo Bridge. I've replayed the entire incident in my mind numerous times to determine how I could have kept him from harm.

"You may recall that on the night that he visited us, Openshaw provided us with a small piece of paper that he had found. It had survived the burning of all the other relevant documents by his Uncle Elias. On the sheet was written the name '*Hudson*'. My interpretation of the note indicated this Hudson was part of the enforcement group that 'cleared' those who had left the K.K.K. and might cause future harm. I believe that Hudson not only 'assisted in clearing' – *murdering*, that is – McCauley, Paramore, and John Swain, the names also listed on that slip of paper, but also all three of the murdered Openshaws – John, his father Joseph, and his uncle, Elias.

"I didn't end my efforts to get at the truth of the matter simply because the killers, Captain Calhoun and the others, had escaped from England on the barque *Lone Star*, which sank on its return voyage to the United States. During my subsequent investigations after John Openshaw's death, I was able to locate this fellow Hudson and determine that he'd long before settled in Dundee after the American Civil War, where he'd married and already established a family consisting of three children. As I've never been able to definitively prove his involvement in the Openshaw murders to the point where he could be charged, he's been able to steer free of the gallows, while I've watched and waited for him to stumble and make a mistake.

"My second message was when I saw that one of the patients was in fact named 'Hudson', and that she was originally from Dundee, Scotland. Could there be a connection? This message went to the same clerk in Sussex County, who was kind enough to use the influence of his position to inquire for me further afield about official information available from Dundee. I learned that a certain Hudson from Dundee who is currently a patient here had initially been institutionalized at the Dundee Royal Lunatic Asylum, and more recently she was transferred here to take advantage of your successful treatments in the treatment of depression.

"The notes in her file, Dr. Hardy, indicated that her condition was partly attributable to discovering that her husband had involved in *'terrible deeds in his past'*. Can there be any doubt that she bears the guilt of finding that her husband was the roving executioner for the *Ku Klux Klan*?

"But Holmes," I said, "if you knew which of the two remaining female patients was Hudson's wife, why did you split our forces? Why didn't we simply guard the woman known as 'Emma'?

"Because, Watson," he replied, "*Miss Openshaw didn't know which was which!* The files were locked and the patient names were false. Unless she chooses to tell us, we may never even know how she was able to determine that Hudson's wife had been placed in residence here. After she vanished from the hospital where she was receiving treatment, Miss Openshaw's whereabouts have been unknown. No doubt she has been slowly and patiently tracking and executing the men – and apparently their relations as well – who were responsible for the deaths of her family. Perhaps somewhere along the way there was an exchange of funds in the right palm that gave her the information as to where poor Hudson's wife was to be found.

"In any case, somehow Miss Openshaw learned that the woman that she sought was here in York, and in her mental state, she must have felt the woman's murder would in some small part exact a portion of her revenge and satisfy that lust. As you indicated, Dr. Hardy, it is a challenge to find and keep employees here at the hospital. I'm certain that she found it quite easy to obtain a position. Unfortunately, once she started here, she discovered that all of the female patients were being treated under pseudonyms, and thus she decided that her only course of action was to systematically eliminate all five of them in order to make sure that the job was completed.

"I placed you to guard Emma, Watson, while Dr. Hardy and I watched over Ruth simply because, in truth, I thought that there was a better chance that Ruth would be tonight's victim because her room was closer to Miss Openshaw's. Instead, she skipped over that one to attack where you were on guard."

"Which of the surviving residents, 'Ruth' or 'Emma', is the true Mrs. Hudson?" I asked.

He glanced toward Miss Openshaw, who now looked suddenly alert once more. Even caught as she was, I believe that she hoped to discover which of the two women sleeping in another part of the building was her true prey, in case there was even the most remote of chances that she could still get free and finish the job.

Holmes shook his head. "That isn't anything that I need to disclose at this time. Just know, Miss Openshaw, that the woman is safe."

Miss Openshaw settled back and gave a small shrug. "I suppose that will have to do, then. I've managed to find so many of the others." And with that, she slipped a small bottle from within her sleeve. Before we could stop her, she had twisted off the cap and raised it to her lips. In a second she had drunk it all and, with a shudder, cast the little bottle to the floor.

"To be certain that it's completely effective," she said, her voice already constricted, "I've ingested what is an excessively lethal dose of cyanide. Mr. Holmes, I was aware of your involvement with the death of my brother many years ago, and I toyed with seeking revenge on you as well for letting him die. Perhaps I should have done so sooner. I do believe that I underestimated your true talents – "

Suddenly she convulsed and collapsed onto the bed. I dashed to her side, verifying that life had indeed left her. Looking at Holmes, William, and the stunned constable, I slowly shook my head, indicating there was nothing that could be done for her.

William sent for a nurse and aide to attend the body, and then the four of us returned to his office. After the day that we'd just experienced, the offered brandy was most welcome.

After quite a long while of silence, Holmes finally stood. "Watson, I suggest that we retire to our rooms at the hotel to get some rest before returning to London tomorrow."

"Actually," I countered, "William had already asked that we stay on for a few days longer. Once this is all sorted out, he owes me a chance to get even from our last golf outing. And while I know that you aren't interested in chasing a little ball down the grass, you can accompany us for a little exercise."

Holmes smiled. "You know that exercise without purpose does not appeal to me. But nevertheless, I may take the opportunity to study more of the history of that bit of land, and the numerous lives that were ended somewhere near your fairways."

The Adventure of the
Chocolate Pot
by Hugh Ashton

Sherlock Holmes was a man of many interests – indeed, I do not recall ever making the acquaintance of any man whose breadth of vision and intellectual scope extended so widely. Nor were these interests of a superficial nature, but in the majority of cases the knowledge that he acquired was of such a depth that he might have passed as a professor of the subject, employed in one of our Universities.

Sometimes these interests were of a passing nature, lasting for only a few months, but in that short space of time, he would have become an expert in that field, and the comprehension thus obtained would remain with him, often to be used in the solution of a case many years later.

An example of this was his interest in the markings of bullets which had been discharged from a firearm. Holmes was of the opinion, which he attempted to verify, that the rifling within the barrels of guns, though theoretically identical, being of the same model and sourced from the same manufacturer, nonetheless exhibited individual characteristics, much as do the whorls and loops of our fingerprints, as theorised by Faulds in his paper of 1880, and with whom Holmes was in later communication.

However, to Scotland Yard, Holmes's theories on the individuality of bullets remained an unproven theory and he was unable to convince even the officer whom he considered to be the finest of the official force, Inspector Stanley Hopkins, of the validity of his suppositions.

Another of Holmes's multifarious interests in which displayed an uncommon skill was acting. He informed me once that he had entertained a notion to become an actor, but that his family had disapproved of his choice of future career.

"However," he informed me one evening as we were sitting in our chairs following dinner, "I took part in several amateur productions at University, and secretly took some instruction in the dramatic art from a professional actor. Much of what I learned, principally that relating to the stage and the theatre, was of little interest to me in my present profession, but some of the fundamental principles of the thespian art, such as how to inhabit another's character, and the mechanical aspects of disguise and so on, have never left me, and indeed have proved of the greatest value to me in my work."

I had many opportunities to witness the skill with which he made use of this past instruction, and to my mind, the case I am about to describe is one of the finest of such incidents, as well as demonstrating his ability to acquire a high degree of expertise in a subject at short notice.

The case had its beginning one spring morning when London was covered by a fine grey mist, rather than the yellow fogs that had plagued us all winter. Though it was not actually raining, it was a day that a Scotchman would describe as "*dreich*", and the coat of the client who sat in the chair by the fire, telling us of his problems, was pearled with a thousand shining beads of moisture. His hat had not entirely protected his head from the weather, and he gratefully accepted my offer of a towel to dry his longish silver hair.

"No, thank you," he had said when I had offered to relieve him of his outer garment and have it dried. "Even in a room such as this, which is admirably heated, I find myself to be cold. At my age it is hard for me to keep warm, and the coat will dry very satisfactorily by the fire."

Sir Barnabas Elkinstone, as he introduced himself, had come from Hampshire to visit Holmes. Since my friend was at that time not currently engaged on any case that he considered of any importance or interest (though any of the three cases on which he found himself employed would have furnished a Scotland Yard detective with a firm foundation on which to build a future career), he consented to see Sir Barnabas and to listen to his story.

"I live a quiet life in Elkinstone Manor, a little outside Winchester," he told us. "The house has been in my family for generations, but my wife died childless some years ago, and on my death the estate will now pass to a distant cousin living in Australia. What will become of it then, I do not like to imagine. But," and he seemed to recover himself from a sad reverie, "that is hardly to the point of what I am about to tell you."

"It is never certain," Holmes answered him, "what may or may not be to the point of a case. But please proceed, sir."

"Very well, then. My hobby – indeed, you might almost consider it to be a passion," and here he gave an embarrassed tittering laugh, "is the collecting of antique silver. I am considered by some to be an expert on the development of fluting in the ornamentation of silver tableware during the later years of the last century, and my thoughts on the matter have been published in several places. Perhaps you have seen them?" he enquired hopefully.

"Alas," Holmes replied with a faint smile, "they have so far escaped my notice."

"No matter," said our visitor. "I fear that I sometimes expect the whole world to share my hobbies. In any event, my nearest neighbour shares my interest, and if my interest is to be described as a passion, his may almost be described as a mania.

"He is immensely wealthy, and a good portion of his wealth has been spent on his collection of Jacobean and Stuart silver, which is acknowledged to be one of the finest in the land. He has occasionally made use of my services as a judge of the authenticity and quality of a piece when he has been contemplating a purchase to add to his collection. The pieces that he has selected are usually of the finest quality, and are often priced beyond the reach of my more modest purse.

"However, to the best of my knowledge, some of these pieces have not been offered for sale by auction – at least in this country. I receive the catalogues of all the major auction houses who deal with these things, and I would know immediately if they were for sale.

"Now, in my collection are several pieces which have been in my family for a few hundred years, and are reckoned by experts to be the finest examples of their kind. When he has visited the Manor, my neighbor – "

"May we know this neighbour's name?" Holmes asked.

The other sighed. "I was hoping that I could give this account while preserving his anonymity. It is not a pleasant story that I have to tell, and I have no wish to besmirch a man's name unnecessarily."

"Without a name," Holmes told him firmly, "I am unable to discover any relevant facts, and without such facts, I am unable to proceed with my investigations. The name, sir, or I shall be forced to decline your case."

"Very well, then. The man in question is a Mr. Samuel Berenson." Holmes made no reply to this information, but merely raised his eyebrows. "He has, as I said, visited my home on a number of occasions, and has admired many of the pieces, which may best be described as heirlooms. Indeed, his interest goes far beyond admiration, and would be better described as covetousness. He has on more than one occasion offered me a considerable sum of money for some of these pieces. I have, of course, refused in every case of this nature."

"Was the sum offered a fair price, in your opinion?"

"Oh, very much so. Indeed, I would say that it is nearly double the price one would expect to pay a dealer for such a piece – provided always that such an item found its way into the market. However, while being nowhere as wealthy as Berenson, I am in no urgent need of the money, and refused emphatically. Besides this, there is also the matter of the historic and family value of the silver, with many of the pieces being stamped with the Elkinstone arms. There are indeed three separate occasions on which he has offered me money for a particularly delicate Queen Anne chocolate pot, which is said by some to be the finest of its kind in existence, and each time I have declined to accept his offer."

"And his reaction when you refused?"

"He appeared to be angry, Mr. Holmes. It was, perhaps, not readily apparent in his face, but I was able to mark the workings of his hands, as they clenched and unclenched into fists."

"And has that anger been expressed in other ways?"

"Not outwardly, at least. He continues to be a good neighbour who seems to desire nothing but friendship, but the other day my butler, Widdenthorpe, informed me that he had been approached by Berenson with a request to purloin the chocolate pot, and present it to Berenson in consideration of a fee. Naturally, the good fellow refused."

"It would seem a somewhat clumsy way to accomplish his ends," remarked Holmes. "Unless your Widdenthorpe has some skills in these matters, such a robbery committed from the inside of a household almost invariably leads to the detection of the culprit, and in the case of the robbery having been instigated from the outside, as in this case, to the detection of the prime mover in the affair."

"I can assure you that Widdenthorpe lacks these criminal skills," we were assured. "He has been in the service of the family since he was a boy, and is as honest as the day is long."

"In that case, Sir Barnabas, I am unsure as to what action you wish me to take on your behalf."

"But do you not see, Mr. Holmes?" exclaimed our visitor, in a state of great excitement. "Berenson now appears to be determined to lay his hands on my silver, by fair means or foul. I may, of course, forbid him my house, but I consider that he would treat that as a hostile act, and I fear that it would spur him on to greater outrages. I wish you, sir, to appeal to Berenson's better nature, and to persuade him of the futility of his quest."

"Do you not think that this matter would be better handled by the police than Mr. Holmes?" I asked him.

"Other than the report by Widdenthorpe that he has been asked to commit a felony, I cannot see that any crime has been committed, and it is merely my word against that of Berenson. No sir, I do not see that the police would wish to be involved in this affair. I consider that the words of Mr. Sherlock Holmes would have more effect than an official warning."

"You do me too much honour, sir," Holmes remarked, with a self-deprecatory smile. "Allow me to look into the matter at more length, and I will let you know whether I decide to carry out your wishes."

Our visitor left us, and Holmes turned to me with a faint smile on his face. "Well, Watson, what do you make of all this?"

"The collector's mania is a strange one, to be sure. I feel that Sir Barnabas was correct in describing it as a passion. I take it that we may take the butler's account of affairs as being correct?"

"Let us do so for the moment," Holmes agreed. "What are your impressions of our visitor?"

"I would take him to be a typical country gentleman, with a consuming interest in his hobby."

"Quite so. And for the moment, let us regard him in precisely that light until we have sufficient cause to do otherwise. But what of the neighbour, Berenson? What do we know of him?"

"The name is familiar, but I am unsure why."

"Let us look in the Index." Holmes searched out a languid hand towards the shelf containing the scrapbooks in which he collected information about those members of society in which he had an interest – that is to say, those who were in one fashion or another, breakers of the law. "Here we are. Berenson, Samuel. Though he has never been prosecuted in a court of law, rumours regarding possible sharp practice in his business affairs have continued to circulate."

"Now I seem to remember some details," I told Holmes. "Was he not the man who owns a number of flour mills? If I recall correctly, he was accused of bribery when his company purchased a rival, against the wishes of a majority of the directors, but the case never came to court."

"You have it correctly, Watson. Bravo. He was, I believe, recommended for a knighthood immediately prior to the incident you just mentioned, but this was withdrawn following the scandal. It is still unclear why he wasn't prosecuted, but it's more than likely that while he was skirting the limits of legality, no law could be proved to have been broken."

"And this case to which we have just been introduced would seem to be another example of such an act which, while not strictly illegal, would appear to be at the very least highly immoral. Do you intend to take up the matter and perform the task that Sir Barnabas requested?"

"Given the *dramatis personæ*, I may well do just that. I have had my eye on Berenson for some time, in connection with some other little affairs connected with antique silver. He is a sly one, and nothing could be proved, but there have been too many coincidences for my liking."

With these words, Holmes retired to his bedroom and emerged some fifteen minutes later, to all intents and purposes a different man.

"You know my methods, Watson," he said to me in a voice which lacked much of the refinement with which I usually associated it. "Pray, tell me what you see of the man in front of you."

I examined Holmes carefully. "I would mark you as a man who has come down in the world. Your boots, for example, are of good quality – not of the best handmade type, to be sure, but were still quite expensive when new. They have been allowed to grow old and shabby, however, and, together with the rest of the garb, display a once-prosperous state which sadly, no longer exists. A tradesman, I would say, with a predisposition to drink, as witness the hip-flask protruding from your pocket, and this failing may be the cause of your current distress. As to what sort of trade, I could not say."

Holmes clapped his hands. "An excellent summary," he said in the accents in which he had first posed his question to me. "You behold before you Mr. Ezra Littleboy, once of Jellicoe's, the Bond Street jeweller, but as you rightly observe, brought low by drink." His voice reverted to its usual accents. "However, I am sadly ignorant of some of the details relating to antique silver, and I must therefore request you to acquire the following volumes, which are out of print, but should be available from second-hand booksellers. You may find Cecil Court to be the most promising area." He handed me a list of some half-dozen titles, all dealing with antique silver. "It is better that I as Sherlock Holmes, or in my present character, not be seen in pursuit of these volumes."

"And where will you be?" I asked.

"Oh," he replied airily, "making discreet enquiries among some distant acquaintances – that is, I know of them by reputation – regarding Mr. Berenson. Pray inform Mrs. Hudson that I expect to return in time for dinner. A beefsteak would be welcome, I think."

With a tip of his battered bowler, he was gone. I passed on his message and made my way to Cecil Court, where I was able to purchase five of the six requested volumes, from four different shops. The sixth appeared to be unobtainable, though one of the booksellers expressed an opinion that a friend of his in Edinburgh might be able to oblige in the matter.

I returned in some triumph to Baker Street to await the return of Sherlock Holmes, who arrived some thirty minutes after me. He, too, wore a look of satisfaction.

"I perceive your day has also been well spent," he greeted me, indicating the pile of books on the table beside me. "To be frank, I hadn't expected more than three of these titles to be available. To have discovered five of the six is good work indeed."

"And may I ask how you have progressed?"

"In a few minutes. Allow me to restore myself to my proper state."

Some time later, Holmes was seated in his favourite armchair, smoking his pipe as he recounted the day's adventures.

"I had some notion of where I might find these men whom I sought. They frequent the public houses at the fringes of the City – appropriately, perhaps, since these men are on the fringes of respectability and legality. It was a relatively simple matter for me to gain their confidence regarding

Mr. Samuel Berenson. He is, in their expressive phrase, 'a wrong 'un', though they freely admit that no legal proceedings against him have ever borne fruit. I also dropped heavy hints that I had access to some valuable antique silver to which I had few claims of rightful possession, and it does appear that from time to time Berenson has been known to make purchases in the past without enquiring too deeply into the legality of possession by the seller."

"Outrageous!" I exclaimed. "That a man in his position should encourage theft and larceny!"

"The world of art is a murky one, Watson. Were we to make a close examination of the provenance of many of the works in our National Gallery, we would, I am sure, be more than a little surprised. And now," he added, as Mrs. Hudson entered bearing a tray, "for our beefsteaks."

The next day saw us at breakfast when a telegram was brought to us by the page, Billy. Holmes ripped it open.

"Bradshaw, Watson. The next train to take us to Winchester, if you would. Billy, take this to the telegraph office." He scribbled a few words on a piece of paper and handed it to the page.

"What is it?" I asked as I turned the pages of Bradshaw.

"Murder!" exclaimed Holmes, his eyes gleaming. "See for yourself."

He held the telegram in front of me, and I read, *Essential you come as soon as possible. Shocking Murder here. Elkinstone.*"

"Who would have thought, that on the very day after he visited us, that there would arise such an opportunity? The train, Watson?"

"There is an express leaving Waterloo in a little over an hour."

"Excellent. I must dress and prepare for the journey." He had barely emerged from his room when Inspector Lestrade of Scotland Yard was admitted.

"If you are not too engaged, Mr. Holmes, I would appreciate your accompanying me to the scene of a dastardly crime that was committed last night. On several occasions, I confess that you have observed some signs which escaped my notice, and enabled me to deduce the identity of the perpetrator."

"Impossible, Lestrade. Watson and I are on our way to Winchester."

"The crime of which I spoke has been committed near Winchester," Lestrade said in some astonishment.

"At Elkinstone Manor?" Holmes asked him, a sly smile on his face.

Lestrade started. "How in the world did you know that, Mr. Holmes?"

By way of answer, Holmes reached in his pocket and pulled out the telegram we had received that morning. "I will acquaint you with my knowledge of the case while we are travelling to Winchester," he told Lestrade, "and you, for your part, may explain all that you know."

As the express sped us towards our destination, Holmes told the police agent of our visitor of the previous day, and Lestrade in his turn informed us that the victim of the murder was the butler, Widdenthorpe, of whom Sir Barnabas had spoken to us. His body had been discovered early in the morning by one of the maids who had come into the room to lay the fire. The room itself was the one in which Sir Barnabas kept his collection of silver, and with one exception, the cases were locked. One item of the collection was reported to be missing.

"I think we will discover the missing item to be a Queen Anne chocolate pot," Holmes told Lestrade.

"Very likely so," answered the police detective, and continued with his account. The dead man's skull had been nearly crushed with a blunt instrument, the nature of which was unknown, as there was no trace of it to be found. The French windows leading to the garden were opened, and faint traces of footprints had been found leading across the flowerbeds.

"But by now, they will have been washed away," Lestrade remarked regretfully, indicating the rain, which was falling steadily.

At the time that the murder had been discovered, Sir Barnabas had been absent from the house, but had returned within thirty minutes of the discovery, having spent the night at his London club, and arriving in Winchester by the earliest train.

"The main suspect must be Samuel Berenson," I said. "Living close by, and knowing the house, and indeed, the collection, he must have seized his opportunity to purloin the silver. It is quite possible that he observed Sir Barnabas leaving the house yesterday, maybe even with the knowledge that the master of the house would be absent."

"I think you have hit upon it, Doctor," Lestrade told me. "Putting together what I have been told by the Hampshire Constabulary and what Mr. Holmes has been telling me, I'm certain that you're in the right here."

"Let us not jump to conclusions, Inspector," said Holmes. "I agree that at first sight Mr. Berenson would appear to be the thief, but I can see one major flaw in this otherwise admirable theory."

"That being?" I asked.

"I credit you and Lestrade here with sufficient intelligence to deduce it for yourselves," Holmes said, and lapsed into silence.

On arrival at Winchester Station, we discovered that the local police force had already ordered an open trap for us to carry us to the manor. Happily the weather had cleared a little, and it was no longer raining. We were escorted by a local constable, who seemed to be in awe of the great personages with whom he was travelling, and hardly opened his mouth for the first fifteen minutes of our journey, save to offer conventional greetings.

"Are you a local man?" Holmes asked him, obviously attempting to put him at his ease.

"Why, yes, sir. Born and bred in the shade of Elkinstone Manor."

"So you are acquainted with the inhabitants of the Manor?"

"Hardly that, sir. I wouldn't be knowing the family, now would I, sir, with my father being only an under-keeper on the estate? And the inside servants keep themselves to themselves very much. I might sometimes meet some of the footmen in the Red Lion on their days off, but not to speak to beyond passing the time of day."

"I see," said Holmes. "And what of Mr. Berenson?"

"Well, sir, Mr. Berenson is a different kettle of fish, as you might say, sir. If you meet him in the lane, he's willing enough to give you a good morning or a good afternoon as it might be, but I wouldn't call him a friendly soul for all that. Hard to say why," continued the young policeman. "And then there were stories of what he'd done in London in his business."

"Very interesting, is it not, Mr. Holmes?" Lestrade commented. "The case against Berenson seems to be tightening." He addressed himself to the young constable. "Have you any idea why your inspector has not arrested Mr. Berenson yet?"

"No, sir. I'm afraid my inspector doesn't tell me that sort of thing, sir."

"And quite right too," said Holmes. "These things can lead to hurtful gossip."

In a few minutes, we had turned off the main road up a drive leading to a handsome mansion, which had a look of the seventeenth century about it.

"Elkinstone Manor," announced the local constable. "Inspector Leighton will be meeting you."

As we stepped from the trap, a broad, ruddy-faced man in tweeds introduced himself as Inspector Leighton. "Inspector, Mr. Holmes, Doctor Watson," he greeted us. "Shall we go in and see the body?"

"If you have no objection," Holmes answered him, "I would much prefer to see the garden first, particularly the area outside the scene of the crime."

Leighton looked at Lestrade enquiringly. The latter shrugged. "Mr. Holmes has had some good luck when we have worked together and he has followed his own nose. I strongly recommend that we allow him this freedom in this case."

"It has hardly been a matter of good luck, Lestrade," Holmes commented acidly, "but I thank you for your support." Leighton led the way to a set of French windows, and Holmes stooped to examine the ground.

"Dear, dear, Inspector," he remarked to Leighton. "Your men have trampled the ground like a herd of elephants. There is remarkably little to be seen here other than the marks of official police boots."

The other appeared only slightly discomfited. "I do not see what you might expect to see here, Mr. Holmes, given the amount of rain that has fallen in the past few hours."

"Tut, man," my friend exclaimed. "While a little rain may obscure some of the more obvious clues, there is always something to be learned from the examination of the ground in the first hours following an event. However," and here he bent to retrieve something from the ground, and slip it into an envelope that he retrieved from his pocket, "we may now enter the room, following the supposed path of the killer. These windows were locked, I take it?"

"Yes, sir. According to the servants, they were locked last night."

Holmes bent to examine the lock, using his lens to do so.

With his eyes firmly fixed on the ground, he led the way into the room, where the body of the unfortunate butler still lay, the head surrounded by a ghastly halo of scarlet blood.

Holmes regarded the gory scene with equanimity. "Yes," he murmured, as if to himself. "A blunt instrument, such as a club or a life-preserver."

"One of my constables discovered what we believe to be the weapon, sir," Leighton told him with some pride in his voice. "A poker, covered with blood and hair, which has been identified as one belonging to the Manor. It was found on the path leading to Mr. Berenson's house."

"Indeed?" said Holmes. "That is well done."

He turned to the display cabinets, which held a glittering array of antique silver. One of the cabinets was open, and it was clear from a conspicuous gap in the arrangement that a piece was missing. "A-ha," Holmes continued, moving to the cabinet in question. "No doubt this once contained a Queen Anne chocolate pot."

"So we have been led to believe," said Lestrade.

"Have you no theories on the case, Mr. Holmes?" asked Leighton.

"At present, none, until we meet Berenson."

"Then you suspect Berenson of committing this murder?" Lestrade asked him.

"I did not say that," Holmes answered him. "It is essential that we meet Berenson as soon as possible."

246

"Where is Sir Barnabas Elkinstone?" Lestrade asked Leighton.

"He appears to have been overcome by the events of the previous night," replied the Hampshire policeman. "The doctor is presently attending him."

"And we shall no doubt be attending him in the near future," remarked Holmes. "In which direction is Berenson's house?" Having received an answer, he started to stride off across the parkland, not bothering to look behind him to ascertain whether we were following him or not.

I immediately started off in his wake, and Lestrade shrugged and followed suit. The country inspector, though obviously mystified by the actions of my friend, had no option but to do the same.

I caught up with Holmes, and asked him, "Do you really intend Lestrade to arrest Berenson on the basis of what you expect to discover at his house?"

"On the contrary, Watson," Holmes smiled. "However, I must see for myself what I have only so far heard by rumour."

Another ten minutes' walking brought us to the stately Georgian mansion which had been purchased by Samuel Berenson following his retirement from business. Holmes rang the bell and gave his name to the servant who answered it, not bothering to mention the names of his companions.

"If you gentlemen would care to wait in the library, I will see if Mr. Berenson is available," we were told. "May I enquire the subject of your visit?"

"Certainly. It concerns his neighbour, Sir Barnabas Elkinstone."

"Very good, sir." He retired, and we were left to examine the room to which we had been conducted, which was named as a library, but in truth seemed to act as a museum, housing a collection of antique silver which to my eyes outshone even the collection that we had just left at Elkinstone Manor.

While we were examining these *objets*, a strange creaking sound could be heard, and as our eyes turned towards the door, in which we beheld a frail elderly figure, seated in a bath-chair pushed by the footman who had admitted us.

"Mr. Holmes, I believe?" the old man enquired of my friend in a quavering voice. "I have long enjoyed the accounts of your cases as written by your friend. And you must be he," he added, turning to me. "Doctor Watson. A pleasure to make your acquaintance. And these two gentlemen are . . . ?"

Holmes introduced the two police inspectors.

247

"Dear me! I hope you have not come to arrest me?" Berenson, for this was indeed he, started to laugh, but his laughter was soon replaced by a fit of coughing. "Forgive me," he requested when this had subsided. "It is simply that I find the idea somewhat amusing. Now, you mentioned that your business was with my neighbour, Sir Barnabas. Perhaps you would care to enlighten me."

Holmes informed him not only of the murder which had been committed, but also of the visit that Sir Barnabas had paid to Baker Street on the previous day.

Again, the old man burst into fits of coughing laughter, at which we stood astonished at the reaction of a man whose response to the news of a murder was laughter. "And so you believed that I would rob my neighbour of his prized chocolate pot, and kill his butler while I was about it?" Lestrade had the grace to stand abashed and mutter something that might have been taken as an apology. "No, my dear fellow, I freely admit that I coveted that piece, and I offered Sir Barnabas a handsome sum for it on more than one occasion. However, in my present condition, I could not even make my way unattended to Elkinstone Manor, and the idea of my taking a weapon against the admirable Widdenthorpe must surely seem absurd to you."

"But you offered Widdenthorpe money to purloin the item, did you not?" I asked.

The old man regarded me with a fixed gaze. "I did indeed," he replied. "However, I was under no illusion that he would be tempted by my offer, and my main purpose in making it was to display to Sir Barnabas the strength of my interest in the piece." He sighed. "Believe me, Sir Barnabas would have done well to accept my offer. He no doubt omitted to tell you, sir," addressing himself to Holmes, "of the fact that he is deeply in debt as the result of the investments in his collection. The sum I offered him would have gone a long way towards paying off that debt, and I would be happy to pay it. For all the words that may have passed between us in the past, I am sorry for his misfortune."

"I see," said Holmes. "May I?" He produced a cigarette case.

"I must implore you not to use tobacco in this house, sir. My lungs are particularly delicate, so much so that no servant of mine is permitted to smoke, either inside or outside the house. Is that not so, James?" he asked the footman who had been standing silently behind his master's bath-chair.

"Indeed so," came the reply. "There is no-one in this household who touches tobacco in any form."

"Of course," went on the old man, "even though it is clear that I cannot be the murderer of poor Widdenthorpe, one of my servants may well have committed the crime, either on his own initiative, or at my behest. Is that not so, James?" addressing the footman once more.

"From what you have told us, that is not possible," Holmes retorted smartly, saving the servant the embarrassment of answering. "I am sure that James and his fellow-servants will be delighted to learn that they are not objects of suspicion."

The footman allowed a faint smile to cross his face. "Thank you, sir. That is indeed most gratifying."

"We may pay you a further visit," Holmes informed the old man, who had fallen into a hall-laughing, half-coughing fit once more. "But for now, I must thank you for your help, and will bid you *adieu.*"

"Why," Lestrade asked Holmes as we made our way across the fields to Elkinstone Manor, "do you not wish to question the servants?"

"Because of this." Holmes produced the envelope into which he had placed his find from the garden. "A cigarette end, of an unusual type. You are aware, Lestrade of my contributions to the detective art with relation to such matters?"

"Very well, but I don't see that this will help us catch the murderer."

"On the contrary, it is the noose round his neck."

On our return to the Manor, Holmes made his way to Sir Barnabas's room, where the baronet was still recuperating from the shock of recent events.

"I have only a few things to ask you," Holmes told him. "May I ask whether your collection, specifically the missing piece, was insured?"

"Naturally. I shall be making a claim for the theft of the chocolate pot."

"And the amount for which it was insured? Would that be equal to the amount offered to you by Berenson for the piece?"

"Slightly in excess of that," was the answer.

"And finally, apart from Berenson, were any other offers made for the pot by any other collector?"

The baronet frowned in thought. "Lowenstein of California once wrote me a letter offering to buy it, I recall. Mathis of Basingstoke expressed an interest, and McPherson of Edinburgh likewise. Lord Goring and the Duke of Shropshire have at times expressed a mild interest. Other than that, I cannot recall any others. There are very few who would have the knowledge to appreciate the piece, or the purse to afford it."

"Thank you." To my great surprise, and that of the two police officers, Holmes proposed an immediate return to London.

"I believe I will have the murderer for you in forty-eight hours," he told the astonished Lestrade. "I will send for you when it is time to make the arrest."

On the train returning to London, Holmes opened one of the books on antique silverware that I had previously purchased for him and immersed himself in it. On arrival at Waterloo, we took our leave of Lestrade and made our way to Baker Street, calling on the way at Leahy's in the Strand, where Holmes replenished his stock of pipe-tobacco.

Once returned, Holmes ensconced himself in his chair, pipe to hand, and a pile of books by his side, which he proceeded to devour. A call to dinner failed to rouse him.

"I must study," he told me. "At this moment, it is more important than food." However, at half-past ten he rose from his chair, clamped a thick slice of roast beef between two slices of bread, and ate it hungrily.

"I am for bed," I told him as he returned to his chair and picked up the next volume. He replied by means of a wordless grunt without even looking up, and I took myself to my bedroom.

In the morning, the air was blue with the fumes from Holmes's pipe. He himself was nowhere to be seen, and an inspection of his room showed it to be empty, and the bed unslept in. Mrs. Hudson hadn't seen him that morning, but I assured her that Holmes was unlikely to be in any danger.

A little before luncheon, he returned, dressed in his previous disguise of Ezra Littleboy, the former jeweller's assistant, and in a high good humour.

"We have our man, Watson," he exclaimed. "I lack the final proof that will send him to the gallows, but I expect to be able to obtain that readily enough."

Following our meal, Holmes once again disappeared into his room, and emerged in a different guise. "And now?" he asked me.

Before me stood the very image of a servant in a good house – a senior footman, perhaps, whose honesty might be in question. His whole deportment and manner proclaimed it, and I said as much to a delighted Holmes.

"Exactly the impression I wish to give. Now, I must be off. Pray request Lestrade to be at the King's Head Public House in Shoreditch at seven o'clock this evening, in the saloon bar, together with a couple of stout constables to be stationed outside in case of trouble. I trust you will accompany Lestrade."

"I would not miss the *dénouement* of this case for the world," I smiled. "You have succeeded admirably in shrouding what at first seemed to be a simple case in an impenetrable mystery."

As Holmes had required of me, I took his request to Scotland Yard, where Lestrade received it with a smile.

"And whom does he suspect?" he asked me. I was forced to reply that I had no conception of the course that Holmes had been pursuing.

250

"Your Mr. Holmes does enjoy his little secrets, does he not? I was sure that we had Berenson by the heels, but it is clear that even if he is the mind behind the crime, it couldn't possibly be he who committed the murder."

I spent the afternoon at Scotland Yard, passing the time in conversation with one of the police surgeons with whom I had come into contact in the past, and discussing various ways in which our profession might be developed to be of further service in the apprehension and conviction of lawbreakers.

At a little after six, I rejoined Lestrade, and in company with two constables, as requested, we set out for Shoreditch, where we soon discovered the King's Head Public House, the saloon bar of which we entered, leaving the constables outside, with instructions to keep out of sight as far as possible, but to be on the alert for the sound of Lestrade's whistle.

It was immediately obvious that we were far from being the usual type of customer who frequented the establishment. Our fellow-drinkers appeared to be those on the far side of the cusp of respectability, and indeed, Lestrade was able to identify several by name as those with whom he had had professional dealings in the past.

At two minutes past seven, Holmes entered, dressed as I had seen him earlier that day. His disguise was so complete that Lestrade failed to recognise him, and I was forced to surreptitiously identify him for the policeman's benefit.

After a few minutes more, another man entered and joined Holmes at his corner table. It was clear that the beard and moustache that he wore were false, and that the shabby coat that he wore was not his usual wear, to judge by the state and the quality of his boots.

Holmes was smoking his briar pipe, and the stranger in his turn pulled out a silver cigarette case. In a short time, the distinctive smell of Turkish tobacco wafted over to us, as Holmes and his companion discoursed in low voices.

Lestrade and I naturally strained our ears to discern the content of their conversation, in as unobtrusive a manner as possible, and I repeat here what I was able to make out.

Stranger: Your note to me this morning was most disturbing.

Holmes (with a slight smile): It was intended to be.

Stranger: No jury will believe you. My word against yours. They will never send me to prison.

Holmes: You are correct there. You will be hanged for what you did.

Stranger: It was never my intention to kill poor Widdenthorpe. I entered the room, the doors being [Here there was a rattle of glasses from the bar, and I was unable to make out the following words]. I must have made a noise, and the poor man entered, gripping a poker. Presumably he considered he had discovered a housebreaker at work.

Holmes (amused): So he had.

Stranger: It was him against me. In the brief struggle, I was able to wrest the poker from his grasp, and somehow I struck him over the head with it. He fell senseless.

Holmes: Whereupon you beat him savagely many times on the head, did you not?.

Stranger: I panicked. I did not know what I was doing. Then I came to myself and realised that I still did not have the item for which I had come. I opened the case, removed the chocolate pot, and left the house.

Holmes: Lighting a cigarette as you did so, no doubt in an attempt to calm yourself.

Stranger: How do you come to know that? And what do you want of me?

Holmes: Justice, Baron, justice.

At this point Lestrade leaped to his feet and blew his whistle. He made a move towards the clearly petrified companion of Sherlock Holmes as the two constables entered the room, to the consternation of the clientele, many of whom started towards the door.

Holmes leaned forward and tugged at the other's false beard, which came away in his hand to reveal a face well-known to readers of Society magazines.

252

Laying his hands on Holmes's companion, Lestrade declared, "I arrest you, Baron Dowson, for the murder of Charles Widdenthorpe. Will you come quietly, or must I use these?" He produced a pair of handcuffs from his pocket. At this, the other customers of the King's Head quietly moved as far away from our little circle as possible, a proceeding that Holmes regarded with amusement.

"I will come with you," said the Baron, for it was he, despite his advanced age, one of the most photographed men about town, and the doyen of many glittering *soirées*. "But," turning to Holmes, "since when have the police used a man's domestic servants as spies and tattletales?"

"I am no servant," Holmes replied calmly. "My name, Sherlock Holmes, may, however, be familiar to you."

"Oh, well. In that case . . . ." the Baron grumbled.

"Let's have you down at the Yard," Lestrade told him, with little more ceremony than he would have used had he been arresting one of the "regulars" who stood around the edges of the room, wide-eyed.

When we had returned to Baker Street, I asked Holmes how he had managed to track down the murderer so quickly.

"There were one or two clues that Lestrade and that good country inspector completely failed to take into account. First, we had the fact that although it was reported that the French windows to the room had been locked, there was no sign of forced entry. We can only conclude that they were in fact unlocked when he entered. As we walked to those windows, I could detect no other obvious signs of footprints or forcing at any other window, which implies that the perpetrator knew that the doors to the room where he would find the silver pot would be unlocked.

"Then there were the footprints on the ground outside. Though, as I remarked, the local police had done their best to destroy the evidence, there were still signs of a pair of shoes, as opposed to police boots, entering and leaving the room. On the way out, the creator of these footprints had smoked a cigarette of a very distinctive type. I instantly recognised the tobacco as being of Turkish origin, and the maker's name, Leahy's, was printed on the paper. As you know, I called at Leahy's and they identified that type of cigarette as being specially made for only a few customers – a half-dozen at most.

"Of those half-dozen, who was the most likely candidate? From my conversations as Ezra Littleboy, I had established the names of the foremost collectors of antique silver. I also obtained such a list, as you heard, from Sir Barnabas. One name was on my list but not of the list of Sir Barnabas – that of Baron Dowson. Why?

"On learning from Berenson that Sir Barnabas was in financial difficulties, and from Sir Barnabas himself that his collection was insured,

I was able to tie together two threads, and conclude he had arranged for Baron Dowson, known to at times undertake proceedings of a somewhat adventurous nature, to purloin the prize of Sir Barnabas's collection, so that the insurance might be collected, without Sir Barnabas having to expose his financial difficulties to the public, which would otherwise have been the case were the chocolate pot to be offered for sale, no matter how discreetly."

"And the Baron would perform this dastardly deed himself?"

"It would appeal to his nature, as well as having the added advantage that the fewer who know of this plot, the closer the secret.

"Following my identification of the thief, whom I might justifiably assume was also the murderer, I determined to convict Dowson out of his own mouth. By posing as a servant of Sir Barnabas, and leaving a note for him, together with some very heavy hints that I knew all, I lured him to a place where he was expecting to pay money in exchange for my silence. With a few facts based on my deductions, as you saw, he was convinced that I was an eyewitness to the murder. The pattern of the bloodstains on the floor told me how the murder had been committed – with a single blow to strike the victim down, and then with a flurry of frenzied violent strikes to the head, shattering the skull and indicating a sense of panic on the part of the murderer, rather than the more dispassionate approach of a hardened criminal. I have no doubt had I persisted with the conversation, Dowson would have been willing to part with a large sum to keep my mouth closed."

"But did you not suspect Berenson at first?"

Holmes laughed. "There is one excellent reason, other than Berenson's physical condition, why I knew it could not be he. The man is a collector who loves display. He is far from being the secretive miser of legend. A rogue in business, perhaps, but an honest rogue, if you take my meaning. If he acquired that bauble, he would wish to display it. No, there is no way that he would be the thief."

Dowson was sent for trial, where he pleaded guilty to murder, and was sentenced to be hanged, there being no extenuating circumstances. Following Holmes's report to Scotland Yard, Sir Barnabas Elkinstone was arrested and charged with insurance fraud, but was found dead in his bed the morning that he was to stand trial. A verdict of accidental death was returned.

Sherlock Holmes visited Baron Dowson in prison the night before he was hanged, and on that occasion, the condemned man paid Holmes the handsome tribute to his thespian powers that I have mentioned elsewhere.

The Cat's Meat Lady
of Cavendish Square
by David Marcum

The early afternoon light – what little that I could see of it through my window – seemed to be fading earlier than I would have expected for mid-September, and I sensed rather than knew for certain that the evening would be a foggy one. Perhaps I had also perceived, beneath the level of conscious thought, that the sounds from pedestrians and vehicular traffic – always quiet at this end of Queen Anne Street – were somehow even more muted.

I stretched my back, feeling each of my fifty years as that tedious day wound forward toward its conclusion. I had only been back in practice for a short while following my recent marriage, and I hadn't properly taken into account that my previously active lifestyle – from joining my friend Sherlock Holmes's interesting and frequent investigations to simply stepping out when the mood hit me for a visit to the tobacconists or a favorite coffee shop along Baker Street – would leave me feeling much more confined than I would have liked as patient after patient filled my new waiting room.

I had maintained successful practices before, both in Kensington and Paddington, but I was younger then, and there was a certain amount of traveling to patients' homes that was a daily requirement. Now, I found that my reputation had somewhat proceeded me, which changed the rules of the game. Being known for my association with Holmes, as well as having gained a certain unexpected and unwelcome notoriety in connection with the publication of narratives of a few dozen of his cases, had caused a great influx of patients to my new establishment – rather more than I would have expected. Or welcomed, truth be told.

From the time that my new bride and I had moved to Queen Anne Street, just east of Harley Street, and opened the door to my ground-floor office, the patient list had been quite steady. I fully expected it to decrease to a more manageable level as people tired of trying to get a look at me – "*Oh, are you* that *Doctor Watson?*" – as if I were some new animal on display at the zoo. I had seen far too many of those that had no real complaints at all. Instead, they gained admittance to my sanctum with some fabricated little cough or rash, and then spent the time looking not-so-subtly around the room to see if I had any artifacts from those cases that they'd read about in *The Strand*. In spite of my slight irritation, I was tempted to track down an old dog skull and leave it on the mantel, as it would have been a special thrill for them to speculate about that fourteen-year-old investigation which had been so popular when recently published. (When I had mentioned this thought to my wife, she had rightly discouraged me.)

Even as I sighed at the thought of being trapped in this cage – at least until the novelty had worn off – I considered how much my wife approved of the success. She was thrilled as a steady stream of patients arrived from the very first day, and so far showed no signs of diminishing. I knew that the flow was bound to decrease over time, and had explained it to her, but the idea didn't seem find firm footing in her mind. I also understood that she was very happy that my time was being used in the consulting room and not in further assistance to Holmes, for they had unfortunately gotten off on something of the wrong foot.

Less than three months before, in the weeks leading up to my marriage, one of Holmes's investigations had turned from almost comical to violent in the blink of an eye. An American confidence trickster had attempted to lure an eccentric old man away from his lodgings with a convoluted tale, a variation on the type of scheme that Holmes and I had encountered before. We had confronted him, and the fellow had made a little speech about getting caught, but only as a distraction, for he suddenly pulled a revolver from his coat and quickly fired two shots. Clearly we were getting careless and over-confident. One of the bullets went wild, but the other grazed my thigh – a superficial wound, as it turned out, but it burned like hot fire in the initial moments, and produced an impressive amount of blood that certainly gave the impression of a nicked artery.

Holmes had clubbed my assailant across the head with a gun-butt before confirming that I would survive. Later, he commented as we waited for the police that he should have been more prepared when dealing with a criminal whose *sobriquet* was "Killer". Still, it was no great pesterment, and I attempted to avoid any mention of it whatsoever to my fiancé – until an unexpected wince as I climbed into a hansom did not go unnoticed, and she soon had the whole story from me. Since that time, it had been no great secret that she felt that assisting Holmes was – to a large degree – a thing of the past. I did not agree, but for the moment that battle had so far been avoided.

Her expectation, however, was put to the test when my next patient made her entrance, for she turned out not to be a patient at all, but rather someone who wished to share a story, hoping that it might be brought to the attention of Holmes himself.

The page knocked and opened the door to announce a Mrs. Fawley. Then he stepped aside, revealing a woman in her sixties, plainly and perhaps too warmly dressed in a wool skirt and heavy jacket. Her whitened hair still showed streaks of blonde, and while her skin was darkened by the sun and lined by the wind, one could find obvious signs of the beauty that she had been in her youth. Her hands looked rough, with short blunted nails and various old scratches and scars. However, the fingers were long and rather elegant. When she spoke, her choice of words indicated that she'd had a good education, though her voice was somewhat strident, as if long overused. The reason was soon apparent as she began to converse.

"I'm a cat's meat lady," she began without any wasted pleasantries. "My grandson is outside, watching my cart." She glanced around, as if to ascertain whether I had a cat. "You aren't a customer," she added in a rather accusatory tone.

I nodded in agreement. While many in London kept cats to fulfil the very necessary function of pest control, I had never done so in any of my own homes, finding other (chemical) means to deal with the problem. Mrs. Hudson had occasionally kept cats, but whenever she did so, there was an uneasy tension throughout the house, as we all – Holmes included – had an unspoken expectation that the poor beast would be found some morning, abruptly deceased and stiffened from a misguided curious encounter with one of my friend's chemical experiments. It had never happened, but I think that both Holmes and I felt a secret relief whenever Mrs. Hudson decided that whatever rodent invasion that had occurred was concluded for the time being and the cat could move on to a new home.

At the time I write this, cat's meat men (and women) are rarer than they once were, and even during their heyday one didn't see them at all except in the larger cities – country folk having no need to pay someone to bring cat food by their home every day. Among the many street sellers that one regularly encounters – the costermongers and vendors of hot potatoes and chestnuts and the like – it was not unusual at all to also find purveyors of scrap horse meat for sale to cats, sold from carts pushed by people like my visitor along very defined routes. I've read that at one time there were over a thousand of them wandering the streets of London on any given day, having found a most unique way of earning an income, and usefully helping to dispose of the thousands of regularly slaughtered horses that had reached the end of their usefulness.

I understood now Mrs. Fawley's weathered appearance and roughened voice, for she spent her days crying "Meat! Meat!" while pushing her cart in all weather, and using those elegant hands to cut up chunks of otherwise unusable muscle, tendon, and offal.

I confirmed that I didn't keep a cat, and she eyed me suspiciously, as if I'd admitted to a crime. But then she pursed her lips and said, "No matter. There are enough people that do that I'll keep busy."

257

Not knowing yet what her story was, I was beginning to suspect that Mrs. Fawley was not one of the sensation-seekers who had appeared at my door simply to say that we'd met. Yet, as I attempted to see if I could identify a medical complaint, and even as I opened my mouth to ask for the reason of her visit, she spoke and explained why she was here.

"My grandson says that you're the doctor that knows Sherlock Holmes."

So I was wrong, I thought. She *was* curious about my famous friend. But then she went on, and I understood that she wasn't a reader of my published efforts at all, but rather someone who had a problem.

"It's really my grandson that should be talking to you," she said. "The first part of the story is his, but I didn't think that he'd be let inside, and in any case someone has to watch the cart." She then began to provide a few particulars of the matter, but I soon realized that Holmes should hear the story as well and raised a hand to stop her, explaining my reasoning. She nodded, and I stepped out to the hallway, where I telephoned Holmes, hoping to find him at home. He was, and promised to be around in a quarter-of-an-hour or less, as the distance from Baker Street to my new practice is quite short.

I returned to the consulting room, informing her that Holmes would arrive very soon. Then, indicating that we should include her grandson, I explained that we could have my page, Jack, take over the watching of her cart, if she had no objections. She nodded, and I led her back out to the street, asking Jack to join us as we passed him. Outside we found a lad of about ten, standing behind one of the typical cat's meat carts, resembling (for those in the countryside who haven't seen them) something very much like a two-wheeled hand barrow, with the wooden tub containing rather odorous meat, and a stained cutting board attached across the end near the handles where the meat could be sectioned and put onto cheap wooden skewers. Mrs. Fawley's grandson, introduced to me as Oliver, hadn't been idle while we were inside. Two passers-by were purchasing his wares, another was waiting his turn, and three stray cats were sitting to one side, watching the goings-on with singularly fixed intensity. A bit farther down the street, a pair of stray dogs were doing the same.

When the final man completed his transaction – having bought three skewers in exchange for a few coins, and then tossing the contents of one of them to the nearby cats before walking away with the rest – Mrs. Fawley explained to Oliver that he would be joining us inside, and the two of them quickly and efficiently buttoned up the hand barrow and pulled it up close to my door. I noticed with a bit of amusement that Jack looked disappointed, as he'd apparently hoped to carry out a few transactions of his own. However, he positioned himself stalwartly beside the cart and prepared to defend it from all possible attackers, both man and beast. With a smile, I closed the front door and led Mrs. Fawley and Oliver to my study, deeper in the house. I rang for tea, and we had just gotten situated when the front bell rang.

I went to open it myself, finding Holmes leaning over and making intent observations of the hand barrow, his nose twitching at the close proximity to the odors emanating from underneath the cover. Jack looked a bit less enthusiastic than he had just a few minutes before, and I told him that he needn't stand immediately beside the cart. He nodded with a thankful look on his face. Holmes finished his examination and stood with a smile. "I'm glad that I was available," he said. "I had only just returned a few minutes before." He passed me and I shut the door. He lowered his voice and continued. "Things are in hand with the Catterick blackmailing scheme, and the Grimsargh Devil has been quiet for over a week. The other six or eight matters that I have on hand just now are all at the waiting stage. This couldn't have come at a better time."

As we passed down the hall, my wife descended from upstairs, and I could see the quickly masked look of surprise on her face upon observing Holmes. He spoke to her, inquiring as to her health and, when she had joined us, she indicated that she was well, asking after Holmes in a similar fashion. Then, with these pleasantries accomplished, we excused ourselves and entered my study. I glanced back as I shut the door to see her frowning.

Inside, I introduced Holmes to Mrs. Fawley and Oliver. Holmes declined my offer of tea and made himself comfortable in the chair to the right of the fireplace which he had claimed during his many previous visits. Then, with me on the opposite side and my visitors seated in between, Holmes indicated that he was ready to hear Mrs. Fawley's narrative.

"It's really Oliver's story," she said. "He's the one who first told me about the glove."

Holmes glanced at the boy, but the woman continued to speak. "It was three days ago – on Monday – when Oliver came home and told me about a glove that was stuck on top of one of the fence posts around Cavendish Square Gardens. I was feeling poorly that day, and after we picked up the meat and got it ready, he took out the cart, staying to the usual route – usually starting at Devonshire Street, but sometimes as far up as Marylebone Road, then working south along Harley Street and to either side for a block or so, before ending up on Wigmore Street along the north side of the Gardens."

"Those are the gardens in Cavendish Square," Holmes clarified.

259

"That's right. That's as much as we can cover in a day, and we have just enough of the meat to supply our regulars, along with the walk-up trade. Besides, if we wander much further, we start treading on the other dealer's routes."

"And does Oliver often go out on his own?" I asked.

"More in the last year or so," answered Mrs. Fawley, giving a glance of pride at the little fellow. He smiled. "He's big enough now to push the cart, and the wrong sort don't bother him. All of us vendors know one another, and they help keep an eye on him. He understands the business well enough, having been raised to it since coming to me when he was four – when his parents died six years ago during that December storm when the Chain Pier in Brighton was destroyed."

"And the glove?" asked Holmes. "Describe it."

"He said it wasn't very big – more like something that a child would wear – and of a peculiar lime-green shade."

One might have expected Holmes to be impatient at this prosaic beginning, but I had told him enough of the rest of the woman's story, including a certain name familiar to both of us, for him to make his way from Baker Street to my fireside. He looked at young Oliver. "Do you concur?"

The boy nodded, and I was impressed that he comprehended Holmes's question – a credit to whatever education that was being facilitated by his grandmother. Now that Oliver was engaged in the telling, Holmes continued asking him questions directly. "Upon which corner of the Square did this occur?"

"Where it meets Harley Street."

"The northwest." I pictured it in my mind's eye, as I had passed through there countless times, while on various errands and during evening rambles. It was only around the corner, a block to the south from my Queen Anne Street residence. And I would likely never forget the night of 5 April, 1894, when Holmes and I had been dropped by a cab at that same corner, the starting point of our strange and cautious path as he led me through alleys and mews and narrow passages to the rear of Camden House, in Baker Street, where we captured Colonel Sebastian Moran, who was so intent on his efforts to kill Holmes with an air-gun that he didn't perceive us observing him from the nearby shadows.

Holmes clearly recalled it as well. "The fence there isn't tall – no more than four feet or so."

Oliver nodded. The glove would have been about eye-level to him.

"Did you take it down?" continued Holmes. "Were you able to get a close look at it? Was there anything unusual about it – stains, or tears, or something hidden inside?"

260

Oliver shook his head. "I left it on the spike where I saw it," he explained. "I didn't know why it was there, but it wasn't my business – I thought that maybe someone had stuck it there as a lark. Or it could have been that it was lost, and someone picked it up and put it there so it would be found. I thought that it wouldn't be there for long no matter what, because someone would take it one way or another. And it didn't stay there long at all. Right then was when I saw the woman."

"Ah," said Holmes. "Tell us about her."

"I saw her," Oliver answered, "about the same time that I noticed the glove. She seemed like a lady. Her clothes were nice, and I thought then that she might live nearby. She didn't have a coat or shawl or hat, even though it was damp that day, and looked as if she'd just been inside. Just as I saw her, she gave a little scream and ran toward it, snatching it down from the fence and holding it to her face, and crying into it as if someone had died."

"And then what did she do?"

"She just cried some more, but only for a few seconds or so, until a man and woman walking by noticed her. They seemed harmless enough – just an old toff and his wife. I've seen them around there before. They looked at each other and then went over and asked if she needed help. She hadn't seen them until then, and they surprised her. She gave another scream and jumped back, looking from one to another as if they'd tried to hurt her. Then she turned and went off in a hurry to one of the houses, straight across from where she'd taken the glove. She rushed up to the front door, threw it open, and ran inside. The door slammed, and the old woman asked the man if they ought to help, but he just shook his head and led her into the Gardens."

"The glove was small, you say – like a child's. Could the woman have been a governess? Or the mother?"

"The mother, I think," replied Oliver. "She was crying too hard to be a nanny. And that's what grand-mum thinks, from when we saw her again the next day."

Holmes shifted his attention back to Mrs. Fawley. "The day before yesterday," Holmes confirmed. "Tuesday."

She nodded. "I was feeling better, so we started out as usual. I didn't give the glove any thought at all – at least until it crossed my mind when we came in sight of the Square. It was then that Oliver pointed out the woman, the same one as the day before he said, running across the street toward the fence, just after we turned from Harley Street. We weren't close enough to say for certain, but there was something on top of one of the fence posts that was a bright lime-green, the same as the glove of the day before.

"We watched as she grabbed it and gave a cry that we could hear from across the street. Then, without waiting, she turned right around and ran back toward one of the houses. She was nearly run down by a hansom, but she reached our side of the street and went right by us and into Number 15."

Holmes nodded and said, almost to himself, "Between Harley Street and Dean's Mews, across from the drinking fountain."

"That's right," agreed Oliver with wide eyes.

"Did anything else happen?"

They both shook their heads. "No," said Mrs. Fawley. "We talked about knocking on the door, to see if we could help, but there was nothing that we could do. We set up by the pathway into the garden where we usually stand and stayed for another half-hour until all the meat was gone. Then we went back to our rooms in Welbeck Street, across from Bentinck Street. We talked about what we'd seen and decided to get to the Square early yesterday afternoon, to see if anything else ended up on the fence, and if we could get a look at who was putting these things there."

"Ah, yes," said Holmes. "Enter John Wilmslow."

Mrs. Fawley nodded. "Last evening, he put a little boot on the post. I recognized him from when he was in the newspapers a few years ago, and wondered why he was part of this."

Oliver looked mildly puzzled. I wasn't surprised, as he would have been too young to hear about John Wilmslow during the short time when he was something of a London celebrity. The man had seemingly burst from nowhere just a few years earlier, having spent the previous decades in Tangiers accumulating a vast fortune as a metal-trader. Originally from Liverpool, he'd been born the son of a dock worker. He'd followed his father into that trade, and within a month he had fled the country on the same night that he and his father became involved in a drunken brawl outside a waterfront tavern. The fight had left one man dead, stabbed in the back. Wilmslow Senior had attempted to place the blame upon his own son John, but several eyewitnesses had definitely seen the father commit the killing, affirming that the son was totally without blame.

Nevertheless, in spite of his established innocence, John Wilmslow had vanished, turning up a year or so later in North Africa with a sizeable amount of currency in the form of pounds, rubles, gold-marks, and dollars, origins unknown. He began investing in mines and processing facilities, and extending his reach into other profitable areas, and it was rumored that his methods were legal when that would actually suffice. And yet, a blind eye was turned, especially in that part of the world, and when his own personal wealth and success began to make money for others in England, his methods were actively encouraged.

262

He had reappeared in London in the early spring of 1899, a rugged and dashing man of about fifty who had seemingly tired of his African experiences. He'd rented an unassuming little house in Hampstead, really nothing more than a cottage that was part of a larger estate, located behind a fortress-like wall near the Heath, and began to make appearances at various parties and social events. His appearance was guaranteed to add acclaim to any venue at which he deigned to appear. His lean figure and dark good looks cut quite a swath through the social set, and the casual public's fascination with him seemed to have no limits. However, there were those who knew a bit more about him than what was touted in the press, and they were rather wary of the man. He exuded an aura of danger, as if he were a cornered beast that had so far refrained from attacking – although the attack was inevitable.

Wilmslow had first come to Holmes's attention – and mine as well – by way of Holmes's brother, Mycroft. We had been requested – although "summoned" might be more accurate – to Mycroft's anonymous Whitehall office on a cool day in late April 1899, just a few months after Wilmslow's return to England. I think that we both expected that Mycroft wished to hear details about the little matter of the third footprint of Sutton Coldfield, in which it will be recalled that Holmes was able, through the use of an electromagnet, to show where the hijacked armaments had been buried in a seemingly innocent farmer's field before they could be spirited out of the country. Inspector Lyford of the Warwickshire Constabulary had implied at the time that there seemed to be an interest in the case in that obscure part of the government from which Mycroft's reach extended the most.

It was with thoughts of that affair in our minds that we found ourselves facing Holmes's older brother across his vast and singularly empty desk. I believe that Holmes was as surprised as I when Mycroft began by saying, "You were unsuccessful in burning all of Milverton's papers."

As a doctor, as a soldier, as a husband, and as an associate of Sherlock Holmes, I've learned that sometimes it's best to remain silent. I also resisted the temptation to turn and look at Holmes, seated to my right. I sensed without seeing him that he was suddenly wary – both at the assertion that we had failed somehow, and also that Mycroft appeared to know our secret. As far as I knew, neither of us had revealed to anyone the truth of what happened on that January night, just a few months earlier, when we had burgled our way into Charles Augustus Milverton's house in Hampstead, intending to steal and destroy the master blackmailer's documents from his safe, and instead witnessing his brutal murder while we hid nearby behind the drapes. The man's executioner, a much-wronged woman who had our complete sympathy, had ground her heel into Milverton's dead face before departing, never aware of our presence. Holmes had immediately rushed to the hallway door, locking it so that the rest of the awakened house couldn't disturb us – at least for a moment – and then set about carrying Milverton's foul documents from the open safe to the fire, where he tossed them, great heaping masses up on the coals.

Even as time was running away from us, and with the expectation that the man's servants would decide to stop pounding on the door to Milverton's study and instead begin their wary approach from the garden, Holmes waited, tarrying far longer than I felt was safe, in order to make sure that the vile papers were irretrievably burning beyond recovery. Only when he was certain that there was no hope of salvaging even a fragment did he lead me outside and through the black night to the garden wall. Even then our escape was almost ruined, as one of the servants unexpectedly came up underneath me just as I topped the wall, grabbing my foot until I kicked myself loose.

We fled across Hampstead Heath, sometimes along the paths, and sometimes taking to the shadows to avoid other late-night wanderers. Our dark clothes helped to conceal us. Finally we felt safe enough to approach a lighted thoroughfare and find a cab to return us to Baker Street. The following morning, our old friend Inspector Lestrade of Scotland Yard had stopped by to see if Holmes might be enticed into investigating the crime. He mistakenly believed that the two men who had burned the blackmailer's papers, as identified by Milverton's servant, were also the murderers. Holmes and Lestrade were both amused that the description of one of the men who had fled from the house looked very much like me. I feigned laughter as well, but in truth I did not share their merriment. Holmes then declined to assist Lestrade, stating that his sympathies were with the killer, and that was the end of the matter. And yet, we now found ourselves called on the carpet before Mycroft Holmes, who appeared to know all.

Holmes didn't bother to deny it. Instead, he replied, "Impossible. There wasn't a scrap left in the safe, and what was in the fire was certainly beyond retrieval." Then, he frowned. "Of course, while it isn't logical, Milverton could have had other hidey-holes."

Mycroft nodded, growling, "Certainly he did. At his other residence, for instance."

At this, both Holmes and I showed astonishment. Then Holmes said, "I'm not aware that he owned any other property."

"He did not. But there is a second smaller residence on the grounds of the *same* property. The two of you entered the main house, located at the corner of East Heath Road and Well Road. But there is another building to the south – also inside the wall, but located on Cannon Lane, with its own direct opening to the street. Apparently Milverton was afraid to sleep in his own house at night so, once he'd finished whatever business he had to transact – and he carried out much of his filthy occupation in the darkness after most people have gone to bed – he would retreat in secret across his gardens to the smaller building, which he had fixed up as something of a fortress. Only there would the reptile feel safe enough to sleep."

"Forgive me, Mycroft," interrupted Holmes, "but my curiosity will abide no longer. I won't bother to deny it, but exactly how did you know of our presence at Milverton's house on that fateful night?"

"Because the papers were burned."

"That sounds suspiciously like something that I would say to vex Watson," replied Holmes. "Might you elaborate?"

"I knew because I have had the story of what happened that night directly from the poor lady who removed Milverton from the board. She told me of how she ended him, and then how she immediately departed. And yet, the papers were burned. The servants were a scurvy crew, worthy of their captain, and they would have kept the papers and delayed calling the police if the thought had only occurred to them. Instead, one of them precipitously sent for the authorities, who arrived within mere minutes. Yet there was no time for the papers to have been burned so completely if they hadn't been tossed into the fire at nearly the exact same time that the man was killed. Clearly if my friend did not burn them, someone else did – someone already there for that purpose.

"I was already aware that, just a week before, you had both become involved in the ongoing efforts to rescue Lady Eva Brackwell from Milverton's clutches. In fact, it was I who suggested your combined participation. After hearing the circumstances of that night, it was the inescapable conclusion that you two were the men on the scene, as reported to the police by the servants. The description of the two of you – especially of you, Doctor – was unmistakable. In fact, I have some inkling that Lestrade has his own suspicions as to the true identity of the two men who fled into the night, but he has happily turned a blind eye, and isn't wasting any time looking in that direction – or in *any* direction, for that matter.

"I trust, Doctor, that you received no injury from when one of Milverton's myrmidons affixed himself to your ankle, or when you fell from the wall. It was just good luck for all concerned that you picked that particular night for a spot of burglary. And yet, there was no way that you could know that there were other papers, and they have fallen into other hands."

Mycroft went on to explain that Milverton had apparently kept his most valued papers hidden in the smaller house off Cannon Lane. He had been able to piece this together after one of the most noted names in the land received a blackmail letter just three days before. "The blackmailer has made no secret of his identity – for like Milverton, he likes to deal directly with his victims. The letter came from John Wilmslow, so recently returned from Africa, and the darling of both the press and an ignorantly indulgent society."

He explained that upon his return to England, Wilmslow had taken the Cannon Lane house, "apparently in all innocence, as Milverton's heirs had no reason not to lease it – and they certainly didn't realize that it contained Milverton's most secret treasures. But to a mind such as Wilmslow's, searching the building and discovering Milverton's cache would have been second-nature." It was then that Mycroft gave us a short *précis* of the man's past.

"And what sort of mischief is he causing?" asked Holmes.

"It is known in the higher circles as 'The Gnosall Infatuation'. I can reveal very little, except to state that Rupprecht of Bavaria, while traveling in England a few years ago, visited Gnosall, where he was . . . indiscrete. His temporary fascination with an innkeeper's daughter, and the issues that resulted – both figurative and literal – have a direct bearing on the British throne, with serious connections to the Jacobite succession and the 1701 Act of Settlement."

Little more needs to be said regarding this matter – and in fact, little is allowed to be recorded. Holmes was tasked with retrieving the remainder of Milverton's documents from Wilmslow, and I was with him when he used the threat of a long jail sentence and the might of the British Government to back him up. Without comment – in fact, Wilmslow probably uttered less than ten words during the entire interview – the man had surrendered all of the documents that he had found hidden in Milverton's cottage.

During Holmes's investigation, it was learned that the Gnosall letters weren't Wilmslow's only irons in the fire. He had taken on an apprentice in the short time since he'd returned to England, a certain spurious Count Negretto Sylvius, and he left this ill-equipped man to take the blame in relation to the poor young woman from Gnosall, Miss Minnie Warrender, who had been so cruelly used. Holmes was able to recover all of Milverton's documents. The Government declined to prosecute, and Wilmslow left for the Continent within days. Still, Mycroft assured us that he was being kept on a short leash, without his knowledge, and on several subsequent occasions we received word when Wilmslow slipped back into

England for short visits in order to carry out some bit of business. And now, apparently, he was back again.

Holmes pinched his lip, no doubt recalling our past encounter with Wilmslow, and considering what Mrs. Fawley had told him. Then, "Two small gloves, and now what looks like a boot. And did the woman from Number 15 retrieve that in the same manner?"

"She did. We were there in plenty of time to see the fellow, this Mr. Wilmslow – we had placed the cart near the fence post that he has used, so that he was easy to spot – and I saw that the curtain of the house opposite kept moving, as if someone there was watching. As soon as he left the boot and walked off along Wigmore Street, toward the Post Office and out of sight, the door opened and the lady ran across, grabbed the boot with a cry, and then ran back inside, slamming the door."

Holmes looked at me. "The conclusion seems obvious, although I hesitate to settle on anything definite without more facts."

I nodded, silently agreeing that to all appearances the scoundrel seemed to be sending a message to the woman, a reminder of sorts, that her child was being held captive, although for what purpose was not clear. Mrs. Fawley appeared to be in agreement. "He has her child," she declared.

"Possibly, although it doesn't do to jump to conclusions."

Oliver wiggled in his chair. "I followed him," he said. "The man that left the boot."

Holmes raised an eyebrow. "Indeed. Where did he go?"

"He walked straight west, almost to Portman Square. Then he turned into Seymour Mews. He went all the way through, and into one of the houses that opens into Duke Street – Number 4, just across from Duke's Mews."

Holmes nodded. "You've done nearly all the work then, Oliver. I couldn't have asked for better from one of the Irregulars."

Apparently the boy knew those children to whom Holmes referred. He sat up a little straighter, his pride evident, and his grandmother gave him an affectionate glance.

"Is there anything else to report?" asked Holmes.

Both shook their heads, and Oliver frowned, as if he should have been able to provide some other additional fact. Holmes tapped his lip for a moment, and then glanced at my mantel clock. "Assuming that another item of clothing will be placed on the fence today at the usual time, we have several hours. I will ask questions and set other inquiries into motion." He looked at Mrs. Fawley. "Would you have any objection if I joined you at your cart this afternoon?"

"Not at all."

"Excellent. I'll be suitably attired so as not to attract attention. Watson, are you free?"

I nodded, having already been thinking of how I would close my practice early for the afternoon – and how I could explain it to my wife.

"Place yourself along Wigmore Street, fifty feet or so west of Harley Street. When Wilmslow delivers his daily message, be ready to precede him back toward Seymour Mews, while being aware that today he may veer off in an entirely different direction. I hope to have more facts in hand by then, and we'll confront him in his lair."

With that, he thanked Mrs. Fawley and Oliver and I showed them to the street, where I found Jack kneeling in front of their cart, attempting to make friends with several stray cats lined up before him, completely uninterested in his offers of affection, their eyes solely upon the odorous covered cart by my steps.

Back inside, I rejoined Holmes in my study, where I poured us each a brandy. He took it, but I could see that he was impatient to depart.

"There is every chance," I said, "that last night's performance was Wilmslow's last. We don't know how long he's been leaving items of clothing before he was observed. In fact, whatever this is about might already be concluded."

Holmes nodded, tipped up the brandy, and then stood, handing me the glass. "Precisely why I should be on my way." He stepped toward the door and then paused. Looking back, he reminded me, "Bring your gun." Then he departed.

There was no need for that reminder, and he knew it. I had learned soon after I began assisting him on his investigations, over two decades earlier, that it was unwise to step into the street without being armed, for Holmes had cultivated a number of dangerous enemies, and the longer that I associated with him, the more that they became my enemies as well. Additionally, one never knew when a simple peaceful day, or an unimportant errand, might suddenly turn into a life-of-death situation, with no time for useless wishes that my faithful service revolver was in my pocket.

No sooner had Holmes departed than I heard a soft knock on my study door. It was my wife, and even though she simply asked if everything was all right, I knew that she was really seeking further information regarding Holmes's visit. I recounted Mrs. Fawley's arrival, and what she and her grandson had seen. At the mention of the items of children's clothing, and the heartrending cries of the woman who retrieved them, she quickly understood the gravity of the situation, and she encouraged me to do all that I could to help. I was relieved.

I walked with her toward the front of the house and we parted at the door to my consulting room – she to return upstairs, and I to resume the yoke of my practice.

By a quarter-after-four, the last of the patients had been seen, and I had a quick bite to eat before retrieving my gun. I let my wife know that I was departing, and then stepped outside. As I had anticipated, a fog had descended upon the capital, giving everything a muted yellow aspect as light from the early-lit gas-lamps was diffused and sounds were muffled by the water vapor hanging in the air. I adjusted the collar of my coat and set off along Queen Anne Street, walking until it terminated in Welbeck Street. I turned south, passing Bentinck Street along the way, and wondered in which of the houses that Mrs. Fawley and Oliver resided.

Then, at Wigmore Street, I turned back a bit toward Cavendish Square, aiming for a teashop along the north side where I could wait until needed. With a warm cup, I found a seat in the window facing east along the street, where I could see just into the Square. The gas-lamps there were numerous, and helped to burn off some of the mist that otherwise might have obstructed my view. Mrs. Fawley – for that was surely her near the distinctive cats-mean cart – was already in place near the water fountain. Standing nearby was a boy, and also a tall figure, clearly from his clothing another purveyor of cat's meat – and though unrecognizable as such, certainly Sherlock Holmes.

I had carried a newspaper with me, but I never opened it, instead pondering the unusual story that we'd heard earlier that day, and considering what Wilmslow hoped to accomplish. Leaving the items of children's clothing on the fence, to be retrieved by the obviously grieving and fearful woman, seemed extraordinarily cruel, and I wondered if it was part of his plan, in some attempt to force something from her, to make things much worse than if he simply sent a message.

I found that I was checking my watch too frequently as five o'clock approached, and I forced myself to wait patiently. Eventually, as they always do, the minutes passed and I noticed a man walking along the opposite side of the street, his had pulled low, as if he wished to avoid recognition. Although I couldn't see his face, he had appeared at approximately the correct time, and was headed in the right direction. Believing this to be Wilmslow, on his way to deposit the latest parcel, I finished my tea, nodded to the shop's owner with whom I had a passing acquaintance, and went outside, placing myself near the building. I unfolded the newspaper, pretending to look at an advertisement, while keeping my eyes fixed on the northwest corner of the Square.

The man was walking slowly, but he did eventually reach his destination, where he fished out something from his overcoat pocket and

269

affixed it to the fence post, not ten feet from my friend and the others around the cat's meat cart. Then the man, certainly Wilmslow, turned quickly and started back my way, moving with much more speed and certainty than he had during his initial approach. As he got closer, I could see a woman running across Wigmore Street to the fence, her hands already outstretched towards the item there, as if afraid someone would retrieve it before she could. Then I could watch no further, as I had to turn myself and start along toward Seymour Mews to the west, staying in front of my quarry.

I would never dare to claim myself as the equal to Sherlock Holmes in any of the activities that he has perfected in his profession, but I will assert that over the course of more than twenty years accompanying him and providing assistance when I could that I haven't been an entirely hopeless pupil. Holmes wouldn't have tolerated me for so long, I think – at least as an associate in his investigations – if I wasn't able to provide some useful assistance in addition to simple stubborn support. Early on, he had taught me the rudiments of following someone, and while I could not claim to be as accomplished as he, I was no slouch about it either. He and I had worked together for so long that we could follow someone as a team, knowing what the other would do, and sharing back-and-forth the duties so as not to cause our prey to be suspicious. Likewise, I could do the same on my own, and it was no hardship at all to stay ahead of Wilmslow while giving him no reason to believe that he was under my observation. And it didn't hurt that I had a good idea of where he was headed.

He was, however, suspicious of being followed, as he often stopped to supposedly glance in a shop window, while instead awkwardly looking back to see who was behind him. There was no sign of Holmes in his vendor disguise, but I knew that he was certainly coming along steadily, perhaps by a side street, and possibly already in some other article of clothing so that he would look completely different from the tall man who had been at Mrs. Fawley's cart. I knew better than to look for him, and I casually continued along Wigmore Street, sometimes letting Wilmslow get closer, and sometimes pulling away as if I were completely unaware of his existence.

I passed the entrance to Seymour Mews and was almost to Portman Square when I stopped to tie my shoe. From that position, I could see Wilmslow turn into the mews. In less than a minute, a boy went in as well, whom I recognized as one of Holmes's Irregulars. The back way was stoppered. I went back to Duke Street, where I stopped several houses down from Number 4. Holmes was sheltering in a nearby doorway and he beckoned me over, where we lit a couple of cigarettes and he caught me up on his afternoon.

"Wilmslow has been in London for nearly two weeks," he explained softly. "I learned from Mycroft, who has received continuous reports over the last few years about Wilmslow's movements, that he returned under the name 'Williams' – close enough to his own, I suppose – and took rooms at the Langham. However, after a week, he vanished, and his whereabouts have since been unknown – until now. I spoke with the landlady of Number 4, across the street, earlier today, and she said that Mr. Williams rented a bedroom and sitting room on the second floor front on the same day that Wilmslow vanished. He moved in with very little in the way of possessions and has been a model tenant, only venturing out a couple of times a day, and usually returning not long after he departs. If not for the fact that he appears to be in hiding, she would have no qualms about him. He is paid up for two more weeks, including meals, which she takes up to him in his rooms. Of course, I determined that there is no sign of a child."

I nodded. "Does he then have the items of clothing with him?"

Holmes shook his head. "Unlikely. The landlady has seen no indications, although that isn't conclusive. I suspect that he's retrieving them somehow during one of his short daily trips, and then subsequently taking them down the street, as we just saw, to leave them on the fence for the woman to find."

"And what did you learn about her?" I asked, for I knew that Holmes wouldn't have ignored that aspect of the case.

"Mycroft informed me that she is Delores Fairchild, the daughter of Sir Edwin Pritchett, who lives at No. 15 Cavendish Square. She is married, and has been living on the Continent for over two years, following a falling-out with her father, who didn't approve of her husband. She returned suddenly a little over a week ago. The servants confided this to me when, in the guise of a knife-sharpener, I made myself useful earlier this afternoon, and was subsequently rewarded with a bit of food and tea, and the company of the staff around their below-stairs table."

"She has returned from the Continent?" I said. "Is there a connection to Wilmslow, who has been out of England since early 1899?"

"Without a doubt. You could not have known, for there was no reason that you should, that Wilmslow has lived there under the name 'Fairchild' in Provence since he left our shores. By piecing together a few facts that I learned from the staff in Sir Edwin's kitchen, I found that his estranged daughter Delores has been living in France since she met and married a man named Fairchild two years ago. They have a child that Sir Edwin has never seen. In fact, his daughter hadn't been home since her marriage, and only turned up a week ago – without the child, a daughter, whom she said was still in France – to make her peace with her father. I was informed that she has been greatly upset ever since, all ascribed to missing her little girl."

I pondered these new facts. "Has Wilmslow then stolen the child away from her mother, and fled with her to England? What point could he have for tormenting his wife so?"

"Ah, I suspect that there is possibly another interpretation. Perhaps the best way to verify it is to ask Wilmslow himself." And with that he cast his cigarette aside into the street and led me across to the doorway of No. 4. It was one of those houses that are left unlocked to both tenants and their visitors, and we simply entered through the doorway and made our way up the narrow stairs. Holmes knocked firmly upon one of the doors and we heard decisive footsteps approach. Then the door was pulled open, and we found ourselves facing a rather angry man.

"I saw you just now, standing there across the street," he growled. "What do you want, Mr. Sherlock Holmes?"

"Ah, Mr. Wilmslow," said Holmes. "I see that you remember me after we negotiated the return of Milverton's additional papers, prior to your sudden departure from England."

"Please, Mr. Holmes," Wilmslow replied, with an unexpected slight desperate tinge to his tone – not what I had expected He frowned. "This is not a good time."

Holmes raised an eyebrow. "You fear for your daughter's safety, then?"

Wilmslow was taken aback, but he apparently knew enough about Holmes to realize that keeping secrets was futile. "I do. I came to London to carry out some business. I'd hoped to be in and out in very quickly, but somehow my enemies had discovered the name under which I've been living in France. Soon after I'd arrived in London, they sent a message to my wife in my name, luring both her and my daughter here on a false pretext. She was met in Canterbury and, almost as soon as she stepped ashore, my daughter was taken. They gave her to understand that Eliza would remain unharmed if she told no one, and if they received what they wanted from me. They told her that I would be informed of their demands, and then they vanished. My wife didn't know where to turn. Instead of returning to France, she made her way to London."

Holmes looked to each side and then replied in a soft tone, "Perhaps we should discuss this inside. It's possible that one of your enemies has taken an adjacent room and is listening with interest as we speak."

Wilmslow nodded and stepped aside. We entered and found a meagre room with a table and two wooden chairs centered before a small coal fireplace, and little else. Through an open doorway I could see a bed and a plain deal table beside it.

Our host indicated that we should each take the two chairs, as he was too nervous to sit. Then he paced before us, elaborating upon his story.

"I was staying at the Langham when they let me know that my daughter was their captive. Each day they have left an item of her clothing for me at the front desk – her hat and scarf, her gloves, and then her boots. They have given me a week, and then they implied that they would move on to . . . to harming her physically." At this, he turned away, covering his eyes, and unable to speak for a moment.

"You have been seen placing items of clothing on the fence across from your father-in-law's house," Holmes explained after a moment. "Every afternoon, about five o'clock. You were recognized, although clearly you tried to do so without drawing unnecessary attention to yourself. Presumably this is to send a message to your wife."

Wilmslow turned back to us, his eyes red. "After my wife arrived in London, she went to the Langham to find me. I had just received the message from my enemies, outlining their demands, and was frantically trying to work out a way to save my daughter when she arrived. I was fearful that somehow Delores would be taken as well, and that she too would be used against me. We agreed that she should stay at her father's home for the duration.

"While some know that I am married, most people don't realize that my wife is Sir Edwin Pritchett's daughter – especially because he essentially disowned her after our wedding. By having her stay at his home, we thought that she could remain in safety, with her whereabouts a mystery until this is all over. My wife agreed, but was adamant that I keep her informed as to what was happening. However, I was afraid to visit her each day, or to send a message that might be intercepted, giving away her location. My enemies had indicated that they would send me a piece of Eliza's clothing each day, and when I mentioned that fact, my wife insisted that I somehow pass those along to her. We agreed that I would leave them on the fence around Cavendish Square, directly across the street, and then quickly depart. She would see them from the window and know that all was still well."

"Your wife has been retrieving the items almost as soon as you walked away," I explained.

Wilmslow shook his head. "I warned her to stay inside."

"Why are you here in Duke Street?" asked Holmes. "Why aren't you still at the Langham?"

"I have continued to reserve the rooms there," he answered, "but I shifted my base of operations here, to this place, in order to have freedom of movement – and yet, I am paralyzed, unable to determine a course of action as the time slips by. I visit the Langham every day in order to retrieve the item of my daughter's clothing, and to check for messages. So far there has been nothing except for the clothes. Tomorrow is the seventh day, and then I expect to receive the promised message regarding the specifics of how to deliver what is demanded of me."

"And that would be . . . ?"

Wilmslow shut his eyes. "They want the remainder of Milverton's papers."

Holmes nodded. "I thought as much. And did you convey that you no longer have them?"

He shook his head. "They wouldn't believe me. They notified me by a note left at the front desk that they had my daughter, and what they demanded in return for her freedom. They gave me a week to retrieve the papers from wherever that I have supposedly hidden them. I am to be notified tomorrow of how delivery shall be accomplished."

"Do you receive the items of clothing at the desk, or are they left in your room?"

"At the desk."

"Have you tried to see who leaves the clothing there?"

"I have not. I was warned not to, and in any case, it's likely to be a faceless minion. I suppose that I could try to follow this person back to the source, but what difference would it make? I know who has her, and to do so might endanger her. This sort of thing isn't my strength. I made my fortune through sometimes brutal business deals. I have no finesse. And there is no one that I can trust to do it for me."

"You state that you have no finesse, and yet your efforts to blackmail certain royal personages in relation to Milverton's papers that you discovered in your rental cottage showed a certain boldness."

"That was not as it appeared, Mr. Holmes," said Wilmslow with a sudden amount of spirit. "I found those papers and realized that the knowledge within them conveyed to their holder a bit of power. I dropped a word here and there while trying to solidify a business deal. It wasn't the right thing to do, I'll admit, but I needed leverage when dealing with the Bavarians, and this was a secret that they wanted kept. But I didn't realize what a hornet's nest I'd found, or how it might affect the British Crown, and you then approached me and accused me of blackmail. I realized that was exactly what I'd been doing, and I simply chose to wash my hands of the whole business. I gave you the papers – without a fuss as you'll recall – and decided to write off my whole attempt to return to England as a wasted effort. I moved to France, lived under another name while still maintaining my business interests, and then I met my wife – herself something of an outcast from Britain. We are perfect for each other, and have been immensely happy. I've continued to run my various enterprises, which required the occasional visit to London, but I assure you that I've kept to the straight-and-narrow path ever since. And now I'm faced with this situation."

He paused to take a deep breath, and Holmes said, "There is really just one further matter to confirm – the identity of these enemies to whom you have referred. I've received something of an intense education this afternoon as to the rivalries currently influencing the imports of metals, and how it relates to the build-up of armaments here at home and among our Continental neighbors. The men who are terrorizing you can only be Clawson and his partners."

Wilmslow's eyes widened slightly, but he nodded. "They seek a number of concessions in Tangiers, and my own interests are in their way. They managed to find Count Negretto Sylvius, who worked for me a short time while I was living in England. He knew enough about my business to help them get on my trail, and to find my weak spots."

Holmes nodded. "I thought as much. I'm gratified to hear that your motivations in the spring of 1899, while still questionable, were not as bad as I had believed, and that you've followed a better path since then. I may say that I used part of the afternoon to verify independently a substantial portion of what you've just told us. It also gave me a chance to examine your biggest competitors, the Clawson brood – father and sons. I've taken the liberty of initiating some steps that should result in a favorable outcome. Would you be willing to join Watson and me on a short trip to Mayfair?"

Wilmslow seemed overwhelmed as he tried to keep up with Holmes's statements. I felt much the same way, but I dimly perceived that Holmes's calmness was an indicator that the entire matter was well in hand and that the conclusion was within sight.

Holmes stood and looked around. "Do you have anything of value here? I doubt that you'll need to return."

Wilmslow simply shook his head, and then he grabbed his coat and had, following us out and down the stairs. We walked to Manchester Square, where a growler was waiting, apparently previously reserved by Holmes. We climbed in and Holmes gave an address in Park Lane. No doubt we could have walked there in just a few minutes, but Wilmslow, having ceded control of the situation to Holmes, had rather collapsed, and it was a mercy to him that he could ride to our destination.

The fog was much thicker than when we'd entered Wilmslow's rooms, and the going was quite slow. Yet we kept to the back streets and had no difficulties. It wasn't long before we pulled up in front of a fine mansion with what would have been a good view of Hyde Park, if one could have seen across the street. We had no sooner stepped to the pavement than several policemen appeared out of the mist, walking toward us from the south, led by our old friend Inspector Gregson. He offered his large hand to each of us, Wilmslow included, and stated, "More men are around back. I don't expect any trouble from these types, but one never knows when someone will panic." He glanced at Wilmslow, whose eyes had widened at the thought of endangering his daughter. "One of them might flee," amended Gregson to ease Wilmslow's fears, but the effort wasn't very effective.

What happened next is soon told. The solid authority of the police gained us entrance to the house, and documents allowing a legal search were presented. A butler attempted to defend the gate, and then fled with documents in hand to a deeper part of the house, a constable at his side. Policemen spread to all parts of the building, while the elder Mr. Clawson, an obese and unpleasant man with curiously arranged hair combed forward from the rear and stiffened somehow over his ears like shellacked wings, propelled himself from somewhere in the rear, his two sons beside him like a shabby pack of poorly trained hyenas, words of outrage on his blue lips. However, these died as soon he perceived Wilmslow's grim presence. The old man's words faded away, but the silence was quickly broken by shouts of triumph from upstairs. Forgetting Clawson and everyone else, Wilmslow dashed up the stairs, only to return moments later with a sleepy young girl clutched in his arms. I took her and gently made a quick examination, determining that she appeared to be unharmed, except for having difficulties in fully awakening. "She may be slightly drugged," I hypothesized.

For Wilmslow, who had been standing slightly behind me, that mere suggestion was enough to translate thought into deed. He pivoted smoothly and landed a shattering punch on Clawson's jaw. The man dropped like a sack of laundry, and no one, not even the villain's sons, made a move to defend him. When it was clear that he was unconscious, I stopped to make sure that he wasn't dead, and then indicated that he could be taken into custody. He was lifted unceremoniously by two burly constables and dragged through his front door. His money didn't help him a bit, and he died in prison.

With a promise to provide further details the next day, we said goodbye to Gregson and returned to our waiting growler. I have no memory of our short journey, as I kept an eye on both Wilmslow and his daughter. Within just a few minutes, we had arrived back at Cavendish Square, and soon the small family was reunited. Watching from the front door was Sir Edwin, who gruffly welcomed Wilmslow inside. Before he shut the door, Sir Edwin caught Holmes's eye and nodded, apparently recognizing him and acknowledging what he had accomplished.

Having dismissed the cab, we strolled down to Welbeck Street, and then to Mrs. Fawley's rooms. Holmes explained that he had verified their location during the time that he spend helping them sell cat's meat in Cavendish Square. It took but a few minutes to relate the barest details of the plot, providing enough information to satisfy them both, and to thank them for their assistance. Holmes praised Oliver for being observant enough to help right a wrong. "With your grandmother's permission," Holmes added, "I may call upon you from time to time when I need your skills in an investigation."

The boy nodded enthusiastically, and then looked toward his grandmother to see if she agreed. She smiled and nodded as well, although just once.

Outside, Holmes and I walked north along Welbeck Street. At the intersection with Queen Anne Street, Holmes wished me a good evening and made as if to continue north toward Baker Street, but I asked that he join my wife and me for a late dinner. He was somewhat reluctant, but I insisted. As we progressed along the quiet street, our view occluded by the fog except for a few feet in any direction, he succinctly explained how he had verified the details of Wilmslow's recent life, by way of his brother's government resources. Additionally, Holmes himself had made an effort over the last few years to stay caught up with Wilmslow, so that making the connection to the Clawsons hadn't been much of a leap. The idea that Wilmslow wasn't tormenting his wife with the child's clothing, but was instead using it to somehow pass long information about the child, had been one of the several theories that he'd listed in his own mind when hearing of the matter, and as events progressed, the truth became obvious.

We had reached my front door as Holmes was explaining his intention to renew his interest in Count Negretto Sylvius. I let us in and, after getting Holmes settled in the study, I went to inform my wife of our guest. She was worried about the child's safety, and I quickly gave her to understand that all was well, and that she would learn the specifics over dinner.

And she did. Holmes was rather reticent and uncharacteristically modest at first, but my wife would have all the details, and by the time the story was told, she realized just how Holmes's deft management of the affair had been able to accomplish a happy ending. I think that it was that night when a great deal of her resentment toward my friend began to be resolved. As I watched the two of them talk, he with respect at her intelligent questions, and she with a genuine interest in his work, I contentedly sipped my after-dinner coffee, trying not to remember that the next day I would be back in the consulting room, without the likely promise of another interesting case anytime soon.

Fortunately, I was incorrect.

The Unveiled Lodger
by Mark Mower

"You may be surprised to learn that we are about to be reacquainted with a former client, Watson – and one I did not expect to hear from again. You will no doubt recall the victim of the Abbas Parva tragedy in Berkshire?"

I stopped cleaning my old service revolver and placed it on the newspaper to my side. "Indeed. That would be the veiled lodger, Mrs. Eugenia Ronder."

"The very woman. She conspired with her lover, Leonardo the circus strongman, to kill her brute of a husband, and in the execution of their plan was savagely mauled by a North African lion."

I shivered at the recollection of her horribly disfigured features. "I take it that the letter you hold is from the lady herself? Is she still boarding in South Brixton?"

Holmes waved the letter above his head in a somewhat jubilant fashion. "The letter is from the former circus performer, but she has moved on from the humble abode of her landlady, Mrs. Merrilow. In fact, she has quite a story to tell. Remind me, when did we originally encounter poor Eugenia?"

"I believe it was towards the end of 1896."

"Then it is a good six years since she relayed her sorry tale. And I seem to remember that were it not for our intervention, she may very well have resorted to the poison bottle."

"Yes, and I'm glad to hear that she has survived to this point. At the time she looked to be ailing rapidly."

He took to his seat in front of the fire and relit the churchwarden which had been abandoned sometime earlier. "She has experienced something of a turnaround in her fortunes. Ordinarily I would provide you with a synopsis of what she has said, but I'm afraid that time will not allow for that. The letter indicates that she is to visit us at ten o'clock this morning, and the cab drawing up outside suggests she is extremely punctual!"

His supposition proved to be correct, for it was less than two minutes later that Mrs. Hudson gave a gentle knock on the sitting room door and entered to announce the arrival of a "Mrs. Eugenia Cullen". I smiled momentarily, believing already that I understood the nature of her changed fortunes.

The woman who stood before us was tall, full-figured, and elegant. Beneath a stylish black overcoat, she was wearing a white puffed blouse, complete with lace collar and broad purple ribbon tie. Her matching velvet skirt was fluted towards the hem, and on her head she wore a veiled hat trimmed with violets, feathers, and red-lace ribbons. The thick purple veil covering her face was cut off close to her upper lip, and she retained the perfectly-shaped mouth and delicately-rounded chin I had seen all those years before.

Holmes wasted no time in greeting our client and taking her coat, before inviting Mrs. Cullen to take a seat close to the fire. She seemed eager to talk, declining the offer of a tea and quickly removing her gloves, which she placed delicately on the arm of the chair before looking directly towards Holmes. I could scarcely believe that this was the same woman I had once seen sitting in a broken arm-chair in the shadowy corner of a threadbare room in South Brixton.

"Gentlemen, it is so good to see you both again. Mr. Holmes, you must have been a little taken aback to receive my letter – especially as my previous note to you contained but a short message and a bottle of Prussic Acid!"

Holmes smiled uneasily. "We are pleased to have you with us, and I am delighted to hear that the world has been good to you since we last met. Your prompt arrival has prevented me from providing Dr. Watson with any details of your changed fortunes, so I wonder if you would be kind enough to explain to us all that has happened since those dark days in South Brixton?"

Our client displayed no reticence in responding to his request. "I'm happy to do so. At the time, I was very close to believing that my life had no meaning. My confession to you helped to change all of that. I determined that I would lay aside my misery and find a path to some sort of contentment. Little did I know just how quickly my prayers would be answered!

"Secreted away in Mrs. Merrilow's lodging room, I had the gift of time. So much so that I began to read and write in order to fill every waking hour. I zealously consumed all manner of books, magazines, and periodicals. I took to writing short fictional stories about love, life, and the circus, and was successful in getting many of these published. And I looked for any opportunity to enrich my life within the confines of those four walls.

"One day I chanced upon a private advertisement in one of the broadsheets. It read simply: '*Widowed older gentleman who loves books, but has recently lost his sight, requires live-in lady reader who shares his passion for the written word.*' At first I believed this to be a scandalous

280

attempt to woe vulnerable women into promiscuity, but the more I pondered the announcement, the greater was my desire to find out whether it was in fact genuine.

"I replied to the advertisement and was delighted to receive an invitation to visit a Mr. Henry Cullen at an address in Arlington Street. The gentleman concerned was most charming, and as part of my interview asked me to read aloud to him from a story of my choosing. I had with me one of my own published tales, the rendition of which brought poor Mr. Cullen to tears – moved, as he said he was, by the heartache of lost love and the pleasing nature of my voice. In short, I was offered, and took up, the position as advertised. A few days later, having given notice to a tearful Mrs. Merrilow, I found myself lodged within the townhouse occupying an airy upstairs bedroom with a splendid view of Green Park.

"Now, I wouldn't wish you to think that there was anything improper about the arrangement to which I had agreed. The spacious home already had a staff of four, comprised of a housekeeper, maidservant, scullery maid, and gardener. Mr. Cullen's bedroom was on the ground floor. With his deteriorating eyesight, he had come to rely on them almost exclusively and rarely left the house or ventured upstairs. At that time, he was a little over sixty years-of-age, but youthful in his countenance and sprightly in his movements. He had worked previously as a literary agent and his extensive library of books – housed within an expansive study next to his bedroom – bore testimony to his lifelong love of literature. My role was straightforward. I would read to him between the hours of ten and eleven o'clock each morning, from two until four most afternoons, and conclude each evening with a narration for one hour prior to Mr. Cullen's bedtime at ten o'clock.

"My visual appearance mattered not to my employer. In fact, had it not been for the tittle-tattle of the scullery maid, he may well have remained unaware that I had any form of facial disfigurement. I was received well enough by the other staff and was free to go about my business with a minimum of interference. When not reading to Mr. Cullen in the study, I spent all of my free time in the upstairs room. On the rare occasions that I needed to leave the house, I would accompany Mr. Cullen into town in a hired carriage. This arrangement worked well, as we were able to provide a measure of support to each other.

"It doesn't take a great detective to work out what happened next. Such is the nature of the human condition. Spending many hours together and enjoying intimate moments through our shared love of romantic literature, Henry and I became inseparable. So much so that one day he asked me to stop reading and made me a proposal of marriage. I didn't take the offer lightly, nor did I attempt to take advantage of the situation.

281

I explained that I would provide him with the details of my previous marriage and the death of my husband. In return, I asked only that he share with me what had happened to his wife.

"He agreed to the declaration of openness and we each told our stories. Mine, you know. In Henry's case, the tale was more traditional. He had married Henrietta at thirty-one years of age. She was ten years younger. For the first six or seven years they had been happy enough, although Henrietta desired to have children. And when she was at last blessed with the birth of a healthy baby boy, the poor woman had not the strength to go on and died that same evening. Henry was racked with grief and couldn't bring himself to look favourably upon the child. He made arrangements for the young Charles Cullen to be taken to an orphanage in Watford, and provided a substantial endowment to enable him to be taken care of until he reached adulthood. Since that time, he has never seen his son.

"We agreed that our past lives did not alter our feelings for each other and set a date for the wedding. I have now been happily married to Henry for some three years."

Holmes and I expressed our congratulations. Once more, I asked Mrs. Cullen if she would like something by way of refreshment.

"Perhaps a small sherry?" was her reply.

I rose from my chair, only to hear our client reconsider her choice. "Actually, Dr. Watson, if it would not be too much trouble, I think I might prefer a *large* glass of sherry. You see, I have not yet told you everything."

I acceded to her request and poured her a fair measure of Madeira. When she had taken a couple of sips of the fortified wine, she resumed her narrative.

"My husband has been the most supportive and devoted companion I could ever have wished for. So much so, that he soon became aware of how troubled I was about the injuries to my face. Our wedding had been a small, private affair, with only a handful of invited guests. I was able to wear a specially commissioned wedding veil to disguise my looks. Thereafter, Henry asked me if I would be interested in consulting a specialist surgeon to see what could be done to reconstruct my features. I had not previously considered that anything of this nature could be attempted, so readily agreed to the idea.

"Henry knew of a surgeon at Guy's Hospital who had successfully undertaken a number of operations to remove flaps of skin from one part of a patient's body in order to sew these over damaged tissue elsewhere. The hospital itself claimed to have completed the first of these *skin grafts* as far back as 1817."

I could attest to this and gently interposed: "That's correct, Mrs. Cullen. One of this country's finest surgeons, Sir Astley Paston Cooper, undertook that operation. And you may know that in the previous decade, other surgeons have pioneered different techniques for cosmetically reconstructing facial tissue – most notably, the Americans, John Roe and George Monks, and James Israel, a doctor from Germany."

"Indeed. I was told that while the surgery was still largely experimental – and not without risks – it offered some hope to patients with conditions like mine. On that basis, and with Henry's backing, I agreed to undergo a number of operations over a six-month period. And while the enhancements could never be described as picture-perfect, I have been delighted with the results."

With this, she began to lift the veil from her chin. I braced myself for whatever vision might appear, but soon found myself transfixed by the remodelled features within my gaze. Gone was the grisly ruin and horror of a missing face. Her pretty brown eyes were now framed within more familiar features. The detail was still crude and unnatural looking, but the improvement was overwhelming. Like Holmes, I was temporarily spellbound.

When I at last found the words to reply, I could only congratulate her. "That is remarkable! Truly remarkable!" This was more than a medical curiosity, for it was clear that it had restored Mrs. Cullen's confidence and something of her personality.

"Thank you. I now feel comfortable to carry out my duties within the home without wearing a veil and use one only to travel. The servants are used to my odd features, and do not confront me with that look of horror to which I had become accustomed whenever my face had been exposed previously. And it is a measure of my self-assurance that I now feel relaxed enough for the skin of my face to be touched by my dear husband."

It was a heartfelt disclosure which moved me greatly. Holmes, too, seemed somewhat emotive in his response, but business-like as ever. "As my colleague has articulated, this is an incredible transformation. And I can see that it has had the most profound effect on your disposition. But your letter hinted at a *darker matter* which has come to light recently?"

Mrs. Cullen let the veil fall across her face once more. "You are quite correct, Mr. Holmes. And it is really for that reason that I thought to consult you. The matter has nothing to do with my surgery, and is more curious than alarming. Nevertheless, I believe that something is amiss and would welcome your enquiries into the matter."

"We would be pleased to assist you in any way that we can. So I would be grateful if you could furnish us with the pertinent facts."

Mrs. Cullen finished what remained of her sherry and then responded. "It was about a month or so ago that I had occasion to go into the potting shed which is inhabited most often by our young gardener, Eric Rayner. I was looking for a spare pot into which I hoped to transplant some of my favourite bulbs to protect them over the winter months. Eric keeps a supply of small containers on a workbench just inside the door. I picked up what I thought was a suitably sized pot, only to find a small folded note within it. While I felt certain that the note contained some sort of message or direction, I couldn't discern what it meant."

Holmes was immediately inquisitive. "Was the note written in a different language or a hand you could not read?"

"No. It contained a series of numbers, separated occasionally by a space, but laid out as if to form some sequence or sentence. I considered that it might be a map direction or even a code to unlock a safety deposit box, but could make nothing of it. In any case, I was not particularly concerned by the discovery, just a little curious."

"Did you keep the note or write down its contents?" I asked.

"No. Well, not on that occasion. But I will come onto that. Now, it was only a couple of days later that another odd thing occurred, this time within the house. I should explain that when we need to, my husband and I will venture into town, most typically on a Thursday. That particular day we had just returned in the carriage. Henry went into the study which adjoins our downstairs bedroom to put his chequebook in the bureau for safe-keeping. While he stores no valuables there, it does contain all of our legal papers. Having opened the bureau, he believed that someone had rifled through the documents – nothing was missing, but being fastidious in his administration now that he cannot see, knew from touch that things were not as he had left them."

"I am sure that is most telling," said Holmes. "Did either of you consult the staff about your suspicions?"

Mrs. Cullen frowned. "No. I would have done, but Henry was reluctant to make a fuss. He said that if it occurred again, he would have a word with our housekeeper, Mrs. Strickland."

"I see. And was there any reoccurrence?"

"Not that I know of. But then we come onto another matter which did make me wonder if some scheme was being plotted within the house. Last week, we had once again ventured into town on the Thursday. The trip normally leaves both of us weary, so we had turned in early that night, leaving Mrs. Strickland to oversee the arrangements for securing the house. Ordinarily she closes the curtains and extinguishes all of the lamps, leaving Eric to bolt the doors.

"I awoke close to midnight with something of a dry throat and decided to get a glass of water from the kitchen. Stepping into my carpet slippers and wrapping my dressing gown around me, I lit a candle and made my way quietly through the house. When I entered the kitchen, I could feel quite a draught and was surprised to see that one of the hurricane lamps had been lit and the back door was ajar. While it was foolish of me to do so, I stepped outside the kitchen and looked around. I could see a light on in the potting shed and felt somewhat relieved, realising that it was probably Eric who was still up.

"In the still of the night, I thought I heard two voices, but as I moved closer to the shed could hear nothing further. By this time I was halfway across the lawn, some fifteen feet from the shed. With the candle held out in front of me, I saw Eric come out carrying a small lamp. He turned back to shut the door of the shed and then addressed me directly, asking if there was something wrong. I did not feel able to challenge him, and merely replied that I had been concerned to find the back door open. He apologised and explained that he had forgotten to put a new pair of shears back into the potting shed and was in the process of doing so before heading off to bed.

"Ordinarily I would have taken him at his word, for he has always been a most reliable employee. But there was something in his voice which made me doubt him. Not wishing to alert him to this, I made my way back into the kitchen. But instead of going straight back to bed, stepped into the parlour and moved the curtains aside to get a good look at the front entrance. As I did so, I saw a tall figure in a white shirt and dark frockcoat climb over one of the iron gates in the drive and head off left down Arlington Street. It was the confirmation I needed that Eric had been lying."

Holmes looked at Mrs. Cullen most solemnly. "This sounds like a very grave business. Did anything else occur that night?"

"No. I climbed back into bed and slept fitfully until the early hours. The following morning, I quizzed Eric once again, giving him every opportunity to amend his account, but he maintained that he had been alone that night. Of course I didn't reveal that I had seen his compatriot leaving via the front gate. And the matter did not end there.

"A little later that morning, I was busy sewing in the parlour and glanced from the window to see Lizzie, our scullery maid, heading down the gravel drive to the front gates. On the other side of the entrance was the same man I had seen only hours earlier. While my eyesight is not perfect, I was able to discern more of his features. He was close to six feet in height, with dark hair and a handsome face, and immaculately turned out. He was wearing a double-breasted jacket, waistcoat, trousers, and black tie, complete with hat and gloves. I guessed him to be an under-butler of some kind. I watched as he chatted briefly to Lizzie, before then handing her what looked like an envelope.

"When Lizzie came through the back door, I was waiting and said that I had seen the man at the entrance. She explained that he had rung the bell at the gate and when she had gone out to ask what he wanted, had been given a letter which was to be passed to Eric. I was curious to know whether she had seen him on any previous occasion. While she answered in the negative, she did confirm that Mrs. Strickland had intercepted at least one letter some weeks earlier. Without wishing to appear overly dramatic, I asked Lizzie to pass me the envelope, saying that I would deal with the matter and requesting that she say nothing to Eric."

Holmes interjected. "Did you trust that she would adhere to your request?"

Mrs. Cullen had no qualms. "Lizzie is a straightforward, hardworking girl of whom I have grown very fond. She does not always think before she speaks, but is loyal and dependable. I have never doubted her integrity and know that she is highly regarded by Mrs. Strickland, who would also be quick to act if she felt Lizzie was not wholly trustworthy. Aside from that, it would be fair to say that there is no great affection between Lizzie and Eric. She is constantly scolding him for entering the house with muddy boots and creating extra work for her. The two have never been close."

"I see. And what of this envelope? Did you attempt to open it?"

"Indeed, I did. The envelope wasn't sealed, so I opened it and removed the note. And when I had copied its contents, returned the note and placed the envelope to one side."

"Excellent!" exclaimed Holmes. "And did you ensure delivery of the note to Eric?"

Our guest chuckled. "Yes. He normally takes a break from his gardening duties at lunchtime. I found him in the potting shed eating a sandwich and explained that the letter had been hand delivered. He looked a little unsettled, but thanked me and took the envelope, without saying anything of the sender."

"Fascinating. Now, do you have the copy you made of the note?"

"Most certainly. In fact, I can do better than that, for I also have another of the cryptic notes which I found in the potting shed only two days ago. Eric had requested some time off to visit his mother in Tooting, and I took the opportunity to search the shed in his absence. I found this new note screwed up in the bottom of a log basket. Fearing that there was indeed some nefarious scheme at hand, I took the precaution of writing to you and requesting this consultation."

286

She rose from her seat and walked across to the coat stand near the door. Retrieving both notes from an outside pocket of her overcoat, she passed the papers to Holmes who began to scrutinise them most intently. When he had done so, he passed one across to me, saying that it was the earlier of the two. In casting a glance over the missive I could not see how he had managed to ascertain this, but let the matter rest. In fact, I couldn't make anything of the note at all, which read:

12,15,15,11   6,15,18   23,9,12,12   20,15   19,5,5   23,8,15   9,14,8,5,18,9,20,19 – 3,3

"Pretty clear, eh Watson? This second note gives us some further indications of the plan in operation, but I will need to clarify a few facts before acting." He passed me the second note, which ran as follows:

12,5,1,22,5   2,1,3,11   4,15,15,18   15,16,5,14   20,8,21,18,19   5,22,5 – 3,3

Once again, I had not the faintest idea what was being communicated but nodded sagely. Mrs. Cullen was clearly intrigued.

"Gentlemen, you have the better of me, for I could discern nothing from the numbers. So what does it all mean?"

"You may rest assured that we will get to the bottom of this. I can tell you that there is no great mystery involved, but it is indeed fortunate that you have brought this to my attention at this time. This being a Wednesday, I will need the rest of today and possibly some time tomorrow morning to tie up a few loose ends. Watson and I will then make the trip across to Arlington Street tomorrow evening, when I will explain all. I trust that you and your husband will be home from town by six o'clock?"

"Of course. I will make arrangements for you to dine with us at that time."

Rather unexpectedly, Holmes declined the offer. "Thank you, but it is essential that no one is informed of our planned arrival. In fact, I wonder if there is any way we could be ushered into the house without alerting the staff?"

Our guest was not in the least perturbed. "That is easily done. We have a side entrance to the property which leads into the study adjoining our bedroom. This is accessible through a locked gate which sits on the south side of the house. Only Henry and I ever use the entrance, which is not visible from the servants' quarters. I will ensure that both the gate and the door are left unlocked shortly before six o'clock tomorrow."

287

"Thank you. That will assist us greatly in what could prove to be a lively evening." So saying, Holmes rose from his chair, indicating that the consultation was over. Mrs. Cullen seemed content with what had been proposed and, having thanked us for our time, departed a few minutes later.

My head was full of questions about what Holmes had made of the letters and why he had planned such a clandestine visit to Arlington Street. I knew that his passing reference to the potential for a "lively evening" signalled that there was likely to be an element of danger. But in terms of further detail, I was to be disappointed, for with the departure of our client, Holmes had already donned his hat and coat and was making for the stairs.

It wasn't until lunchtime the following day that I finally caught up with my good friend. I had been busy attending to half-a-dozen house calls that morning and called in at Baker Street shortly before one o'clock. Mrs. Hudson was most accommodating in offering me a sandwich of thickly-cut bread and cold sliced beef. As I entered the upstairs sitting room, I noted that Holmes had already finished his luncheon and was sat before the fire, drawing on his churchwarden.

"Ah, Watson! I see that you have finished work for the day and are already prepared for our planned visit to Arlington Street."

Knowing of Holmes's methods, I realised that the absence of my medical bag told him I had already stopped off at my home. And the bulge in the right hand pocket of my overcoat provided him with confirmation that I had thought to bring with me the service revolver that I'd cleaned thoroughly the day before. As my hand momentarily brushed the flap of the pocket, I saw that he had followed my line of reasoning and was smiling broadly.

"I have made very good progress on the case – a simple affair, but a timely intervention. I doubt that you'll need your revolver, but it is as well to be prepared. The man we're dealing with is both clever and determined, and fully prepared to kill those who stand in his way."

I was surprised at the disclosure. "Then there is murder afoot?"

"I believe so. But we are two or three steps ahead of our would-be killer."

"So you know who he is?"

"Of course, as you would if you had deciphered the coded notes."

I felt a twinge of embarrassment as I admitted that the numbers had meant nothing to me and I had been reluctant to say as much in front of our client.

Holmes grinned once again. "Well, you have plenty of time to make up for that this afternoon. The notes are still there on the table. I have one more pressing visit to attend to, and will return by five o'clock. By then, I expect you to have cracked the code and be in a position to confirm what you believe to be the plot at hand!"

He left me a few minutes later, saying that he was to visit a property in Pimlico. I resigned myself to an afternoon of mental concentration, determined to show Holmes that I could make sense of it all. As it turned out, being left alone with only my own thoughts for company, I had it cracked within ten minutes and could but smirk at the simplicity of the case.

True to his word, Holmes returned to 221b a good hour before we needed to be at Arlington Street. It was mild outside and we agreed to walk the mile-and-a-half to the Cullen's townhouse. On the way, I was able to explain what I had deciphered and what I believed to be the bare bones of the case. I was reassured to learn that Holmes concurred with every part of my synopsis.

"Splendid! I have but a few additional details to add based on what I have been able to find out since yesterday. I will share those with you when we explain everything to Mrs. Cullen."

It was a pleasant walk to our destination. We had some time to spare when we got to Arlington Street and spent a short while sat on a park bench beneath a gas-lamp within Green Park. At five minutes to six, we approached the side entrance to the townhouse, having entered through the small gate.

As we stepped into the study, we were greeted immediately by our client. Mrs. Cullen wore no veil and seemed quite relaxed. She quickly introduced us to her husband, a tall, well-groomed gentleman with a pleasing countenance and upright stature. He welcomed us into his home and said that certain preparations had been made. Eric Rayner had been sent into town to purchase a new garden fork and was expected back around six-thirty. Lizzie the scullery maid had been similarly tasked to pick up a roll of dress fabric from a shop in Piccadilly. Elizabeth Cleary, the maidservant, was taking a half-day holiday to visit an aged aunt in Brighton, which left only Mrs. Strickland. She was busy preparing the Cullen's evening meal and was, in any case, the most trusted of their employees.

Holmes expressed his gratitude: "Thank you. All of that will assist us in our endeavours this evening, particularly the absence of your gardener. With that in mind, would it be possible for me to take a quick look within the potting shed before we outline the nature of this affair?"

"Most certainly, Mr. Holmes. Eugenia will be able to guide you there on a route which isn't visible from the kitchen."

Our client responded accordingly and, with a lamp taken from a table within the study, led Holmes through a door and off into the house. In the time they were gone, Henry Cullen and I chatted amiably about art and literature, and he confessed to being a great admirer of my narratives.

Holmes returned some ten minutes later. With the four of us seated around the fireplace, my colleague began to sketch out the facts as he had uncovered them.

"It is as well that you came to us yesterday, Mrs. Cullen, for I can confirm that your gardener is immersed in a plot to kill both you and your husband. My quick search of the potting shed revealed a sum of money hidden within a tool chest – no doubt some advance payment for young Eric's complicity in this affair. I also found a new cudgel placed conveniently on the workbench inside the door, which may have been purchased during Eric's recent trip to Tooting. I believe that to be the weapon which our assailant is planning to use tonight when he enters the house, intent on assaulting you."

The Cullen's looked horrified at the revelation. It was Henry who spoke first. "Why would Eric want to kill us? If his intention is to steal from the house, he could easily have done that earlier today when we were in town."

"This isn't a simple case of robbery, although it is most likely that the events planned for this evening are to be made to look like a straightforward case of burglary. And I should emphasise that Eric will not be the man wielding the cudgel. That role is to be undertaken by your own son, Charles Cullen . . . ."

The shock of the pair was palpable. Henry Cullen was immediately tearful. His wife was breathing heavily and struggling to voice any sort of response. When at last she did speak, it was to Henry that she addressed her concern. "My love, it isn't my place to judge you for the way you treated your son all those years ago, but I suppose it was inevitable that one day Charles might attempt to make contact with you. We couldn't have known that his intentions would be quite so iniquitous."

Her husband could only agree. "I fear that I have very nearly been the architect of my own demise. But how can you be so sure that Charles is the person behind all of this?"

"The evidence is set out on the two coded messages received by your gardener. Doctor Watson can explain what they spelt out."

I was a little surprised to be asked to elaborate, but relished the opportunity, retrieving the two notes from inside my jacket. "Your son used a simple letter-to-number cipher to communicate with the gardener, where the letter '*A*' would be represented by the number '*1*', '*B*' by the digit '*2*' and so on. Translated, the earlier of the two notes reads: '*Look for will to see who inherits'* and is signed off with the initials '*CC*'. It helps to explain why the papers in your bureau were searched through a month or so ago."

Henry Cullen interjected. "Heaven's above! The will leaves all of my possessions to Eugenia, but in the event that anything should happen to her, the estate would pass to Charles as my only living relative. It was a change to the will which we discussed and agreed only six months ago. So having learnt of the provisions in the will, you believe that Charles is prepared to kill us both in order to inherit?"

"Indeed. And the second note tells us when. Translated, it reads, *'Leave back door open Thurs Eve'* and is again signed '*CC*'. We believe that Charles is planning to visit the house tonight when everyone has gone to bed, including your gardener. The latter could then claim that he was tucked up in bed during the attack and not involved in the plot."

Mrs. Cullen asked, "How can you be sure? This all seems so far-fetched."

Holmes then explained. "The notes suggested that it was Charles who was behind all of the strange events of the past month. But I needed further proof. After you left Baker Street yesterday, I travelled to Watford. You had mentioned that the infant Charles had been placed in an orphanage there. The only institution of that nature in Watford is the London Orphan Asylum. Consulting their records, I was able to confirm that a 'Charles Cullen' had been a pupil and boarder there for some years. And having reached the age of twenty-one had left the asylum – the records showing that he entered domestic service working for a family at an address in Pimlico.

"I made my way there this morning and enquired after Charles. The butler explained that in his time working for the family, the lad had proved to be industrious and quick to learn, eventually becoming an under-footman within the house. Some nine months ago, he secured a position as a footman elsewhere and handed in his notice, the butler being disappointed to lose him. He is now employed in a house only four doors away from here, further along Arlington Street."

"That would seem to confirm the matter," agreed Mrs. Cullen. "I suppose it was all part of his plan to get closer to his father."

"It would seem so. And I think we can easily surmise that he became acquainted with Eric Rayner to further pursue that objective. Having someone within the house meant that he didn't have to risk exposure. And it's possible that he learned of the planned changes to the will from the gardener, who may have overheard your conversations."

"That is quite possible," agreed Mr. Cullen. "I have been a fool, Mr. Holmes, an absolute fool. Is it any wonder that the boy hates me so much?"

Holmes looked sympathetic. "I cannot answer that. But I can ensure that your son is prevented from committing the most heinous of crimes tonight. Watson and I will remain here in this study while you dine and play out the evening as you would ordinarily. You are to give the staff no hint that anything is afoot. And when everyone has retired to bed, we will be vigilant in waiting for your son to put in an appearance."

The couple seemed content with the plan. Mrs. Cullen then suggested that the door of the study be locked from the inside to prevent any of the staff from inadvertently discovering the two of us. We retained the key to enable us to make our way through the house later that night. She agreed to inform the housekeeper that the windows in the study had been secured and the curtains drawn.

Left alone, Holmes and I helped ourselves to some brandy and settled down for the evening, conversing in hushed tones. At ten o'clock we heard the Cullens retiring for the night in the room next door. Sometime later, there was the sound of footsteps ascending the stairs, which we guessed to be the female servants heading for bed. It was only much later, at around eleven-thirty, that we heard a final footfall – a signal that the gardener had turned in.

We allowed another fifteen minutes to elapse before quietly unlocking the study door and tip-toeing our way through to the kitchen. It was a clear moonlit night, making it easy to see. Having taken in the layout, we decided to position ourselves within the pantry to the left of the back door. Charles Cullen couldn't enter the house without passing within a couple of feet of the pantry door, which was open sufficiently to enable us to watch his movements. I already had my revolver to hand.

We had but a short time to wait for the young footman to arrive. There was the distinct sound of the door knob being turned and the light tread of the intruder as he stepped into the kitchen, closing the door behind him. We watched as our quarry took three or four paces beyond the pantry. I could see that in his right hand that he was carrying the cudgel.

Holmes decided to act immediately, silently opening the pantry door and stepping into the room behind Cullen. Quietly but clearly, he said, "Put the cudgel down, Mr. Cullen. There are two of us, and my colleague is armed with a revolver."

Charles Cullen froze momentarily and then turned around slowly. His face betrayed a mixture of astonishment and anger. His eyes were fixed on Holmes, who stood ahead of me. I raised the revolver and stepped forward. Realising that he couldn't take on both of us, Cullen let his arm fall and dropped the cudgel on the floor. "Who are you? You aren't employed in this house."

"My name is Sherlock Holmes. I'm acting for your father and step-mother to stop you from committing murder."

Cullen snorted unexpectedly. "I can guess the rest. And I imagine this must be the renowned Dr. Watson? How bitterly ironic! My plotting was inspired by the tales of your adventures. It seems that my literary heroes have sought to outfox me – probably with the help of that half-witted gardener."

There was no doubting that the tall, eloquent, and evidently well-read, young man stood before us was Henry Cullen's son. The angry expression had disappeared, replaced by a boyish smirk.

"Of course, you have rather placed the cart before the horse, Mr. Holmes. If you hope to have me arrested for attempted murder, I will of course deny that that was my intention. Having stopped me at this point, there is no evidence to prove that I had anything more than burglary in mind."

He was wholly unaware that someone else had entered the kitchen behind him. When Henry Cullen spoke, the young man was startled and turned quickly to face his father.

"You will not be arrested, Charles. Having seen to it that you were incarcerated for the first twenty-one years of your life, I'm not prepared to see you languish in a prison cell for the remainder of your days. I blame myself for all that has happened, and can understand why you feel such contempt for me."

It was a heartfelt admission which was met with a cold and vicious response. "Don't you dare patronise me! Not now, not ever! I would rather dance at the end of a hangman's noose than acknowledge your paternity. All I wanted was your money, which I understand you would rather leave to a scar-faced harridan – "

There was to be no rapprochement beyond this episode. While the young footman was to face no charges for his conduct that night, he returned to his place of employment vowing never to speak to his father again. Eric Rayner was dismissed the next day and warned about ever returning to Arlington Street. And while Mr. and Mrs. Cullen were grateful for what Holmes and I had done, they could not hide their deep distress at the events which had unfolded that night.

Mrs. Eugenia Cullen continued to send short notes and Christmas cards to Holmes and me for some years after this. As a writer, her romantic stories had brought her some small fame, although she shunned public attention. With the passing of her husband in the spring of 1903, she once again became something of a recluse, refusing to leave the house and relying on the support of her loyal household staff. When she eventually died in June 1908, she ensured that all of them were well provided for. A small obituary in *The Times* marked her departure and described her broader legacy. The whole of her estate, then estimated to be worth around £350,000, was to be left to a charity which housed and cared for injured, sick, and aged circus animals.

The League of
Unhappy Orphans
by Leslie Charteris and Denis Green

Sherlock Holmes and The Saint
An Introduction by Ian Dickerson

Everyone has a story to tell about how they first met Sherlock Holmes. For me it was a Penguin paperback reprint my brother introduced me to in my pre-teen years. I read it, and went on to read all the original stories, but it didn't appeal to me in the way it appealed to others. This is probably because I discovered the adventures of The Saint long before I discovered Sherlock Holmes.

The Saint, for those readers who may need a little more education, was also known as Simon Templar and was a modern day Robin Hood who first appeared in 1928. Not unlike Holmes, he has appeared in books, films, TV shows, and comics. He was created by Leslie Charteris, a young man born in Singapore to a Chinese father and an English mother, who was just twenty years old when he wrote that first Saint adventure. He'd always wanted to be a writer – his first piece was published when he was just nine years of age – and he followed that Saint story, his third novel, with two further books, neither of which featured Simon Templar.

However, there's a notable similarity between the heroes of his early novels, and Charteris, recognising this, and being somewhat fed up of creating variations on the same theme, returned to writing adventures for The Saint. Short stories for a weekly magazine, *The Thriller*, and a change of publisher to the mainstream Hodder & Stoughton, helped him on his way to becoming a best-seller and something of a pop culture sensation in Great Britain.

But he was ambitious. Always fond of the USA, he started to spend more time over there, and it was the 1935 novel – and fifteenth Saint book – *The Saint in New York*, that made him a transatlantic success. He spent some time in Hollywood, writing for the movies and keeping an eye on The Saint films that were then in production at RKO studios. Whilst there, he struck up what would become a lifelong friendship with Denis Green, a British actor and writer, and his new wife, Mary.

Fast forward a couple of years . . . . Leslie was on the west coast of the States, still writing Saint stories to pay the bills, writing the occasional non-Saint piece for magazines, and getting increasingly frustrated with RKO who, he felt, weren't doing him, or his creation, justice. Denis Green, meanwhile, had established himself as a stage actor, and had embarked on a promising radio career both in front of and behind the microphone.

Charteris was also interested in radio. He had a belief that his creation could be adapted for every medium and was determined to try and prove it. In 1940, he commissioned a pilot programme to show how The Saint would work on radio, casting his friend Denis Green as Simon Templar. Unfortunately, it didn't sell, but just three years later, he tried again, commissioning a number of writers – including Green – to create or adapt Saint adventures for radio.

They also didn't sell, and after struggling to find a network or sponsor for The Saint on the radio, he handed the problem over to established radio show packager and producer, James L. Saphier. Charteris was able to solve one problem, however: At the behest of advertising agency Young & Rubicam, who represented the show's sponsors, Petri Wine, Denis Green had been sounded out about writing for *The New Adventures of Sherlock Holmes*, a weekly radio series that was then broadcasting on the Mutual Network.

Green confessed to his friend that, whilst he could write good radio dialogue, he simply hadn't a clue about plotting. He was, as his wife would later recall, a reluctant writer: "He didn't really like to write. He would wait until the last minute. He would put it off as long as possible by scrubbing the kitchen stove or wash the bathroom – anything before he sat down at the typewriter. I had a very clean house." Charteris offered a solution: They would go into partnership, with him creating the stories and Green writing the dialogue.

But there was another problem: *The New Adventures of Sherlock Holmes* aired on one of the radio networks that Leslie hoped might be interested in the adventures of The Saint, and it would not look good, he thought, for him to be involved with a rival production. Leslie adopted the pseudonym of *Bruce Taylor*, (as you will see at the end of the following script,) taking inspiration taking inspiration from the surname of the show's producer Glenhall Taylor and that of Rathbone's co-star, Nigel Bruce.

The Taylor/Green partnership was initiated with "The Strange Case of the Aluminum Crutch", which aired on July 24th, 1944, and would ultimately run until the following March, with *Bruce Taylor*'s final contribution to the Holmes Canon being "The Secret of Stonehenge", which aired on March 19th, 1945 – thirty-five episodes in all.

Bruce Taylor's short radio career came to an end in short because Charteris shifted his focus elsewhere. Thanks to Saphier, The Saint found a home on the NBC airwaves, and aside from the constant demand for literary Saint adventures, he was exploring the possibilities of launching a Saint magazine. He was replaced by noted writer and critic Anthony Boucher, who would establish a very successful writing partnership with Denis Green.

Fast forward quite a few more years – to 1988 to be precise: A young chap called Dickerson, a long standing member of *The Saint Club*, discovers a new TV series of The Saint is going into production. Suitably inspired, he writes to the then-secretary of the Club, suggesting that it was time the world was reminded of The Saint, and The Saint Club in particular. Unbeknownst to him, the secretary passes his letter on to Leslie Charteris himself. The teenaged Dickerson and the aging author struck up a friendship which involved, amongst other things, many fine lunches, followed by lazy chats over various libations. Some of those conversations featured the words "Sherlock" and "Holmes".

It was when Leslie died, in 1993, that I really got to know his widow, Audrey. We often spoke at length about many things, and from time to time discussed Leslie and the Holmes scripts, as well as her own career as an actress.

When she died in 2014, Leslie's family asked me to go through their flat in Dublin. Pretty much the first thing I found was a stack of radio scripts, many of which had been written by *Bruce Taylor* and Denis Green.

I was, needless to say, rather delighted. More so when his family gave me permission to get them into print. Back in the 1940's, no one foresaw an afterlife for shows such as this, and no recordings exist of this particular Sherlock Holmes adventure. So here you have the only documentation around of Charteris and Green's "The League of Unhappy Orphans" . . . .

Ian Dickerson

The League of Unhappy Orphans

Originally Broadcast on October 23rd, 1944

CHARACTERS
- SHERLOCK HOLMES
- DR. JOHN H. WATSON
- INSPECTOR LESTRADE
- DONALD GRANT
- HAROLD LATIMER
- MRS. LATIMER
- JACK
- POLICEMAN

Tonight's story was suggested by an incident in the Sir Arthur Conan Doyle story, "The Naval Treaty"

BILL FORMAN (ANNOUNCER): Petri Wine brings you –

MUSIC: THEME – FADE ON CUE:

FORMAN: Basil Rathbone and Nigel Bruce in *The New Adventures of Sherlock Holmes*.

MUSIC: THEME – FULL FINISH

OPENING COMMERCIAL

FORMAN: The Petri family – the family that took time to bring you good wine – invites you to listen to Doctor Watson tell us about another exciting adventure he shared with the world's most famous detective, Sherlock Holmes. And *I'd* like to tell you about one of the world's most famous wines – port wine. You've heard of port wine, of course, but you really don't *know* about port wine until you've tried a *Petri* California Port. Petri Port is a deep red in color. It's full-bodied, rich. As that Petri Port gurgles from the bottle into your glass you can smell its fragrance – the fragrance of plump luscious grapes. And as you sip it – you know that the flavor of Petri port comes right from the heart of those grapes. In my opinion, you've never tasted a more delicious wine. Try that Petri Port some evening right after dinner, or serve it later in the evening – with cheese and crackers, with fruit, or

298

by itself. The very fact that you serve a Petri Port establishes you immediately as a person who knows. Yes, and you can serve that Petri Port proudly. . . . because that name "*Petri*" on the label is the proudest name in the history of American Wines.

MUSIC: *SCOTCH POEM*

FORMAN: And now, once again, we find ourselves on the patio of Doctor Watson's California ranch house. Good evening, Doctor.

WATSON: Evening, Mr. Forman.

FORMAN I'm glad to see you home again, Doctor. We certainly missed you last week.

WATSON: Thank you, Mr. Forman, though I must say you did a splendid job without me, young fella me lad, splendid. That's why I telephoned you from Canada.

FORMAN: It was good to hear your voice, although I must say it sounded a little incongruous to hear the operator say, "Doctor Watson calling – Long distance."

WATSON: And why did that seem incongruous, Mr. Forman?

FORMAN: Well after all, Doctor, one hardly associates a telephone with Baker Street.

WATSON: Why not? We had one.

FORMAN: Really? I never knew that.

WATSON: Oh yes . . . and in the adventure I'm going to tell you tonight, the telephone plays an important part.

FORMAN: I know the address was 221b Baker Street, but what was your telephone number, Doctor?

WATSON: It was an unlisted number, Mr. Forman. (CHUCKLING) But I suppose it'll be safe to give it out after all these years. It was Paddington 1234. I confess I was rather against the instrument when Holmes had it installed in 1903. As a matter of interest, he was one of the very first subscribers when the London Post Office took over the service. But to get on with my story: On the morning our adventure started, I came down to breakfast rather later than usual. I'd been out on an urgent case in the middle of the night, and in consequence I'm afraid I wasn't in the best of tempers. Holmes was seated at his side-table, clad in his dressing gown, working hard over a chemical experiment. A large curved retort was boiling furiously in the blueish flame of a Bunsen burner. I was just cracking my second boiled (FADING) egg when the great man spoke . . . .

HOLMES: You entered at a crisis, Watson. Had this litmus paper remained blue, all would have been well. As you see, it is red – that means a man's life.

WATSON: I didn't know you were working on a case, Holmes.

HOLMES: My connection with it now ceases. I shall forward my findings to Inspector Lestrade and forget the case as speedily as possible. By the way, old fellow, why are you in such a shocking temper this morning?

WATSON: I wasn't aware that I'd given any indication of my mood.

HOLMES: (INTERRUPTING) Oh, come now, Watson. On normal mornings, you are quite an artist with a boiled egg. This morning you positively assaulted it with your spoon. And you were very testy with Mrs. Hudson.

WATSON: Well, if you must know, I was up half the night with a patient. That wretched telephone you insisted on having is a curse to a doctor. Can't even get a decent night's rest any more.

HOLMES: You're an incurable die-hard. I predict that the telephone will prove an invaluable adjunct in your profession.

SOUND EFFECT: PHONE RINGS

HOLMES: (FADING A LITTLE) Talk of the devil.

SOUND EFFECT: RECEIVER BEING UNHOOKED

HOLMES: (OFF A LITTLE) Hello . . . hello? Doctor Watson? Yes. Just a moment . . . (COMING ON) For you, old fellow.

WATSON: (GRUMBLING) A man hasn't got any privacy any more. (INTO PHONE) Yes, who is it? Who? . . . Speak a little louder, will you . . . Nurse Bramber . . . yes. She is? . . . Splendid. Then there's no need for me to come? . . . Good . . . And the temperature? . . . . Pulse? . . . Good, then I'll see her tomorrow.

SOUND EFFECT: RECEIVER BEING REPLACED

HOLMES: An example, I think, of where the telephone saved you a journey, Watson?

WATSON: (GRUDGINGLY) Yes, I must admit it did. But if we hadn't had the machine installed, I wouldn't have been routed out of bed in the middle of the night.

SOUND EFFECT: DOOR BELL RING (OFF)

WATSON: I wonder who that can be?

HOLMES: Probably Mr. Donald Grant.

WATSON: Donald Grant? Who's he?

HOLMES: I received this letter from him in the morning post.

SOUND EFFECT: CRACKLE OF PAPER

WATSON: Hmm (AFTER A MOMENT. READING) "*I propose to call on you at eleven-thirty tomorrow morning on a matter of the gravest importance. Donald Grant.*" And it's headed the Charing Cross Hotel. Sounds as if he's a visitor to London.

HOLMES: You are assuming that no person would stay at a railway hotel unless they were out-of-towners, I suppose?

WATSON: Exactly.

HOLMES: A reasonable deduction . . . .

301

SOUND EFFECT: KNOCK ON DOOR

HOLMES: Come in, come in.

SOUND EFFECT: DOOR OPEN

HOLMES: Mr. Donald Grant, I presume?

GRANT: (JOVIAL, MIDDLE-AGED, SCOTCH ACCENT) (FADING IN) Yes, sir. You are Mr. Sherlock Holmes.

HOLMES: Yes, and this is my friend and colleague, Doctor Watson.

GRANT: Colleague? Then I can talk freely in front of him?

HOLMES: Absolutely. Sit down, won't you.

GRANT: Thank you. (AFTER A MOMENT) Up in Greenock, where I come from, I've heard quite a bit of talk about you, Mr. Holmes.

HOLMES: Nothing derogatory, I trust?

WATSON: Holmes, don't fish for compliments. Would Mr. Grant be here if he'd heard anything but good about you?

HOLMES: Supposing you tell us your problem, sir?

GRANT: Look, Mr. Holmes, I'm a business man, and before I engage you on this case, I'd like to have some idea of your charges.

WATSON: (OUTRAGED) Well, really, sir! Mr. Holmes is not in the habit of haggling over money.

HOLMES: My dear Watson. Mr. Grant is a business man, and I am in business. He's perfectly entitled to ask my fee. Tell me the services you desire of me, Mr. Grant and I'll name it. If it's too steep for you, go elsewhere and no harm done. How's that?

GRANT: That's the way I like to do business – fair and straight from the shoulder, Well, gentleman, Here's my story: I've spent most of my life as a mining engineer, apprenticed in Glasgow, but practicing all over the world. South America, Alaska, Australia, are as much home

302

to me as Greenock. My last venture was in French West Africa, where I contracted a bad case of blackwater fever.

WATSON: Blackwater fever? You're lucky to be alive, Mr. Grant. Almost invariably a fatal disease. I remember Doctor McCutcheon telling me –

HOLMES: Yes, Watson, but Mr. Grant luckily is alive, so I suggest we let him finish his story.

WATSON: (HURT) I was only trying to explain just what blackwater fever is.

HOLMES: I doubt if Mr. Grant needs reminding. Please continue, sir.

GRANT: During all my years abroad, I was in partnership with a man by the name of George Colman – a splendid man, and it was a very happy and profitable association for me. When my health failed ten years ago, and I was forced to return to Scotland, I sold my interest in the partnership back to Colman. Two years ago, he himself died of the same fever.

WATSON: You see, Holmes? Almost invariably fatal.

GRANT: Colman had a daughter, Pamela, and after I retired, he sent her to England to be educated, and she became largely my care. Her mother died many years ago, and on her father's death, she became my ward under the terms of his will.

HOLMES: I see. Is she living with you now?

GRANT: She was – until a month ago – when she ran away with a young fella by the name of Harold Latimer. Mr. Holmes, I must find her. That's why I've come to you.

WATSON: Why did she run away, Mr. Grant?

GRANT: Oh, it's a simple-enough story. He was apprenticed to me. I've been operating in Greenock as a consulting engineer since my return. Pamela was living with me happily enough until young Latimer came on the scene six months ago.

HOLMES: You didn't like the boy, I take it?

GRANT: I'd nothing against him personally – then. He was industrious and quick to learn, but it took me some weeks to realize the reason he used to come to my house to study at nights was to gain the opportunity of being near Pamela.

WATSON: And you disapproved of his attentions, I suppose?

GRANT: Yes, I did, Doctor Watson. Pamela's only twenty, and she could have made an excellent match for herself. Her father left her a very comfortable fortune, and I felt she shouldn't rush into marriage with a youngster earning thirty shillings a week.

HOLMES: Marriage was mentioned then?

GRANT: I didn't give them much of an opportunity. I forbade Latimer to see her again.

HOLMES: Hmm. And that precipitated their flight, I suppose?

GRANT: Yes, Mr. Holmes. One day I found a note from her saying she had run away with him. That upset me greatly, but you can imagine my feelings when I discovered my safe had been broken open and several valuable bonds had been stolen.

WATSON: And you suspect young Latimer of stealing them?

GRANT: No doubt about that. As a matter of fact, only a few nights before, we were discussing the mechanism of safe locks, and fool that I was, I demonstrated with my own safe. Obviously, he memorized the combination.

HOLMES: Who do these bonds belong to?

GRANT: At the moment, to the Colman estate. They would come to Pamela on her twenty-first birthday.

HOLMES: And when will that be?

GRANT: In two weeks' time.

HOLMES: Exactly what bonds were they?

GRANT: Stock in Colman's French West African Mining Concession.

HOLMES: Negotiable stock?

GRANT: Negotiable in two weeks when Pamela comes of age. Of course, you can see the young scoundrel's plan. He's keeping her prisoner until she's twenty-one. Then he'll marry her and cash in on the stock. Mr. Holmes, you've got to find them for me.

HOLMES: Mr. Grant, why didn't you report your loss to the police?

GRANT: I don't want public scandal to touch my old friend's daughter. After all, the theft must have been committed with her connivance.

WATSON: Have you any idea where the couple is now?

GRANT: I know they're in London.

HOLMES: How do you know that?

GRANT: Well, sir, ever since her disappearance, I have been running advertisements in the personal columns of all the prominent papers in the country. Several weeks ago, I received a letter from Pamela, telling me that she had no intention of returning.

HOLMES: And the postmark on the letter?

GRANT: London. So of course, since my arrival, I've been walking the streets searching for them – a hopeless task, you might think. But yesterday I saw them.

HOLMES: You saw them? Where?

GRANT: I was walking along Tottenham Court Road when I saw Harold Latimer striding along ahead of me. I followed him for quite some time until finally he went into quite a shabby-looking lodging house in Gordon Square.

WATSON: What did you do then?

305

GRANT: After he had gone in, I looked the house over . . . .

SOUND EFFECT: HEAVY KNOCKING ON DOOR

GRANT: (CALLING) Open up! Come on, can't you? Open this door!

SOUND EFFECT: MORE HAMMERING ON DOOR

GRANT: (SHOUTING) Let me in!

SOUND EFFECT: DOOR OPENING

WOMAN: (FADING IN) (MIDDLE AGED, MIDDLE-CLASS, MIDDLE ACCENT) Don't have to knock the door down, do you? What d'you want?

GRANT: I want to see Miss Colman . . . and Mr. Latimer.

WOMAN: .Well there's' no one here by that name.

GRANT: There is! I just saw Latimer come in this house, and I saw Miss Colman at that window there.

WOMAN: Are you sure you're quite right in the head?

GRANT: (EXPLODING) Of course I'm right in the head!

WOMAN: Then you ought to have your eyes examined, because there's no one here by those names, and that front room you just pointed to has been empty for a week.

GRANT: You're lying!

WOMAN: (BRIDLING) Don't you speak to me like that! I'm a respectable woman and I run a respectable boarding house, and I tell you there's no one here by those names, so be off with you!

SOUND EFFECT: FRONT DOOR BEING SLAMMED

GRANT: (FURIOUSLY) Well, of all the . . . .

GRANT: (SHOUTING) You come back here! You're trying to hide them! Let me in or I'll call a policeman . . . .

SOUND EFFECT: MORE BATTERING ON DOOR

POLICEMAN: Well, what do you say to that, missis?

WOMAN: (OBSTINATELY) I say they're not here.

POLICEMAN: That's easily settled. Let's take a look.

WOMAN: You can't search my house without a warrant.

POLICEMAN: Won't take me long to get one. What you got to hide anyway?

WOMAN: All right. Come in. First time I've let police inside my house. I'm very particular about my lodgers. Always have been, and that's why I've never had any trouble.

SOUND EFFECT: FOOTSTEPS. DOOR OPEN

WOMAN: There now! Perhaps you'll believe me – the room's not occupied.

SOUND EFFECT: FOOTSTEPS STOP

POLICEMAN: Looks as if you was seein' things, mister.

GRANT: (OFF A LITTLE) Nonsense. Look over here . . . a kettle still boiling on the gas ring, plates and cups all ready for tea. It's obvious – you covered up for them while they made their escape through the back door. What have you got to say to that?

WOMAN: (SULLENLY) What if I did? The paid their rent regular and told me they didn't want to be disturbed. Sweet young couple as you'd find in a month of Sundays. When this man came knocking on the door, they told me to keep him waiting until they got out the back

307

door. Why shouldn't I try and help them? (FADING) You'd have done the same yourself, Constable.

GRANT: And that's how they escaped me, Mr. Holmes. They slipped out the back way while that wretched woman was delaying me at the front.

HOLMES: What was the address of this boarding house?

GRANT: 47 Gordon Square.

HOLMES: Thank you, Mr. Grant. I accept your case.

GRANT: And your fee?

HOLMES: Fifty guineas if I succeed in finding them.

GRANT: That seems a little steep, Mr. Holmes.

HOLMES: Nothing if I fail.

GRANT: All right, I'll pay it. Now, what d'you want me to do first?

HOLMES: Go back to y our hotel and wait until you hear from me. Good day, sir, and I hope that before many hours, I may have news for you.

WATSON: Good-bye, Mr. Grant.

GRANT: (Fading) Thank you, gentlemen, and I shall hope to hear from you soon.

SOUND EFFECT: DOOR CLOSES

WATSON: Doesn't seem a very interesting case, Holmes. I'm surprised you accepted it.

HOLMES: On the contrary, I find some peculiarly intriguing angles to it. Now, dear fellow, I have some work for you to do. I want you to get in touch with the Baker Street Irregulars.

WATSON: That band of street urchins?

HOLMES: Yes.

WATSON: How can they help you in this case?

HOLMES: The young couple left their lodgings at a few seconds notice yesterday. They must have some baggage – therefore they must have taken a cab. Tell the boys to find out the cabbie who drove a young couple from somewhere near 47 Gordon Square, and bring him to me, Pay the boys their usual shilling a piece, of course. Then send this telegram to our friend Dubois in Paris.

WATSON: Where does Dubois fit into the picture?

HOLMES: The Colman mining interests are in French West Africa. I want further information on the subject. Here's the telegram.

WATSON: Very well, Holmes. (FADING) I still don't understand your interest in this case.

HOLMES: (TO HIMSELF) Dear old Watson. He's so delightfully –

SOUND EFFECT: TELEPHONE RINGS, RECEIVER BEING LIFTED

HOLMES: (AFTER A MOMENT) Hello ?

WOMAN'S VOICE: (ON FILTER) (SINISTER) Paddington One – two – three – four? Sherlock Holmes?

HOLMES: Yes.

VOICE: Mr. Holmes? Mr. Sherlock Holmes?

HOLMES: Speaking. What can I do for you?

VOICE: You are trying to find Pamela Colman and Harold Latimer. If you value your life, drop the case. Drop it at once.

HOLMES: Who is this speaking? Who are you?

VOICE: Someone who does not wish to see you die.

HOLMES: Tell me who's speaking.

309

VOICE: I am speaking for all of us. For the League.

HOLMES: The league? What league?

VOICE: Only the most powerful league in the world and also one of the most dangerous – The League of Unhappy Orphans!

MUSIC: UP STRONG AND INTO:

FORMAN: Doctor Watson's story will continue in just a few seconds . . . and I'd like to take those few seconds, if you don't mind, to tell you about another famous after-dinner wine . . . Petri California Muscatel. Petri Muscatel is a rich ember wine that's just perfect served after your dessert, or for that matter, in *place* of a dessert. That's because Petri Muscatel has captured the wonderful flavor of muscat grapes – and you know how delicious they are! Women particularly like the flavor of Petri Muscatel . . . which makes it an ideal wine to serve when friends drop in in the afternoon . . . or later in the evening. If you'll just try a Petri Muscatel, I'm sure it will strengthen your conviction that the best wines you ever tested are *Petri* Wines!

MUSIC: *SCOTCH POEM*

FORMAN: And now, back to tonight's new Sherlock Holmes adventure. Mr. Donald Grant has invoked the aid of the great detective in finding his ward, Pamela Colman, who has run away with Harold Latimer – a flight that was accompanied by the theft of some valuable bonds. Almost immediately after Holmes had accepted the case, he received a strange and threatening telephone call. As we rejoin our story, it is several hours later, and Holmes is receiving a report from a young street urchin – a member of his band of unofficial helpers, (FADING) The Baker Street Irregulars . . . .

HOLMES: Well, Jack, were you able to locate the cab driver who picked up the young couple as they left Gordon Square earlier today?

JACK: (COCKNEY) Yes sir, Mr. 'Olmes. We found 'im.

HOLMES: Splendid, Jack. Where did he drive them to?

JACK: He picks up the couple on the corner of Gordon Square and Gower Street. Carrying a couple of bags, they were, and seemed all sort of flustered like, the cabbie said.

HOLMES: That's undoubtedly the same pair. Go on.

JACK: They tell him to drive to Bayswater. They didn't go to a house there. Just 'ad him drop 'em on the corner of Kensington Garden Square and Clark Street. He left 'em there, standing on the pavement with their bags beside 'em.

HOLMES: Hmm. We can presume they were within walking distance of their present lodgings. Where's the cabbie now, Jack?

JACK: Right outside, sir. He drove a bunch of us 'ere. Want me to bring 'im up?

HOLMES: No, Jack. I want you to go back to the cabbie and tell him to drive you to the exact spot where he left the young couple earlier. He can wait for you boys while you explore every house nearby, until you get news of the pair. When you do, jump in the cab, come back here, and report to me. Understood, Jack?

JACK: (FADING) Right, sir.

HOLMES: And Jack . . . .

JACK: (FADING BACK) Yes, sir?

HOLMES: I suppose it's possible the boys may be hungry after the trip?

JACK: (LAUGHING) Not 'alf they won't, sir.

HOLMES: Then Mrs. Hudson will have a meal ready for you all when you return.

JACK: Coo . . . Thank you, Mr. 'Olmes.

SOUND EFFECT: DOOR OPEN

WATSON: (FADING IN) Holmes, here's a telegram for you. Just arrived. Hello, Jack.

311

JACK: 'Ello, Doctor Watson. (FADING) I'll be going, sir.

HOLMES: (CALLING) Good luck, Jack.

JACK: (OFF) Thank you, sir. . . and don't worry. We'll find 'im.

SOUND EFFECT: DOOR CLOSE. CRACKLE OF PAPER

WATSON: Did the Baker Street Irregulars find any trace of the missing couple?

HOLMES: Yes, they found the cabbie who drove them, and now . . . . (EXCLAIMING) Splendid! Splendid!

WATSON: What's splendid? Who's your telegram from?

HOLMES: Our friend Monsieur Dubois, in Paris. It throws a very interesting light on our case.

SOUND EFFECT: TELEPHONE RINGS

WATSON: (FADING A LITTLE) I only hope that isn't a call for me.

SOUND EFFECT: RECEIVER BEING LIFTED

HOLMES: (AFTER A MOMENT – ON TELEPHONE) Hello?

WOMAN: Sherlock Holmes?

HOLMES: Speaking.

WOMAN: This is your last warning. Stop trying to find Pamela Colman and Harold Latimer if you value your life.

HOLMES: Now look, madam –

WOMAN: There is nothing more to be said. You have received your last warning from The League of Unhappy Orphans.

MUSIC: BRIDGE

312

HOLMES: Well, Jack, what luck this time? You've been gone nearly four hours.

JACK: (EXCITEDLY) I found 'em, Mr. 'Olmes. Took me four hours, but I found 'em myself.

WATSON: You did? Good boy!

HOLMES: Splendid, Jack.

JACK: They're at 17 Kensington Garden Square. First floor front. We all of us started off on the Square, and I struck lucky, the eleventh house I tried.

HOLMES: As a matter of interest, Jack, what was your method of approach?

JACK: (BEWILDERED) Method of . . . .

WATSON: (LAUGHING) Mr. Holmes means . . . how did you get your information?

JACK: (COMPREHENDING) Oh. I just gave 'em the tale. Said I was looking for my poor old mum. That she'd left me, an' I know she'd moved somewhere round there. When I got to the eleventh house, the old girl said no one that sounded like my mum had come along, but there was a young couple had just moved in. So I asks their name – just to be sure – an' she ups and says Miss Colman and Mr. Latimer. Just the names you give me.

HOLMES: Very enterprising of you, Jack. You're a smart boy. Here's five shillings for you.

JACK: Coo! Thanks, guv'nor.

HOLMES: And now, go downstairs and get the rest of the boys. Mrs. Hudson has that spread waiting for you.

JACK: I'll get the boys . . . but I couldn't eat a thing, Mr. 'Olmes.

WATSON: Why, Jack, that's very unlike you. What's wrong?

JACK: Nothing's wrong, Doctor. It's just that every 'ouse I go to, the old girl's make me 'ave something to eat. Said I looked kind-of thin.

WATSON: (LAUGHING) Then you'll just have to watch the others tuck in.

JACK: (FADING) Yes, Doctor.

SOUND EFFECT: DOOR OPENS

JACK: (OFF) Oh . . . beg your pardon, sir.

WATSON: Hello, Mr. Grant.

GRANT: (FADING IN) I'm sorry to interrupt you, Mr. Holmes, but I got so restless waiting at my hotel. I just had to come 'round and see how things are going.

HOLMES: You arrive at a most propitious moment, Mr. Grant. The missing couple have been found.

GRANT: They're found? Wonderful. Where are they?

HOLMES: 17 Kensington Garden Square, Bayswater. First floor front.

GRANT: (EXCITEDLY) Mr. Holmes . . . everything I heard about you is true. I'm most grateful . . . Have you a pen?

WATSON: On the desk there.

GRANT: (FADING A LITTLE) I'll write you my cheque for fifty guineas.

SOUND EFFECT: SCRATCHING OF PEN

HOLMES: No need for that, Mr. Grant, until you have verified my information.

GRANT: I have implicit faith in you, Mr. Holmes.

HOLMES: I would suggest that we come with you, though. I like to see my cases through to their logical end.

314

GRANT: I appreciate that, Mr. Holmes. But in this case, I'm perfectly capable of taking care of that ruffian myself. In fact, I'd prefer to be alone. It's going to be a rather embarrassing business. Here's your cheque.

HOLMES: Thank you, Mr. Grant. Well . . . Good day, sir.

WATSON: Good day.

GRANT: Good-bye, gentlemen, and my heartfelt thanks. (FADING) I shall spread your fame even more in Greenock.

SOUND EFFECT: DOOR CLOSE

WATSON: (LAUGHING) That's the easiest fee I've ever seen you earn, Holmes. Why, you haven't even left this room.

HOLMES: No, but we're leaving it now, Grab your hat and coat, old fellow.

WATSON: But where are we going? The case is finished.

HOLMES: Oh no it isn't! We're going to Scotland Yard to pick up Lestrade, and then the three of us will pay a visit to 17 Kensington Gardens Square.

MUSIC: BRIDGE

SOUND EFFECT: KNOCKING ON DOOR, REPEATED AFTER A MOMENT

WATSON: Gloomy looking house, I must say.

HOLMES: Yes. I wonder why nobody answers this door.

LESTRADE: Probably because there's nobody there. It looks to me, Mr. Holmes, as if you're wasting my time.

HOLMES: I assure you I'm not, Lestrade. Just have a little patience.

SOUND EFFECT: KNOCKING ON DOOR

315

WATSON: (AFTER A MOMENT) Hello . . . . there's Grant . . . coming 'round from the back of the house.

HOLMES: (RAISING HIS VOICE) Good evening, Mr. Grant.

GRANT: (FADING IN. SURPRISED) Mr. Holmes, I didn't expect to find you here.

HOLMES: I'm very conscientious. I just wanted to make sure I'd earned my fee. Have you found the couple?

GRANT: No, I can't get any answer. They must be out. Why don't you come back to my hotel and we can all try again later? Your friend also. I don't know what his name is . . . ?

HOLMES: Allow me to introduce you. This is –

WATSON: (SUDDENLY) Holmes! Look! That window. There is smoke coming out of it!

LESTRADE: Good Lord! The house is on fire!

HOLMES: Quick, Watson! Your shoulder to this door –

SOUND EFFECT: HEAVY BLOWS ON DOOR, FOLLOWED BY SPLINTERING WOODWORK

HOLMES: Go on in, Watson! Lestrade – remember the instructions I have given you. Drastic measures if necessary. Keep your eyes peeled, and don't let anyone in – or out!

LESTRADE: Right, Mr. Holmes.

SOUND EFFECT: RUNNING FOOTSTEPS ON STAIRS

WATSON: (AFTER A MOMENT. PANTING WITH EXERTION) This smoke . . . it's suffocating . . . .

HOLMES: One more door . . . Come on . . . .

SOUND EFFECT: SPLINTERING OF WOODWORK

HOLMES: That's it . . . .

SOUND EFFECT: FOOTSTEPS STOP. FAINT CRACKLE OF FLAMES

WATSON: Good Lord! Those curtains – they're blazing!

HOLMES: I'll get them down. Grab a blanket off the bed, will you? Meanwhile . . . .

SOUND EFFECT: CURTAINS BEING RIPPED

WATSON: Careful, Holmes! Here's the blanket!

SOUND EFFECT: BLANKET BEING BEATEN ON FLOOR

HOLMES: That's it . . . and I think we'll add the water from this jug for good measure . . . .

SOUND EFFECT: JUG OF WATER BEING THROWN ON FLOOR. FAINT HISS OF WATER.

HOLMES: That does it, I think.

WATSON: Holmes, look – Through the smoke . . . Three people, bound and gagged on the sofa there – right next to the curtains!

HOLMES: Exactly. Here . . . let's untie them . . . the gag first. (AFTER A MOMENT) How are you, Mr. Harold Latimer?

LATIMER: (YOUNG) Where is he?

HOLMES: And now the legs . . . there. If you're looking for Mr. Grant, you'll find him at the front door, in the company of –

LATIMER: (FADING) Look after the women, will you –

WATSON: (CALLING) Latimer! Come back here!

HOLMES: I shouldn't worry about him, Watson. Meanwhile, help me untie the ladies . . . .

317

WATSON: That boy could get away! I'm going after him!

SOUND EFFECT: RUNNING FOOTSTEPS

WATSON: (AFTER A MOMENT. CALLING) Latimer! It's no good trying to run away! Lestrade! Get him!

GRANT: (FADING IN) Get away from me, you blackguard!

SOUND EFFECT: SCUFFLING

LESTRADE: Stop that! Stop it, d'you hear?

LATIMER: Just let me get my hands on him!

WATSON: Hold on to him, Lestrade!

SOUND EFFECT: HEAVIER SCUFFLING

GRANT: Get a policeman! He'll kill me!

LESTRADE: What d'you mean "get a policeman"? I'm a –

WATSON: Look out, Grant! He's got an arm free!

SOUND EFFECT: RESOUNDING CRACK ON JAW, FOLLOWED BY A GROAN AND FALLING BODY

WATSON: You infernal young scoundrel! Hitting a man three times your age!

LESTRADE: I have to warn you, young fella, that I'm a police officer, and you're committing assault and battery right under my very –

HOLMES: (FADING IN) Ah, I see you've taken care of Mr. Grant, Harold. I'm sorry I missed it. Watson, Lestrade. Stop struggling with Latimer.

WATSON: But he nearly killed poor Grant.

HOLMES: I shouldn't blame him if he completed the job.

318

WATSON: But . . . but . . . .

LATIMER: Are the women all right, Mr. Holmes?

HOLMES: Perfectly. A little flustered naturally. I suggest you go back and calm them.

LATIMER: I can't tell you how grateful I am for your saving us, Mr. Holmes.

HOLMES: Before you go, my dear boy, just two questions.

LATIMER: Yes, Mr. Holmes?

HOLMES: The papers you removed from the safe – they really contained the proof of Grant's intentions regarding the mining concession, didn't they?

LATIMER: That's right, Mr. Holmes – though I can't think how you knew it.

HOLMES: One other question: Why did your Mother call herself "The League of Unhappy Orphans" on the telephone?

LATIMER: (LAUGHING) That was Pamela's idea. I've often kidded her by calling her a poor little unhappy orphan.

HOLMES: (CHUCKLING) I see. Now run along, my boy. We'll join you in a few minutes.

LATIMER: (FADING) Very well, Mr. Holmes.

LESTRADE: Do you mind telling me what's going on, Mr. Holmes? I'm completely bewildered.

WATSON: So am I.

HOLMES: Now, Lestrade, you will have company on your way back to the Yard. The recumbent Mr. Grant there is guilty of arson and attempted murder.

LESTRADE: But what was his motive?

WATSON: Yes . . . and why did he come to you?

HOLMES: He came to me to find his victims for him. You see, the Colman mining concession expires in a few days, unless renewed by some member of the family – in other words, Pamela. My telegram from Dubois solicited this fact. Grant was planning to pick up the concession himself, and exploit it with a syndicate.

WATSON: And young Latimer discovered the plans?

HOLMES: Exactly. That's what he stole from the safe.

LESTRADE: I wish I knew what you gentlemen were talking about. It doesn't make any sense to me.

HOLMES: Let me clear up the matter for Watson first, Lestrade. You'll hear the whole story later, when I prefer charges. What bothers you, Watson?

WATSON: The other woman upstairs, tied up in that room – who's she?

HOLMES: Latimer's mother. She was chaperoning the couple until they got married. She, of course, was the supposed landlady in Gordon Square, as well as the sinister voice on the telephone. A versatile lady. I can't help feeling she could have been a magnificent actress.

WATSON: Buy why did she try and frighten you away with that Unhappy Orphan nonsense?

HOLMES: Because they know I was working for Grant, and naturally they didn't want me to discover them.

WATSON: Couldn't they have gone to the police?

LESTRADE: (SADLY) No one ever comes to us, Dr. Watson – not with anything interesting, they don't.

HOLMES: Never mind, Lestrade. You shall take the credit for this case.

WATSON: When did you first suspect Grant?

320

HOLMES: When he produced the theory that Latimer was a fortune-hunter. If the boy had been after an heiress, obviously he would have waited until Pamela became of age, and then married her legitimately.

LESTRADE: Sounds like a very unusual case to me, Mr. Holmes.

HOLMES: Unusual, my dear Lestrade? It's unique.

LESTRADE: Why?

HOLMES: It's the first time in my career that a crook has paid me fifty guineas to catch him!

MUSIC: UP STRONG TO FINISH.

FORMAN: Doctor, that was quite an eventful story. Did everything work out well between Mr. Latimer and Pamela?

WATSON: Oh yes. Pamela managed to renew her mining concession in time . . . and of course, she married Mr. Latimer.

FORMAN: Well, good for them.

WATSON: Mr. Forman, I can see that you like a happy ending to your stories. (CHUCKLES)

FORMAN: Yep . . . I'm a happy-ending man. I not only like happy endings to my stories, but I like happy endings to my meals, too.

WATSON: What do you mean?

FORMAN: Well, after a good dinner . . . I like a good glass of Petri California Port . . . that's a happy ending for *any* meal. But you ought to know – (LAUGH)

WATSON: Yes, I do.

FORMAN: And you know *why* Petri Port and *all* the Petri Wines taste so darned good. It's because the Petri Family has been making wine for generations. They know how. You see, the Petri family has been

321

making wine ever since they started the Petri business . . . way back in the eighteen-hundreds. And because the Petri family has always owned and operated the business . . . well, everything they've ever learned about the art of turning luscious grapes into delicious wine, they've been able to keep in the family . . . handing that skill and experience on down from father to son, from father to son. So it's no wonder that every drop of Petri wine is truly good wine. No matter what type of wine you prefer, you can never go wrong with a Petri Wine . . . because Petri took time to bring you good wine. . . . . And what story do you have up your sleeve for us next week, Doctor?

WATSON: A strange one, Mr. Forman. It takes place in a haunted chateau in the south of France. And its owner is the last kind of person you'd expect to find there.

FORMAN: Why, Doctor?

WATSON: Because in spite of the old world locale and the ancient atmosphere, she's what you Americans call . . . a pistol packing momma! Well, that's what you'll hear next week. Right now, if I may, I'd like to say a word to every young woman listening in. You young ladies know about the job our Navy is doing. That job isn't over yet by a long sight. I don't have to tell you about that, but have you ever really thought about personally helping to do that job? Have you tried to find out what it means to join the *WAVES*? Not only find out how much you're needed . . . but find out how much the *WAVES* can do for you? It's a wonderful career for a girl. You not only have the personal satisfaction that goes with helping to win this war . . . but you'll have fun, and excitement, and wonderful friends. If you're twenty to thirty-six years old, you have at least two years of high school, and no children under eighteen . . . why not drop in at your nearest Navy recruiting station, or write for *The Story of You in Navy Blue*. Write to *WAVES*, Washington, 25, D.C. Get the facts. You'll really be pleasantly surprised.

FORMAN: Tonight's Sherlock Holmes adventure is written by Denis Green and Bruce Taylor, and is based on an incident in the Sir Arthur Conan Doyle story "The Naval Treaty". Mr. Rathbone appears through the courtesy of Metro-Goldwyn-Mayer, and Mr. Bruce through the courtesy of Universal Pictures, where they are now starring in the *Sherlock Holmes* series.

MUSIC: THEME UP AND DOWN UNDER

FORMAN: (OUT) The Petri Wine Company of San Francisco, California invites you to tune in again next week, same time, same station.

MUSIC: HIT JINGLE

SINGERS: *Oh, the Petri family took the time, to bring you such good wine, so when you eat and when you cook, Remember Petri Wine!*

FORMAN: Yes, Petri Wine made by the Petri Vine Company, San Francisco, California.

SINGERS: *Pet – Pet – Petri . . . Wine.*

FORMAN: This is Bill Forman saying goodnight for the Petri family. *Sherlock Holmes* comes to you from the Don Lee studios in Hollywood. This is the Mutual Broadcasting Network!

The Adventure of the
Three Fables
by Jane Rubino

When I first set out to publish a few sketches designed to illustrate the singular talents of Sherlock Holmes, I had not anticipated how far I would have to withhold particular facts, or even entire cases, and often those facts and those cases which were most likely to satisfy the public's unbecoming appetite for sensation. Those appetites, I am sorry to say, were indulged by others, agents who bartered in gossip and secrets. These mercenary scoundrels were not deterred by honor or restraint, and their trade wasn't solely confined to their victims. At times, my reputation was a casualty as well, for in bringing to light what I had endeavored to keep in the dark, they cast a shade on my reputation by portraying me as an artful chronicler, one whose accounts must be viewed with doubt or disdain. Yet, when exposure might be the ruin of an exalted household, or lead to some grave political consequence, or place an innocent life in jeopardy, I was obliged to hold back, or to dissemble, or to wait until the passage of time allowed for some discreet revision or abolished all necessity for concealment.

So it was in the matter of Isadora Klein. And so, for the sake of my friend's reputation and my own – and because circumstances now leave me free to do so – I will put forth the hitherto unpublished sequel to her tale.

Many years before this problem came to Holmes's notice, the death of the aged Sugar King, Fredrick Klein, had left Isadora Klein a very young, very lovely, and very wealthy widow. Freed from confinement to her late husband's estate in Pernambuco, the lady returned to her native Spain for a time, and at last settled in London, where she directed her late husband's business interests from the finest house on Grosvenor Square and amused herself with a succession of young lovers

One of these paramours had been Douglas Maberley, the most handsome, engaging, high-spirited member of London's *beau monde*. His tempestuous affair with Mrs. Klein had so far outlasted the ones before it that he was persuaded she loved him and proposed – indeed, demanded – marriage. The lady's reply was to mock his presumption, inform him that their dalliance had come to an end, and discard him for wealthier and more illustrious prey.

Maberley refused to be cast aside, and continued to pursue Mrs. Klein so relentlessly that at last she took the extreme measure of retaining the notorious Spencer John gang to bring home to the lad once and for all that she was done with him. The gang called up a ruffian named Stockdale who, with one of his minions, seized Maberley as he attempted to force his way into Mrs. Klein's residence, beat him mercilessly beneath the lady's window, and then tossed him, bleeding, into the gutter. Crushed and degraded, the discarded lover crawled off to a minor government post in Italy to lick his wounds and plot his revenge. Alas, Maberley's injuries sent him into an irreversible decline, and upon his death-bed, he penned a scandalous *roman a clef* that rendered Mrs. Klein in a most sinister shade. One copy of this dark fable was sent to the lady herself and with it – so that she might feel the twist of the knife – a note stating that there was a second copy which would go to his publisher.

My introduction to the matter came a month after these events, with the dramatic entrance of Steve Dixie into the Baker Street sitting room. Dixie, another of Stockdale's minions, had been dispatched to warn Holmes against answering an appeal from Maberley's widowed mother. A fortnight after her return from Italy, where Mrs. Maberley had attended her son's death-bed and arranged for his remains to be returned to England, the lady had received a curious proposal: If she would part with her home, taking away nothing but her clothing and personal effects, she would be paid five-hundred pounds above what she had given for it. As chance would have it, the lady's late husband had been one of Holmes's early clients, and so it was to Holmes that she submitted this strange offer with a plea for his opinion and advice.

The party behind the offer was none other than Mrs. Klein. Fearing that the publication of Maberley's *exposé* would thwart an anticipated proposal of marriage from the young Duke of Lomond, Mrs. Klein set out to lay her hands on the second copy. When she discovered that it had not reached Maberley's publisher, she concluded that it must be among personal effects forwarded to his mother – hence the scheme to take possession of that lady's home and all of its contents. Had Holmes searched Maberley's trunks when he had interviewed his client, he would have turned up the manuscript. Had he even posted a guard or two inside the lady's home, he might have apprehended the ruffians sent by Mrs. Klein to recover it. But Holmes had done neither. Mrs. Klein got hold of the document which she promptly destroyed, and my demoralized friend could do no better than to exact a restitution of five-thousand pounds which he delivered to Mrs. Maberley, telling her only that "the responsible party deeply regrets the misadventure, and hopes that you will accept this compensation."

The poor lady seemed resigned to this imperfect resolution. "It had once been a dream of mine to travel 'round the world," she said. "I will wait until poor Douglas' coffin arrives from Italy, so that I may put him to rest in England, and after that – God knows, there is nothing more to keep me here." And then, she added, "I am sure that you did your best." It was not meant as a rebuke, but I daresay he felt its sting.

So ended the case. But only the first half of it.

Upon a cold morning some weeks after Mrs. Maberley's ordeal, I had finished a number of morning calls and with nothing to engage me until later in the day, I decided to stop at my old rooms at Baker Street. There, I found Holmes lounging upon the settee in his mouse-colored dressing gown, scraping his bow back and forth across the violin on his lap. For the past week, Mrs. Klein's engagement to the Duke of Lomond had eclipsed all other news, and I saw her lovely photograph looking up from the litter of newspapers scattered around the carpet.

"You are between cases, I see."

"I am. Have no fear, Doctor," he added, with a smile. "I will not revert to old habits. The years seem to have given me a better tolerance for *ennui*."

"Holmes, you could not have done better."

He laid aside his violin, gathered the papers into a great ball and pitched it into the grate. "I could not have done worse," he said.

A sharp peal at the bell cut short my reply. From below, we heard a muttered exchange and then a lumbering step upon the stair. "Well, here is something that may bring an end to your *ennui*."

"And something out of the common if it has thrown brother Mycroft from his orbit."

A moment later, the door swung open and the massive figure of Mycroft Holmes stepped into the room, working his way out of his overcoat as he made his way to the settee.

"It was badly done, Sherlock," he declared as he sat. "And see how I am put out as a result."

"I see that you are put out," said Holmes, as he settled into an armchair. "And that I am not your first call this morning."

Mycroft clasped his hands upon his girth and waited for his brother to continue.

"At this time of day," said Holmes, "you would have just arrived at Whitehall. Something has kept you from a routine that a fellow could set his watch upon. There was a summons and an urgent one – urgent enough for you to come directly from the lady to lay the matter before me."

"The lady?"

"The *noble* lady. Your rooms, your club, Whitehall – that is where a gentleman would have gone to consult with you. So you were summoned,

326

and by someone whose rank calls for the morning attire that you last donned – as I see from the strain upon your waistcoat – some eight pounds ago. So now, what was badly done?"

"The Maberley affair! Why did you not search the boy's luggage? Why did you leave his mother unprotected? What if those papers might have prevented the engagement!"

"Ah. It was the Dowager Duchess of Lomond, then?"

"She is beside herself."

"So would I be if a son of mine were to marry Mrs. Klein."

"But, Holmes," I protested, "you had said that her Grace did not object to the match."

"I believe that I said the duchess *might* not object to the difference in age – "

"Not object!" Mycroft gave a snort of disgust. "A firm upper lip to keep the scandalmongers at bay. She most strenuously objects, and not to the lady's colorful history alone. The Duke is an only child and scarcely twenty-two! Why choose a woman so much older? What if his marriage is childless? The next in line is her late husband's wastrel of a nephew!"

Holmes shrugged his shoulders. "At, I believe, thirty-eight, Mrs. Klein is – "

"Forty-one! A year younger than the duchess herself!"

"Still, forty-one does not necessarily exclude the prospect of an heir. In any case, the lady's age is immaterial, so long as the Duke is of age to marry where he likes. Clearly, he likes Mrs. Klein enough to overlook her seniority and her past. I am afraid that her Grace can do no better than to hope that the lady may either present her husband with an heir in a timely fashion, or to die in a timely fashion and leave him free to make a more fruitful match."

"The duchess does not take your flippant view of the matter. She is quite desperate."

"I confess that I'm surprised that you take any view of the matter at all, Mycroft. Society intrigues are outside of your field."

"But those that may have political consequences are not. There are appetites other than Mrs. Klein's taste in paramours. Universal appetites, and for a commodity over which Mrs. Klein exercises considerable control. She manages all of her late husband's interests, you know."

"The sugar trade," said Holmes.

"We English are the largest consumers of sugar in all the world! Think of it – table sugar, biscuits, jams, confections – "

"I don't need to think of it, Mycroft. I yield to your authority on the subject."

"England must satisfy an appetite for what she does not produce, and so is at the mercy of those who do. And for those who do, fickle nature dictates whether it will be feast or famine. In the governing of what makes its way to our table, there is more at stake in the sugar trade than in the commerce of butter or tea."

"And as the Duke is an M.P., and – young as he is – one who already seems destined for higher office – you believe that his wife may exercise influence over policy?"

"Why else would she single him out? Yes, Lomond is rich and clever, with an excellent pedigree, but if Mrs. Klein wanted nothing more than title and fortune, she might have had them long before this."

"I understand your apprehensions, Mycroft, but what can I do? The Duke has proposed marriage, the engagement has been announced and a wedding date is fixed. The Duke is a Roman Catholic, so there will be no divorce after they are married, and there can be no withdrawal of his offer beforehand without the risk of a very public suit for breach of promise. Surely, her Grace would not want *that* scandal splashed across those society papers."

"Those same papers report that, out of respect for the gentleman's Parliamentary obligations, there will be no wedding before October, four months from now," I added. "Given the lady's history, there is the chance that her caprice will run its course well before then, and *she* will break things off, or commit some indiscretion that would make a suit for breach the lesser of two scandals."

"I would not have dragged myself here this morning if the wedding was four months from now, Doctor. According to her Grace, her son informed her yesterday that Mrs. Klein has had a change of heart and wants to marry right away – as soon as it can be managed."

Holmes leaned forward in his chair, all trace of languor gone. "She wants to fix him immediately. What reason did she give?"

"None – at least none that the young man confided to her Grace. If your old nemesis Charles Milverton were alive – oh, do not attempt to disown your role in *that* matter, Sherlock. I am not Lestrade – I would be inclined toward blackmail – that she wants to hurry him to the altar before something comes forward that would allow for a retraction of the Duke's offer."

"Such as what? Letters? Photographs?" Holmes shook his head. "The Duke would never see them. She would have paid."

"She could not have paid off Maberley's publisher," Mycroft grumbled. "How could you have let her make off with the manuscript? You made a complete hash of the business, Sherlock!"

"Yes, I made a hash of it. Though, lately, I have wondered what it really was about his fable that alarmed her so?"

"Certainly, her numerous affairs – " I said.

"Pooh!" Holmes interrupted with a wave of his hand. "The Duke would have to be blind as a mole to be ignorant of them, and yet he offered her marriage."

"Maberley's vicious portrait of the lady herself."

"Mrs. Klein would persuade the Duke that this was merely the vindictive exaggeration of a rejected suitor. No, the facts – the lady's behavior – argue for something more damning. Think, Watson – the lady read the first manuscript, the one that Maberley sent her from Italy. If it contained no more than an inventory of her love affairs and a shade upon her character, why would she go to such lengths to get her hands on the second one? Why offer to buy Mrs. Maberley's home? Why enter a devil's bargain with the Spencer John gang who might as easily turn on her as do her bidding? Recall her words to us, Watson – that if Maberley's novel were published, it would be the ruin of her life's ambitions."

"But, surely, she has no reason to fear the ruin of her ambitions now. She destroyed both copies of the manuscript, and Douglas Maberley is dead. If there was a secret – well, that is dead as well."

"Secrets rarely die, Doctor," said Mycroft. "They just lie dormant. They wait. Whatever reason there may be for Mrs. Klein's desire to marry immediately – if it is something that may put an end to the match, you must root it out, it or I cannot answer for her Grace. She will do anything to have the engagement broken off, even something that is quite out of *her* field." He pushed himself up from the settee. "Come, Sherlock – use your powers! Maberley and Milverton were not the sole custodians of society's skeletons. Try that fellow Pike. He may have something useful."

"Very well," said Holmes. "What do you say, Watson – are you engaged this morning?"

"No, I have no calls until later this afternoon."

"Then allow me to introduce you to one of the queerest fellows in London."

"You did not meet the gentleman in the course of our first encounter with Mrs. Klein," said Holmes as our cab rattled toward the St. James Street Club. "But I daresay you know him by way of the morsels that make their way onto the scandal sheets. Odd as it may seem, he is like Mycroft, after a fashion – he has no energy at all, but possesses an amazing talent for gathering and cataloguing information. His *métier* is the social realm, rather than the political one. When I presented to Pike the strange offer made to Mrs. Maberley, I knew only, from my interrogation of Stockdale's wife, that the offer had come from a rich woman. It was Pike who drew upon his vast knowledge of London's *beau monde* and recalled that a young man named 'Maberley' had been among Isadora Klein's many lovers. Ah, here we are!"

At the St. James Club, we presented our cards and after a few moments were ushered into a lavishly furnished chamber set aside for Langdale Pike. Here, this strange creature held court and conducted a robust trade in the buying and selling of salacious tidbits that made their way into the blind paragraphs of the garbage press.

"Sherlock Holmes!" called a high, reedy voice as we entered this retreat. Across the room, Langdale Pike lounged upon a broad, high-backed armchair, his slippered feet resting on an ottoman, while cigar smoke coiled around his head. He was a slight, pallid creature whose white complexion contrasted sharply with a pair of piercing blue eyes and shock of ruddy hair, and though the hand extended to me was as fragile as a girl's, the handshake was firm. On either side of his armchair were small end tables, one piled high with papers and note-books, and the other bearing a silver basket filled to overflowing with visiting cards.

"''*Will you walk into my parlor,*" said a spider to a fly?'" he crooned as we sat. "It isn't the Knightsbridge business, and I don't believe it is the engagement of Princess Alice. No, no, you come to chat about another engagement, I think, of a noble young man to a very *sweet* lady. A lady we discussed only last month. Am I correct?"

"You are."

"You are the second person this week to do so."

"Who was the first? Was it a woman?"

Pike shook his finger at Holmes and smiled. "Have you nothing for me?"

"The engagement of Miss deMerville was not broken off because of the gentleman's injuries."

"Of course not. But what did the trick, then?"

"A book. Nothing that you can take possession of at this stage, but a certain Miss Winter – Kitty Winter – has an intimate knowledge of its contents. She was released from prison six weeks ago. Perhaps I may arrange an introduction."

Pike drew a pencil from his pocket and scribbled Miss Winter's name on one of the sheets upon the side table. "Yes, my visitor was a woman. She called last week, just after the engagement was announced. But I must be discreet – let us just say that she is a fond mother, and a very unhappy one."

"Who is not fond of Isadora Klein. And who would not be unhappy to see the match broken off?"

330

Pike shrugged his shoulders.

"Yesterday, Mrs. Klein decided that she wants to be married, not in October, but immediately."

Pike raised his eyebrows. "Immediately! Oh, dear. I *am* in your debt for that little morsel. You're quite certain? And why, pray?"

"Why, indeed?"

"Well, of course, she does not grow younger, but how much older will she be four months from now?" Pike drew on his cigar and sent a languid jet of smoke above our heads "But she has the Duke entirely under her spell, and so if she wants to marry three days from now, she will have her way."

"Unless something occurs to break the spell and give him cause to rescind his offer."

Pike conceded this point with a nod. "What might that be, I wonder? I might venture a guess, of course, but even an educated guess is a guess notwithstanding. A shocking habit."

"Have you no theory?"

"My dear Holmes, a theory is fashioned from data. Now, how does one gather data?" Pike blew rings of smoke into the air. "Perhaps by choosing, from among the many questions that might be asked, the one most likely to take us from the theoretical to the material. For example, one might ask why the lady wants to marry the Duke immediately. Or, one might ask why she wants to marry him at all."

"Because she is ambitious. She will be a duchess. She will move in the very best society. She will gain, by way of a young, malleable husband, some influence in the political sphere."

"Yes, yes. But perhaps her desires are more – *elementary*, shall we say? Lomond is young and handsome and quite rich. It would be a very different story if he were young, handsome, and poor."

"Like Douglas Maberley?"

"Maberley. Have you read any of his novels? Trash, delightful trash. I have often thought that I had a turn in that direction. I have even sketched out a premise or two. Would you like to hear one? Once upon a time, a young girl from a prominent Spanish line falls in love with a dashing fellow, handsome, young, and – alas! – poor. They set out to elope, but they are apprehended. For his part in the plot, the young man is beaten and left for dead. As for the girl – well, she is locked away until her family can arrange to exile her to the custody of relations living on a family estate in . . . let us say South America. There, she is pressed into an unhappy marriage with an old fellow. One of those barons of commerce – coffee, tobacco. Sugar, perhaps. After two years of misery as a wife, she has the good fortune to become a widow – a lovely, wealthy, independent widow.

331

She returns to Spain, travels her native land for many years – gossip has her searching for her former love, but who knows? I haven't worked that part out yet. Perhaps he is dead. Perhaps she is too, after a fashion. Dead to all feeling. It is quite sad, what tragedies inflicted upon us in youth will do to the heart – they will harden it or they will break it, or they will twist it until it resembles something not like a heart at all."

"*Le belle dame sans merci,*" Holmes murmured, gravely.

"Perhaps a child might have softened her heart, but alas – that baron of commerce was quite old, and barely two years after he stood at the altar, he was laid in his grave. And she? What shall I do with her? I know! I will bring her to London. But," he added, with a sigh, "I don't see how I can bring my tale to a happy end. There are many too affairs, too many men. Young men, as her first love had been, lovers who remain young, even as she does not. And then, after many years, she comes upon one who is very much like her first love – why he might *be* that first love, reincarnate. She has found what had lost more than twenty years before."

"And he is a young, handsome fellow," said Holmes. "But not a poor one."

"Ah! I see that you are a fabulist as well! Yes, he is rich. Young as well, perhaps young enough to be her son. I think I will even give him a title. Something to pass down to *their* son, in good time. Of course, before we arrive at that good time, there must be the conflict that is so necessary in such fables. Some opposition to the match. Parties who would wish to break it off."

Pike extinguished his cigar on the cover of a notebook. "I haven't taken my tale any further. I have ideas, of course, and hear whispers. I feel their quiver, but for now they remain at the outer reach of my somewhat purple plot. Theories. Surmise and conjecture. And whether covering fact or fiction, theories can get stretched quite thin, don't you agree? I, myself, prefer paper and ink."

"What did you make of him, Watson?" Holmes asked as we left the St. James Club.

"He is a queer fellow, certainly. You took him by surprise when you told him that Mrs. Klein wants to marry immediately."

"And Pike is rarely taken by surprise. But his tale – what did you make of that?"

"An interesting fiction."

"And one that stretches only so far."

"Not far enough to reach Mrs. Klein's decision to advance the wedding date," I said. "What is your theory?"

332

Holmes shrugged his shoulders. "Lomond is the only son of a very long and distinguished line, and both Mycroft and Pike mention the significance of an heir. If an arrival should be forthcoming, it would better serve the ambitions of the lady, and the rights of the issue, to have that arrival occur after marriage, rather than before. It is," he added, "only a provisional theory."

"How will you test it?"

"The lady's *volte-face* is quite abrupt – too much so for its motive to have reached beyond her household, but may be less of a mystery within it."

"You don't mean to get engaged to the housemaid, do you?"

Holmes chuckled, and shook his head. "No – I believe I have a less precarious alternative open to me, thank Heaven! But I must not keep you from your patients, Doctor. Call at Baker Street tomorrow morning. Perhaps by then I will be able to add a chapter to Pike's intriguing tale."

The remainder of my day, and into the early hours of the next one were spent at the bedside of a patient. It wasn't until nearly two in the morning that his fever broke and he was resting comfortably enough for me to return home and try for a few hours of sleep.

A moonless sky, combined with a steady drizzle and dense fog slowed my cab to a crawl. It happened that the route took us along Baker Street, and as it passed my old address, I saw a faint glow of lamp-light in the vicinity of the sitting room window. Behind the shade, Holmes's tall, spare silhouette paced back and forth with an impatient energy. He had told me to call in the morning, but it was clear that he had not gone to bed, and so I decided that there was no point in waiting until dawn to hear what progress he had made with the case.

I would not disturb the household at this hour, but took out the latch-key that Holmes insisted I keep in my possession. To my surprise, the door wasn't locked, an oversight that gave me some concern, for Mrs. Hudson had always been the most careful and conscientious of landladies.

I locked the door behind me and was ascending the stair when I heard Holmes call down in a low voice. "Watson?"

"Yes."

"When I asked you to call in the morning, I didn't expect you so far before breakfast."

"I beg your pardon," I said. "I saw the light. Did you know that the door was left – "

"Yes," he said, somewhat sharply. And then, in a tone of resignation, he added, "I suppose there is no help for it. If you locked the door, be so good as to go down and unlock it again."

333

I did as I was told, and went upstairs once more.

"Just leave the sitting room door ajar if you please. Excellent weather!" he said, as he waved me toward the armchair.

"Excellent? It's black as pitch and the fog is thick as cheese!"

"Precisely. If a fellow wants to be invisible, this is the night for it."

"Are you expecting someone at this hour? Not a client, surely."

"No. Ah! Here he is."

I had always reckoned my hearing to be acute, and yet I hadn't heard the door below, and scarcely detected the slow, cautious step ascending the stair.

A moment later, the sitting room door swung wide and a tall, broad figure appeared at the threshold. He wore a long gray overcoat, a derby that was pulled low upon his forehead, and a muffler drawn up to the bridge of his nose, so that only two alert dark eyes peered into the room, and then settled upon me.

Holmes gave a shrug that clearly stated, "It could not be helped," and beckoned the man into the room.

The visitor closed the door behind him and then unbuttoned his coat and removed his hat, muffler, and gloves, and I saw the black visage and powerful figure of the bruiser, Steve Dixie.

"Sit down, Watson," Holmes said, for I leapt from my chair at the sight of the ruffian. "You dress for the fog, I see," Holmes said to Dixie. "I was just telling Watson here that a fellow might be invisible on such a night."

Our visitor studied my astonished stare and grinned. "I'm afraid you may want to charge Holmes once again of using you but not trusting you. I read all your tales, you see, Doctor."

The voice well-modulated, the accent that of an educated American – Gone was coarse vernacular and the bullying demeanor.

"To be fair," said Holmes. "You did lay it on rather thick."

"So did you."

"'Masser' Holmes?'"

"I seem to recall some remark about a scent bottle," countered the visitor.

"*Touché*. But in my own defense, I had not expected friend Watson to call that morning any more than I did on this one, and preserving your *incognito* was more important than preserving what good opinion his readers may hold of me. You're late – I expected you hours ago."

"It's been a long day at Grosvenor Square. Two long days, in fact."

"So, I hear. Well, take a chair by the fire. I don't think any of us would be the worse for a brandy and soda. Watson, allow me to introduce Steven Bell, though I am afraid that he must remain Steve Dixie so far as the public are concerned. A hint of his true identity would put his life in jeopardy and undo the work of a year."

"True identity?" I said, as I shook the massive hand extended to me.

"Detective Bell is a Pinkerton man," said Holmes.

"You were very convincing."

"Thank you." Bell sank into a chair and took the glass of brandy from Holmes. "To whatever brings us justice," he said by way of a toast. "Jack Spencer's wanted on my side of the Atlantic as well as yours, Doctor. But he's sharp as a raven and slippery as mud. I almost had my hands on his gang when they made ready to move fifty-thousand in bank notes."

"Counterfeit?" I said.

"As good as I've seen. Better than Prescott's work, and he was a master of the trade."

"What happened?"

"One of Spencer's men, a young fool named Perkins, made off with a set of plates that he tried to sell to a rival gang. They had him knifed in broad daylight right outside the Holborn Bar as a warning to the rest of us, and then decided to hold back the notes until matters cooled. The Harrow Weald job was good for a quick thousand – "

"Isadora Klein paid them steal some papers from the home of a Mrs. Maberley."

Bell nodded. "They put Barney Stockdale and his missus on it. When Mrs. Maberley brought Holmes into the business, it was my good luck, because Steve Dixie was the one sent to warn him off. Holmes and I have both been working on the Spencer John gang for some time, and we can get a few lines to one another if we're careful, but there is a risk in meeting face to face."

"So when you barged in here that day, it was a rendezvous?"

"It was meant to be. But when I saw you here, I didn't know if Holmes took you into his confidence, so I figured it was best to play it out as Steve Dixie. The rest you know – Mrs. Klein got her papers and Stockdales got ten months each. She'll see to it they're not any the worse for the lag, and I'm the better for it, because their arrest left her wanting a household factotum, and Jack Spencer pressed her to take Steve Dixie."

"It wasn't wise of the lady to place herself in their debt," Holmes observed.

"No. And she may come to regret it. As for my role, I'm little more than a sharp eye and – well, 'muscle' is what we call it in my part of the world. I put off any young men who might come around and muddle things up with the Duke, run errands, and act go-between if she needs to get word to Jack Spencer. I lock up the house after the Duke leaves – he calls nearly every night – and take special care to see that the drawing room is secure, because that's where the wedding gifts are laid out." Bell shook his head. "The engagement's barely a week old and already her drawing room's crammed with loot – I'd no idea a second marriage brought in so much plunder."

"And you cast an inventory of the – loot – to draw the gang to the surface," said Holmes. "Though I'm not certain that butter dishes and grape scissors are a sufficient lure."

"No, but there is the wedding present the Duke promised her. A family heirloom he vowed to hand over just before they marry, so that she might wear it down the aisle. A diamond-and-pearl necklace said to be worth a hundred-thousand."

"That's better."

"He brought it to her when he called tonight."

"Better still, perhaps. And that would seem to be confirmation that the wedding will be soon?"

Bell nodded. "And it's got them all thrown below stairs. Until yesterday, a four-month engagement and all that went with it seemed to suit her fine – all the callers and dressmakers and photographers from the society papers, and planning for a grand wedding in October. The housekeeper – she's been with Mrs. Klein longest – once said that Mrs. Klein was pushed into the match with Klein and there was no jubilee, just a quick tying of the knot at the consulate in Pernambuco."

"So she has been making up for what she had missed with her first experiment," said Holmes.

"Until yesterday."

"Then proceed from there, Bell, and leave nothing out."

"Yesterday morning, Mrs. Klein and Alice – her maid – were in the drawing room. They'd just taken in a fresh stock of spoils – a tea set, a silver tray with the Lomond crest, some filigree trinket boxes, a French writing desk. Another table was needed to lay it all out, and so Alice and I were sent up to search the spare rooms for one that might suit. We'd just got back to the drawing room when we heard a shriek from inside and ran in to see the gifts scattered on the carpet, the writing desk overturned, the tea set in pieces – and there stood Mrs. Klein, white as a block of marble, staring at a sheet of paper in her hand, and muttering as if to herself, 'There was a third one! *A third one!*' Alice spoke her name, and Mrs. Klein seemed to collect herself. She tossed the paper into the grate and strode out of the room. 'I'll sweep up the china, Miss Alice,' I said. 'Go see to your mistress.' As soon as she left the room, I went for the note before the flames got it."

Bell rose and drew from his breast pocket a handkerchief folded around what remained of a sheet of pale blue writing paper, creased in the middle and scorched all around the edges, with the top portion burned away. Holmes took this object between two fingers, ran his eyes over it, and then laid it under a lamp and examined it more closely with his magnifying lens, while Bell and I looked over his shoulder. The fragment of paper had been of good quality, and on the portion that had remained intact, were several lines of writing:

> *must now curse herself for allowing, in a rare unguarded moment, the secret she had kept to herself for so many years to escape her lips. With that one lapse, she had placed herself in his power. The secret that would have made no difference to me, my Lady, will make all the difference in the world to your new captive – whether under your spell or under your thumb, he knows his duty, and when he knows the truth, the spell will give way and you*

"It looks like something copied from one of those trash novels," said Bell.

"Not any novel, Bell. Douglas Maberley's novel."

"Maberley's novel!" I cried. "But, Holmes, there were only two copies, one that he sent to Mrs. Klein from Italy, and the second that was stolen at Harrow Weald. And Mrs. Klein destroyed both."

"So we were told by Mrs. Klein and so she may have believed. You're certain, Bell, that you heard her say 'A third one!'?"

"Clear as my name."

"But where is this third copy, then?" I asked.

"With whomever sent this." Holmes turned his gaze upon the bit of singed paper once more. "See the crease? Folded only once, it wouldn't easily slip into an envelope."

"There was no envelope," said Bell. "It didn't come with the post that was brought up an hour before. It must have come in with one of the wedding gifts."

"And one of them, you said, was a tray with the Lomond crest."

"Yes. The Dowager's been putting on a good show, but below stairs they say she'd go to any length, short of murder, to have the match broken off."

"So I hear." Holmes dropped back into his chair and gave Bell a brief sketch of our interviews with Mycroft Holmes and Pike.

"I would have thought the Dowager'd stop short of going to the likes of Langdale Pike," said Bell.

"Could Pike have this third copy of the Maberley's work," I asked, "and given it – or a page from it – to the duchess?"

"He would *give* nothing," Holmes interrupted. "He would have named his price."

"Which she could well afford. But how do we know that this really *is* Maberley's work? Perhaps Pike himself wrote it. He said that he had read Maberley's novels, and had a turn for melodrama. He may have produced something in Maberley's style – "

"No, it is Maberley's work. Observe how the pronouns shift back and forth, the same quirk of grammar that we also saw upon the fragment that his mother preserved. And it is not from a published work. A rejected suitor might be careless with his pronouns, but no editor would have allowed such clumsiness into a published work."

"Maberley's work, perhaps, but not his handwriting."

"No, his hand was cramped and uneven and this is regular and neat. Almost too regular and neat – the writer made no effort to reproduce Maberley's hand, only to disguise his – or her – own."

"Because Mrs. Klein might recognize it?"

"Perhaps. Or perhaps because she would not. It may be that the writer's object is to let Mrs. Klein know that a third copy of Maberley's work, and whatever secrets it contains, are in the hands of another. Pray, Bell, continue with your account. What happened after you recovered this note?"

"I'd just swept up the broken china and set the room to rights when Mrs. Klein summoned me. She gave me a note to deliver to the Duke's residence in town. He was to come in the evening, but it seems she wanted him straight away. From there, I was to hunt up Jack Spencer and give him a message. Another of Steve Dixie's chores, to act the go-between because her communication with him is never in writing."

Holmes leaned forward in his chair. "And what was this message?"

"That she had a job for him. He was to be at the kitchen area the following night at midnight. Tonight."

"A few hours ago. The household staff retire before midnight?"

"Well before."

"And did Spencer keep the appointment?"

Bell nodded.

"Pray, continue."

"Jack Spencer's got a half-dozen fox-holes all around London, and I was four hours tracking him down. When I got back to Grosvenor Square, the Duke was there and had been for hours, and at tea. Alice – who keeps her ear to the wall – told us that she heard the mistress pressing him to marry her as soon as possible."

"And she evidently carried her point, or her Grace wouldn't have summoned Mycroft this morning."

338

"And the Duke wouldn't have brought his wedding gift to Mrs. Klein when he dined with her tonight." said Bell.

"The necklace?"

Bell nodded.

"Did you see it?"

"Yes. She was wearing it after the Duke left, when she called me in to say that she would secure the house herself and I might retire."

"Leaving a clear field for her rendezvous with Spencer."

"Yes. It's why I was late. I made a show of going up to my room and when the last of the servants retired, I crept down to the kitchen and tucked myself away in the pantry."

"You took a great risk, Bell," said Holmes, gravely.

"I know it. One sneeze or shuffle would have been the end of me. I had to close the pantry door behind me, so I couldn't make out all that was said, though they spoke for a half-an-hour, perhaps more. I did hear Spencer say, 'Not before dawn – I'll need two or three hours at least to call in my men.' And then Mrs. Klein said, 'What happens to her is of no consequence – do what you must, only bring it to me and you shall be paid,' was her reply, and then she said, 'All I ask is that you make it look like burglary.'"

"Burgle the duchess' residence?" I exclaimed. "Why, even the Spencer John gang couldn't plan *that* operation in a few hours. She must have at least a dozen household staff and one of the finest addresses in town, not some lonely country neighborhood, and – "

I did not finish my sentence, for Holmes leaped from his chair and dashed from the room. I heard his footsteps clattering up to the lumber rooms, and after a few minutes of thumping and scraping above, he returned with a battered cardboard box which he dropped upon the carpet.

"Once again, Doctor, you are a conductor of light." Holmes threw off the lid and began to rummage through bundles of papers and envelopes. "The good doctor has often frowned upon my habit of preserving so many relics of my cases," he said to Bell. "But what is irrelevant today may be of great importance a month hence. What can you tell me, Bell" he continued as he sorted through a packet of envelopes, "of that china tea set that your mistress received yesterday?"

Bell and I exchanged a baffled look. "The pattern was dark blue on white – flowers and bees, with a tracing of gold on the spout and top."

"That sheet of paper – if folded in half – would it fit into the pot?"

"Yes, I imagine so."

"That pattern you describe," Holmes said, as he plucked an envelope from the packet, and drew out a single sheet of pale blue paper, "is one that might be found some twenty years ago on a Crown Derby tea set. And the lady who sent this appeal to me, the day before Steve Dixie made his dramatic entrance into these rooms, possessed such an item."

"Mrs. Maberley!" I cried.

"Mrs. Maberley," said Holmes, gravely. "And that lady does live in a lonely country neighborhood."

"But surely she has left England by now."

"I hope that she has, but I will not allow myself to be caught off guard again. You have both had a long day behind you – "

"And a long one ahead," I said. "If there's a chance to bring an end to the gang, I'm with you as well."

"Good. You're armed, I trust, Bell? Have you your pistol, Watson?"

"Yes."

"I will wire the inspector from the station. He was a smug fellow as I recall, but at least he can have a few men at the Three Gables in case the gang arrives before us."

It was still quite dark when we set out, and our journey was a silent one for the most part. Bell and I exchanged a few words, but Holmes said nothing, only sat in somber introspection, completely absorbed by the new and ominous turn the case had taken.

It wasn't yet dawn when we arrived at Harrow, where we were met by the same rotund inspector who had investigated the Three Gables burglary weeks before. Only the gravity of the matter before us prevented me from laughing at the fellow's expression when a man he had known only as the bruiser Steve Dixie, was presented to him as Pinkerton detective, Steven Bell.

"I wasn'y happy to have the gang slip through my net," said he, "and so I am glad for another chance at them." And then, replying to my friend's inquiry about Mrs. Maberley he said, "No, she hasn't left England, Mr. Holmes. Waiting for her boy's remains to arrive has kept her here – he is to be put in the ground this morning, in fact – and then I believe she will go. How many will there be, do you think?"

"Jack Spencer, and at least two others. Three, perhaps."

"Well, we are four, and I've posted three more at the copse behind the house."

"Excellent," said Holmes. "As for us, we will have to make our ambush at that recess in the high hedge. It isn't the ideal screen, but it will have to do."

We made our way to Mrs. Maberley's home and, passing through the gate, crept around to a small hollow where the hedge that surrounded the house formed a right angle. "Perhaps I should wake the household, and

340

have the ladies taken away," said the inspector in a low voice. "There is only Mrs. Maberley and her girl – "

Holmes raised his hand for silence, and pointed to the glow of a lamp in the front hall. The door opened and Mrs. Maberley stepped out, followed by her servant girl, and then turned to lock the door. Arm in arm, the two women walked down the path and through the gate and then disappeared in the direction of the lane.

"Where can she be going at this hour?" I whispered.

"To St. Mary's, I expect," said the inspector. "She wanted no ceremony, there will only be the vicar and a few to help at the grave site. It is for the best if it gets her and the girl out of the way."

The black sky and early morning chill made for a melancholy vigil, and a precarious one, for after an hour had passed, daybreak began to lift away the dark that had provided much of our scant ambush.

"How much longer, do you think?" whispered the inspector.

"They make their own time," was Bell's reply.

"This won't do for a hiding-place once it is full daylight. If they mean to come at all – "

"Hush!" Holmes nodded toward the hedge at the far side of the house. It appeared to flutter and then a breach formed and a crouched figure darted through the opening, followed by a second and then a third. My hand stole into my pocket and gripped the butt of my revolver and beside me I sensed that Bell was doing the same.

The three figures weren't twenty-five feet from us when we saw the tallest of the three – Spencer, I was certain – advance toward the sitting room's ground floor window and examine it with the self-command of one who knows exactly what he has set out to do. He produced a sturdy object the size of a stout club and, gripping it with both hands, he struck the long ground floor window again and again with the butt of this object. In less than a minute, he had knocked out all of the glass. Then, one after another, the three crept through the aperture and disappeared into the house.

"We must move!" whispered the inspector.

"No," said Holmes. "The women aren't in the house. We can take them when they come out again. You saw what they were carrying, Inspector?"

"Truncheons."

"No, torches," said Bell, grimly. "It is an intimidation I know well. Once they have the papers, they will set fire to the house as a warning to Mrs. Maberley."

"I doubt that they know she's gone," said Holmes, grimly. "You said that Mrs. Klein told Spencer that what happened to the lady was of no consequence. They come prepared to do murder as well as burglary and arson."

For nearly half-an-hour more we waited, Holmes rigid as marble while the inspector chafed and muttered that we must apprehend them at once. At last, the three villains emerged and huddled together in urgent conversation. Their angry gestures, and the few words we were able to catch, betrayed frustration that they had found neither the papers nor the occupant. The leader then seemed to come to a resolution, and ordering the others to light their torches, and lighting his own, he stepped back from the shattered window, and made ready to pitch the blazing object into the sitting room.

"Now!" Holmes ordered.

"Stop where you are!" cried the inspector, and we sprang to our feet as the three turned upon us, the torches held aloft.

Bell stepped forward to confront a powerfully-built figure, whose dark eyes were set ablaze by the reflected flame. "What – is that you, Steve Dixie?" he roared.

"Is that you, Jack Spencer?" Bell replied.

"Don't try to bolt," the inspector warned the culprits. "I've three men ready to cut you off at the other side of the hedge. Now, just drop those torches in the grass, and then raise up your hands."

The two confederates looked to Spencer, who scowled, dropped his torch, and then rolled it with his boot until it was extinguished by the damp ground. The other two followed suit, and it was at this moment that the inspector's men pushed through the hedge behind them, dragging a fourth confederate in their custody. Their sudden appearance was just enough distraction for Spencer to whisk a small revolver from his breast and fire a single shot before Holmes sprang at him, crashed the butt of his own weapon down upon the villain's wrist, then pressed its barrel to the man's forehead.

"It's the four of you to our seven," barked the inspector. "Get the darbies on them and then search their pockets for weapons and see what they made off with. Were you struck, Di – that is, Detective Bell?"

I turned to see Bell gripping his bleeding shoulder. "A scratch, and well worth it."

"'*Detective*?'" roared Spencer, and the villain directed a string of foul oaths at the Pinkerton man. "I'll see you in Hell!"

"You'll have a good, long wait, Jack Spencer," was Bell's retort.

"It is an arrest that will do you credit, Inspector," said Holmes, as the four were placed in handcuffs. "If you will allow the doctor to bring our American colleague into the house so that he might look after Bell's injuries, I'll wait with you until the police van arrives."

Bell and I made our way through the shattered window, and I lit the lamps and had Bell sit on the couch. I helped him ease off his coat, and then cut away the sleeve of his shirt to examine the wound. The bullet had left a deep gash in his flesh, but hadn't hit bone, and I unlocked the front door for Holmes and then searched the kitchen and pantry for towels and a basin soap and water. I returned to the patient and offered him my flask as I began to clean the wound.

"Are you shocked, Doctor?"

"By the sight of blood?"

"No – that it's as red as yours."

"Don't be ridiculous, Bell. Take another pull on that flask and keep quiet."

Holmes entered and looked around at the clutter of broken glass and overturned furniture and scattered papers that the scoundrels had left in their wake.

"How is the patient, Doctor?"

"He'll be fine."

"Ah!" he said, with a nod toward the shattered window. "There is Mrs. Maberley and her girl."

A constable had been posted at the gate to drive off the idlers who had begun to collect at the scene. I glanced out and saw the man address Mrs. Maberley, who listened, white-faced, and then took her young servant by the hand and hurried toward the house.

"Mr. Holmes!" she cried, as she entered, and looked around at the disarray. "The constable said there has been another burglary!"

"Yes, madam." And then, noting her startled expression when she saw the wounded Pinkerton man. "I believe you may have seen this gentleman about last month. Allow me to introduce Detective Bell."

The lady's surprise was evident but she recovered herself, and immediately sent the girl to fetch bandages and adhesive plaster. "And my sewing basket," she added. "I have nothing for suturing but some good silk thread. It will have to do." When these items were brought up, Mrs. Maberley sent the girl to the kitchen to prepare tea, and then set a chair beside the couch and assisted me in mending Bell's wound. She was a capable nurse, steady and efficient, not troubled by the unsightly wound or the blood.

"I have had practice, Doctor," she said, in reply to my praise. "For a month, I was day-and-night at my son's bedside and watched my splendid boy sink into a broken, raving, delirious creature, until his lungs, or his heart, or his magnificent spirit, gave out at last."

343

"And yet," observed Holmes, "even such a trying vigil must have allowed you some periods of respite, when you might occupy yourself with correspondence, or needlework. Or reading, perhaps."

"Yes."

"You came upon a manuscript – a rather sensational, dramatic tale, the fable of a young man's downfall that results from his passionate love affair with an older woman. Perhaps you thought it was a forgotten draft of one of your son's earlier novels, but as you read on, you realized that it was a recent work, the sad history of his own ruin at the hands of a – " Holmes shrugged his shoulders.

"A fiend," the woman murmured.

"A fiend. When we first spoke, I asked if your son's tragedy had been the result of a love affair – a woman – and you replied, 'Or a fiend.' Now when you said that, you hadn't yet unpacked your son's personal effects that had been sent from Italy. You didn't know that a copy of this same manuscript lay among them, a manuscript that burglars had been hired to steal. You – quite foolishly – attempted to intercept the thieves as they made off with it and were, in fact, able to recover a single page. One line from that page, I recall: '*she smiled, like the heartless fiend that she was.*' Now if you weren't aware of this copy, packed among your son's belongings, how extraordinary that you should use the very term from its text. Unless, of course, you *had* read it before – not the stolen manuscript, which was the last of *three* copies, but one that you came upon it Italy and read during those quiet intervals at your son's bedside."

"Yes. I didn't know that Douglas had other copies of that unhappy work, but one must have turned up after I left Italy, and was placed in a trunk with his other effects that were sent here. I had already recognized it to be a veiled account of Douglas's own life, though I didn't know the identity of the woman. And then, in this very room, Mr. Holmes, you got Susan Stockdale to admit that she had been paid to spy upon me by a rich woman. And when you gave me five-thousand pounds from an anonymous party as compensation for the burglary, I didn't need to be a detective to understand that it could only have come from this same rich woman, who must be the woman in my poor boy's manuscript, the fiend who had broken his heart."

"But you still didn't know her identity."

"No, not until last week, when I read an item in the newspaper – the engagement of Mrs. Isadora Klein to the young Duke of Lomond. There had been a chapter in the manuscript where the woman discards her poor lover so that she might take up with a rich one. A prince," she added, with a wry smile. "Could this Isadora Klein be the fiend who had dealt so

344

mercilessly with my son? I was determined to know the truth. I even thought of consulting you once more, Mr. Holmes – "

"Had I not failed you so miserably," said my friend.

The lady sighed. "Or I might appeal to one whom Douglas had occasionally mentioned when he lived in town, a strange creature who is a human repository of all of London's gossip."

"Langdale Pike."

"Yes. A *very* strange creature, but he knew the entire history of my poor son's love affair with Isadora Klein. And now I was certain that my son's unhappy fable was no more than the thinnest coating of fiction over fact, and that it was Isadora Klein who had – " The lady choked back a sob. "Who had sent my son to his grave, so that she might take up with the Duke."

"And so you sent her a wedding present," said Holmes.

"Yes."

"A Crown Derby tea set. With a sheet of paper inside the teapot, a sheet upon which you may have written a line or two, hinting that there was another manuscript, and then, to confirm this, you copied out a passage from the novel, a passage that I think Mrs. Klein wouldn't want her young fiancé to read."

"I daresay not."

"Detective Bell was able to recover that sheet of paper from the fire, but only a few lines survived, lines that alluded to a secret – a secret that was the true reason Mrs. Klein was so desperate to have all copies of the document destroyed."

"There is a passage in the manuscript – a particularly unhappy passage – when the lady has a moment of weakness and tells the young man of her past. I have it here." From her bosom, the lady drew a sheet of folded foolscap, and handed to Holmes. He ran his eyes over it and then gave a defeated sigh and showed the paper to Bell and me. Upon the page, several paragraphs had been written in Maberley's cramped, uneven hand, but we were only able to make out a few words and phrases, as it was, for the most part, blotched and indecipherable. "I didn't want to leave Italy without something of his, so I removed this page from the manuscript I had been reading." She took the sheet, and replaced it in her bosom. "It would be legible, if his tears, and my own, hadn't stained it so."

"But you know what was written."

"I know it by heart."

"Because you had read it in Italy. And you copied it from memory, and placed it in the tea set that you sent to Mrs. Klein."

The lady nodded. "Yesterday evening, my son arrived from Italy and this morning, he was put in his grave. I wanted it done very early – there was no point in prolonging my misery. He was my only child. The Duke is an only child. Did you know that? The only child of a long and distinguished line."

"Yes."

"We are not so very different from aristocracy – our hopes are all the same, even the Duke. Young – and, I daresay, smitten as he is – his hopes are the same as my late husband's were. What do you suppose they are?"

"The welfare of your children, I imagine," said Holmes, gently.

She conceded his point with a nod. "Perhaps I should approach the question differently. How many love affairs has Mrs. Klein had, do you suppose? And for how many years? So many men. It is a subject upon which I can claim no authority, and yet, one would think that mere probability would have called for the occasional dose of pennyroyal, or a discreet visit to Switzerland or France. Unless it wasn't necessary. Unless some incident in her youth made it unnecessary."

"She cannot have a child," said Holmes, gravely.

"In that passage in the manuscript, the woman reveals a love affair. Her first love, and one that resulted in an inconvenience. The young man was dealt with, and a surgeon was called in to dispense with the inconvenience, but the consequence was that she was left unable to bear a child. It would have made no difference to Douglas, but it will make all the difference in the world to the Duke. He may be young, but he is the last of a long and distinguished line, and he knows his duty. You said that the hopes of a parent are for the welfare of their children, Mr. Holmes, but first there must *be* children. She can never have what I had, and what she took from me."

"Mrs. Klein destroyed two copies of the manuscript, one sent to her by your son, and the second that was stolen from this house. Pray, what became of the third copy, the one you had read at his bedside?"

"It is with Douglas. I laid it in the coffin beside him in Italy, and this morning his coffin was laid in the ground."

Not until noon were we able to leave Harrow Weald, and not before Mrs. Maberley, with extraordinary kindness, urged Bell to remain until he had made a complete recovery. "You may have my son's room. It is the most comfortable, and, as the doctor has said, I am a very capable nurse."

"You're very kind," said Bell. "But I'm no stranger to rough treatment, and a good look at Spencer and his men in a cell is all I need to put me on the mend."

The arrival of the lady's attorney and a kindly neighbor gave us an opening to make our exit, and leaving her to the care of Mr. Sutro and Miss

346

Westphail, we first stopped at the police station at Harrow so that Bell might look upon Jack Spencer and his men.

"Those below Spencer will turn on one another before they are brought to trial," he said, as we made our way to the railway station. "And on Mrs. Klein as well. She ordered them to make the business look like a burglary, but they took it too far – attempted arson, attempted murder. I know the Spencer John gang, and they won't take on her share of the blame."

"They may say what they like," Holmes replied, grimly. "She wouldn't put such a scheme in place without also ensuring that she would have the earliest notice of its success, or failure. By now, she must know that her scheme has gone awry. I daresay she will be gone from London before we return. No, I think we must be satisfied that the young Duke has had a very narrow escape, although a costly one."

"A broken heart," I said.

"Oh, something more material than a broken heart," was Holmes's reply. "Recall her instructions to Jack Spencer – that what happened to Mrs. Maberley was of no consequence and that he was to do whatever he must."

Holmes studied our puzzled expressions for a moment. "It wasn't the attack of Mrs. Maberley's home that was to look like a burglary – it was the attack on Mrs. Klein's. A necklace worth a hundred-thousand is a very handsome payment for the elimination of that last obstacle to such an advantageous marriage, don't you agree? But, of course, she couldn't simply hand it over – how would she explain its loss to the Duke? She must appear to be the victim of a burglary."

"And so, she has it, I suppose, wherever she's gone."

"I think, when she has time to reflect upon what she had hoped for, and what she has lost, she will find those gems to be very cold comfort."

"Have you nothing for me?" said Langdale Pike, when Holmes called upon him the next day.

"Douglas Maberley left behind three manuscripts, drafts of his next novel which was to be a *roman a clef* of his affair with Mrs. Klein."

"Mrs. Klein. I hear that she has broken with the Duke and returned to Pernambuco. And that she took a little memento of their brief engagement with her. So," he murmured, as he lit a cigar, "what became of these interesting works?"

"Two were destroyed by Mrs. Klein."

"And the third?"

"Lies in Douglas Maberley's coffin."

"Oh dear. Well, you know the tale of Rossetti's poems. He laid them in his wife's coffin, and seven years later, he dug them up again."

"Secrets rarely die," said Holmes. "They just lie dormant. They wait."

NOTE

For some years, there has been a trend in popular fiction toward continuations, alternative histories, and re-imaginings, and there is probably no story in The Canon that is in greater need of some re-tooling than "The Adventure of the Three Gables". It's hard to reconcile the story's cringeworthy racism with the wonderful humanity of "The Yellow Face", and readers find themselves either rationalizing the work as Conan Doyle's attempt to keep up with the times (It was published in 1926) when the advent of more hard-boiled detective fiction was taking root, or arguing that it wasn't the work of Conan Doyle at all.

It is not only in the matter of his language and conduct that Holmes fails to shine – he is neglectful and lazy, and the tale's only sparks of "color and life" come from the supporting cast: Susan, the inspector, Isadora Klein, Steve Dixie, and even the off-stage Langdale Pike.

As for the bit at the end, and the allusion to Rossetti's buried poems – quite true. According to most accounts of the escapade, Rossetti was abetted by the Victorian era rapscallion, Charles Augustus Howell, who was the inspiration for Doyle's Charles Augustus Milverton.

JR

The Cobbler's Treasure
by Dick Gillman

Chapter I – Commander Thorn Returns

I has stopped to visit with my friend Sherlock Holmes one afternoon in late September 1903 when the intriguing case of "The Cobbler's Treasure" was revealed to us. Replete after a tasty luncheon comprising a generous portion of "Toad in the Hole", served with a rich onion gravy, carrots, and roasted potatoes, we settled back to enjoy a pipe. I looked towards my friend who had taken his pipe from his lips and was now using the stem to conduct some musical piece that he was reprising in his head.

"Tell me, is the piece that so interests you one that I would appreciate?"

Holmes inclined his head slightly, replaced the pipe stem between his lips, and drew strongly upon it before answering. "I doubt it, Watson. As I recall, you consider the music of the Baroque period, and particularly that of the Venetian master Vivaldi, somewhat frivolous."

I pursed my lips on hearing this, saying, "Not so, for I appreciate many of his pieces, but you must admit, some are a little over-exuberant."

On hearing this, Holmes leapt from his chair and raced for his violin, crying, "Exuberant? Great heavens! Any man who can profoundly influence the work of J. S. Bach cannot be criticised for his exuberance!" Picking up his beloved Stradivarius, he began to play energetically . . . but he barely managed to bow a few bars before the strident ringing of the bell in the hallway below interrupted his exertions.

Carefully replacing the violin within its case, Holmes stood stock still like a setter, almost aquiver, as he strained to hear any snippet of conversation from the hallway beneath. Throwing himself back into his armchair, he now sat, alert, as he listened to the footfalls on the stairs. One clearly belonged to his landlady, whilst the other was a crisp, almost-military step. Holmes rubbed his hands together in glee as he waited for the sitting room door to open.

Within seconds, a faint knock announced the arrival of Mrs. Hudson and beside her, a tall fellow whose appearance was, I thought, familiar to me. He was aged, I would say, around forty years, lean, with greying hair and sharp, chiseled features. The way he held himself seemed to confirm my impression a military man. With a jolt, I suddenly remembered his identity, and Holmes pre-empted the landlady's introduction by saying,

"Thank you, Mrs. Hudson. We know who this gentleman is." He then turned to our visitor. "Good afternoon, Commander Thorn. Please, be seated. I trust that this is not a reprise of our previous meeting in July, and that I am not to be whisked away, almost in irons, to The Admiralty?"

Thorn pursed his lips and then slowly shook his head before a thin smile lit his face. "Indeed not, Mr. Holmes, although my masters find themselves requiring your assistance once more."

Holmes nodded, and I could see from his expression that he held no malice towards the man seated before him. Reaching for his briar, he re-lit it before saying, "My brother's hand is undoubtedly in this, but please continue."

Commander Thorn leant forward a little as he spoke. "As you say, your brother is aware of my visit to Baker Street." Thorn paused and then resumed. "I've been informed that you were of some service, about a year ago, when you assisted in the detention of a person who had an interest in matters at Weymouth."

Holmes drew strongly upon his pipe and then wagged the stem towards Thorn, saying, "Come, Commander, you may speak openly here. It was not I, but my friend Watson, who stood bravely before the fellow – unarmed, I might add – to enable his capture."

Thorn glanced in my direction and then slowly nodded. "I see. Then I shall lay my cards upon the table. From your enquiries, you will have understood that the Whitehead Company is the sole supplier of torpedoes to the Royal Navy. As the science of modern submarine warfare gathers pace, they are at the forefront of research into improvements in both the performance and guidance of these weapons."

Thorn paused, seeming to consider how to proceed. "It is the improvements made to the guidance system, the gyroscope in particular, that is of concern to my department. It has come to our attention that sensitive information regarding such research has been passed to a foreign power – a power that, we fear, is rapidly gathering strength."

I frowned as I considered the implications of what Thorn had said, asking, "I'm unsure as to how a gyroscope can be of use in a torpedo, Commander? I had a gyroscope as a child and found it to be simply an intriguing toy."

Before Commander Thorn could reply, Holmes lent forward, saying, "It is much more, Watson, but tell me, Commander: How might we be of service?"

Thorn frowned. His expression now most serious. "There is the body of a young man that was recovered from the Thames lying in the mortuary at Tower Bridge. I would be very much obliged if you might examine it."

351

Thorn was silent for a moment. "It appears that he may have taken his own life by drowning but I – we would value your opinion."

Holmes took his pipe from his lips, asking, "Of what interest might this person be to the Admiralty?"

I looked towards Thorn, who now clasped his hands in his lap. "The young man, George Miller, was a promising engineering draftsman and worked at the Admiralty. By way of his position, he had access to all new designs furnished by Whitehead."

Holmes pursed his lips. "You suspect him of passing on information?"

Thorn sat silent for a moment. "It is a possibility, nothing more."

Holmes sat back, looking directly towards Thorn before replying, "But I think that there is more. What is your connection with this George Miller, Commander?" As he said this, Holmes held a finger aloft and slowly wagged it as a clear signal that he would accept no deception.

Thorn again remained silent and then, with brows drawn and an earnest look upon his face, he said quietly, "He is the son of an officer who served under me and was killed during the Boxer Rebellion. Whether I feel some misplaced guilt – I am unsure. However, I confess that I had some influence in obtaining George's position at the Admiralty."

Holmes slowly blew out a stream of blue smoke towards the already almond-coloured ceiling before adding, "And now, perhaps, a dark cloud hangs over both you and young Miller?"

Thorn looked directly towards Holmes and gave the slightest of nods. "Nothing has been said, Mr. Holmes, but there has been a subtle change in the way that I'm addressed and the nature of my given duties." Thorn fell silent, his head slightly bowed.

Holmes rose and, uncharacteristically, he briefly touched Thorn's shoulder, saying, "Watson and I will examine Miller's body and send our findings directly to you. Now, if you might take your leave, we will at once journey to Tower Bridge." Thorn looked relieved on hearing this and with a brief nod to us both, he departed.

True to his word, Holmes tapped out the dottle from his briar on the fender and strode across the room, picking up his coat, hat, and stick as he went. On reaching the door, he didn't turn but called over his shoulder, "Come along, Watson. Ever the laggard!"

I took no offence at this remark, as I knew it to be in jest and simply a ruse designed to encourage me follow him with a little more haste. On collecting my own outer garments and reaching Baker Street, I found that Holmes had already summoned a hansom and was waving his stick enthusiastically in my direction. Climbing somewhat stiffly aboard, I found myself travelling at some speed down Baker Street towards the north tower of the famous bridge, and to the mortuary beneath it.

This, I recalled, was our second visit to this particular mortuary within a month. It had been created within the tower's structure to receive the bodies which, due to the tidal nature and currents in the Thames, had ended up being washed up close by. From our previous visit, we had also discovered that it served to receive the bodies recovered from the Thames brought by the launches of the river police.

With the cab sliding to a halt on the granite cobbles, Holmes leapt out and then tossed the cabby a shilling. Looking around him, he then turned towards the left-hand stone archway beneath the tower. I followed at my own pace and, on opening the stout, wooden door, descended a flight of whitewashed steps. These led down to a small, vaulted room where, at right angles, stood the mortuary proper with its two slabs.

A wide-eyed mortuary attendant looked somewhat startled by our rapid entrance but, on recognising Holmes, simply pointed towards the left-hand slab. Here, its occupant was draped to the shoulders with a drab, grey, mortuary sheet. Holmes nodded in thanks to the attendant before carefully drawing down the sheet. Exposed before us was the lifeless body of a young man illuminated by the pale, yellow glow given out by the double-burnered gaslight that hissed and flickered above us.

Holmes carefully circled the body for a full minute, taking in every detail, like some ever-watchful garden bird. Once satisfied, he then took out his glass and examined, most carefully, the young man laid before him. After examining the limbs, Holmes seemed to pay particular attention to the back of the head before gently summoning me to help him roll the body onto its side. I noticed that as we did this, a small amount of river water was expressed from the mouth of the corpse.

Having done this, Holmes then turned his attention to the pile of clothes that stood on a small table at some little distance. For my part, I took the opportunity to further examine the body myself. The young man was of average height and aged, I would say, less than twenty-five years. Dark-haired and clean-shaven, he appeared to have been in good health at the time of his death. Other than some small abrasions to his limbs and torso, which I took to have been caused by his immersion and recovery from the water, there appeared to be no other injuries.

It was as I turned toward Holmes that I observed him placing a small sample envelope into his jacket pocket. I moved to his side, asking quietly, "You have found something of interest?"

He gave the slightest of nods and then handed me a small, blue poison bottle which I took and then, gingerly, opened. As I raised the stopper warily towards my nose, the acrid odour of a strong acid was unmistakeable. I hastily replaced the stopper and, as I returned it to Holmes, I saw that he held in his palm a length of string of some twelve inches and a flaccid, child's rubber balloon. Looking towards me, he raised an eyebrow and then gave me a questioning look before replacing the items on the small table.

Moving back to the body, Holmes again briefly looked inside Miller's mouth as though in confirmation. With a nod towards the mortuary attendant, we returned to the kerb and sought a cab for our return to Baker Street.

It was during our journey that I ventured to ask Holmes what else he had discovered. Reaching into his jacket pocket, he produced the sample envelope and from it he shook out a few small clusters of some hard, dull grey substance. Peering closely at it, I asked, "What is that? It looks somewhat metallic."

Holmes nodded. "Just so. I suspect that it is zinc, but I must confirm it at Baker Street."

Nothing further was said and for the remainder of the journey, Holmes sat back in the cab, deep in thought.

No sooner had we reached the sitting room than Holmes busied himself, gathering glassware and reagents from his collection of chemical apparatus. After but a few minutes of experimentation, he sat back with a smile of satisfaction upon his face. "The small sample that I gathered from Miller's jacket pocket was, indeed, zinc. A simple test of its reactivity with other metal salts was conclusive."

I stood tight-lipped as I considered this, for I had no inkling as to the significance of the find. Holmes now smiled thinly, saying, "But that is not all that I gleaned, for within the concealed ticket pocket of his jacket was this."

Holmes now held out what appeared to simply be two small sheets of blotting paper. Taking them, I separated the sheets to find within a small piece, upon which was printed a number *"157"* and *"J. Abrams"*. "What might this be?" I asked. "I take it that it is not a cloakroom ticket."

Holmes chuckled, saying, "Indeed not. I believe it to be a receipt for an item left for repair or, perhaps, a pawnbroker's ticket. However, looking at the quality of the young man's clothes and observing that he was clearly well-fed, I think that the former is most likely."

Upon saying that, Holmes now stood and took up a telegram pad, upon which he scribbled before ringing for Billy, the page boy.

I didn't question as to whom the telegram had been sent, but surmised it was in relation to the ticket from Miller's pocket.

Chapter II – A Visit to Whitechapel

It was the following morning that a reply to Holmes's telegram arrived. When I dropped by, he was sitting in his armchair, reading his copy of *The Times*. On the dining table was the battlefield of his place setting. The usual disarray of scattered cutlery with accompanying smears of both marmalade and butter were in evidence upon Mrs. Hudson's fine damask tablecloth. I regarded it with some despair as a gentle knock at the door announced her entrance. Holding the small telegram envelope before her, she approached Holmes, who dropped his paper and pounced forward, almost tearing the envelope from her grasp. I sighed and gave Mrs. Hudson a knowing look as she left, shaking her head.

Holmes seemed elated by the missive, crying, "Whitechapel!" and then moving to the bookcase which contained the modest library of reference works. Taking from it a trade gazetteer, he rapidly thumbed through it before announcing, "Ha! There are a dozen possibilities, but only two in Whitechapel. Come along, Watson! We seek either a watchmaker or a cobbler." I was a little mystified by this outburst but, managing to have one final swallow of coffee, I hastily followed my friend down the stairs and into the bright sunlight of Baker Street.

Holmes wasted little time in attracting the attention of the driver of a passing cab, calling up to him, "Charlotte Street, Whitechapel, if you please."

I was no stranger to the squalor of London, but there were areas within Whitechapel where the grinding poverty was almost indescribable. Indeed, as we travelled eastwards, I was fearful of what we might find in Charlotte Street.

The cab eventually stopped outside St Mary's Station in Whitechapel Road. Climbing down, I looked towards the driver, who then threw out his arm to point, saying, "There you go, gents. That's Charlotte Street – and I ain't taking my cab down there." Without a word, Holmes tossed the cabbie a florin and strode off in the direction indicated.

Charlotte Street was indeed grim – a forbidding row of four-storey, terraced dwellings that were the home to a multitude of what might hesitantly be described as the more well-to-do residents of Whitechapel. Curious faces peered at us through the panes of grimy windows and from shadowed alleyways as we made our way southwards. At one point, a well-built man made as if to approach, but a nod from Holmes and raising his stick in salute was sufficient to curb the fellow's curiosity.

After some fifty yards or so, the quality of the housing had improved somewhat, and at one corner we found a small watchmaker's shop. Here, iron grills were in place part-way up the windows, and a further set of stout iron bars were positioned behind the glass of the shop door. On entering, and after a brief enquiry of the watchmaker which resulted in a shake of the head, we were on our way once more.

As we walked further down Charlotte Street, I asked, "So it is a receipt for a cobbler. I take it that your telegram was to Thorn?"

Holmes nodded. "Yes. The only address that the Admiralty had for Miller was his mother's home in Richmond. However, through conversations with a colleague of the young man, it has been suggested that we might enquire in Whitechapel."

I considered this for a moment before replying, "There is a good deal of difference between the two areas. I would imagine that one might find it somewhat easier to become anonymous in Whitechapel than the leafy suburbs of Richmond."

Holmes nodded, replying, "Indeed – and here, I believe, are the premises we seek." With that, he raised his stick, pointing towards a shop on the other side of the street. Here the signage declared that this was the premises of "*J. Abrams – Boot and Shoe Repairs*".

To our dismay, the shop was securely fastened and a small card in the corner of the glazed door read, "*Closed – To Re-open on Wednesday*".

Holmes's lips, I saw, were now pressed tightly together in frustration. Reaching for his notebook, he quickly wrote a note before tearing the page from it and posting it through the letterbox in the shop door. Turning on his heel, he strode away, clearly irritated.

It was later in the afternoon of the same day, as we sat at leisure, that the doorbell in the hallway below rang. Holmes lowered his broadsheet and was immediately alert. As we listened, the footfalls of Mrs. Hudson were accompanied by the steady, almost-weary, plod of another.

Within seconds, a faint knock on the door announced the arrival of a fellow whose appearance was, I thought, somewhat curious. The man standing beside Mrs. Hudson was of middle years, tall, dark-haired, and bearded with an open face. He was dressed in a rather well-worn dark jacket and trousers, but with a pair of fine, black, patent shoes.

Holmes rose and dismissed her before she could introduce our visitor. Sitting once more, Holmes then turned to our guest, saying, "Welcome, Mr. Abrams. Please be seated. I take it that your shop remains closed. Are the byways of Whitechapel now so smooth that your services are not required?"

I gave Holmes a hard, questioning look and watched as our clearly confused visitor sat, somewhat unsteadily, upon our velvet sofa. Then, "Why . . . err . . . yes and no, Mr. Holmes, for I am never short of business."

Holmes smiled and then turned slightly towards me, with his arm outstretched, saying, "This is my friend, Dr. John Watson. You have noticed, Watson, that Mr. Abrams is an able cobbler who serves the Jewish community in Whitechapel?"

Abrams nodded and sat wide-eyed, before asking, "How . . . ?"

Holmes smiled once more. "You have, no doubt, made your way here in response to my missive. However, whilst others may call at Baker Street, your identity is unmistakeable. Your waistcoat shows some abrasion where your leather apron is fastened about your waist, and the fine workmanship of your own shoes is at odds with your rather work-weary attire."

Holmes's eyes sparkled as he continued. "A mere glance at your calloused hands show that your employment involves some element of manual labour, and the scars to your thumb and forefinger bear witness to your use of a cobbler's needle and awl. You are the proprietor of your business, as you are able to close your shop as you please." Holmes paused, adding, "An employee would not be released from his labours until the end of his working day."

Abrams blinked as Holmes drew strongly upon his pipe before continuing, "Abrams is a Jewish surname with links to the Jewish, English, and Dutch communities . . . but your watch fob bears the six-pointed star of Solomon's Seal. Whitechapel is the largest Jewish community in London, and the location of your place of work was confirmed by the colour of the *2d* bus ticket protruding from your waistcoat pocket – tuppence being the appropriate fare for the five miles from Whitechapel to Baker Street."

Holmes sat back and placed the pipe to his lips before asking, "Now is this not so, Mr. Abrams?"

Abrams smiled and gave a brief nod. "All that you say is true, Mr. Holmes. Before I left Charlotte Street, I was concerned that your note to call here might be some prank, but as I closed my door, I happened upon Rabbi Lionel Cohen. I mentioned your name to him and he reassured me that all was in order."

Holmes sat back, his eyes half-closed, saying softly, "Ah, yes, Rabbi Cohen." Holmes now reached into his waistcoat pocket and produced from it the small, printed receipt, saying, "I take it that this relates to an item that was brought to your shop for repair, as I described in my note?"

Abrams took the receipt and nodded – a look of disbelief now passed across his face. Taking a deep breath, Abrams began. "Some five days ago, the landlord of a lodging house in Romford Street came into my shop with a pair of opera shoes belonging to one of his lodgers and he asked me to replace the heel on the right shoe. This I agreed to do, but as the heel seemed to have been crudely fitted, I told him that it would need to be replaced at the cost of a shilling."

357

Abrams again paused and then reached into his jacket pocket, removing from it what appeared to be a very small, velvet bag. "It was as I removed the old heel that I found this." Abrams leaned forward and passed the bag to Holmes. I craned my neck and peered towards my friend as he carefully untied the bag and tipped its contents into the palm of his hand.

My eyes opened wide as I cried, "A diamond!" Holmes now held before him a fine jewel that sparkled like fire in the afternoon sunlight. "Is it real?" I stammered.

John Abrams nodded. "Oh yes, Doctor. As Mr. Holmes mentioned, Abrams is a Jewish name, and one that is associated with Holland. My father was Johannes Abrams, and our family home was within the 'diamond quarter' of Amsterdam."

Abrams now looked saddened as he recalled, "Many years ago, we fled from there to London. From an early age, I was familiar with the diamond trade, but I had no desire to join the family business. Instead, I was apprenticed to a saddler and shoemaker." Abrams pursed his lips, adding, "Shortly before my father died, he gave me some stones that he had managed to bring with him to England, and with the money from their sale, I was able to set myself up in business."

I frowned, saying almost to myself, "That is a most peculiar place to keep safe such a valuable item."

Abrams nodded. "Quite so, Doctor. I have kept it on my person for safe keeping, but the tale has now becomes even stranger, for the ticket you have produced is for this very pair of shoes! The morning after I had agreed to repair the shoes, I received an urgent telegram from a Mr. George Miller imploring – nay, *ordering* me – not to proceed with the repair, and that he would come to my shop that very afternoon to collect them."

On hearing this, I sat bolt upright. Holmes leant forward, bright-eyed, asking, "I take it that this Mr. Miller did not appear?"

"No, Mr. Holmes, not that day nor the next. I have left it until I closed the shop today, but as he hasn't made an appearance and, after speaking to Rabbi Cohen and receiving your note, I decided to come to you." Abrams then frowned and shook his head. "I don't know what to do. I am hoping that my story is of some interest and that I might leave the diamond with you?" Abrams paused, adding, somewhat eagerly, "If you are in agreement, Mr. Holmes . . . and . . . and should Mr. Miller call at my shop, I shall direct him to you, here, in Baker Street."

Holmes expression darkened as he heard this. He then nodded, saying, "Yes, of course. It is indeed an intriguing puzzle, Mr. Abrams, and it has certainly piqued my interest. Do you have a full address for this Mr. Miller?"

Abrams searched in his jacket pocket and pulled from it a small, printed bill. Upon it, I noted, had been written in a good hand the address, "*15 Romford Street*". "I didn't presume to call upon the gentleman myself, given what I had found . . . ."

Holmes rose, pocketed the diamond and, on extending his hand, uttered, "Quite so. I will bid you 'Good day', Mr. Abrams, and I will make enquiries." At this, Abrams rose and, clearly relieved, departed with just a simple nod to us both.

I sat back, struck a Vesta against my silver match case, and re-lit my pipe. After taking several long draws upon it, I frowned, asking, "This is indeed a strange business. Why would anyone consider secreting a diamond in the heel of his shoe?"

Holmes frowned as he returned to his chair and picked up his briar. "Clearly there is the element of concealment, and also a means of transporting an item of value with some security." Holmes now drew on his pipe and then wagged the stem in my direction, saying, "The fact that the diamond is always carried about the person implies two things. Firstly, as Abrams mentioned, there may not be an adequate place of safety for it at the home address. Secondly, it is perhaps carried in case of an emergency, or for its intrinsic value, as currency."

I frowned and gave this some thought before asking, "Is this common practice? I have never heard of it."

Holmes's face was without expression as he replied, "I know it to be so in some circles. Imagine that you travel, perhaps covertly, between nations. Diamonds are valued highly in almost all cultures. Untraceable, unlike letters of credit, they may be easily converted into currency."

I rubbed my chin as I turned over in my mind what Holmes had said. "Are you suggesting, then, that this man Miller might, perhaps, be a smuggler?"

Holmes held his forefinger to his lips, saying "I think not, given that it was a single stone, but it may well be that he inhabits a world more familiar to my brother." On saying this, Holmes now raised an eyebrow and smiled thinly. "I believe that it would be unwise to leave this matter untouched, even for another day, for we know the reason why Mr. Miller hasn't returned to retrieve his most valuable property. Come, Watson. Romford Street awaits!"

Chapter III – A Grim Discovery

Swiftly finding a cab and returning to Whitechapel, we were soon striding down Romford Street in search of the late George Miller's lodgings. Looking above each of the doorways, it took only a few minutes to discover the small, cast-iron plate that indicated that the door before us was, indeed, Number Fifteen. Holmes raised his stick and rapped soundly. After a few moments, a surprisingly well-groomed man opened the door, asking, "Yes?"

Holmes touched his hat and then proffered his card, saying, "Good evening. My name is Sherlock Holmes, and this is Doctor Watson. We're seeking a Mister Miller. Might he be in residence?"

The man's questioning look hardened as he read Holmes's card and, on looking up, replied, "Unless you have come to settle his rent, I will bid you a good evening, for it seems that he has up and left. He said he was just going away for a couple of days on business, but he's been gone more than twice that, and he owes me five shillings!"

Holmes smiled, reached into his pocket, and withdrew from it a sovereign. Holding it before him, Holmes said, "I'm happy to pay what is owed, but I would like to see his room. Of course, I would also be willing to compensate you for your time and trouble."

The fellow before us was wide-eyed as he ogled the coin in Holmes's grasp. Throwing the door fully open, he beamed a welcome as he reached for it. "This way, gents. His room is on the first floor."

Leading the way, we passed along a short corridor with tired, papered decorations above a stained pine dado rail. Whilst shabby, it was clean to the touch. The fellow before us slowly climbed the narrow staircase which turned back on itself as it reached the next floor. Reaching into his trouser pocket, he produced a small bunch of keys, saying, "Here you are, sirs. Number Six. I'll leave you for a few minutes to have a look around."

Holmes nodded and smiled in thanks, asking, "Was Mr. Miller here long, Mr – ?"

"Weaver, sir. Matthew Weaver, I am the landlord. He was here for about a month, never no trouble nor nothing."

Holmes again smiled. "Was it you that took his shoes to Mr. Abrams, the cobbler?"

The man's eyes opened wide as he nodded. "Bless me, how did you know that? Yes, sir. He said that he was going away for a couple of days on business, but after two days had passed, I knocked on the door here and as I didn't get no reply, I unlocked it, as I was concerned-like. Everything seemed to be in its place but I sees that he had left out a pair of trousers to be pressed." Weaver smiled, adding, "My wife does a bit of washing and such for our guests. Anyways, I sees these posh shoes, and just as I was going to push them back under the bed, I notices that the heel on one of them was a bit loose."

Weaver paused, adding in explanation, "I does odd jobs, see, to earn a bit on the side, and I know that Mr. Miller was a bit particular with his clothes, so off I trots to Mr. Abrams."

Holmes frowned. "And you haven't seen him since?"

Weaver shook his head. "No sir, I ain't, but the wife says that one evening last week, late-like, he nipped up to his room and then comes running downstairs and hammers on our door wanting to know where his shoes is. I was out, down at the Bull's Head, so she tells him what I's done, gives him the cobbler's ticket, and off he goes." With a scowl, Weaver continued, "I reckon's he's done a moonlight! Anyways, give me a shout when you've seen enough." At that, Weaver seemed to simply shrug and left us to examine Miller's room and its contents.

In truth, it seemed very much like the many other rented premises that I would see, almost daily, when called to a home visit. The room itself, whilst clean, was barely ten feet square. The small window, opposite the door, looked out onto Romford Street but did little to relieve the room's dismal aspect. For furniture there was but a single bed, a washstand with a bowl and jug, and a small wardrobe. A desk and chair stood beneath the window, and upon the bare floorboards beside the bed was a rag rug that had seen better days.

Holmes lit the stub of candle beside the bed and then opened the wardrobe. For my part, I examined the desk as best I could, using the fading light from the window. Upon it I noticed a railway timetable, and as I examined it, a map of part of the Underground that had been folded within fell to the floor. As I retrieved it, I observed that a section of one line had been coloured and annotated. Thinking this to be of some interest, I placed it to one side.

The desk had a single drawer and held all that one would expect: A small bottle of ink which was firmly corked, two dip pens and a few spare nibs, and a small amount of writing paper and envelopes. It was as I lifted the sheets of writing paper that I observed the corner of a notebook peeping out from beneath. Taking it, I moved a little closer to the window to gain as much illumination as I could and riffled through the pages.

The first few held some figures, accounts which, I assumed, were Miller's day-to-day out-goings and income. Beside these, he had a few scribbled comments which seemed to display his melancholy concerning his lack of funds. The rest of the book appeared to be blank until I reached the final two pages. Here there were what appeared to be several attempts at the beginning of a letter. On reading these, my hand went to my mouth, and I couldn't help but exclaim, "Oh Lord!"

Holmes swiftly turned and I held out the pages to him. Moving closer to the candle, Holmes read aloud:

361

Dearest Mother,

*I hope you are well. In truth, I cannot say the same for myself,
for I find that I have become a disgrace to the family through
my own stupidity. I have been drawn into actions that I
heartily regret and must now ensure that no blame or taint
can fall upon you or upon father's good name*

Holmes paused. I could see from his expression that he had been
moved by these words. Looking again, he now read, in silence, the other
attempts to write what was, in effect, a suicide note. Holmes closed the
book, his voice void of emotion, saying, "It is not unexpected, Watson. I
would imagine that even now his mother has received the full letter and is
grieving."

I nodded and then proceeded to show Holmes the annotated
Underground railway map that I'd discovered. He raised an eyebrow,
nodded, and then placed the map, together with the notebook, within his
inside coat pocket. This, I noticed, already contained a folded newspaper.

It was just as Holmes had refastened his coat that the landlord re-
appeared in the doorway, asking, "Finished gents? I imagine that I'll have
to sell all the clothes and the like for the rest of the month's rent."

Holmes now stepped forward, taking another sovereign from his
pocket. "That will be un-necessary, Mr. Weaver. I will arrange for Miller's
belongings to be collected tomorrow, if that is convenient?"

Weaver pursed his lips. "Yes. I'll be at home, sir, and be glad to have
the room cleared." Holmes nodded and strode down the stairs without
another word.

A short walk to the Commercial Road found us hailing a hansom and
returning to Baker Street, Holmes having not uttered a single word other
than to give directions to the cabbie. Once there, he dashed off a telegram
and then proceeded to throw himself into his armchair. It was only after
some half-an-hour of silence and the beginning of our second pipes that
Holmes spoke. "It appears, Watson, that the fears of Commander Thorn
have been confirmed. If there is a way to mitigate the effects of Miller's
actions and some way to exonerate Thorn, then we must find it. I fear that
he may well become tarnished, simply by association"

Holmes sat back and drew strongly upon his pipe. "Let us now
consider what we have discovered from our visit to Romford Street."
Reaching down beside his chair, he placed the map of the Underground,
the notebook, and also the newspaper that I had observed in his coat pocket
upon his slender knees.

362

Holmes frowned. "For there to have been secrets passed, there must have been meetings between Miller and some third party – or at least a delivery of information."

I nodded in agreement but was puzzled by his reference to a "delivery". "Do you believe that the information from the Admiralty was posted?"

Holmes pursed his lips. "It's a possibility, for the newspaper that I discovered had circled entries within the personal column which may well relate to meeting places. However, I'm fascinated by what we found at the mortuary and in Miller's wardrobe at Romford Street."

I looked blankly, as I was unaware of any further evidence that had been obtained, other than that which now adorned his lap.

Holmes had a twinkle in his eye as he asked, "Tell me, Watson. What can you recall from your chemistry lectures on the reaction of zinc with, say . . . Sulphuric Acid?"

Pursing my lips, I replied, "Well, the products of such a reaction would be the sulphate of zinc and hydrogen . . . ." It was at that moment that I suddenly made the connection with what we had found amongst Miller's possessions at the mortuary. "The rubber balloon – and the string!" I cried out.

Holmes nodded. "Amongst Miller's effects were a small bottle of acid, and also a few grains of zinc in his jacket pocket, but how were they to be used? At Romford Street, I also found a small cardboard tube and some gummed paper within the wardrobe. Clearly this was meant to contain the drawings that he was passing."

I gave this some thought before stating, "Surely you cannot be saying that Miller delivered the drawings by placing them within a cardboard tube attached to a rubber balloon filled with hydrogen gas? Such an arrangement would be at the mercy of the elements and would drift wherever the prevailing wind might take it!"

Holmes nodded slowly and then blew out a thin stream of smoke. "There must be some method of guidance to determine the direction of flight. As you say, the balloon couldn't be released in the open." He frowned and took from his lap the Underground map that I had discovered. Opening it out, he traced the path of the line that had been coloured with a red pencil. At a point along the line, a red cross had been drawn. "This is most curious, for the marked location is between stations. I would imagine it to be some small distance from the rear of The National Portrait Gallery."

My own grasp of the siting of London landmarks was far from extensive and I relied upon Holmes's own encyclopaedic knowledge in this matter.

363

Sitting back, Holmes now drew up his knees tightly towards his chest and closed his eyes. I knew now that any further conversation with my friend would go unheard as he withdrew from the world. Taking my leave and with an unheard "Good Night", I made my way home.

The following morning, as I stopped in to visit, I noticed that Holmes had already eaten. His plate and cutlery had been brusquely pushed to one side as he stood at the table, poring over both the notebook and the newspaper.

For my part, I rang the bell to inform Mrs. Hudson that I would like a cup of coffee, if she didn't mind.

Taking his pipe from his mouth, Holmes tapped the stem against an entry that had been circled in the personal column of *The Times*. I saw from the date that this was a copy from the week previous. "What do you make of this?"

I peered at the circled item, reading aloud, *"Friday, Six p.m. G.M."* I pursed my lips before saying, "Well, it seems as though Miller was confirming that his item had been included within this edition and that he intended to meet somebody."

Holmes nodded, replying, "I believe that you're half-correct in what you say . . . but I think, perhaps, it was a notification that something was to be ready for collection at that time."

I considered this for a moment before blurting out, "A balloon! But where? We've already determined that it couldn't be released in the open."

"Quite so. It's imperative that we investigate what is to be found at the precise position shown on the map." Deep in thought, Holmes now retreated to his armchair with the notebook. As for myself, I was indeed grateful for the appearance of Mrs. Hudson and her breakfast tray.

I had just finished the coffee and was dabbing my lips with a napkin when Holmes said, "Charing Cross Station." What importance this location had was a mystery to me, but I followed my friend's lead.

A cab was quickly obtained and it was as we rode toward our destination, I ventured to ask why we were heading into the city. Holmes turned towards me and smiled. "Miller worked in the Admiralty Building, and the nearest Underground station is Charing Cross, a mere two-hundred yards from his place of work."

I nodded, but I was still somewhat bemused, and my blank expression seemed to exasperate my friend. "The plans, Watson! If you were stealing secret documents, you would not wish to have them about your person any longer than was absolutely necessary!"

Holmes could see that I still hadn't grasped the import of what he had tried to explain, and he sighed loudly. "The position marked on the railway map is but a short distance from the station. Whatever he was doing with the balloon happened there."

Within minutes, the cab had drawn up beside the station and Holmes headed off towards the gallery at the trot. I tossed the cabbie a shilling and was quite breathless as I caught up. Holmes seemed to have little regard for my fatigue as he looked about him. "This area, at the rear of the gallery, was once Hemmings Row, which was demolished – but not that!" His face lit up, his arm outstretched and pointing before him. As I watched, he began running towards a short, square structure of brick and Portland stone.

I followed at my own pace. Before us was what appeared to be a house, but in miniature. It stood some twelve-feet-by-six-feet and had brick filled "windows" with Portland stone ledges and cap stones. In height, it was some eight feet tall and a stout, iron door was built into one end. As to the roof, the gable ends were in place, but it was as though the traditional apex of slates had been replaced with a similarly shaped wide steel mesh.

Handing me his stick and then grasping the brickwork, Holmes reached up and stood on the window ledge. From this position, he then proceeded to examine the mesh before descending to examine the iron door of this strange structure.

I was about to ask him the purpose of the building when a veritable cloud of steam and sulphurous smoke emerged from its meshed roof. "Venting!" I cried.

Holmes had a wry smile on his face as he then charged off in the direction of the nearby Underground station.

Chapter IV – Charing Cross

The hotel and station of Charing Cross that abutted the Strand was indeed a fine building of considerable size. The hotel built above the station loomed skyward over several floors, its red brick walls punctuated by Portland stone-dressed windows. In front of the hotel stood the ornate Queen Eleanor's Memorial Cross, some seventy feet high, erected in 1865 – this brick-and-stone edifice being something of a nod to the original thirteenth-century structure which had stood close by.

Finding the entrance and steps to the Underground station, surrounded by ornate cast-iron fencing, we then descended some twenty or so feet to the cream tiled and white-washed atrium of the station proper. Paying our two-pence fare, we passed through the turnstile before making our way along the stone paved platform of this tiled, arched cavern. Holmes, I noticed, was casually walking towards the farthest end of the

365

platform when, suddenly, he disappeared from view. I was immediately concerned and increased my pace slightly, but not sufficiently to attract attention.

As I reached the limit of the platform, I could make out a small flight of steps leading down to the tracks and a dimly illuminated figure beyond, beckoning to me. Taking care, I followed and, mindful of the signal linkages and other railway paraphernalia, I slowly trailed after Holmes, who now stood, gazing upwards, some thirty or so yards from the station proper.

As I watched, he suddenly seemed to increase in illumination as he stood, stock-still to one side of the iron rails. "Here, Watson. It was here that Miller inflated and then released his balloon with its precious cargo." I looked upwards and saw above me a brick-lined chimney shaft with a small balcony and mesh cover. I realised then that I was gazing at the internal structure of the small building in Hemmings Row.

Holmes now ducked backwards into an arched, brick niche used by the railway staff as a place of safety from any approaching train. In the shadows, Holmes struck a Vesta and looked around him within the confines of the niche. Reaching down, he retrieved a small item and held it beside the flickering match flame. Within his gloved hand was a small, blue, uncorked bottle. I looked towards him and saw a grim smile before he extinguished the match and then returned to the platform.

Little was said during our return to Baker Street, and it was only as we sat and considered what had been discovered that I plucked up the courage to ask, "What do you imagine prompted Miller to take his own life?"

Holmes had his eyes half-closed. He slowly took his briar from his lips before replying, "I believe it was most probably guilt. Miller had, for some reason, made the decision to betray his country. However, in doing so he inadvertently implicated Thorn, a man who may, himself, have had his own feelings of guilt. Miller realised his error and was aware that, if discovered, he would bring shame upon his family name and his widowed mother." Holmes paused and drew once more upon his pipe. "Fearing that the repair to his shoe would reveal the hidden gem and, perhaps, be brought to the attention of the authorities, may have been sufficient to push him, literally, over the edge. All would come to light and a devastating scandal would ensue with reputations ruined."

I sat and thought about this for some minutes before asking, "What then is to be done? No more secrets will be passed, but what of Thorn? By his influence in finding Miller a position, he may well have a shadow cast upon him. Trust, once lost in the position he holds, may never be regained."

Holmes nodded slowly. "I must not allow Thorn to fall from grace, for I'm sure that his intentions were, indeed, honourable. I need to speak to him once more." Reaching for a telegram pad, Holmes scribbled before ringing for Billy.

It was mid-morning the following day when the bell in the hallway below announced our visitor. The measured, military step on the stairs identified who was to be our guest.

Within moments, the gentle tap on the sitting room door was followed by the appearance of Mrs. Hudson, accompanied by the tall figure of Commander Thorn. With a smile and a nod to her, Holmes directed Thorn to be seated. Looking towards him, I could readily see that the strain of this affair was telling upon the fellow. Dark circles had appeared around his eyes, and his expression seemed to be permanently strained.

Sitting forward, he asked, "Your telegram was brief, Mr. Holmes. Tell me, have you discovered anything regarding young Miller?"

Holmes nodded and then gazed fixedly at Thorn as he asked, "Has his death become public knowledge? Your answer is vitally important."

Thorn slowly shook his head. "No. His absence has been marked officially, as 'On Leave', and those in his department are none the wiser."

Holmes sat back before recounting all that had been revealed from our visit to Tower Bridge mortuary and then Romford Street. I could see that Thorn was both shocked and dismayed by what he heard. It was clear that he understood how this would undoubtedly affect his own career. His body slumped as Holmes recounted our meeting with Abrams. He was then shown the diamond.

In truth, Thorn looked a beaten man, but Holmes then leant forward, saying, "It is a sad tale, but I believe that all may not be lost, Commander." At this, Thorn's head rose slightly from its resting place upon his chest. "I require you to do two things. First, you must arrange for Miller's effects to be collected from his lodgings at 15 Romford Street in Whitechapel. You must make haste, as we do not wish for his disappearance to become common knowledge. The landlord, a Mr. Weaver, is a man who may well have a loose tongue."

As I watched, Thorn took a small, leather-bound notebook from his jacket pocket and made a note of the name and address. "And secondly, Mr. Holmes?"

"I require you to accompany Dr. Watson and me to Charing Cross Station tomorrow evening. I will advise you of the hour, and be sure to bring your service revolver."

Thorn's eyes opened wide on hearing this, but he nodded in agreement. Holmes now rose and extended his hand, saying, "Take heart,

Thorn. You will emerge from this a little scarred, but your service to your country will stand you in good stead."

Thorn blinked, stood and with a puzzled look upon his face, bade us a "Good morning," and left.

No sooner had the door closed than Holmes clapped his hands and then rubbed them together in delight. I was mystified by his apparent jollity after such a harrowing encounter. Looking toward me, he was bright-eyed, crying. "The game's afoot, Watson, for we are to take the fellow who has orchestrated this dilemma!"

Holmes then stepped to the table and rummaged for the copy of *The Times* that had been annotated by Miller. "Ha! Now for the lure!" Reaching for the telegram pad, Holmes took unusual care to write a single sentence upon it before tearing off the top sheet and ringing for Billy.

I frowned on seeing this and gave Holmes a questioning look, but as I did so, he moved past me, gathered his outer garments, and went down the stairs without uttering a single word.

It was perhaps an hour later that he returned, bright-eyed and with a small, brown paper wrapped parcel beneath his arm. He didn't even acknowledge my presence, but instead disappeared into his bedroom, closing the door rather too quickly behind him. I knew not to disturb him and passed some time reading an intriguing article in the August edition of *The Lancet*. In time Holmes re-appeared, and he looked particularly pleased with himself. My questioning glance produced nothing more than a raised eyebrow, and so I returned to my reading.

After my arrival the following afternoon, Holmes did little except mope, the only moment of animation being his trip downstairs to purchase a copy of *The Times*. On his return, he flung the paper onto the dining table before tearing at the pages until he found the item he was searching for. Satisfied, he returned to his chair with a wolfish grin upon his lips.

I could only purse my lips and then move to the table to try and make some sense of the scattered pages before me. As I scanned the tightly packed type of the uppermost page, my pipe almost fell from my mouth as one particular item leapt out at me. There, in the "Personal" column was an entry, "*Thursday, Six p.m. G.M.*".

I looked towards my friend. The wry smile on Holmes's face told all. He nodded, saying, "Yes, Watson. The fly has been cast, and I believe we will catch a fine trout this evening. I must inform Thorn."

With a telegram sent to Commander Thorn to meet us at Charing Cross Station at a quarter-to-six, Holmes readied himself for the task ahead. On the table had been spread out a newspaper, and upon it had been placed a small, blue-glass poison bottle and its accompanying cork, a small funnel, and a heap of grey metal beads that I knew to be zinc.

Beside this was a thin cardboard tube, similar to that which had been discovered at Romford Street. The tube was attached by a small piece of string to an uninflated, child's rubber balloon. Holmes sat for a few moments whilst he took up some strong Sulphuric Acid from his own supply and then filled and firmly corked the small poison bottle. This he placed carefully in his overcoat pocket together with an envelope containing the zinc granules.

Then he took a sheet of writing paper from his desk and busily penned what appeared to be a letter. I was indeed curious, as when he had finished and had blotted it, he proceeded to roll it tightly and insert it into the cardboard tube before sealing it with gummed tape. I didn't enquire as to the letter's content, and he didn't offer any explanation as he placed that too into his overcoat pocket.

That night, Holmes's face showed little emotion as we made our way down the stairs to Baker Street before summoning a cab for our journey. The weight of exonerating Thorn appeared to be weighing heavily upon my friend.

Chapter V – The Lure is Taken!

By half-past-five, we were at the entrance to Charing Cross Station. Holmes made ready to descend once more to the tracks whilst asking me to stand watch and wait for Thorn. After some ten minutes or so, he was back, and a look of quiet expectancy had now brightened his countenance.

Within moments of Holmes's return, the now-familiar figure of Thorn, with his crisp, military step, approached from the direction of the Admiralty building. After a brief handshake, followed by Holmes outlining his intentions, we casually began walking in the direction of the vent.

Thorn made his way toward a newspaper seller who stood at the corner of The National Portrait Gallery, purchasing a paper before sitting on a bench some twenty feet away from the vent. For our part, Holmes and I stood some little distance away, whereupon he began a rather animated conversation as to which fishing flies provide a modicum of success. I was facing Holmes but could see, over his shoulder, that a balloon now bobbed happily beneath the roof-mesh of the vent.

It was as he expounded upon the merits of a dry Damsel fly that I noticed him stiffen slightly. I found it indeed difficult to avoid the temptation to turn and follow his gaze but I resisted manfully. As Holmes continued with his discourse, a short, dapper fellow dressed in a formal overcoat, top hat, and carrying a somewhat incongruous, hook-ended walking stick passed me by. Looking around briefly, he then disappeared from view and, as I watched, I saw the balloon being retrieved by means of the hooked stick.

Holmes had heard the scrape of the iron door to the vent being opened and hastened towards it, with Thorn close on his heels. I followed and was just in time to see the fellow locking the vent door.

"Good evening, Mr. Yamamoto. I see that you have retrieved my note." On hearing Holmes's words, the fellow spun round and his right hand plunged into his overcoat pocket. Holmes then spoke sharply. "I would strongly advise against acting foolishly. My companion, Commander Thorn of the Naval Intelligence Deparment, would not hesitate to fire.

I looked towards Thorn who had already drawn his pistol. His face was cold and without emotion as he faced Yamamoto. The diminutive figure nodded slightly and took his empty hand from his coat pocket and turned towards my friend.

"Good evening, Mr. Holmes. I think that we met at the Spithead review when I was a guest onboard the *HMS Illustrious*."

Holmes nodded. "Indeed so. You were the Japanese naval attaché, and I believe that the Imperial Japanese Navy now has a similarly fine vessel – the battleship *Mikasa* – which, I believe, bears a truly remarkable – in fact, an uncanny – resemblance to the *Illustrious.* " Yamamoto smiled and bowed in agreement.

Holmes was now firm as he asked, "To avoid any unpleasantness, the cardboard tube, if you please?"

I thought for a moment that the fellow was going to refuse Holmes's request, but a single look towards a resolute Thorn was sufficient for Yamamoto to reach into his opposite coat pocket and produce the cardboard tube and the now limp balloon.

Holmes reached out his hand, took the tube and, after removing the gummed tape, he withdrew a single sheet of paper. "Thank you. I fear that you will receive no further communications from George Miller, though not as a result of your own actions."

Holmes paused for a moment and his voice was now cold as he continued. "Miller chose to end this affair in the only way that he thought honourable."

Unrolling the piece of paper, Holmes now read aloud his handwritten copy of the note that Miller had drafted to his mother. When he had finished, he asked, "You understand the significance of this, Yamamoto?" The Japanese nodded, sombrely.

Holmes then continued, "Your diplomatic immunity protects you at present, but I have little doubt that, within the hour, you will be declared '*persona non-grata*' and expelled from Great Britain at the very earliest opportunity."

Pocketing the tube and without a further word, Holmes turned on his heel and left. I nodded toward an incredulous Thorn and followed my friend as he strode away, beckoning to the driver of an oncoming cab.

On our return to Baker Street, nothing further was said and I left for my own home in Queen Anne Street. It was after I'd stopped by the following morning that a telegram arrived from Thorn which confirmed that Yamamoto had, indeed, been expeditiously informed of his status and was now required to quit our shores within forty-eight hours. Having read it, Holmes tossed it to one side, unmoved by its content.

"What do you intend to do with the diamond?" I enquired.

Holmes put down his coffee cup and then sat back. "I have given this some considerable thought, Watson. I'm vehemently opposed to persons benefitting from their misdeeds. However, I'm of the opinion that, as there is no provenance to the stone, there is a slim possibility that Miller purchased it legitimately."

On hearing this I frowned, feeling that this was unlikely in the extreme. Holmes continued, "I suggest, Watson, that the stone be sold and the revenue from it invested to provide Miller's mother with some small pension, although nothing can replace the tragic loss of both a husband and a son."

I considered Holmes suggestion for a moment before giving a single nod. Whilst I was not completely at ease with the thought of any benefit ensuing from Miller's illegal activities, I agreed that no further hardship should fall upon Mrs. Miller.

In the days that followed, no mention was made in the press of Yamamoto's departure. However, Holmes received a note, with an assurance from Mycroft Holmes that Thorn would remain in post, his reputation intact.

As regards further contact with Thorn, an envelope arrived containing his card which bore, on its reverse, the words "*With grateful thanks*" and his signature. Within the envelope was also a cutting from a local Richmond newspaper which reported the funeral of George Miller. On reading this, Holmes was content and considered the case to be at an end.

The Adventure of the
Wells Beach Ruffians
by Derrick Belanger

Dear Watson,

I hope all is well with you and that you are enjoying your retirement as much as I am. I write to you from across the pond in the small oceanside community of Wells, Maine. I'm sure you recall that during my hiatus, I spent some time north of here in the Bay of Fundy studying tidal patterns. I always enjoyed the New England coast and decided to spend a sojourn here working on my *The Whole Art of Detection*.

Old Martha is watching the cottage while I'm away. She has proved to be much more resourceful than you or I ever knew, my friend. Let me just say that while I'm across the Atlantic, I know that my home is safe with her keeping watch over matters.

Do you remember how at the end of our time together in Baker Street, you would joke with me that mysteries had a way of finding me? That no matter where we would try to escape for some seclusion, we would somehow stumble upon a case? You may have hit on something, my friend, for even thousands of miles from home, I still find myself presented with interesting adventures. It is a recent one which has prompted me to put my pen to paper and write you this missive, for this adventure led me to meet two gentlemen whose friendship reminded me of ours.

I was sitting in the bar at the Beach Plum, the hotel where I'm staying. I had only just arrived that morning and registered under the name of Mäkinen, pretending to be a Finnish traveller. Because of your popular narratives, it is difficult for me to find a locale where my name is unknown. Therefore, I always use an alias when traveling, whether it is to Manchester or to Marrakech.

It was late morning when I took my seat at the counter and ordered a whisky. There was only one other man in the establishment at the time, sitting a few seats down from me. The bartender, a jolly bald-headed bushy-browed fellow named Thomas, asked me where I was from. I told him I was from Espoo in Finland and had escaped on a sojourn to complete some important writing. The other fellow at the bar, a grisly-faced old timer with salty white hair and an unkempt beard with swirls like the sea, let out a loud seal-like bark at my explanation. "You're as much a Finn," he started, then paused, took a swig of his whisky, and concluded, "You're

372

as much a Finn as I'm a saint." The bartender laughed heartily at this pronouncement.

"What do you mean, sir?" I asked somewhat indignantly.

"Look in the mirror," he commanded, then counted down on his hand, "Jet black hair mixed in with white, grey eyes, a beak like a hawk, gaunt face . . . sound like any Finn you know, Tom?"

The bartender eyed me over. "Can't say he does, Hal, but I also can't say I know many Finns." Thomas turned his plump form to me and while he kept his happy countenance, his eyes were questioning. "What's your angle, stranger?" he asked in a friendly fashion. I'm sure that many people had come through his tavern, hiding their identity.

"Your friend is correct," I said with a smile on my face. It was clear that the two men met me no ill will. They enjoyed that they had caught me in a lie, and I admit that I too was enjoying myself. It is rare to find someone who uses their powers of observation. "I am an actor," I explained revealing a half-truth, "and I'm studying for a role as a sailor in Maine. I humbly admit my disguise was a poor choice." I turned to Hal and couldn't help saying to him, "I'm impressed that you saw through my ruse so quickly. You are a real Sherlock Holmes, my friend." I motioned for Thomas to poor the man another whisky.

He thanked me and said, "You are kind, sir, but it don't take Sherlock Holmes to see you don't have the fair hair and blue eyes of the Nordics. Fact is, if I was a Sherlock Holmes, I could track down those ruffians who beat up Jamison today."

"I heard about that," Thomas said, with a sad shake of his jowls. He was pouring out two more glasses of whisky which he handed over to Hal and to me. He then continued, "What's this world coming to? And after losing his son and all."

As you can imagine, Watson, my interest was piqued. I asked the men about this Jamison.

"It's a sad story . . . ." He paused, not knowing how to address me.

"Charles," I finished for him. "Mr. Charles Croft."

"Ah," he nodded acknowledging what he believed to be my true name. "It's a sad story, Charlie. Jamison's name should be Job with all the misfortune he's endured. All had been fine in the man's life. He was a fisherman, and a good one. Had a house and his own boat. Wasn't a rich man, but none of us are."

"Aye, we're poor but we don't know it," confirmed Thomas in a tone meant to be serious. "If we got a roof over our head and a woman in our bed then we don't need much else." We all raised our glasses to this wise proclamation.

Hal lowered his glass and his voice took on a somber tone. "Then tragedy struck as it often does, in threes. Jamison's wife caught pneumonia and passed. Soon after that, while the poor man was still grieving, we had a bad storm hit the area. Winds were something fierce. Jamison's boat was tossed about like a toy in the storm and by the time the winds had ceased, there wasn't much left of his ship except for splinters."

"Didn't have no insurance, the daft fool," barked Thomas.

"Didn't have much money," explained Hal, almost apologizing for Jamison. "The man wasn't much of a fisherman. His son was, though. The family business had been improving before the storm hit. With the boat destroyed, his son joined a larger fishing boat out of Kennebunk. He explained to his dad that he'd send home money from his jobs and soon they'd be able to buy another boat and start over. It wasn't to be, though."

Thomas stepped away from us to dry some glasses which I noted were already dry. The poor man had turned his face away, greatly saddened by the story.

Even Hal choked up on this last part. "Then . . . Then just a few weeks later . . . his poor son was lost at sea. They never did find the body."

Hal stopped and we sat in silence for a moment. He nursed his drink quietly, taking a moment to mourn his friend.

"Since then," Hal started, speaking much softer, "Jamison hasn't been quite right in the head. He spends the day from sun-up to sun-down wandering the beach, and looking out across the ocean, hoping that his son will return. The town – we take care of him. Some of the ladies bring him food, and the boys, we watch out for him, make sure no one gives him any trouble when they hear him muttering to himself on the beach."

"Your friend has been burdened with grief that none should have to endure," I solemnly lamented. The two men nodded in agreement. "Pray tell, what further burden was put on Jamison today."

"Monsters assaulted him, that's what," Hal spat.

"Monsters?" I asked, feigning shock. "In this town?"

"There are monsters here, but not from this town, mind you. We have good folk here. Not the hooligans I saw today."

"What happened?" I asked, keeping an edge in my voice indicating curiosity and fear.

"Let me tell you, Charlie," Hal started. He leaned his right elbow on the table and turned his face to look directly at me, drawing me in to his tale with his sharp emerald eyes. "This morning I was on my usual early morning walk over to Esther's. I own a trinket shop and make my money selling souvenirs to tourists. Most of my money is made this time of year, as the city folk come in on vacation. Esther, she's a sweet young girl with a pretty smile who the tourists like. I notice my register has much more money in it when she has a shift. As much as I like her, she is a wild one, out all night dancing at the halls. I always have to wake her in the morning to get her ready for her shift. So this morning, I was going over to see her when I hear this hollering from the beach, some poor soul screaming for his life."

"My word! And that was Jamison?" I asked.

"Yes, the poor fella, I heard him yelling 'Help! Help!' Course I didn't know it was him because the tide was out, and he was a good distance from the shore. I started running to the sound. I wasn't sure what was going on, I thought maybe someone had hit their head on a rock or drowned."

"With all that shouting, did a lot of people come to Jamison's aid?"

"Naw, it was just me. Esther lives at the south end of the beach. It's a bit rocky there, and though there might be a beachcomber or two around, most are in the central area. It was early, so no one was on the beach yet. Everyone was still inside, and so I doubt that anyone else heard him.

"Anyway, when I came across Jamison, the poor fool was hunched over, kneeling on the ground, clutching his chest. I saw some figures off in the distance, but it was a misty, and so I couldn't really see nothing. At that point, Jamison hadn't told me who attacked him, so I didn't know what had happened."

"Did Jamison tell you what happened?"

"Of course he did. I wouldn't have known how many people attacked him if he didn't. I asked the man what was wrong, and he looks at me through gritted teeth and wheezes, 'Hal! Thank Christ it's you. They just attacked me, Hal. For no reason. Two of them.'

"I looked around the beach and from all angles. I remembered the shapes I saw running off, but they were long gone. I helped the poor man to his feet and together we limped back to the mainland."

"Did you happen to note which direction the men were running?"

"Well, it was foggy, but they were running down the beach away from town. By the time I got Jamison to the doctor, I figured the two would've been long gone. Plus with the tide coming in, it's not like I'd have had any tracks to follow."

I nodded and took a sip of my whisky. I wanted to ask the sorts of questions that I could when clients had visited us in 221b. Here, I had to work to get information out of Hal. I couldn't question him, for as an outsider, it would raise too much suspicion. Fortunately, Thomas was just as curious as I was, and he asked the follow-up question.

"Did he describe the attackers?" Thomas asked as he took a seat at the bar across from Hal.

"Jamison didn't get a good look at them," lamented Hal. "He said he was just looking for his son, combing the beach to see if he could find him.

He saw some figures in the mist and called out to them. The two men then ran up to him quickly and one of them punched him hard in the gut. The other kicked him hard. That's when he called for help. They got a few more good hits in before running off. I must have spooked them when they heard me coming."

"Strangers attacking a defenseless man," complained Thomas. "What is this world coming to?"

"Is Jamison all right?" I asked. I found myself concerned for the man after all that he'd endured.

"He's at home resting. The doctor checked him out. He has some bruised ribs, but nothing broken. I expect he'll be up soon as he can to go back out to the beach and search for his son."

"What about the police?" asked Thomas. "Surely they're out looking for the assailants."

Hal shook his head. "They took a statement from me and Jamison. In fact it was Solomon who took our statements. Tom, you know, the new guy from Old Orchard. He took the attack seriously, but as he explained, he don't have much to go on. Neither one of us got a good look at the men. If it was winter, it would be easy enough to find two strangers, but in the summer, the tourists outnumber the locals."

"The police had better be looking," complained Thomas. "I don't care if they ain't got much to go on. Those two will strike again. Mark my word."

"Believe me, I agree with you. If I could only get my hands on those two – " snarled Hal, and he put out his hands and moved them to show he would wring their necks.

"What if you could?" I asked nonchalantly.

Both Thomas and Hal turned to me quickly. They exchanged those knowing glances of true friends questioning how I could make such an offer. "What do you mean?" asked Thomas.

I took the last drink of my whisky and slammed my glass on the counter. "I mean, from what you've told us, I think the ruffians are going to return. Tonight." Again, the two friends exchanged questioning glances.

"What makes you think that?" Hal asked with a hint of malice in his voice. Clearly he wondered how I, as an outsider, could know such a thing.

"Call it a hunch," I answered cooly. I stood from the bar and tossed a few dollars down to cover my drinks and my tip. "But if you gentlemen can meet me back here at six this evening, I believe that I can help you catch those men."

"My shift ends at five," answered Thomas.

"My shop closes at six, but I suppose I can have Esther close up and then I can return later to count out the register."

376

"Then it is agreed," I said with a smile. "Six o'clock it is. Oh, and Hal, one last question: What was the name of Jamison's son?"

"It's Roger. Is that important?"

"I believe that it is."

Well, Watson, after I left the Sea Plum, I spent the day as I had planned, working on my writing and conducting research. I did pay a visit to Jamison to see if he could shed any more light on the identity of the two men who assaulted him. The man isn't of sound mind, so it took an effort to get him to focus on my questions.

The man was much younger than I anticipated, probably in his early forties, but looking like he was in his sixties. His face was badly bruised from the assault. I informed him that I had spoken to Hal and thought I might be able to help catch his attackers.

Jamison's cottage was much tidier than I had anticipated, most likely because of the community support that he was receiving. I was expecting to see a home much like our rooms in Baker Street on some of my worst days, but the floor was clean, although the couch had some newspapers scattered near it, probably because that's what Jamison had been reading as he was laid up.

He invited me to sit and asked how he could help catch his assailants.

"Tell me," I started, "what did you notice about the two men who attacked you?"

"They were on me so quickly, and with the fog, I didn't really see them," he answered apologetically. I had to lean in to hear him as he spoke softly.

"Come now, there must be something. Even if you didn't see them, did you hear anything, or even smell something out of the ordinary?"

"I can't say much about the men. The ocean has a strong smell, and the crash of the waves is about all I can remember, except for the sound of their feet slopping in the mud." He paused and lowered his head. I thought he was drifting off, but then he sat up, rigid. "They looked like sailors to me. They were dressed in dark grey pants and button shirts. I believe they wore hats. One of them had a beard. Brown hair, I think."

"That's very good. Now, tell me, did they attack you before or after you called your son's name?"

His eyes were distant, and when I mentioned his son, they welled up, and he walked to his window looking out at the path which led down to the beach, to where he desperately wanted to search for Roger.

"Please, Mr. Jamison," I said, hoping to refocus the man.

"After," he practically whispered. "I saw the sailors and I thought – I hoped . . . ." He choked on his words. "Hoped that my boy had returned."

377

Sensing that the man was drifting away, I asked him what he could tell me of the town. He had lived in Wells all of his life, as had his parents and grandparents before him. He came from a family of fishermen, and while I had tried to move his focus away from his son, I could tell that I had disturbed him. He felt disappointment that his family line should end with him.

I didn't want to cause him any harm and felt that my line of questioning had unfortunately pained him. I noticed that one of the news papers on his floor was *The New York Times*. I asked him how he came about getting the paper from a town so far away, and he explained that the sailors and their wives had been bringing him newspapers from their travels. He always enjoyed reading the news. I asked him if I could look through his papers. Fortunately, he had a bundle of them, as a few women who clean his house were due that day, but since he had been attacked they had assured him they'd let him rest up and do the cleaning the following day. This left Jamison with a stack of various newspapers from the prior week.

Since they were going to be tossed away, he let me take them with me. This was a bit of auspicious luck, Watson, for I had planned on taking the train to York to visit a private library where I could read up on the area's news. Jamison had saved me much work, and I thanked him for it.

We spent some time discussing the New England and the parts of Canada closest to Maine. I told him of my time in Fundy and my research on the bay. He was fascinated by the tidal patterns of the area, and by the time I left, the man was in high spirits. Though I'm sure it was fleeting, I was glad I could bring a moment of solace to someone who had suffered so greatly.

Soon after, I returned to my room, and quickly learned from the news all that I needed to discover. I sent a short missive off to the local police, and then spent the remainder of the afternoon revising a chapter in *The Whole Art of Detection*.

As scheduled, I met Hal and Thomas in the bar at six p.m. It was quite busy when I arrived, with most of the tables taken and all the stools at the bar filled. Hal and Thomas were seated at the last two stools on the left side of the bar. They were deep in conversation, and before I interrupted them, I watched them for a moment. Their interactions, facial expressions, and their reactions to one another reminded me of the way we used to converse in Baker Street. I felt a pang of jealousy, I admit, my friend, for I realized how much that friendship was missing from my life. I finally decided to walk over and interrupt them.

378

"Well Charlie, are we going to get those hooligans?" asked Thomas. He took the last gulp of his beer and set the glass on the counter. Hal did the same.

You really think they'll be back?" asked Hal.

"I do." I looked up at the clock on the wall and noted the time. "Hal, if you will lead the way, then you can have your revenge on the ruffians, but we must leave now. Otherwise, we could be too late."

The two men rose at my urging and we left the bar. We walked along the boardwalk listening to the waves crash off in the distance. Thomas was wheezing a little as he tried to keep pace with Hal and me. Hal, for his age, was moving at a good clip. The hour was late, but it being July, there was plenty of light in the sky. We cast long shadows as we traversed, the motion of the ocean sounding in the distance. "It's the tide, aye," Hal said confidently to me.

"I beg your pardon?" I asked Hal.

"That's why you think they'll be back. The tide is low again. It's at the same level it was when Jamison stumbled on those men. For some reason, the tide had something to do with the attack, didn't it?"

"Why Hal, I am impressed," I said, honestly.

"As you said," he ribbed. "I'm a regular Sherlock Holmes. I figured that part out. I just can't figure out why they'd come back."

"These gentlemen will help explain," I answered as we came across two young constables standing on the boardwalk just at its southern end.

"What's all this, Charlie?" asked Thomas when he saw the officers.

"Thomas, I'd like you to meet – " I started, but he interrupted me.

"This is a small town, Charlie. We know Don and Eric," Thomas explained, addressing the two officers by name.

"Good to see you, Hal," said Don. Both officers were in their twenties and had similar physiques – tall, broad shoulders, muscular bodies. Don was a touch older and had blonde hair. Eric's hair was auburn. Hal accepted Don's hand and they shook.

"You're here to arrest Jamison's attackers," said Thomas. "Do us a favor and let me and Hal have the first crack at them before you haul them away." He shook his fists menacingly and even jabbed at the air.

"I'm afraid this is much bigger than just hooligans beating on Jamison," answered Don. "If what this Charles tells me is true, these are wanted men. Big time criminals."

"Really? Well I'm all ears to hear about it," Hal said turning to me. I could tell he wondered how I knew all that I knew.

"Gentlemen, I'm afraid that we can't tarry. We don't want to miss our prey. If you will lead the way, Hal, I'll explain everything when we arrive."

379

It didn't take long for us to walk over to the section of the beach where Hal found Jamison that morning. We stood in the muddy sand for a moment. I could taste the salt upon my lips. All we could hear was the rumble of the waves. As Hal had explained, this section of the beach was away from the hotels, and so there weren't people about at that hour.

I was going to begin to explain to Hal all that had transpired when Eric, the police officer, yelled, "There they are!" My eyes aren't what they used to be, and so I only saw some blurry shapes off in the distance. Eric removed his sidearm, dashed off, and we all followed close at his heels.

As we approached, we saw two men dressed as Jamison had described them, in sailor's outfits though, they were now grimy and disheveled. They were carrying a large trunk between them. The man in front dropped the trunk and reached into his pocket. The other man yelled, "Roger, no!" But it was too late.

The first man, Roger, had taken out a pistol and shot at us. The bullet went far. Don and Eric returned fire, and the man clutched his chest and collapsed onto the sand.

The other man dropped his end of the trunk, fell to his knees, and held his hands up. "I surrender! Please, don't shoot."

Well, Watson, after that, it didn't take long for us to surround the man and for the officers to put him in handcuffs. "Yes, arrest me," he pleaded. "Just don't shoot."

"Don't shoot!" growled Hal menacingly. "You oughta end up like your friend there." He took a step toward the cowering man and lifted his fist in the air ready to strike. The officers weren't stopping him.

"No, please!" the man cowered, his body shaking he looked up at the police, hoping they would offer him some protection. "You have to believe me! I didn't mean to hurt anyone. No one was supposed to get hurt. It was supposed to be a simple plan."

Hal stepped forward, and if I hadn't intervened he would have surely struck the prisoner. "Just a minute, Hal. This man is none other than Simon Wright, the last at-large member of a team of jewel thieves who struck a number of homes in the Berkshires."

"That's right," Simon said remorsefully. He looked to us with pain in his eyes, and ran his hands through his disheveled blonde locks. "We were only taking from those that had plenty while we had so little. We were servants – drivers, cooks, and laborers. We all dreamed of making some real money one day. It wasn't fair for us all to be working twelve-hour days while our bosses sat in the lap of luxury."

"So you decided to steal from your employers?" I asked.

"Yes, sure, it was Eric's idea." He glanced over at his friend's corpse and shuddered. "He had grand plans, that one. All we needed to do was

380

take a little from the wealthy. They wouldn't even notice it was gone. If we pooled it together then we'd have enough so that we'd be well enough off, not enough to live in a mansion mind you, but enough for us to live comfortably, in a town like this." He looked to Wells, off in the distance.

"How'd you end up here? Berkshires is a long way to travel," commented Hal with a snort.

"The plan was to take the jewels a little at a time until we amassed a decent enough fortune. Then, over the course of a few months, we'd all quit our jobs. It'd be spread out enough that no one would suspect a thing. After that, we'd move up to Nova Scotia. Roger had a connection there, said he could get the jewels sold off to people in Europe. Then, we'd split the bounty and all go our separate ways.

"It would've worked except the Wharton family discovered their missing jewelry. We aren't hardened criminals, so our man Jeffries – well, when they interrogated the staff, he caved. He admitted to stealing the jewels, but he also told them about us. We had to leave as soon as we could. Unfortunately, only Roger and I managed to get away."

"I still don't see why you came here," said Thomas.

"We didn't intend to stop here," explained Simon. "We were just trying to get up past the border into Canada. We were traveling at night, trying to keep close to shore so we wouldn't get lost, but also far enough out to avoid any rocks. Our boat was small, so we weren't too worried. Last night, as we were traveling here, we saw a vessel out in the distance which appeared to turn towards us. We panicked, thinking it was the police.

"Then, Roger had an idea. He was a sailor at one point and knew a bit about tides and shores. He figured we'd go in just enough to dump the trunk of jewels and then come back at low tide to collect it. I know it sounds crazy, but that's what we did. We dumped the trunk with the jewels overboard and Roger did something, I'm not sure what, to mark the location.

"The boat that spooked us ended up turning away, and we discovered it was just a schooner navigating around some rocky outposts. We cursed our luck, but Roger assured me he knew where the trunk was and, after we found a secluded place to tether the boat, we could come back in the morning and get the jewels."

"That's when Jamison found you," said Hal.

"Who?" asked Simon, truly puzzled.

"The man that you assaulted," I explained.

"Oh, that's his name. We didn't mean to hurt him. We were out looking for the jewels when we heard someone call Roger's name. We thought it was the police. When we saw it was just one person we went to attack him, so we wouldn't be arrested. Then we heard someone else approaching and we ran back to our hiding spot. That's when Roger got the idea to buy the gun. We were scared. We didn't know if we'd been spotted. Still don't know how your friend knew it was us."

"Ironically," I explained, "Jamison was looking for someone else named Roger."

"Of all the rotten luck," spat Simon bitterly, his sadness turning to anger.

The police had heard enough. They arranged for recovery of the chest and escorted Simon to the shore while Thomas and Hal carried the body of the dead man. I noticed that they were subdued. They grumbled no more about hurting Simon. Seeing the body and the criminal in cuffs was enough to appease their appetite for revenge.

The next day as I was having lunch at the bar, Hal saw me at the counter and joined me. Both he and Thomas thanked me warmly for helping to catch Simon, and they treated me by covering the cost of my lunch.

"You know, Charlie," said Hal, putting down his whisky cocktail, "that was quite a hunch you had about those crooks. Care to explain it?"

I lowered my lobster sandwich and agreed to answer his question. "As you already surmised, Hal, the time of the assault was at low tide. Then, I had to think, why would two people assault this man? Several reasons come to mind. The first possibility would be to rob him. However, the locale seemed odd for thieves. Robbing a man on the boardwalk seemed to make much more sense than robbing someone close to the sea, a place where people do not tend to carry money. Another possibility was that the two ruffians were specifically looking for Jamison to attack him for some reason. The fact that it was Jamison who came across the villains and not the other way around seemed to discredit that possibility. So then the final possibility, the most likely one, was that the men were looking for something and attacked Jamison because he stumbled upon them. Since the two men were searching for something and were scared off before they could retrieve it, I surmised that they would return for their item at the next opportunity, that being when the tide was at its lowest."

"Not bad," said Hal. He took a sip of his drink and then asked, "How'd you know to get the police involved?"

"Ah, I read in the paper about a robbery in the Berkshires and knew that two criminals were still at large, and that the stolen jewelry hadn't been reclaimed. One of the wanted men was named Roger, the name that Jamison was calling when the two men attacked him. When I looked at the pieces of information, I worked out that these two men must have been the ones who attacked poor Jamison."

Thomas and Hal gave each other knowing looks and smirked at my explanation. "You should have been a detective," said Thomas.

"Yeah," agreed Hal. "You're a regular Sherlock Holmes. Aren't you Charlie – or should I say, *Mr. Holmes.*"

I admit Watson, I was taken aback by the men knowing my identity.

Hal chuckled and then said, "Don't worry, your secret's safe with us. We thank you for what you did for Jamison."

Well, Watson, the two men were good to their word. I spent my sojourn in Wells and each day lunched with my new friends. We talked about all sorts of things each day – the weather, sports, news in the states and abroad. They never brought up any of our cases, Watson. The men were true to their word and I was able to get several chapters written and edited during my stay.

Hal is something of an anomaly. His mind is sharp, and he is able to observe and deduce, but much like my brother, he prefers to notice things from a distance and not get involved. The police have missed out on a brilliant mind. I wish that he had chosen a different career instead of being a proprietor of a trinket store. Thomas is a good man. He may not have the gift of observation, but he is a great storyteller, and I learned much from him about local lore. I appreciated both of their kind temperaments. Being with them made me miss our time together.

I hope you have had a chuckle at this case stumbling its way to me, your humble friend. If another doesn't interrupt my leaving, I'm due to check out tomorrow and make my way back to Boston for my return trip. I write to you, for upon my arrival, I'd like to stay a few days in London and see you, old friend. It's been far too long. I'd like to hear about your own travels, and perhaps even a case will find us while we're together.

Sincerely,

Your dear friend,

Sherlock Holmes

The Adventure of the Doctor's Hand

by Michael Mallory

It will come as no surprise to those who know me (an admittedly small confederacy which is becoming smaller with each passing year) that I am not much experienced in the state of being nonplussed. During my years as a consulting detective in the teeming hive of humanity called London, I can recall only one or two times in which I was genuinely overcome by a sense of puzzlement. Since my retreat to the south downs of Sussex, nearly two decades ago, there have been no such reoccurrences . . . at least until the crisp September afternoon in the year of 1922, when a knock came to the door of my cottage. My housekeeper was in the village shopping for vegetables and (hopefully) a bit of fresh meat at the time, so I answered it myself. I was expecting to see a lad from the town of Eastbourne whom I had recently engaged to assist me in my final honey harvest of the year. To my great surprise my caller was my old friend, compatriot, and flatmate Dr. John Watson, whom I had not seen in some four months.

He didn't extend a hand to me. Instead, he grinned broadly and said, "Well, Holmes, aren't you going to invite me in?" As I stepped back to do so, I noticed that he had gained some measure of girth since last we clapped eyes upon each other, and the hair protruding from under his tweed cap was considerably snowier than his moustache, which remained brown and was bushier than I recall. But it was Watson nonetheless.

"I cannot begin to fathom what has brought you here," I said, "unless it is to report the quality of the curry served at the Saxon's Head Inn, of which I have never partaken, or obtain my opinion as to whether you should seek medical attention for the tremor in your right hand."

His smile further broadened. "Good old Holmes," he said. "I will not bother asking how you deduced I supped on curry at the public house, or how you know that I suffer from a trembling hand, which is hidden in my pocket, since I am confident you will tell me without prompting."

"The fact that you did not immediately offer your hand to me was my first clue that something about it was wrong, but the determining factors are those two tiny yellow spots on your trousers representing the bits of curry you dropped onto your lap while dining. One such spot I might understand, even for someone as fastidious and skilled with his hands as

384

you. Two such, though, can only mean you were having difficulty guiding the food to your mouth while eating, indicating a shaking hand."

He withdrew it from his pocket and the tremor was quite noticeable.

"I am hoping that it is temporary," he said. "My self-diagnosis is that it may be nothing more than a pinched nerve, or perhaps a late-blooming symptom of my old shoulder wound. If it doesn't subside on its own, I shall seek a second opinion."

"Watson, I care not if your hand dances the Viennese Waltz," I said, reaching for it and shaking it gently, lest it produce discomfort for him. "May I offer you some mead? It is made from my own honey. A publican in the village ferments it for me." I poured a glass from a recently opened bottle and handed it to my friend, who took it with his left hand, of course, and sipped it gingerly. A look of approval overtook his face and he took a heartier swig. "Don't have too much, though," I cautioned, "since it is of higher alcohol content than you may be used to." After pouring a glass for myself, I bade him to take a seat on the sofa and then took my chair across from him and said, "Now, then, my friend, how are you?"

For nearly an hour we spoke of our lives — his in London with a wife (who at this moment in time was in the north of England visiting a friend), and mine in Sussex, where my view of the ocean offers my mind the sort of peaceful repose I once achieved only through a hypodermic needle. Watson told me that while his tremor didn't affect his ability to write, since placing the pen nib to paper steadied his hand, holding any kind of medical instrument was out of the question.

"That hardly matters, though, since I haven't engaged in full practise for some years," he said. "If a shaky hand from an old wound is what I must endure in old age, at least I have achieved old age, and in comfort. That is more than I can say for some, including the man who saved my life in Afghanistan. Overall I have been very fortunate."

After I refilled our glasses, I said, "You know, Watson, I cannot help but think that you didn't travel all the way from London simply to talk philosophy of life."

"Quite right. I came here because I have a new client for you."

"I have retired from the detection game, as you well know. My only clients now buzz and pollinate flowers."

"Even so, you may wish to take this case. It is for, shall we say, a special client."

I studied his face. The utter seriousness of his expression told me all I needed to know. "By which you mean *you*," I deduced.

"Is it that evident?"

"You do appear to be bowing under a weight that might burden Atlas. There is nothing seriously amiss, I hope."

"That remains to be seen. It is why I have come to you for help."

I leaned back in my chair. "Very well. More than anyone, you know my methods. Proceed."

He smiled wanly and said, "Rather than starting at the beginning, I must first tell you of the problem, and then return to the event which I believe caused it. You may recall that the army agency, Cox and Company at Charing Cross, is home to both my personal banking accounts and certain items housed within its vaults — one of which is my old military dispatch box. I'm certain you have heard me speak of it."

"That is the box containing your records of our adventures together?"

"It is. Some of them I have fully written up but have chosen not to offer for publication, while other pages contain notes for cases that will remain sequestered because they contain sensitive material that might create distress among those involved or their families, even after all these years. Those I plan to destroy."

"If you have come here to ask for my permission, Watson, you have it."

"There is more to it than that. Last week . . . Tuesday, to be precise, at half-past-three . . . I finally got around to visiting Cox. I presented myself to the assistant manager, a chap named Cavens, and requested the retrieval of my dispatch box from the storage vaults. As is their custom, I offered my card and my signature as proof of my identity. I thought I detected a strange reaction on the fellow's face, but he disappeared into the bowels of the building as per my request. He returned some minutes later with the disconcerting news that my dispatch box was missing."

"Misplaced, or wrongly stored, perhaps?"

"Alas, no. This time Cavens brought with him a young subordinate named Foxley, who informed me I had already requested the dispatch box and taken it out of the premises some twelve weeks earlier!"

"Which, I assume, you did not," I offered.

"Holmes, while I may be experiencing an occasional lapse of memory befitting someone who has just marked his seventieth birthday, I am hardly so enfeebled as to forget such a withdrawal. Under further questioning, I got Foxley to admit that he handed over the box to a man who identified himself as my agent after the man presented a letter requesting the box be released to him."

"It would appear that Cox and Company employs less stringent security regulations than their reputation suggests."

"That is just it – they *did* adhere to their security rules, checking the letter against samples of my handwriting on file, including my signature. According to young Foxley, it was a perfect match. I am the victim of a theft and forgery scheme."

386

"So it would appear," I commented. "Who knew where your box was stored?"

Watson sighed heavily, almost with shame. "That brings me to the motivating event of which I earlier spoke," he said. "The fact is anyone who reads my stories in *The Strand*, particularly this past February's issue, would know where the box was stored. Not only that, they would know what it contained. Do you remember that business many years ago involving the death of the wife of an American politician whose body was found on a bridge in Hampshire?"

"Of course. Thor Bridge, to be precise. What of it?"

"I finally got around to writing the account. However, I submitted it to Greenhough Smith, the editor of *The Strand*, he told me it was too short, which I could not understand, as it was the same length as my others. However, I opted to comply with his request for additional wordage. Since there was nothing more of the tale itself that required telling, I added a prologue of sorts in which I mentioned my dispatch box, where it was sequestered, and hinted at what it contained."

"Did your prologue include any details about the contents of the box?" I asked.

"A few," he said. "That Phillimore business, for instance, and the vanished ship, the *Alicia*."

"Both of which disappeared, as has your dispatch box."

"If you are implying that the *Alicia* will arrive in port decades late, piloted by Phillimore, who will be found reading my notes, I might presume the mead has gone to your head, not mine."

"Nothing of the sort," I told him, unable to suppress a chuckle. "Did you also refer to any of the sensitive materials?"

"Only that they were controversial in nature and might cause consternation should they become known. I provided no details or names. Good heavens, do you think the box might have been taken by someone involved in one of those cases so as to prevent its release?"

"That is one possibility," I told him. "So is the converse – that it was removed to gain access to the information which could then be used to blackmail a participant in a case."

"Good Lord. Will you help me, Holmes? I know it will necessitate your coming to London, but I can turn to no one else."

"Among the advantages to farming bees is that they do not require daily feeding," I said. "I daresay they will hardly notice my absence for upwards of a week. Of course I will accompany you to London."

It appeared as though a weight had suddenly been lifted from his shoulders, and this time he took my hand and pumped. "I knew you would not let me down. We can leave at once."

387

Stealing a glance at my watch, I said, "Cox and Company would already be closing for the day by the time the afternoon train arrived in the city, meaning the earliest we could pay a call would be tomorrow. I suggest we wait until then and take the first train in the morning. Until then, I offer you the comforts of my humble home."

"Rooming together like old times, eh, Holmes?" he said, smiling.

"With some differences, Watson. I no longer play the violin, for instance. A touch of rheumatism in the wrist prevents it."

After a late, but ultimately restful, night, we arose and breakfasted through the efforts of my housekeeper Martha, who was more than surprised to find a visitor. Watson continued to comment on the quiet of Sussex, even after we were train-bound to London. Once we arrived at Victoria Station, I began to perceive why. During my absence, London had not only become more crowded, but the horse-drawn vehicles of my tenure in the city had largely been replaced by an armada of motorcars, which added a layer of cacophony to hubbub.

Upon arriving (*via* motorized cab) at the offices of Cox and Company in Charing Cross, Watson led the way inside and demanded to see Foxley, who was summoned up out of the vaults like a valuable book at the British Library. He was a young man whose florid face betrayed a touch of dismay upon our confronting him. "Are you who I think you are?" he asked, looking at me.

"That is, of course, impossible to determine, not having direct access into your mind," I replied, "but my name is Sherlock Holmes."

"Crikey."

At my request, we were led to a small office in the back which contained a desk and two wooden guest chairs, which Watson and I took while Foxley remained standing. "Am I in trouble?" he asked.

"Not unless you have done something to warrant it," I said. "Tell me of the man who came here some time prior to last Tuesday the twelfth and requested release of the dispatch box."

"Well, sir, there's not a lot I can tell you, except that he had a letter in Dr. Watson's handwriting saying it was all right to comply with the request."

"Exactly when did he appear?"

"I can't recall the precise date, sir, though I know it was at the beginning of June, not long after I'd taken employment here."

"I see. What did the man look like?"

"I can't exactly remember that, either. Not young, but not a greybeard either."

"What colour was his beard, then?" Watson asked.

"Oh, no sir, he didn't have a beard at all," Foxley replied. "I was simply using an expression. He was older, but not real old, if you know what I mean."

"Have you seen him since?" I asked the lad.

"I don't think so. I'm sorry, sir, but so many people come through here that it's hard to remember them all."

"The letter, then — did it match the signature for Watson you have on file?"

"Oh, yes, sir, and the handwriting was the same, too. Otherwise I wouldn't have handed over the box."

"I should very much like to see that signature card. Would you fetch it, please?" Foxley rushed out of the office only to return a minute later, holding a rather worn card, which he handed to me. Even though I easily recognized the writing, I showed it to Watson who nodded. I then asked him to write his name on a fresh piece of paper, which was provided by Foxley, and comparing the new signature with the file signature brought a smile to my lips. "These signatures are indeed made by the same hand," I said, "but even a casual perusal of them reveals they are not identical."

"Handwriting changes over time," Watson said.

"True, though it is apt to change more significantly for those who do not write very often. For a man who writes as much as you do, I would expect less difference. No, Watson, despite your conviction that you hold and wield a pen as steady as ever despite your tremor, I'm afraid it is having an effect. Not a crippling one, but noticeable." Turning then to young Foxley, I asked how many people within the bank knew specifically where the dispatch box was located.

"I don't know, sir," he responded. "I hope you aren't thinking that this was an inside job."

"I haven't yet formed a conclusion of any kind. I am merely gathering information. Let me be blunt, Mr. Foxley: Did you remove the dispatch box yourself and then fabricate the story of a man coming for it?"

"No sir!" he cried, looking alarmed.

"Do you know of or suspect anyone working within these walls who might have done the same?"

"No sir, I do not. All I know is that its disappearance is my fault. It's not like I took it, and it's not like I know who did, but I was still the one who released it so that makes it my fault. Like I said, I'd only just started here, and maybe I wasn't as diligent as I could have been in confirming the identity of the caller, but I don't wish to be made redundant over the mistake."

"I have no intention of pressing for such action," I told him. "Your refreshingly honest testimony has been quite helpful."

389

Once we were out of the bank and hailing another cab to transport us to his home in Queen Anne Street, Watson commented, "I really don't know what we learned in there, Holmes, though I take it that you don't suspect the lad or anyone else at Cox."

"Had Foxley or an associate wanted the box or its contents, they could have taken it at any time, surreptitiously opened it, found the information they sought, and returned it to its place without your knowing it had ever been touched. No, I believe the boy when he says someone came for it, just as I believe his contrition about handing it over is genuine."

"Then we're back at the beginning."

"Not quite," I told him. "Whoever it was that forged the letter presented to Foxley had a sample of your writing from years past, prior to the slight alteration in your penmanship caused by the tremor. We must think of who that might be."

"Really, Holmes, I can hardly be expected to remember every person to whom I have written a letter."

I said nothing else as we waited for a cab to pull up to the kerb. Once ensconced inside, I continued my silence, instead devoting the time to my thoughts, which were interrupted a few moments later by Watson's utterance of, "Good God, so many victims of that terrible war." I glanced up to see through the window a man wearing the tattered remnants of a military uniform walking on crutches, to compensate for the absence of his right leg. "So many of them on the streets of London," my friend commented. "It is truly enough to break one's heart. I returned from service with a slight weakness in the shoulder and a few isolated scars. But these poor fellows, good men who put themselves in harm's way for King and country, were all fighting to preserve our civilization — only to come back maimed, missing an arm or a leg or a face, or simply facing never-ending struggle like my lifesaving former orderly, Murray. But I can only do so much, even for a man to whom I owe everything. Where is the justice, Holmes?"

"Justice is as fickle a mistress as she is blind."

We each retreated into our private thoughts until the cab turned onto Queen Anne Street and pulled to the kerb to let us out. After we had settled in his study, he said, "I cannot offer anything as exotic as home-produced mead, but would you be interested in a brandy?"

I accepted the drink and sat on his sofa while Watson put logs into the fireplace and lit the tinder. "Allow me to offer you my hospitality in return," he said. "My wife isn't expected to return for another three days, during which time I can offer you quarters here."

Thanking him, I accepted the snifter of brandy, and then asked, "How well do you trust your publishing house?"

"I'm sorry?"

"The magazine . . . how well do you trust its staff?"

"Good heavens, Holmes, you can't suspect anyone at *The Strand*. I have worked with Greenhough Smith for more than three decades. I trust him implicitly. What has brought about this sudden suspicion of my editor?"

"It is not so sudden. I was ruminating on it in the cab. We are looking for a person who has access to your handwriting from before your tremor took hold, are we not? Who would have more access to it than someone to whom you have been submitting handwritten manuscripts for over thirty years?"

"I cannot believe Smith or anyone else there could have done this."

"A visit to the magazine offices should provide illumination."

"We only just got here, Holmes. I confess I am no longer accustomed to charging about the city and countryside. Besides, I can reach Smith by telephone." Pulling himself out of his chair, he walked to a small table near the entryway on which sat a telephone and dialed a number. A few moments later he said, "Hello, Smith? This is John Watson. Fine, thank you. Do you have a moment? You recall that you have asked me to introduce you to Sherlock Holmes if he became available? He is here, hold on a moment." Watson then held out the receiver for me.

Taking it, I said, "Mr. Smith? This is Sherlock Holmes."

"Mr. Holmes," said a voice that remained robust even through the tininess of the telephone line. "How lovely to finally speak with you. I hope you'll forgive me for wondering at times over the years whether you were, in fact, a real person and not simply a figment of Watson's imagination."

"I am quite real, I assure you, and I would like to pay a call on you at your office, if that is possible."

"Yes, of course. I would be honoured by such a visit."

"Could I come at once?"

"Yes, fine, I shall be here." Then his voice became quieter as he said, "There is another reason I am glad to hear from you, Mr. Holmes. There is a matter I wish to discuss with you, something private and rather delicate concerning our mutual friend."

"I see. Very well, I shall see you within the hour."

After receiving the address, 8 Southampton Street, I replaced the receiver and turned back to Watson. "At least let me finish my brandy before we set out," he said with a sigh.

"Actually, there is no need for you to accompany me this time," I told him. "I shall be more effective in extracting information from the man on my own. Besides, there is another stop I wish to make while I'm out. I shan't be long. In return for your hospitality, Watson, I will treat us both to dinner at Simpson's."

I left Watson happily contemplating the chops at our favorite restaurant and took the first public transport I saw that offered a pathway to Southampton Street (that ran just north of the Strand, which, in turn, I assume provided the publication with its name). Entering the magazine offices, I asked for Greenhough Smith and was ushered into a room containing a large desk and shelves of periodicals. Behind the desk was a sturdily-built man with a large moustache, greying hair, and eyeglasses — and whose fingertips looked as though they had been dyed with blue ink. "Mr. Holmes," he said, leaping up from his chair and extending his hand. "H. Greenhough Smith, your servant, sir. I would recognize you anywhere, thanks to the late Mr. Paget. His likeness was remarkable. Please, sit down." As I did so, Smith stepped around the desk and closed his office door, then returned to his chair. "What is it that brings you here today?"

"I have a question about manuscripts," I replied.

"Ah, I see. Are you by any chance thinking of offering some of your own for publication?"

I laughed lightly. "No, in truth that had not occurred to me, though I have written a book on bee culture."

"Should you ever decide to pick up the pen for periodical publication, I would very much like the honour of having first look at the material."

"I shall remember that. My question, Mr. Smith, is how many people on staff here at the magazine actually see an author's manuscript before it is printed."

"Oh, well, there is me, of course, the proofreader, and ultimately our typesetter and the artist, if the piece warrants an illustration. Why do you ask?"

"I am trying to discern who might have learned about a certain military dispatch box before the reading public."

"Military dispatch . . . oh, you must mean that reference John made in his last story. As I have said, myself, the proofreader, the typesetter, and in that instance Mr. Gilbert, the illustrator. We published that tale in two consecutive issues, February and March. The business of the dispatch box, though, would have appeared in the February issue, as it was in the additional text I requested."

"He told me you claimed the piece was too short."

"Yes, well, the story in and of itself was not lacking, but at the very last moment we lost an advertiser, which left a third-page blank space in the issue. Since we had already decided at which point to split the story, I needed more prose to fill the gap. Knowing how reliable John is, I asked

392

him to contribute more words. Have I satisfactorily answered your question?"

"Nearly so. How long have your proofreader and typesetter been with you?"

"Oh, for years. Both are valuable and trusted members of the staff."

"And well compensated, I trust?"

Smith's expression turned quizzical. "Are you here on behalf of Dr. Watson to request a higher payment?"

"No, I am not. I am seeking to ascertain whether any member of your staff would need additional income by, say, engaging in forgery – even blackmail."

"Mr. Holmes, I assure you, if I knew of any such matters by a member of this magazine, he would no longer be a member of this magazine." He then stopped speaking and an expression of thoughtful concern coloured his face. "Forgery . . . by Gad, that must be the explanation," he said as though to himself.

"Does that word have some significance to you?"

Smith opened a desk drawer and pulled out a thin manuscript, which he handed to me. I recognized the handwriting immediately as that of my friend's. It bore the redundant title *The Adventure of the Adventurous Vicar*. "This pertains to the delicate matter I mentioned to you over the telephone," he said. "I received this some weeks ago, eager as always to obtain a new contribution from the doctor. Then I read it. It is quite simply . . . unpublishable. This has caused me no little vexation, given the long-standing relationship between *The Strand* and John Watson. I have been in a quandary as to how to tell him the story was substandard without damaging, if not severing altogether, that relationship. Frankly, Mr. Holmes, I was afraid that something had happened to John, something physical or emotional to cause such deterioration of his work. But when you mentioned forgery just now, that possibility entered my mind. You will agree, however, that the document you hold is rendered in John's handwriting."

As I read the opening lines of the story, I could not stifle a laugh. *I can't rightly exactly recall when this singular adventure took place,"* they began, *"but it was still in the rein of Her Majesty Queen Victoria. I'd been the friend, confidante, and fellow adventurer of Sherlock Holmes for quite a number of years, though at times I felt more like his batman, always at his beck and call."*

"I have read enough," I said, handing the manuscript back. "While there are a few superficial similarities to Watson's manner of composition, if not his adherence to proper spelling, I assure you he did not set these words to paper. Did this arrive with a cover letter? One that perhaps includes instructions not to send the cheque for the story to Watson's address in Queen Anne Street, but rather to a third party, such as an agent?"

"By Gad, you must have psychical abilities as well," Smith said, producing the letter from his desk. "How did you know that?"

"Because it makes perfect sense that it would. The man who wrote the inferior story and the letter did so in an attempt to earn money from it, a plan that would be circumvented were the money to go directly to Watson."

The address provided in the letter, which was also written in a facsimile of Watson's hand and ostensibly signed by him, was located in an unsavoury section of the East End of London. After committing the address to memory I handed the letter back, rose, and said, "Thank you, Mr. Smith. You have been most helpful."

"No, Mr. Holmes, thank you. It is such a relief to me knowing that Watson was not actually responsible for this codswallop, and that I don't have to confront him over it. Do you happen to know who is behind it?"

"I do."

"I hope you will bring him to justice."

"That is my intent."

"Excellent. I bid you good day then, Mr. Holmes, and please don't forget what I said about writing your own stories."

Before returning to Queen Anne Street, I visited the small apartment I continued to lease near the Diogenes Club which was stocked with emergency clothing and supplies relating to my former trade. Today all that I required was a change of shirt and stockings and the contents of a small box hidden under a floorboard. Since there were at least two months' worth of dust on the floor and furniture, the woman that I employed to clean the place had either opted for employment elsewhere or had recently suffered some misfortune that prevented her from working. That, however, was a question I would have to investigate and resolve at a later date.

I was prepared to find Watson in a state of impatience when I returned. Instead, I discovered him nodding in his chair. I decided to let him sleep, and as he did, I studied his right hand which wasn't trembling at all. This didn't surprise me.

It was nearly an hour before he awakened, time I spent washing up and changing clothes. "I trust that you had a good rest," I said, which caused him some embarrassment. "Do not worry, Watson. When a formerly active man suddenly finds himself without activity, sleep is often the result. You will be happy to know that I expect to have the matter of your missing dispatch box concluded by tomorrow."

"Really? You know where it is?"

"I'm confident that I do. My ears having been opened."

"Your ears?"

"Yes. In the past, you have heard me say that I'd been a blind fool for having failed to recognize a clue or piece of evidence, but in this instance, it is my ears that have failed me. I repeatedly heard something to which I should have immediately responded but allowed to breeze by. Perhaps being away from my farm has resulted in a lack of buzzing in my ears that interferes with my hearing."

"At least tell me what you have deduced."

"Tomorrow, Watson, all will be explained. For this evening, all I ask is that you trust me and set worry aside."

My wish came true as my friend once more became the Watson of memory throughout dinner at Simpsons, and later back in his home: Jovial, energetic, seeming to relish talking about my old cases as much as he obviously enjoyed setting them for publication. It was a little after midnight when I declared the evening to be over and he walked me to the spare bedroom. "God, what an evening," he said. "I feel like writing it all down while it remains fresh in my memory."

"Should you choose to do so, you will experience no objection from your hand," I said.

"Great Scott!" he cried. "The tremor is all but gone!"

"I cannot offer a medical cause, since that is your bailiwick and not mine, though I should think the trouble has always been a combination of anxiety, tension, and even fearfulness."

"Fearfulness, Holmes? Need I remind you I was a soldier of Her Majesty's Army?"

"Not at all, though even a soldier must face the daunting, if not fearsome, challenge of growing old . . . if he is fortunate enough, of course. Good night, Watson."

The next morning found him setting out muffins and soft-boiled eggs, bacon, and a pot of strong tea. "I'm not the cook my wife is," he said, "but in a pinch I can function quite well."

After breakfasting, I laid out to him where we must go in order to retrieve his dispatch box, and, as I expected, he vehemently resisted my conclusion.

"Surely you must have miscalculated this time, Holmes," he protested. "I cannot believe that he would be responsible for this."

"There is but one way to determine the truth. Will you come?"

"Yes, of course, though I fear . . . I mean, I expect that you are wrong."

Hiring a motorcar was the quickest way to get us to our destination, the district of Shoreditch, and within the half-hour we were deposited in front of a squalid, brick-terraced building. "Here?" Watson asked.

"I'm afraid so."

"Good God."

Going inside, and crossing the borders of a territorial war being waged by two small urchins on the ground floor, we took the stairs to the first floor and went to a room marked *13*. Delivering a quick rap to the door, we waited until a man's voice called through, "Just a minute." A moment later the door opened with a rusty moan.

It was difficult to assess who exhibited the most extreme reaction, the thin, grey-haired, somewhat weather-beaten man who opened the door, or Watson upon recognizing him.

"Your name is Murray?" I asked, and the man nodded. "I am Sherlock Holmes, and I believe that you have something belonging to your former commanding officer."

"So it's true," Watson said, with a tone of sad resignation as he faced the orderly who had saved his life on the battlefield. "I was hoping that Holmes was in error."

"We should like to come in," I said, and the man stepped back to allow it, but kept his eyes on the floor as he did so. The flat was tiny — barely able to contain the three of us — and sparsely furnished, but neat and tidy. "Is the dispatch box here?"

"Yes, sir," Murray said.

"Look at me, Lance-corporal!" Watson commanded, and his former servant's head snapped up, though his entire body was quaking. "Why did you steal my box from the bank?"

"I'm ashamed to say, sir. I'm ashamed."

"Let me hazard an explanation, then," I said. "That you are a man of limited means is self-evident. Twice in the last two days, Watson has mentioned you and your condition, references that I failed to hear, as it were, but which I came to realize implied he has recently been in contact with you. I presume, Murray, you sought him out to ask for personal assistance."

"Yes, sir."

"And when he didn't provide it, you decided to use him to try and help yourself, isn't that right?"

"Sir, things haven't gone easily for me since I left the service," Murray said, "but I was always able to pay my own way. At least I was until the end of last year when I was sacked from my job on the docks. They said I was too old to work – but I'm only sixty-four! I tried to find other employment, but there just aren't very many things I can do out of uniform. When the only thing I had left to eat was my pride, I finally swallowed it too and went to see the surgeon-captain here. He gave me ten quid, which didn't last long, but I didn't want to keep coming back like a right royal beggar, even as I was growing desperate. Then one day I passed this news vendor and saw a magazine cover reading, '*A New Sherlock Holmes Adventure by John H. Watson*' on the cover. I spent a precious sixpence on it with the thought that maybe I should try to write the story of us together in Maiwand, and my saving him, and sell it to the magazine.

"But hunger does terrible things to a man, and soon I started thinking things like how I was the reason the doctor's still around to write these stories, so maybe he owed me something. When I read the story, though, that part about the dispatch box gave me another idea and . . . I guess my desperation got the better of me. Instead of writing my own story, I thought I might try writing one as though *by* the doctor. I still had some old letters from you in my trunk and practised the handwriting until it looked real. You remember, Captain, how I used to occasionally sign your name to things – with your permission of course – and no one ever knew the difference?"

"I remember it now, Murray," Watson said.

"Well, I put on my best clothes and took a letter that I'd made to that bank, and got the box. I used the notes inside, but soon found out writing isn't as easy as forgery. I had a hard time coming up with something, but I finally finished it and sent it in. I never heard back from them. Maybe the magazine figured out it wasn't real." Murray glanced in my direction. "How'd you know it was me though, sir?" he asked. "I never included my name in any of the faked letters, not even the envelope."

"You identified yourself in a sentence in which you, writing in the guise of Watson, confessed to sometimes feeling like a *batman*," I told him. "A batman is a military orderly, and in order to understand what the position feels like, one must have actually been an officer's servant, as you were to Watson."

"I can't tell you how sorry I am, Captain," Murray said. "I await your judgment and discipline."

"We're about forty years beyond that, lance-corporal. Forty years that I wouldn't have enjoyed if not for you. If you return the dispatch box to me, I shall endeavour to forget this ever happened."

"Yes sir." Murray scuttled into an adjoining bedroom and returned moments later with the tin dispatch box. "Sorry about the lock, sir. I had to force it open. But everything that was in there is still there. You can inspect it for yourself, sir."

"No, I believe you," Watson said. "I will not pretend that I am not disappointed with you, Murray. But I see no reason to further complicate

397

things, and add to your misery, by proffering charges. I would like to do something to help you, but I'm not a wealthy man. I no longer have my income as a surgeon."

"Watson, I nearly forgot to tell you," I interjected. "While I was out yesterday, I put a classified notice in the *Times* offering a reward for the return of your box, simply as a measure of precaution. Since Murray has indeed returned the box, I think it is fair that he should get the reward." I pulled a roll of banknotes from my pocket and counted out a hundred pounds, then handed them to the man whose eyes widened like twin moons. Suddenly snapping to attention, he saluted me, a gesture I returned with a slight bow, never having worn the uniform of the Kingdom.

We left Murray before the spectacle of tears broke out. In the taxi back to Queen Anne Street, holding his precious box on his lap, Watson asked, "Did you really advertise in the newspaper offering a reward?"

"No," I replied, "though sometimes bending the truth a little is what is required to bring a downtrodden man back to full attention."

"Still, that was remarkably generous of you – giving a hundred pounds to someone you'd never met before."

"When I was in my private room yesterday, I pulled a cashbox up from its hiding place and discovered it contained much more than I remembered."

"Even so, you had no personal connection with the man. It's not like he saved *your* life."

"Are you certain of that, Watson? Try to imagine how different *my* life would have been had you died on the battlefield before we ever met. What would *I* have become? Would I have joined my brother in the civil service – or worse, become a police inspector? It might be argued that the fellow saved us both."

Watson endeavoured to have me stay another night with him, but I had honey to harvest. I bade him a fond goodbye and returned on the four o'clock train. Despite my rewarding Murray with a hundred pounds and paying for supper at Simpson's, I still carried more than two-hundred that I had pulled from my cashbox — quite the unexpected payment for my work on the case.

After a week, my daily routine and duties pushed adventure of the missing dispatch box further out of my mind. In fact, I thought little about it until the following March, at which time I received a package from Watson containing a copy of his latest literary effort for *The Strand Magazine*, a recounting of the strange case of one Professor Presbury — who managed to make quite the monkey of himself — and a letter.

398

My dear Holmes, (it began)

I must first thank you for the case of mead you sent us for Christmas. I gave two bottles of it to Greenhough Smith, who is presently begging me for another. He sends his best regards, incidentally, and entreats you not to forget the proposition he made to you . . . whatever that may have been.

I have returned my dispatch box to Cox and Co. . . . which is now Cox and Kings, though not because of anything pertaining to my records . . . with instructions that it not be released again to anyone but myself, in person, or an agent who holds a missive containing a special password that only the bank and I know. I have removed the sensitive documents and, after a long and difficult argument with myself, have indeed destroyed them. I simply do not wish to risk their being made public at some point in the future. The other stories and notes remain, and whether they shall ever see the light of day will be up to the executor of my will (who shall be in possession of the secret password of which I spoke).

You may be interested to learn that I have embarked on a new professional venture: I have sold a series of stories to a motion picture company. The deal was quite lucrative, and acting upon the suggestion of my wife I'm turning over a portion of the proceeds to a newly-formed organization that helps former military men who require assistance. I suggested that Murray be engaged as a salaried officer in the charity, in charge of disbursements. He is excited about his new duties and is so far handling them well. He is a good chap who suffered a momentary lapse of conscience.

The tremor in my hand is mostly gone, returning only when I am excessively tired or upset — two conditions I take pains to avoid.

The long and the short of it, Holmes, is that I'm still alive, and I plan to remain so for as long as life sees fit to accommodate my demands of it.

I pray all is well with you and your bees.
Do not become a stranger

Yrs.
Watson

After reading the letter again, I placed it in a file wherein I keep important papers and decided that it was time for me to pay tribute to and honour my good friend in the only way I could think of, being so many miles away on the Sussex coast.

I would visit the Saxon's Head public house in the village that very evening and order a plate of curry.

The Case of the
Purloined Talisman
by John Lawrence

The following details an undisclosed case in the illustrious career of Sherlock Holmes, the legendary consulting detective. The existence of this remarkable document was revealed only recently by a solicitor in the firm once retained by Dr. John H. Watson. A sealed tan envelope had been entrusted to the firm by Dr. Watson shortly after it was written in 1925, and, as stipulated by Dr. Watson, had remained sealed in the firm's safe until the appointed date for its disclosure, a century after the end of the Great War. The envelope was opened recently and found to contain the following letter and manuscript, which are presented here for the first time. – J.L.

London, 14 August, 1925
To Londoners of the Twenty-first Century:

I have requested that my solicitor safeguard the accompanying document and that its existence not be disclosed until the centennial of the end of the Great War, 11 November, 2018. Following that date, the envelope and its contents may be divulged and conveyed to The Strand Magazine *or its literary successor for publication.*

Herein lies an extraordinary case undertaken by Mr. Sherlock Holmes whose nature is so delicate that it must not be publicly disclosed until long after I, and all other participants in the story, have gone to our rewards. I thank you for your willingness to conform to what must appear to be an eccentric request, but once the manuscript is revealed, the reason for a century of concealment will become evident. I only pray the world was able to avoid the grave outcome the story portends.

Very respectfully yours,
John H. Watson, M.D.
London

T he Great War had ended nearly five years earlier, and yet London still maintained a discernible air of gaiety, triumph, and relief. The horror associated with the "war to end all wars" had receded, and Britons were quite convinced that nothing comparable could again be contemplated.

Having nearly reached the advanced age of seventy-one, I had long since pared down my medical practice and was content to spend my days in less strenuous activities. Upon occasion, however, I would have the opportunity to visit with my dearest companion of so many decades and adventures, Sherlock Holmes, either at his home in Sussex or on those increasingly rare occasions when he would venture to London.

It was one of those visits in late 1923 that served as the occasion of one of our most remarkable adventures, one whose impact may well be impossible to determine for years to come. I had returned only a few days earlier from a trip to Morocco during a lull in the Berber uprising and was still recovering from the fatigue of the journey when I received a wire from Holmes asking if I might meet him at Waterloo Station. I was delighted at the prospect of seeing my old friend, and was waiting on the platform when his train arrived.

"Good to see you, Watson!" Holmes called cheerily as he stepped off the train and strode across the crowded platform to greet me.

"Holmes!" I said, grasping his hand in both of mine and giving it a good shake. "It is so good to see you! I trust your journey was uneventful."

"Quite enjoyable," he assured, eying me carefully, a slight smile turning up the ends of those thin lips. "And I presume that Morocco agreed with you – except for your over-indulgence in the highly spiced foods, your lack of adequate house staff, and your constant concerns for your personal safety." I smiled patiently at yet again being the object of his astonishing deductive powers.

"Holmes, you never change, do you?" I remarked. "It is very good to be dissected by you like a cadaver on a slab." His powers of observation and deduction certainly didn't seem to have deteriorated in the months since our last visit. "All right, explain to me how you come to know so much of my recent activities in North Africa."

"Surely it's obvious," he said, flicking his long fingers towards my face. "There is white powder caked around the corner of your mouth, suggesting recent consumption of a calcium compound intended to relieve gastric distress – doubtless caused by your diet of tagines and hariras common in Morocco. Your lack of house staff is obvious by the flecks of dried food on your sleeve – perhaps some of that harira? – and by the mud you have allowed to accumulate on your boots, all of which surely would have been cleaned by any competent servant.

"As to your safety concerns, I note that you are carrying a cane of unusual heft. The elaborately carved bone handle is clearly of Tuareg origins, designed by those 'blue people' for self-protection. Certainly such

402

a formidable instrument isn't required to assist you in walking – indeed, your gait seems quite normal – so you must have chosen the cane to serve as a club if needed against some ungrateful, feloniously-inclined urchin."

"But how did you know of my journey to Morocco?" I wondered aloud.

"Ah," said Holmes, smiling faintly. "You had sent me a note announcing your trip!"

He paused to allow me to admire his exhibition of deductive skills, and to give me an opportunity to acknowledge that he was right on every count. "Well done," I said, as he surely had expected.

He looked away, shaking his head slightly, and said over his shoulder, "Actually, it was all quite obvious – or, as you would write in one of your little stories, 'Elementary',"

He looked somewhat older than on the occasion of our last visit, but he remained whip-thin and from his grip, I could tell, as strong as ever. His hair, combed straight backwards, was thinning on the top, and his gray side-whiskers were trimmed shorter, in keeping with recent style. The lines on his thin face were more pronounced, running down from the edges of his beaked nose, past his thin mouth, towards his long, pointed chin. The hollows under his cheekbones were somewhat deeper, and there was a flap of slack skin under his chin that comes to us all, thanks to the merciless force of gravity. His eyes remained bright and sharp, but the lids above them were slightly more hooded and drooped, accentuating the hawk-like appearance that I had always perceived in his countenance.

We hailed a cab and were taken to the venerable Brown's Hotel in Mayfair, where his as-yet undisclosed client had reserved rooms for him. It always seemed odd to be in London with Holmes and not return to our former quarters at Baker Street, abandoned two decades earlier, but the warmth and elegance of Brown's compensated in nearly every respect.

"You have a reservation for me," he informed the youthful clerk at the front desk. "My name is 'Holmes'."

"Ah, yes, Mr. Sherlock Holmes," the young man said. "I believe my grandfather had mentioned your name when I was a child!"

Holmes's eyebrows arched slightly and his mouth pursed, but otherwise he displayed little in response to the clerk's remark, although I could barely suppress a smile. We deposited Holmes's luggage in his comfortable room and soon found ourselves at the nearby Goat Tavern. I quickly brought Holmes up to date with the details of my limited practice as he polished off his tea and a slice of lemon cake before reaching for his pipe and shag tobacco. "And you?" I asked. "Are you continuing to enjoy life as an apiarist?"

"I find my Sussex bees most enjoyable," he said. "I'm pleased to say that I have become great friends with Manley, whom you might know as author of *Honey Production in the British Isles*."

"Actually, no," I replied with a hint of exasperation. "I'm unfamiliar with that particular volume or its author."

"Well, never mind," Holmes said impatiently. "Watson, I've been asked to undertake a rather unique mission abroad, one in which I could very well use some expert assistance." A tiny smile spread across his normally expressionless countenance. "Perhaps something that might interest you – if you aren't too busy, of course."

Even at this late date, I almost hesitate to identify the eminent figure who had engaged Holmes, for it wasn't the Foreign Office, but rather a controversial member of Commons. We soon engaged a motorcar to carry us along the Embankment to a clandestine meeting near Whitehall. The name of Holmes's client was certainly known to me, but largely in a disparaging way, given his controversial record in government during the Great War. "Don't jump to conclusions," Holmes counseled. "The key point here is the validity of the mission, not the reputation or popularity of the man behind it."

Soon we were s being escorted into an office in the shadow of the tower containing Big Ben and seated across the desk from our distinguished employer, the Honorable Winston Churchill, MP, late the wartime Lord of the Admiralty and a man in fear not only for his country's safety but his own life as well. Tensions with Ireland were at fever pitch once again – indeed, the distinguished diplomat and soldier Sir Henry Wilson had been assassinated outside his own London home by I.R.A. fanatics the previous June, and concerns about the durability of The League of Nations and The Treaty of Versailles were growing with each passing month.

"The whole map of Europe has been changed by the cataclysm that has swept the world," Churchill had recently declared. The rising menace of the Russian *Bolsheviki* threatened even greater instability for Eastern Europe, and perhaps for England as well. Mounting disruptions in India and Egypt, instigated by the calls for independence by the nationalist agitator Gandhi, jeopardized the future of the Empire itself.

Despite his thinning red hair, round form, and oddly cherubic look, no one would mistake the mercurial Churchill for anything but a gravely engaged statesman. Of course, I knew of his reputation as a hard-driving advocate for the Empire and promoter of stronger defences, but for all the world, across the table he seemed more like a frantic Puck with a cigar clenched tightly in his mouth.

"Mr. Holmes, Dr. Watson," he nodded in our direction slightly as he spoke our names, "these are grave times indeed. I recall the great service that you both provided to Britain on the eve of the Great War, apprehending that scoundrel Van Bork," Churchill said. "Now your country requires your services as never before. Were your brother Mycroft in better health," he looked at Holmes, "there would be no need for your involvement. But as it is," his shoulders involuntarily hunched, "we have no one else to whom we might turn."

"I am flattered to be of service," Holmes murmured. "May I ask to whom you allude when you reference 'we'? Are you speaking on behalf of the government – (He knew that Churchill was not a member of the government, so that was not likely.) – the King – (Even less so, as Churchill was not a favorite of the monarch.) – or some . . . *other interest?*"

"I am speaking in the interest of *all* of the above, sir, whether they are aware of it or not!" Churchill replied curtly, waving his hand above his head and vaguely in the direction of the Palace of Westminster. "Your client is England itself! My honorable colleagues in the current government fail to comprehend the risks or the dangers, but I assure you, sir, the peril is grave, and becoming more so daily."

"Indeed," replied Holmes, his lips pursing slightly. "Pray explain what service I may provide to you and England."

"Germany," said Churchill decisively. "The danger is Germany. The country is coming apart at the seams, a phoenix rising from the ashes, straining to pull itself free from its moorings," he fulminated, mixing metaphors and syntax. "Few in this country appreciate the gravity of recent developments. And certainly, few in there!" he cried, pointing to Barry's massive tower with its huge clock looming over the House of Commons.

"I want you, Mr. Holmes – I *need* you – to help me to wake England out of its stupor, to encourage our countrymen to embrace rearmament, to begin preparing for the next war which is coming as surely as we are sitting here!" he declared. He slapped the tabletop with his bare hand for emphasis before sticking his fat cigar back into his rubbery mouth and hunching forward closer to Holmes's face.

Churchill described an assignment that would take Holmes into southern Germany to conduct reconnaissance of the noisy band of National Socialist extremists – or *Nazis* – who had taken root in Bavaria. Their incendiary rhetoric attributed the post-war humiliation of the German nation to treason by Jews, a group with which Churchill had developed close alliances. These fanatics, led by a cashiered army corporal who had served the Kaiser during the War, were inflaming their countrymen and denouncing the concessions made in Versailles treaty, especially the payment of millions of pounds in reparations to the allies and the hated War Guilt Clause. "He is either a maniac or the most dangerous person in the world," Churchill said of the Nazi leader, Adolf Hitler, "and perhaps both! I need you to tell me."

The portrait of life in Germany that he painted was far more insidious than that being portrayed in the British press, as was the incendiary tone of the Nazi propaganda. Between this Nazi hysteria on the right, and the rise of the Bolsheviks in Russia on the left, it seemed in the opinion of our distinguished host that, however inconceivable, another war might well be unavoidable,

"You see, Mr. Holmes," he explained, "conventional diplomacy, and even my own scholarly writings, simply fail to achieve the necessary impact. In my current diminished role. I am unable to summon the powers of our military or our intelligence services. I must turn to you, as a private consulting spy, if you will, to help expose the true nature of the Nazi plans. Only then will we wake up this naïve and pacifistic nation to the dangers looming before us."

But that was not all. Churchill was also deeply concerned with enemies that he believed were operating in England, clandestinely aiding the Germans' plans for global conquest. "They are everywhere, spinning their webs, seducing the innocents with false promises of peace," he intoned, sounding both menacing and slightly deranged "They are here in London!" he declared, lowering his voice dramatically "You have heard of Oswald Mosley? We must expose them – and *root them out*!"

He again stuck his cigar in his rubbery mouth and arched his eyebrows. His face emerged from a cloud of acrid smoke as he leaned as close to Holmes and me as possible. "Well," he asked as his exhaled smoke enveloped his bulbous head. The effect was remarkable! "Can England count on the two of you? Can *I* count on you?"

During his long career, Holmes had been no stranger to taking commissions from governments, both British and foreign alike, and on occasion they were of a distinctly clandestine nature. Few challenges, however, seemed to address a scenario as filled with diplomatic intrigue and peril as the one Churchill had outlined.

"The assignment certainly has many points of interest," remarked Holmes after we had bade *adieu* to our new client. With a report from an unimpeachable source like Sherlock Holmes, Churchill surmised, he could rouse his fellow parliamentarians from their torpor in order to begin preparations for the inevitable tempest. However, the Nazis were not to be trifled with – a slip, any intemperate comment, could easily expose Holmes's true identify and subject him to serious danger!

My immediate reaction to the proposition was negative in the extreme. "Holmes, if I may say so, you aren't the man physically that you once were," I remonstrated. In his prime, Holmes had been a formidable master of the Japanese art of *baritsu*, able to defend himself against adversaries of far greater stature. But after decades of strenuous activity and injury (and mountains of shag tobacco), Holmes didn't move as confidently as he once was able. He would have a difficult time protecting himself against an aggrieved, jack-boot-wearing brown shirt in Bavaria. He stuck out his lower lip as we rumbled along the cobbled streets, his heavy lids half-closed on his slate-gray eyes. "I believe that I can stay a step of two ahead of Corporal Hitler's thugs," he said, a slight smile crossing his lips. "And I shall have you along, Watson, if things get really sticky!"

After returning to Brown's, Holmes instructed, "Hurry home and pack for a short trip, Watson, and don't forget your service revolver. Our client will not countenance delay." Holmes passed the remainder of the day immersed in a number of books on the World War, German history, and recent political machinations in Bavaria. Returning to Brown's late in the afternoon, I found him sprawled on the floor, surrounded by open journals, newspapers, and pads of paper upon which he had been scribbling notes.

"Yes, I believe we are ready for our travels," Holmes declared. "We shall take the boat train in the morning to France. I've booked us a comfortable coach on the train to Munich and rooms in a fine hotel in that city." He turned to me. "Are you prepared for our departure?" he queried.

"I suppose so," I replied. I eyed him carefully. "Are you not a bit hesitant undertaking this mission on the instructions of Churchill? Granted, he has a fine military record, but his judgment is suspect. Remember that dreadful Gallipoli failure in Turkey!"

"True, true, not his finest hour," Holmes responded, "although he was hardly alone in bearing responsibility for the catastrophe. In any event, in this case I believe that he has a clearer eye and sounder appreciation of the threat than many who remain in high positions in the Government." We spent a relaxing evening playing whist while I recounted my recent adventures in Fez and Marrakech.

Early the next morning, I met Holmes at Victoria Station, and we boarded the train for Dover. The journey was passed in near silence with Holmes deep in thought, his head tilted back, eyes closed. But for his long fingers drumming steadily on the brim of his hat, which he held in his lap, one might have thought him asleep. We transferred to the ferry for the uneventful trip across the Channel, that magnificent moat that had keep England secure from invaders for a thousand years – although the recent innovation of hurling bombs from airplanes had seriously eroded our much-vaunted isolation from unpleasantness on the Continent.

407

Not until we had boarded the train at the Gare de l'Est in Paris and begun the journey across France to southern Germany did Holmes speak of his intentions. He poked his head outside the compartment to ensure that no one was lurking in the passageway and then closed the door firmly. The rumbling of the wheels over the rails provided us an additional measure of security from anyone attempting to overhear out conversation, but he still drew close to me and spoke in a measured whisper.

"Watson, this may well be our most significant case," he began, "but also our most dangerous! This Hitler must be taken very seriously, despite his ridiculous rhetoric. I doubt very much that he is the fool that some imagine. His recent speeches show him to be a formidable orator. His supporters number in the thousands, perhaps tens-of-thousands, and they are heavily armed and prone to violence. I fear, as does the Bavarian government, that he will initiate a mutinous action within weeks, perhaps days, that could destabilize all of Germany. We need not speculate about how grave a challenge that would present."

Our train pulled into the Munich station early in the morning and we proceeded to our rented rooms on the *Landwehrstraße*. Holmes quickly disappeared into the crowded streets while I made dining arrangements with the hotel-keeper. It required only a few conversations and a quick look at the newspapers – my German remained passable – to appreciate how grave the atmosphere in the city had become. A state of emergency had been declared by the Prime Minister of Bavaria in late September as fears of political violence swirled through the city. With Hitler and his armed legions threatening the fragile government, the air was thick with intrigue.

Holmes returned late in the afternoon, his face grim and his manner furtive. He turned off the lights in the room and motioned me to the window. "Watch the street, Watson," he asked. "Careful now – don't allow the curtains to move."

"What am I looking for?" I beseeched.

"Do you see anyone following me? Is anyone hiding in the shadows, looking up at these rooms?" he queried.

I could see no one, but Holmes's high state of agitation alarmed me. We had been in numerous tight situations over the years, but his manner seemed one of unusual caution.

"I don't think that you were followed," I counseled. "Or at least if you were, I don't see anyone watching the hotel." Holmes stepped towards his bedroom. "See here," I said. "I really think that it's about time that you shared with me your plan for this expedition – especially if, as it seems, I am also to be endangered by my participation."

Silently, he waved me into the darkened room and bade me sit on a chair opposite to him. Only the orange glow of the tobacco in the bowl of his pipe assured me he was present in the room at all. Soon my eyes adjusted to the dark and I could see that he was sitting quite close to me, hunched up with his chest near his knees, his left hand slowly rubbing his long jaw.

"Bad business, Watson," he remarked softly. "Bad business. I doubt very much that even Churchill is remotely aware of the state to which things have deteriorated here. He certainly was right to enlist us in this mission.

"I have been to a meeting tonight of some of the most dastardly criminals I've ever encountered," he began. "These men have no principles, no honor. They live only to intimidate, to destroy, and to dominate. They are far worse than the petty burglar or blackmailer, for their intended victim isn't a helpless widow or a confused lover, but rather an unsuspecting world!"

"Holmes!" I cried. "Do you mean the Nazi gangsters?"

"Precisely," he responded. "I have spent the last several hours learning of their nefarious plot, which is about to be sprung."

"But what is their objective?" I asked.

"Nothing short of revolution!" Holmes replied. "The destruction of the Weimar Government. Indeed, their initial plan was to launch their uprising in Berlin itself, but they called that off when they realized that the odds against success were too great. Now they intend to overthrow the government of Bavaria first, and then expand their anarchy and perfidy across Germany.

"Their leader, this Hitler, is a curious fellow," he mused. "A painter, of all things, and not without some talent. A minor military figure of no significance whatsoever, and yet, a master of incitement – brutally possessed, even demonic. His words seem to grab hold of the masses, who would clearly follow him into battle – as they undoubtedly will."

"But why is no one arming to prevent this uprising?" I asked.

"That is the question Churchill sent us here to uncover, for he believes – as do only a few of our countrymen – that the Nazis' appetite extends well beyond Bavaria or even Berlin. Perhaps," his voice went soft, "even to the cliffs of Dover and beyond."

"Outrageous!" I cried. But here we were in a strange city, a foreign country, with no allies. How were we to halt a revolution? I wondered. "What are we to do?"

Holmes grew thoughtful, his long chin in his hand. "As a practical matter, how do we prevent the *putsch*, which seems imminent?" Holmes mused. "How indeed?"

The following morning, Holmes was gone before I rose, so I dressed and breakfasted, and then took a walk along the Isar River before returning to my room shortly before noon. Holmes returned soon thereafter, and his face was set with a grim look.

"I have met with von Knilling," he said, referring to the Bavarian Prime Minister. "He seems at his wits' end. The prospect of violence is growing by the hour, and his government appears nearly powerless to prevent it."

"Surely he is prepared to meet the rascals head-on," I protested.

"Yes, but the damage to his government, to the nation, may be impossible to contain," said Holmes. "I fear that our activities may not remain so secret after this evening. You must arrange for our tickets back to France and then across the Channel tomorrow. It may be too dangerous for us to remain in Munich much longer."

As the day progressed, Holmes scurried about the city while I visited the concierge to arrange our passage back to London. We shared tea and excellent cakes at a charming café at four o'clock, and we then returned to our rooms where Holmes began applying a mixture of prosthetics, beeswax, and face colorations, transforming himself into a person that even I could scarcely recognize. From several paper bags, he removed a pair of well-worn wool trousers, a shirt and a rough coat, and scuffed boots. Within minutes, he was indistinguishable from an everyday resident of the German city. We ate an early dinner in the hotel's excellent restaurant, and then Holmes slipped into the street and was swallowed up by the increasingly turbulent atmosphere of Munich.

For one of the few times in our association, I ignored Holmes's direct instructions. Given the unfamiliar city and the risk of danger, I felt my presence was warranted, as was the service revolver that I had brought on Holmes's instruction. At a careful distance, and employing the tricks of stealth that Holmes himself had taught me, I followed him through the darkening streets. Crossing the Ludwingsbrüke, Holmes hurried to the Au-Haidhausen district where loomed his destination, the enormous *Bürgerbräukeller* beer hall.

The hall was well populated and the sounds of music and merriment floated out despite the doors and windows that were closed against the November chill. Far more bracing than the air, however, were the dozens, perhaps hundreds, of Nazis in their characteristic brown shirts menacingly milling about outside the Bürgerbräukeller.

I watched from a distance as Holmes maneuvered through their ranks and quickly slipped inside. After waiting a few minutes, I followed him into the cavernous room that reeked of beer and hummed with the laughter

410

and arguments of thousands of inebriated Bavarians and the dreadful "*oom-pah*" orchestra that no civilized ear could find pleasing.

I was weaving through the crowd when I suddenly felt someone drawing me close. "Watson!" hissed Holmes into my ear. "You shouldn't have come! The danger is too great!"

"Balderdash," I whispered back, although whispering was hardly required in the raucous room. "I cannot abandon you to such risk! Did you not see the small army of brown shirts outside?"

"And the members of the local government inside!" Holmes responded, pointing to a large table where Kahr, Seisser, and Lossow were huddled over their steins of beer, clearly evaluating the deepening sense of crisis. "They are at enormous jeopardy if – "

Holmes's words were cut off as the doors to the *Bürgerbräukeller* crashed open and a band of the brown shirted agitators burst into the chamber. At the head of the intruders was the now-familiar visage of Adolf Hitler, a lock of dark hair falling over his forehead and a small moustache giving him a distinct if slightly ridiculous appearance. He was accompanied by his chief lieutenants, the heavily scarred Ernst Roehm, the bloated Hermann Göring, and the bushy-browed Rudolph Hess.

Suddenly Hitler shouted, "The national revolution has broken out! Nobody is allowed to leave!" He punctuated his declaration by pulling a revolver from inside his shirt and firing a single shot into the Bürgerbräukeller's ceiling. The effect was electric: The music and laughter halted, replaced by expressions of shock and outrage. The shot was the signal for sympathizers inside the hall to spring into action, as well they did, seizing the Bavarian leaders and hustling them to a grim fate.

"Holmes!" I cried in the direction of my friend. "This could be the beginning of the collapse of Weimer!" But he was gone, having vanished into the teeming crowd. In the confusion, I decided to follow his instructions, easing my way outdoors and making my way back to our hotel. For a long while, I sat up waiting for him, but I unwillingly drifted off to sleep in the stuffed chair.

"Wake up, Watson," I heard murmured roughly in my ear. It was Holmes, and his appearance was alarming, He remained in the costume and make-up, but now he was dirty and haggard, with a ragged cut that ran down his left cheek, just missing his eye. The knuckles on one hand were red and torn, and a bandage on his left hand was stained with dark red blood. His shirt was ripped, as was one knee of his trousers. I noted the cuckoo clock on the mantel read two o'clock in the morning, just as its little door flew open and a carved bird popped out uttering a double chirp.

"Good Lord!" I exclaimed. "What has happened to you?"

"Oh, nothing too serious," he calmly replied. "I couldn't have hoped for a better seat to the evening's very consequential activities. But I should say that the storm clouds gathering in Munich have every likelihood of darkening all of the continent in the not-too-distant future, and very likely our island as well."

While I ministered to his wounds – washing and bandaging the cuts with sterile gauze that I had fortunately packed – Holmes filled me in on the events that had transpired after I had retreated from the *Bürgerbräukeller*.

"The Nazis presumed to declare an end to the current government of Bavaria," Holmes explained. "The three officials in the beer hall were taken into custody, and a call went out for other bands of Nazis to seize government buildings throughout the city. Hitler whipped the mob into a terrifying frenzy. His closing words were – 'Either the German revolution begins tonight, or we will all be dead by dawn!' Very theatrical!"

An involuntary shudder shook his thin shoulders as he pulled his woolen scarf up tighter around his neck. "It was quite alarming, Watson," he muttered. "Even preposterous. This ridiculous megalomaniac! And yet, I fear what we have witnessed is far more the prologue to a long and tragic nightmare than the *denouement* of a low-brow melodrama."

He quickly stood and gathered his coat and hat. "I must return to the agitation," he declared, although it was still hours before sunrise. "I will be cautious, but whether I return or not, Watson, you must be on the train to France in the morning." I opened my mouth to protest, but Holmes was out the door before I could reach him.

Holmes's fears of growing violence were more than prescient. In the pre-dawn hours, a band of the Nazis attempted to lay siege to the *Reichswehr* barracks and then the Defence Ministry, where a cordon of police blocked their way. From my hotel, I could hear a furious gun battle between the two groups. When it was over, I soon learned that four officers lay dead in the street along with sixteen members of Hitler's legions. Hitler himself, along with other leaders in the abortive *putsch*, had been rounded up and sent off to prison where, one could only hope, they would soon hang for their acts of treason.

Fortunately, the disorder did not disrupt the travel plans that I'd made. I anxiously waited for Holmes to appear at the train station. Just a few minutes before the scheduled departure, he rushed onto the platform where I was waiting with our tickets. We clambered aboard as the train began to depart the station.

"I've sent a wire to Churchill advising him we're returning to London," he reported. "I promised him a full report within a few days of our return."

I looked at his battered face and injured hand. "You certainly will require assistance preparing such a report so quickly," I said as the train picked up momentum and we mercifully began speeding towards the French frontier. "I'm afraid I must check on several patients upon my return," I added, hoping he would understand my time was not entirely at his disposal.

"Not a problem on either account," he assured. "Churchill has extended my stay at Brown's Hotel and has thoughtfully engaged a temporary assistant to help me. She will meet me at Brown's, and you may take whatever time that you require attending to your patients."

We quickly found our compartment where we sat in silence for most of the trip, reflecting on how close we had come to being trapped in the spreading political conflagration. I didn't draw a relaxed breath until we were safely on board the ferry back to Dover.

Ensconced once again in great comfort at Brown's, Holmes quickly prepared to draft his report to Churchill, who eagerly awaited our bird's eye account of the Munich uprising. The assistant arranged by Churchill was a Miss Edwena Hunt, a most attractive and efficient young woman, with blonde hair, a slight limp, and exquisite taste in clothing. She arrived promptly in the morning and proved a devoted aide to the famous detective.

As we sat drinking our morning coffee and reading *The Times* a few days later, there was a knock on the door. Holmes was poring over his draft report and showed little signs of rising to open it, and so I strode across the room. There, once again, was the ever-attentive Miss Hunt, along with an unfamiliar young man holding a well-wrapped box.

"Mr. Holmes," she said, as they stepped into the room. "I encountered this fellow in the lobby. He claims that you've been expecting this."

Holmes seemed excited by the young man's arrival and quickly strode to the door, not even pausing when he knocked some papers and a pencil off his desk. Miss Hunt quickly stooped to pick them up and then carefully straightened up the pages strewn over the desk.

The messenger was casually dressed, the growth of a few days covering his chin. He extended the package to Holmes and stepped backward, his soft cap in hand.

"Ah! Franz, good!" Holmes said, taking the box. "Watson, you remember Franz, one of the 'Irregulars'?" he said, referencing the young urchins who had run errands and provided intelligence to Holmes during the hey-day of his career.

"Guv'nor," said Franz, tipping his head towards Holmes, his crooked smile revealing broken and yellowed teeth. "A real pleasure to see you again!" Somewhere in that grizzled face was the young boy who had scampered up and down the stairs at Baker Street all those years past, but I couldn't recognize him. Holmes handed him a few coins and, with a tip of his hat, he clambered down the stairs and back into the bustle of Albemarle Street.

"Well, it is a relief that this package has arrived safely," said Holmes, as he tore at the tape and string sealing the brown paper wrapping. In a moment, he lifted a plain, brown cardboard box perhaps two-feet square. I could see the excitement in his eyes as he set it on a low table and lifted the lid, allowing a bright red cloth to partially spill onto the floor.

Pulling the rest of the material out of the box, Holmes revealed to my horror a white circle in the middle of the red banner, and in the center of the white patch, the horrid black swastika of the Bavarian Nazis.

"Holmes!" I cried, "I am appalled! I'm horrified! A Nazi flag? In Brown's Hotel?"

It was clear Miss Hunt shared my surprise at the contents of the box, which she regarded with keen attention. Holmes stuffed the flag back into the box, thanked Miss Hunt for her assistance, and escorted her from the room, instructing her not to mention the contents of the package to anyone. Once she had departed, he again withdrew the despicable banner and held it out in front of him, a smile of deep satisfaction spreading across his face. He examined the flag carefully, holding it close to his face and grunting a satisfied recognition. Finally, he turned back to me and saw the look of horror on my face.

"Ah, Watson," he said, carefully laying the object on the table. "You see, this isn't just any flag. You see this?" He pointed a long finger at dark red splotches that flicked across the white portion of the flag. "This is the *Blutfahne*." I remained perplexed. "The 'Blood Flag', certain to become a priceless talisman to the Nazi leaders," Holmes continued. "Especially Hitler.

"I saw this flag carried into battle the other night by the Nazis in Munch. When the police fired on them near the Defence Ministry, unwisely creating sixteen undeserved martyrs, the flag bearer was among the gravely wounded. He collapsed on top of this flag, staining the cloth with his blood, here – " He pointed to a red spot and then to others. " – and here, and here. Hitler, I have heard, has let it be known from his prison cell that he prizes this flag more than any relic of the *putsch*. I have no doubt that madman will do anything to recover it."

"But how did you come by the . . . *Blut*-whatever?" I asked.

"All in good time," Holmes soothingly purred. "All in good time. Meanwhile, I have here in my hands a most valued artifact of the lunatic Nazis, and their mustachioed leader is sitting in a Bavarian jail wondering what became of it! I shall keep it here," he motioned towards a trunk near the fireplace, "for safekeeping until I deliver it to our friends at the Defence Ministry." He quickly folded the flag, returned it to its cardboard box, and locked it inside the trunk.

The next morning, Holmes was still triumphant when I arrived for breakfast, which soon appeared along with Miss Hunt.

"You seem in an excellent mood, Mr. Holmes," she cheerfully said as we sat down to steaming plates of eggs, bangers, and toast. "Are you so enthused over the arrival of yesterday's package?"

"Oh yes, Miss Hunt," he replied. "I'm afraid I cannot speak about it too much, even to you," he added, this latter comment spoken in a theatrical *sotto voce*, although no one else was in the room. "I must visit Whitehall later today to describe it to some members of the government. It may seem an inconsequential souvenir, but I assure you, the contents of that box may well involve questions of war!"

"*War!*" she cried with great alarm as she stood up, her hand flying up to her mouth. "But no one believes there is a risk of war, do they? Why, we just ended such a terrible conflict! I – I am distressed just at the thought of another one!" She buried her attractive face in her hands, and as her knees buckled slightly, I sprang forward to steady her.

"There, there," Holmes comforted. "I'm sure that I spoke too dramatically. There has been a slight ripple of agitation on the Continent, but the likelihood of conflict is quite minimal. League of Nations and all. But I must hurry. The sooner I speak with these officials, the better our country will be served." He disappeared into his bedchamber and re-emerged carrying his satchel, bade us farewell, and disappeared out the door.

My mind was hardly on my patients that morning – one with the croup, another with symptoms of measles – as I kept an eye on the clock. At one-thirty, I closed the office and headed back to Brown's as planned, arriving ahead of Holmes. I was alarmed to find the door to his room slightly ajar, and when I entered, I immediately drew in my breath.

The sitting room seemed as though a typhoon had blown through it, with papers and other items strewn haphazardly around. Boxes and drawers had been opened, their contents tossed indifferently on the floor and the furniture upended. Lying on the floor was the distraught Miss Hunt, surrounded by papers and the contents of the desk, the bureau, and even her own handbag.

"Good Lord!" I shouted and rushed to her assistance, tearing the gag from her face and pulling on the cords that bound her wrists. As I did so, I noticed as well a nasty bruise upon her forehead from which a small amount of blood was still flowing, evidently the result of a blow from a blunt instrument. Fortunately, she seemed more terrified than badly injured as I knelt by her side, frantically untying the knots that bound her.

"Oh, Dr. Watson, thank goodness you have come!" she cried, big tears running down her soft cheeks and her shoulders heaving. "This is all my fault!"

"Don't be silly," I counseled, fetching her a glass of water, although she might well have appreciated something considerably stronger. "What happened here? And are you alright?"

"Oh, yes, I am now," she gasped as she sat on the sofa. "I had come by early to straighten up Mr. Holmes's rooms a bit. You know, with his injured hand, he really cannot do so himself. They arrived soon afterwards, pushing their way into the room when I answered their knock. As I attempted to call the concierge, one hit me here – " She pointed to the abrasion on her forehead. " – and they bound me with these ropes. They refused to believe that I didn't know what they were asking about, and they proceeded to create this unfortunate mess."

Just then, Holmes burst into the room and quickly surveyed the disorder that only hours before had been his comfortable quarters. We quickly filled him in on Miss Hunt's terrifying account of the past several hours.

"Hmm, do you have the ropes that they used to bind you?" he asked. Miss Hunt handed them over and Holmes scrutinized their length, their material, and the remaining knots.

"How many men?" he asked.

"Three, I think," she responded, "and they talked to someone in the hall, so at least four. They went through everything. It took over an hour! Oh, Mr. Holmes, do you know what they were searching for!"

"I have no doubt," he declared. "I pray they didn't injure you." He held her hands tenderly and closely examined her hands and wrists where the intruders had bound her. "No damage, thank goodness," he said, shifting his examination to the bruise on her forehead. "And this bruise is superficial – no concussion. Don't you agree, Watson? What a relief that you weren't injured more seriously!"

"Indeed!" I added.

"Well, they were out of luck because I had the object of their burglary with me," he explained, patting his satchel. "I'm delivering it this very evening to the Defence Ministry. I fear these hooligans are to be disappointed should they return tomorrow.

"I am deeply sorry for your troubles," he smiled at Miss Hunt as he gathered up the contents of her handbag and handed it to her. Reaching into his satchel, he withdrew a small box wrapped in blue paper with a red silk bow "Perhaps this small gift will compensate you for your very unnerving day," he said, handing it to her. "A souvenir of our recent journey to the Continent. I hope it helps soothe you following this most disgraceful assault."

"Why, Mr. Holmes!" she cried, pulling at the ribbon and tearing the paper. As she opened the box, she uttered a tiny gasp and lifted out a glittering crystal bottle.

"It is the newest perfume in France," he declared, watching her face eagerly for her reaction. "Chanel No. 5. I don't know whether there was a 1, 2, 3, or 4, but No. 5 is 'the rave' in Paris. I do hope that you will accept it in appreciation for the devoted care you've extended to me over these past days."

"Mr. Holmes, your thoughtfulness and generosity are remarkable," she replied. "I'm sure it is an extraordinary fragrance. Do you mind if I try some now?"

"I should be deeply disappointed, indeed, if you did not!" he answered reaching for the bottle. His pocketknife cut loose the sealing tape and then he extended his hand to the lady. "Allow me." She gave her hand to him and as he gently pulled it towards him, dousing her forearm with a generous dollop of Chanel No 5.

"Oh! Perhaps a bit more than required," he laughed. "But a truly remarkable fragrance, don't you think?"

"Oh, yes, Mr. Holmes, I cannot possibly thank you enough," she said as she wiped off the excess perfume with her forearm. She flashed him a sweet smile that, given my own experience with women, I took as an indication that the young lady was indeed a bit smitten with the world's most famous detective.

"Now you should take your leave for the evening. I must complete some work before delivering this wretched flag to Whitehall. After this outrageous intrusion, I shall be relieved to be done with it," he declared.

"But I must help you clean the room," she protested. "I feel the mess is in part my fault, as I unwittingly provided the intruders their entry."

"Certainly not!" he proclaimed. "You bear no responsibility for this intrusion at all." He helped her to her feet, gathered her coat and hat for her, and gently eased her towards the door. "As they say, '*Störe dich nicht!*'"

Miss Hunt smiled wanly. "Thank you, Mr. Holmes," she said, "but I am afraid I do not understand that language."

"Hah! Of course not," Holmes responded. "A remnant of my recent trip. In German, it means '*Don't disturb yourself*'." He ushered her out the door with a self-satisfied smile, which told me he was pleased with the response his gift had received.

"Remarkable, indeed!" I exclaimed after Miss Hunt had left. "What an extraordinary gift!"

"Now, now, surely Miss Hunt is deserving of a special thanks for her many services, not to mention her terrible ordeal," Holmes replied. "I don't think one small bottle of perfume is a terrible extravagance. Besides – " He suddenly became quite serious. " – the game, as you would say, is afoot, and we must prepare for the resolution!"

"What 'game'?" I exclaimed. "What 'resolution'? Have you devised a plan to apprehend Miss Hunt's attackers without even knowing their identity?"

"The 'plan,' dear chap, is in that bag," he said, drawing the Nazi flag from the satchel. "You didn't think that I would be so foolish as to leave it unguarded in this room! The key to resolving this case should arrive within minutes. In the meanwhile, let me close my eyes for a time, and when our guests arrive, please show them in."

What guests? I wondered. What role were they to play? Why did Holmes still have that flag, which I thought he would already have delivered to the Defence Ministry or Churchill? As he sat motionless in the stuffed chair, his eyes closed and his eyelids occasionally fluttering, I tried to reconstruct the chaotic journey of the past few days – from Whitehall to a beer hall in Munich, to barely escaping the growing violence in Bavaria, to a purloined, blood-stained Nazi flag in the sitting room at Brown's and now, the terrible assault on Miss Hunt. I welcomed the knock on the door that signaled the arrival of our guest.

Holmes bounded out of the chair with an alacrity for which I would scarcely have given him credit, given his age and recent injuries. He was at the door in an instant and threw it open.

"Ah, thank you, thank you, Carruthers," he called to the slender man who appeared in the doorway. "And welcome to you as well," he said to a tan-and-white dog of impressive size that bounded into the room. In an instant, the dog's massive paws were on Holmes's chest as it lapped at the detective's face, which he turned away to avoid its enthused slobbering.

"He's Ollie, he is," said Carruthers, introducing the hound. "That's short for 'Olfactory'. That means 'smell', you know."

Holmes murmured his familiarity with the term.

"I tell you, Mr. Holmes, this dog has a nose on him like no dog I've ever trained," Carruthers continued. "Blood, sweat, a scent on a glove or shoe – nothing gets past that nose, it don't."

"Well, Ollie, we shall put your nose to the test today," declared Holmes once Carruthers had departed. "He will assure that our little souvenir from Munich remains secure. Later this evening, we shall depart with my memento, which will never return to this room. I certainly don't

418

want to risk another intrusion by whomever was searching my room and tying up our poor Miss Hunt like a Christmas goose!"

Ollie's arrival did little to dispel my utter confusion. For the next half-hour or so, with the dog curled up at his feet, Holmes and I sat by the glowing fireplace as he reviewed the text of his final report for Churchill. He finished his study, stuffed the papers into his bag, and sat back in his chair, his long fingers were supporting his nose while his thumbs hooked under his pointed chin, the thumbs and forefingers forming a diamond and his lids closed. The only sound in the room was the ticking of the mantel clock.

The late afternoon light outside had begun to grow dusky when Holmes declared softly, "I think that will do. Ollie, come here my friend." In a louder voice he said, "Come, Watson. Let us prepare to deliver this dastardly flag to the proper authorities. The sooner it is out of these rooms for good, the better."

The hound had stood up and lazily walked to the chair where Holmes sat. Holmes reached across to the small desk, opened a drawer, and withdrew a small vial. Removing the top, he held it out for Ollie to sniff. "Here you go, Ollie," he offered as the dog wandered over to investigate the contents. When he got close, his head started and Holmes withdrew the vial and replaced its cap.

"Now, Ollie," he said, intently staring at the hound. "Show me!"

Ollie stood immobile for a few moments, and then turned to a door on the far wall of the room that had been locked shut since we had first arrived. He froze, not moving a hair whilst Holmes followed his gaze to the door.

Suddenly Holmes pulled a silver police whistle from his pocket and blew it three times, emitting a piercing shriek that chilled my bones. At the same moment, he grabbed my Moroccan walking stick from where it rested next to my chair and strode to the door on which Ollie remained fixated. Without warning, Holmes raised the heavy end of the cane above his head and brought it down forcefully on the doorknob, smashing the glass handle and the lock attached to it. Seizing the door, he yanked it open.

He swiftly reached into the dark recess and pulled through the doorway a flustered and angry Edwena Hunt, writhing against his steel-like grip and with a shocked look on her face. She shrieked and swung at Holmes with her free hand, pummeling him again and again, but he held her tightly and kept pulling until she tumbled onto the floor.

"There we are, Miss Hunt!" Holmes cried, brandishing my stick like a club over the enraged woman. "You are unmasked!"

The door of the hotel room flew open and several young men in police uniforms rapidly filed in, led by a tall young man with sandy hair and trim moustache who bent down next to Miss Hunt, grasped her by her left arm, and forcing her to stand. "Edwena Hunt," he declared, "I am Inspector Trilling of Scotland Yard. You are under arrest."

"On what charge?" she angrily demanded, trying to twist out of his grip.

"On the charge of espionage against the Crown!"

"Espionage?" she cried, forcing a sharp laugh. "On behalf of whom?"

"On behalf of the Nazi fanatic, Hitler," Holmes interjected. "It will do you no good to feign ignorance."

"We have the incontrovertible facts, thanks to Mr. Holmes here – and our colleague, Ollie," Trilling added, nodding to the hound. He forced handcuffs on her wrists as she struggled vainly.

My head was spinning with the gravity of what had just occurred. "Wait," I pleaded, sitting down in one of the chairs. "Miss Hunt is . . . a spy . . . *for the Nazis?*"

"She is not Miss Hunt," Holmes seethed. "She is Anna Stanzhofler, a disciple of the Nazi rabble, sent to spy on me in hopes of thwarting my services to those in the British government who recognize Nazism as a venal and dangerous ideology."

"But it is inconceivable Churchill would send a spy to assist you!" I protested.

"Churchill did arrange through an agency for Miss Edwena Hunt to assist me during my stay in London," he explained, "but apparently a Mosley agent in Whitehall must have learned of the arrangement and arranged for her to be absconded-with on her way to Brown's. I fear that Miss Hunt's current whereabouts remain unknown, although we must hope for the best. Miss Stanzhofler was then substituted to impersonate her while conducting nefarious spying activities."

Holmes looked over at the furious German agent. "I was hardly likely to grant an unknown person – even an attractive young lady – unfettered access to my room without a far more thorough background check than Miss Stanzhofler had evidently anticipated.

"The Nazis had learned of our recent trip to Bavaria," he said, holding up the stained flag. "They dispatched the ersatz Miss Hunt to see what they could learn of my activities and my report to Churchill. It was, I confess, a deception I perceived quite readily. However, when the flag arrived and I saw Miss Hunt's reaction, I realized that it would serve as the bait I needed to lure the spy network here in London into exposing itself!

"Some consultation ensued with our friends at Scotland Yard, who were able to confirm my suspicions. Have I got it about right, Miss

Stanzhofler?" he asked the seething woman, holding the bloodstained flag where she could see it clearly.

"The *Blutfahne!*" the fake Miss Hunt hissed, her eyes flashing. "Give it to me!" She lunged for the flag, but the police held her tight and Holmes moved the flag away from her grasp. "You do not deserve even to touch it!" she shrieked.

"I have a good mind to toss it into the fire and be done with it," he responded, "but Whitehall has uses for it. Not that you will be in any position to inform your colleagues. Ah, your colleagues!" Holmes strode to the window and opened the sash. "Have you got them?" he called out to those in the street below.

"Yes, Mr. Holmes," came a voice from the street. "Four of them came running out of the hotel when you blew the whistle, and we got them all, three by the front door and one by the rear."

"I had Twilling here station several Scotland Yard men outside the front and back entrances of the hotel," he smiled, "knowing that the conspirators would flee when they heard the police whistle and the commotion caused by your apprehension." He pointed his long finger down to the group of officers gathered on the street who were holding the angry prisoners in their clutches.

"Should you find yourself free and again engaged in the business of espionage," Holmes said to the spy, "which I very much doubt will be the fate that awaits you, I suggest that you pay greater attention to details, for your amateurish blunders quickly alerted me to your little masquerade.

"The ropes your associates used to bind you were too loosely tied to be credible restraints," he explained. "When I examined your wrists and applied the perfume, I saw no signs of chafing that would surely have been expected had you made a genuine effort to free yourself. And that bump on your forehead . . . ." He shook his head disapprovingly. "I'm afraid it was far too gentle a knock, probably self-inflicted, which is why it raised only a superficial welt.

"In addition, the cut was still oozing blood when I examined you, which indicated that the attack had occurred only minutes before Watson and I arrived. Had it been an hour or so since you had been assaulted, as you reported, the blood surely would have coagulated by the time I examined you. Tsk, tsk, not at all convincing." Holmes turned to me and I nodded my agreement about the freshness of the wound although, in the excitement of discovering her predicament, I confess to having ignored the implication.

Trilling's' men grasped the spy by her arm and escorted her out of the room. Holmes carefully folded the Nazi talisman and placed it back in the box and handed it to the inspector. "Now this is your responsibility," he declared, "and I would appreciate your delivering it to the Defence Ministry at your earliest opportunity. I prefer never to see it again." I watched Trilling and his prisoner depart, then glanced at Holmes, at the smashed door to the adjacent room, at my ruined walking stick, and finally at Ollie, who was happily chewing on one of Holmes silk slippers.

"I must be getting too old for such adventures," I admitted to Holmes. "At a minimum, I would have thought I might have suspected some part of this bizarre case, but I must admit, she had me utterly fooled. I am as confused and surprised as I was during the earliest days of our association."

"Don't be hard on yourself, Watson," Holmes counseled, carefully clapping me gently on my good shoulder. "A pretty face can easily interfere with rational thought, I understand. Come, let us venture off to The Globe for an early dinner, and I shall lay the entire case out for you."

Soon, bolstered by a fine *pinot grigio* and *primo plato* of grilled fish, Holmes began to clear away the fog that still swirled about the case.

"Churchill has been desperate to raise the alarm of the rising German threat," he said, "but the resistance within the government has been ferocious. They are tired of war, of death, of fear itself. They seek tranquility at any cost, he fears, and are prepared to embrace false hopes to avoid the trauma of rearmament and conflict."

Our journey fortuitously had coincided with the beer hall *putsch*, providing us with incontrovertible evidence of the capacity of Hitler and his thugs to rally thousands of frustrated Bavarians. Upon our return to London, Holmes had spent a morning dropping hints of his escapade at clubs frequented by known German sympathizers, including the young parliamentarian Churchill had mentioned, Oswald Mosley. In effect, Holmes used himself as bait to expose an underground cell of British devotees of the fascist cause. A day later, Miss Hunt had appeared at our door, ready to care for the wounded detective.

"I was instantaneously skeptical of Miss Hunt when she appeared," he said as our lamb chops arrived, along with a fine claret, and he began slashing through them. "I have an instinctive suspicion about anyone who conveniently arrives in my presence as a case is afoot. Churchill had arranged for a young lady to assist me whilst in London, but of course he had never actually met Miss Hunt. So I had no reason to accept that she was who she presented herself to be without some checking.

"My motto, as you know, Watson, is to 'assume *nothing*'," he said, spearing a juicy cube of lamb and taking a long drink of wine. "It wasn't difficult to find holes in her story, especially when I took the liberty of visiting the placement agency that had referred the young lady. The manager was pleased to hear that she was proving satisfactory for my needs, especially given the car accident that had left her with a slight limp.

"Miss Stanzhofler's masquerade was quite thorough in that respect, as you noticed, but I noted that the wear on her shoe heels was even. The differently worn heels of anyone with a genuine limp undoubtedly would have been quite distinguishable.

"She also struck me as too well informed about my habits – my . . . 'quirks,' if you will – for someone that I had never met," he said, adding slyly, "and she remarkably claimed *not* to have read your little stories. She made a few mistakes that revealed her as a fraud.

"For example, I took the liberty of checking the contents of her purse when I picked it up after the assault and discovered several pamphlets printed in German. When this imposter claimed not to understand the fragmentary words I spoke to her in German, my suspicions were further aroused. Surely a young woman who read German pamphlets would have understood such simple terms. And yet this woman implausibly denied all understanding of the language."

He took a deep swallow of the claret and continued. "She spent far too much time examining my rooms on those occasions when she was announcing the arrival of a guest. Remember when she picked up those papers and pencil that had fallen on the floor the other day?" he asked. "She stole a few moments to read over the papers as she was rearranging them on my desk. If she was so curious, might she not also have sought to overhear the conversations that occurred after she had departed? After a good deal of searching, I discovered that my suspicions were correct.

"I was very curious about that door in my suite that evidently was locked from the other side. Where did it go? Clearly into a communicating room, because there would be little reason to lock a closet that opened only to this suite. My suspicion was confirmed in a discussion with the hotel manager, who reported the door led to a small room with its own access to the corridor, typically used by servants accompanying a guest staying in the suite that I'm occupying. Anyone wishing to overhear my conversations need only enter that room silently from the corridor and listen at the door to hear our conversations as clearly as if she had been standing next to us. Of course, it was difficult to know if, or when, Miss Stanzhofler might sequester herself in the room to learn of our plans to deliver the flag to the authorities. So a plan was needed.

"Even before our departure for the Continent, I had been contemplating how to maneuver the Nazis in London into revealing themselves, and the *Blutfahne* unexpectedly provided me the perfect means. When I saw the wounded demonstrator, Heinrich Trambauer, fall bleeding on this Nazi banner in Munich, an idea immediately struck me.

423

Hitler, who reportedly holds a fanatic's obsession with the occult, likely would regard such a talisman as having incalculable value and go to great lengths to retrieve it. I believe it is fair to say the entire strategy had occurred to me even before the flag had fallen to the ground in front of the *Feldherrnhalle*."

"So you made arrangements to secure the flag in Bavaria and have it sent to you here in London?" I inquired. "How?"

"I saw the crowd's angry reaction when a police officer grabbed it from the Nazis," he explained. "I hurried to the local police headquarters to speak with a high-ranking officer, an old friend whom I had assisted some years ago on a case involving a prominent nobleman in Bavaria and a certain – ahem, '*singer*' – in a local club.

"'I should be greatly indebted to you if this flag were to find its way to me,' I told him. 'I must have it, even if only briefly. It may well provide us an essential opportunity against these zealots who threaten your country as well as mine!" He readily agreed, and when the flag, bloodied as it was, appeared in his office later in the day, he immediately boxed it and sent it to me here in London, where it was delivered by the one-time Irregular, Franz, with whom you were recently reacquainted."

"But if you knew that Miss Hunt, or whatever her name is, was a spy, why didn't you just arrest her?" I asked.

"I needed proof, and I needed her to lure her henchmen to reveal themselves, which is why I loudly proclaimed my intention to deliver the flag to the Defence Ministry tonight. I had to force her hand. Such a disclosure, I was quite certain, would lead her to enlist her own crew of musclemen to intercept me and ensure that the flag didn't make it to my intended destination."

"Well, if you suspected she was a spy, why did you give such expensive perfume to her?"

"No young lady can say 'no' to perfume, Watson, of that I was quite confident," Holmes declared. "Yet if she was fond of it, so, too, was my loyal friend Ollie, whose perceptive nose could detect it easily through the locked door leading to the anteroom. I needed to be certain that Miss Stanzhofler was in place to overhear my loud announcement that we were departing. I had little doubt she would signal her compatriots to prepare to subdue me and abscond with the flag.

"By the way," he added, "I must apologize for damaging your walking stick, which proved quite effective in exposing her hiding place."

He speared another piece of lamb and smiled.

"I think that Churchill will be pleased to learn that we've rounded up the most dangerous band of German spies operating in London, and all because they risked their necks to recover a stained flag," Holmes said with an air of satisfaction.

We concluded our dinner and took a cab back to the hotel for a nightcap. "England and the world are a bit safer tonight, Watson," Holmes declared. "A deadly team of maniacal Nazis is safely under lock and key at the Old Bailey, Hitler and his group of fanatics are in jail in Munich, the flag is safely in the hands of Scotland Yard and on its way to the Defence Ministry, and Europe is on notice that the menace of German nationalism far from extinguished. I certainly hope that the government will at last heed Mr. Churchill's call for a bigger navy, a new air force, and rearmament now that the intentions of the Nazis are so unmistakable. Of one thing we can be almost certain: No British statesman will advocate appeasement with so unstable a tyrant as Hitler!"

Several weeks later, after Holmes had returned to his bees and I to my patients, we heard disturbing news. Evidently a Mosley sympathizer in the Foreign Office, perhaps the same one who had likely tipped off the Nazi saboteurs about Miss Hunt, had pinched the *Blutfahne* and returned it to the Nazis in hopes of appeasing their maniacal hostility towards England. The icon indeed soon resurfaced in the hands of Nazi officials in Bavaria, where it was being revered as symbol of fanatical nationalism. Even more inexplicably, a few months later, Hitler was surprisingly released after just nine months in Landsberg prison, during which he produced his monstrous autobiography published just weeks ago. Undoubtedly, he has now resumed his struggle to revitalize German militarism, which I fear will not end well for Europe.

"This loss disheartens me more than I can say," Holmes bitterly admitted. "I fear Whitehall's sloppy security cost England an item of great symbolic value that will be exploited by very dangerous extremists. And I'm gravely concerned that we have, within our own government, those who still fail to appreciate the grave danger these Nazi hooligans pose to our security."

The conclusion of the case, however was not without one bright spot. In return for a promise of leniency in sentencing, Miss Stanzhofler agreed to intercede to secure the release of the real Miss Edwena Hunt, who had been held in a dank basement at the Isle of Dogs in the East End. The young woman was shaken but unhurt by her alarming experience and quickly departed London for the quiet of her parents' home in Berwick-upon-Tweed.

"Holmes, your service has been invaluable," I assured him. "Surely the culpability lies entirely with Whitehall. One can only hope that your work has raised sufficient concern to prepare for any dangers the flag and its fanatical followers will unleash."

Given the continuing instability in Continental politics as I write this account in 1925, I have decided to sequester this report on our adventure in Bavaria. I very much hope the readers of the Twenty-First Century will recognize the great debt they owe to the prowess of Sherlock Holmes for identifying the dangers at grave risk to his own safety. Most fervently, I pray that they proved able to avoid the terrible conflagration that this adventure seems to foreshadow.

About the Contributors

Hugh Ashton was born in the U.K., and moved to Japan in 1988, where he remained until 2016, living with his wife Yoshiko in the historic city of Kamakura, a little to the south of Yokohama. He and Yoshiko have now moved to Lichfield, a small cathedral city in the Midlands of the U.K., the birthplace of Samuel Johnson, and one-time home of Erasmus Darwin. In the past, he has worked in the technology and financial services industries, which have provided him with material for some of his books set in the 21st century. He currently works as a writer: Novelist, freelance editor, and copywriter, (his work for large Japanese corporations has appeared in international business journals), and journalist, as well as producing industry reports on various aspects of the financial services industry. Recently, however, his lifelong interest in Sherlock Holmes has developed into an acclaimed series of adventures featuring the world's most famous detective, written in the style of the originals. In addition to these, he has also published historical and alternate historical novels, short stories, and thrillers. Together with artist Andy Boerger, he has produced the *Sherlock Ferret* series of stories for children, featuring the world's cutest detective.

Brian Belanger is a publisher and editor, but is best known for his freelance illustration and cover design work. His distinctive style can be seen on several MX Publishing covers, including *Silent Meridian* by Elizabeth Crowen, *Sherlock Holmes and the Menacing Melbournian* by Allan Mitchell, *Sherlock Holmes and A Quantity of Debt* by David Marcum, *Welcome to Undershaw* by Luke Benjamen Kuhns, and many more. Brian is the co-founder of Belanger Books LLC, where he illustrates the popular *MacDougall Twins with Sherlock Holmes* young reader series (#1 bestsellers on Amazon.com UK). A prolific creator, he also designs t-shirts, mugs, stickers, and other merchandise on his personal art site: *www.redbubble.com/people/zhahadun*.

Derrick Belanger is an educator and also the author of the #1 bestselling book in its category, *Sherlock Holmes: The Adventure of the Peculiar Provenance*, which was in the top 200 bestselling books on Amazon. He also is the author of *The MacDougall Twins with Sherlock Holmes* books, and he edited the Sir Arthur Conan Doyle horror anthology *A Study in Terror: Sir Arthur Conan Doyle's Revolutionary Stories of Fear and the Supernatural*. Mr. Belanger co-owns the publishing company Belanger Books, which released the Sherlock Holmes anthologies *Beyond Watson*, *Holmes Away From Home: Adventures from the Great Hiatus* Volumes 1 and 2, *Sherlock Holmes: Before Baker Street*, and *Sherlock Holmes: Adventures in the Realms of H.G. Wells* Volumes I and 2. Derrick resides in Colorado and continues compiling unpublished works by Dr. John H. Watson.

Lizzy Butler has been the Fundraising, Community, and Events Manager at the Stepping Stones School, located in Hyndhead, Surrey, since early 2019.

Bob Byrne was a columnist for *Sherlock Magazine* and has contributed to *Sherlock Holmes Mystery Magazine* and the Sherlock Holmes short story collection *Curious Incidents*. He publishes two free online newsletters: *Baker Street Essays* and *The Solar Pons Gazette*, both of which can be found at *www.SolarPons.com*, the only website dedicated to August Derleth's successor to the Great Detective. Bob's column, *The Public Life of Sherlock Holmes*, appears every Monday morning at *www.BlackGate.com* and explores Holmes, hard boiled, and other mystery matters, and whatever other topics come to mind by the deadline. His mystery-themed blog is *Almost Holmes*.

Leslie Charteris was born in Singapore on May 12th, 1907. With his mother and brother, he moved to England in 1919 and attended Rossall School in Lancashire before moving on to Cambridge University to study law. His studies there came to a halt when a publisher accepted his first novel. His third one, entitled *Meet the Tiger*, was written when he was twenty years old and published in September 1928. It introduced the world to Simon Templar, *aka* The Saint. He continued to write about The Saint until 1983 when the last book, *Salvage for The Saint*, was published. The books, which have been translated into over thirty languages, number nearly a hundred and have sold over forty-million copies around the world. They've inspired, to date, fifteen feature films, three television series, ten radio series, and a comic strip that was written by Charteris and syndicated around the world for over a decade. He enjoyed travelling, but settled for long periods in Hollywood, Florida, and finally in Surrey, England. He was awarded the Cartier Diamond Dagger by the *Crime Writers' Association* in 1992, in recognition of a lifetime of achievement. He died the following year.

Ian Dickerson was just nine years old when he discovered The Saint. Shortly after that, he discovered Sherlock Holmes. The Saint won, for a while anyway. He struck up a friendship with The Saint's creator, Leslie Charteris, and his family. With their permission, he spent six weeks studying the Leslie Charteris collection at Boston University and went on to write, direct, and produce documentaries on the making of *The Saint* and *Return of The Saint,* which have been released on DVD. He oversaw the recent reprints of almost fifty of the original Saint books in both the US and UK, and was a co-producer on the 2017 TV movie of *The Saint*. When he discovered that Charteris had written Sherlock Holmes stories as well – well, there was the excuse he needed to revisit The Canon. He's consequently written and edited three books on Holmes' radio adventures. For the sake of what little sanity he has, Ian has also written about a wide range of subjects, none of which come with a halo, including talking mashed potatoes, Lord Grade, and satellite links. Ian lives in Hampshire with his wife and two children. And an awful lot of books by Leslie Charteris. Not quite so many by Conan Doyle, though.

Sir Arthur Conan Doyle (1859-1930) *Holmes Chronicler Emeritus*. If not for him, this anthology would not exist. Author, physician, patriot, sportsman, spiritualist, husband and father, and advocate for the oppressed. He is remembered and honored for the purposes of this collection by being the man who introduced Sherlock Holmes to the world. Through fifty-six Holmes short stories, four novels, and additional Apocryphal entries, Doyle revolutionized mystery stories and also greatly influenced and improved police forensic methods and techniques for the betterment of all. *Steel True Blade Straight.*

Steve Emecz's main field is technology, in which he has been working for about twenty years. Steve is a regular trade show speaker on the subject of eCommerce, and his tech career has taken him to more than fifty countries – so he's no stranger to planes and airports. He wrote two novels (one a bestseller) in the 1990's, and a screenplay in 2001. Shortly after, he set up MX Publishing, specialising in NLP books. In 2008, MX published its first Sherlock Holmes book, and MX has gone on to become the largest specialist Holmes publisher in the world. MX is a social enterprise and supports three main causes. The first is Happy Life, a children's rescue project in Nairobi, Kenya, where he and his wife, Sharon, spend every Christmas at the rescue centre in Kasarani. In 2014, they wrote a short book about the project, *The Happy Life Story*. The second is the Stepping Stones School, of which Steve is a patron. Stepping Stones is located at Undershaw, Sir Arthur Conan Doyle's former home. Steve has been a mentor for the World Food Programme for the last several years, supporting their innovation bootcamps and giving 1-2-1 mentoring to several projects.

Mark A. Gagen BSI is co-founder of Wessex Press, sponsor of the popular *From Gillette to Brett* conferences, and publisher of *The Sherlock Holmes Reference Library* and many other fine Sherlockian titles. A life-long Holmes enthusiast, he is a member of *The Baker Street Irregulars* and *The Illustrious Clients of Indianapolis*. A graphic artist by profession, his work is often seen on the covers of *The Baker Street Journal* and various BSI books.

Jayantika Ganguly BSI is the General Secretary and Editor of the *Sherlock Holmes Society of India*, a member of the *Sherlock Holmes Society of London*, and the *Czech Sherlock Holmes Society*. She is the author of *The Holmes Sutra* (MX 2014). She is a corporate lawyer working with one of the Big Six law firms.

Dick Gillman is an English writer and acrylic artist living in Brittany, France with his wife Alex, Truffle, their Black Labrador, and Jean-Claude, their Breton cat. During his retirement from teaching, he has written over twenty Sherlock Holmes short stories which are published as both e-books and paperbacks. His contribution to the superb MX Sherlock Holmes collection, published in October 2015, was entitled "The Man on Westminster Bridge" and had the privilege of being chosen as the anchor story in *The MX Book of New Sherlock Holmes Stories – Part II (1890-1895)*.

Denis Green was born in London, England in April 1905. He grew up mostly in London's Savoy Theatre where his father, Richard Green, was a principal in many Gilbert and Sullivan productions, A Flying Officer with RAF until 1924, he then spent four years managing a tea estate in North India before making his stage debut in *Hamlet* with Leslie Howard in 1928. He made his first visit to America in 1931 and established a respectable stage career before appearing in films – including minor roles in the first two Rathbone and Bruce Holmes films – and developing a career in front of and behind the microphone during the golden age of radio. Green and Leslie Charteris met in 1938 and struck up a lifelong friendship. Always busy, be it on stage, radio, film or television, Green passed away at the age of fifty in New York.

John Atkinson Grimshaw (1836-1893) was born in Leeds, England. His amazing paintings, usually featuring twilight or night scenes illuminated by gas-lamps or moonlight, are easily recognizable, and are often used on the covers of books about The Great Detective to set the mood, as shadowy figures move in the distance through misty mysterious settings and over rain-slicked streets.

Arthur Hall was born in Aston, Birmingham, UK, in 1944. He discovered his interest in writing during his schooldays, along with a love of fictional adventure and suspense. His first novel, *Sole Contact*, was an espionage story about an ultra-secret government department known as "Sector Three", and was followed, to date, by three sequels. Other works include five Sherlock Holmes novels, *The Demon of the Dusk*, *The One Hundred Percent Society*, *The Secret Assassin*, *The Phantom Killer*, and *In Pursuit of the Dead*, as well as a collection of short stories, and a modern detective novel. He lives in the West Midlands, United Kingdom.

431

Paula Hammond has written over sixty fiction and non-fiction books, as well as short stories, comics, poetry, and scripts for educational DVD's. When not glued to the keyboard, she can usually be found prowling round second-hand books shops or hunkered down in a hide, soaking up the joys of the natural world.

Roger Johnson BSI, ASH is a retired librarian, now working as a volunteer assistant at the Essex Police Museum. In his spare time, he is commissioning editor of *The Sherlock Holmes Journal*, an occasional lecturer, and a frequent contributor to *The Writings about the Writings*. His sole work of Holmesian pastiche was published in 1997 in Mike Ashley's anthology *The Mammoth Book of New Sherlock Holmes Adventures*, and he has the greatest respect for the many authors who have contributed new tales to the present mighty trilogy. Like his wife, Jean Upton, he is a member of both *The Baker Street Irregulars* and *The Adventuresses of Sherlock Holmes*.

John Lawrence served for thirty-eight years as a staff member in the U.S. House of Representatives, the last eight as Chief of Staff to Speaker Nancy Pelosi (2005-2013). He has been a Visiting Professor at the University of California's Washington Center since 2013. He is the author of *The Class of '74: Congress After Watergate and the Roots of Partisanship* (2018), and has a Ph.D. in history from the University of California (Berkeley).

David L. Leal PhD, is Professor of Government and Mexican American Studies at the University of Texas at Austin. He is also an Associate Member of Nuffield College at the University of Oxford and a Senior Fellow of the Hoover Institution at Stanford University. His research interests include the political implications of demographic change in the United States, and he has published dozens of academic journal articles and edited nine books on these and other topics. He has taught classes on Immigration Politics, Latino Politics, Politics and Religion, Mexican American Public Policy Studies, and Introduction to American Government. In the spring of 2019, he taught British Politics and Government, which had the good fortune (if that is the right word) of taking place parallel with so many Brexit developments. He is also the author of three articles in *The Baker Street Journal* as well as letters to the editor of the *TLS: The Times Literary Supplement*, *Sherlock Holmes Journal*, and *The Baker Street Journal*. As a member of the British Studies Program at UT-Austin, he has given several talks on Sherlockian and Wodehousian topics. He most recently wrote a chapter, "Arthur Conan Doyle and Spiritualism," for the program's latest book in its *Adventures with Britannia* series (Harry Ransom Center/IB Tauris/Bloomsbury). He is the founder and Warden of "MA, PhD, Etc," the BSI professional scion society for higher education, and he is a member of *The Fourth Garrideb*, *The Sherlock Holmes Society of London*, *The Clients of Adrian Mulliner*, and *His Last Bow (Tie)*.

John Lescroart is a New York Times bestselling author known for his series of legal and crime thriller novels featuring the characters Dismas Hardy, Abe Glitsky, and Wyatt Hunt. His novels have sold more than ten-million copies, have been translated into twenty-two languages in more than seventy-five countries, and eighteen of his books have been on *The New York Times* bestseller list. Libraries Unlimited has included him in its publication "The 100 Most Popular Thriller and Suspense Authors". Lescroart was born in Houston, Texas, and graduated from Junípero Serra High School in San Mateo, California (Class of 1966). He earned a B.A. in English with Honors at UC Berkeley in 1970. Before becoming a full-time writer in 1994, Lescroart was a self-described "Jack of all trades", who worked as a word processor for law firms as well as a bartender, moving man, house painter, editor, advertising director, computer programmer, and fundraising executive. Through his twenties, he was also a full-time singer-songwriter-guitarist, and performed under the name Johnny Capo, with Johnny Capo and his Real Good Band. In addition to nearly thirty novels, Lescroart has written several screenplays, and he is an original founding member of the group *International Thriller Writers*. John's blog at *JohnLescroart.com* is updated regularly with writing tips, insights on his books, recipes, recommendations, book give-aways, and more! Please also find John on Twitter and Facebook.

Michael Mallory is the Derringer-winning author of the "Amelia Watson" (The Second Mrs. Watson) series and "Dave Beauchamp" mystery series, and more than one-hundred-twenty-five short stories. An entertainment journalist by day, he has written eight nonfiction books on pop culture and more than six-hundred newspaper and magazine articles. Based in Los Angeles, Mike is also an occasional actor on television.

David Marcum plays *The Game* with deadly seriousness. He first discovered Sherlock Holmes in 1975 at the age of ten, and since that time, he has collected, read, and chronologicized literally thousands of traditional Holmes pastiches in the form of novels, short stories, radio and television episodes, movies and scripts, comics, fan-fiction, and unpublished manuscripts. He is the author of over sixty Sherlockian pastiches, some published in anthologies and magazines such as *The Strand*, and others collected in his own books, *The Papers of Sherlock Holmes, Sherlock Holmes and A Quantity of Debt*, and *Sherlock Holmes – Tangled Skeins*. He has edited fifty books, including several dozen traditional Sherlockian anthologies, such as the ongoing series *The MX Book of New Sherlock Holmes Stories*, which he created in 2015. This collection is now up to 21 volumes, with several more in preparation. He was responsible for bringing back August Derleth's Solar Pons for a new generation, first with his collection of authorized Pons stories, *The Papers of Solar Pons*, and then by editing the reissued authorized versions of the original Pons books. He is now doing the same for the adventures of Dr. Thorndyke. He has contributed numerous essays to various publications, and is a member of a number of Sherlockian groups and Scions. He is a licensed Civil Engineer, living in Tennessee with his wife and son. His irregular Sherlockian blog, *A Seventeen Step Program*, addresses various topics related to his favorite book friends (as his son used to call them when he was small), and can be found at *http://17stepprogram.blogspot.com/* Since the age of nineteen, he has worn a deerstalker as his regular-and-only hat. In 2013, he and his deerstalker were finally able make his first trip-of-a-lifetime Holmes Pilgrimage to England, with return Pilgrimages in 2015 and 2016, where you may have spotted him. If you ever run into him and his deerstalker out and about, feel free to say hello!

Steve Mason has been the Third Mate (President) of *The Crew of the Barque* Lone Star scion society in Dallas/Fort Worth for over seven years. He is also the Chair of the Communications Committee for *The Beacon Society*, a national educational scion society. With Joe Fay and Rusty Mason, he produces the *Baker Street Elementary* comic strip each week, the first adventures of Sherlock Holmes and John Watson.

Mark Mower is a member of the *Crime Writers' Association, The Sherlock Holmes Society of London*, and *The Solar Pons Society of London*. He writes true crime stories and fictional mysteries. His first two volumes of Holmes pastiches were entitled *A Farewell to Baker Street* and *Sherlock Holmes: The Baker Street Case-Files* (both with MX Publishing) and, to date, he has contributed chapters to six parts of the ongoing *The MX Book of New Sherlock Holmes Stories*. He has also had stories in two anthologies by Belanger Books:

433

Holmes Away From Home: Adventures from the Great Hiatus – Volume II – 1893-1894 (2016) and *Sherlock Holmes: Before Baker Street* (2017). More are bound to follow. Mark's non-fiction works include *Bloody British History: Norwich* (The History Press, 2014), *Suffolk Murders* (The History Press, 2011) and *Zeppelin Over Suffolk* (Pen & Sword Books, 2008).

Sidney Paget (1860-1908), a few of whose illustrations are used within this anthology, was born in London, and like his two older brothers, became a famed illustrator and painter. He completed over three-hundred-and-fifty drawings for the Sherlock Holmes stories that were first published in *The Strand* magazine, defining Holmes's image forever after in the public mind.

Richard K. Radek, the author of *The Sequestered Adventures of Sherlock Holmes* series, is a native of Evanston, Illinois (USA), and a graduate of Northern Illinois University. He is a prominent arbitrator, certified educator, and author of many legal articles and awards. A long time student of The Canon, Mr. Radek writes traditional, period-authentic Holmes adventures, faithful to the style and chronology of the original Doyle tales. One hallmark of his work is the accuracy of the historical detail Mr. Radek instills in the plots, persona, and settings of his Holmes stories. Another is the wit and wry humor woven in and interspersed. The result is a body of work that can be appreciated by the entire spectrum of Holmes aficionados, from the novice only just learning about Sherlock who wants an entertaining story, to the most discriminating experts who can appreciate the many, sometimes subtle, Holmesian insights Mr. Radek hides in the stories. In the main, Mr. Radek's tales are great fun to read.

Jane Rubino is the author of A Jersey Shore mystery series, featuring a Jane Austen-loving amateur sleuth and a Sherlock Holmes-quoting detective, *Knight Errant, Lady Vernon and Her Daughter,* (a novel-length adaptation of Jane Austen's novella *Lady Susan,* co-authored with her daughter Caitlen Rubino-Bradway, *What Would Austen Do?,* also co-authored with her daughter, a short story in the anthology *Jane Austen Made Me Do It, The Rucastles' Pawn, The Copper Beeches from Violet Turner's POV,* and, of course, there's the Sherlockian novel in the drawer – who doesn't have one? Jane lives on a barrier island at the New Jersey shore.

Geri Schear is a novelist and short story writer. Her work has been published in literary journals in the U.S. and Ireland. Her first novel, *A Biased Judgement: The Diaries of Sherlock Holmes 1897* was released to critical acclaim in 2014. The sequel, *Sherlock Holmes and the Other Woman* was published in 2015, and *Return to Reichenbach* in 2016. She lives in Kells, Ireland.

Vincent Starrett (1886–1974) was a Canadian-born American writer, newspaperman, and bibliophile. Born in Canada, his father moved the family to Chicago in 1889. In 1907, he began working for the *Chicago Daily News* as reporter, feature writer, and columnist. In 1920, he wrote the Sherlock Holmes pastiche "The Adventure of the Unique 'Hamlet'", and his most famous work, *The Private Life of Sherlock Holmes,* was published in 1933. He wrote the book column, "Books Alive", for *The Chicago Tribune,* which ran for twenty-five years before retiring it in 1967. Starrett was one of the founders of *The Hounds of the Baskerville (sic),* a Chicago scion of *The Baker Street Irregulars.*

Joseph W. Svec III is retired from Oceanography, Satellite Test Engineering, and college teaching. He has lived on a forty-foot cruising sailboat, on a ranch in the Sierra Nevada

Foothills, in a country rose-garden cottage, and currently lives in the shadow of a castle with his childhood sweetheart and several long coated German shepherds. He enjoys writing, gardening, creating dioramas, world travel, and enjoying time with his sweetheart.

D.J. Tyrer is the person behind Atlantean Publishing, was placed second in the Writing Magazine "Local Reporter" competition, and has been widely published in anthologies and magazines around the world, such as *Disturbance* (Laurel Highlands), *Mysteries of Suspense* (Zimbell House), *History and Mystery, Oh My!* (Mystery & Horror LLC), and *Love 'Em, Shoot 'Em* (Wolfsinger), and issues of *Awesome Tales*, and in addition, has a novella available in paperback and on the Kindle, *The Yellow House* (Dunhams Manor) and a comic horror e-novelette, *A Trip to the Middle of the World*, available from Alban Lake through Infinite Realms Bookstore.
His website is: *https://djtyrer.blogspot.co.uk/*
The Atlantean Publishing website is at *https://atlanteanpublishing.wordpress.com/*

Peter Coe Verbica grew up on a commercial cattle ranch in Northern California, where he learned the value of a strong work ethic. He works for the Wealth Management Group of a global investment bank, and is an Adjunct Professor in the Economics Department at SJSU. He is the author of numerous books, including *Left at the Gate and Other Poems, Hard-Won Cowboy Wisdom (Not Necessarily in Order of Importance), A Key to the Grove and Other Poems*, and *The Missing Tales of Sherlock Holmes (as Compiled by Peter Coe Verbica, JD)*. Mr. Verbica obtained a JD from Santa Clara University School of Law, an MS from Massachusetts Institute of Technology, and a BA in English from Santa Clara University. He is the co-inventor on a number of patents, has served as a Managing Member of three venture capital firms, and the CFO of one of the portfolio companies. He is an unabashed advocate of cowboy culture and enjoys creative writing, hiking, and tennis. He is married with four daughters. For more information, or to contact the author, please go to *www.hardwoncowboywisdom.com*.

The following contributors appear
in the companion volumes:
The MX Book of New Sherlock Holmes Stories
Part XIX – 2020 Annual (1882-1890)
Part XX – 2020 Annual (1891-1897)

Ian Ableson is an ecologist by training and a writer by choice. When not reading or writing, he can reliably be found scowling at a clipboard while ankle-deep in a marsh somewhere in Michigan. His love for the stories of Arthur Conan Doyle started when his grandfather gave him a copy of *The Original Illustrated Sherlock Holmes* when he was in high school, and he's proud to have been able to contribute to the continuation of the tales of Sherlock Holmes and Dr. Watson.

Deanna Baran lives in a remote part of Texas where cowboys may still be seen in their natural habitat. A librarian and former museum curator, she writes in between cups of tea, playing *Go*, and trading postcards with people around the world.

S.F. Bennett has, at various times, been an actor, a lecturer, a journalist, a historian, an author and a potter. Whilst some of those things still apply, she has always been an avid collector, concentrating mainly on ephemera and other related items concerning Sherlock Holmes and British science-fiction of the 1970's. To date, she has written articles on aspects of The Canon for *The Baker Street Journal*, *The Sherlock Holmes Journal*, and *The Torr*, the journal of *The Sherlock Holmes Society of the West Country*. When not collecting, she can be found writing science-fiction and mystery stories, and has contributed to several anthologies of new Sherlock Holmes pastiches. Her first novel was *The Secret Diary of Mycroft Holmes: The Thoughts and Reminiscences of Sherlock Holmes's Elder Brother, 1880-1888* (2017). She is also the author of *A Study In Postcards: Sherlock Holmes in the Golden Age of the Picture Postcard* (*Sherlock Holmes Society of London*, 2019).

Andrew Bryant was born in Bridgend, Wales, and now lives in Burlington, Ontario. His previous publications include *Poetry Toronto*, *Prism International*, *Existere*, *On Spec*, *The Dalhousie Review*, and *The Toronto Star*. His first Holmes story was published in *The MX Book of New Sherlock Holmes Stories - Part XIII*, with the second in *Part XVI*. The two stories in this collection are the third and fourth. Andrew's interest in Holmes stems from watching the Basil Rathbone and Nigel Bruce films as a child, followed by collecting The Canon, and a fascinating visit to 221B Baker Street.

Thomas A. Burns, Jr. is the author of the *Natalie McMasters Mysteries*. He was born and grew up in New Jersey, attended Xavier High School in Manhattan, earned B.S degrees in Zoology and Microbiology at Michigan State University, and a M.S. in Microbiology at North Carolina State University. He currently resides in Wendell, North Carolina. As a kid, Tom started reading mysteries with The Hardy Boys, Ken Holt and Rick Brant, and graduated to the classic stories by authors such as A. Conan Doyle, Dorothy Sayers, John Dickson Carr, Erle Stanley Gardner, and Rex Stout, to name a few. Tom has written fiction as a hobby all of his life, starting with The Man from U.N.C.L.E. stories in marble-backed copybooks in grade school. He built a career as technical, science, and medical writer and editor for nearly thirty years in industry and government. Now that he's truly on his own as a novelist, he's excited to publish his own mystery series, as well as to contribute stories about his second-most-favorite detective, Sherlock Holmes, to *The MX anthology of New Sherlock Holmes Stories*.

Nick Cardillo has been a devotee of Sherlock Holmes since the age of six. His first published short story, "The Adventure of the Traveling Corpse" appeared in *The MX Book of New Sherlock Holmes Stories – Part VI: 2017 Annual*, and he has written subsequent stories for both MX Publishing and Belanger Books. In 2018, Nick completed his first anthology of new Sherlock Holmes adventures entitled *The Feats of Sherlock Holmes*. Nick is a fan of The Golden Age of Detective Fiction, Hammer Horror, and Doctor Who. He writes film reviews and analyses at *Sacred-Celluloid.blogspot.com*. He is a student at Susquehanna University in Selinsgrove, PA.

Chris Chan is a writer, educator, and historian. He works as a researcher and "International Goodwill Ambassador" for Agatha Christie Ltd. His true crime articles, reviews, and short fiction have appeared (or will soon appear) in *The Strand*, *The Wisconsin Magazine of History*, *Mystery Weekly*, *Gilbert!*, *Nerd HQ*, Akashic Books' *Mondays are Murder* web series, *The Baker Street Journal*, and *Sherlock Holmes Mystery Magazine*.

Craig Stephen Copland confesses that he discovered Sherlock Holmes when, sometime in the muddled early 1960's, he pinched his older brother's copy of the immortal stories and was forever afterward thoroughly hooked. He is very grateful to his high school English teachers in Toronto who inculcated in him a love of literature and writing, and even inspired him to be an English major at the University of Toronto. There he was blessed to sit at the feet of both Northrup Frye and Marshall McLuhan, and other great literary professors, who led him to believe that he was called to be a high school English teacher. It was his good fortune to come to his pecuniary senses, abandon that goal, and pursue a varied professional career that took him to over one-hundred countries and endless adventures. He considers himself to have been and to continue to be one of the luckiest men on God's good earth. A few years back he took a step in the direction of Sherlockian studies and joined the *Sherlock Holmes Society of Canada* – also known as *The Toronto Bootmakers*. In May of 2014, this esteemed group of scholars announced a contest for the writing of a new Sherlock Holmes mystery. Although he had never tried his hand at fiction before, Craig entered and was pleasantly surprised to be selected as one of the winners. Having enjoyed the experience, he decided to write more of the same, and is now on a mission to write a new Sherlock Holmes mystery that is related to and inspired by each of the sixty stories in the original Canon. He currently lives and writes in Toronto and Dubai, and looks forward to finally settling down when he turns ninety.

Harry DeMaio is a *nom de plume* of Harry B. DeMaio, successful author of several books on Information Security and Business Networks, as well as the twelve-volume *Casebooks of Octavius Bear*. He is also a published author for Belanger Books and *The MX Sherlock Holmes* series edited by David Marcum. A retired business executive, former consultant, information security specialist, pilot, disk jockey, and graduate school adjunct professor, he whiles away his time traveling and writing preposterous books, articles, and stories. He has appeared on many radio and TV shows and is an accomplished, frequent public speaker. Former New York City natives, he and his extremely patient and helpful wife, Virginia, and their Bichon Frisé, Woof, live in Cincinnati (and several other parallel universes.) They have two sons living in Scottsdale, Arizona and Cortlandt Manor, New York, both of whom are quite successful and quite normal, thus putting the lie to the theory that insanity is hereditary. His e-mail is *hdemaio@zoomtown.com* You can also find him on Facebook. His website is *www.octaviusbearslair.com* His books are available on Amazon, Barnes and Noble, directly from MX Publishing, and at other fine bookstores.

Anna Elliott is an author of historical fiction and fantasy. Her first series, *The Twilight of Avalon* trilogy, is a retelling of the Trystan and Isolde legend. She wrote her second series, *The Pride and Prejudice Chronicles*, chiefly to satisfy her own curiosity about what might have happened to Elizabeth Bennet, Mr. Darcy, and all the other wonderful cast of characters after the official end of Jane Austen's classic work. She enjoys stories about strong women, and loves exploring the multitude of ways women can find their unique strengths. She was delighted to lend a hand with the "Sherlock and Lucy" series, and this story, firstly because she loves Sherlock Holmes as much as her father, co-author Charles Veley, does, and second because it almost never happens that someone with a dilemma shouts, "Quick, we need an author of historical fiction!" Anna lives in the Washington, D.C .area with her husband and three children.

Matthew J. Elliott is the author of *Big Trouble in Mother Russia* (2016), the official sequel to the cult movie *Big Trouble in Little China, Lost in Time and Space: An Unofficial Guide to the Uncharted Journeys of Doctor Who* (2014), *Sherlock Holmes on the Air* (2012), *Sherlock Holmes in Pursuit* (2013), *The Immortals: An Unauthorized Guide to* Sherlock *and* Elementary (2013), and *The Throne Eternal* (2014). His articles, fiction, and reviews have appeared in the magazines *Scarlet Street, Total DVD, SHERLOCK,* and *Sherlock Holmes Mystery Magazine,* and the collections *The Game's Afoot, Curious Incidents 2, Gaslight Grimoire, The Mammoth Book of Best British Crime 8,* and *The MX Book of New Sherlock Holmes Stories – Part III: 1896-1929.* He has scripted over 260 radio plays, including episodes of *Doctor Who, The Further Adventures of Sherlock*

Holmes, *The Twilight Zone*, *The New Adventures of Mickey Spillane's Mike Hammer*, *Fangoria's Dreadtime Stories*, and award-winning adaptations of *The Hound of the Baskervilles* and *The War of the Worlds*. He is the only radio dramatist to adapt all sixty original stories from The Canon for the series *The Classic Adventures of Sherlock Holmes*. Matthew is a writer and performer on *RiffTrax.com*, the online comedy experience from the creators of cult sci-fi TV series *Mystery Science Theater 3000* (*MST3K* to the initiated). He's also written a few comic books.

Sonia Fetherston BSI is a member of the illustrious *Baker Street Irregulars*. For almost thirty years, she's been a frequent contributor to Sherlockian anthologies, including Calabash Press's acclaimed *Case Files* series, and Wildside Press's *About* series. Sonia's byline often appears in the pages of *The Baker Street Journal*, *The Journal* of the *Sherlock Holmes Society of London*, *Canadian Holmes*, and the Sydney Passengers' *Log*. Her work earned her the coveted Morley-Montgomery Award from the *Baker Street Irregulars*, and the Derek Murdoch Memorial Award from *The Bootmakers of Toronto*. Sonia is author of *Prince of the Realm: The Most Irregular James Bliss Austin* (BSI Press, 2014). She's at work on another biography for the BSI, this time about Julian Wolff.

David Friend lives in Wales, Great Britain, where he divides his time between watching old detective films and thinking about old detective films. Now thirty, he's been scribbling out stories for twenty years and hopes, some day, to write something half-decent. Most of what he pens is set in an old-timey world of non-stop adventure with debonair sleuths, kick-ass damsels, criminal masterminds, and narrow escapes, and he wishes he could live there.

Tim Gambrell lives in Exeter, Devon, with his wife, two young sons, three cats, and now only four chickens. He has previously contributed two stories to *The MX Book of New Sherlock Holmes Stories*: "The Yellow Star of Cairo" in Vol. XIII, and "The Haunting of Bottomly's Grandmother" in Vol. XVI. He also contributed a story to *Sherlock Holmes and Dr Watson: The Early Adventures*, Vol. III, from Belanger Books, and has a further tale in Vol. II of the forthcoming collection *Sherlock Holmes and The Occult Detectives*, also from Belanger Books. Outside of the world of Holmes, Tim has written extensively for Doctor Who spin-off ranges. His books include two linked novels from Candy Jar Books: *Lethbridge-Stewart: The Laughing Gnome – Lucy Wilson & The Bledoe Cadets*, and *The Lucy Wilson Mysteries: The Brigadier and The Bledoe Cadets* (both 2019), and *Lethbridge-Stewart: Bloodlines – An Ordinary Man* (Candy Jar, 2020, written with Andy Frankham-Allen). He's also written a novella, *The Way of The Bry'hunee* (2019) for the Erimem range from Thebes Publishing. Tim's short fiction includes stories in *Lethbridge-Stewart: The HAVOC Files 3* (Candy Jar, 2017, revised edition 2020), *Bernice Summerfield: True Stories* (Big Finish, 2017) and *Relics . . . An Anthology* (Red Ted Books, 2018), plus a number of charity anthologies.

Dick Gillman – *In addition to a story in this volume, Dick also has stories in Part XIX*

Arthur Hall – *In addition to two stories in this volume, Arthur also has stories in Parts XIX and XX*

Stephen Herczeg is an IT Geek, writer, actor, and film-maker based in Canberra Australia. He has been writing for over twenty years and has completed a couple of dodgy novels, sixteen feature-length screenplays, and numerous short stories and scripts. Stephen was very successful in 2017's International Horror Hotel screenplay competition, with his scripts *TITAN* winning the Sci-Fi category and *Dark are the Woods* placing second in the horror category. His work has featured in *Sproutlings – A Compendium of Little Fictions* from Hunter Anthologies, the *Hells Bells* Christmas horror anthology published by the Australasian Horror Writers Association, and the *Below the Stairs*, *Trickster's Treats*, *Shades of Santa*, *Behind the Mask*, and *Beyond the Infinite* anthologies from OzHorror.Con, *The Body Horror Book*, *Anemone Enemy*, and *Petrified Punks* from Oscillate Wildly Press, and *Sherlock Holmes In the Realms of H.G. Wells* and *Sherlock Holmes: Adventures Beyond the Canon* from Belanger Books.

Christopher James was born in 1975 in Paisley, Scotland. Educated at Newcastle and UEA, he was a winner of the UK's National Poetry Competition in 2008. He has written two full length Sherlock Holmes novels, *The Adventure of the Ruby Elephant* and *The Jeweller of Florence*, both published by MX, and is working on a third.

Steven Philip Jones has written over sixty graphic novels and comic books including the horror series *Lovecraftian*, *Curious Cases of Sherlock Holmes*, the original series *Nightlinger*, *Street Heroes 2005*, adaptations of *Dracula*, several H. P. Lovecraft stories, and the 1985 film *Re-animator*. Steven is also the author of several novels and nonfiction books including *The Clive Cussler Adventures: A Critical Review*, *Comics Writing: Communicating With Comic Book* , *King of Harlem*, *Bushwackers*, *The House With the Witch's Hat*, *Talisman: The Knightmare Knife*, and *Henrietta Hex: Shadows From the Past.* Steven's other writing credits include a number of scripts for radio dramas that have been broadcast internationally. A graduate of the University of Iowa, Steven has a Bachelor of Arts in Journalism and Religion, and was accepted into Iowa's Writer's Workshop – M.F.A. program.

Susan Knight's most recent collection of short stories, *Mrs Hudson Investigates*, was issued by MX Publishing in November 2019. She is the author of two other non-Sherlockian, story collections, as well as three novels, a book of non-fiction, and several plays. She lives in Dublin where she teaches Creative Writing. She is currently working on a new Mrs Hudson novel set in Ireland.

David Marcum – *In addition to a story in this volume, David also has stories in Parts XIX and XX*

Jacquelynn Morris, ASH, BSI, JHWS, is a member of several Sherlock Holmes societies in the Mid-Atlantic area of the U.S.A., but her home group is Watson's Tin Box in Maryland. She is the founder of *A Scintillation of Scions*, an annual Sherlock Holmes symposium. She has been published in the BSI Manuscript Series, *The Wrong Passage*, as well as in *About Sixty* and *About Being a Sherlockian* (Wildside Press). Jacquelynn was the U.S. liaison for the Undershaw Preservation Trust for several years, until Undershaw was purchased to become part of Stepping Stones School.

James Moffett is a Masters graduate in Professional Writing, with a specialisation in novel and non-fiction writing. He also has an extensive background in media studies. James began developing a passion for writing when contributing to his University's student magazine. His interest in the literary character of Sherlock Holmes was deep-rooted in his youth. He released his first publication of eight interconnected short stories titled *The Trials of Sherlock Holmes* in 2017, along with previous contributions to *The MX Book of New Sherlock Holmes Stories.*

Mark Mower – *In addition to a story in this volume, Mark also has a story in Part XX*

Will Murray is the author of over seventy novels, including forty *Destroyer* novels and seven posthumous *Doc Savage* collaborations with Lester Dent, under the name Kenneth Robeson, for Bantam Books in the 1990's. Since 2011, he has written a number of additional Doc Savage adventures for Altus Press, two of which co-starred The Shadow, as well as a solo Pat Savage novel. His 2015 Tarzan novel, *Return to Pal-Ul-Don*, was followed by *King Kong vs. Tarzan* in 2016. Murray has written short stories featuring such classic characters as Batman, Superman, Wonder Woman, Spider-Man, Ant-Man, the Hulk, Honey West, the Spider, the Avenger, the Green Hornet, the Phantom, and Cthulhu. A previous Murray Sherlock Holmes story appeared in Moonstone's *Sherlock Holmes: The Crossovers Casebook*, and another in *Sherlock Holmes and Doctor Was Not*, involving H. P. Lovecraft's Dr. Herbert West. Additionally, his Sherlock Holmes stories have appeared in *The MX Book of New Sherlock Holmes Stories*. His most recent book is *Tarzan, Conqueror of Mars*.

Robert Perret is a writer, librarian, and devout Sherlockian living on the Palouse. His Sherlockian publications include "The Canaries of Clee Hills Mine" in *An Improbable Truth: The Paranormal Adventures of Sherlock Holmes*, "For King and Country" in *The Science of Deduction*, and "How Hope Learned the Trick" in *NonBinary Review*. He considers himself to be a pan-Sherlockian and a one-man Scion out on the lonely moors of Idaho. Robert has recently authored a yet-unpublished scholarly article tentatively entitled "A Study in Scholarship: The Case of the *Baker Street Journal*'. His is the author of *Dead ringers: Sherlock Holmes Stories* (2019). More information is available at *www.robertperret.com*

Gayle Lange Puhl has been a Sherlockian since Christmas of 1965. She has had articles published in *The Devon County Chronicle*, *The Baker Street Journal*, and *The Serpentine Muse*, plus her local newspaper. She has created Sherlockian jewelry, a 2006 calendar entitled "If Watson Wrote For TV", and has painted a limited series of Holmes-related nesting dolls. She co-founded the scion *Friends of the Great Grimpen Mire* and the Janesville, Wisconsin-based *The Original Tree Worshipers*. In January 2016, she was awarded the "Outstanding Creative Writer" award by the Janesville Art Alliance for her first book *Sherlock Holmes and the Folk Tale Mysteries*. She is semi-retired and lives in Evansville, Wisconsin. Ms. Puhl has one daughter, Gayla, and four grandchildren.

Tracy J. Revels, a Sherlockian from the age of eleven, is a professor of history at Wofford College in Spartanburg, South Carolina. She is a member of *The Survivors of the Gloria Scott* and *The Studious Scarlets Society*, and is a past recipient of the Beacon Society Award. Almost every semester, she teaches a class that covers The Canon, either to college students or to senior citizens. She is also the author of three supernatural Sherlockian pastiches with MX (*Shadowfall*, *Shadowblood*, and *Shadowwraith*), and a regular contributor to her scion's newsletter. She also has some notoriety as an author of very silly skits: For proof, see "The Adventure of the Adversarial Adventuress" and "Occupy Baker Street" on YouTube. When not studying Sherlock, she can be found researching the history of her native state, and has written books on Florida in the Civil War and on the development of Florida's tourism industry.

Roger Riccard of Los Angeles, California, U.S.A., is a descendant of the Roses of Kilravock in Highland Scotland. He is the author of two previous Sherlock Holmes novels, *The Case of the Poisoned Lilly* and *The Case of the Twain Papers*, a series of short stories

440

in two volumes, *Sherlock Holmes: Adventures for the Twelve Days of Christmas* and *Further Adventures for the Twelve Days of Christmas*, and the new series *A Sherlock Holmes Alphabet of Cases,* all of which are published by Baker Street Studios. He has another novel and a non-fiction Holmes reference work in various stages of completion. He became a Sherlock Holmes enthusiast as a teenager (many, many years ago), and, like all fans of The Great Detective, yearned for more stories after reading The Canon over and over. It was the Granada Television performances of Jeremy Brett and Edward Hardwicke, and the encouragement of his wife, Rosilyn, that at last inspired him to write his own Holmes adventures, using the Granada actor portrayals as his guide. He has been called "The best pastiche writer since Val Andrews" by the *Sherlockian E-Times.*

Brenda Seabrooke's stories have been published in sixteen reviews, journals, and anthologies. She has received grants from the National Endowment for the Arts and Emerson College's Robbie Macauley Award. She is the author of twenty-three books for young readers including *Scones and Bones on Baker Street: Sherlock's (maybe!) Dog and the Dirt Dilemma*, and *The Rascal in the Castle: Sherlock's (possible!) Dog and the Queen's Revenge.* Brenda states: "It was fun to write from Dr. Watson's point of view and not have to worry about fleas, smelly pits, ralphing, or scratching at inopportune times."

Matthew Simmonds hails from Bedford, in the South East of England, and has been a confirmed devotee of Sir Arthur Conan Doyle's most famous creation since first watching Jeremy Brett's incomparable portrayal of the world's first consulting detective, on a Tuesday evening in April, 1984, while curled up on the sofa with his father. He has written numerous short stories, and his first novel, *Sherlock Holmes: The Adventure of The Pigtail Twist*, was published in 2018. A sequel is nearly complete, which he hopes to publish in the near future. Matthew currently co-owns Harrison & Simmonds, the fifth-generation family business, a renowned County tobacconist, pipe, and gift shop on Bedford High Street.

Robert V. Stapleton was born and brought up in Leeds, Yorkshire, England, and studied at Durham University. After working in various parts of the country as an Anglican parish priest, he is now retired and lives with his wife in North Yorkshire. As a member of his local writing group, he now has time to develop his other life as a writer of adventure stories. He has recently had a number of short stories published, and he is hoping to have a couple of completed novels published at some time in the future.

Kevin P. Thornton is a seven-time Arthur Ellis Award Nominee. He is a former director of the local Heritage Society and Library, and he has been a soldier in Africa, a contractor for the Canadian Military in Afghanistan, a newspaper and magazine columnist, a Director of both the *Crime Writers of Canada* and the *Writers' Guild of Alberta*, a founding member of *Northword Literary Magazine*, and is either a current or former member of *The Mystery Writers of America*, *The Crime Writers Association*, *The Calgary Crime Writers*, *The International Thriller Writers*, *The International Association of Crime Writers*, *The Keys* – a Catholic Writers group founded by Monsignor Knox and G.K. Chesterton – as well as, somewhat inexplicably, *The Mesdames of Mayhem* and *Sisters in Crime*. If you ask, he will join. Born in Kenya, Kevin has lived or worked in South Africa, Dubai, England, Afghanistan, New Zealand, Ontario, and now Northern Alberta. He lives on his wits and his wit, and is doing better than expected. He is not one to willingly split infinitives, and while never pedantic, is on occasion known to be ever so slightly punctilious.

·

Christopher Todd has been a nurse for four decades, was a radio production director and copywriter for twenty years, and has been an ordained Episcopal priest for eighteen years, as well as an interim Lutheran pastor and jail chaplain for eight years. He has been a Sherlockian since he was twelve, was a member of *The Noble Bachelors of St. Louis*, has been published in *The Baker Street Journal* and cited three times in *The World Bibliography of Sherlock Holmes and Dr. Watson*. His numerous careers and widespread interests color his blog at *preacherofthenight.blogspot.com*. He lives in the Florida Keys with his wife and is indoctrinating his grandkids in his faith and in Sherlock Holmes, possibly in that order.

Thomas A. (Tom) Turley was born in Virginia, grew up in Tennessee, and lives now in Montgomery, Alabama. He and his wife Paula have two grown children and one beautiful granddaughter. Although Tom has a Ph.D. in British history, he spent most of his career as an archivist with the State of Alabama. Approaching retirement, he returned to a youthful hobby: Writing fiction. Tom's first story, "The Devil's Claw", appeared in *The Book of Villains*, a 2011 Main Street Rag anthology. His pastiche "Sherlock Holmes and the Adventure of the Tainted Canister" (2014) is available as an e-book and an audiobook from MX Publishing. It was also published in *The Art of Sherlock Holmes – USA Edition 1* (2019), in company with a painting by artist Angela Fegan. Three of Tom's stories, "A Scandal in Serbia", "A Ghost from Christmas Past", and "The Solitary Violinist" have appeared in MX Publishing's ongoing anthology of traditional pastiches (Parts VI, VII, and XVIII). The latter two were praised by *Publishers Weekly* in its reviews of the relevant MX volumes. "Ghost" was also included in *The Art of Sherlock Holmes, West Palm Beach Edition* (2019), paired with a painting by artist Nune Asatryan. Tom's latest short story, "A Game of Skittles", appears in MX Publishing' spring 2020 anthology, *Part XIX*. Later this year, Tom should complete a collection of historical pastiches entitled *Sherlock Holmes and the Crowned Heads of Europe*. The first story chronologically, "Sherlock Holmes and the Case of the Dying Emperor", is already available from MX Publishing as an e-book. Set in Berlin in 1888, during the brief reign of Emperor Frederick III (son-in-law of Queen Victoria and father of the notorious "Kaiser Bill"), it inaugurates Sherlock Holmes's espionage campaign against the German Empire, which ended only in August 1914 with "His Last Bow". When completed, *Sherlock Holmes and the Crowned Heads of Europe* will also include "A Scandal in Serbia" and two new stories on the last dynastic tragedies that befell the House of Habsburg. Tom's non-literary interests include hiking, ship modeling, classical music, and University of Tennessee athletics (not a popular pursuit in Alabama!). Interested readers can contact him through MX Publishing or his Goodreads and Amazon author's pages.

Charles Veley has loved Sherlock Holmes since boyhood. As a father, he read the entire Canon to his then-ten-year-old daughter at evening story time. Now, this very same daughter, grown up to become acclaimed historical novelist Anna Elliott, has worked with him to develop new adventures in the *Sherlock Holmes and Lucy James Mystery Series*. Charles is also a fan of Gilbert & Sullivan, and wrote *The Pirates of Finance*, a new musical in the G&S tradition that won an award at the New York Musical Theatre Festival in 2013. Other than the Sherlock and Lucy series, all of the books on his Amazon Author Page were written when he was a full-time author during the late Seventies and early Eighties. He currently works for United Technologies Corporation, where his main focus is on creating sustainability and value for the company's large real estate development projects.

Peter Co Verbica – *In addition to a story in this volume, Peter also has a story in Part XIX*

I.A. Watson is a novelist and jobbing writer from Yorkshire who cut his teeth on writing Sherlock Holmes stories and has even won an award for one. His works include *Holmes and Houdini, Labours of Hercules, St. George and the Dragon* Volumes 1 and 2, and *Women of Myth,* and the non-fiction essay book *Where Stories Dwell.* He pens short detective stories as a means of avoiding writing things that pay better. A full list of his sixty-plus published works appears at:
http://www.chillwater.org.uk/writing/iawatsonhome.htm

Matthew White is an up-and-coming author from Richmond, Virginia in the USA. He has been a passionate devotee of Sherlock Holmes since childhood. He can be reached at *matthewwhite.writer@gmail.com.*

Sean Wright BSI makes his home in Santa Clarita, a charming city at the entrance of the high desert in Southern California. For sixteen years, features and articles under his byline appeared in *The Tidings* – now *The Angelus News* – publications of the Roman Catholic Archdiocese of Los Angeles. Continuing his education in 2007, Mr. Wright graduated *summa cum laude* from Grand Canyon University, attaining a Bachelor of Arts degree in Christian Studies. He then attained a Master of Arts degree, also in Christian Studies. Once active in the entertainment industry, in an abortive attempt to revive dramatic radio in 1976 with his beloved mentor the late Daws Butler directing, Mr. Wright co-produced and wrote the syndicated *New Radio Adventures of Sherlock Holmes* starring the late Edward Mulhare as the Great Detective. Mr. Wright has written for several television quiz shows and remains proud of his work for *The Quiz Kid's Challenge* and the popular TV quiz show *Jeopardy!* for which The Academy of Television Arts and Sciences honored him in 1985 with an Emmy nomination in the field of writing. Honored with membership in *The Baker Street Irregulars* as "The Manor House Case" after founding *The Non-Canonical Calabashes, The Sherlock Holmes Society of Los Angeles* in 1970, Mr. Wright has written for *The Baker Street Journal* and *Mystery Magazine.* Since 1971, he has conducted lectures on Sherlock Holmes's influence on literature and cinema for libraries, colleges, and private organizations, including MENSA. Mr. Wright's whimsical *Sherlock Holmes Cookbook* (Drake) created with John Farrell BSI, was published in 1976 and a mystery novel, *Enter the Lion: a Posthumous Memoir of Mycroft Holmes* (Hawthorne), "edited" with Michael Hodel BSI, followed in 1979. As director general of The Plot Thickens Mystery Company, Mr. Wright originated hosting "mystery parties" in homes, restaurants, and offices, as well as producing and directing the very first "Mystery Train" tours on Amtrak beginning in 1982.

The MX Book of New Sherlock Holmes Stories
Edited by David Marcum
(MX Publishing, 2015-)

"This is the finest volume of Sherlockian fiction I have ever read, and I have read, literally, thousands." – Philip K. Jones

"Beyond Impressive . . . This is a splendid venture for a great cause!
– Roger Johnson, Editor, *The Sherlock Holmes Journal,*
The Sherlock Holmes Society of London

Part I: 1881-1889
Part II: 1890-1895
Part III: 1896-1929
Part IV: 2016 Annual
Part V: Christmas Adventures
Part VI: 2017 Annual
Part VII: Eliminate the Impossible (1880-1891)
Part VIII – Eliminate the Impossible (1892-1905)
Part IX – 2018 Annual (1879-1895)
Part X – 2018 Annual (1896-1916)
Part XI – Some Untold Cases (1880-1891)
Part XII – Some Untold Cases (1894-1902)
Part XIII – 2019 Annual (1881-1890)
Part XIV – 2019 Annual (1891-1897)
Part XV – 2019 Annual (1898-1917)
Part XVI – Whatever Remains . . . Must be the Truth (1881-1890)
Part XVII – Whatever Remains . . . Must be the Truth (1891-1898)
Part XVIII – Whatever Remains . . . Must be the Truth (1898-1925)
Part XIX – 2020 Annual (1882-1890)
Part XX – 2020 Annual (1891-1897)
Part XXI – 2020 Annual (1898-1923)

In Preparation
Part XXII – Some More Untold Cases

. . . and more to come!

The MX Book of New Sherlock Holmes Stories
Edited by David Marcum
(MX Publishing, 2015-   )

Publishers Weekly says:

Part VI: *The traditional pastiche is alive and well . . . .*

Part VII: *Sherlockians eager for faithful-to-the-canon plots and characters will be delighted.*

Part VIII: *The imagination of the contributors in coming up with variations on the volume's theme is matched by their ingenious resolutions.*

Part IX: *The 18 stories . . . will satisfy fans of Conan Doyle's originals. Sherlockians will rejoice that more volumes are on the way.*

Part X: *. . . new Sherlock Holmes adventures of consistently high quality.*

Part XI: *. . . an essential volume for Sherlock Holmes fans.*

Part XII: *. . . continues to amaze with the number of high-quality pastiches . . .*

Part XIII: *. . . Amazingly, Marcum has found 22 superb pastiches . . . This is more catnip for fans of stories faithful to Conan Doyle's original*

Part XIV: *. . . this standout anthology of 21 short stories written in the spirit of Conan Doyle's originals.*

Part XV: *Stories pitting Sherlock Holmes against seemingly supernatural phenomena highlight Marcum's 15th anthology of superior short pastiches.*

Part XVI: *Marcum has once again done fans of Conan Doyle's originals a service.*

Part XVII: *This is yet another impressive array of new but traditional Holmes stories.*

Part XVIII: *Sherlockians will again be grateful to Marcum and MX for high-quality new Holmes tales.*

The MX Book of New Sherlock Holmes Stories

Edited by David Marcum

(MX Publishing, 2015-   )

MX Publishing

MX Publishing is the world's largest specialist Sherlock Holmes publisher, with several hundred titles and over a hundred authors creating the latest in Sherlock Holmes fiction and non-fiction.

From traditional short stories and novels to travel guides and quiz books, MX Publishing caters to all Holmes fans.

The collection includes leading titles such as *Benedict Cumberbatch In Transition* and *The Norwood Author*, which won the 2011 *Tony Howlett Award* (Sherlock Holmes Book of the Year).

MX Publishing also has one of the largest communities of Holmes fans on *Facebook*, with regular contributions from dozens of authors.

www.mxpublishing.co.uk (UK) and *www.mxpublishing.com* (USA)

www.ingramcontent.com/pod-product-compliance
Lightning Source LLC
Chambersburg PA
CBHW020919020726
47495CB00002B/258